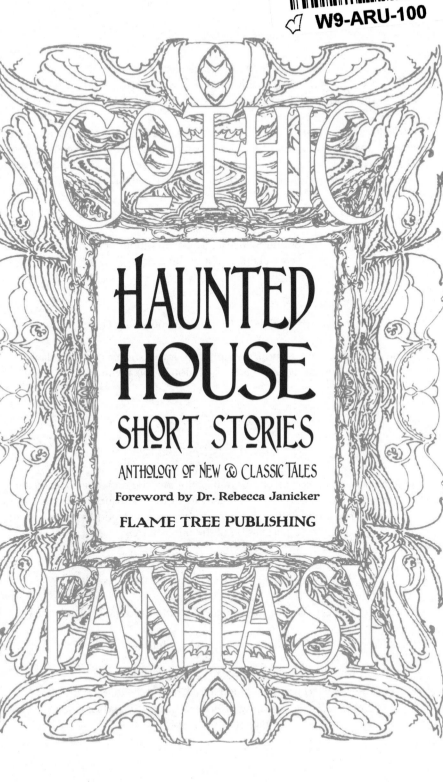

GOTHIC

HAUNTED HOUSE

SHORT STORIES

ANTHOLOGY OF NEW & CLASSIC TALES

Foreword by Dr. Rebecca Janicker

FLAME TREE PUBLISHING

FANTASY

This is a FLAME TREE Book

Publisher & Creative Director: Nick Wells
Project Editor: Gillian Whitaker
Editorial Board: Josie Mitchell, Taylor Bentley, Catherine Taylor

Publisher's Note: Due to the historical nature of the classic text, we're aware that there may be some language used which has the potential to cause offence to the modern reader. However, wishing overall to preserve the integrity of the text, rather than imposing contemporary sensibilities, we have left it unaltered.

FLAME TREE PUBLISHING
6 Melbray Mews, Fulham,
London SW6 3NS, United Kingdom
www.flametreepublishing.com

First published 2019

Stories by modern authors are subject to international copyright law, and are licensed for publication in this volume.

21 23 22
3 5 7 9 10 8 6 4

ISBN: 978-1-78755-266-1

The cover image is created by Flame Tree Studio based on artwork by Slava Gerj and Gabor Ruszkai.

A copy of the CIP data for this book is available from the British Library.

Printed and bound in China

See our new fiction imprint
FLAME TREE PRESS | FICTION WITHOUT FRONTIERS
New and original writing in Horror, Crime, SF and Fantasy
flametreepress.com

GOTHIC

HAUNTED HOUSE

SHORT STORIES

ANTHOLOGY OF NEW & CLASSIC TALES

Foreword by Dr. Rebecca Janicker

FLAME TREE PUBLISHING

FANTASY

Contents

Foreword: Haunted House Short Stories

REPLETE with secrecy and evocative of dread, the haunted house looms large in the field of supernatural fiction. A sub-genre of the Gothic, which emerged in the eighteenth century as a response to the failure of Enlightenment thinking to account for the existence of evil, haunted house stories use place as a focal point for engaging with themes of human transgression and paranormal angst. For, despite its ostensible disregard for reality, the Gothic has grappled with real-world issues such as social injustice and abuses of power from its very inception. Scholars have observed that a key Gothic theme is the *return of the repressed* – the incursion of the past into the present – which is an impulse epitomised by the act of haunting. Ghostly activity thus represents a failure to keep the past buried and it is the grisly details of these hidden crimes, as well as their inevitable unearthing, that pervades such tales.

Atmosphere and setting were the lifeblood of the European Gothic. In the first Gothic novel, Horace Walpole's *The Castle of Otranto* (1764), the gloomy and intimidating edifice of the title was vital to the novel's popularity. Encompassing themes of usurpation and tyranny, the eponymous castle provides a symbolic backdrop against which past wrongs are redressed. Ghostly activity confirms the extent to which the castle is troubled by its violent past. Other celebrated Gothic authors, including the likes of Mrs Ann Radcliffe and Matthew Lewis, were soon to follow suit in utilising the inherent power of wild vistas and ancient ruins to infuse their own tales with the requisite Gothic mood of supernatural terror. Though a twentieth-century tale by an American author, H. P. Lovecraft's 'The Rats in the Walls', with its lurid depictions of the horrors lurking beneath a centuries-old dwelling in England, nonetheless owes a clear debt to European Gothic.

The literary device of the haunted castle laid the foundations for other types of troubled space. Many established conventions of British Gothic had to be adapted once the genre was transplanted to the New World and setting was chief amongst them. Given its status as a new nation, America lacked the medieval architecture so integral to European Gothic and thus replaced the grandiose castle with the domestic dwelling. Yet the stories lost none of their power to disturb. Following Sigmund Freud, the 'uncanny' pertains to a fearful sense that something, or someone, is both familiar and unfamiliar at the same time. Haunted house stories have special potency because the home is so familiar – the place in which we should feel safest – and a threat to the home, which renders it unfamiliar, is fundamentally destabilising. In this collection, the protagonist of Joseph Sheridan Le Fanu's 'An Account of the Strange Disturbances in Aungier Street' finds the comfort of his lodgings undermined by a ghostly presence.

The Gothic is a highly malleable form and, as time goes on, new kinds of haunted spaces arise to address new problems. For horror titan Stephen King, the haunted house can be understood simply as the 'Bad Place' and, from a Danish guest house in 'Number 13' by M. R. James to an empty plot of land in a Boston neighbourhood in 'The Vacant Lot' by Mary E. Wilkins Freeman, this tome incorporates a diverse range of places troubled by ghostly activity. Indeed, Edith Nesbit's 'The Ebony Frame' pushes the boundaries even further with its depiction of a haunted painting. From its origins in the spooky fortresses of the Old World, to its rebirth as a domestic form across the Atlantic, the haunted house story has endured to absorb and disturb new generations of readers.

Dr. Rebecca Janicker

Publisher's Note

There's nothing quite like a good haunted house story, steeped in suspense, to really send chills up your spine. The long-formed parallel between the haunted house of the mind and the physical space of the home has meant such stories hold a rich place in the horror genre. Not only does the setting allow full atmospheric possibility – from the gloomy mansion in Poe's 'The Fall of the House of Usher' to the vine-consumed house in 'The Giant Wistaria' by Charlotte Perkins Gilman – but fresh terror can be found from the spirits anchored to those spaces. Whether they helplessly exist or actively disturb, in half bridging the gap to the living world these lingering presences are an uncanny reminder of things past, and true to form prove difficult to dislodge.

Haunted House Short Stories aims to bring familiar and new material to this well-trodden theme. We've included both tales that are subtle – the residual energies of a building visible only in the cracks – as well as those with undeniable apparitions and malevolent forces at work. In such stories there can be a true breadth of location too: not only the typical houses, mansions, castles, but also the playhouse, the gaolhouse, the public house, hotels…all of which have at some point in literature served as effective accommodation for the paranormal.

In keeping with other books in our successful Gothic Fantasy anthology series, the tales in this book combine contemporary work with classic stories that helped shape the genre. Masterful tales from M.R. James and Edith Wharton, for example, sit comfortably alongside the creeping horror of Ramsey Campbell's 'At Lorn Hall' and the gloriously macabre stories received by submission.

Our submissions process seems to bring ever more great stories our way, and we have thoroughly enjoyed the various takes on the theme this time, from demonic birdhouses to a re-imagining of Hansel and Gretel. Expect mysterious rooms that can never be found again, ghostly replays of past events, and supernatural insects in this collection's real mix of content and writing techniques, which we've tried to preserve as best as possible by retaining the US and UK spellings used originally by the authors. Altogether, we hope the selection provides an absorbing anthology: one to read by the fire on a dark night, when the shadows of a room will never seem so deliciously unnerving; the soft creaks of the floorboards never so weighted with presence.

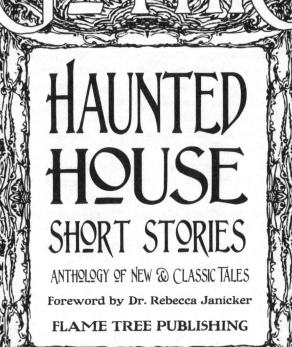

GOTHIC

HAUNTED HOUSE

SHORT STORIES

ANTHOLOGY OF NEW & CLASSIC TALES

Foreword by Dr. Rebecca Janicker

FLAME TREE PUBLISHING

FANTASY

How Fear Departed From The Long Gallery

E.F. Benson

CHURCH-PEVERIL is a house so beset and frequented by spectres, both visible and audible, that none of the family which it shelters under its acre and a half of green copper roofs takes psychical phenomena with any seriousness. For to the Peverils the appearance of a ghost is a matter of hardly greater significance than is the appearance of the post to those who live in more ordinary houses. It arrives, that is to say, practically every day, it knocks (or makes other noises), it is observed coming up the drive (or in other places). I myself, when staying there, have seen the present Mrs. Peveril, who is rather short-sighted, peer into the dusk, while we were taking our coffee on the terrace after dinner, and say to her daughter:

"My dear, was not that the Blue Lady who has just gone into the shrubbery. I hope she won't frighten Flo. Whistle for Flo, dear."

(Flo, it may be remarked, is the youngest and most precious of many dachshunds.)

Blanche Peveril gave a cursory whistle, and crunched the sugar left unmelted at the bottom of her coffee-cup between her very white teeth.

"Oh, darling, Flo isn't so silly as to mind," she said. "Poor blue Aunt Barbara is such a bore!"

"Whenever I meet her she always looks as if she wanted to speak to me, but when I say, 'What is it, Aunt Barbara?' she never utters, but only points somewhere towards the house, which is so vague. I believe there was something she wanted to confess about two hundred years ago, but she has forgotten what it is."

Here Flo gave two or three short pleased barks, and came out of the shrubbery wagging her tail, and capering round what appeared to me to be a perfectly empty space on the lawn.

"There! Flo has made friends with her," said Mrs. Peveril. "I wonder why she dresses in that very stupid shade of blue."

From this it may be gathered that even with regard to psychical phenomena there is some truth in the proverb that speaks of familiarity. But the Peverils do not exactly treat their ghosts with contempt, since most of that delightful family never despised anybody except such people as avowedly did not care for hunting or shooting, or golf or skating. And as all of their ghosts are of their family, it seems reasonable to suppose that they all, even the poor Blue Lady, excelled at one time in field-sports. So far, then, they harbour no such unkindness or contempt, but only pity. Of one Peveril, indeed, who broke his neck in vainly attempting to ride up the main staircase on a thoroughbred mare after some monstrous and violent deed in the back-garden, they are very fond, and Blanche comes downstairs in the morning with an eye unusually bright when she can announce that Master Anthony was "very loud" last night. He (apart from the fact of his having been so foul a ruffian) was a tremendous fellow across country, and they like these indications of the continuance of his superb vitality. In fact, it is supposed to be a compliment, when you go to stay at Church-Peveril, to be assigned a bedroom which is frequented by defunct members of the family. It means that you are worthy to look on the august and villainous dead, and you will find yourself shown into some vaulted or tapestried chamber, without benefit of electric light, and are told that great-great-grandmamma Bridget occasionally has vague business by the fireplace, but it is better not to talk to her, and that you will hear Master Anthony 'awfully well' if he attempts the front staircase any time before morning. There you are left for your night's repose, and, having quakingly undressed, begin reluctantly to put out your candles. It is draughty in these great chambers, and the solemn tapestry swings and bellows and subsides, and the firelight dances on the forms of huntsmen and warriors and stern pursuits. Then you climb into your bed, a bed so huge that you feel as if the desert of Sahara was spread for you, and pray, like the mariners who sailed with St. Paul, for day. And, all the time, you are aware that Freddy and Harry and Blanche and possibly even Mrs. Peveril are quite capable of dressing up and making disquieting tappings outside your door, so that when you open it some inconjecturable horror fronts you. For myself, I stick steadily to the assertion that I have an obscure valvular disease of the heart, and so sleep undisturbed in the new wing of the house where Aunt Barbara, and great-great-grandmamma Bridget and Master Anthony never penetrate. I forget the details of great-great-grandmamma Bridget, but she certainly cut the throat of some distant relation before she disembowelled herself with the axe that had been used at Agincourt. Before that she had led a very sultry life, crammed with amazing incident.

But there is one ghost at Church-Peveril at which the family never laugh, in which they feel no friendly and amused interest, and of which they only speak just as much as is necessary for the safety of their guests. More properly it should be described as two ghosts, for the 'haunt' in question is that of two very young children, who were twins. These, not without reason, the family take very seriously indeed. The story of them, as told me by Mrs. Peveril, is as follows:

In the year 1602, the same being the last of Queen Elizabeth's reign, a certain Dick Peveril was greatly in favour at Court. He was brother to Master Joseph Peveril, then owner of the family house and lands, who two years previously, at the respectable age of seventy-four, became father of twin boys, first-born of his progeny. It is known that the royal and ancient virgin had said to handsome Dick, who was nearly forty years his brother's junior, "'Tis pity that you are not master of Church-Peveril," and these words probably suggested to him a sinister design. Be that as it may, handsome Dick, who very adequately sustained the family reputation for wickedness, set off to ride down to Yorkshire, and found that, very conveniently, his brother Joseph had just been seized with an apoplexy, which appeared to be the result of a continued spell of hot weather combined with the necessity of quenching his thirst with an augmented amount of sack, and had actually died while handsome Dick, with God knows what thoughts in his mind, was journeying northwards. Thus it came about that he arrived at Church-Peveril just in time for his brother's funeral. It was with great propriety that he attended the obsequies, and returned to spend a sympathetic day or two of mourning with his widowed sister-in-law, who was but a faint-hearted dame, little fit to be mated with such hawks as these. On the second night of his stay, he did that which the Peverils regret to this day. He entered the room where the twins slept with their nurse, and quietly strangled the latter as she slept. Then he took the twins and put them into the fire which warms the long gallery. The weather, which up to the day of Joseph's death had been so hot, had changed suddenly to bitter cold, and the fire was heaped high with burning logs and was exultant with flame. In the core of this conflagration he struck out a cremation-chamber, and into that he threw the two children, stamping them down with his riding-boots. They could just walk, but they could not walk out of that ardent place. It is said that he laughed as he added more logs. Thus he became master of Church-Peveril.

The crime was never brought home to him, but he lived no longer than a year in the enjoyment of his blood-stained inheritance. When he lay a-dying he made his confession to the priest who attended him, but his spirit struggled forth from its fleshly coil before Absolution could be given him. On that very night there began in Church-Peveril the haunting which to this day is but seldom spoken of by the family, and then only in low tones and with serious mien. For only an hour or two after handsome Dick's death, one of the servants passing the door of the long gallery heard from within peals of the loud laughter so jovial and yet so sinister which he had thought would never be heard in the house again. In a moment of that cold courage which is so nearly akin to mortal terror he opened the door and entered, expecting to see he knew not what manifestation of him who lay dead in the room below. Instead he saw two little white-robed figures toddling towards him hand in hand across the moon-lit floor.

The watchers in the room below ran upstairs startled by the crash of his fallen body, and found him lying in the grip of some dread convulsion. Just before morning he regained consciousness and told his tale. Then pointing with trembling and ash-grey finger towards the door, he screamed aloud, and so fell back dead.

During the next fifty years this strange and terrible legend of the twin-babies became fixed and consolidated. Their appearance, luckily for those who inhabit the house, was exceedingly rare, and during these years they seem to have been seen four or five times only. On each occasion they appeared at night, between sunset and sunrise, always in the same long gallery, and always as two toddling children scarcely able to walk. And on each occasion the luckless individual who saw them died either speedily or terribly, or with both speed and terror, after the accursed vision had appeared to him. Sometimes he might live for a few months: he was lucky if he died, as did the servant who first saw them, in a few hours. Vastly more awful was the fate of a certain Mrs. Canning, who had the ill-luck to see them in the middle of the next century, or to be quite accurate, in the year 1760. By this time the hours and the place of their appearance were well known, and, as up till a year ago, visitors were warned not to go between sunset and sunrise into the long gallery.

But Mrs. Canning, a brilliantly clever and beautiful woman, admirer also and friend of the notorious sceptic M. Voltaire, wilfully went and sat night after night, in spite of all protestations, in the haunted place. For four evenings she saw nothing, but on the fifth she had her will, for the door in the middle of the gallery opened, and there came toddling towards her the ill-omened innocent little pair. It seemed that even then she was not frightened, but she thought it good, poor wretch, to mock at them, telling them it was time for them to get back into the fire. They gave no word in answer, but turned away from her crying and sobbing. Immediately after they disappeared from her vision and she rustled downstairs to where the family and guests in the house were waiting for her, with the triumphant announcement that she has seen them both, and must needs write to M. Voltaire, saying that she had spoken to spirits made manifest. It would make him laugh. But when some months later the whole news reached him he did not laugh at all.

Mrs. Canning was one of the great beauties of her day, and in the year 1760 she was at the height and zenith of her blossoming. The chief beauty, if it is possible to single out one point where all was so exquisite, lay in the dazzling colour and incomparable brilliance of her complexion. She was now just thirty years of age, but, in spite of the excesses of her life, retained the snow and roses of girlhood, and she courted the bright light of day which other women shunned, for it but showed to great advantage the splendour of her skin. In consequence she was very considerably dismayed one morning, about a fortnight after her strange experience in the long gallery, to observe on her left cheek, an inch or two below her turquoise-coloured eyes, a little greyish patch of skin, about as big as a threepenny piece. It was in vain that she applied her accustomed washes and unguents: vain, too, were the arts of her fardeuse and of her medical adviser. For a week she kept herself secluded, martyring herself with solitude and unaccustomed physics, and for result at the end of the week she had no amelioration to comfort herself with: instead this woeful grey patch had doubled itself in size. Thereafter the nameless disease, whatever it was, developed in new and terrible ways. From the centre of the discoloured place there sprouted forth little lichen-like tendrils of greenish-grey, and another patch appeared on her lower lip. This, too, soon vegetated, and one morning, on opening her eyes to the horror of a new day, she found that her vision was strangely blurred. She sprang to her looking-glass, and what she saw caused her to shriek aloud with horror. From under her upper eye-lid a fresh growth had sprung up, mushroom-like, in the night, and its filaments extended downwards, screening the pupil of her eye. Soon after, her tongue and throat were attacked: the air passages became obstructed, and death by suffocation was merciful after such suffering.

More terrible yet was the case of a certain Colonel Blantyre who fired at the children with his revolver. What he went through is not to be recorded here.

It is this haunting, then, that the Peverils take quite seriously, and every guest on his arrival in the house is told that the long gallery must not be entered after nightfall on any pretext whatever. By day, however, it is a delightful room and intrinsically merits description, apart from the fact that the due understanding of its geography is necessary for the account that here follows. It is full eighty feet in length, and is lit by a row of six tall windows looking over the gardens at the back of the house. A door communicates with the landing at the top of the main staircase, and about half-way down the gallery in the wall facing the windows is another door communicating with the back staircase and servants' quarters, and thus the gallery forms a constant place of passage for them in going to the rooms on the first landing. It was through this door that the baby-figures came when they appeared to Mrs. Canning, and on several other occasions they have been known to make their entry here, for the room out of which handsome Dick took them lies just beyond at the top of the back stairs. Further on again in the gallery is the fireplace into which he thrust them, and at the far end a large bow-window looks straight down the avenue. Above this fireplace there hangs with grim significance a portrait of handsome Dick, in the insolent beauty of early manhood, attributed to Holbein, and a dozen other portraits of great merit face the windows. During the day this is the most frequented sitting-room in the house, for its other visitors never appear there then, nor does it then ever resound with the harsh jovial laugh of handsome Dick, which sometimes, after dark has fallen, is heard by passers-by on the landing outside. But Blanche does not grow bright-eyed when she hears it: she shuts her ears and hastens to put a greater distance between her and the sound of that atrocious mirth.

But during the day the long gallery is frequented by many occupants, and much laughter in no wise sinister or saturnine resounds there. When summer lies hot over the land, those occupants lounge in the deep window seats, and when winter spreads his icy fingers and blows shrilly between his frozen palms, congregate round the fireplace at the far end, and perch, in companies of cheerful chatterers, upon sofa and chair, and chair-back and floor. Often have I sat there on long August evenings up till dressing-time, but never have I been there when anyone has seemed disposed to linger over-late without hearing the warning: "It is close on sunset: shall we go?" Later on in the shorter autumn days they often have tea laid there, and sometimes it has happened that, even while merriment was most uproarious, Mrs. Peveril has suddenly looked out of the window and said, "My dears, it is getting so late: let us finish our nonsense downstairs in the hall." And then for a moment a curious hush always falls on loquacious family and guests alike, and as if some bad news had just been known, we all make our silent way out of the place.

But the spirits of the Peverils (of the living ones, that is to say) are the most mercurial imaginable, and the blight which the thought of handsome Dick and his doings casts over them passes away again with amazing rapidity.

A typical party, large, young, and peculiarly cheerful, was staying at Church-Peveril shortly after Christmas last year, and as usual on December 31, Mrs. Peveril was giving her annual New Year's Eve ball. The house was quite full, and she had commandeered as well the greater part of the Peveril Arms to provide sleeping-quarters for the overflow from the house. For some days past a black and windless frost had stopped all hunting, but it is an ill windlessness that blows no good (if so mixed a metaphor may be forgiven), and the lake below the house had for the last day or two been covered with an adequate and admirable sheet of ice. Everyone in the house had been occupied all the morning of that day in performing swift and violent manoeuvres on the elusive surface, and as soon as lunch was over we all, with one exception, hurried out again. This one exception was Madge Dalrymple, who had had the misfortune to fall rather badly earlier in the day, but hoped, by resting her injured knee, instead of joining the skaters again, to be able to dance that evening. The hope, it is true, was the most sanguine sort, for she could but hobble ignobly back to the house, but with the breezy optimism which characterises the Peverils (she is Blanche's first cousin), she remarked that it would be but tepid enjoyment that she could, in her present state, derive from further skating, and thus she sacrificed little, but might gain much.

Accordingly, after a rapid cup of coffee which was served in the long gallery, we left Madge comfortably reclined on the big sofa at right-angles to the fireplace, with an attractive book to beguile the tedium till tea. Being of the family, she knew all about handsome Dick and the babies, and the fate of Mrs. Canning and Colonel Blantyre, but as we went out I heard Blanche say to her, "Don't run it too fine, dear," and Madge had replied, "No; I'll go away well before sunset." And so we left her alone in the long gallery.

Madge read her attractive book for some minutes, but failing to get absorbed in it, put it down and limped across to the window. Though it was still but little after two, it was but a dim and uncertain light that entered, for the crystalline brightness of the morning had given place to a veiled obscurity produced by flocks of thick clouds which were coming sluggishly up from the north-east. Already the whole sky was overcast with them, and occasionally a few snowflakes fluttered waveringly down past the long windows. From the darkness and bitter cold of the afternoon, it seemed to her that there was like to be a heavy snowfall before long, and these outward signs were echoed inwardly in her by that muffled drowsiness of the brain, which to those who are sensitive to the pressures and lightness of weather portends storm. Madge was peculiarly the prey of such external influences: to her a brisk morning gave an ineffable brightness and briskness of spirit, and correspondingly the approach of heavy weather produced a somnolence in sensation that both drowsed and depressed her.

It was in such mood as this that she limped back again to the sofa beside the log-fire. The whole house was comfortably heated by water-pipes, and though the fire of logs and peat, an adorable mixture, had been allowed to burn low, the room was very warm. Idly she watched the dwindling flames, not opening her book again, but lying on the sofa with face towards the fireplace, intending drowsily and not immediately to go to her own room and spend the hours, until the return of the skaters made gaiety in the house again, in writing one or two neglected letters. Still drowsily she began thinking over what she had to communicate: one letter several days overdue should go to her mother, who was immensely interested in the psychical affairs of the family. She would tell her how Master Anthony had been prodigiously active on the staircase a night or two ago, and how the Blue Lady, regardless of the severity of the weather, had been seen by Mrs. Peveril that morning, strolling about. It was rather interesting: the Blue Lady had gone down the laurel walk and had been seen by her to enter the stables, where, at the moment, Freddy Peveril was inspecting the frost-bound hunters. Identically then, a sudden panic had spread through the stables, and the horses had whinnied and kicked, and shied, and sweated. Of the fatal twins nothing had been seen for many years past, but, as her mother knew, the Peverils never used the long gallery after dark.

Then for a moment she sat up, remembering that she was in the long gallery now. But it was still but a little after half-past two, and if she went to her room in half an hour, she would have ample time to write this and another letter before tea. Till then she would read her book. But she found she had left it on the windowsill, and it seemed scarcely worthwhile to get it. She felt exceedingly drowsy.

The sofa where she lay had been lately recovered, in a greyish green shade of velvet, somewhat the colour of lichen. It was of very thick soft texture, and she luxuriously stretched her arms out, one on each side of her body, and pressed her fingers into the nap. How horrible that story of Mrs. Canning was: the growth on her face was of the colour of lichen. And then without further transition or blurring of thought Madge fell asleep.

She dreamed. She dreamed that she awoke and found herself exactly where she had gone to sleep, and in exactly the same attitude. The flames from the logs had burned up again, and leaped on the walls, fitfully illuminating the picture of handsome Dick above the fireplace. In her dream she knew exactly what she had done today, and for what reason she was lying here now instead of being out with the rest of the skaters. She remembered also (still dreaming), that she was going to write a letter or two before tea, and prepared to get up in order to go to her room. As she half-rose she caught sight of her own arms lying out on each side of her on the grey velvet sofa.

But she could not see where her hands ended, and where the grey velvet began: her fingers seemed to have melted into the stuff. She could see her wrists quite clearly, and a blue vein on the backs of her hands, and here and there a knuckle. Then, in her dream, she remembered the last thought which had been in her mind before she fell asleep, namely the growth of the lichen-coloured vegetation on the face and the eyes and the throat of Mrs. Canning. At that thought the strangling terror of real nightmare began: she knew that she was being transformed into this grey stuff, and she was absolutely unable to move. Soon the grey would spread up her arms, and over her feet; when they came in from skating they would find here nothing but a huge misshapen cushion of lichen-coloured velvet, and that would be she. The horror grew more acute, and then by a violent effort she shook herself free of the clutches of this very evil dream, and she awoke.

For a minute or two she lay there, conscious only of the tremendous relief at finding herself awake. She felt again with her fingers the pleasant touch of the velvet, and drew them backwards and forwards, assuring herself that she was not, as her dream had suggested, melting into greyness and softness. But she was still, in spite of the violence of her awakening, very sleepy, and lay there till, looking down, she was aware that she could not see her hands at all. It was very nearly dark.

At that moment a sudden flicker of flame came from the dying fire, and a flare of burning gas from the peat flooded the room. The portrait of handsome Dick looked evilly down on her, and her hands were visible again. And then a panic worse than the panic of her dreams seized her.

Daylight had altogether faded, and she knew that she was alone in the dark in the terrible gallery.

This panic was of the nature of nightmare, for she felt unable to move for terror. But it was worse than nightmare because she knew she was awake. And then the full cause of this frozen fear dawned on her; she knew with the certainty of absolute conviction that she was about to see the twin-babies.

She felt a sudden moisture break out on her face, and within her mouth her tongue and throat went suddenly dry, and she felt her tongue grate along the inner surface of her teeth. All power of movement had slipped from her limbs, leaving them dead and inert, and she stared with wide eyes into the blackness. The spurt of flame from the peat had burned itself out again, and darkness encompassed her.

Then on the wall opposite her, facing the windows, there grew a faint light of dusky crimson.

For a moment she thought it but heralded the approach of the awful vision, then hope revived in her heart, and she remembered that thick clouds had overcast the sky before she went to sleep, and guessed that this light came from the sun not yet quite sunk and set. This sudden revival of hope gave her the necessary stimulus, and she sprang off the sofa where she lay. She looked out of the window and saw the dull glow on the horizon. But before she could take a step forward it was obscured again. A tiny sparkle of light came from the hearth which did no more than illuminate the tiles of the fireplace, and snow falling heavily tapped at the window panes. There was neither light nor sound except these.

But the courage that had come to her, giving her the power of movement, had not quite deserted her, and she began feeling her way down the gallery. And then she found that she was lost. She stumbled against a chair, and, recovering herself, stumbled against another. Then a table barred her way, and, turning swiftly aside, she found herself up against the back of a sofa.

Once more she turned and saw the dim gleam of the firelight on the side opposite to that on which she expected it. In her blind gropings she must have reversed her direction. But which way was she to go now. She seemed blocked in by furniture. And all the time insistent and imminent was the fact that the two innocent terrible ghosts were about to appear to her.

Then she began to pray. "Lighten our darkness, O Lord," she said to herself. But she could not remember how the prayer continued, and she had sore need of it. There was something about the perils of the night. All this time she felt about her with groping, fluttering hands. The fire-glimmer which should have been on her left was on her right again; therefore she must turn herself round again. "Lighten our darkness," she whispered, and then aloud she repeated, "Lighten our darkness."

She stumbled up against a screen, and could not remember the existence of any such screen.

Hastily she felt beside it with blind hands, and touched something soft and velvety. Was it the sofa on which she had lain? If so, where was the head of it. It had a head and a back and feet – it was like a person, all covered with grey lichen. Then she lost her head completely. All that remained to her was to pray; she was lost, lost in this awful place, where no one came in the dark except the babies that cried. And she heard her voice rising from whisper to speech, and speech to scream. She shrieked out the holy words, she yelled them as if blaspheming as she groped among tables and chairs and the pleasant things of ordinary life which had become so terrible.

Then came a sudden and an awful answer to her screamed prayer. Once more a pocket of inflammable gas in the peat on the hearth was reached by the smouldering embers, and the room started into light. She saw the evil eyes of handsome Dick, she saw the little ghostly snowflakes falling thickly outside. And she saw where she was, just opposite the door through which the terrible twins made their entrance. Then the flame went out again, and left her in blackness once more. But she had gained something, for she had her geography now. The centre of the room was bare of furniture, and one swift dart would take her to the door of the landing above the main staircase and into safety. In that gleam she had been able to see the handle of the door, bright-brassed, luminous like a star. She would go straight for it; it was but a matter of a few seconds now.

She took a long breath, partly of relief, partly to satisfy the demands of her galloping heart.

But the breath was only half-taken when she was stricken once more into the immobility of nightmare.

There came a little whisper, it was no more than that, from the door opposite which she stood, and through which the twin-babies entered. It was not quite dark outside it, for she could see that the door was opening. And there stood in the opening two little white figures, side by side. They came towards her slowly, shufflingly. She could not see face or form at all distinctly, but the two little white figures were advancing. She knew them to be the ghosts of terror, innocent of the awful doom they were bound to bring, even as she was innocent. With the inconceivable rapidity of thought, she made up her mind what to do. She had not hurt them or laughed at them, and they, they were but babies when the wicked and bloody deed had sent them to their burning death. Surely the spirits of these children would not be inaccessible to the cry of one who was of the same blood as they, who had committed no fault that merited the doom they brought. If she entreated them they might have mercy, they might forebear to bring the curse on her, they might allow her to pass out of the place without blight, without the sentence of death, or the shadow of things worse than death upon her.

It was but for the space of a moment that she hesitated, then she sank down on to her knees, and stretched out her hands towards them.

"Oh, my dears," she said, "I only fell asleep. I have done no more wrong than that—"

She paused a moment, and her tender girl's heart thought no more of herself, but only of them, those little innocent spirits on whom so awful a doom was laid, that they should bring death where other children bring laughter, and doom for delight. But all those who had seen them before had dreaded and feared them, or had mocked at them.

Then, as the enlightenment of pity dawned on her, her fear fell from her like the wrinkled sheath that holds the sweet folded buds of Spring.

"Dears, I am so sorry for you," she said. "It is not your fault that you must bring me what you must bring, but I am not afraid any longer. I am only sorry for you. God bless you, you poor darlings."

She raised her head and looked at them. Though it was so dark, she could now see their faces, though all was dim and wavering, like the light of pale flames shaken by a draught. But the faces were not miserable or fierce – they smiled at her with shy little baby smiles. And as she looked they grew faint, fading slowly away like wreaths of vapour in frosty air.

Madge did not at once move when they had vanished, for instead of fear there was wrapped round her a wonderful sense of peace, so happy and serene that she would not willingly stir, and so perhaps disturb it. But before long she got up, and feeling her way, but without any sense of nightmare pressing her on, or frenzy of fear to spur her, she went out of the long gallery, to find Blanche just coming upstairs whistling and swinging her skates.

"How's the leg, dear," she asked. "You're not limping any more."

Till that moment Madge had not thought of it.

"I think it must be all right," she said; "I had forgotten it, anyhow. Blanche, dear, you won't be frightened for me, will you, but – but I have seen the twins."

For a moment Blanche's face whitened with terror.

"What?" she said in a whisper.

"Yes, I saw them just now. But they were kind, they smiled at me, and I was so sorry for them. And somehow I am sure I have nothing to fear."

It seems that Madge was right, for nothing has come to touch her. Something, her attitude to them, we must suppose, her pity, her sympathy, touched and dissolved and annihilated the curse.

Indeed, I was at Church-Peveril only last week, arriving there after dark. Just as I passed the gallery door, Blanche came out.

"Ah, there you are," she said: "I've just been seeing the twins. They looked too sweet and stopped nearly ten minutes. Let us have tea at once."

The Room in the Tower

E.F. Benson

IT IS PROBABLE that everybody who is at all a constant dreamer has had at least one experience of an event or a sequence of circumstances which have come to his mind in sleep being subsequently realised in the material world. But, in my opinion, so far from this being a strange thing, it would be far odder if this fulfilment did not occasionally happen, since our dreams are, as a rule, concerned with people whom we know and places with which we are familiar, such as might very naturally occur in the awake and daylit world. True, these dreams are often broken into by some absurd and fantastic incident, which puts them out of court in regard to their subsequent fulfilment, but on the mere calculation of chances, it does not appear in the least unlikely that a dream imagined by anyone who dreams constantly should occasionally come true. Not long ago, for instance, I experienced such a fulfilment of a dream which seems to me in no way remarkable and to have no kind of psychical significance. The manner of it was as follows.

A certain friend of mine, living abroad, is amiable enough to write to me about once in a fortnight. Thus, when fourteen days or thereabouts have elapsed since I last heard from him, my mind, probably, either consciously or subconsciously, is expectant of a letter from him. One night last week I dreamed that as I was going upstairs to dress for dinner I heard, as I often heard, the sound of the postman's knock on my front door, and diverted my direction downstairs instead. There, among other correspondence, was a letter from him. Thereafter the fantastic entered, for on opening it I found inside the ace of diamonds, and scribbled across it in his well-known handwriting, "I am sending you this for safe custody, as you know it is running an unreasonable risk to keep aces in Italy."

The next evening I was just preparing to go upstairs to dress when I heard the postman's knock, and did precisely as I had done in my dream. There, among other letters, was one from my friend. Only it did not contain the ace of diamonds. Had it done so, I should have attached more weight to the matter, which, as it stands, seems to me a perfectly ordinary coincidence. No doubt I consciously or subconsciously expected a letter from him, and this suggested to me my dream. Similarly, the fact that my friend had not written to me for a fortnight suggested to him that he should do so. But occasionally it is not so easy to find such an explanation, and for the following story I can find no explanation at all. It came out of the dark, and into the dark it has gone again.

All my life I have been a habitual dreamer: the nights are few, that is to say, when I do not find on awaking in the morning that some mental experience has been mine, and sometimes, all night long, apparently, a series of the most dazzling adventures befall me. Almost without exception these adventures are pleasant, though often merely trivial. It is of an exception that I am going to speak.

It was when I was about sixteen that a certain dream first came to me, and this is how it befell. It opened with my being set down at the door of a big red-brick house, where, I understood, I was going to stay. The servant who opened the door told me that tea was being served in the garden, and led me through a low dark-panelled hall, with a large open fireplace, on to a cheerful green lawn set round with flower beds. There were grouped about the tea-table a small party of people, but they were all strangers to me except one, who was a schoolfellow called Jack Stone, clearly the son of the house, and he introduced me to his mother and father and a couple of sisters. I was, I remember, somewhat astonished to find myself here, for the boy in question was scarcely known to me, and I rather disliked what I knew of him; moreover, he had left school nearly a year before. The afternoon was very hot, and an intolerable oppression reigned. On the far side of the lawn ran a red-brick wall, with an iron gate in its centre, outside which stood a walnut tree. We sat in the shadow of the house opposite a row of long windows, inside which I could see a table with cloth laid, glimmering with glass and silver. This garden front of the house was very long, and at one end of it stood a tower of three storeys, which looked to me much older than the rest of the building.

Before long, Mrs. Stone, who, like the rest of the party, had sat in absolute silence, said to me, "Jack will show you your room: I have given you the room in the tower."

Quite inexplicably my heart sank at her words. I felt as if I had known that I should have the room in the tower, and that it contained something dreadful and significant. Jack instantly got up, and I understood that I had to follow him. In silence we passed through the hall, and mounted a great oak staircase with many corners, and arrived at a small landing with two doors set in it. He pushed one of these open for me to enter, and without coming in himself, closed it after me. Then I knew that my conjecture had been right: there was something awful in the room, and with the terror of nightmare growing swiftly and enveloping me, I awoke in a spasm of terror.

Now that dream or variations on it occurred to me intermittently for fifteen years. Most often it came in exactly this form, the arrival, the tea laid out on the lawn, the deadly silence succeeded by that one deadly sentence, the mounting with Jack Stone up to the room in the tower where horror dwelt, and it always came to a close in the nightmare of terror at that which was in the room, though I never saw what it was. At other times I experienced variations on this same theme. Occasionally, for instance, we would be sitting at dinner in the dining-room, into the windows of which I had looked on the first night when the dream of this house visited me, but wherever we were, there was the same silence, the same sense of dreadful oppression and foreboding. And the silence I knew would always be broken by Mrs. Stone saying to me, "Jack will show you your room: I have given you the room in the tower." Upon which (this was invariable) I had to follow him up the oak staircase with many corners, and enter the place that I dreaded more and more each time that I visited it in sleep. Or, again, I would find myself playing cards still in silence in a drawing-room lit with immense chandeliers, that gave a blinding illumination. What the game was I have no idea; what I remember, with a sense of miserable anticipation, was that soon Mrs. Stone would get up and say to me, "Jack will show you your room: I have given you the room in the tower." This drawing-room where we played cards was next to the dining-room, and, as I have said, was always brilliantly illuminated, whereas the rest of the house was full of dusk and shadows. And yet, how often, in spite of those bouquets of lights, have I not pored over the cards that were dealt me, scarcely able for some reason to see them. Their designs, too, were strange: there were no red suits, but all were black, and among them there were certain cards which were black all over. I hated and dreaded those.

As this dream continued to recur, I got to know the greater part of the house. There was a smoking-room beyond the drawing-room, at the end of a passage with a green baize door. It was always very dark there, and as often as I went there I passed somebody whom I could not see in the doorway coming out. Curious developments, too, took place in the characters that peopled the dream as might happen to living persons. Mrs. Stone, for instance, who, when I first saw her, had been black-haired, became gray, and instead of rising briskly, as she had done at first when she said, "Jack will show you your room: I have given you the room in the tower," got up very feebly, as if the strength was leaving her limbs. Jack also grew up, and became a rather ill-looking young man, with a brown moustache, while one of the sisters ceased to appear, and I understood she was married.

Then it so happened that I was not visited by this dream for six months or more, and I began to hope, in such inexplicable dread did I hold it, that it had passed away for good. But one night after this interval I again found myself being shown out onto the lawn for tea, and Mrs. Stone was not there, while the others were all dressed in black. At once I guessed the reason, and my heart leaped at the thought that perhaps this time I should not have to sleep in the room in the tower, and though we usually all sat in silence, on this occasion the sense of relief made me talk and laugh as I had never yet done. But even then matters were not altogether comfortable, for no one else spoke, but they all looked secretly at each other. And soon the foolish stream of my talk ran dry, and gradually an apprehension worse than anything I had previously known gained on me as the light slowly faded.

Suddenly a voice which I knew well broke the stillness, the voice of Mrs. Stone, saying, "Jack will show you your room: I have given you the room in the tower." It seemed to come from near the gate in the red-brick wall that bounded the lawn, and looking up, I saw that the grass outside was sown thick with gravestones. A curious greyish light shone from them, and I could read the lettering on the grave nearest me, and it was, "In evil memory of Julia Stone." And as usual Jack got up, and again I followed him through the hall and up the staircase with many corners. On this occasion it was darker than usual, and when I passed into the room in the tower I could only just see the furniture, the position of which was already familiar to me. Also there was a dreadful odour of decay in the room, and I woke screaming.

The dream, with such variations and developments as I have mentioned, went on at intervals for fifteen years. Sometimes I would dream it two or three nights in succession; once, as I have said, there was an intermission of six months, but taking a reasonable average, I should say that I dreamed it quite as often as once in a month. It had, as is plain, something of nightmare about it, since it always ended in the same appalling terror, which so far from getting less, seemed to me to gather fresh fear every time that I experienced it. There was, too, a strange and dreadful consistency about it. The characters in it, as I have mentioned, got regularly older, death and marriage visited this silent family, and I never in the dream, after Mrs. Stone had died, set eyes on her again. But it was always her voice that told me that the room in the tower was prepared for me, and whether we had tea out on the lawn, or the scene was laid in one of the rooms overlooking it, I could always see her gravestone standing just outside the iron gate. It was the same, too, with the married daughter; usually she was not present, but once or twice she returned again, in company with a man, whom I took to be her husband. He, too, like the rest of them, was always silent. But, owing to the constant repetition of the dream, I had ceased to attach, in my waking hours, any significance to it. I never met Jack Stone again during all those years, nor did I ever see a house that resembled this dark house of my dream. And then something happened.

I had been in London in this year, up till the end of the July, and during the first week in August went down to stay with a friend in a house he had taken for the summer months, in the Ashdown Forest district of Sussex. I left London early, for John Clinton was to meet me at Forest Row Station, and we were going to spend the day golfing, and go to his house in the evening. He had his motor with him, and we set off, about five of the afternoon, after a thoroughly delightful day, for the drive, the distance being some ten miles. As it was still so early we did not have tea at the club house, but waited till we should get home. As we drove, the weather, which up till then had been, though hot, deliciously fresh, seemed to me to alter in quality, and become very stagnant and oppressive, and I felt that indefinable sense of ominous apprehension that I am accustomed to before thunder. John, however, did not share my views, attributing my loss of lightness to the fact that I had lost both my matches. Events proved, however, that I was right, though I do not think that the thunderstorm that broke that night was the sole cause of my depression.

Our way lay through deep high-banked lanes, and before we had gone very far I fell asleep, and was only awakened by the stopping of the motor. And with a sudden thrill, partly of fear but chiefly of curiosity, I found myself standing in the doorway of my house of dream. We went, I half wondering whether or not I was dreaming still, through a low oak-panelled hall, and out onto the lawn, where tea was laid in the shadow of the house. It was set in flower beds, a red-brick wall, with a gate in it, bounded one side, and out beyond that was a space of rough grass with a walnut tree. The facade of the house was very long, and at one end stood a three-storied tower, markedly older than the rest.

Here for the moment all resemblance to the repeated dream ceased. There was no silent and somehow terrible family, but a large assembly of exceedingly cheerful persons, all of whom were known to me. And in spite of the horror with which the dream itself had always filled me, I felt nothing of it now that the scene of it was thus reproduced before me. But I felt intensest curiosity as to what was going to happen.

Tea pursued its cheerful course, and before long Mrs. Clinton got up. And at that moment I think I knew what she was going to say. She spoke to me, and what she said was:

"Jack will show you your room: I have given you the room in the tower."

At that, for half a second, the horror of the dream took hold of me again. But it quickly passed, and again I felt nothing more than the most intense curiosity. It was not very long before it was amply satisfied.

John turned to me.

"Right up at the top of the house," he said, "but I think you'll be comfortable. We're absolutely full up. Would you like to go and see it now? By Jove, I believe that you are right, and that we are going to have a thunderstorm. How dark it has become."

I got up and followed him. We passed through the hall, and up the perfectly familiar staircase. Then he opened the door, and I went in. And at that moment sheer unreasoning terror again possessed me. I did not know what I feared: I simply feared. Then like a sudden recollection, when one remembers a name which has long escaped the memory, I knew what I feared. I feared Mrs. Stone, whose grave with the sinister inscription, 'In evil memory', I had so often seen in my dream, just beyond the lawn which lay below my window. And then once more the fear passed so completely that I wondered what there was to fear, and I found myself, sober and quiet and sane, in the room in the tower, the name of which I had so often heard in my dream, and the scene of which was so familiar.

I looked around it with a certain sense of proprietorship, and found that nothing had been changed from the dreaming nights in which I knew it so well. Just to the left of the door was the bed, lengthways along the wall, with the head of it in the angle. In a line with it was the fireplace and a small bookcase; opposite the door the outer wall was pierced by two lattice-paned windows, between which stood the dressing-table, while ranged along the fourth wall was the washing-stand and a big cupboard. My luggage had already been unpacked, for the furniture of dressing and undressing lay orderly on the wash-stand and toilet-table, while my dinner clothes were spread out on the coverlet of the bed. And then, with a sudden start of unexplained dismay, I saw that there were two rather conspicuous objects which I had not seen before in my dreams: one a life-sized oil painting of Mrs. Stone, the other a black-and-white sketch of Jack Stone, representing him as he had appeared to me only a week before in the last of the series of these repeated dreams, a rather secret and evil-looking man of about thirty. His picture hung between the windows, looking straight across the room to the other portrait, which hung at the side of the bed. At that I looked next, and as I looked I felt once more the horror of nightmare seize me.

It represented Mrs. Stone as I had seen her last in my dreams: old and withered and white-haired. But in spite of the evident feebleness of body, a dreadful exuberance and vitality shone through the envelope of flesh, an exuberance wholly malign, a vitality that foamed and frothed with unimaginable evil. Evil beamed from the narrow, leering eyes; it laughed in the demon-like mouth. The whole face was instinct with some secret and appalling mirth; the hands, clasped together on the knee, seemed shaking with suppressed and nameless glee. Then I saw also that it was signed in the left-hand bottom corner, and wondering who the artist could be, I looked more closely, and read the inscription, 'Julia Stone by Julia Stone'.

There came a tap at the door, and John Clinton entered.

"Got everything you want?" he asked.

"Rather more than I want," said I, pointing to the picture.

He laughed.

"Hard-featured old lady," he said. "By herself, too, I remember. Anyhow she can't have flattered herself much."

"But don't you see?" said I. "It's scarcely a human face at all. It's the face of some witch, of some devil."

He looked at it more closely.

"Yes; it isn't very pleasant," he said. "Scarcely a bedside manner, eh? Yes; I can imagine getting the nightmare if I went to sleep with that close by my bed. I'll have it taken down if you like."

"I really wish you would," I said. He rang the bell, and with the help of a servant we detached the picture and carried it out onto the landing, and put it with its face to the wall.

"By Jove, the old lady is a weight," said John, mopping his forehead. "I wonder if she had something on her mind."

The extraordinary weight of the picture had struck me too. I was about to reply, when I caught sight of my own hand. There was blood on it, in considerable quantities, covering the whole palm.

"I've cut myself somehow," said I.

John gave a little startled exclamation.

"Why, I have too," he said.

Simultaneously the footman took out his handkerchief and wiped his hand with it. I saw that there was blood also on his handkerchief.

John and I went back into the tower room and washed the blood off; but neither on his hand nor on mine was there the slightest trace of a scratch or cut. It seemed to me that, having ascertained this, we both, by a sort of tacit consent, did not allude to it again. Something in my case had dimly occurred to me that I did not wish to think about. It was but a conjecture, but I fancied that I knew the same thing had occurred to him.

The heat and oppression of the air, for the storm we had expected was still undischarged, increased very much after dinner, and for some time most of the party, among whom were John Clinton and myself, sat outside on the path bounding the lawn, where we had had tea. The night was absolutely dark, and no twinkle of star or moon ray could penetrate the pall of cloud that overset the sky. By degrees our assembly thinned, the women went up to bed, men dispersed to the smoking or billiard room, and by eleven o'clock my host and I were the only two left. All the evening I thought that he had something on his mind, and as soon as we were alone he spoke.

"The man who helped us with the picture had blood on his hand, too, did you notice?" he said.

"I asked him just now if he had cut himself, and he said he supposed he had, but that he could find no mark of it. Now where did that blood come from?"

By dint of telling myself that I was not going to think about it, I had succeeded in not doing so, and I did not want, especially just at bedtime, to be reminded of it.

"I don't know," said I, "and I don't really care so long as the picture of Mrs. Stone is not by my bed."

He got up.

"But it's odd," he said. "Ha! Now you'll see another odd thing."

A dog of his, an Irish terrier by breed, had come out of the house as we talked. The door behind us into the hall was open, and a bright oblong of light shone across the lawn to the iron gate which led on to the rough grass outside, where the walnut tree stood. I saw that the dog had all his hackles up, bristling with rage and fright; his lips were curled back from his teeth, as if he was ready to spring at something, and he was growling to himself. He took not the slightest notice of his master or me, but stiffly and tensely walked across the grass to the iron gate. There he stood for a moment, looking through the bars and still growling. Then of a sudden his courage seemed to desert him: he gave one long howl, and scuttled back to the house with a curious crouching sort of movement.

"He does that half-a-dozen times a day." said John. "He sees something which he both hates and fears."

I walked to the gate and looked over it. Something was moving on the grass outside, and soon a sound which I could not instantly identify came to my ears. Then I remembered what it was: it was the purring of a cat. I lit a match, and saw the purrer, a big blue Persian, walking round and round in a little circle just outside the gate, stepping high and ecstatically, with tail carried aloft like a banner. Its eyes were bright and shining, and every now and then it put its head down and sniffed at the grass.

I laughed.

"The end of that mystery, I am afraid." I said. "Here's a large cat having Walpurgis night all alone."

"Yes, that's Darius," said John. "He spends half the day and all night there. But that's not the end of the dog mystery, for Toby and he are the best of friends, but the beginning of the cat mystery. What's the cat doing there? And why is Darius pleased, while Toby is terror-stricken?"

At that moment I remembered the rather horrible detail of my dreams when I saw through the gate, just where the cat was now, the white tombstone with the sinister inscription. But before I could answer the rain began, as suddenly and heavily as if a tap had been turned on, and simultaneously the big cat squeezed through the bars of the gate, and came leaping across the lawn to the house for shelter. Then it sat in the doorway, looking out eagerly into the dark. It spat and struck at John with its paw, as he pushed it in, in order to close the door.

Somehow, with the portrait of Julia Stone in the passage outside, the room in the tower had absolutely no alarm for me, and as I went to bed, feeling very sleepy and heavy, I had nothing more than interest for the curious incident about our bleeding hands, and the conduct of the cat and dog. The last thing I looked at before I put out my light was the square empty space by my bed where the portrait had been. Here the paper was of its original full tint of dark red: over the rest of the walls it had faded. Then I blew out my candle and instantly fell asleep.

My awaking was equally instantaneous, and I sat bolt upright in bed under the impression that some bright light had been flashed in my face, though it was now absolutely pitch dark. I knew exactly where I was, in the room which I had dreaded in dreams, but no horror that I ever felt when asleep approached the fear that now invaded and froze my brain. Immediately after a peal of thunder crackled just above the house, but the probability that it was only a flash of lightning which awoke me gave no reassurance to my galloping heart. Something I knew was in the room with me, and instinctively I put out my right hand, which was nearest the wall, to keep it away. And my hand touched the edge of a picture-frame hanging close to me.

I sprang out of bed, upsetting the small table that stood by it, and I heard my watch, candle, and matches clatter onto the floor. But for the moment there was no need of light, for a blinding flash leaped out of the clouds, and showed me that by my bed again hung the picture of Mrs. Stone. And instantly the room went into blackness again. But in that flash I saw another thing also, namely a figure that leaned over the end of my bed, watching me. It was dressed in some close-clinging white garment, spotted and stained with mould, and the face was that of the portrait.

Overhead the thunder cracked and roared, and when it ceased and the deathly stillness succeeded, I heard the rustle of movement coming nearer me, and, more horrible yet, perceived an odour of corruption and decay. And then a hand was laid on the side of my neck, and close beside my ear I heard quick-taken, eager breathing. Yet I knew that this thing, though it could be perceived by touch, by smell, by eye and by ear, was still not of this earth, but something that had passed out of the body and had power to make itself manifest. Then a voice, already familiar to me, spoke.

"I knew you would come to the room in the tower," it said. "I have been long waiting for you. At last you have come. Tonight I shall feast; before long we will feast together."

And the quick breathing came closer to me; I could feel it on my neck.

At that the terror, which I think had paralyzed me for the moment, gave way to the wild instinct of self-preservation. I hit wildly with both arms, kicking out at the same moment, and heard a little animal-squeal, and something soft dropped with a thud beside me. I took a couple of steps forward, nearly tripping up over whatever it was that lay there, and by the merest good luck found the handle of the door. In another second I ran out on the landing, and had banged the door behind me. Almost at the same moment I heard a door open somewhere below, and John Clinton, candle in hand, came running upstairs.

"What is it?" he said. "I sleep just below you, and heard a noise as if – Good heavens, there's blood on your shoulder."

I stood there, so he told me afterwards, swaying from side to side, white as a sheet, with the mark on my shoulder as if a hand covered with blood had been laid there.

"It's in there," I said, pointing. "She, you know. The portrait is in there, too, hanging up on the place we took it from."

At that he laughed.

"My dear fellow, this is mere nightmare," he said.

He pushed by me, and opened the door, I standing there simply inert with terror, unable to stop him, unable to move.

"Phew! What an awful smell," he said.

Then there was silence; he had passed out of my sight behind the open door. Next moment he came out again, as white as myself, and instantly shut it.

"Yes, the portrait's there," he said, "and on the floor is a thing – a thing spotted with earth, like what they bury people in. Come away, quick, come away."

How I got downstairs I hardly know. An awful shuddering and nausea of the spirit rather than of the flesh had seized me, and more than once he had to place my feet upon the steps, while every now and then he cast glances of terror and apprehension up the stairs. But in time we came to his dressing-room on the floor below, and there I told him what I have here described.

The sequel can be made short; indeed, some of my readers have perhaps already guessed what it was, if they remember that inexplicable affair of the churchyard at West Fawley, some eight years ago, where an attempt was made three times to bury the body of a certain woman who had committed suicide. On each occasion the coffin was found in the course of a few days again protruding from the ground. After the third attempt, in order that the thing should not be talked about, the body was buried elsewhere in unconsecrated ground. Where it was buried was just outside the iron gate of the garden belonging to the house where this woman had lived. She had committed suicide in a room at the top of the tower in that house. Her name was Julia Stone.

Subsequently the body was again secretly dug up, and the coffin was found to be full of blood.

The Spook House

Ambrose Bierce

ON THE ROAD leading north from Manchester, in eastern Kentucky, to Booneville, twenty miles away, stood, in 1862, a wooden plantation house of a somewhat better quality than most of the dwellings in that region. The house was destroyed by fire in the year following – probably by some stragglers from the retreating column of General George W. Morgan, when he was driven from Cumberland Gap to the Ohio river by General Kirby Smith. At the time of its destruction, it had for four or five years been vacant. The fields about it were overgrown with brambles, the fences gone, even the few negro quarters, and out-houses generally, fallen partly into ruin by neglect and pillage; for the negroes and poor whites of the vicinity found in the building and fences an abundant supply of fuel, of which they availed themselves without hesitation, openly and by daylight. By daylight alone; after nightfall no human being except passing strangers ever went near the place.

It was known as the 'Spook House'. That it was tenanted by evil spirits, visible, audible and active, no one in all that region doubted any more than he doubted what he was told of Sundays by the traveling preacher. Its owner's opinion of the matter was unknown; he and his family had disappeared one night and no trace of them had ever been found. They left everything – household goods, clothing, provisions, the horses in the stable, the cows in the field, the negroes in the quarters – all as it stood; nothing was missing – except a man, a woman, three girls, a boy and a babe! It was not altogether surprising that a plantation where seven human beings could be simultaneously effaced and nobody the wiser should be under some suspicion.

One night in June, 1859, two citizens of Frankfort, Col. J. C. McArdle, a lawyer, and Judge Myron Veigh, of the State Militia, were driving from Booneville to Manchester. Their business was so important that they decided to push on, despite the darkness and the mutterings of an approaching storm, which eventually broke upon them just as they arrived opposite the 'Spook House'. The lightning was so incessant that they easily found their way through the gateway and into a shed, where they hitched and unharnessed their team. They then went to the house, through the rain, and knocked at all the doors without getting any response. Attributing this to the continuous uproar of the thunder they pushed at one of the doors, which yielded. They entered without further ceremony and closed the door. That instant they were in darkness and silence. Not a gleam of the lightning's unceasing blaze penetrated the windows or crevices; not a whisper of the awful tumult without reached them there. It was as if they had suddenly been stricken blind and deaf, and McArdle afterward said that for a moment he believed himself to have been killed by a stroke of lightning as he crossed the threshold. The rest of this adventure can as well be related in his own words, from the Frankfort Advocate of August 6, 1876:

"When I had somewhat recovered from the dazing effect of the transition from uproar to silence, my first impulse was to reopen the door which I had closed, and from the knob of which I was not conscious of having removed my hand; I felt it distinctly, still in the clasp of my fingers. My notion was to ascertain by stepping again into the storm whether I had been deprived of sight and hearing. I turned the doorknob and pulled open the door. It led into another room!

"This apartment was suffused with a faint greenish light, the source of which I could not determine, making everything distinctly visible, though nothing was sharply defined. Everything, I say, but in truth the only objects within the blank stone walls of that room were human corpses. In number they were perhaps eight or ten – it may well be understood that I did not truly count them. They were of different ages, or rather sizes, from infancy up, and of both sexes. All were prostrate on the floor, excepting one, apparently a young woman, who sat up, her back supported by an angle of the wall. A babe was clasped in the arms of another and older woman. A half-grown lad lay face downward across the legs of a full-bearded man. One or two were nearly naked, and the hand of a young girl held the fragment of a gown which she had torn open at the breast. The bodies were in various stages of decay, all greatly shrunken in face and figure. Some were but little more than skeletons.

"While I stood stupefied with horror by this ghastly spectacle and still holding open the door, by some unaccountable perversity my attention was diverted from the shocking scene and concerned itself with trifles and details. Perhaps my mind, with an instinct of self-preservation, sought relief in matters which would relax its dangerous tension. Among other things, I observed that the door that I was holding open was of heavy iron plates, riveted. Equidistant from one another and from the top and bottom, three strong bolts protruded from the beveled edge. I turned the knob and they were retracted flush with the edge; released it, and they shot out. It was a spring lock. On the inside there was no knob, nor any kind of projection – a smooth surface of iron.

"While noting these things with an interest and attention which it now astonishes me to recall I felt myself thrust aside, and Judge Veigh, whom in the intensity and vicissitudes of my feelings I had altogether forgotten, pushed by me into the room. 'For God's sake,' I cried, 'do not go in there! Let us get out of this dreadful place!'

"He gave no heed to my entreaties, but (as fearless a gentleman as lived in all the South) walked quickly to the center of the room, knelt beside one of the bodies for a closer examination and tenderly raised its blackened and shriveled head in his hands. A strong disagreeable odor came through the doorway, completely overpowering me. My senses reeled; I felt myself falling, and in clutching at the edge of the door for support pushed it shut with a sharp click!

"I remember no more: six weeks later I recovered my reason in a hotel at Manchester, whither I had been taken by strangers the next day. For all these weeks I had suffered from a nervous fever, attended with constant delirium. I had been found lying in the road several miles away from the house; but how I had escaped from it to get there I never knew. On recovery, or as soon as my physicians permitted me to talk, I inquired the fate of Judge Veigh, whom (to quiet me, as I now know) they represented as well and at home.

"No one believed a word of my story, and who can wonder? And who can imagine my grief when, arriving at my home in Frankfort two months later, I learned that Judge Veigh had never been heard of since that night? I then regretted bitterly the pride which since the first few days after the recovery of my reason had forbidden me to repeat my discredited story and insist upon its truth.

"With all that afterward occurred – the examination of the house; the failure to find any room corresponding to that which I have described; the attempt to have me adjudged insane, and my triumph over my accusers – the readers of the Advocate are familiar. After all these years I am still confident that excavations which I have neither the legal right to undertake nor the wealth to make would disclose the secret of the disappearance of my unhappy friend, and possibly of the former occupants and owners of the deserted and now destroyed house. I do not despair of yet bringing about such a search, and it is a source of deep grief to me that it has been delayed by the undeserved hostility and unwise incredulity of the family and friends of the late Judge Veigh."

Colonel McArdle died in Frankfort on the thirteenth day of December, in the year 1879.

The Shadow in the Corner

Mary Elizabeth Braddon

WILDHEATH GRANGE stood a little way back from the road, with a barren stretch of heath behind it, and a few tall fir-trees, with straggling wind-tossed heads, for its only shelter. It was a lonely house on a lonely road, little better than a lane, leading across a desolate waste of sandy fields to the sea-shore; and it was a house that bore a bad name among the natives of the village of Holcroft, which was the nearest place where humanity might be found.

It was a good old house, nevertheless, substantially built in the days when there was no stint of stone and timber – a good old grey stone house with many gables, deep window-seats, and a wide staircase, long dark passages, hidden doors in queer corners, closets as large as some modern rooms, and cellars in which a company of soldiers might have lain perdu.

This spacious old mansion was given over to rats and mice, loneliness, echoes, and the occupation of three elderly people: Michael Bascom, whose forebears had been landowners of importance in the neighbourhood, and his two servants, Daniel Skegg and his wife, who had served the owner of that grim old house ever since he left the university, where he had lived fifteen years of his life – five as student, and ten as professor of natural science.

At three-and-thirty Michael Bascom had seemed a middle-aged man; at fifty-six he looked and moved and spoke like an old man. During that interval of twenty-three years he had lived alone in Wildheath Grange, and the country people told each other that the house had made him what he was. This was a fanciful and superstitious notion on their part, doubtless, yet it would not have been difficult to have traced a certain affinity between the dull grey building and the man who lived in it. Both seemed alike remote from the common cares and interests of humanity; both had an air of settled melancholy, engendered by perpetual solitude; both had the same faded complexion, the same look of slow decay.

Yet lonely as Michael Bascom's life was at Wildheath Grange, he would not on any account have altered its tenor. He had been glad to exchange the comparative seclusion of college rooms for the unbroken solitude of Wildheath. He was a fanatic in his love of scientific research, and his quiet days were filled to the brim with labours that seldom failed to interest and satisfy him. There were periods of depression, occasional moments of doubt, when the goal towards which he strove seemed unattainable, and his spirit fainted within him. Happily such times were rare with him. He had a dogged power of continuity which ought to have carried him to the highest pinnacle of achievement, and which perhaps might ultimately have won for him a grand name and a world-wide renown, but for a catastrophe which burdened the declining years of his harmless life with an unconquerable remorse.

One autumn morning – when he had lived just three-and-twenty years at Wildheath, and had only lately begun to perceive that his faithful butler and body servant, who was middle-aged when he first employed him, was actually getting old – Mr. Bascom's breakfast meditations over the latest treatise on the atomic theory were interrupted by an abrupt demand from that very Daniel Skegg. The man was accustomed to wait upon his master in the most absolute silence, and his sudden breaking out into speech was almost as startling as if the bust of Socrates above the bookcase had burst into human language.

"It's no use," said Daniel; "my missus must have a girl!"

"A what?" demanded Mr. Bascom, without taking his eyes from the line he had been reading.

"A girl – a girl to trot about and wash up, and help the old lady. She's getting weak on her legs, poor soul. We've none of us grown younger in the last twenty years."

"Twenty years!" echoed Michael Bascom scornfully. "What is twenty years in the formation of a strata – what even in the growth of an oak – the cooling of a volcano!"

"Not much, perhaps, but it's apt to tell upon the bones of a human being."

"The manganese staining to be seen upon some skulls would certainly indicate—" began the scientist dreamily.

"I wish my bones were only as free from rheumatics as they were twenty years ago," pursued Daniel testily; "and then, perhaps, I should make light of twenty years. Howsoever, the long and the short of it is, my missus must have a girl. She can't go on trotting up and down these everlasting passages, and standing in that stone scullery year after year, just as if she was a young woman. She must have a girl to help."

"Let her have twenty girls," said Mr. Bascom, going back to his book.

"What's the use of talking like that, sir. Twenty girls, indeed! We shall have rare work to get one."

"Because the neighbourhood is sparsely populated?" interrogated Mr. Bascom, still reading.

"No, sir. Because this house is known to be haunted."

Michael Bascom laid down his book, and turned a look of grave reproach upon his servant.

"Skegg," he said in a severe voice, "I thought you had lived long enough with me to be superior to any folly of that kind."

"I don't say that I believe in ghosts," answered Daniel with a semi-apologetic air; "but the country people do. There's not a mortal among 'em that will venture across our threshold after nightfall."

"Merely because Anthony Bascom, who led a wild life in London, and lost his money and land, came home here broken-hearted, and is supposed to have destroyed himself in this house – the only remnant of property that was left him out of a fine estate."

"Supposed to have destroyed himself!" cried Skegg; "Why the fact is as well known as the death of Queen Elizabeth, or the great fire of London. Why, wasn't he buried at the cross-roads between here and Holcroft?"

"An idle tradition, for which you could produce no substantial proof," retorted Mr. Bascom.

"I don't know about proof; but the country people believe it as firmly as they believe their Gospel."

"If their faith in the Gospel was a little stronger they need not trouble themselves about Anthony Bascom."

"Well," grumbled Daniel, as he began to clear the table, "a girl of some kind we must get, but she'll have to be a foreigner, or a girl that's hard driven for a place."

When Daniel Skegg said a foreigner, he did not mean the native of some distant clime, but a girl who had not been born and bred at Holcroft. Daniel had been raised and reared in that insignificant hamlet, and, small and dull as it was, he considered the world beyond it only margin.

Michael Bascom was too deep in the atomic theory to give a second thought to the necessities of an old servant. Mrs. Skegg was an individual with whom he rarely came in contact. She lived for the most part in a gloomy region at the north end of the house, where she ruled over the solitude of a kitchen, that looked like a cathedral, and numerous offices of the sculler, larder, and pantry class, where she carried on a perpetual warfare with spiders and beetles, and wore her old life out in the labour of sweeping and scrubbing. She was a woman of severe aspect, dogmatic piety, and a bitter tongue. She was a good plain cook, and ministered diligently to her master's wants. He was not an epicure, but liked his life to be smooth and easy, and the equilibrium of his mental power would have been disturbed by a bad dinner.

He heard no more about the proposed addition to his household for a space of ten days, when Daniel Skegg again startled him amidst his studious repose by the abrupt announcement:

"I've got a girl!"

"Oh," said Michael Bascom; "have you?" and he went on with his book.

This time he was reading an essay on phosphorus and its functions in relation to the human brain.

"Yes," pursued Daniel in his usual grumbling tone; "she was a waif and stray, or I shouldn't have got her. If she'd been a native she'd never have come to us."

"I hope she's respectable," said Michael.

"Respectable! That's the only fault she has, poor thing. She's too good for the place. She's never been in service before, but she says she's willing to work, and I daresay my old woman will be able to break her in. Her father was a small tradesman at Yarmouth. He died a month ago, and left this poor thing homeless. Mrs. Midge, at Holcroft, is her aunt, and she said to the girl, Come and stay with me till you get a place; and the girl has been staying with Mrs. Midge for the last three weeks, trying to hear of a place. When Mrs. Midge heard that my missus wanted a girl to help, she thought it would be the very thing for her niece Maria. Luckily Maria had heard nothing about this house, so the poor innocent dropped me a curtsey, and said she'd be thankful to come, and would do her best to learn her duty. She'd had an easy time of it with her father, who had educated her above her station, like a fool as he was," growled Daniel.

"By your own account I'm afraid you've made a bad bargain," said Michael. "You don't want a young lady to clean kettles and pans."

"If she was a young duchess my old woman would make her work," retorted Skegg decisively.

"And pray where are you going to put this girl?" asked Mr. Bascom, rather irritably; "I can't have a strange young woman tramping up and down the passages outside my room. You know what a wretched sleeper I am, Skegg. A mouse behind the wainscot is enough to wake me."

"I've thought of that," answered the butler, with his look of ineffable wisdom. "I'm not going to put her on your floor. She's to sleep in the attics."

"Which room?"

"The big one at the north end of the house. That's the only ceiling that doesn't let water. She might as well sleep in a shower-bath as in any of the other attics."

"The room at the north end," repeated Mr. Bascom thoughtfully; "isn't that—?"

"Of course it is," snapped Skegg; "but she doesn't know anything about it."

Mr. Bascom went back to his books, and forgot all about the orphan from Yarmouth, until one morning on entering his study he was startled by the appearance of a strange girl, in a neat black and white cotton gown, busy dusting the volumes which were stacked in blocks upon his spacious writing table – and doing it with such deft and careful hands that he had no inclination to be angry at this unwonted liberty. Old Mrs. Skegg had religiously refrained from all such dusting, on the plea that she did not wish to interfere with the master's ways. One of the master's ways, therefore, had been to inhale a good deal of dust in the course of his studies.

The girl was a slim little thing, with a pale and somewhat old-fashioned face, flaxen hair, braided under a neat muslin cap, a very fair complexion, and light blue eyes. They were the lightest blue eyes Michael Bascom had ever seen, but there was a sweetness and gentleness in their expression which atoned for their insipid colour.

"I hope you do not object to my dusting your books, sir," she said, dropping a curtsey.

She spoke with a quaint precision which struck Michael Bascom as a pretty thing in its way.

"No; I don't object to cleanliness, so long as my books and papers are not disturbed. If you take a volume off my desk, replace it on the spot you took it from. That's all I ask."

"I will be very careful, sir."

"When did you come here?"

"Only this morning, sir."

The student seated himself at his desk, and the girl withdrew, drifting out of the room as noiselessly as a flower blown across the threshold. Michael Bascom looked after her curiously. He had seen very little of youthful womanhood in his dry-as-dust career, and he wondered at this girl as at a creature of a species hitherto unknown to him. How fairly and delicately she was fashioned; what a translucent skin; what soft and pleasing accents issued from those rose-tinted lips. A pretty thing, assuredly, this kitchen wench! A pity that in all this busy world there could be no better work found for her than the scouring of pots and pans.

Absorbed in considerations about dry bones, Mr. Bascom thought no more of the pale-faced handmaiden. He saw her no more about his rooms. Whatever work she did there was done early in the morning, before the scholar's breakfast.

She had been a week in the house, when he met her one day in the hall. He was struck by the change in her appearance.

The girlish lips had lost their rose-bud hue; the pale blue eyes had a frightened look, and there were dark rings round them, as in one whose nights had been sleepless, or troubled by evil dreams.

Michael Bascom was so startled by an undefinable look in the girl's face that, reserved as he was by habit and nature, he expanded so far as to ask her what ailed her.

"There is something amiss, I am sure," he said. "What is it?"

"Nothing, sir," she faltered, looking still more scared at his question. "Indeed, it is nothing; or nothing worth troubling you about."

"Nonsense. Do you suppose, because I live among books, I have no sympathy with my fellow-creatures? Tell me what is wrong with you, child. You have been grieving about the father you have lately lost, I suppose."

"No, sir; it is not that. I shall never leave off being sorry for that. It is a grief which will last me all my life."

"What, there is something else then?" asked Michael impatiently. "I see; you are not happy here. Hard work does not suit you. I thought as much."

"Oh, sir, please don't think that," cried the girl, very earnestly. "Indeed, I am glad to work – glad to be in service; it is only —"

She faltered and broke down, the tears rolling slowly from her sorrowful eyes, despite her effort to keep them back.

"Only what?" cried Michael, growing angry. "The girl is full of secrets and mysteries. What do you mean, wench?"

"I – I know it is very foolish, sir; but I am afraid of the room where I sleep."

"Afraid! Why?"

"Shall I tell you the truth, sir? Will you promise not to be angry?"

"I will not be angry if you will only speak plainly; but you provoke me by these hesitations and suppressions."

"And please, sir, do not tell Mrs. Skegg that I have told you. She would scold me; or perhaps even send me away."

"Mrs. Skegg shall not scold you. Go on, child."

"You may not know the room where I sleep, sir; it is a large room at one end of the house, looking towards the sea. I can see the dark line of water from the window, and I wonder sometimes to think that it is the same ocean I used to see when I was a child at Yarmouth. It is very lonely, sir, at the top of the house. Mr. and Mrs. Skegg sleep in a little room near the kitchen, you know, sir, and I am quite alone on the top floor."

"Skegg told me you had been educated in advance of your position in life, Maria. I should have thought the first effect of a good education would have been to make you superior to any foolish fancies about empty rooms."

"Oh, pray, sir, do not think it is any fault in my education. Father took such pains with me; he spared no expense in giving me as good an education as a tradesman's daughter need wish for. And he was a religious man, sir. He did not believe" – here she paused, with a suppressed shudder – "in the spirits of the dead appearing to the living, since the days of miracles, when the ghost of Samuel appeared to Saul. He never put any foolish ideas into my head, sir. I hadn't a thought of fear when I first lay down to rest in the big lonely room upstairs."

"Well, what then?"

"But on the very first night," the girl went on breathlessly, "I felt weighed down in my sleep as if there were some heavy burden laid upon my chest. It was not a bad dream, but it was a sense of trouble that followed me all through my sleep; and just at daybreak – it begins to be light a little after six – I woke suddenly, with the cold perspiration pouring down my face, and knew that there was something dreadful in the room."

"What do you mean by something dreadful. Did you see anything?"

"Not much, sir; but it froze the blood in my veins, and I knew it was this that had been following me and weighing upon me all through my sleep. In the corner, between the fire-place and the wardrobe, I saw a shadow – a dim, shapeless shadow—"

"Produced by an angle of the wardrobe, I daresay."

"No, sir; I could see the shadow of the wardrobe, distinct and sharp, as if it had been painted on the wall. This shadow was in the corner – a strange, shapeless mass; or, if it had any shape at all, it seemed—"

"What?" asked Michael eagerly.

"The shape of a dead body hanging against the wall!"

Michael Bascom grew strangely pale, yet he affected utter incredulity.

"Poor child," he said kindly; "you have been fretting about your father until your nerves are in a weak state, and you are full of fancies. A shadow in the corner, indeed; why, at daybreak, every corner is full of shadows. My old coat, flung upon a chair, will make you as good a ghost as you need care to see."

"Oh, sir, I have tried to think it is my fancy. But I have had the same burden weighing me down every night. I have seen the same shadow every morning."

"But when broad daylight comes, can you not see what stuff your shadow is made of?"

"No, sir: the shadow goes before it is broad daylight."

"Of course, just like other shadows. Come, come, get these silly notions out of your head, or you will never do for the work-a-day world. I could easily speak to Mrs. Skegg, and make her give you another room, if I wanted to encourage you in your folly. But that would be about the worst thing I could do for you. Besides, she tells me that all the other rooms on that floor are damp; and, no doubt, if she shifted you into one of them, you would discover another shadow in another corner, and get rheumatism into the bargain. No, my good girl, you must try to prove yourself the better for a superior education."

"I will do my best, sir," Maria answered meekly, dropping a curtsey.

Maria went back to the kitchen sorely depressed. It was a dreary life she led at Wildheath Grange – dreary by day, awful by night; for the vague burden and the shapeless shadow, which seemed so slight a matter to the elderly scholar, were unspeakably terrible to her. Nobody had told her that the house was haunted, yet she walked about those echoing passages wrapped round with a cloud of fear. She had no pity from Daniel Skegg and his wife. Those two pious souls had made up their minds that the character of the house should be upheld, so far as Maria went. To her, as a foreigner, the Grange should be maintained to be an immaculate dwelling, tainted by no sulphurous blast from the underworld. A willing, biddable girl had become a necessary element in the existence of Mrs. Skegg. That girl had been found, and that girl must be kept. Any fancies of a supernatural character must be put down with a high hand.

"Ghosts, indeed!" cried the amiable Skegg. "Read your Bible, Maria, and don't talk no more about ghosts."

"There are ghosts in the Bible," said Maria, with a shiver at the recollection of certain awful passages in the Scripture she knew so well.

"Ah, they was in their right place, or they wouldn't ha' been there," retorted Mrs. Skegg. "You ain't agoin' to pick holes in your Bible, I hope, Maria, at your time of life."

Maria sat down quietly in her corner by the kitchen fire, and turned over the leaves of her dead father's Bible till she came to the chapters they two had loved best and oftenest read together. He had been a simple-minded, straightforward man, the Yarmouth cabinet-maker – a man full of aspirations after good, innately refined, instinctively religious. He and his motherless girl had spent their lives alone together, in the neat little home which Maria had so soon learnt to cherish and beautify; and they had loved each other with an almost romantic love. They had had the same tastes, the same ideas. Very little had sufficed to make them happy. But inexorable death parted father and daughter, in one of those sharp, sudden partings which are like the shock of an earthquake – instantaneous ruin, desolation, and despair.

Maria's fragile form had bent before the tempest. She had lived through a trouble that might have crushed a stronger nature. Her deep religious convictions, and her belief that this cruel parting would not be for ever, had sustained her. She faced life, and its cares and duties, with a gentle patience which was the noblest form of courage.

Michael Bascom told himself that the servant-girl's foolish fancy about the room that had been given her was not a matter of serious consideration. Yet the idea dwelt in his mind unpleasantly, and disturbed him at his labours. The exact sciences require the complete power of a man's brain, his utmost attention; and on this particular evening Michael found that he was only giving his work a part of his attention. The girl's pale face, the girl's tremulous tones, thrust themselves into the foreground of his thoughts.

He closed his book with a fretful sigh, wheeled his large arm-chair round to the fire, and gave himself up to contemplation. To attempt study with so disturbed a mind was useless. It was a dull grey evening, early in November; the student's reading-lamp was lighted, but the shutters were not yet shut, nor the curtains drawn. He could see the leaden sky outside his windows, the fir-tree tops tossing in the angry wind. He could hear the wintry blast whistling amidst the gables, before it rushed off seaward with a savage howl that sounded like a war-whoop.

Michael Bascom shivered, and drew nearer the fire.

"It's childish, foolish nonsense," he said to himself, "yet it's strange she should have that fancy about the shadow, for they say Anthony Bascom destroyed himself in that room. I remember hearing it when I was a boy, from an old servant whose mother was housekeeper at the great house in Anthony's time. I never heard how he died, poor fellow – whether he poisoned himself, or shot himself, or cut his throat; but I've been told that was the room. Old Skegg has heard it too. I could see that by his manner when he told me the girl was to sleep there."

He sat for a long time, till the grey of evening outside his study windows changed to the black of night, and the war-whoop of the wind died away to a low complaining murmur. He sat looking into the fire, and letting his thoughts wander back to the past and the traditions he had heard in his boyhood.

That was a sad, foolish story of his great-uncle, Anthony Bascom: the pitiful story of a wasted fortune and a wasted life. A riotous collegiate career at Cambridge, a racing-stable at Newmarket, an imprudent marriage, a dissipated life in London, a runaway wife; an estate forfeited to Jew money-lenders, and then the fatal end.

Michael had often heard that dismal story: how, when Anthony Bascom's fair false wife had left him, when his credit was exhausted, and his friends had grown tired of him, and all was gone except Wildheath Grange, Anthony, the broken-down man of fashion, had come to that lonely house unexpectedly one night, and had ordered his bed to be got ready for him in the room where he used to sleep when he came to the place for the wild duck shooting, in his boyhood. His old blunderbuss was still hanging over the mantelpiece, where he had left it when he came into the property, and could afford to buy the newest thing in fowling-pieces. He had not been to Wildheath for fifteen years; nay, for a good many of those years he had almost forgotten that the drear old house belonged to him.

The woman who had been housekeeper at Bascom Park, till house and lands had passed into the hands of the Jews, was at this time the sole occupant of Wildheath. She cooked some supper for her master, and made him as comfortable as she could in the long untenanted dining-room; but she was distressed to find, when she cleared the table after he had gone upstairs to bed, that he had eaten hardly anything.

Next morning she got his breakfast ready in the same room, which she managed to make brighter and cheerier than it had looked overnight. Brooms, dusting-brushes, and a good fire did much to improve the aspect of things. But the morning wore on to noon, and the old housekeeper listened in vain for her master's footfall on the stairs. Noon waned to late afternoon. She had made no attempt to disturb him, thinking that he had worn himself out by a tedious journey on horseback, and that he was sleeping the sleep of exhaustion. But when the brief November day clouded with the first shadows of twilight, the old woman grew seriously alarmed, and went upstairs to her master's door, where she waited in vain for any reply to her repeated calls and knockings.

The door was locked on the inside, and the housekeeper was not strong enough to break it open. She rushed downstairs again full of fear, and ran bare-headed out into the lonely road. There was no habitation nearer than the turnpike on the old coach road, from which this side road branched off to the sea. There was scanty hope of a chance passer-by. The old woman ran along the road, hardly knowing whither she was going or what she was going to do, but with a vague idea that she must get somebody to help her.

Chance favoured her. A cart, laden with sea-weed, came lumbering slowly along from the level line of sands yonder where the land melted into water. A heavy lumbering farm-labourer walked beside the cart.

"For God's sake, come in and burst open my master's door!" she entreated, seizing the man by the arm. "He's lying dead, or in a fit, and I can't get to help him."

"All right, missus," answered the man, as if such an invitation were a matter of daily occurrence. "Whoa, Dobbin; stond still, horse, and be donged to thee."

Dobbin was glad enough to be brought to anchor on the patch of waste grass in front of the Grange garden. His master followed the housekeeper upstairs, and shattered the old-fashioned box-lock with one blow of his ponderous fist.

The old woman's worst fear was realised. Anthony Bascom was dead. But the mode and manner of his death Michael had never been able to learn. The housekeeper's daughter, who told him the story, was an old woman when he was a boy. She had only shaken her head, and looked unutterable things, when he questioned her too closely. She had never even admitted that the old squire had committed suicide. Yet the tradition of his self-destruction was rooted in the minds of the natives of Holcroft: and there was a settled belief that his ghost, at certain times and seasons, haunted Wildheath Grange.

Now Michael Bascom was a stern materialist. For him the universe with all its inhabitants was a great machine, governed by inexorable laws. To such a man the idea of a ghost was simply absurd – as absurd as the assertion that two and two make five, or that a circle can be formed of a straight line. Yet he had a kind of dilettante interest in the idea of a mind which could believe in ghosts. The subject offered an amusing psychological study. This poor little pale girl, now, had evidently got some supernatural terror into her head, which could only be conquered by rational treatment.

"I know what I ought to do," Michael Bascom said to himself suddenly. "I'll occupy that room myself tonight, and demonstrate to this foolish girl that her notion about the shadow is nothing more than a silly fancy, bred of timidity and low spirits. An ounce of proof is better than a pound of argument. If I can prove to her that I have spent a night in the room, and seen no such shadow, she will understand what an idle thing superstition is."

Daniel came in presently to shut the shutters.

"Tell your wife to make up my bed in the room where Maria has been sleeping, and to put her into one of the rooms on the first floor for tonight, Skegg," said Mr. Bascom.

"Sir?"

Mr. Bascom repeated his order.

"That silly wench has been complaining to you about her room," Skegg exclaimed indignantly. "She doesn't deserve to be well fed and cared for in a comfortable home. She ought to go to the workhouse."

"Don't be angry with the poor girl, Skegg. She has taken a foolish fancy into her head, and I want to show her how silly she is," said Mr. Bascom.

"And you want to sleep in his – in that room yourself," said the butler.

"Precisely."

"Well," mused Skegg, "if he does walk – which I don't believe – he was your own flesh and blood; and I don't suppose he'll do you any hurt."

When Daniel Skegg went back to the kitchen he railed mercilessly at poor Maria, who sat pale and silent in her corner by the hearth, darning old Mrs. Skegg's grey worsted stockings, which were the roughest and harshest armour that ever human foot clothed itself withal.

"Was there ever such a whimsical, fine, lady-like miss," demanded Daniel, "to come into a gentleman's house, and drive him out of his own bedroom to sleep in an attic, with her nonsenses and vagaries." If this was the result of being educated above one's station, Daniel declared that he was thankful he had never got so far in his schooling as to read words of two syllables without spelling. Education might be hanged for him, if this was all it led to.

"I am very sorry," faltered Maria, weeping silently over her work. "Indeed, Mr. Skegg, I made no complaint. My master questioned me, and I told him the truth. That was all."

"All!" exclaimed Mr. Skegg irately; "All, indeed! I should think it was enough."

Poor Maria held her peace. Her mind, fluttered by Daniel's unkindness, had wandered away from that bleak big kitchen to the lost home of the past – the snug little parlour where she and her father had sat beside the cosy hearth on such a night as this; she with her smart work-box and her plain sewing, he with the newspaper he loved to read; the petted cat purring on the rug, the kettle singing on the bright brass trivet, the tea-tray pleasantly suggestive of the most comfortable meal in the day.

Oh, those happy nights, that dear companionship! Were they really gone for ever, leaving nothing behind them but unkindness and servitude?

Michael Bascom retired later than usual that night. He was in the habit of sitting at his books long after every other lamp but his own had been extinguished. The Skeggs had subsided into silence and darkness in their drear ground-floor bed-chamber. Tonight his studies were of a peculiarly interesting kind, and belonged to the order of recreative reading rather than of hard work. He was deep in the history of that mysterious people who had their dwelling-place in the Swiss lakes, and was much exercised by certain speculations and theories about them.

The old eight-day clock on the stairs was striking two as Michael slowly ascended, candle in hand, to the hitherto unknown region of the attics. At the top of the staircase he found himself facing a dark narrow passage which led northwards, a passage that was in itself sufficient to strike terror to a superstitious mind, so black and uncanny did it look.

"Poor child," mused Mr. Bascom, thinking of Maria; "this attic floor is rather dreary, and for a young mind prone to fancies—"

He had opened the door of the north room by this time, and stood looking about him.

It was a large room, with a ceiling that sloped on one side, but was fairly lofty upon the other; an old-fashioned room, full of old-fashioned furniture – big, ponderous, clumsy – associated with a day that was gone and people that were dead. A walnut-wood wardrobe stared him in the face – a wardrobe with brass handles, which gleamed out of the darkness like diabolical eyes. There was a tall four-post bedstead, which had been cut down on one side to accommodate the slope of the ceiling, and which had a misshapen and deformed aspect in consequence. There was an old mahogany bureau that smelt of secrets. There were some heavy old chairs with rush bottoms, mouldy with age, and much worn. There was a corner washstand, with a big basin and a small jug – the odds and ends of past years. Carpet there was none, save a narrow strip beside the bed.

"It is a dismal room," mused Michael, with the same touch of pity for Maria's weakness which he had felt on the landing just now.

To him it mattered nothing where he slept; but having let himself down to a lower level by his interest in the Swiss lake-people, he was in a manner humanised by the lightness of his evening's reading, and was even inclined to compassionate the weaknesses of a foolish girl.

He went to bed, determined to sleep his soundest. The bed was comfortable, well supplied with blankets, rather luxurious than otherwise, and the scholar had that agreeable sense of fatigue which promises profound and restful slumber.

He dropped off to sleep quickly, but woke with a start ten minutes afterwards. What was this consciousness of a burden of care that had awakened him – this sense of all-pervading trouble that weighed upon his spirits and oppressed his heart – this icy horror of some terrible crisis in life through which he must inevitably pass? To him these feelings were as novel as they were painful. His life had flowed on with smooth and sluggish tide, unbroken by so much as a ripple of sorrow. Yet tonight he felt all the pangs of unavailing remorse; the agonising memory of a life wasted; the stings of humiliation and disgrace, shame, ruin; a hideous death, which he had doomed himself to die by his own hand. These were the horrors that pressed him round and weighed him down as he lay in Anthony Bascom's room.

Yes, even he, the man who could recognise nothing in nature, or in nature's God, better or higher than an irresponsible and invariable machine governed by mechanical laws, was fain to admit that here he found himself face to face with a psychological mystery. This trouble, which came between him and sleep, was the trouble that had pursued Anthony Bascom on the last night of his life. So had the suicide felt as he lay in that lonely room, perhaps striving to rest his wearied brain with one last earthly sleep before he passed to the unknown intermediate land where all is darkness and slumber. And that troubled mind had haunted the room ever since. It was not the ghost of the man's body that returned to the spot where he had suffered and perished, but the ghost of his mind – his very self; no meaningless simulacrum of the clothes he were, and the figure that filled them.

Michael Bascom was not the man to abandon his high ground of sceptical philosophy without a struggle. He tried his hardest to conquer this oppression that weighed upon mind and sense. Again and again he succeeded in composing himself to sleep, but only to wake again and again to the same torturing thoughts, the same remorse, the same despair. So the night passed in unutterable weariness; for though he told himself that the trouble was not his trouble, that there was no reality in the burden, no reason for the remorse, these vivid fancies were as painful as realities, and took as strong a hold upon him.

The first streak of light crept in at the window – dim, and cold, and grey; then came twilight, and he looked at the corner between the wardrobe and the door.

Yes; there was the shadow: not the shadow of the wardrobe only – that was clear enough, but a vague and shapeless something which darkened the dull brown wall; so faint, so shadow, that he could form no conjecture as to its nature, or the thing it represented. He determined to watch this shadow till broad daylight; but the weariness of the night had exhausted him, and before the first dimness of dawn had passed away he had fallen fast asleep, and was tasting the blessed balm of undisturbed slumber. When he woke the winter sun was shining in at the lattice, and the room had lost its gloomy aspect. It looked old-fashioned, and grey, and brown, and shabby; but the depth of its gloom had fled with the shadows and the darkness of night.

Mr. Bascom rose refreshed by a sound sleep, which had lasted nearly three hours. He remembered the wretched feelings which had gone before that renovating slumber; but he recalled his strange sensations only to despise them, and he despised himself for having attached any importance to them.

"Indigestion very likely," he told himself; "or perhaps mere fancy, engendered of that foolish girl's story. The wisest of us is more under the dominion of imagination than he would care to confess. Well, Maria shall not sleep in this room any more. There is no particular reason why she should, and she shall not be made unhappy to please old Skegg and his wife."

When he had dressed himself in his usual leisurely way, Mr. Bascom walked up to the corner where he had seen or imagined the shadow, and examined the spot carefully.

At first sight he could discover nothing of a mysterious character. There was no door in the papered wall, no trace of a door that had been there in the past. There was no trap-door in the worm-eaten boards. There was no dark ineradicable stain to hint at murder. There was not the faintest suggestion of a secret or a mystery.

He looked up at the ceiling. That was sound enough, save for a dirty patch here and there where the rain had blistered it.

Yes; there was something – an insignificant thing, yet with a suggestion of grimness which startled him.

About a foot below the ceiling he saw a large iron hook projecting from the wall, just above the spot where he had seen the shadow of a vaguely defined form. He mounted on a chair the better to examine this hook, and to understand, if he could, the purpose for which it had been put there.

It was old and rusty. It must have been there for many years. Who could have placed it there, and why? It was not the kind of hook upon which one would hang a picture or one's garments. It was placed in an obscure corner. Had Anthony Bascom put it there on the night he died; or did he find it there ready for a fatal use?

"If I were a superstitious man," thought Michael, "I should be inclined to believe that Anthony Bascom hung himself from that rusty old hook."

"Sleep well, sir?" asked Daniel, as he waited upon his master at breakfast.

"Admirably," answered Michael, determined not to gratify the man's curiosity.

He had always resented the idea that Wildheath Grange was haunted.

"Oh, indeed, sir. You were so late that I fancied—"

"Late, yes! I slept so well that I overshot my usual hour for waking. But, by-the-way, Skegg, as that poor girl objects to the room, let her sleep somewhere else. It can't make any difference to us, and it may make some difference to her."

"Humph!" muttered Daniel in his grumpy way; "you didn't see anything queer up there, did you?"

"See anything? Of course not."

"Well, then, why should she see things? It's all her silly fiddle-faddle."

"Never mind, let her sleep in another room."

"There ain't another room on the top floor that's dry."

"Then let her sleep on the floor below. She creeps about quietly enough, poor little timid thing. She won't disturb me."

Daniel grunted, and his master understood the grunt to mean obedient assent; but here Mr. Bascom was unhappily mistaken. The proverbial obstinacy of the pig family is as nothing compared with the obstinacy of a cross-grained old man, whose narrow mind has never been illuminated by education. Daniel was beginning to feel jealous of his master's compassionate interest in the orphan girl. She was a sort of gentle clinging thing that might creep into an elderly bachelor's heart unawares, and make herself a comfortable nest there.

"We shall have fine carryings-on, and me and my old woman will be nowhere, if I don't put down my heel pretty strong upon this nonsense," Daniel muttered to himself, as he carried the breakfast-tray to the pantry.

Maria met him in the passage.

"Well, Mr. Skegg, what did my master say?" she asked breathlessly.

"Did he see anything strange in the room?"

"No, girl. What should he see? He said you were a fool."

"Nothing disturbed him? And he slept there peacefully?" faltered Maria.

"Never slept better in his life. Now don't you begin to feel ashamed of yourself?"

"Yes," she answered meekly; "I am ashamed of being so full of fancies. I will go back to my room tonight, Mr. Skegg, if you like, and I will never complain of it again."

"I hope you won't," snapped Skegg; "you've given us trouble enough already."

Maria sighed, and went about her work in saddest silence. The day wore slowly on, like all other days in that lifeless old house. The scholar sat in his study; Maria moved softly from room to room, sweeping and dusting in the cheerless solitude. The midday sun faded into the grey of afternoon, and evening came down like a blight upon the dull old house.

Throughout that day Maria and her master never met. Anyone who had been so far interested in the girl as to observe her appearance would have seen that she was unusually pale, and that her eyes had a resolute look, as of one who was resolved to face a painful ordeal. She ate hardly anything all day. She was curiously silent. Skegg and his wife put down both these symptoms to temper.

"She won't eat and she won't talk," said Daniel to the partner of his joys. "That means sulkiness, and I never allowed sulkiness to master me when I was a young man, and you tried it on as a young woman, and I'm not going to be conquered by sulkiness in my old age."

Bedtime came, and Maria bade the Skeggs a civil goodnight, and went up to her lonely garret without a murmur.

The next morning came, and Mrs. Skegg looked in vain for her patient hand-maiden, when she wanted Maria's services in preparing the breakfast.

"The wench sleeps sound enough this morning," said the old woman. "Go and call her, Daniel. My poor legs can't stand them stairs."

"Your poor legs are getting uncommon useless," muttered Daniel testily, as he went to do his wife's behest.

He knocked at the door, and called Maria – once, twice, thrice, many times; but there was no reply. He tried the door, and found it locked. He shook the door violently, cold with fear.

Then he told himself that the girl had played him a trick. She had stolen away before daybreak, and left the door locked to frighten him. But, no; this could not be, for he could see the key in the lock when he knelt down and put his eye to the keyhole. The key prevented his seeing into the room.

"She's in there, laughing in her sleeve at me," he told himself; "but I'll soon be even with her."

There was a heavy bar on the staircase, which was intended to secure the shutters of the window that lighted the stairs. It was a detached bar, and always stood in a corner near the window, which it was but rarely employed to fasten. Daniel ran down to the landing, and seized upon this massive iron bar, and then ran back to the garret door.

One blow from the heavy bar shattered the old lock, which was the same lock the carter had broken with his strong fist seventy years before. The door flew open, and Daniel went into the attic which he had chosen for the stranger's bed-chamber.

Maria was hanging from the hook in the wall. She had contrived to cover her face decently with her handkerchief. She had hanged herself deliberately about an hour before Daniel found her, in the early grey of morning. The doctor, who was summoned from Holcroft, was able to declare the time at which she had slain herself, but there was no one who could say what sudden access of terror had impelled her to the desperate act, or under what slow torture of nervous apprehension her mind had given way. The coroner's jury returned the customary merciful verdict of 'Temporary insanity'.

The girl's melancholy fate darkened the rest of Michael Bascom's life. He fled from Wildheath Grange as from an accursed spot, and from the Skeggs as from the murderers of a harmless innocent girl. He ended his days at Oxford, where he found the society of congenial minds, and the books he loved. But the memory of Maria's sad face, and sadder death, was his abiding sorrow. Out of that deep shadow his soul was never lifted.

The Truth, the Whole Truth, and Nothing but the Truth

Rhoda Broughton

Mrs. de Wynt to Mrs. Montresor
18, Eccleston Square, May 5th.

My dearest Cecilia,

Talk of the friendships of Orestes and Pylades, of Julie and Claire, what are they to ours? Did Pylades ever go ventre à terre, half over London on a day more broiling than any but an âine damnée could even imagine, in order that Orestes might be comfortably housed for the season?

Did Claire ever hold sweet converse with from fifty to one hundred house agents, in order that Julie might have three windows to her drawing-room and a pretty portière? You see I am determined not to be done out of my full meed of gratitude.

Well, my friend, I had no idea till yesterday how closely we were packed in this great smoky beehive, as tightly as herrings in a barrel. Don't be frightened, however. By dint of squeezing and crowding, we have managed to make room for two more herrings in our barrel, and those two are yourself and your other self, i.e. your husband. Let me begin at the beginning. After having looked over, I verily believe, every undesirable residence in West London; after having seen nothing intermediate between what was suited to the means of a duke, and what was suited to the needs of a chimney-sweep; after having felt bed-ticking, and explored kitchen-ranges till my brain reeled under my accumulated experience, I arrived at about half-past five yesterday afternoon at 32, —Street, May Fair.

"Failure No. 253, I don't doubt," I said to myself, as I toiled up the steps with my soul athirst for afternoon tea, and feeling as ill-tempered as you please. So much for my spirit of prophecy.

Fate, I have noticed, is often fond of contradicting us flat, and giving the lie to our little predictions. Once inside, I thought I had got into a small compartment of Heaven by mistake.

Fresh as a daisy, clean as a cherry, bright as a seraph's face, it is all these, and a hundred more, only that my limited stock of similes is exhausted. Two drawing-rooms as pretty as ever woman crammed with people she did not care two straws about; white curtains with rose-coloured ones underneath, festooned in the sweetest way; marvellously, immorally becoming, my dear, as I ascertained entirely for your benefit, in the mirrors, of which there are about a dozen and a half; Persian mats, easy chairs, and lounges suited to every possible physical conformation, from the Apollo Belvedere to Miss Biffin; and a thousand of the important little trivialities that make up the sum of a woman's life: peacock fans, Japanese screens, naked boys and décolletée shepherdesses; not to speak of a family of china pugs, with blue ribbons round their necks, which ought of themselves to have added fifty pounds a year to the rent. Apropos, I asked, in fear and trembling, what the rent might be – "Three hundred pounds a year". A feather would have knocked me down. I could hardly believe my ears, and made the woman repeat it several times, that there might be no mistake. To this hour it is a mystery to me.

With that suspiciousness which is so characteristic of you, you will immediately begin to hint that there must be some terrible unaccountable smell, or some odious inexplicable noise haunting the reception rooms. Nothing of the kind, the woman assured me, and she did not look as if she were telling stories. You will next suggest – remembering the rose-coloured curtains – that its last occupant was a member of the demimonde. Wrong again. Its last occupant was an elderly and unexceptionable Indian officer, without a liver, and with a most lawful wife. They did not stay long, it is true, but then, as the housekeeper told me, he was a deplorable old hypochondriac, who never could bear to stay a fortnight in any one place. So lay aside that scepticism, which is your besetting sin, and give unfeigned thanks to St Brigitta, or St Gengulpha, or St Catherine of Siena, or whoever is your tutelar saint, for having provided you with a palace at the cost of a hovel, and for having sent you such an invaluable friend as

Your attached,
Elizabeth de Wynt.

P.S. – I am so sorry I shall not be in town to witness your first raptures, but dear Artie looks so pale and thin and tall after the whooping-cough, that I am sending him off at once to the sea, and as I cannot bear the child out of my sight, I am going into banishment likewise.

Mrs. Montresor to Mrs. de Wynt
32, —Street, May Fair, May 14th.

Dearest Bessy,
Why did not dear little Artie defer his whooping-cough convalescence till August? It is very odd, to me, the perverse way in which children always fix upon the most inconvenient times and seasons for their diseases. Here we are installed in our Paradise, and have searched high and low, in every hole and corner, for the serpent, without succeeding in catching a glimpse of his spotted tail. Most things in this world are disappointing, but 32, —Street, May Fair, is not. The mystery of the rent is still a mystery. I have been for my first ride in the Row this morning; my horse was a little fidgety; I am half afraid that my nerve is not what it was. I saw heaps of people I knew. Do you recollect Florence Watson? What a wealth of red hair she had last year! Well, that same wealth is black as the raven's wing this year! I wonder how people can make such walking impositions of themselves, don't you? Adela comes to us next week; I am so glad. It is dull driving by oneself of an afternoon; and I always think that one young woman alone in a brougham, or with only a dog beside her, does not look good. We sent round our cards a fortnight before we came up, and have been already deluged with callers. Considering that we have been

two years exiled from civilised life, and that London memories are not generally of the longest, we shall do pretty well, I think. Ralph Gordon came to see me on Sunday; he is in the – the Hussars now. He has grown up such a dear fellow, and so good-looking! Just my style, large and fair and whiskerless! Most men nowadays make themselves as like monkeys, or Scotch terriers, as they possibly can. I intend to be quite a mother to him. Dresses are gored to as indecent an extent as ever; short skirts are rampant. I am sorry; I hate them. They make tall women look lank, and short ones insignificant. A knock! Peace is a word that might as well be expunged from one's London dictionary.

Yours affectionately,
Cecilia Montresor

Mrs. de Wynt to Mrs. Montresor
The Lord Warden, Dover, May 18th.

Dearest Cecilia,

You will perceive that I am about to devote only one small sheet of note-paper to you. This is from no dearth of time, Heaven knows! time is a drug in the market here, but from a total dearth of ideas. Any ideas that I ever have, come to me from without, from external objects; I am not clever enough to generate any within myself. My life here is not an eminently suggestive one. It is spent digging with a wooden spade, and eating prawns. Those are my employments at least; my relaxation is going down to the Pier, to see the Calais boat come in. When one is miserable oneself, it is decidedly consolatory to see someone more miserable still; and wretched and bored, and reluctant vegetable as I am, I am not sea-sick. I always feel my spirits rise after having seen that peevish, draggled procession of blue, green and yellow fellow-Christians file past me. There is a wind here always, in comparison of which the wind that behaved so violently to the corners of Job's house was a mere zephyr. There are heights to climb which require more daring perseverance than ever Wolfe displayed, with his paltry heights of Abraham. There are glaring white houses, glaring white roads, glaring white cliffs. If anyone knew how unpatriotically I detest the chalk-cliffs of Albion! Having grumbled through my two little pages – I have actually been reduced to writing very large in order to fill even them – I will send off my dreary little billet. How I wish I could get into the envelope myself too, and whirl up with it to dear, beautiful, filthy London. Not more heavily could Madame de Staël have sighed for Paris from among the shades of Coppet.

Your disconsolate,
Bessy

Mrs. Montresor to Mrs. de Wynt
32, —Street, May Fair, May 27th.

Oh, my dearest Bessy, how I wish we were out of this dreadful, dreadful house! Please don't think me very ungrateful for saying this, after your taking such pains to provide us with a Heaven upon earth, as you thought.

What has happened could, of course, have been neither foretold, nor guarded against, by any human being. About ten days ago, Benson (my maid) came to me with a very long face, and said, "If you please, 'm, did you know that this house was haunted?" I was so startled: you know what a coward I am. I said, "Good Heavens! No! Is it?" "Well, 'm, I'm pretty nigh sure it is," she said, and the expression of her countenance was about as lively as an undertaker's; and then she told me that cook had been that morning to order groceries from a shop in the neighbourhood, and on her giving the man the direction where to send the things to, he had said, with a very peculiar smile, "No. 32, —Street, eh? H'm? I wonder how long you'll stand it; last lot held out just a fortnight." He looked so odd that she asked him what he meant, but he only said, "Oh! Nothing! Only that parties never do stay long at 32." He had known parties go in one day, and out the next, and during the last four years he had never known any remain over the month. Feeling a good deal alarmed by this information, she naturally inquired the reason; but he declined to give it, saying that if she had not found it out for herself, she had much better leave it alone, as it would only frighten her out of her wits; and on her insisting and urging him, she could only extract from him, that the house had such a villainously bad name, that the owners were glad to let it for a mere song. You know how firmly I believe in apparitions, and what an unutterable fear I have of them: anything material, tangible, that I can lay hold of – anything of the same fibre, blood, and bone as myself, I could, I think, confront bravely enough; but the mere thought of being brought face to face with the 'bodiless dead', makes my brain unsteady. The moment Henry came in, I ran to him, and told him; but he pooh-poohed the whole story, laughed at me, and asked whether we should turn out of the prettiest house in London, at the very height of the season, because a grocer said it had a bad name. Most good things that had ever been in the world had had a bad name in their day; and, moreover, the man had probably a motive for taking away the house's character, some friend for whom he coveted the charming situation and the low rent. He derided my 'babyish fears', as he called them, to such an extent that I felt half ashamed, and yet not quite comfortable either; and then came the usual rush of London engagements, during which one has no time to think of anything but how to speak, and act, and look for the moment then present. Adela was to arrive yesterday, and in the morning our weekly hamper of flowers, fruit, and vegetables arrived from home. I always dress the flower vases myself, servants are so tasteless; and as I was arranging them, it occurred to me – you know Adela's passion for flowers – to carry up one particular cornucopia of roses and mignonette and set it on her toilet-table, as a pleasant surprise for her. As I came downstairs, I had seen the housemaid – a fresh, round-faced country girl – go into the room, which was being prepared for Adela, with a pair of sheets that had been airing over her arm. I went upstairs very slowly, as my cornucopia was full of water, and I was afraid of spilling some. I turned the handle of the bedroom-door and entered, keeping my eyes fixed on my flowers, to see how they bore the transit, and whether any of them had fallen out. Suddenly a sort of shiver passed over me; and feeling frightened – I did not know why – I looked up quickly. The girl was standing by the bed, leaning forward a little with her hands clenched in each other, rigid, every nerve tense; her eyes, wide open, starting out of her head, and a look of unutterable stony horror in them; her cheeks and mouth not pale, but livid as those of one that died awhile ago in mortal pain. As I looked at her, her lips moved a little, and an awful hoarse voice, not like hers in the least, said, "Oh! My God, I have seen it!" and then she fell down suddenly, like a log, with a heavy noise. Hearing the noise, loudly audible all through the thin walls and floors of a London house, Benson came running in, and between us we managed to lift her on to the bed, and tried to bring her to herself by rubbing her feet and hands, and holding strong salts to her nostrils. And all the while we kept glancing over our shoulders, in a vague cold terror of seeing some awful, shapeless apparition. Two long hours she lay in a state of utter unconsciousness. Meanwhile Harry, who had been down to his club, returned. At the end of two hours we succeeded in bringing her back to sensation and life, but only to make the awful discovery that she was raving mad. She became so violent that it required all the combined strength of Harry and Phillips (our butler) to hold her down in the bed. Of course, we sent off instantly for a doctor, who on her growing a little calmer towards evening, removed her in a cab to his own house. He has just been here to tell me that she is now pretty quiet, not from any return to sanity, but from sheer exhaustion. We are, of course, utterly in the dark as to what she saw, and her ravings are far too disconnected and unintelligible to afford us the slightest clue. I feel so completely shattered and upset by this awful occurrence, that you will excuse me, dear, I'm sure, if I write incoherently. One thing I need hardly tell you, and that is, that no earthly consideration would induce me to allow Adela to occupy that terrible room. I shudder and run by quickly as I pass the door.

Yours, in great agitation,
Cecilia

Mrs. de Wynt to Mrs. Montresor
The Lord Warden, Dover, May 28th.

Dearest Cecilia,

Yours just come; how very dreadful! But I am still unconvinced as to house being in fault. You know I feel a sort of godmother to it, and responsible for its good behaviour. Don't you think that what the girl had might have been a fit? Why not? I myself have a cousin who is subject to seizures of the kind, and immediately on being attacked his whole body becomes rigid, his eyes glassy and staring, his complexion livid, exactly as in the case you describe. Or, if not a fit, are you sure that she has not been subject to fits of madness? Please be sure and ascertain whether there is not insanity in her family. It is so common nowadays, and so much on the increase, that nothing is more likely. You know my utter disbelief in ghosts. I am convinced that most of them, if run to earth, would turn out about as genuine as the famed Cock Lane one. But even allowing the possibility, nay, the actual unquestioned existence of ghosts in the abstract, is it likely that there should be anything to be seen so horribly fear-inspiring, as to send a perfectly sane person in one instant raving mad, which you, after three weeks' residence in the house, have never caught a glimpse of? According to your hypothesis, your whole household ought, by this time, to be stark staring mad. Let me implore you not to give way to a panic which may, possibly, probably prove utterly groundless. Oh, how I wish I were with you, to make you listen to reason!

Artie ought to be the best prop ever woman's old age was furnished with, to indemnify me for all he and his whooping-cough have made me suffer. Write immediately, please, and tell me how the poor patient progresses. Oh, had I the wings of a dove! I shall be on wires till I hear again.

Yours,
Bessy

Mrs. Montresor to Mrs. de Wynt
No. 5, Bolton Street, Piccadilly, June 12th.

Dearest Bessy,

You will see that we have left that terrible, hateful, fatal house. How I wish we had escaped from it sooner! Oh, my dear Bessy, I shall never be the same woman again if I live to be a hundred. Let me try to be coherent, and to tell you connectedly what has happened. And first, as to the housemaid, she has been removed to a lunatic asylum, where she remains in much the same state. She has had several lucid intervals, and during them has been closely, pressingly questioned as to what it was she saw; but she has maintained an absolute, hopeless silence, and only shudders, moans, and hides her face in her hands when the subject is broached. Three days ago I went to see her, and on my return was sitting resting in the drawing-room, before going to dress for dinner, talking to Adela about my visit, when Ralph Gordon walked in. He has always been walking in the last ten days, and Adela has always flushed up and looked very happy, poor little cat, whenever he made his appearance. He looked very handsome, dear fellow, just come in from the park; seemed in tremendous spirits, and was as sceptical as even you could be, as to the ghostly origin of Sarah's seizure. "Let me come here tonight and sleep in that room; do, Mrs. Montresor," he said, looking very eager and excited. "With the gas lit and a poker, I'll engage to exorcise every demon that shows his ugly nose; even if I should find –

*"Seven white ghostisses
Sitting on seven white postisses."*

"You don't mean really?" I asked, incredulously. "Don't I? That's all," he answered emphatically.

"I should like nothing better. Well, is it a bargain?" Adela turned quite pale. "Oh, don't," she said, hurriedly, "please, don't! Why should you run such a risk? How do you know that you might not be sent mad too?" He laughed very heartily, and coloured a little with pleasure at seeing the interest she took in his safety. "Never fear," he said, "it would take more than a whole squadron of departed ones, with the old gentleman at their head, to send me crazy." He was so eager, so persistent, so thoroughly in earnest, that I yielded at last, though with a certain strong reluctance, to his entreaties. Adela's blue eyes filled with tears, and she walked away hastily to the conservatory, and stood picking bits of heliotrope to hide them. Nevertheless, Ralph got his own way; it was so difficult to refuse him anything. We gave up all our engagements for the evening, and he did the same with his. At about ten o'clock he arrived, accompanied by a friend and brother officer, Captain Burton, who was anxious to see the result of the experiment. "Let me go up at once, he said, looking very happy and animated. "I don't know when I have felt in such good tune; a new sensation is a luxury not to be had every day of one's life; turn the gas up as high as it will go; provide a good stout poker, and leave the issue to Providence and me." We did as he bid. "It's all ready now," Henry said, coming downstairs after having obeyed his orders; "the room is nearly as light as day. Well, good luck to you, old fellow!" "Goodbye, Miss Bruce," Ralph said, going over to Adela, and taking her hand with a look, half laughing, half sentimental –

"Fare thee well, and if for ever then for ever, fare thee well, that is my last dying speech and confession. Now mind," he went on, standing by the table, and addressing us all; "if I ring once, don't come. I may be flurried, and lay hold of the bell without thinking; if I ring twice, come." Then he went, jumping up the stairs three steps at a time, and humming a tune. As for us, we sat in different attitudes of expectation and listening about the drawing-room. At first we tried to talk a little, but it would not do; our whole souls seemed to have passed into our ears. The clock's ticking sounded as loud as a great church bell close to one's ear. Addy lay on the sofa, with her dear little white face hidden in the cushions. So we sat for exactly an hour; but it seemed like two years, and just as the clock began to strike eleven, a sharp ting, ting, ting, rang clear and shrill through the house. "Let us go," said Addy, starting up and running to the door. "Let us go," I cried too, following her. But Captain Burton stood in the way, and intercepted our progress. "No," he said, decisively, "you must not go; remember Gordon told us distinctly, if he rang once not to come. I know the sort of fellow he is, and that nothing would annoy him more than having his directions disregarded."

"Oh, nonsense!" Addy cried passionately, "he would never have rung if he had not seen something dreadful; do, do let us go!" she ended, clasping her hands. But she was overruled, and we all went back to our seats. Ten minutes more of suspense, next door to unendurable; I felt a lump in my throat, a gasping for breath; ten minutes on the clock, but a thousand centuries on our hearts. Then again, loud, sudden, violent, the bell rang! We made a simultaneous rush to the door. I don't think we were one second flying upstairs. Addy was first. Almost simultaneously she and I burst into the room. There he was, standing in the middle of the floor, rigid, petrified, with that same look – that look that is burnt into my heart in letters of fire – of awful, unspeakable, stony fear on his brave young face. For one instant he stood thus; then stretching out his arms stiffly before him, he groaned in a terrible, husky voice, "Oh, my God! I have seen it!" and fell down dead. Yes, dead. Not in a swoon or in a fit, but dead. Vainly we tried to bring back the life to that strong young heart; it will never come back again till that day when the earth and the sea give up the dead that are therein. I cannot see the page for the tears that are blinding me; he was such a dear fellow! I can't write any more today.

Your broken-hearted
Cecilia

Sanctuary

Rebecca Buchanan

EMILY was screaming again.

Moyra grimaced, and glanced up at the ceiling. She could hear furniture scraping across the floor. A lamp crashed against a wall, glass shattering. Loud *bang-bang-bang*s as Emily's door slammed open and then shut, again and again.

Her gaze moved to one of the parlor windows, which looked out on a quiet mountain lake. The window beside it showed a fierce nighttime storm, wild lightning jumping between the clouds.

The storm. It was always a storm which set her off, bringing back all the bad memories and the pain.

Friday gripped her hand more tightly, shaking.

Moyra smiled down at the little boy, offering what reassurance she could. Thirty years, and he had never left her side. Thirty years since he had appeared at the front door, pale and traumatized and mute. She had ushered him inside, wrapped him in a blanket, and sat him down in the kitchen for a glass of milk and a warm slice of apple pie.

A few of the other children had gathered in the doorway, so she had poured more milk and cut more pieces of pie.

Many of those children were gone now, but a few still lingered.

Thirty years and he had never spoken a word, so she just called him Friday, for the day of the week when he had arrived. (He didn't seem to mind.)

At least, she thought it had been a Friday. It was easy to lose track.

Another resounding *bang*, and then the soft sound of a child weeping.

Moyra waited a moment, nodded, and began to climb the stairs. Her knees protested and her hips protested and she was sucking air hard by the time she reached the second floor. She had to stop and press her hand against the wall, giving her body a chance to recover.

At least the climb down the stairs would be easier.

Friday squeezed her hand again, his eyes wide and solemn.

Another reassuring smile and they continued down the hallway.

The door to Emily's room hung half-open. The frame had split in one corner and there was a wide crack down the middle of the door. The damage this time, at least, was minor and would soon heal.

Moyra pushed the door open all the way and leaned in. "Emily?" She peered around. The lamp had already repaired itself and was back on top of the dresser. The rocking chair still lay on its side and the nightstand was on the wrong side of the room. Wide shreds of wallpaper were slowly reattaching themselves, though, and the feathers from the pillows were sliding across the floor, gathering into neat piles.

Emily herself sat on the floor at the foot of the bed, her knees curled up and her face tucked in tight.

Motioning for Friday to stay in the doorway, Moyra pulled her hand free, stepped around a few piles of feathers, and sat down on the bed.

She let Emily cry.

When the girl finally lifted her head to scrub angrily at her cheeks, Moyra leaned over and gently rubbed her hair.

Emily sighed. "Sorry."

"Never apologize, my dear. Never. You take as long as you need and do whatever you need to do. It's your pain, and you work through it however you need to."

Emily dragged the back of her hand across her face again and looked up at Moyra. "Okay." Her lips trembled in a half-smile. "Pie?"

Moyra patted her head again. "Absolutely. What kind would you like? Peach? Rhubarb?"

"Potato?"

"I'm sure there are still potatoes in the pantry. Peas and carrots, too. Would you like to come down and help me make it?"

Emily glanced around the room. Moyra did the same. The wallpaper was fully restored, the crack in the door was gone, and the feathers were back inside the pillow and on the bed again. The rocking chair had returned to its corner and, as she watched, the nightstand slid back into place.

Emily nodded once, a quick, firm jerk of her chin. "Okay. Friday, you wanna help, too?"

Clutching the doorframe, the little boy nodded slowly.

Moyra pushed herself to her feet, took each child by the hand, and headed back down the hallway towards the stairs. "Do you know, I bet there's some asparagus in the pantry, too. Perhaps we could make some of that, too, and Tobias—"

Loud, rapid knocks at the front door.

Moyra paused, feeling Friday skitter behind her.

Those knocks were not the sounds a child would make. And, in most cases, the door just opened to let the child in, anyway. They never had to ask.

Another series of hurried *rap-rap-rap*s.

Well, then.

Straightening her shoulders, taking the children more firmly by the hand, Moyra slowly descended the stairs. It was easier, but still made her hips twinge. When they reached the first floor, she shooed them towards the kitchen. Emily left her reluctantly, but Friday hung on tight.

A voice called out from behind the door. Male. Youngish. "Hello? Anyone home? I'm sorry, but my car broke down and I can't get a signal. Hello?"

Moyra cast a grateful look at the walls around her, then turned the knob and pulled the door open.

It was dusk on the far side, and winter to judge by the thick, hard layer of snow and ice that ended at the bottom of the porch. More snow dripped off the man who stood shivering in front of her, his glasses fogging in the warmth from the house.

"Hey. Thank you. I am so sorry to bother you—"

"But your car broke down and your phone doesn't work." There had been no cell phones in her day, when she was still out and about in the world, but she had learned of them from some of the children who came, stayed for a while, and moved on; phones and many other things. "I'm not surprised. We don't need them around here, so they tend not to work."

The man blinked at her in confusion. "Pardon?"

"Why don't you come in and warm up? We were just about to make some potato pie, and maybe asparagus. Would you care to join us?"

"Uh, yeah, sure." The man stepped inside, shrugging out of his coat and hanging it on the tall rack. The door swung shut behind him. "If I could use your phone first."

"We don't have one. Never needed it." She stuck out her hand. "I'm Moyra."

"Grayson. Doctor James Grayson," he answered, automatically stripping off his gloves and returning the gesture. He stuffed the gloves inside his coat. "I'm sorry, did you say no phone?"

"That's correct." Friday still holding her hand, Moyra led the doctor past the parlor and dining room and into the kitchen, where Emily sat at the table. The girl frowned at the strange man. Moyra raised her eyebrows and pursed her lips, motioning Emily towards the large walk-in pantry. "Doctor of what?"

"Oh, psychology. I was on my way to a conference and I seem to have gotten turned around."

"Mmm." Moyra set the tea kettle on the stovetop, then turned as Emily passed her a basket of fresh carrots and another of peas. Three large potatoes, a thick slab of butter, a block of cheese, and a crust already in its pie tin followed. Moyra spread everything out on the kitchen island, handed the cheese grater to Emily and another knife to Doctor Grayson, and began to chop. Friday sat curled up against her leg.

"So, could you direct me back to the main road?" Grayson hesitated, then grabbed a carrot. His slices were awkward and uneven.

"No. I doubt it's there anymore."

"Pardon?"

"The house has a tendency to move around. Emily, could you grab some thyme and rosemary?"

"Sure." The girl hopped over to the back kitchen door and opened it to reveal a warm summer afternoon. Rolling green hills spread off into the distance. Emily grabbed two small pots from among the dozen that sat on the back porch railing and carried them inside. The door closed quietly behind her.

Grayson stared, his mouth hanging open.

"Doctor, if you would be so kind." When he continued to stare stupidly, she waved her knife at the plants. "Cut off a bit and mince it. For the pie. Please."

Swallowing hard, Grayson broke off a few stems of thyme and rosemary. His gaze jumped wildly around the room, the knife usually missing as he chopped haphazardly. A flush spread up his throat and across his cheeks, and sweat beaded along the edge of his forehead.

Gradually the flush faded and the sweat dried. He stopped chopping, eyes fixing on Moyra. "That was a trick of some kind. You have a projection screen or something back there. Like, a green house with a fake window or something."

"No." Moyra looked past him towards the door and the hallway beyond. "Hovering is rude. Either come in and introduce yourselves or go back to doing whatever."

Grayson spun on his heel, Emily snickering at his expression.

The children stood in or near the door, their styles of clothing and the expressions on their faces varying widely. Robert, in his blue jeans and denim jacket, looked curious. Beside him, Etta hugged her dolly and glowered. Andy stood further back, barefoot and dressed only in his pajamas; he looked frightened. His sister Agatha, who had died trying to protect him, wrapped her arms around him from behind.

"In or out, make up your minds."

Andy and Agatha retreated up the stairs.

Robert raised his hand in greeting. "Hey. How's it going?" His voice was soft, almost lyrical. He poked Etta in the arm. "Say hi."

The little girl buried her face sullenly in the doll's knit hair. "Hi," she muttered.

"Dinner will be ready soon. You're welcome to join us, if you want."

Robert nodded, rolling his shoulders in a half-shrug. He turned, went down the hallway, and opened the front door. There was a beach outside now, and a sparkling blue-green ocean. Robert pulled the door shut and Moyra could hear the faint squeak as he settled onto the porch swing.

Etta continued to stare sullenly for a long moment, then spun and ran up the stairs.

Grayson was flushed and sweating again.

Moyra tossed the finely chopped potatoes, carrot slices, and peas into the crust. The crudely minced thyme and rosemary followed, and the handfuls of cheese that Emily had grated. "Robert was born Rachel," Moyra explained. Anger edged her words, though she tried to hold it back. Friday didn't like it when she was angry; it frightened him. She drew a deep breath. "His parents didn't approve so they handed him over to a minister who promised to *cure* him. Robert doesn't remember exactly what happened, but he does know that the minister hid his body under the church."

She heard Grayson swallow.

"Etta was kidnapped by a pedophile. He kept her for a year before he got bored and murdered her." She turned, slid the pie into the oven, and pulled a bundle of fresh asparagus out of the pantry.

Emily stood still, her head down.

"Andy and Agatha's mother was an alcoholic. She flew into a rage one day when Andy stole the wrong kind of whiskey. Agatha tried to protect him, like she always did, so their mother killed them both." She laid a hand on Emily's shoulder. "Could you make the asparagus? Doctor Grayson and I will be in the parlor."

The tea kettle that never needed to be filled let out a loud whistle.

Grayson jumped, dropping his knife. It clattered across the kitchen island.

"What sort of tea do you like, Doctor?"

"Uh. Uh. I – I like – like spicy. Spicy orange." His voice cracked.

Moyra smiled, the same reassuring smile she offered Friday when he was particularly frightened. She lifted a clear glass jar out of the cupboard, the leaves inside every shade of red and orange and yellow. She set it on a tray beside the kettle. "What a coincidence. We happen to have spicy orange on-hand. Let's adjourn to the parlor until the pie is ready, shall we?"

Grayson nodded dumbly. His feet shuffled along the floor as he followed her to the front parlor, his eyes wide.

He jumped again as they passed the stairs. There was a thump and the door to the storage space rattled.

"I'm sorry, is there – is there someone *under the stairs?*"

Moyra set the tray on the low table, her hips flashing in pain as she bent over. "Oh, yes. That's Tobias. When he was alive, his parents kept him locked under the staircase for, well, years. When his older brother set fire to the house, Tobias wasn't able to get out."

Grayson gaped at her.

She gingerly sat down on the couch, Friday cuddling up beside her. "He comes out every now and then, usually when I make asparagus. It's his favorite. He stays out longer each time, so I have hope that he won't be here much longer."

"Much longer...."

"Yes. That he'll move on."

Hands opening and closing, Grayson edged into the room. He studied the half-dozen windows, each of which looked out on a different landscape: sand dunes, a meadow of wildflowers, a jungle filled with colorful birds. "To *where*, exactly?"

"Oh, I have no idea." She poured tea into each cup, adding a few dollops of honey to her own. "Well, no certainty, at any rate. I do have *ideas*. So did my predecessor, Mr. Coleman. Delightful man. We worked together for nearly a year before he passed on. He was a firm believer in reincarnation, except when he wasn't. It was his theory that the children remained here until they healed and then they could be reborn with a clean slate, as it were, unencumbered by the pain of their previous death."

"I don't—" He loudly cleared his throat and settled into a plush chair across from her. His eyes skipped to Friday and back to her again. "I don't believe that. This."

Moyra frowned. "Believe what?"

"*This!*" He waved his arms around. "Any of this! All of this! You're – this is a *cult*. Or you're trafficking these children. None of what you said is true. Couldn't possibly *be* true."

"Oh, dear. You're one of *those* people. Purely rational, purely logical. Or, at least that's what you tell yourself. But really, somewhere in there – even if it's way deep down – you still believe."

"I don't—"

"Of course you do. You still believe in the weird and the wonderful and the horrible. The house never would have chosen you if you didn't. Being a psychologist is an added benefit. That means you have empathy and, presumably, coping skills. And you will need them. Both of them. The empathy and the coping skills, I mean."

Grayson ran a hand over his scalp. "I don't. I really *don't* believe any of this."

"Mm. I disagree. You're here. You are clearly frightened, but you are also intrigued. Curious. You haven't run. You're sitting here drinking tea, waiting for the potato pie to finish baking."

He studied her, expression moving from offended to hesitant to quizzical to bemused to cautiously interested. "So why am I here? Or, why do *you* think I'm here?"

She blew on her tea and took a sip. Sweet orange, followed by a hot bite. "Me. I am old. I have been here for...oh, dear. Well over sixty years. I don't have much longer. How long I can't really say for certain. But the house knows I'm dying, and that a new caretaker will be needed soon."

Grayson huffed a laugh, scratching at the back of his neck. "So, this is a sentient house filled with the spirits of murdered children. And you look after them. And I'm expected not only to believe all of this, but to take over for you and stay here for the rest of *my* life."

"Yes."

This time he did laugh. Pressing his hands to his thighs, he pushed himself to his feet. "You people are insane. I'm leaving." He turned away.

"Your choice, of course. Once you leave, though, the house will never reappear. Not to you. Other people have said no, or left after only a short while." He paused on the threshold of the parlor, half turned away from her. "I was the third person the house chose to succeed Mr. Coleman. I was the only one who stayed. I have never regretted it. You won't, either."

He turned back towards her.

"You are a healer, Dr. Grayson. Why else would you have chosen psychology? There is a lot of pain in the world. There are a lot of *children* in pain. You have the chance to help some of them, children you would not otherwise ever have the opportunity to aid. Here, they can heal. They can rage and scream and cry and paint and bake and watch the sunrise and do whatever else they need to do to heal. And you can help them."

He watched her for long moments, his face carefully blank. Then he shook his head, pulled his jacket off the rack, and opened the door. He paused, looking back towards her. He appeared to be on the verge of saying something, but then shook his head again. He crossed the threshold and closed the door.

Moyra sighed, disappointment making her shoulders curve inward. "Drat," she whispered.

A low murmur of voices. The squeak of the porch swing.

She held her breath, straining to listen. Beside her, Friday inched forward on the couch, his attention focused on the outer wall and the porch beyond.

Moyra could not make out specific words, but the tone was friendly. Robert seemed to ask a question, Grayson answered, and they both laughed.

She sipped her tea, and waited.

The windows changed again: a great waterfall against shiny black rock, a knotted oak tree dripping honey, a wide grassy plain dotted with gazelles.

The oven pinged.

Moyra set aside her tea cup and returned to the kitchen with Friday. She found Emily pulling out the potato pie and setting it on the stovetop to cool. A pan full of garlic-seasoned asparagus sat next to it, steam rising into the air.

Moyra leaned over and inhaled the delightful scents. Beside her, Friday rose up on his tiptoes to do the same. "Mmm. Delicious. Why don't you two set the table. Enough for everyone, just in case they decide to join us."

Emily grinned and yanked open the cupboard. She pulled out plates and cups, carefully handing a few at a time to Friday, while Moyra fished the utensils out of the drawer.

She studiously ignored the sound of the under-stairs door swinging open, and the soft shuffle of feet. When she was sure that Tobias had reached the kitchen doorway, she gently asked him to fetch the napkins from the linen drawer. More shuffling steps. He moved into her line of sight, his chin tucked in tight, his eyes down. Just as gently, she thanked him for helping and then led him into the dining room, cloth napkins clutched in his hands.

They were just sitting down to eat, the potato pie and asparagus and jug of cold milk arranged in the middle of the table, when the front door opened again. Robert came in, met her eyes, and shook his head.

Moyra felt her shoulders tighten. Disappointment curdled her stomach. "Well, for his sake, I hope the house settled somewhere near his car."

Robert settled down across from her. She served Friday and Tobias first, on either side of her, than passed the potato pie around. She was just dumping a large spoonful on her own plate when Etta appeared and clambered onto the chair beside Emily.

Robert scooped up some potato pie. "Think Andy and Agatha will come down?"

"Not likely, I'm afraid. Not tonight." She looked around the table, smiling at each child in turn. "Perhaps tomorrow. And we'll be waiting for them when they do."

The Haunted and the Haunters
or, The House and the Brain
Edward Bulwer-Lytton

A FRIEND of mine, who is a man of letters and a philosopher, said to me one day, as if between jest and earnest – "Fancy! Since we last met, I have discovered a haunted house in the midst of London."

"Really haunted? – And by what? Ghosts?"

"Well, I can't answer these questions – all I know is this – six weeks ago I and my wife were in search of a furnished apartment. Passing a quiet street, we saw on the window of one of the houses a bill, 'Apartments Furnished'. The situation suited us: we entered the house – liked the rooms – engaged them by the week – and left them the third day. No power on earth could have reconciled my wife to stay longer, and I don't wonder at it."

"What did you see?"

"Excuse me – I have no desire to be ridiculed as a superstitious dreamer – nor, on the other hand, could I ask you to accept on my affirmation what you would hold to be incredible without the evidence of your own senses. Let me only say this, it was not so much what we saw or heard (in which you might fairly suppose that we were the dupes of our own excited fancy, or the victims of imposture in others) that drove us away, as it was an undefinable terror which seized both of us whenever we passed by the door of a certain unfurnished room, in which we neither saw nor heard anything. And the strangest marvel of all was, that for once in my life I agreed with my wife – silly woman though she be – and allowed, after the third night, that it was impossible to stay a fourth in that house. Accordingly, on the fourth morning, I summoned the woman who kept the house and attended on us, and told her that the rooms did not quite suit us, and we would not stay out our week. She said, dryly: 'I know why; you have stayed longer than any other lodger; few ever stayed a second night; none before you, a third. But I take it they have been very kind to you.'

"'They – who?' I asked, affecting a smile.

"'Why, they who haunt the house, whoever they are. I don't mind them; I remember them many years ago, when I lived in this house, not as a servant; but I know they will be the death of me some day. I don't care – I'm old, and must die soon, anyhow; and then I shall be with them, and in this house still.' The woman spoke with so dreary a calmness, that really it was a sort of awe that prevented my conversing with her farther. I paid for my week, and too happy were I and my wife to get off so cheaply."

"You excite my curiosity," said I; "nothing I should like better than to sleep in a haunted house. Pray give me the address of the one which you left so ignominiously."

My friend gave me the address; and when we parted, I walked straight towards the house thus indicated.

It is situated on the north side of Oxford Street, in a dull but respectable thoroughfare. I found the house shut up – no bill at the window, and no response to my knock. As I was turning away, a beer-boy, collecting pewter pots at the neighbouring areas, said to me, "Do you want anyone in that house, sir?"

"Yes, I heard it was to let."

"Let! Why, the woman who kept it is dead – has been dead these three weeks, and no one can be found to stay there, though Mr. J— offered ever so much. He offered mother, who chars for him, one pound a week just to open and shut the windows, and she would not."

"Would not! And why?"

"The house is haunted; and the old woman who kept it was found dead in her bed, with her eyes wide open. They say the devil strangled her."

"Pooh! You speak of Mr. J—. Is he the owner of the house?"

"Yes."

"Where does he live?"

"In G— Street, No.—."

"What is he? – In any business?"

"No, sir – nothing particular; a single gentleman."

I gave the pot-boy the gratuity earned by his liberal information, and proceeded to Mr. J—, in G— Street, which was close by the street that boasted the haunted house. I was lucky enough to find Mr. J— at home – an elderly man, with intelligent countenance and prepossessing manners.

I communicated my name and my business frankly. I said I heard the house was considered to be haunted – that I had a strong desire to examine a house with so equivocal a reputation – that I should be greatly obliged if he would allow me to hire it, though only for a night. I was willing to pay for that privilege whatever he might be inclined to ask. "Sir," said Mr. J—, with great courtesy, "the house is at your service, for as short or as long a time as you please. Rent is out of the question – the obligation will be on my side should you be able to discover the cause of the strange phenomena which at present deprive it of all value. I cannot let it, for I cannot even get a servant to keep it in order or answer the door. Unluckily the house is haunted, if I may use that expression, not only by night, but by day; though at night the disturbances are of a more unpleasant and sometimes of a more alarming character.

"The poor old woman who died in it three weeks ago was a pauper whom I took out of a workhouse, for in her childhood she had been known to some of my family, and had once been in such good circumstances that she had rented that house of my uncle. She was a woman of superior education and strong mind, and was the only person I could ever induce to remain in the house. Indeed, since her death, which was sudden, and the coroner's inquest, which gave it a notoriety in the neighbourhood, I have so despaired of finding any person to take charge of it, much more a tenant, that I would willingly let it rent-free for a year to anyone who would pay its rates and taxes."

"How long is it since the house acquired this sinister character?"

"That I can scarcely tell you, but very many years since. The old woman I spoke of said it was haunted when she rented it between thirty and forty years ago. The fact is that my life has been spent in the East Indies and in the civil service of the Company. I returned to England last year on inheriting the fortune of an uncle, amongst whose possessions was the house in question. I found it shut up and uninhabited. I was told that it was haunted, that no one would inhabit it. I smiled at what seemed to me so idle a story. I spent some money in repainting and roofing it – added to its old-fashioned furniture a few modern articles – advertised it, and obtained a lodger for a year. He was a colonel retired on half-pay. He came in with his family, a son and a daughter, and four or five servants: they all left the house the next day, and although they deponed that they had all seen something different, that something was equally terrible to all. I really could not in conscience sue, or even blame, the colonel for breach of agreement.

"Then I put in the old woman I have spoken of, and she was empowered to let the house in apartments. I never had one lodger who stayed more than three days. I do not tell you their stories – to no two lodgers have there been exactly the same phenomena repeated. It is better that you should judge for yourself, than enter the house with an imagination influenced by previous narratives; only be prepared to see and to hear something or other, and take whatever precautions you yourself please."

"Have you never had a curiosity yourself to pass a night in that house?"

"Yes. I passed not a night, but three hours in broad daylight alone in that house. My curiosity is not satisfied, but it is quenched. I have no desire to renew the experiment. You cannot complain, you see, sir, that I am not sufficiently candid; and unless your interest be exceedingly eager and your nerves unusually strong, I honestly add that I advise you not to pass a night in that house."

"My interest is exceedingly keen," said I, "and though only a coward will boast of his nerves in situations wholly unfamiliar to him, yet my nerves have been seasoned in such variety of danger that I have the right to rely on them – even in a haunted house."

Mr. J— said very little more; he took the keys of the house out of his bureau, gave them to me, and thanking him cordially for his frankness, and his urbane concession to my wish, I carried off my prize.

Impatient for the experiment, as soon as I reached home I summoned my confidential servant – a young man of gay spirits, fearless temper, and as free from superstitious prejudice as anyone I could think of.

"F—," said I, "you remember in Germany how disappointed we were at not finding a ghost in that old castle, which was said to be haunted by a headless apparition? Well, I have heard of a house in London which, I have reason to hope, is decidedly haunted. I mean to sleep there tonight. From what I hear, there is no doubt that something will allow itself to be seen or to be heard – something, perhaps, excessively horrible. Do you think, if I take you with me, I may rely on your presence of mind, whatever may happen?"

"Oh, sir! Pray trust me," answered F—, grinning with delight.

"Very well – then here are the keys of the house – this is the address. Go now – select for me any bedroom you please; and since the house has not been inhabited for weeks, make up a good fire – air the bed well – see, of course, that there are candles as well as fuel. Take with you my revolver and my dagger – so much for my weapons – arm yourself equally well; and if we are not a match for a dozen ghosts, we shall be but a sorry couple of Englishmen."

I was engaged for the rest of the day on business so urgent that I had not leisure to think much on the nocturnal adventure to which I had plighted my honour. I dined alone, and very late, and while dining, read, as is my habit. The volume I selected was one of Macaulay's Essays. I thought to myself that I would take the book with me; there was so much of healthfulness in the style, and practical life in the subjects, that it would serve as an antidote against the influences of superstitious fancy.

Accordingly, about half-past nine, I put the book into my pocket, and strolled leisurely towards the haunted house. I took with me a favourite dog – an exceedingly sharp, bold, and vigilant bull-terrier – a dog fond of prowling about strange ghostly corners and passages at night in search of rats – a dog of dogs for a ghost.

It was a summer night, but chilly, the sky somewhat gloomy and overcast. Still, there was a moon – faint and sickly, but still a moon – and if the clouds permitted, after midnight it would be brighter.

I reached the house, knocked, and my servant opened with a cheerful smile.

"All right, sir, and very comfortable."

"Oh!" said I, rather disappointed; "have you not seen nor heard anything remarkable?"

"Well, sir, I must own I have heard something queer."

"What? – What?"

"The sound of feet pattering behind me; and once or twice small noises like whispers close at my ear – nothing more."

"You are not at all frightened?"

"I! Not a bit of it, sir"; and the man's bold look reassured me on one point – viz. that, happen what might, he would not desert me.

We were in the hall, the street-door closed, and my attention was now drawn to my dog. He had at first ran in eagerly enough, but had sneaked back to the door, and was scratching and whining to get out. After patting him on the head, and encouraging him gently, the dog seemed to reconcile himself to the situation and followed me and F— through the house, but keeping close at my heels instead of hurrying inquisitively in advance, which was his usual and normal habit in all strange places. We first visited the subterranean apartments, the kitchen and other offices, and especially the cellars, in which last there were two or three bottles of wine still left in a bin, covered with cobwebs, and evidently, by their appearance, undisturbed for many years. It was clear that the ghosts were not wine-bibbers.

For the rest we discovered nothing of interest. There was a gloomy little backyard, with very high walls. The stones of this yard were very damp – and what with the damp, and what with the dust and smoke-grime on the pavement, our feet left a slight impression where we passed. And now appeared the first strange phenomenon witnessed by myself in this strange abode. I saw, just before me, the print of a foot suddenly form itself, as it were. I stopped, caught hold of my servant, and pointed to it. In advance of that footprint as suddenly dropped another. We both saw it. I advanced quickly to the place; the footprint kept advancing before me, a small footprint – the foot of a child: the impression was too faint thoroughly to distinguish the shape, but it seemed to us both that it was the print of a naked foot. This phenomenon ceased when we arrived at the opposite wall, nor did it repeat itself on returning.

We remounted the stairs, and entered the rooms on the ground floor, a dining parlour, a small back-parlour, and a still smaller third room that had been probably appropriated to a footman – all still as death. We then visited the drawing-rooms, which seemed fresh and new. In the front room I seated myself in an armchair. F— placed on the table the candlestick with which he had lighted us. I told him to shut the door. As he turned to do so, a chair opposite to me moved from the wall quickly and noiselessly, and dropped itself about a yard from my own chair, immediately fronting it.

"Why, this is better than the turning-tables," said I, with a half-laugh – and as I laughed, my dog put back his head and howled.

F—, coming back, had not observed the movement of the chair. He employed himself now in stilling the dog. I continued to gaze on the chair, and fancied I saw on it a pale blue misty outline of a human figure, but an outline so indistinct that I could only distrust my own vision. The dog now was quiet.

"Put back that chair opposite to me," said I to F—; "put it back to the wall."

F— obeyed. "Was that you, sir?" said he, turning abruptly.

"I – what!"

"Why, something struck me. I felt it sharply on the shoulder – just here."

"No," said I. "But we have jugglers present, and though we may not discover their tricks, we shall catch them before they frighten us."

We did not stay long in the drawing rooms – in fact, they felt so damp and so chilly that I was glad to get to the fire upstairs. We locked the doors of the drawing rooms – a precaution which, I should observe, we had taken with all the rooms we had searched below. The bedroom my servant had selected for me was the best on the floor – a large one, with two windows fronting the street. The four-posted bed, which took up no inconsiderable space, was opposite to the fire, which burned clear and bright; a door in the wall to the left, between the bed and the window, communicated with the room which my servant appropriated to himself.

This last was a small room with a sofa-bed, and had no communication with the landing-place – no other door but that which conducted to the bedroom I was to occupy. On either side of my fireplace was a cupboard, without locks, flushed with the wall, and covered with the same dull-brown paper. We examined these cupboards – only hooks to suspend female dresses – nothing else; we sounded the walls – evidently solid – the outer walls of the building. Having finished the survey of these apartments, warmed myself a few moments, and lighted my cigar, I then, still accompanied by F—, went forth to complete my reconnoitre. In the landing-place there was another door; it was closed firmly. "Sir," said my servant in surprise, "I unlocked this door with all the others when I first came; it cannot have got locked from the inside, for it is a—"

Before he had finished his sentence the door, which neither of us then was touching, opened quietly of itself. We looked at each other a single instant. The same thought seized both – some human agency might be detected here. I rushed in first, my servant followed. A small blank dreary room without furniture – a few empty boxes and hampers in a corner – a small window – the shutters closed – not even a fireplace – no other door but that by which we had entered – no carpet on the floor, and the floor seemed very old, uneven, worm-eaten, mended here and there, as was shown by the whiter patches on the wood; but no living being, and no visible place in which a living being could have hidden. As we stood gazing around, the door by which we had entered closed as quietly as it had before opened: we were imprisoned.

For the first time I felt a creep of undefinable horror. Not so my servant. "Why, they don't think to trap us, sir; I could break that trumpery door with a kick of my foot."

"Try first if it will open to your hand," said I, shaking off the vague apprehension that had seized me, "while I open the shutters and see what is without."

I unbarred the shutters – the window looked on the little backyard I have before described; there was no ledge without – nothing but sheer descent. No man getting out of that window would have found any footing till he had fallen on the stones below.

F—, meanwhile, was vainly attempting to open the door. He now turned round to me, and asked my permission to use force. And I should here state, in justice to the servant, that, far from evincing any superstitious terrors, his nerve, composure, and even gaiety amidst circumstances so extraordinary compelled my admiration, and made me congratulate myself on having secured a companion in every way fitted to the occasion. I willingly gave him the permission he required. But though he was a remarkably strong man, his force was as idle as his milder efforts; the door did not even shake to his stoutest kick. Breathless and painting, he desisted. I then tried the door myself, equally in vain.

As I ceased from the effort, again that creep of horror came over me; but this time it was more cold and stubborn. I felt as if some strange and ghastly exhalation were rising up from the chinks of that rugged floor, and filling the atmosphere with a venomous influence hostile to human life. The door now very slowly and quietly opened as of its own accord. We precipitated ourselves into the landing-place. We both saw a large pale light – as large as the human figure, but shapeless and unsubstantial – move before us, and ascend the stairs that led from the landing into the attics. I followed the light, and my servant followed me. It entered, to the right of the landing, a small garret, of which the door stood open. I entered in the same instant. The light then collapsed into a small globule, exceedingly brilliant and vivid; rested a moment on a bed in the corner, quivered, and vanished. We approached the bed and examined it – a half-tester, such as is commonly found in attics devoted to servants. On the drawers that stood near it we perceived an old faded silk kerchief, with the needle still left in a rent half repaired. The kerchief was covered with dust; probably it had belonged to the old woman who had last died in that house, and this might have been her sleeping-room.

I had sufficient curiosity to open the drawers; there were a few odds and ends of female dress, and two letters tied round with a narrow ribbon of faded yellow. I took the liberty to possess myself of the letters. We found nothing else in the room worth noticing – nor did the light reappear; but we distinctly heard, as we turned to go, a pattering footfall on the floor – just before us. We went through the other attics (in all, four), the footfall still preceding us. Nothing to be seen – nothing but the footfall heard. I had the letters in my hand; just as I was descending the stairs I distinctly felt my wrist seized, and a faint, soft effort made to draw the letters from my clasp. I only held them the more tightly, and the effort ceased.

We regained the bedchamber appropriated to myself, and I then remarked that my dog had not followed us when we had left it. He was thrusting himself close to the fire, and trembling. I was impatient to examine the letters; and while I read them, my servant opened a little box in which he had deposited the weapons I had ordered him to bring, took them out, placed them on a table close at my bedhead, and then occupied himself in soothing the dog, who, however, seemed to heed him very little.

The letters were short – they were dated; the dates exactly thirty-five years ago. They were evidently from a lover to his mistress, or a husband to some young wife. Not only the terms of expression, but a distinct reference to a former voyage indicated the writer to have been a seafarer. The spelling and handwriting were those of a man imperfectly educated, but still the language itself was forcible. In the expressions of endearment there was a kind of rough wild love; but here and there were dark unintelligible hints at some secret not of love – some secret that seemed to crime. "We ought to love each other," was one of the sentences I remember, "for how everyone else would execrate us if all was known." Again: "Don't let anyone be in the same room with you at night – you talk in your sleep." And again: "What's done can't be undone; and I tell you there's nothing against us unless the dead could come to life." Here there was underlined in a better handwriting (a female's), "They do!" At the end of the letter latest in date the same female hand had written these words: "Lost at sea the 4th of June, the same day as—"

I put down the letters, and began to muse over their contents.

Fearing, however, that the train of thought into which I fell might unsteady my nerves, I fully determined to keep my mind in a fit state to cope with whatever of marvellous the advancing night might bring forth. I roused myself – laid the letters on the table – stirred up the fire, which was still bright and cheering – and opened my volume of Macaulay. I read quietly enough till about half-past eleven. I then threw myself dressed upon the bed, and told my servant he might retire to his own room, but must keep himself awake. I bade him leave open the door between the two rooms. Thus alone, I kept two candles burning on the table by my bedhead. I placed my watch beside the weapons, and calmly resumed my Macaulay.

Opposite to me the fire burned clear; and on the hearth-rug, seemingly asleep, lay the dog. In about twenty minutes I felt an exceedingly cold air pass by my cheek, like a sudden draught. I fancied the door to my right, communicating with the landing-place, must have got open; but no – it was closed. I then turned my glance to my left, and saw the flame of the candles violently swayed as by a wind. At the same moment the watch beside the revolver softly slid from the table – softly, softly – no visible hand – it was gone. I sprang up, seizing the revolver with the one hand, the dagger with the other; I was not willing that my weapons should share the fate of the watch. Thus armed, I looked round the floor – no sign of the watch. Three slow, loud, distinct knocks were now heard at the bedhead; my servant called out, "Is that you, sir?"

"No; be on your guard."

The dog now roused himself and sat on his haunches, his ears moving quickly backwards and forwards. He kept his eyes fixed on me with a look so strange that he concentrated all my attention on himself. Slowly he rose up, all his hair bristling, and stood perfectly rigid, and with the same wild stare. I had no time, however, to examine the dog. Presently my servant emerged from his room; and if ever I saw horror in the human face, it was then. I should not have recognised him had we met in the streets, so altered was every lineament. He passed by me quickly, saying in a whisper that seemed scarcely to come from his lips, "Run – run! It is after me!" He gained the door to the landing, pulled it open, and rushed forth. I followed him into the landing involuntarily, calling him to stop; but, without heeding me, he bounded down the stairs, clinging to the balusters, and taking several steps at a time. I heard, where I stood, the street door open – heard it again clap to. I was left alone in the haunted house.

It was but for a moment that I remained undecided whether or not to follow my servant; pride and curiosity alike forbade so dastardly a flight. I re-entered my room, closing the door after me, and proceeded cautiously into the interior chamber. I encountered nothing to justify my servant's terror. I again carefully examined the walls, to see if there were any concealed door. I could find no trace of one – not even a seam in the dull-brown paper with which the room was hung. How, then, had the Thing, whatever it was, which had so scared him, obtained ingress except through my own chamber?

I returned to my room, shut and locked the door that opened upon the interior one, and stood on the hearth, expectant and prepared. I now perceived that the dog had slunk into an angle of the wall, and was pressing himself close against it, as if literally trying to force his way into it. I approached the animal and spoke to it; the poor brute was evidently beside itself with terror. It showed all its teeth, the slaver dropping from its jaws, and would certainly have bitten me if I had touched it. It did not seem to recognise me. Whoever has seen at the Zoological Gardens a rabbit fascinated by a serpent, cowering in a corner, may form some idea of the anguish which the dog exhibited. Finding all efforts to soothe the animal in vain, and fearing that his bite might be as venomous in that state as if in the madness of hydrophobia, I left him alone, placed my weapons on the table beside the fire, seated myself, and recommenced my Macaulay.

Perhaps in order not to appear seeking credit for a courage, or rather a coolness, which the reader may conceive I exaggerate, I may be pardoned if I pause to indulge in one or two egotistical remarks.

As I hold presence of mind, or what is called courage, to be precisely proportioned to familiarity with the circumstance that lead to it, so I should say that I had been long sufficiently familiar with all experiments that appertain to the Marvellous. I had witnessed many very extraordinary phenomena in various parts of the world – phenomena that would be either totally disbelieved if I stated them, or ascribed to supernatural agencies. Now, my theory is that the Supernatural is the Impossible, and that what is called supernatural is only a something in the laws of nature of which we have been hitherto ignorant. Therefore, if a ghost rise before me, I have not the right to say, "So, then, the supernatural is possible," but rather, "So, then, the apparition of a ghost is, contrary to received opinion, within the laws of nature – i.e. not supernatural."

Now, in all that I had hitherto witnessed, and indeed in all the wonders which the amateurs of mystery in our age record as facts, a material living agency is always required. On the Continent you will find still magicians who assert that they can raise spirits. Assume for the moment that they assert truly, still the living material form of the magician is present; and he is the material agency by which from some constitutional peculiarities, certain strange phenomena are represented to your natural senses.

Accept again, as truthful, the tales of Spirit Manifestation in America – musical or other sounds – writings on paper, produced by no discernible hand – articles of furniture moved without apparent human agency – or the actual sight and touch of hands, to which no bodies seem to belong – still there must be found the medium or living being, with constitutional peculiarities capable of obtaining these signs. In fine, in all such marvels, supposing even that there is no imposture, there must be a human being like ourselves, by whom, or through whom, the effects presented to human beings are produced. It is so with the now familiar phenomena of mesmerism or electro-biology; the mind of the person operated on is affected through a material living agent. Nor, supposing it true that a mesmerised patient can respond to the will or passes of a mesmeriser a hundred miles distant, is the response less occasioned by a material being; it may be through a material fluid – call it Electric, call it Odic, call it what you will – which has the power of traversing space and passing obstacles, that the material effect is communicated from one to the other.

Hence all that I had hitherto witnessed, or expected to witness, in this strange house, I believed to be occasioned through some agency or medium as mortal as myself; and this idea necessarily prevented the awe with which those who regard as supernatural things that are not within the ordinary operations of nature, might have been impressed by the adventures of that memorable night.

As, then, it was my conjecture that all that was presented, or would be presented, to my senses, must originate in some human being gifted by constitution with the power so to present them, and having some motive so to do, I felt an interest in my theory which, in its way, was rather philosophical than superstitious. And I can sincerely say that I was in as tranquil a temper for observation as any practical experimentalist could be in awaiting the effects of some rare though perhaps perilous chemical combination. Of course, the more I kept my mind detached from fancy, the more the temper fitted for observation would be obtained; and I therefore riveted eye and thought on the strong daylight sense in the page of my Macaulay.

I now became aware that something interposed between the page and the light – the page was overshadowed; I looked up, and I saw what I shall find it very difficult, perhaps impossible, to describe.

It was a Darkness shaping itself out of the air in very undefined outline. I cannot say it was of a human form, and yet it had more resemblance to a human form, or rather shadow, than anything else. As it stood, wholly apart and distinct from the air and the light around it, its dimensions seemed gigantic, the summit nearly touching the ceiling. While I gazed, a feeling of intense cold seized me. An iceberg before me could not more have chilled me; nor could the cold of an iceberg have been more purely physical. I feel convinced that it was not the cold caused by fear. As I continued to gaze, I thought – but this I cannot say with precision – that I distinguished two eyes looking down on me from the height. One moment I seemed to distinguish them clearly, the next they seemed gone; but still two rays of a pale-blue light frequently shot through the darkness, as from the height on which I half-believed, half-doubted, that I had encountered the eyes.

I strove to speak – my voice utterly failed me; I could only think to myself, "Is this fear? It is not fear!" I strove to rise – in vain; I felt as if weighed down by an irresistible force. Indeed, my impression was that of an immense and overwhelming Power opposed to my volition; that sense of utter inadequacy to cope with a force beyond men's, which one may feel physically in a storm at sea, in a conflagration, or when confronting some terrible wild beast, or rather, perhaps, the shark of the ocean, I felt morally. Opposed to my will was another will, as far superior to its strength as storm, fire, and shark are superior in material force to the force of men.

And now, as this impression grew on me, now came, at last, horror – horror to a degree that no words can convey. Still I retained pride, if not courage; and in my own mind I said, "This is horror, but it is not fear; unless I fear, I cannot be harmed; my reason rejects this thing; it is an illusion – I do not fear." With a violent effort I succeeded at last in stretching out my hand towards the weapon on the table; as I did so, on the arm and shoulder I received a strange shock, and my arm fell to my side powerless. And now, to add to my horror, the light began slowly to wane from the candles – they were not, as it were, extinguished, but their flame seemed very gradually withdrawn; it was the same with the fire – the light was extracted from the fuel; in a few minutes the room was in utter darkness.

The dread that came over me, to be thus in the dark with that dark Thing, whose power was so intensely felt, brought a reaction of nerve. In fact, terror had reached that climax, that either my senses must have deserted me, or I must have burst through the spell. I did burst through it. I found voice, though the voice was a shriek. I remember that I broke forth with words like these – "I do not fear, my soul does not fear"; and at the same time I found the strength to rise. Still in that profound gloom I rushed to one of the windows – tore aside the curtain – flung open the shutters; my first thought was – LIGHT. And when I saw the moon high, clear, and calm, I felt a joy that almost compensated for the previous terror. There was the moon, there was also the light from the gas-lamps in the deserted slumberous street. I turned to look back into the room; the moon penetrated its shadow very palely and partially – but still there was light. The dark Thing, whatever it might be, was gone – except that I could yet see a dim shadow which seemed the shadow of that shade, against the opposite wall.

My eye now rested on the table, and from under the table (which was without cloth or cover – an old mahogany round table) there rose a hand, visible as far as the wrist. It was a hand, seemingly, as much of flesh and blood as my own, but the hand of an aged person – lean, wrinkled, small too – a woman's hand.

That hand very softly closed on the two letters that lay on the table: hand and letters both vanished. There then came the same three loud measured knocks I had heard at the bedhead before this extraordinary drama had commenced.

As those sounds slowly ceased, I felt the whole room vibrate sensibly; and at the far end there rose, as from the floor, sparks or globules like bubbles of light, many-coloured – green, yellow, fire-red, azure. Up and down, to and fro, hither, thither, as tiny will-o'-the-wisps, the sparks moved, slow or swift, each at its own caprice. A chair (as in the drawing-room below) was now advanced from the wall without apparent agency, and placed at the opposite side of the table. Suddenly, as forth from the chair, there grew a shape – a woman's shape. It was distinct as a shape of life – ghastly as a shape of death. The face was that of youth, with a strange mournful beauty; the throat and shoulders were bare, the rest of the form in a loose robe of cloudy white. It began sleeking its long yellow hair, which fell over its shoulders; its eyes were not turned towards me, but to the door; it seemed listening, watching, waiting. The shadow of the shade in the background grew darker; and again I thought I beheld the eyes gleaming out from the summit of the shadow – eyes fixed upon that shape.

As if from the door, though it did not open, there grew out another shape equally distinct, equally ghastly – a man's shape – a young man's. It was in the dress of the last century, or rather in a likeness of such dress; for both the male shape and the female, though defined, were evidently unsubstantial, impalpable – simulacra – phantasms; and there was something incongruous, grotesque, yet fearful, in the contrast between the elaborate finery, the courtly precision of that old-fashioned fashioned garb, with its ruffles and lace and buckles, and the corpse-like aspect and ghost-like stillness of the fitting wearer. Just as the male shape approached the female, the dark Shadow started from the wall, all three for a moment wrapped in darkness. When the pale light returned, the two phantoms were as if in the grasp of the Shadow that towered between them; and there was a bloodstain on the breast of the female; and the phantom-male was leaning on its phantom-sword, and blood seemed trickling fast from the ruffles, from the lace; and the darkness of the intermediate Shadow swallowed them up – they were gone. And again the bubbles of light shot, and sailed, and undulated, growing thicker and thicker and more wildly confused in their movements.

The closet-door to the right of the fireplace now opened, and from the aperture there came the form of a woman, aged. In her hand she held letters – the very letters over which I had seen the Hand close; and behind her I heard a footstep. She turned round as if to listen, then she opened the letters and seemed to read; and over her shoulder I saw a livid face, the face as of a man long drowned – bloated, bleached – seaweed tangled in its dripping hair; and at her feet lay a form as of a corpse and beside the corpse there cowered a child, a miserable, squalid child, with famine in its cheeks and fear in its eyes. And as I looked in the old woman's face, the wrinkles and lines vanished, and it became a face of youth – hard-eyed, stony, but still youth; and the Shadow darted forth, and darkened over these phantoms as it had darkened over the last.

Nothing now was left but the Shadow, and on that my eyes were intently fixed, till again eyes grew out of the Shadow – malignant, serpent eyes. And the bubbles of light again rose and fell, and in their disordered, irregular, turbulent maze, mingled with the wan moon-light. And now from these globules themselves as from the shell of an egg, monstrous things burst out; the air grew filled with them; larvae so bloodless and so hideous that I can in no way describe them except to remind the reader of the swarming life which the solar microscope brings before his eyes in a drop of water – things transparent, supple, agile, chasing each other, devouring each other – forms like nought ever beheld by the naked eye. As the shapes were without symmetry, so their movements were without order. In their very vagrancies there was no sport; they came round me and round, thicker and faster and swifter, swarming over my head, crawling over my right arm, which was outstretched in involuntary command against all evil beings.

Sometimes I felt myself touched, but not by them; invisible hands touched me. Once I felt the clutch as of cold soft fingers at my throat. I was still equally conscious that if I gave way to fear I should be in bodily peril; and I concentrated all my faculties in the single focus of resisting, stubborn will. And I turned my sight from the Shadow – above all, from those strange serpent eyes – eyes that had now become distinctly visible. For there, though in nought else around me, I was aware that there was a will, and a will of intense, creative, working evil, which might crush down my own.

The pale atmosphere in the room began now to redden as if in the air of some near conflagration. The larvae grew lurid as things that live in fire. Again the room vibrated; again were heard the three measured knocks; and again all things were swallowed up in the darkness of the dark Shadow, as if out of that darkness all had come, into that darkness all returned.

As the gloom receded, the Shadow was wholly gone. Slowly as it had been withdrawn, the flame grew again into the candles on the table, again into the fuel in the grate. The whole room came once more calmly, healthfully into sight.

The two doors were still closed, the door communicating with the servants' room still locked. In the corner of the wall, into which he had so convulsively niched himself, lay the dog. I called to him – no movement; I approached – the animal was dead; his eyes protruded; his tongue out of his mouth; the froth gathered round his jaws. I took him in my arms; I brought him to the fire; I felt acute grief for the loss of my poor favourite – acute self-reproach; I accused myself of his death; I imagined he had died of fright. But what was my surprise on finding that his neck was actually broken – actually twisted out of the vertebrae. Had this been done in the dark? – Must it not have been by a hand human as mine? – Must there not have been a human agency all the while in that room? Good cause to suspect it. I cannot tell. I cannot do more than state the fact fairly; the reader may draw his own inference.

Another surprising circumstance – my watch was restored to the table from which it had been so mysteriously withdrawn; but it had stopped at the very moment it was so withdrawn; nor, despite all the skill of the watchmaker, has it ever gone since – that is, it will go in a strange erratic way for a few hours, and then comes to a dead stop – it is worthless.

Nothing more chanced for the rest of the night. Nor, indeed, had I long to wait before the dawn broke. Not till it was broad daylight did I quit the haunted house. Before I did so, I revisited the little blind room in which my servant and myself had been for a time imprisoned. I had a strong impression – for which I could not account – that from that room had originated the mechanism of the phenomena – if I may use the term – which had been experienced in my chamber. And though I entered it now in the clear day, with the sun peering through the filmy window, I still felt, as I stood on its floor, the creep of the horror which I had first there experienced the night before, and which had been so aggravated by what had passed in my own chamber. I could not, indeed, bear to stay more than half a minute within those walls. I descended the stairs, and again I heard the footfall before me; and when I opened the street door, I thought I could distinguish a very low laugh. I gained my own home, expecting to find my runaway servant there. But he had not presented himself; nor did I hear more of him for three days, when I received a letter from him, dated from Liverpool, to this effect:

"*HONOURED SIR, – I humbly entreat your pardon, though I can scarcely hope that you will think I deserve it, unless – which Heaven forbid! – you saw what I did. I feel that it will be years before I can recover myself; and as to being fit for service, it is out of the question. I am therefore going to my brother-in-law at Melbourne. The ship sails tomorrow. Perhaps the long voyage may set me up. I do nothing now but start and tremble, and fancy It is behind me. I humbly beg you, honoured sir, to order my clothes, and whatever wages are due to me, to be sent to my mother's, at Walworth – John knows her address."*

The letter ended with additional apologies, somewhat incoherent, and explanatory details as to effects that had been under the writer's charge.

This flight may perhaps warrant a suspicion that the man wished to go to Australia, and had been somehow or other fraudulently mixed up with the events of the night. I say nothing in refutation of that conjecture; rather, I suggest it as one that would seem to many persons the most probable solution of improbable occurrences. My own theory remained unshaken. I returned in the evening to the house, to bring away in a hack cab the things I had left there, with my poor dog's body. In this task I was not disturbed, nor did any incident worth note befall me, except that still, on ascending and descending the stairs I heard the same footfall in advance. On leaving the house, I went to Mr. J—'s. He was at home. I returned him the keys, told him that my curiosity was sufficiently gratified, and was about to relate quickly what had passed, when he stopped me, and said, though with much politeness, that he had no longer any interest in a mystery which none had ever solved.

I determined at least to tell him of the two letters I had read, as well as of the extraordinary manner in which they had disappeared, and I then inquired if he thought they had been addressed to the woman who had died in the house, and if there were anything in her early history which could possibly confirm the dark suspicions to which the letters gave rise. Mr. J— seemed startled, and, after musing a few moments, answered, "I know but little of the woman's earlier history, except, as I before told you, that her family were known to mine. But you revive some vague reminiscences to her prejudice. I will make inquiries, and inform you of their result. Still, even if we could admit the popular superstition that a person who had been either the perpetrator or the victim of dark crimes in life could revisit, as a restless spirit, the scene in which those crimes had been committed, I should observe that the house was infested by strange sights and sounds before the old woman died – you smile – what would you say?"

"I would say this, that I am convinced, if we could get to the bottom of these mysteries, we should find a living human agency."

"What! You believe it is all an imposture? For what object?"

"Not an imposture in the ordinary sense of the word. If suddenly I were to sink into a deep sleep, from which you could not awake me, but in that sleep could answer questions with an accuracy which I could not pretend to when awake – tell you what money you had in your pocket – nay, describe your very thoughts – it is not necessarily an imposture, any more than it is necessarily supernatural. I should be, unconsciously to myself, under a mesmeric influence, conveyed to me from a distance by a human being who had acquired power over me by previous rapport."

"Granting mesmerism, so far carried, to be a fact, you are right. And you would infer from this that a mesmeriser might produce the extraordinary effects you and others have witnessed over inanimate objects – fill the air with sights and sounds?"

"Or impress our senses with the belief in them – we never having been en rapport with the person acting on us? No. What is commonly called mesmerism could not do this; but there may be a power akin to mesmerism, and superior to it – the power that in the old days was called Magic. That such a power may extend to all inanimate objects of matter, I do not say; but if so, it would not be against nature, only a rare power in nature which might be given to constitutions with certain peculiarities, and cultivated by practice to an extraordinary degree. That such a power might extend over the dead – that is, over certain thoughts and memories that the dead may still retain – and compel, not that which ought properly to be called the soul, and which is far beyond human reach, but rather a phantom of what has been most earth-stained on earth, to make itself apparent to our senses – is a very ancient though obsolete theory, upon which I will hazard no opinion. But I do not conceive the power would be supernatural.

"Let me illustrate what I mean from an experiment which Paracelsus describes as not difficult, and which the author of the 'Curiosities of Literature' cites as credible: A flower perishes; you burn it. Whatever were the elements of that flower while it lived are gone, dispersed, you know not whither; you can never discover nor re-collect them. But you can, by chemistry, out of the burnt dust of that flower, raise a spectrum of the flower, just as it seemed in life. It may be the same with the human being. The soul has so much escaped you as the essence or elements of the flower. Still you may make a spectrum of it. And this phantom, though in the popular superstition it is held to be the soul of the departed, must not be confounded with the true soul; it is but the eidolon of the dead form.

"Hence, like the best-attested stories of ghosts or spirits, the thing that most strikes us is the absence of what we hold to be soul – that is, of superior emancipated intelligence. They come for little or no object – they seldom speak, if they do come; they utter no ideas above that of an ordinary person on earth. These American spirit-seers have published volumes of communications in prose and verse, which they assert to be given in the names of the most illustrious dead – Shakespeare, Bacon – heaven knows whom. Those communications, taking the best, are certainly not a whit of higher order than would be communications from living persons of fair talent and education; they are wondrously inferior to what Bacon, Shakespeare, and Plato said and wrote when on earth.

"Nor, what is more notable, do they ever contain an idea that was not on the earth before. Wonderful, therefore, as such phenomena may be (granting them to be truthful), I see much that philosophy may question, nothing that it is incumbent on philosophy to deny – viz. nothing supernatural. They are but ideas conveyed somehow or other (we have not yet discovered the means) from one mortal brain to another. Whether, in so doing, tables walk of their own accord, or fiend-like shapes appear in a magic circle, or bodyless hands rise and remove material objects, or a Thing of Darkness, such as presented itself to me, freeze our blood – still am I persuaded that these are but agencies conveyed, as by electric wires, to my own brain from the brain of another. In some constitutions there is a natural chemistry, and those may produce chemic wonders – in others a natural fluid, call it electricity, and these produce electric wonders. But they differ in this from Normal Science – they are alike objectless, purposeless, puerile, frivolous. They lead on to no grand results; and therefore the world does not heed, and true sages have not cultivated them. But sure I am, that of all I saw or heard, a man, human as myself, was the remote originator; and I believe unconsciously to himself as to the exact effects produced, for this reason: no two persons, you say, have ever told you that they experienced exactly the same thing. Well, observe, no two persons ever experience exactly the same dream. If this were an ordinary imposture, the machinery would be arranged for results that would but little vary; if it were a supernatural agency permitted by the Almighty, it would surely be for some definite end.

"These phenomena belong to neither class; my persuasion is that they originate in some brain now far distant; that that brain had no distinct volition in anything that occurred; that what does occur reflects but its devious, motley, ever-shifting, half-formed thoughts; in short, that it has been but the dreams of such a brain put into action and invested with a semisubstance. That this brain is of immense power, that it can set matter into movement, that it is malignant and destructive, I believe: some material force must have killed my dog; it might, for aught I know, have sufficed to kill myself, had I been as subjugated by terror as the dog – had my intellect or my spirit given me no countervailing resistance in my will."

"It killed your dog! That is fearful! Indeed, it is strange that no animal can be induced to stay in that house; not even a cat. Rats and mice are never found in it."

"The instincts of the brute creation detect influences deadly to their existence. Man's reason has a sense less subtle, because it has a resisting power more supreme. But enough; do you comprehend my theory?"

"Yes, though imperfectly – and I accept any crotchet (pardon the word), however odd, rather than embrace at once the notion of ghosts and hobgoblins we imbibed in our nurseries. Still, to my unfortunate house the evil is the same. What on earth can I do with the house?"

"I will tell you what I would do. I am convinced from my own internal feelings that the small unfurnished room at right angles to the door of the bedroom which I occupied, forms a starting-point or receptacle for the influences which haunt the house; and I strongly advise you to have the walls opened, the floor removed – nay, the whole room pulled down. I observe that it is detached from the body of the house, built over the small backyard, and could be removed without injury to the rest of the building."

"And you think, if I did that—"

"You would cut off the telegraph wires. Try it. I am so persuaded that I am right, that I will pay half the expense if you will allow me to direct the operations."

"Nay, I am well able to afford the cost; for the rest, allow me to write to you."

About ten days afterwards I received a letter from Mr. J—, telling me that he had visited the house since I had seen him; that he had found the two letters I had described, replaced in the drawer from which I had taken them; that he had read them with misgivings like my own; that he had instituted a cautious inquiry about the woman to whom I rightly conjectured they had been written. It seemed that thirty-six years ago (a year before the date of the letters), she had married against the wish of her relatives, an American of very suspicious character; in fact, he was generally believed to have been a pirate. She herself was the daughter of very respectable tradespeople, and had served in the capacity of a nursery governess before her marriage. She had a brother, a widower, who was considered wealthy, and who had one child of about six years old. A month after the marriage, the body of this brother was found in the Thames, near London Bridge; there seemed some marks of violence about his throat, but they were not deemed sufficient to warrant the inquest in any other verdict than that of 'found drowned'.

The American and his wife took charge of the little boy, the deceased brother having by his will left his sister the guardian of his only child – and in the event of the child's death, the sister inherited. The child died about six months afterwards – it was supposed to have been neglected and ill-treated. The neighbours deposed to have heard it shriek at night. The surgeon who had examined it after death said that it was emaciated as if from want of nourishment, and the body was covered with livid bruises. It seemed that one winter night the child had sought to escape – crept out into the back-yard – tried to scale the wall – fallen back exhausted, and been found at morning on the stones in a dying state. But though there was some evidence of cruelty, there was none of murder; and the aunt and her husband had sought to palliate cruelty by alleging the exceeding stubbornness and perversity of the child, who was declared to be half-witted. Be that as it may, at the orphan's death the aunt inherited her brother's fortune.

Before the first wedded year was out, the American quitted England abruptly, and never returned to it. He obtained a cruising vessel, which was lost in the Atlantic two years afterwards. The widow was left in affluence; but reverses of various kinds had befallen her: a bank broke –

an investment failed – she went into a small business and became insolvent – then she entered into service, sinking lower and lower, from housekeeper down to maid-of-all-work – never long retaining a place, though nothing peculiar against her character was ever alleged. She was considered sober, honest, and peculiarly quiet in her ways; still nothing prospered with her. And so she had dropped into the workhouse, from which Mr. J— had taken her, to be placed in charge of the very house which she had rented as mistress in the first year of her wedded life.

Mr. J— added that he had passed an hour alone in the unfurnished room which I had urged him to destroy, and that his impressions of dread while there were so great, though he had neither heard nor seen anything, that he was eager to have the walls bared and the floors removed as I had suggested. He had engaged persons for the work, and would commence any day I would name.

The day was accordingly fixed. I repaired to the haunted house – we went into the blind dreary room, took up the skirting, and then the floors. Under the rafters, covered with rubbish, was found a trap-door, quite large enough to admit a man. It was closely nailed down, with clamps and rivets of iron. On removing these we descended into a room below, the existence of which had never been suspected. In this room there had been a window and a flue, but they had been bricked over, evidently for many years. By the help of candles we examined this place; it still retained some mouldering furniture – three chairs, an oak settle, a table – all of the fashion of about eighty years ago. There was a chest of drawers against the wall, in which we found, half-rotted away, old-fashioned articles of a man's dress, such as might have been worn eighty or a hundred years ago by a gentleman of some rank – costly steel buckles and buttons, like those yet worn in court dresses – a handsome court sword – in a waistcoat which had once been rich with gold lace, but which was now blackened and foul with damp, we found five guineas, a few silver coins, and an ivory ticket, probably for some place of entertainment long since passed away. But our main discovery was in a kind of iron safe fixed to the wall, the lock of which it cost us much trouble to get picked.

In this safe were three shelves and two small drawers. Ranged on the shelves were several small bottles of crystal, hermetically stopped. They contained colourless volatile essences, of what nature I shall say no more than that they were not poisons – phosphor and ammonia entered into some of them. There were also some very curious glass tubes, and a small pointed rod of iron, with a large lump of rock-crystal, and another of amber – also a loadstone of great power.

In one of the drawers we found a miniature portrait set in gold, and retaining the freshness of its colours most remarkably, considering the length of time it had probably been there. The portrait was that of a man who might be somewhat advanced in middle life, perhaps forty-seven or forty-eight.

It was a most peculiar face – a most impressive face. If you could fancy some mighty serpent transformed into man, preserving in the human lineaments the old serpent type, you would have a better idea of that countenance than long descriptions can convey: the width and flatness of frontal – the tapering elegance of contour disguising the strength of the deadly jaw – the long, large, terrible eye, glittering and green as the emerald – and withal a certain ruthless calm, as if from the consciousness of an immense power. The strange thing was this – the instant I saw the miniature I recognised a startling likeness to one of the rarest portraits in the world – the portrait of a man of a rank only below that of royalty, who in his own day had made a considerable noise. History says little or nothing of him; but search the correspondence of his contemporaries, and you find reference to his wild daring, his bold profligacy, his restless spirit, his taste for the occult sciences. While still in the meridian of life he died and was

 69

buried, so say the chronicles, in a foreign land. He died in time to escape the grasp of the law, for he was accused of crimes which would have given him to the headsman.

After his death, the portraits of him, which had been numerous, for he had been a munificent encourager of art, were bought up and destroyed – it was supposed by his heirs, who might have been glad could they have razed his very name from their splendid line. He had enjoyed a vast wealth; a large portion of this was believed to have been embezzled by a favourite astrologer or soothsayer – at all events, it had unaccountably vanished at the time of his death. One portrait alone of him was supposed to have escaped the general destruction; I had seen it in the house of a collector some months before. It had made on me a wonderful impression, as it does on all who behold it – a face never to be forgotten; and there was that face in the miniature that lay within my hand. True, that in the miniature the man was a few years older than in the portrait I had seen, or than the original was even at the time of his death. But a few years! Why, between the date in which flourished that direful noble and the date in which the miniature was evidently painted, there was an interval of more than two centuries. While I was thus gazing, silent and wondering, Mr. J— said:

"But is it possible? I have known this man."

"How – where?" I cried.

"In India. He was high in the confidence of the Rajah of —, and well-nigh drew him into a revolt which would have lost the Rajah his dominions. The man was a Frenchman – his name de V—, clever, bold, lawless. We insisted on his dismissal and banishment: it must be the same man – no two faces like his – yet this miniature seems nearly a hundred years old."

Mechanically I turned round the miniature to examine the back of it, and on the back was engraved a pentacle; in the middle of the pentacle a ladder, and the third step of the ladder was formed by the date 1765. Examining still more minutely, I detected a spring; this, on being pressed, opened the back of the miniature as a lid. Withinside the lid was engraved "Mariana to thee – Be faithful in life and in death to —." Here follows a name that I will not mention, but it was not unfamiliar to me. I had heard it spoken of by old men in my childhood as the name borne by a dazzling charlatan, who had made a great sensation in London for a year or so, and had fled the country on the charge of a double murder within his own house – that of his mistress and his rival. I said nothing of this to Mr. J—, to whom reluctantly I resigned the miniature.

We had found no difficulty in opening the first drawer within the iron safe; we found great difficulty in opening the second: it was not locked, but it resisted all efforts till we inserted in the chinks the edge of a chisel. When we had thus drawn it forth, we found a very singular apparatus in the nicest order. Upon a small thin book, or rather tablet, was placed a saucer of crystal; this saucer was filled with a clear liquid – on that liquid floated a kind of compass, with a needle shifting rapidly round, but instead of the usual points of a compass were seven strange characters, not very unlike those used by astrologers to denote the planets. A very peculiar, but not strong nor displeasing odour, came from this drawer, which was lined with a wood that we afterwards discovered to be hazel. Whatever the cause of this odour, it produced a material effect on the nerves. We all felt it, even the two workmen who were in the room – a creeping tingling sensation from the tips of the fingers to the roots of the hair. Impatient to examine the tablet, I removed the saucer. As I did so the needle of the compass went round and round with exceeding swiftness, and I felt a shock that ran through my whole frame, so that I dropped the saucer on the floor. The liquid was spilt – the saucer was broken – the compass rolled to the end of the room – and at that instant the walls shook to and fro, as if a giant had swayed and rocked them.

The two workmen were so frightened that they ran up the ladder by which we had descended from the trapdoor; but seeing that nothing more happened, they were easily induced to return.

Meanwhile I had opened the tablet: it was bound in a plain red leather, with a silver clasp; it contained but one sheet of thick vellum, and on that sheet were inscribed, within a double pentacle, words in old monkish Latin, which are literally to be translated thus: – "On all that it can reach within these walls – sentient or inanimate, living or dead – as moves the needle, so work my will! Accursed be the house, and restless be the dwellers therein."

We found no more. Mr. J— burnt the tablet and its anathema. He razed to the foundations the part of the building containing the secret room with the chamber over it. He had then the courage to inhabit the house himself for a month, and a quieter, better-conditioned house could not be found in all London. Subsequently he let it to advantage, and his tenant has made no complaints.

But my story is not yet done. A few days after Mr. J— had removed into the house, I paid him a visit. We were standing by the open window and conversing. A van containing some articles of furniture which he was moving from his former house was at the door. I had just urged on him my theory that all those phenomena regarded as supermundane had emanated from a human brain; adducing the charm, or rather curse, we had found and destroyed in support of my philosophy. Mr. J— was observing in reply, "That even if mesmerism, or whatever analogous power it might be called, could really thus work in the absence of the operator, and produce effects so extraordinary, still could those effects continue when the operator himself was dead? And if the spell had been wrought, and, indeed, the room walled up, more than seventy years ago, the probability was, that the operator had long since departed this life"; Mr. J—, I say, was thus answering, when I caught hold of his arm and pointed to the street below.

A well-dressed man had crossed from the opposite side, and was accosting the carrier in charge of the van. His face, as he stood, was exactly fronting our window. It was the face of the miniature we had discovered; it was the face of the portrait of the noble three centuries ago.

"Good Heavens!" cried Mr. J—, "that is the face of de V—, and scarcely a day older than when I saw it in the Rajah's court in my youth!"

Seized by the same thought, we both hastened downstairs. I was first in the street; but the man had already gone. I caught sight of him, however, not many yards in advance, and in another moment I was by his side.

I had resolved to speak to him, but when I looked into his face I felt as if it were impossible to do so. That eye – the eye of the serpent – fixed and held me spellbound. And withal, about the man's whole person there was a dignity, an air of pride and station and superiority, that would have made anyone, habituated to the usages of the world, hesitate long before venturing upon a liberty or impertinence. And what could I say? What was it I would ask? Thus ashamed of my first impulse, I fell a few paces back, still, however, following the stranger, undecided what else to do. Meanwhile he turned the corner of the street; a plain carriage was in waiting, with a servant out of livery, dressed like a valet-de-place, at the carriage door. In another moment he had stepped into the carriage, and it drove off. I returned to the house. Mr. J— was still at the street door. He had asked the carrier what the stranger had said to him.

"Merely asked whom that house now belonged to."

The same evening I happened to go with a friend to a place in town called the Cosmopolitan Club, a place open to men of all countries, all opinions, all degrees. One orders one's coffee, smokes one's cigar. One is always sure to meet agreeable, sometimes remarkable, persons.

I had not been two minutes in the room before I beheld at a table, conversing with an acquaintance of mine, whom I will designate by the initial G—, the man – the Original of the Miniature. He was now without his hat, and the likeness was yet more startling, only I observed that while he was conversing there was less severity in the countenance; there was even a smile, though a very quiet and very cold one. The dignity of mien I had acknowledged in the street was also more striking; a dignity akin to that which invests some prince of the East – conveying the idea of supreme indifference and habitual, indisputable, indolent, but resistless power.

G— soon after left the stranger, who then took up a scientific journal, which seemed to absorb his attention.

I drew G— aside. "Who and what is that gentleman?"

"That? Oh, a very remarkable man indeed. I met him last year amidst the caves of Petra – the scriptural Edom. He is the best Oriental scholar I know. We joined company, had an adventure with robbers, in which he showed a coolness that saved our lives; afterwards he invited me to spend a day with him in a house he had bought at Damascus – a house buried amongst almond blossoms and roses – the most beautiful thing! He had lived there for some years, quite as an Oriental, in grand style. I half suspect he is a renegade, immensely rich, very odd; by the by, a great mesmeriser. I have seen him with my own eyes produce an effect on inanimate things. If you take a letter from your pocket and throw it to the other end of the room, he will order it to come to his feet, and you will see the letter wriggle itself along the floor till it has obeyed his command. 'Pon my honour, 'tis true: I have seen him affect even the weather, disperse or collect clouds, by means of a glass tube or wand. But he does not like talking of these matters to strangers. He has only just arrived in England; says he has not been here for a great many years; let me introduce him to you."

"Certainly! He is English, then? What is his name?"

"Oh! A very homely one – Richards."

"And what is his birth – his family?"

"How do I know? What does it signify? No doubt some parvenu, but rich – so infernally rich!"

G— drew me up to the stranger, and the introduction was effected. The manners of Mr. Richards were not those of an adventurous traveller. Travellers are in general constitutionally gifted with high animal spirits: they are talkative, eager, imperious. Mr. Richards was calm and subdued in tone, with manners which were made distant by the loftiness of punctilious courtesy – the manners of a former age. I observed that the English he spoke was not exactly of our day. I should even have said that the accent was slightly foreign. But then Mr. Richards remarked that he had been little in the habit for many years of speaking in his native tongue. The conversation fell upon the changes in the aspect of London since he had last visited our metropolis. G— then glanced off to the moral changes – literary, social, political – the great men who were removed from the stage within the last twenty years – the new great men who were coming on. In all this Mr. Richards evinced no interest. He had evidently read none of our living authors, and seemed scarcely acquainted by name with our younger statesmen. Once and only once he laughed; it was when G— asked him whether he had any thoughts of getting into Parliament. And the laugh was inward – sarcastic – sinister – a sneer raised into a laugh. After a few minutes G— left us to talk to some other acquaintances who had just lounged into the room, and I then said quietly:

"I have seen a miniature of you, Mr. Richards, in the house you once inhabited, and perhaps built, if not wholly, at least in part, in — Street. You passed by that house this morning."

Not till I had finished did I raise my eyes to his, and then his fixed my gaze so steadfastly that I could not withdraw it – those fascinating serpent eyes. But involuntarily, and if the words that translated my thought were dragged from me, I added in a low whisper, "I have been a student in the mysteries of life and nature; of those mysteries I have known the occult professors. I have the right to speak to you thus." And I uttered a certain password.

"Well," said he, dryly, "I concede the right – what would you ask?"

"To what extent human will in certain temperaments can extend?"

"To what extent can thought extend? Think, and before you draw breath you are in China!"

"True. But my thought has no power in China."

"Give it expression, and it may have: you may write down a thought which, sooner or later, may alter the whole condition of China. What is a law but a thought? Therefore thought is infinite – therefore thought has power; not in proportion to its value – a bad thought may make a bad law as potent as a good thought can make a good one."

"Yes; what you say confirms my own theory. Through invisible currents one human brain may transmit its ideas to other human brains with the same rapidity as a thought promulgated by visible means. And as thought is imperishable – as it leaves its stamp behind it in the natural world even when the thinker has passed out of this world – so the thought of the living may have power to rouse up and revive of the thoughts which the dead – such as those thoughts were in life – though the thought of the living cannot reach the thoughts which the dead now may entertain. Is it not so?"

"I decline to answer, if, in my judgment, thought has the limit you would fix to it; but proceed. You have a special question you wish to put."

"Intense malignity in an intense will, engendered in a peculiar temperament, and aided by natural means within the reach of science, may produce effects like those ascribed of old to evil magic. It might thus haunt the walls of a human habitation with spectral revivals of all guilty thoughts and guilty deeds once conceived and done within those walls; all, in short, with which the evil will claims rapport and affinity – imperfect, incoherent, fragmentary snatches at the old dramas acted therein years ago. Thoughts thus crossing each other haphazard, as in the nightmare of a vision, growing up into phantom sights and sounds, and all serving to create horror, not because those sights and sounds are really visitations from a world without, but that they are ghastly monstrous renewals of what have been in this world itself, set into malignant play by a malignant mortal.

"And it is through the material agency of that human brain that these things would acquire even a human power – would strike as with the shock of electricity, and might kill, if the thought of the person assailed did not rise superior to the dignity of the original assailer – might kill the most powerful animal if unnerved by fear, but not injure the feeblest man, if, while his flesh crept, his mind stood out fearless. Thus, when in old stories we read of a magician rent to pieces by the fiends he had evoked – or still more, in Eastern legends, that one magician succeeds by arts in destroying another – there may be so far truth, that a material being has clothed, from its own evil propensities certain elements and fluids, usually quiescent or harmless, with awful shape and terrific force – just as the lightning that had lain hidden and innocent in the cloud becomes by natural law suddenly visible, takes a distinct shape to the eye, and can strike destruction on the object to which it is attracted."

"You are not without glimpses of a very mighty secret," said Mr. Richards, composedly. "According to your view, could a mortal obtain the power you speak of, he would necessarily be a malignant and evil being."

"If the power were exercised as I have said, most malignant and most evil – though I believe in the ancient traditions that he could not injure the good. His will could only injure those with whom it has established an affinity, or over whom it forces unresisted sway. I will now imagine an example that may be within the laws of nature, yet seem wild as the fables of a bewildered monk.

"You will remember that Albertus Magnus, after describing minutely the process by which spirits may be invoked and commanded, adds emphatically that the process will instruct and avail only to the few – that a man must be born a magician! – that is, born with a peculiar physical temperament, as a man is born a poet. Rarely are men in whose constitution lurks this occult power of the highest order of intellect; usually in the intellect there is some twist, perversity, or disease. But, on the other hand, they must possess, to an astonishing degree, the faculty to concentrate thought on a single object – the energic faculty that we call will. Therefore, though their intellect be not sound, it is exceedingly forcible for the attainment of what it desires. I will imagine such a person, pre-eminently gifted with this constitution and its concomitant forces. I will place him in the loftier grades of society. I will suppose his desires emphatically those of the sensualist – he has, therefore, a strong love of life. He is an absolute egotist – his will is concentrated in himself – he has fierce passions – he knows no enduring, no holy affections, but he can covet eagerly what for the moment he desires – he can hate implacably what opposes itself to his objects – he can commit fearful crimes, yet feel small remorse – he resorts rather to curses upon others, than to penitence for his misdeeds. Circumstances, to which his constitution guides him, lead him to a rare knowledge of the natural secrets which may serve his egotism. He is a close observer where his passions encourage observation, he is a minute calculator, not from love of truth, but where love of self sharpens his faculties – therefore he can be a man of science.

"I suppose such a being, having by experience learned the power of his arts over others, trying what may be the power of will over his own frame, and studying all that in natural philosophy may increase that power. He loves life, he dreads death; he wills to live on. He cannot restore himself to youth, he cannot entirely stay the progress of death, he cannot make himself immortal in the flesh and blood; but he may arrest for a time so prolonged as to appear incredible, if I said it – that hardening of the parts which constitutes old age. A year may age him no more than an hour ages another. His intense will, scientifically trained into system, operates, in short, over the wear and tear of his own frame. He lives on. That he may not seem a portent and a miracle, he dies from time to time, seemingly, to certain persons. Having schemed the transfer of a wealth that suffices to his wants, he disappears from one corner of the world, and contrives that his obsequies shall be celebrated. He reappears at another corner of the world, where he resides undetected, and does not revisit the scenes of his former career till all who could remember his features are no more. He would be profoundly miserable if he had affections – he has none but for himself. No good man would accept his longevity, and to no men, good or bad, would he or could he communicate its true secret. Such a man might exist; such a man as I have described I see now before me! – Duke of —, in the court of —, dividing time between lust and brawl, alchemists and wizards; – again, in the last century, charlatan and criminal, with name less noble, domiciled in the house at which you gazed today, and flying from the law you had outraged, none knew whither; traveller once more revisiting London, with the same earthly passions which filled your heart when races now no more walked through yonder streets; outlaw from the school of all the nobler and diviner mystics; execrable Image of Life in Death and Death in Life, I warn you back from the cities and homes of healthful men; back to the ruins of departed empires; back to the deserts of nature unredeemed!"

There answered me a whisper so musical, so potently musical, that it seemed to enter into my whole being, and subdue me despite myself. Thus it said:

"I have sought one like you for the last hundred years. Now I have found you, we part not till I know what I desire. The vision that sees through the Past, and cleaves through the veil of the Future, is in you at this hour; never before, never to come again. The vision of no puling fantastic girl, of no sick-bed somnambule, but of a strong man, with a vigorous brain. Soar and look forth!"

As he spoke I felt as if I rose out of myself upon eagle wings. All the weight seemed gone from air – roofless the room, roofless the dome of space. I was not in the body – where I knew not – but aloft over time, over earth.

Again I heard the melodious whisper – "You say right. I have mastered great secrets by the power of Will; true, by Will and by Science I can retard the process of years: but death comes not by age alone. Can I frustrate the accidents which bring death upon the young?"

"No; every accident is a providence. Before a providence snaps every human will."

"Shall I die at last, ages and ages hence, by the slow, though inevitable, growth of time, or by the cause that I call accident?"

"By a cause you call accident."

"Is not the end still remote?" asked the whisper, with a slight tremor.

"Regarded as my life regards time, it is still remote."

"And shall I, before then, mix with the world of men as I did ere I learned these secrets, resume eager interest in their strife and their trouble – battle with ambition, and use the power of the sage to win the power that belongs to kings?"

"You will yet play a part on the earth that will fill earth with commotion and amaze. For wondrous designs have you, a wonder yourself, been permitted to live on through the centuries. All the secrets you have stored will then have their uses – all that now makes you a stranger amidst the generations will contribute then to make you their lord. As the trees and the straws are drawn into a whirlpool – as they spin round, are sucked to the deep, and again tossed aloft by the eddies, so shall races and thrones be plucked into the charm of your vortex. Awful Destroyer – but in destroying, made, against your own will, a Constructor!"

"And that date, too, is far off?"

"Far off; when it comes, think your end in this world is at hand!"

"How and what is the end? Look east, west, south, and north."

"In the north, where you never yet trod towards the point whence your instincts have warned you, there a spectre will seize you. 'Tis Death! I see a ship – it is haunted – 'tis chased – it sails on. Baffled navies sail after that ship. It enters the region of ice. It passes a sky red with meteors. Two moons stand on high, over ice-reefs. I see the ship locked between white defiles – they are ice-rocks. I see the dead strew the decks – stark and livid, green mould on their limbs. All are dead but one man – it is you! But years, though so slowly they come, have then scathed you. There is the coming of age on your brow. and the will is relaxed in the cells of the brain. Still that will, though enfeebled, exceeds all that man knew before you, through the will you live on, gnawed with famine; and nature no longer obeys you in that death-spreading region; the sky is a sky of iron, and the air has iron clamps, and the ice-rocks wedge in the ship. Hark how it cracks and groans. Ice will embed it as amber embeds a straw. And a man has gone forth, living yet, from the ship and its dead; and he has clambered up the spikes of an iceberg, and the two moons gaze down on his form. That man is yourself; and terror is on you – terror; and terror has swallowed your will. And I see swarming up the steep ice-rock, grey grisly things. The bears of the north have scented their quarry – they come near you and nearer, shambling and rolling their bulk. And in that day every moment shall seem to you longer than the centuries through which you have passed. And heed this – after life, moments continued make the bliss or the hell of eternity."

"Hush," said the whisper; "but the day, you assure me, is far off – very far! I go back to the almond and rose of Damascus! Sleep!"

The room swam before my eyes. I became insensible. When I recovered, I found G— holding my hand and smiling. He said, "You who have always declared yourself proof against mesmerism have succumbed at last to my friend Richards."

"Where is Mr. Richards?"

"Gone, when you passed into a trance – saying quietly to me, 'Your friend will not wake for an hour.'"

I asked, as collectedly as I could, where Mr. Richards lodged.

"At the Trafalgar Hotel."

"Give me your arm," said I to G—; "let us call on him; I have something to say."

When we arrived at the hotel, we were told that Mr. Richards had returned twenty minutes before, paid his bill, left directions with his servant (a Greek) to pack his effects and proceed to Malta by the steamer that should leave Southampton the next day. Mr. Richards had merely said of his own movements that he had visits to pay in the neighbourhood of London, and it was uncertain whether he should be able to reach Southampton in time for that steamer; if not, he should follow in the next one.

The waiter asked me my name. On my informing him, he gave me a note that Mr. Richards had left for me, in case I called.

The note was as follows: "I wished you to utter what was in your mind. You obeyed. I have therefore established power over you. For three months from this day you can communicate to no living man what has passed between us – you cannot even show this note to the friend by your side. During three months, silence complete as to me and mine. Do you doubt my power to lay on you this command? Try to disobey me. At the end of the third month, the spell is raised. For the rest I spare you. I shall visit your grave a year and a day after it has received you."

So ends this strange story, which I ask no one to believe. I write it down exactly three months after I received the above note. I could not write it before, nor could I show to G—, in spite of his urgent request, the note which I read under the gas-lamp by his side.

At Lorn Hall

Ramsey Campbell

RANDOLPH hadn't expected the map to misrepresent the route to the motorway quite so much. The roads were considerably straighter on the page. At least it was preferable to being directed by a machine on the dashboard, which would have reminded him of being told by Harriet that he'd gone wrong yet again, even when he knew where he was going. Although it oughtn't to be dark for hours, the April sky beyond a line of lurid hills had begun to resemble a charcoal slab. He was braking as the road meandered between sullen fields of rape when he had to switch the headlights on. The high beams roused swarms of shadows in the hedges and glinted on elongated warnings of bends ahead, and then the light found a signpost. It pointed down a lane to somewhere called Lorn Hall.

He stopped the Volvo and turned on the hazard lights. The sign looked neglected except by birds, which had left traces of their visits, but Lorn Hall sounded like the kind of place he liked to wander around. The children never did, complaining to Harriet if he even tried to take them anywhere like that on the days he had them. They loved being driven in the rain – the stormier the better, however nearly blind it made him feel – and so he couldn't help feeling relieved that they weren't with him to insist. He could shelter in the mansion until the storm passed over. He quelled the twitching of the lights and drove along the lane.

Five minutes' worth of bends enclosed by hulking spiky hedges brought him to a wider stretch of road. As it grew straight he glimpsed railings embedded in the left-hand hedge, rusting the leaves. Over the thorns and metal spikes surrounded by barbs he saw sections of an irregular roof patrolled by crows. Another minute brought him to the gateway of Lorn Hall.

He couldn't have given a name to the style of the high broad house. Perhaps the stone was darkened by the approaching storm, but he thought it would have looked leaden even in sunlight. At the right-hand end of the building a three-storey barrel put him in mind of a clenched fist with bricks for grey knuckles. Far less than halfway from it on the unadorned frontage, a door twice as tall as a man stood beneath a pointed arch reminiscent of a mausoleum. Five sets of windows each grew smaller as they mounted to the roofs, where chimneys towered among an assortment of slate peaks. Even the largest of the ground-floor windows were enmeshed with lattices, and every window was draped with curtains that the gloom lent the look of dusty cobwebs. Apart from an unmarked whitish van parked near the front door there was no sign of life.

The signpost had surely been addressed to sightseers, and the formidable iron gates were bolted open, staining the weedy gravel of the drive. One of the gateposts in the clutch of the hedge had lost its stone globe, which poked its dome bewigged with lichen out of the untended lawn. Ivy overgrew sections of the lawn and spilled onto the drive. The shapes the topiary bushes had been meant to keep were beyond guessing; they looked fattened and deformed by age. If Harriet had been with him she would have insisted on leaving by now, not to mention protesting that the detour was a waste of time. This was another reason he drove up to the house.

Did the curtains stir as he drew up beside the van? He must have seen shadows cast by the headlamps, because the movements at all three windows to the left of the front door had been identical. Nobody had ducked out of sight in the van either. Randolph turned off the lights and the engine, pocketing his keys as he turned to face the mansion. The sky had grown so stuffed with darkness that he didn't immediately see the front door was ajar.

To its left, where he might have looked for a doorbell, a tarnished blotchy plaque said **LORN HALL**. The door displayed no bell or knocker, just a greenish plaque that bore the legend **RESIDENCE OF CROWCROSS**. "Lord Crowcross," Randolph murmured as though it might gain some significance for him if not summon its owner to the door. As he tried to recall ever having previously heard the name he felt a chill touch as thin as a fingernail on the back of his neck. It was a raindrop, which sent him to push the heavy door wide.

The door had lumbered just a few inches across the stone flags when it met an obstruction. Randolph might have fancied that somebody determined but enfeebled was bent on shutting him out, perhaps having dropped to all fours. The hindrance proved to be a greyish walking boot that had toppled over from its place against the wall. Several pairs grey with a mixture of dried mud and dust stood in the gloomy porch. "Don't go any further," Harriet would have been saying by now, "you don't know if you're invited," but Randolph struggled around the door and kicked the boot against the wall. As he made for the archway on the far side of the porch, light greeted him.

Little else did. His approach had triggered a single yellowish bulb that strove to illuminate a large room. Opposite the arch an empty chair upholstered in a pattern so faded it wasn't worth distinguishing stood behind a bulky desk. Apart from a blotter like a plot of moss and earth, the desk was occupied by a pair of cardboard boxes and scattered with a few crumpled pamphlets for local attractions. The box that was inscribed **HONESTY** in an extravagantly cursive script contained three coins adding up to five pounds and so thoroughly stuck to the bottom that they were framed by glue. The carton marked **TOUR** in the same handwriting was cluttered with half a dozen sets of headphones. As Randolph dug in his pockets for change, his host watched him.

The man was in a portrait, which hung on the grey stone wall behind the desk it dwarfed. He stood in tweed and jodhpurs on a hill. With one hand flattened on his hip he seemed less to be surveying the landscape in the foreground of the picture than to be making his claim on it clear. The wide fields scattered with trees led to Lorn Hall. Although his fleshy face looked satisfied in every way, the full almost pouting lips apparently found it redundant to smile. His eyes were as blue as the summer sky above him, and included the viewer in their gaze. Was he less of an artist than he thought, or was he meant to tower over the foreshortened perspective? Randolph had guessed who he was, since the **C** that signed the lower left-hand corner of the canvas was in the familiar handwriting. "My lord," Randolph murmured as he dropped coins in the box.

The clink of metal didn't bring anyone to explain the state of the headphones. They weren't just dusty; as he rummaged through them, a leggy denizen scrabbled out of the box and fell off the desk to scuttle into the shadows. "That's very much more than enough," Harriet would have said to him in the way she did not much more often to their children. If you weren't adventurous you weren't much at all, and the gust of wind that slammed the front door helped Randolph stick to his decision. Having wiped the least dusty set of headphones with a pamphlet for a penal museum, he turned them over in his hands but couldn't find a switch. As he fitted them gingerly over his ears a voice said "You'll excuse my greeting you in person."

Nobody was visible beyond the open door beside the painting, only darkness. The voice seemed close yet oddly distant, pronouncing every consonant but so modulated it implied the speaker hardly cared if he was heard. "Do move on once you've taken in my portrait," he said. "There may be others awaiting their turn."

"There's only me," Randolph pointed out and stared with some defiance at the portrait. If Lord Crowcross had taught himself to paint, he wasn't the ideal choice of teacher. The landscape was a not especially able sketch that might have been copied from a photograph, and the figure was unjustifiably large. The artist appeared to have spent most time on the face, and Randolph was returning its gaze when Crowcross said "Do move on once you've taken in my portrait. There may be others awaiting their turn."

"I already told you I'm on my own," Randolph protested. The headphones must be geared to the listener's position in the house, but the technology seemed incongruous, as out of place as Randolph was determined not to let the commentary make him feel. "I'm on my way," he said and headed for the next room.

He'd barely stepped over the stone threshold when the light went out behind him. "Saving on the bills, are we?" he muttered as he was left in the dark. In another second his arrival roused more lights – one in each corner of an extensive high-ceilinged room. "This is where the family would gather of an evening," Crowcross said in both his ears. "We might entertain our peers here, such as were left. I am afraid our way of life lost favour in my lifetime, and the country is much poorer." The room was furnished with senile obese sofas and equally faded overweight armchairs, all patterned with swarms of letters like the initial on the portrait. A tapestry depicting a hunt occupied most of the wall opposite the windows, which Randolph might have thought were curtained so as to hide the dilapidation from the world. Several decanters close to opaque with dust stood on a sideboard near a massive fireplace, where cobwebbed lumps of coal were piled in the iron cage of the hearth. Had the place been left in this state to remind visitors it had fallen on hard times? Everyone Randolph knew would be ashamed to go in for that trick, whatever their circumstances. Quite a few were desperate to sell their homes, but all his efforts as an estate agent were in vain just now. He turned to find his way out of the room and saw Lord Crowcross watching him.

This time his host was in a painting of the room, though this was clearer from the positions of the furniture than from any care in the depiction. Sketchy figures sat in chairs or sprawled languidly on the couches. Just enough detail had been added to their faces – numerous wrinkles, grey hair – to signify that every one was older than the figure in the middle of the room. He was standing taller than he should in proportion to the others, and his obsessively rendered face appeared to be ignoring them. "Do make your way onwards whenever you're ready," he said without moving his petulant lips. "I fear there are no servants to show you around."

"No wonder the place is in such a state" – or rather the absence of servants was the excuse, and Randolph was tempted to say so. By now Harriet would have been accusing him of risking the children's health. He loitered to make the voice repeat its message, but this wasn't as amusing as he'd expected; he could almost have fancied it was hiding impatience if not contempt. "Let's see what else you've got to show me," he said and tramped out of the room.

All the lights were extinguished at once. He was just able to see that he'd emerged into a broad hallway leading to a staircase wider than his arms could stretch. He smelled damp on stone or wood. By the dim choked glow through doorways on three sides of the hall he made out that the posts at the foot of the steep banisters were carved with cherubs. In the gloom the eyes resembled ebony jewels, but the expressions on the chubby wooden faces were unreadable. "Do continue to the next exhibit," Crowcross prompted him.

Presumably this meant the nearest room. Randolph paced to the left-hand doorway and planted a foot on the threshold, but had to take several steps forward before the light acknowledged him. Fewer than half the bulbs in the elaborate chandelier above the long table lit up. "This is where the family would dine in style," Crowcross said, "apart from the youngest member."

The table was set for ten people. Dusty plates and silver utensils stained with age lay on the extravagantly lacy yellowed tablecloth. Like the upholstery of all the chairs, every plate was marked with **C**. Doilies to which spiders had lent extra patterns were spread on a sideboard, opposite which a painting took most of the place of a tapestry that had left its outline on the stone wall. Although the painting might have depicted a typical dinner at Lorn Hall, Randolph thought it portrayed something else. Of the figures seated at the table, only the one at the head of the table possessed much substance. The familiar face was turned away from his sketchy fellow diners to watch whoever was in the actual room, while a servant with a salver waited on either side of him. "Subsequently the situation was reversed," Crowcross said, "and I made the place my own."

Was the painting meant to remind him of the family he'd lost – to provide companionship in his old age? Randolph was trying to see it in those terms when the pinched voice said "By all means make your way onwards." He could do without a repetition, and he made for the hall. As the chandelier went dark he glimpsed somebody turning the bend of the staircase.

"Excuse me," Randolph called, moving the earpiece away from his right ear, but the other didn't respond. If they were wearing headphones too they might not have heard him. He'd only wanted to ask whether they knew what time the house closed to the public. At least he wasn't alone in it, and he picked his way along the hall to the kitchen, where part of the darkness seemed to remain solid as the weary light woke up.

It was a massive black iron range that dominated the grey room. A dormant fragment of the blackness came to life, waving its feelers as it darted into one of the round holes in the top of the range. How long had the kitchen been out of use? Surely nobody would put up with such conditions now. Chipped blotchy marble surfaces and a pair of freezers – one a head taller than Randolph, its twin lying horizontal – might be responsible for some of the chill that met him. A solitary cleaver lay on a ponderous table, which looked not just scored by centuries of knife strokes but in places hacked to splinters. Randolph looked around for a portrait, but perhaps Crowcross felt the kitchen was undeserving of his presence. "My father enjoyed watching the maids at their work," he said. "Red-handed skivvies, he called them. I did myself. Since then the world has changed so radically that their like have been among the visitors. Perhaps you are of their kind."

"Not at all," Randolph objected and felt absurd, not least because he suspected that Crowcross might have disagreed with him. He was searching for some trace of the people who'd worked here – initials carved on the table, for instance – when Crowcross said "There is no more to see here. Let us move on."

He sounded like a parody of a policeman – an officious one used to being obeyed. Randolph couldn't resist lingering to force him to say it again, and might easily have thought a hint of petulance had crept into the repetition. The light failed before Randolph was entirely out of the kitchen, but he glimpsed a door he'd overlooked in the underside of the staircase. As he reached for the heavy doorknob Crowcross said "Nothing of interest is kept down there. I never understood its appeal for my father."

Perhaps Randolph did, assuming the servants' quarters were below. He wondered how his guide's mother had felt about the arrangement. The scalloped doorknob wouldn't turn even when he applied both hands to it. As he looked for a key in the thick dust along the lintel Crowcross spoke. "I have told you nothing has remained. Let us see where I was a child."

His petulance was unmistakable. No doubt the basement rooms would be unlit in any case. Randolph was making his way past the stairs when he heard whoever else was in the house shuffling along an upper corridor. He wondered if there was more light up there, since the footfalls were surer than his own. They receded out of earshot as he pushed open the door of the turret room.

The room was lit, though nothing like immediately, by a single bare bulb on a cobwebbed flex. The round aloof ceiling caught much of the light, and Randolph suspected that even with the curtains open the room might have seemed like a cell to a child. It was furnished with a desk and a table in proportion, each attended by a starkly straight chair. While the table was set for a solitary meal, it had space for a pile of books: an infant's primer on top, a children's encyclopaedia many decades old at the bottom. Even when Randolph made the children read instead of playing, Harriet rarely agreed with his choice of books. The stone floor was scattered with building blocks, a large wooden jigsaw depicting a pastoral scene, an abacus, a picture book with pages thick as rashers, open to show a string like a scrawny umbilical cord dangling from the belly of a pig spotted with mould. The desk was strewn with exercise books that displayed the evolution of the omnipresent handwriting; one double page swarmed with a **C** well on its way to resembling the letter that seemed almost to infest the mansion. "This is where I spent the years in growing worthy of my name," said Crowcross. "In our day parents hired their delegates and kept them on the premises. Now the care of children is another industry, one more product of the revolution that has overtaken the country by stealth."

Above the desk a painting showed the room much as it was now, if somewhat brighter and more insubstantial. Crowcross stood between rudimentary impressions of the table and the desk. His arms were folded, and he might have been playing a teacher, except that nobody else was in the room – at least, not in the picture of it. "If you have learned everything you feel entitled to know," he said, "let us go up."

Did Randolph want to bother going on, given the condition of the house? Harriet certainly wouldn't have, even if the children weren't with them. He'd had nothing like his money's worth yet, unless he retrieved the payment on his way out. Perhaps the person upstairs might know more about the history of Lorn Hall, and Randolph didn't mind admitting to a guilty fascination, not least with the companion at his ear. "If you have learned everything you feel," Crowcross said and fell silent as Randolph left the room.

He was on the lowest stair when he noticed that the cherub on the banister had no wings. Somebody had chopped them off, leaving unequal stumps, and he couldn't help suspecting that the vandal had been Crowcross, perhaps since he'd found himself alone in Lorn Hall, the last of his line. He had the uneasy notion that Crowcross was about to refer to if not justify the damage. "If you have learned," the voice said before he could let go of the shaky banister.

From the bend in the stairs he saw the upper corridor, just about illuminated by the dimness beyond several doorways. Whoever he'd glimpsed on the stairs wasn't to be seen, and no light suggested they were in a room. Presumably they were at the top of the house by now. Barely glancing at a second mutilated cherub, Randolph made for the nearest room along the corridor.

Its principal item was an enormous four-poster bed. Burdened by plaster sloughed by the ceiling, the canopy sagged like an ancient cobweb. More plaster glistened on an immense dressing-table and an upholstered chair that must once have looked muscular. Most of the light from the few live bulbs in the chandelier fell short of a side room, where Randolph was just able to distinguish a marble bath with blackened taps and a pallid hand gripping the side to haul its owner into view, but that was a crumpled cloth. "You are in the master bedroom,"

Crowcross said tonelessly enough to be addressing an intruder. "Would you expect the master to have left more of a mark?"

His portrait showed him gripping the left-hand bedpost. As well as declaring ownership he gave the impression of awaiting a companion – watching with feigned patience for someone to appear in the doorway at Randolph's back. His imperiousness was somewhat undermined by crumbs of plaster adorning the top of the picture frame. "Will you know what robs a man of mastery?" he said. "Pray accompany me along the corridor." Randolph couldn't help feeling relieved not to be given the tour by his host in the flesh. He suspected the commentary had been recorded late in the man's life – when he was turning senile, perhaps. The chandelier in the next room contained even fewer bulbs, which faltered alight to outline another bed. Its posts were slimmer than its neighbour's, and the canopy was more delicate, which meant it looked close to collapsing under the weight of debris. Had a fall of plaster smashed the dressing-table mirror? Randolph could see only shards of glass among the dusty cosmetic items. "Here you see the private suite of the last Lady Crowcross," the voice said. "I fear that the ways of our family were not to her taste."

He held a bedpost in his left fist, but it was unclear which bedroom he was in. His depiction of himself was virtually identical with the one next door. A figure identifiable as a woman by the long hair draped over the pillow lay in the sketch of a bed. Randolph couldn't judge if Crowcross had given her a face, because where one should be was a dark stain, possibly the result of the age and state of the painting. "Please don't exert yourself to look for any signs of children," Crowcross said. "They were taken long ago. My lady disagreed with the Crowcross methods and found another of our fairer counterparts to plead her case."

"I know the feeling," Randolph said, immediately regretting the response. There was no point in being bitter; he told himself so every time he had the children and whenever he had to give them up. As he caught sight of the bathroom shower, which was so antiquated that the iron cage put him in mind of some medieval punishment, Crowcross said "You'll have none of the little dears about you, I suppose. They must conduct themselves appropriately in this house."

While Randolph thought his and Harriet's children might have passed the test, at least if they'd been with him, he was glad not to have to offer proof. As he made for the corridor he glimpsed a trickle of moisture or some livelier object running down a bar of the shower cage. "That's the style," said Crowcross. "There's nothing worthy of attention here if you've taken in my work."

It almost sounded as though the guide was aware of Randolph's movements. To an extent this was how the commentary operated, but could it really be so specific? He was tempted to learn how it would react if he stayed in the room, but when the lit bulbs flickered in unison as though to urge him onwards he retreated into the corridor.

The adjacent room was the last on this side. Shadows swarmed and fluttered among the dead bulbs as the chandelier struggled to find life. All the furniture was stout and dark, the bedposts included. One corner of the laden canopy had almost torn loose. The room smelled dank, so that Randolph wouldn't have been surprised to see moisture on the stone walls. "This was the sanctum of the eldest Crowcross," the voice said. "His wife's quarters were across the corridor."

Presumably the portrait was meant to demonstrate how the room had become his. He was at the window, holding back the curtain to exhibit or lay claim to a version of the landscape in summer. His eyes were still on his audience; Randolph was beginning to feel as if the gaze never left him. He was meeting it and waiting for the next words when he heard a vehicle start up outside the house. The bedposts shook like dislocated bones as he dashed across the room, and debris shifted with a stony whisper. The gap between the curtains was scarcely a finger's width. They felt capable of leaving handfuls of sodden heavy fabric in his grasp, and he knew where at least some of the smell came from. As he dragged them apart the rings twitched rustily along the metal rail. He craned forward, keeping well clear of the windowsill, which was scattered with dead flies like seeds of some unwelcome growth. The grid of cramped panes was coated with grime and crawling with raindrops, so that he was only just able to make out the grounds. Then, beyond the misshapen bloated topiary, he saw movement – the van near which he'd parked. Its outline wavered as it sped along the drive and picked up speed on the road.

Was Randolph alone in the house now? In that case, how had the driver sneaked past him? As the van disappeared into the rainswept gloom Crowcross said "Will you see the woman's quarters now? Everything is open to you, no matter what your pedigree."

How distasteful was this meant to sound? Randolph might have had enough by now except for the weather. He felt as if he was ensuring he outran the voice by hurrying across the corridor. A few bulbs sputtered alight in their cobwebbed crystal nest to show him yet another dilapidated bed. A hole had rotted in the canopy, dumping plaster on the stained bedclothes. Crowcross was holding a bedpost again, and a careless scribble behind him suggested that someone had just left the sketched bed. "Any little treasures would be barred from all these rooms," he said. "Have any found their way in now? Do keep an eye on their behaviour. We don't want any damage."

"I think you're having a bit of a joke," Randolph said. How senile had the speaker been by the time he'd recorded the commentary? Had he been seeing his home as it used to be? The light stuttered, rousing shadows in the bathroom and enlivening a muddy trickle on the initialled tiles above the marble trough. "If you have had your pleasure," Crowcross said, "the eldest breathed their last next door."

"My pleasure," Randolph retorted, and it was a question too.

The chandelier in the adjacent room lacked several bulbs. In the pensioned light a pair of four-posters occupied much of the cheerless space. Although the canopies were intact, the supports showed their age, some of the thinner ones bowing inwards. "They came here to grow as old as they could," Crowcross said. "Tell any little cherubs that, and how they had to stay together while they did."

Randolph thought the commentary had turned childish in the wrong way, if indeed there was a right one. He'd begun to feel it was no longer addressed to him or any listener, especially once Crowcross muttered "And then older."

The beds were flanked by massive wardrobes almost as dark outside as in. Both were open just enough to let Randolph distinguish shapes within. The figure with a dwarfish puffy head and dangling arms that were longer than its legs was a suit on a padded hanger. Its opposite number resembled a life-size cut-out of a woman drained of colour – just a long white dress, not a shroud. Nobody was about to poke a face around either of the doors, however much Randolph was reminded of a game of hide and seek. He'd never prevented the children from playing that, even if he might have in Lorn Hall. As he did his best to finish peering at the wardrobes Crowcross said "Are you still hoping for diversions? They await your judgement."

Randolph was starting to feel like the butt of a joke he wasn't expected to appreciate, since Crowcross didn't seem to think much of his visitors, let alone their views. When a pair of the lamps in the next room jittered alight, a ball on the billiard table shot into the nearest pocket. Of course only its legs had made it look as large as a billiard ball. Packs of battered cards were strewn across a table patched with baize, and cobwebs had overtaken a game of chess, where chipped marble chessmen lay in the dust beside the board. "This is where games were played," Crowcross said, "by those who had the privilege. Mine was waiting, and in the end I won."

He might have been talking to himself again, and resentfully at that. "We haven't seen your room yet," Randolph said and wondered if all of them had been. "You aren't ashamed of it, are you? It's a bit late to be ashamed."

He was heading for the turret room when Crowcross said "Eager to see where I was visited by dreams? Since then they have had the run of the house."

After a pause the room was illuminated by a stark grubby bulb. A bed with no posts and less than half the size of any of the others stood in the middle of the stone floor. The only other furniture was a wardrobe and a comparably sombre dressing-table with a mirror so low it cut Randolph off above the waist. Perhaps the soft toys huddled on the pillow had at some stage been intended to make the room more welcoming, but that wasn't their effect now. The pair of teddy bears and the lamb with boneless legs had all acquired red clownish mouths that contradicted their expressions. So much paint had been applied that it still resembled fresh blood.

They were in the portrait, where their sketched faces looked disconcertingly human. Perhaps the alterations to the actual toys had been a kind of preliminary study. Crowcross stood at the sunlit window, beyond which a distant figure stooped, hands outstretched. "I used to love watching the keepers trap their prey," Crowcross said. "They are put here for our pleasure and our use."

As Randolph turned away he saw what the painting didn't show. The toys on the pillow almost hid the clasped pair of hands protruding from beneath the quilt, which was blotched with mould. No, they were wings, none too expertly severed from the body – a pair of wooden wings. "This could have been a child's room," Crowcross mused. "We always raised our children to be men."

"Don't we talk about girls? I thought I was supposed to be unreasonable but my dear lord, my wife ought to listen to you," Randolph said and seemed to hear a confused violent noise in response. The window was shuddering under an onslaught of rain. He turned his back to all the eyes watching him – the portrait's and those of the disfigured toys, which were exactly as blank – and heard soft rapid footfalls on the stairs above him.

They were shuffling along the top corridor by the time he reached the staircase. "Excuse me, could you wait?" he shouted, raising the other headphone from his ear as he dashed upstairs so fast that he couldn't have said whether one cherub's face was splintered beyond recognition. Whenever he grabbed the banister, it wobbled with a bony clatter of its uprights. In a few seconds he saw that the top corridor was deserted.

None of the rooms showed a light. Perhaps whoever was about was trying to fix one, since otherwise their presence would have triggered it. Perhaps they were too busy to answer Randolph. Had the driver of the van been in the house at all? Presumably the person Randolph had glimpsed earlier was up here now. They couldn't have gone far, and he made for the turret room in the hope of finding them.

He saw he was alone once the meagre light recognised him. A lectern stood beside an imposing telescope that was pointed at the window. Astronomical charts – some crumpled, others chewed or torn to shreds – lay on the floor. "I never saw the appeal of the stars," Crowcross said, more distantly now. "I've no wish to be reminded of the dead. They say that's how old their light is. I preferred to watch the parade of the world. The glass brought it close enough for my taste."

He could have used the telescope to spy on the grounds and the road. Beyond the blurred fields Randolph saw an endless chain of watery lights being drawn at speed along the horizon. It was the motorway, where he promised himself he'd be soon, but he could finish exploring while he waited for the rain to stop, particularly since the family wasn't with him. He left the turret room with barely a glance at the portrait in which Crowcross appeared to be stroking the barrel of the telescope as if it were a pet animal.

The next room was a library. Shelves of bound sets of fat volumes covered every wall up to the roof. Each volume was embossed with a **C** like a brand at the base of its spine. More than one high shelf had tipped over with the weight of books or the carelessness with which they'd been placed, so that dozens of books were sprawled about the floor in a jumble of dislocated pages. A ladder with rusty wheels towered over several stocky leather armchairs mottled with decay. "This might be tidier," said Crowcross. "Perhaps that could be your job."

What kind of joke was this meant to be? Randolph wondered if the last lord of Lorn Hall could have pulled the books down in a fury at having nowhere to hang his portrait. He couldn't have done much if any reading in here unless there had been more light than the one remaining bulb provided. It was enough to show that Randolph was still alone, and he dodged across the corridor.

An unshaded bulb on a cobwebbed flex took its time over revealing a bedroom. All four bedposts leaned so far inwards that they could have been trying to grasp the light or fend it off. The canopy lay in a heap on the bed. Although Randolph thought he'd glimpsed clothes hanging in the tall black wardrobe as the light came on, once he blinked away the glare he could see nothing except gloom beyond the scrawny gap – no pale garment for somebody bigger than he was, no wads of tissue paper stuffed into the cuffs and collar. "This could be made fit for guests again," Crowcross said. "Would you consider it to be your place?"

He sounded as furtively amused as he looked in his portrait, which showed him standing in the doorway of the room, gazing at whoever was within. It made Randolph glance behind him, even though he knew the corridor was empty. "I wouldn't be a guest of yours," he blurted, only to realise that in a sense he was. Almost too irritated to think, he tramped out of the room.

Next door was a bedroom very reminiscent of its neighbour. The fallen canopy of the four-poster was so rotten it appeared to have begun merging with the quilt. The portrait beyond the bed was virtually identical with the last one, and the light could have been competing at reluctance with its peers. Nothing was visible in the half-open wardrobe except padded hangers like bones fattened by dust. Randolph was about to move on when Crowcross said "This could be made fit for guests again. Would you consider it to be your place?"

The repetition sounded senile, and it seemed to cling to Randolph's brain. As he lurched towards the corridor Crowcross added "Will you make yourself at home?"

It had none of the tone of an invitation, and Randolph wasn't about to linger. Whoever else was upstairs had to be in the last room. "Have you seen all you choose?" Crowcross said while Randolph crossed the corridor. "See the rest, then." The last room stayed dark until Randolph shoved the door wider, and then the lights began to respond – more of them than he thought he'd seen during the rest of the tour. The room was larger than both its neighbours combined, and graced with several chandeliers that he suspected had been replaced by solitary bulbs elsewhere in the house. They were wired low on the walls and lay on the floor, casting more shadow than illumination as he peered about the room.

It was cluttered with retired items. Rolled-up tapestries drooped against the walls, and so did numerous carpets and rugs, suggesting that someone had chosen to rob Lorn Hall of warmth. Several battered grandfather clocks stood like sentries over wooden crates and trunks that must have taken two servants apiece to carry them, even when they were empty of luggage. Smaller clocks perched on rickety pieces of furniture or lurked on the floorboards, and Randolph couldn't help fancying that somebody had tried to leave time up here to die.

Crouching shadows outnumbered the objects he could see, but he appeared to be alone. As he narrowed his eyes Crowcross said "Here is where I liked to hide. Perhaps I still do."

"I would if I were you," Randolph said without having a precise retort in mind. He'd noticed a number of paintings stacked against the wall at the far end of the room. Were they pictures Crowcross had replaced with his own, or examples of his work he didn't want visitors to see? Randolph picked his way across the floor, almost treading on more than one photograph in the dimness – they'd slipped from unsteady heaps of framed pictures which, as far as he could make out, all showed members of the Crowcross family. Even the glass on the topmost pictures in the heaps was shattered. He'd decided to postpone understanding the damage until he was out of the room when he reached the paintings against the wall.

Though the light from the nearest chandelier was obstructed by the clutter, the image on the foremost canvas was plain enough. It portrayed Crowcross in a field, his arms folded, one foot on a prone man's neck. He looked not so much triumphant as complacent. The victim's face was either turned away submissively or buried in the earth, and his only distinguishing feature was the **C** embossed on his naked back. It wasn't a painting from life, Randolph told himself; it was just a symbol or a fantasy, either of which was bad enough. He was about to tilt the canvas forward to expose the next when Crowcross spoke. "The last," he said.

Did he mean a painting or the room, or did the phrase have another significance? Randolph wasn't going to be daunted until he saw what Crowcross had tried to conceal, but as he took hold of a corner of the frame the portrait was invaded by darkness. A light had been extinguished at his back – no, more than one – and too late he realised something else. Because the headphones weren't over his ears any more he'd mistaken the direction of the voice. It was behind him.

The room seemed to swivel giddily as he did. The figure that almost filled the doorway was disconcertingly familiar, and not just from the versions in the paintings; he'd glimpsed it skulking in the wardrobe. It wore a baggy nightshirt no less pallid and discoloured than its skin. Its face was as stiff as it appeared in any of the portraits, and the unblinking eyes were blank as lumps of greyish paint. The face had lolled in every direction it could find, much like the contents of the rest of the visible skin – the bare arms, the legs above the clawed feet. When the puffy white lips parted Randolph thought the mouth was in danger of losing more than its shape. As the figure shuffled forward he heard some of the substance of the unshod feet slopping against the floor. Just as its progress extinguished the rest of the lights it spoke with more enthusiasm than he'd heard from it anywhere else in the house. "Game," it said.

An Eddy on the Floor

Bernard Capes

I HAD the pleasure of an invitation to one of those reunions or séances at the house, in a fashionable quarter, of my distant connection, Lady Barbara Grille, whereat it was my hostess's humour to gather together those many birds of alien feather and incongruous habit that will flock from the hedgerows to the least little flattering crumb of attention. And scarce one of them but thinks the simple feast is spread for him alone. And with so cheap a bait may a title lure.

That reference to so charming a personality should be in this place is a digression. She affects my narrative only inasmuch as I happened to meet at her house a gentleman who for a time exerted a considerable influence over my fortunes.

The next morning after the séance, my landlady entered with a card, which she presented to my consideration:

Major James Shrike.
H. M. Prison, D—

All astonishment, I bade my visitor up.

He entered briskly, fur-collared, hat in hand, and bowed as he stood on the threshold. He was a very short man – snub-nosed; rusty-whiskered; indubitably and unimpressively a cockney in appearance. He might have walked out of a Cruikshank etching.

I was beginning, "May I enquire—" when the other took me up with a vehement frankness that I found engaging at once.

"This is a great intrusion. Will you pardon me? I heard some remarks of yours last night that deeply interested me. I obtained your name and address from our hostess, and took the liberty of —"

"Oh! Pray be seated. Say no more. My kinswoman's introduction is all-sufficient. I am happy in having caught your attention in so motley a crowd."

"She doesn't – forgive the impertinence – take herself seriously enough."

"Lady Barbara? Then you've found her out?"

"Ah! You're not offended?"

"Not in the least."

"Good. It was a motley assemblage, as you say. Yet I'm inclined to think I found my pearl in the oyster. I'm afraid I interrupted – eh?"

"No, no, not at all. Only some idle scribbling. I'd finished."

"You are a poet?"

"Only a lunatic. I haven't taken my degree."

"Ah! It's a noble gift – the gift of song; precious through its rarity."

I caught a note of emotion in my visitor's voice, and glanced at him curiously.

"Surely," I thought, "that vulgar, ruddy little face is transfigured."

"But," said the stranger, coming to earth, "I am lingering beside the mark. I must try to justify my solecism in manners by a straight reference to the object of my visit. That is, in the first instance, a matter of business."

"Business!"

"I am a man with a purpose, seeking the hopefullest means to an end. Plainly: if I could procure you the post of resident doctor at D— gaol, would you be disposed to accept it?"

I looked my utter astonishment.

"I can affect no surprise at yours," said the visitor. "It is perfectly natural. Let me forestall some unnecessary expression of it. My offer seems unaccountable to you, seeing that we never met until last night. But I don't move entirely in the dark. I have ventured in the interval to inform myself as to the details of your career. I was entirely one with much of your expression of opinion as to the treatment of criminals, in which you controverted the crude and unpleasant scepticism of the lady you talked with. Combining the two, I come to the immediate conclusion that you are the man for my purpose."

"You have dumbfounded me. I don't know what to answer. You have views, I know, as to prison treatment. Will you sketch them? Will you talk on, while I try to bring my scattered wits to a focus?"

"Certainly I will. Let me, in the first instance, recall to you a few words of your own. They ran somewhat in this fashion: Is not the man of praetical genius the man who is most apt at solving the little problems of resourcefulness in life? Do you remember them?"

"Perhaps I do, in a cruder form."

"They attracted me at once. It is upon such a postulate I base my practice. Their moral is this: To know the antidote the moment the snake bites. That is to have the intuition of divinity. We shall rise to it some day, no doubt, and climb the hither side of the new Olympus. Who knows? Over the crest the spirit of creation may be ours."

I nodded, still at sea, and the other went on with a smile:

"I once knew a world-famous engineer with whom I used to breakfast occasionally. He had a patent egg-boiler on the table, with a little double-sided ladle underneath to hold the spirit. He complained that his egg was always undercooked. I said, "Why not reverse the ladle so as to bring the deeper cut uppermost?" He was charmed with my perspicacity. The solution had never occurred to him. You remember, too, no doubt, the story of Coleridge and the horse collar. We aim too much at great developments. If we cultivate resourcefulness, the rest will follow. Shall I state my system in nuce? It is to encourage this spirit of resourcefulness."

"Surely the habitual criminal has it in a marked degree?"

"Yes; but abnormally developed in a single direction. His one object is to out-manoeuvre in a game of desperate and immoral chances. The tactical spirit in him has none of the higher ambition. It has felt itself in the degree only that stops at defiance."

"That is perfectly true."

"It is half self-conscious of an individuality that instinctively assumes the hopelessness of a recognition by duller intellects. Leaning to resentment through misguided vanity, it falls 'all oblique'. What is the cure for this? I answer, the teaching of a divine egotism. The subject must be led to a pure devotion to self. What he wishes to respect he must be taught to make beautiful and interesting. The policy of sacrifice to others has so long stunted his moral nature because it is a hypocritical policy. We are responsible to ourselves in the first instance; and to argue an eternal system of blind self-sacrifice is to undervalue the fine gift of individuality. In such he sees but an indefensible policy of force applied to the advantage of the community. He is told to be good – not that he may morally profit, but that others may not suffer inconvenience."

I was beginning to grasp, through my confusion, a certain clue of meaning in my visitor's rapid utterance. The stranger spoke fluently, but in the dry, positive voice that characterises men of will.

"Pray go on," I said; "I am digesting in silence."

"We must endeavour to lead him to respect of self by showing him what his mind is capable of.

I argue on no sectarian, no religious grounds even. Is it possible to make a man's self his most precious possession? Anyhow, I work to that end. A doctor purges before building up with a tonic. I eliminate cant and hypocrisy, and then introduce self-respect. It isn't enough to employ a man's hands only. Initiation in some labour that should prove wholesome and remunerative is a redeeming factor, but it isn't all. His mind must work also, and awaken to its capacities. If it rusts, the body reverts to inhuman instincts."

"May I ask how you—?"

"By intercourse – in my own person or through my officials. I wish to have only those about me who are willing to contribute to my designs, and with whom I can work in absolute harmony. All my officers are chosen to that end. No doubt a dash of constitutional sentimentalism gives colour to my theories. I get it from a human trait in me that circumstances have obliged me to put a hoarding round."

"I begin to gather daylight."

"Quite so. My patients are invited to exchange views with their guardians in a spirit of perfect friendliness; to solve little problems of practical moment; to acquire the pride of self-reliance.

We have competitions, such as certain newspapers open to their readers in a simple form. I draw up the questions myself. The answers give me insight into the mental conditions of the competitors. Upon insight I proceed. I am fortunate in private means, and I am in a position to offer modest prizes to the winners; whenever such a one is discharged, he finds awaiting him the tools most handy to his vocation. I bid him go forth in no pharisaical spirit, and invite him to communicate with me. I wish the shadow of the gaol to extend no further than the road whereon it lies. Henceforth, we are acquaintances with a common interest at heart. Isn't it monstrous that a state-fixed degree of misconduct should earn a man social ostracism? Parents are generally inclined to rule extra tenderness towards a child whose peccadilloes have brought him a whipping. For myself have no faith in police supervision. Give a culprit his term and have done with it. I find the majority who come back to me are ticket-of-leave men. Have I said enough? I offer you the reversion of the post. The present holder of it leaves in a month's time. Please to determine here and at once."

"Very good. I have decided."

"You will accept?"

"Yes."

With my unexpected appointment as doctor to D— gaol, I seemed to have put on the seven-league boots of success. No doubt it was an extraordinary degree of good fortune, even to one who had looked forward with a broad view of confidence; yet, I think, perhaps on account of the very casual nature of my promotion, I never took the post entirely seriously. At the same time I was fully bent on justifying my little cockney patron's choice by a resolute subscription to his theories of prison management.

Major James Shrike inspired me with a curious conceit of impertinent respect. In person the very embodiment of that insignificant vulgarity, without extenuating circumstances, which is the type in caricature of the ultimate cockney, he possessed a force of mind and an earnestness of purpose that absolutely redeemed him on close acquaintanceship. I found him all he had stated himself to be, and something more.

He had a noble object always in view – the employment of sane and humanitarian methods in the treatment of redeemable criminals, and he strove towards it with completely untiring devotion. He was of those who never insist beyond the limits of their own understanding, clear-sighted in discipline, frank in relaxation, an altruist in the larger sense.

His undaunted persistence, as I learned, received ample illustration some few years prior to my acquaintance with him, when – his system being experimental rather than mature – a devastating epidemic of typhoid in the prison had for the time stultified his efforts. He stuck to his post; but so virulent was the outbreak that the prison commissioners judged a complete evacuation of the building and overhauling of the drainage to be necessary. As a consequence, for some eighteen months – during thirteen of which the Governor and his household remained sole inmates of the solitary pile (so sluggishly do we redeem our condemned social bog-lands) – the 'system' stood still for lack of material to mould. At the end of over a year of stagnation, a contract was accepted and workmen put in, and another five months saw the prison reordered for practical purposes.

The interval of forced inactivity must have sorely tried the patience of the Governor. Practical theorists condemned to rust too often eat out their own hearts. Major Shrike never referred to this period, and, indeed, laboriously snubbed any allusion to it.

He was, I have a shrewd notion, something of an officially petted reformer. Anyhow, to his abolition of the insensate barbarism of crank and treadmill in favour of civilizing methods no opposition was offered. Solitary confinement – a punishment outside all nature to a gregarious race – found no advocate in him. "A man's own suffering mind," he argued, "must be, of all moral food, the most poisonous for him to feed on. Surround a scorpion with fire and he stings himself to death, they say. Throw a diseased soul entirely upon its own resources and moral suicide results."

To sum up: his nature embodied humanity without sentimentalism, firmness without obstinacy, individuality without selfishness; his activity was boundless, his devotion to his system so real as to admit no utilitarian sophistries into his scheme of personal benevolence. Before I had been with him a week, I respected him as I had never respected man before.

One evening (it was during the second month of my appointment) we were sitting in his private study – a dark, comfortable room lined with books. It was an occasion on which a new characteristic of the man was offered to my inspection.

A prisoner of a somewhat unusual type had come in that day – a spiritualistic medium, convicted of imposture. To this person I casually referred.

"May I ask how you propose dealing with the newcomer?"

"On the familiar lines."

"But, surely – here we have a man of superior education, of imagination even?"

"No, no, no! A hawker's opportuneness; that describes it. These fellows would make death itself a vulgarity."

"You've no faith in their—"

"Not a tittle. Heaven forfend! A sheet and a turnip are poetry to their manifestations. It's as crude and sour soil for us to work on as any I know. We'll cart it wholesale."

"I take you – excuse my saying so – for a supremely sceptical man."

"As to what?"

"The supernatural." There was no answer during a considerable interval. Presently it came, with deliberate insistence:

"It is a principle with me to oppose bullying. We are here for a definite purpose – his duty plain to any man who wills to read it. There may be disembodied spirits who seek to distress or annoy where they can no longer control. If there are, mine, which is not yet divorced from its means to material action, declines to be influenced by any irresponsible whimsy, emanating from a place whose denizens appear to be actuated by a mere frivolous antagonism to all human order and progress."

"But supposing you, a murderer, to be haunted by the presentment of your victim?"

"I will imagine that to be my case. Well, it makes no difference. My interest is with the great human system, in one of whose veins I am a circulating drop. It is my business to help to keep the system sound, to do my duty without fear or favour. If disease – say a fouled conscience – contaminates me, it is for me to throw off the incubus, not accept it, and transmit the poison. Whatever my lapses of nature, I owe it to the entire system to work for purity in my allotted sphere, and not to allow any microbe bugbear to ride me roughshod, to the detriment of my fellow drops."

I laughed.

"It should be for you," I said, "to learn to shiver, like the boy in the fairytale."

"I cannot," he answered, with a peculiar quiet smile; "and yet prisons, above all places, should be haunted."

Very shortly after his arrival I was called to the cell of the medium, F—. He suffered, by his own statement, from severe pains in the head.

I found the man to be nervous, anaemic; his manner characterised by a sort of hysterical effrontery.

"Send me to the infirmary," he begged. "This isn't punishment, but torture."

"What are your symptoms?"

"I see things; my case has no comparison with others. To a man of my super-sensitiveness close confinement is mere cruelty."

I made a short examination. He was restless under my hands.

"You'll stay where you are," I said.

He broke out into violent abuse, and I left him.

Later in the day I visited him again. He was then white and sullen; but under his mood I could read real excitement of some sort.

"Now, confess to me, my man," I said, "what do you see?"

He eyed me narrowly, with his lips a little shaky.

"Will you have me moved if I tell you?"

"I can give no promise till I know."

He made up his mind after an interval of silence.

"There's something uncanny in my neighbourhood. Who's confined in the next cell – there, to the left?"

"To my knowledge it's empty."

He shook his head incredulously.

"Very well," I said, "I don't mean to bandy words with you"; and I turned to go.

At that he came after me with a frightened choke.

"Doctor, your mission's a merciful one. I'm not trying to sauce you. For God's sake have me moved! I can see further than most, I tell you!"

The fellow's manner gave me pause. He was patently and beyond the pride of concealment terrified.

"What do you see?" I repeated stubbornly.

"It isn't that I see, but I know. The cell's not empty!" I stared at him in considerable wonderment.

"I will make enquiries," I said. "You may take that for a promise. If the cell proves empty, you stop where you are."

I noticed that he dropped his hands with a lost gesture as I left him. I was sufficiently moved to accost the warder who awaited me on the spot.

"Johnson," I said, "is that cell—"

"Empty, sir," answered the man sharply and at once.

Before I could respond, F— came suddenly to the door, which I still held open.

"You lying cur!" he shouted. "You damned lying cur!" The warder thrust the man back with violence.

"Now you, 49," he said, "dry up, and none of your sauce!" and he banged to the door with a sounding slap, and turned to me with a lowering face. The prisoner inside yelped and stormed at the studded panels.

"That cell's empty, sir," repeated Johnson.

"Will you, as a matter of conscience, let me convince myself? I promised the man."

"No, I can't."

"You can't?"

"No, sir."

"This is a piece of stupid discourtesy. You can have no reason, of course?"

"I can't open it – that's all."

"Oh, Johnson! Then I must go to the fountainhead."

"Very well, sir."

Quite baffled by the man's obstinacy, I said no more, but walked off. If my anger was roused, my curiosity was piqued in proportion.

I had no opportunity of interviewing the Governor all day, but at night I visited him by invitation to play a game of piquet.

He was a man without 'incumbrances' – as a severe conservatism designates the *lares* of the cottage – and, at home, lived at his ease and indulged his amusements without comment.

I found him 'tasting' his books, with which the room was well lined, and drawing with relish at an excellent cigar in the intervals of the courses.

He nodded to me, and held out an open volume in his left hand. "Listen to this fellow," he said, tapping the page with his fingers:

> "*The most tolerable sort of Revenge, is for those wrongs which there is no Law to remedy. But then, let a man take heed, the Revenge be such, as there is no law to punish. Else, a man's Enemy, is still before hand, and it is two for one. Some, when they take Revenge, are Desirous the party should know, whence it cometh. This is the more Generous. For the Delight seemeth to be, not so much in doing the Hurt, as in making the Party repent: But Base and Crafty Cowards, are like the Arrow that flyeth in the Dark. Cosmus, Duke of Florence, had a Desperate Saying against Perfidious or Neglecting Friends, as if these Wrongs were unpardonable. You shall read (saith he) that we are commanded to forgive our Enemies: But you never read, that we are commanded to forgive our Friends.*"

"Is he not a rare fellow?"

"Who?" said I.

"Francis Bacon, who screwed his wit to his philosophy, like a hammer-head to its handle, and knocked a nail in at every blow. How many of our friends round about here would be picking oakum now if they had made a gospel of that quotation?"

"You mean they take no heed that the Law may punish for that for which it gives no remedy?"

"Precisely; and specifically as to revenge. The criminal, from the murderer to the petty pilferer, is actuated solely by the spirit of vengeance – vengeance blind and speechless – towards a system that forces him into a position quite outside his natural instincts."

"As to that, we have left Nature in the thicket. It is hopeless hunting for her now."

"We hear her breathing sometimes, my friend. Otherwise Her Majesty's prison locks would rust. But, I grant you, we have grown so unfamiliar with her that we call her simplest manifestations supernatural nowadays."

"That reminds me. I visited F— this afternoon. The man was in a queer way – not foxing, in my opinion. Hysteria, probably."

"Oh! What was the matter with him?"

"The form it took was some absurd prejudice about the next cell – number 47. He swore it was not empty – was quite upset about it – said there was some infernal influence at work in his neighbourhood. Nerves, he finds, I suppose, may revenge themselves on one who has made a habit of playing tricks with them. To satisfy him, I asked Johnson to open the door of the next cell —"

"He refused. It is closed by my orders."

"That settles it, of course. The manner of Johnson's refusal was a bit uncivil, but—"

He had been looking at me intently all this time – so intently that I was conscious of a little embarrassment and confusion. His mouth was set like a dash between brackets, and his eyes glistened. Now his features relaxed, and he gave a short high neigh of a laugh.

"My dear fellow, you must make allowances for the rough old lurcher. He was a soldier. He is all cut and measured out to the regimental pattern. With him Major Shrike, like the king, can do no wrong. Did I ever tell you he served under me in India? He did; and, moreover, I saved his life there."

"In an engagement?"

"Worse – from the bite of a snake. It was a mere question of will. I told him to wake and walk, and he did. They had thought him already in rigor mortis; and, as for him – well, his devotion to me since has been single to the last degree."

"That's as it should be."

"To be sure. And he's quite in my confidence. You must pass over the old beggar's churlishness."

I laughed an assent. And then an odd thing happened. As I spoke, I had walked over to a bookcase on the opposite side of the room to that on which my host stood. Near this bookcase hung a mirror – an oblong affair, set in brass repoussé work – on the wall; and, happening to glance into it as I approached, I caught sight of the Major's reflection as he turned his face to follow my movement.

I say 'turned his face' – a formal description only. What met my startled gaze was an image of some nameless horror – of features grooved, and battered, and shapeless, as if they had been torn by a wild beast.

I gave a little indrawn gasp and turned about. There stood the Major, plainly himself, with a pleasant smile on his face.

"What's up?" said he.

He spoke abstractedly, pulling at his cigar; and I answered rudely, "That's a damned bad looking-glass of yours!"

"I didn't know there was anything wrong with it," he said, still abstracted and apart. And, indeed, when by sheer mental effort I forced myself to look again, there stood my companion as he stood in the room.

I gave a tremulous laugh, muttered something or nothing, and fell to examining the books in the case. But my fingers shook a trifle as I aimlessly pulled out one volume after another.

"Am I getting fanciful?" I thought – "I whose business it is to give practical account of every bugbear of the nerves. Bah! My liver must be out of order. A speck of bile in one's eye may look a flying dragon."

I dismissed the folly from my mind, and set myself resolutely to inspecting the books marshalled before me. Roving amongst them, I pulled out, entirely at random, a thin, worn duodecimo, that was thrust well back at a shelf end, as if it shrank from comparison with its prosperous and portly neighbours. Nothing but chance impelled me to the choice; and I don't know to this day what the ragged volume was about. It opened naturally at a marker that lay in it – a folded slip of paper, yellow with age; and glancing at this, a printed name caught my eye.

With some stir of curiosity, I spread the slip out. It was a title-page to a volume, of poems, presumably; and the author was James Shrike.

I uttered an exclamation, and turned, book in hand.

"An author!" I said. "You an author, Major Shrike!"

To my surprise, he snapped round upon me with something like a glare of fury on his face.

This the more startled me as I believed I had reason to regard him as a man whose principles of conduct had long disciplined a temper that was naturally hasty enough.

Before I could speak to explain, he had come hurriedly across the room and had rudely snatched the paper out of my hand.

"How did this get—" he began; then in a moment came to himself, and apologised for his ill manners.

"I thought every scrap of the stuff had been destroyed," he said, and tore the page into fragments. "It is an ancient effusion, doctor – perhaps the greatest folly of my life; but it's something of a sore subject with me, and I shall be obliged if you'll not refer to it again."

He courted my forgiveness so frankly that the matter passed without embarrassment; and we had our game and spent a genial evening together. But memory of the queer little scene stuck in my mind, and I could not forbear pondering it fitfully.

Surely here was a new side-light that played upon my friend and superior a little fantastically.

Conscious of a certain vague wonder in my mind, I was traversing the prison, lost in thought, after my sociable evening with the Governor, when the fact that dim light was issuing from the open door of cell number 49 brought me to myself and to a pause in the corridor outside.

Then I saw that something was wrong with the cell's inmate, and that my services were required.

The medium was struggling on the floor, in what looked like an epileptic fit, and Johnson and another warder were holding him from doing an injury to himself.

The younger man welcomed my appearance with relief.

"Heard him guggling," he said, "and thought as something were up. You come timely, sir."

More assistance was procured, and I ordered the prisoner's removal to the infirmary. For a minute, before following him, I was left alone with Johnson.

"It came to a climax, then?" I said, looking the man steadily in the face.

"He may be subject to 'em, sir," he replied evasively.

I walked deliberately up to the closed door of the adjoining cell, which was the last on that side of the corridor. Huddled against the massive end wall, and half embedded in it, as it seemed, it lay in a certain shadow, and bore every sign of dust and disuse. Looking closely, I saw that the trap in the door was not only firmly bolted, but screwed into its socket.

I turned and said to the warder quietly – "Is it long since this cell was in use?"

"You're very fond of asking questions," he answered doggedly.

It was evident he would baffle me by impertinence rather than yield a confidence. A queer insistence had seized me – a strange desire to know more about this mysterious chamber. But, for all my curiosity, I flushed at the man's tone.

"You have your orders," I said sternly, "and do well to hold by them. I doubt, nevertheless, if they include impertinence to your superiors."

"I look straight on my duty, sir," he said, a little abashed. "I don't wish to give offence."

He did not, I feel sure. He followed his instinct to throw me off the scent, that was all.

I strode off in a fume, and after attending F— in the infirmary, went promptly to my own quarters.

I was in an odd frame of mind, and for long tramped my sitting-room to and fro, too restless to go to bed, or, as an alternative, to settle down to a book. There was a welling up in my heart of some emotion that I could neither trace nor define. It seemed neighbour to terror, neighbour to an intense fainting pity, yet was nor distinctly either of these. Indeed, where was cause for one, or the subject of the other? F— might have endured mental sufferings which it was only human to help to end, yet F— was a swindling rogue, who, once relieved, merited no further consideration.

It was not on him my sentiments were wasted. Who, then, was responsible for them?

There was a very plain line of demarcation between the legitimate spirit of enquiry and mere apish curiosity. I could recognise it, I have no doubt, as a rule, yet in my then mood, under the influence of a kind of morbid seizure, inquisitiveness took me by the throat. I could not whistle my mind from the chase of a certain graveyard will-o'-wisp; and on it went stumbling and floundering through bog and mire, until it fell into a state of collapse, and was useful for nothing else.

I went to bed and to sleep without difficulty, but I was conscious of myself all the time, and of a shadowless horror that seemed to come stealthily out of corners and to bend over and look at me, and to be nothing but a curtain or a hanging coat when I started and stared.

Over and over again this happened, and my temperature rose by leaps, and suddenly I saw that if I failed to assert myself, and promptly, fever would lap me in a consuming fire. Then in a moment I broke into a profuse perspiration, and sank exhausted into delicious unconsciousness.

Morning found me restored to vigour, but still with the maggot of curiosity in my brain. It worked there all day, and for many subsequent days, and at last it seemed as if my every faculty were honeycombed with its ramifications. Then "this will not do", I thought, but still the tunnelling process went on.

At first I would not acknowledge to myself what all this mental to-do was about. I was ashamed of my new development, in fact, and nervous, too, in a degree of what it might reveal in the matter of moral degeneration; but gradually, as the curious devil mastered me, I grew into such harmony with it that I could shut my eyes no longer to the true purpose of its insistence. It was the closed cell about which my thoughts hovered like crows circling round carrion.

'In the dead waste and middle' of a certain night I awoke with a strange, quick recovery of consciousness. There was the passing of a single expiration, and I had been asleep and was awake. I had gone to bed with no sense of premonition or of resolve in a particular direction; I sat up a monomaniac. It was as if, swelling in the silent hours, the tumour of curiosity had come to a head, and in a moment it was necessary to operate upon it.

I make no excuse for my then condition. I am convinced I was the victim of some undistinguishable force, that I was an agent under the control of the supernatural, if you like.

Some thought had been in my mind of late that in my position it was my duty to unriddle the mystery of the closed cell. This was a sop timidly held out to and rejected by my better reason. I sought – and I knew it in my heart – solution of the puzzle, because it was a puzzle with an atmosphere that vitiated my moral fibre. Now, suddenly, I knew I must act, or, by forcing self-control, imperil my mind's stability.

All strung to a sort of exaltation, I rose noiselessly and dressed myself with rapid, nervous hands. My every faculty was focused upon a solitary point. Without and around there was nothing but shadow and uncertainty. I seemed conscious only of a shaft of light, as it were, traversing the darkness and globing itself in a steady disc of radiance on a lonely door.

Slipping out into the great echoing vault of the prison in stockinged feet, I sped with no hesitation of purpose in the direction of the corridor that was my goal. Surely some resolute Providence guided and encompassed me, for no meeting with the night patrol occurred at any point to embarrass or deter me. Like a ghost myself, I flitted along the stone flags of the passages, hardly waking a murmur from them in my progress.

Without, I knew, a wild and stormy wind thundered on the walls of the prison. Within, where the very atmosphere was self-contained, a cold and solemn peace held like an irrevocable judgement.

I found myself as if in a dream before the sealed door that had for days harassed my waking thoughts. Dim light from a distant gas jet made a patch of yellow upon one of its panels; the rest was buttressed with shadow.

A sense of fear and constriction was upon me as I drew softly from my pocket a screwdriver I had brought with me. It never occurred to me, I swear, that the quest was no business of mine, and that even now I could withdraw from it, and no one be the wiser. But I was afraid – I was afraid. And there was not even the negative comfort of knowing that the neighbouring cell was tenanted. It gaped like a ghostly garret next door to a deserted house.

What reason had I to be there at all, or, being there, to fear? I can no more explain than tell how it was that I, an impartial follower of my vocation, had allowed myself to be tricked by that in the nerves I had made it my interest to study and combat in others.

My hand that held the tool was cold and wet. The stiff little shriek of the first screw, as it turned at first uneasily in its socket, sent a jarring thrill through me. But I persevered, and it came out readily by-and-by, as did the four or five others that held the trap secure.

Then I paused a moment; and, I confess, the quick pant of fear seemed to come grey from my lips. There were sounds about me – the deep breathing of imprisoned men; and I envied the sleepers their hard-wrung repose.

At last, in one access of determination, I put out my hand and sliding back the bolt, hurriedly flung open the trap. An acrid whiff of dust assailed my nostrils as I stepped back a pace and stood expectant of anything – or nothing. What did I wish, or dread, or foresee? The complete absurdity of my behaviour was revealed to me in a moment. I could shake off the incubus here and now, and be a sane man again.

I giggled, with an actual ring of self-contempt in my voice, as I made a forward movement to close the aperture. I advanced my face to it, and inhaled the sluggish air that stole forth, and – God in heaven!

I had staggered back with that cry in my throat, when I felt fingers like iron clamps close on my arm and hold it. The grip, more than the face I turned to look upon in my surging terror, was forcibly human.

It was the warder Johnson who had seized mc, and my heart bounded as I met the cold fury of his eyes.

"Prying!" he said, in a hoarse, savage whisper. "So you will, will you? And now let the devil help you!"

It was not this fellow I feared, though his white face was set like a demon's; and in the thick of my terror I made a feeble attempt to assert my authority.

"Let me go!" I muttered. "What! You dare?"

In his frenzy he shook my arm as a terrier shakes a rat, and, like a dog, he held on, daring me to release myself.

For the moment an instinct half-murderous leapt in me. It sank and was overwhelmed in a slough of some more secret emotion.

"Oh!" I whispered, collapsing, as it were, to the man's fury, even pitifully deprecating it. "What is it? What's there? It drew me – something unnameable."

He gave a snapping laugh like a cough. His rage waxed second by second. There was a maniacal suggestiveness in it; and not much longer, it was evident, could he have it under control. I saw it run and congest in his eyes; and, on the instant of its accumulation, he tore at me with a sudden wild strength, and drove me up against the very door of the secret cell.

The action, the necessity of self-defence, restored me to some measure of dignity and sanity.

"Let me go, you ruffian!" I cried, struggling to free myself from his grasp.

It was useless. He held me madly. There was no beating him off: and, so holding me, he managed to produce a single key from one of his pockets, and to slip it with a rusty clang into the lock of the door.

"You dirty, prying civilian!" he panted at me, as he swayed this way and that with the pull of my body. "You shall have your wish, by G—! You want to see inside, do you? Look, then!"

He dashed open the door as he spoke, and pulled me violently into the opening. A great waft of the cold, dank air came at us, and with it – what?

The warder had jerked his dark lantern from his belt, and now – an arm of his still clasped about one of mine – snapped the slide open.

"Where is it?" he muttered, directing the disc of light round and about the floor of the cell, I ceased struggling. Some counter influence was raising an odd curiosity in me.

"Ah!" he cried, in a stifled voice, "there you are, my friend!". He was setting the light slowly travelling along the stone flags close by the wall over against us, and now, so guiding it, looked askance at me with a small, greedy smile.

"Follow the light, sir," he whispered jeeringly.

I looked, and saw twirling on the floor, in the patch of radiance cast by the lamp, a little eddy of dust, it seemed. This eddy was never still, but went circling in that stagnant place without apparent cause or influence; and, as it circled, it moved slowly on by wall and corner, so that presently in its progress it must reach us where we stood.

Now, draughts will play queer freaks in quiet places, and of this trifling phenomenon I should have taken little note ordinarily. But, I must say at once, that as I gazed upon the odd moving thing my heart seemed to fall in upon itself like a drained artery.

"Johnson!" I cried, "I must get out of this. I don't know what's the matter, or – Why do you hold me? D— it! Man, let me go; let me go, I say!"

As I grappled with him he dropped the lantern with a crash and flung his arms violently about me.

"You don't!" he panted, the muscles of his bent and rigid neck seeming actually to cut into my shoulder-blade. "You don't, by G—! You came of your own accord, and now you shall take your bellyfull!"

It was a struggle for life or death, or, worse, for life and reason. But I was young and wiry, and held my own, if I could do little more. Yet there was something to combat beyond the mere brute strength of the man I struggled with, for I fought in an atmosphere of horror unexplainable, and I knew that inch by inch the thing on the floor was circling round in our direction.

Suddenly in the breathing darkness I felt it close upon us, gave one mortal yell of fear, and, with a last despairing fury, tore myself from the encircling arms, and sprang into the corridor without. As I plunged and leapt, the warder clutched at me, missed, caught a foot on the edge of the door, and, as the latter whirled to with a clap, fell heavily at my feet in a fit. Then, as I stood staring down upon him, steps sounded along the corridor and the voices of scared men hurrying up.

Ill and shaken, and, for the time, little in love with life, yet fearing death as I had never dreaded it before, I spent the rest of that horrible night huddled between my crumpled sheets, fearing to look forth, fearing to think, wild only to be far away, to be housed in some green and innocent hamlet, where I might forget the madness and the terror in learning to walk the unvext paths of placid souls. That unction I could lay to my heart, at least. I had done the manly part by the stricken warder, whom I had attended to his own home, in a row of little tenements that stood south of the prison walls. I had replied to all enquiries with some dignity and spirit, attributing my ruffled condition to an assault on the part of Johnson, when he was already under the shadow of his seizure. I had directed his removal, and grudged him no professional attention that it was in my power to bestow. But afterwards, locked into my room, my whole nervous system broke up like a trodden ant-hill, leaving me conscious of nothing but an aimless scurrying terror and the black swarm of thoughts, so that I verily fancied my reason would give under the strain.

Yet I had more to endure and to triumph over.

Near morning I fell into a troubled sleep, throughout which the drawn twitch of muscle seemed an accent on every word of ill-omen I had ever spelt out of the alphabet of fear. If my body rested, my brain was an open chamber for any toad of ugliness that listed to 'sit at squat' in.

Suddenly I woke to the fact that there was a knocking at my door – that there had been for some little time.

I cried, "Come in!" finding a weak restorative in the mere sound of my own human voice; then, remembering the key was turned, bade the visitor wait until I could come to him.

Scrambling, feeling dazed and white-livered, out of bed, I opened the door, and met one of the warders on the threshold. The man looked scared, and his lips, I noticed, were set in a somewhat boding fashion.

"Can you come at once, sir?" he said. "There's summat wrong with the Governor."

"Wrong? What's the matter with him?"

"Why" – he looked down, rubbed an imaginary protuberance smooth with his foot, and glanced up at me again with a quick, furtive expression – "he's got his face set in the grating of 47, and danged if a man Jack of us can get him to move or speak."

I turned away, feeling sick. I hurriedly pulled on coat and trousers, and hurriedly went off with my summoner, Reason was all absorbed in a wildest phantasy of apprehension.

"Who found him?" I muttered, as we sped on.

"Vokins see him go down the corridor about half after eight, sir, and see him give a start like when he noticed the trap open. It's never been so before in my time. Johnson must ha' done it last night, before he were took."

"Yes, yes."

"The man said the Governor went to shut it, it seemed, and to draw his face to'ards the bars in so doin'. Then he see him a-lookin' through, as he thought; but nat'rally it weren't no business of his'n, and he went off about his work. But when he come anigh agen, fifteen minutes later, there were the Governor in the same position; and he got scared over it, and called out to one or two of us."

"Why didn't one of you ask the Major if anything was wrong?"

"Bless you! We did; and no answer. And we pulled him, compatible with discipline, but—"

"But what?"

"He's stuck."

"Stuck!"

"See for yourself, sir. That's all I ask."

I did, a moment later. A little group was collected about the door of cell 47, and the members of it spoke together in whispers, as if they were frightened men. One young fellow, with a face white in patches, as if it had been floured, slid from them as I approached, and accosted me tremulously.

"Don't go anigh, sir. There's something wrong about the place."

I pulled myself together, forcibly beating down the excitement reawakened by the associations of the spot. In the discomfiture of others' nerves I found my own restoration.

"Don't be an ass!" I said, in a determined voice. "There's nothing here that can't be explained. Make way for me, please!

They parted and let me through, and I saw him. He stood, spruce, frock-coated, dapper, as he always was, with his face pressed against and into the grill, and either hand raised and clenched tightly round a bar of the trap. His posture was as of one caught and striving frantically to release himself; yet the narrowness of the interval between the rails precluded so extravagant an idea. He stood quite motionless – taut and on the strain, as it were – and nothing of his face was visible but the back ridges of his jawbones, showing white through a bush of red whiskers.

"Major Shrike!" I rapped out, and, allowing myself no hesitation, reached forth my hand and grasped his shoulder. The body vibrated under my touch, but he neither answered nor made sign of hearing me. Then I pulled at him forcibly, and ever with increasing strength. His fingers held like steel braces. He seemed glued to the trap, like Theseus to the rock.

Hastily I peered round, to see if I could get a glimpse of his face. I noticed enough to send me back with a little stagger.

"Has none of you got a key to this door?" I asked, reviewing the scared faces about me, than which my own was no less troubled, I feel sure.

"Only the Governor, sir," said the warder who had fetched me. "There's not a man but him amongst us that ever seen this opened."

He was wrong there, I could have told him; but held my tongue, for obvious reasons.

"I want it opened. Will one of you feel in his pockets?"

Not a soul stirred. Even had not sense of discipline precluded, that of a certain inhuman atmosphere made fearful creatures of them all.

"Then," said I, "I must do it myself."

I turned once more to the stiff-strung figure, had actually put hand on it, when an exclamation from Vokins arrested me.

"There's a key – there, sir!" he said – "stickin' out yonder between his feet."

Sure enough there was – Johnson's, no doubt, that had been shot from its socket by the clapping to of the door, and afterwards kicked aside by the warder in his convulsive struggles.

I stooped, only too thankful for the respite, and drew it forth. I had seen it but once before, yet I recognised it at a glance.

Now, I confess, my heart felt ill as I slipped the key into the wards, and a sickness of resentment at the tyranny of Fate in making me its helpless minister surged up in my veins.

Once, with my fingers on the iron loop, I paused, and ventured a fearful side glance at the figure whose crooked elbow almost touched my face; then, strung to the high pitch of inevitability, I shot the lock, pushed at the door, and in the act, made a back leap into the corridor.

Scarcely, in doing so, did I look for the totter and collapse outwards of the rigid form. I had expected to see it fall away, face down, into the cell, as its support swung from it. Yet it was, I swear, as if something from within had relaxed its grasp and given the fearful dead man a swingeing push outwards as the door opened.

It went on its back, with a dusty slap on the stone flags, and from all its spectators – me included – came a sudden drawn sound, like a wind in a keyhole.

What can I say, or how describe it? A dead thing it was – but the face!

Barred with livid scars where the grating rails had crossed it, the rest seemed to have been worked and kneaded into a mere featureless plate of yellow and expressionless flesh.

And it was this I had seen in the glass!

There was an interval following the experience above narrated, during which a certain personality that had once been mine was effaced or suspended, and I seemed a passive creature, innocent of the least desire of independence. It was not that I was actually ill or actually insane.

A merciful Providence set my finer wits slumbering, that was all, leaving me a sufficiency of the grosser faculties that were necessary to the right ordering of my behaviour.

I kept to my room, it is true, and even lay a good deal in bed; but this was more to satisfy the busy scruples of a locum tenens – a practitioner of the neighbourhood, who came daily to the prison to officiate in my absence – than to cosset a complaint that in its inactivity was purely negative. I could review what had happened with a calmness as profound as if I had read of it in a book. I could have wished to continue my duties, indeed, had the power of insistence remained to me. But the saner medicus was acute where I had gone blunt, and bade me to the restful course. He was right. I was mentally stunned, and had I not slept off my lethargy, I should have gone mad in an hour – leapt at a bound, probably, from inertia to flaming lunacy.

I remembered everything, but through a fluffy atmosphere, so to speak. It was as if I looked on bygone pictures through ground glass that softened the ugly outlines.

Sometimes I referred to these to my substitute, who was wise to answer me according to my mood; for the truth left me unruffled, whereas an obvious evasion of it would have distressed me.

"Hammond," I said one day, "I have never yet asked you. How did I give my evidence at the inquest?"

"Like a doctor and a sane man."

"That's good. But it was a difficult course to steer. You conducted the post-mortem. Did any peculiarity in the dead man's face strike you?"

"Nothing but this: that the excessive contraction of the bicipital muscles had brought the features into such forcible contact with the bars as to cause bruising and actual abrasion. He must have been dead some little time when you found him."

"And nothing else? You noticed nothing else in his face – a sort of obliteration of what makes one human, I mean?"

"Oh, dear, no! Nothing but the painful constriction that marks any ordinary fatal attack of angina pectoris. There's a rum breach of promise case in the paper today. You should read it; it'll make you laugh."

I had no more inclination to laugh than to sigh; but I accepted the change of subject with an equanimity now habitual to me.

One morning I sat up in bed, and knew that consciousness was wide awake in me once more. It had slept, and now rose refreshed, but trembling. Looking back, all in a flutter of new responsibility, along the misty path by way of which I had recently loitered, I shook with an awful thankfulness at sight of the pitfalls I had skirted and escaped – of the demons my witlessness had baffled.

The joy of life was in my heart again, but chastened and made pitiful by experience.

Hammond noticed the change in me directly he entered, and congratulated me upon it.

"Go slow at first, old man," he said. "You've fairly sloughed the old skin; but give the sun time to toughen the new one. Walk in it at present, and be content."

I was, in great measure, and I followed his advice. I got leave of absence, and ran down for a month in the country to a certain house we wot of, where kindly ministration to my convalescence was only one of the many blisses to be put to an account of rosy days.

> *Then did my love awake,*
> *Most like a lily-flower,*
> *And as the lovely queene of heaven,*
> *So shone shee in her bower.*

Ah, me! Ah, me! When was it? A year ago, or two-thirds of a lifetime? Alas! 'Age with stealing steps hath clawde me with his erowch.' And will the yews root in my heart, I wonder?

I was well, sane, recovered, when one morning, towards the end of my visit, I received a letter from Hammond, enclosing a packet addressed to me, and jealously sealed and fastened. My friend's communication ran as follows:

There died here yesterday afternoon a warder, Johnson – he who had that apoplectic seizure, you will remember, the night before poor Shrik's exit. I attended him to the end, and, being alone with him an hour before the finish, he took the enclosed from under his pillow, and a solemn oath from me that I would forward it direct to you sealed as you will find it, and permit no other soul to examine or even touch it. I acquit myself of the charge, but, my dear fellow, with an uneasy sense of the responsibility I incur in thus possibly suggesting to you a retrospect of events which you had much best consign to the limbo of the – not inexplainable, but not worth trying to explain. It was patent from what I have gathered that you were in an overstrung and excitable condition at that time, and that your temporary collapse was purely nervous in its character. It seems there was some nonsense abroad in the prison about a certain cell, and that there were fools who thought fit to associate Johnson's attack and the other's death with the opening of that cell's door. I have given the new Governor a tip, and he has stopped all that. We have examined the cell in company, and found it, as one might suppose, a very ordinary chamber. The two men died perfectly natural deaths, and there is the last to be said on the subject. I mention it only from the fear that the enclosed may contain some allusion to the rubbish, a perusal of which might check the wholesome convalescence of your thoughts. If you take my advice, you will throw the packet into the fire unread. At least, if you do examine it, postpone the duty till you feel impervious to any mental trickery, and – bear in mind that you are a worthy member of a particularly matter-of-fact and unemotional profession.

I smiled at the last clause, for I was now in a condition to feel a rather warm shame over my erst weak-knee'd collapse before a sheet and an illuminated turnip. I took the packet to my bedroom, shut the door, and sat myself down by the open window. The garden lay below me, and the dewy meadows beyond. In the one, bees were busy ruffling the ruddy gillyflowers and April stocks; in the other, the hedge twigs were all frosted with Mary buds, as if Spring had brushed them with the fleece of her wings in passing.

I fetched a sigh of content as I broke the seal of the packet and brought out the enclosure.

Somewhere in the garden a little sardonic laugh was clipped to silence. It came from groom or maid, no doubt; yet it thrilled me with an odd feeling of uncanniness, and I shivered slightly.

"Bah!" I said to myself determinedly. "There is a shrewd nip in the wind, for all the show of sunlight"; and I rose, pulled down the window, and resumed my seat.

Then in the closed room, that had become deathly quiet by contrast, I opened and read the dead man's letter.

Sir, I hope you will read what I here put down. I lay it on you as a solemn injunction, for I am a dying man, and I know it. And to who is my death due, and the Governor's death, if not to you, for your pryin' and curiosity, as surely as if you had drove a nife through our harts? Therefore, I say, Read this, and take my burden from me, for it has been a burden; and now it is right that you that interfered should have it on your own mortal shoulders. The Major is dead and I am dying, and in the first of my fit it went on in my head like cimbells that the trap was left open, and that if he passed he would look in and it would get him. For he knew not fear, neither would he submit to bullying by God or devil.

Now I will tell you the truth, and Heaven quit you of your responsibility in our destruction.

There wasn't another man to me like the Governor in all the countries of the world. Once he brought me to life after doctors had given me up for dead; but he willed it, and I lived; and ever afterwards I loved him as a dog loves its master. That was in the Punjab; and I came home to England with him, and was his servant when he got his appointment to the jail here. I tell you he was a proud and fierce man, but under control and tender to those he favoured; and I will tell you also a strange thing about him. Though he was a soldier and an officer, and strict in discipline as made men fear and admire him, his hart at bottom was all for books, and literature, and such-like gentle crafts. I had his confidence, as a man gives his confidence to his dog, and before others. In this way I learnt the bitter sorrow of his life. He had once hoped to be a poet, acknowledged as such before the world. He was by natur' an idelist, as they call it, and God knows what it meant to him to come out of the woods, so to speak, and swet in the dust of cities; but he did it, for his will was of tempered steel. He buried his dreams in the clouds and came down to earth greatly resolved, but with one undying hate. It is not good to hate as he could, and worse to be hated by such as him; and I will tell you the story, and what it led to.

It was when he was a subaltern that he made up his mind to the plunge. For years he had placed all his hopes and confidents in a book of verses he had wrote, and added to, and improved during that time. A little encouragement, a little word of praise, was all he looked for, and then he was redy to buckle to again, profitin' by advice, and do better. He put all the love and beauty of his hart into that book, and at last, after doubt, and anguish, and much diffidents, he published it, and give it to the world. Sir, it fell what they call still-born from the press. It was like a green leaf flutterin' down in a dead wood. To a proud and hopeful man, bubblin' with music, the pain of neglect, when he come to relise it, was terrible. But nothing was said, and there was nothing to say. In silence he had to endure and suffer.

But one day, during manoovers, there came to the camp a grey-faced man, a newspaper correspondent, and young Shrike nocked up a friendship with him. Now how it come about I cannot tell, but so it did that this skip-kennel wormed the lad's sorrow out of him, and his confidents, swore he'd been damnabilly used, and that when he got back he'd crack up the book himself in his own paper. He was a fool for his pains, and a serpent in his croolty. The notice come out as promised, and, my God! the author was laughed and mocked at from beginning to end. Even confidentses he had given to the creature was twisted to his ridicule, and his very appearance joked over. And the mess got wind of it, and made a rare story for the dog days.

He bore it like a soldier and that he became hart and liver from the moment. But he put something to the account of the grey-faced man and locked it up in his breast.

He come across him again years afterwards in India, and told him very politely that he hadn't forgotten him, and didn't intend to. But he was anigh losin' sight of him there for ever and a day, for the creature took cholera, or what looked like it, and rubbed shoulders with death and the devil before he pulled through. And he come across him again over here, and that was the last of him, as you shall see presently.

Once, after I knew the Major (he were Captain then), I was a-brushin' his coat, and he stood a long while before the glass. Then he twisted upon me, with a smile on his mouth, and says he – "The dog was right, Johnson: this isn't the face of a poet. I was a presumtious ass, and born to east up figgers with a pen behind my ear."

"Captain," I says, "if you was skinned, you'd look like any other man without his. The quality of a soul isn't expressed by a coat."

"Well," he answers, "my soul's pretty clean-swept, I think, save for one Bluebeard chamber in it that's been kep' locked ever so many years. It's nice and dirty by this time, I expect," he says, Then the grin comes on his mouth again. "I'll open it some day," he says, "and look. There's something in it about comparing me to a dancing dervish, with the wind in my petticuts. Perhaps I'll get the chance to set somebody else dancing by-and-by."

He did, and took it, and the Bluebeard chamber come to be opened in this very jail.

It was when the system was lying fallow, so to speak, and the prison was deserted. Nobody was there but him and me and the echoes from the empty courts. The contract for restoration hadn't been signed, and for months, and more than a year, we lay idle, nothing bein' done.

Near the beginnin' of this period, one day comes, for the third time of the Major's seein' him, the grey-faced man. "Let bygones be bygones," he says. "I was a good friend to you, though you didn't know it; and now, I expect, you're in the way to thank me."

"I am," says the Major.

"Of course," he answers. "Where would be your fame and reputation as one of the leadin' prison reformers of the day if you had kep' on in that timing nonsense?"

"Have you come for my thanks?" says the Governor.

"I've come, says the grey-faced man, "to examine and report upon your system."

"For your paper?"

"Possibly; but to satisfy myself of its efficacy, in the first instance."

"You aren't commissioned, then?"

"No; I come on my own responsibility."

"Without consultation with anyone?"

"Absolutely without. I haven't even a wife to advise me," he says, with a yellow grin. What once passed for cholera had set the bile on his skin like paint, and he had caught a manner of coughing behind his hand like a toast-master.

"I know," says the Major, looking him steady in the face, "that what you say about me and my affairs is sure to be actuated by conscientious motives."

"Ah," he answers. "You're sore about that review still, I see."

"Not at all," says the Major; "and, in proof, I invite you to be my guest for the night, and tomorrow I'll show you over the prison and explain my system."

The creature cried, "Done!" and they set to and discussed jail matters in great earnestness. I couldn't guess the Governor's intentions, but, somehow, his manner troubled me. And yet I can remember only one point of his talk. He were always dead against making public show of his birds. "They're there for reformation, not ignominy" he'd say. Prisons in the old days were often, with the asylum and the work'us, made the holiday showplaces of towns. I've heard of one Justice of the Peace, up North, who, to save himself trouble, used to sign a lot of blank orders for leave to view, so that applicants needn't bother him when they wanted to go over. They've changed all that, and the Governor were instrumental in the change.

"It's against my rule," he said that night, "to exhibit to a stranger without a Government permit; but, seein' the place is empty, and for old remembrance sake, I'll make an exception in your favour, and you shall learn all I can show you of the inside of a prison."

Now this was natural enough; but I was uneasy.

He treated his guest royly; so much that when we assembled the next mornin' for the inspection, the grey-faced man were shaky as a wet dog. But the Major were all set prim and dry, like the soldier he was.

We went straight away down corridor B, and at cell 47 we stopped.

"We will begin our inspection here," said the Governor. "Johnson, open the door."

I had the keys of the row; fitted in the right one, and pushed open the door.

"After you, sir," said the Major; and the creature walked in, and he shut the door on him.

I think he smelt a rat at once, for he began beating on the wood and calling out to us. But the Major only turned round to me with his face like a stone.

"Take that key from the bunch," he said, "and give it to me."

I obeyed, all in a tremble, and he took and put it in his pocket.

"My God, Major." I whispered, "what are you going to do with him?"

"Silence, sir!" he said; "How dare you question your superior officer!"

And the noise inside grew louder.

The Governor, he listened to it a moment like music; then he unbolted and flung open the trap, and the creature's face came at it like a wild beast's.

"Sir," said the Major to it, "you can't better understand my system than by experiencing it. What an article for your paper you could write already – almost as pungint a one as that in which you ruined the hopes and prospects of a young cockney poet."

The man mouthed at the bars. He was half-mad, I think, in that one minute.

"Let me out!" he screamed. "This is a hidius joke! Let me out!"

"When you are quite quiet – deathly quiet," said the Major, "you shall come out. Not before"; and he shut the trap in its face very softly.

"Come, Johnson, march!" he said, and took the lead, and we walked out of the prison.

I was like to faint, but I dared not disobey, and the man's screeching followed us all down the empty corridors and halls, until we shut the first great door on it.

It may have gone on for hours, alone in that awful emptiness. The creature was a reptile, but the thought sickened my heart.

And from that hour till his death, live months later, he rotted and maddened in his dreadful tomb.

There was more, but I pushed the ghastly confession from me at this point in uncontrollable loathing and terror. Was it possible – possible, that injured sanity could so falsify its victim's even tradition of decency?

"Oh!" I muttered, "what a disease is ambition! Who takes one step towards it puts his foot on Alsirat!"

It was minutes before my shocked nerves were equal to a resumption of the task; but at last I took it up again, with a groan.

I don't think at first I realised the full mischief the Governor intended to do. At least, I hoped he only meant to give the man a good fright and then let him go. I might have known better. How could he ever release him without ruining himself?

The next morning he summoned me to attend him. There was a strange new look of triumph in his face, and in his hand he held a heavy hunting-crop. I pray to God he acted in madness, but my duty and obedience was to him.

"There is sport towards, Johnson," he said. "My dervish has got to dance."

I followed him quiet. We listened when I opened the jail door, but the place was silent as the grave. But from the cell, when we reached it, came a low, whispering sound.

The Governor slipped the trap and looked through.

"All right," he said, and put the key in the door and flung it open.

He were sittin' crouched on the ground, and he looked up at us vacant-like. His face were all fallen down, as it were, and his mouth never ceased to shake and whisper.

The Major shut the door and posted me in a corner. Then he moved to the creature with his whip.

"Up!" he cried. "Up, you dervish, and dance to us!" and he brought the thong with a smack across his shoulders.

The creature leapt under the blow, and then to his feet with a cry, and the Major whipped him till he danced. All round the cell he drove him, lashing and cutting – and again, and many times again, until the poor thing rolled on the floor whimpering and sobbing. I shall have to give an account of this some day. I shall have to whip my master with a red-hot serpent round the blazing furnace of the pit, and I shall do it with agony, because here my love and my obedience was to him.

When it was finished, he bade me put down food and drink that I had brought with me, and come away with him; and we went, leaving him rolling on the floor of the cell, and shut him alone in the empty prison until we should come again at the same time tomorrow.

So day by day this went on, and the dancing three or four times a week, until at last the whip could be left behind, for the man would scream and begin to dance at the mere turning of the key in the lock. And he danced for four months, but not the fifth.

Nobody official came near us all this time. The prison stood lonely as a deserted ruin where dark things have been done.

Once, with fear and trembling, I asked my master how he would account for the inmate of 47 if he was suddenly called upon by authority to open the cell; and he answered, smiling – "I should say it was my mad brother. By his own account, he showed me a brother's love, you know. It would be thought a liberty; but the authorities, I think, would stretch a point for me. But if I got sufficient notice, I should clear out the cell."

I asked him how, with my eyes rather than my lips, and he answered me only with a look.

And all this time he was, outside the prison, living the life of a good man – helping the needy, ministering to the poor. He even entertained occasionally, and had more than one noisy party in his house.

But the fifth month the creature danced no more. He was a dumb, silent animal then, with matted hair and beard; and when one entered he would only look up at one pitifully, as if he said, "My long punishment is nearly ended." How it came that no enquiry was ever made about him I know not, but none ever was.

Perhaps he was one of the wandering gentry that nobody ever knows where they are next. He was unmarried, and had apparently not told of his intended journey to a soul.

And at the last he died in the night. We found him lying stiff and stark in the morning, and scratched with a piece of black crust on a stone of the wall these strange words: 'An Eddy on the Floor'. Just that – nothing else.

Then the Governor came and looked down, and was silent. Suddenly he caught me by the shoulder.

"Johnson," he cried, "if it was to do again, I would do it! I repent of nothing. But he has paid the penalty, and we call quits. May he rest in peace!"

"Amen!" I answered low. Yet I knew our turn must come for this.

We buried him in quicklime under the wall where the murderers lie, and I made the cell trim and rubbed out the writing, and the Governor locked all up and took away the key. But he locked in more than he bargained for.

For months the place was left to itself, and neither of us went anigh 47. Then one day the workmen was to be put in, and the Major he took me round with him for a last examination of the place before they come.

He hesitated a bit outside a particular cell; but at last he drove in the key and kicked open the door.

"My God!" he say's, "he's dancing still!". My heart was thumpin', I tell you, as I looked over his shoulder. What did we see? What you well understand, sir; but, for all it was no more than that, we knew as well as if it was shouted in our ears that it was him, dancin'. It went round by the walls and drew towards us, and as it stole near I screamed out, "An Eddy on the floor!" and seized and dragged the Major out and clapped to the door behind us.

"Oh!" I said, "in another moment it would have had us."

He looked at me gloomily.

"Johnson," he said, "I'm not to be frightened or coerced. He may dance, but he shall dance alone. Get a screwdriver and some screws and fasten up this trap. No one from this time looks into this cell."

I did as he bid me, swetin'; and I swear all the time I wrought I dreaded a hand would come through the trap and clutch mine.

On one pretex' or another, from that day till the night you meddled with it, he kep' that cell as close shut as a tomb. And he went his ways, discardin' the past from that time forth. Now and again an over-sensitive prisoner in the next cell would complain of feelin' uncomfortable. If possible, he would be removed to another; if not, he was damn'd for his fancies. And so it might be goin' on to now, if you hadn't pried and interfered. I don't blame you at this moment, sir. Likely you were an instrument in the hands of Providence; only, as the instrument, you must now take the burden of the truth on your own shoulders. I am a dying man, but I cannot die till I have confessed. Per'aps you may find it in your hart some day to give up a prayer for me – but it must be for the Major as well.

Your obedient servant.

J. Johnson

What comment of my own can I append to this wild narrative? Professionally, and apart from personal experiences, I should rule it the composition of an epileptic. That a noted journalist, nameless as he was and is to me, however nomadic in habit, could disappear from human ken, and his fellows rest content to leave him unaccounted for, seems a tax upon credulity so stupendous that I cannot seriously endorse the statement.

Yet, also – there is that little matter of my personal experience.

No. 252 Rue M. le Prince

Ralph Adams Cram

WHEN IN MAY, 1886, I found myself at last in Paris, I naturally determined to throw myself on the charity of an old chum of mine, Eugene Marie d'Ardeche, who had forsaken Boston a year or more ago on receiving word of the death of an aunt who had left him such property as she possessed. I fancy this windfall surprised him not a little, for the relations between the aunt and nephew had never been cordial, judging from Eugene's remarks touching the lady, who was, it seems, a more or less wicked and witch-like old person, with a penchant for black magic, at least such was the common report.

Why she should leave all her property to d'Ardeche, no one could tell, unless it was that she felt his rather hobbledehoy tendencies towards Buddhism and occultism might some day lead him to her own unhallowed height of questionable illumination. To be sure d'Ardeche reviled her as a bad old woman, being himself in that state of enthusiastic exaltation which sometimes accompanies a boyish fancy for occultism; but in spite of his distant and repellent attitude, Mlle. Blaye de Tartas made him her sole heir, to the violent wrath of a questionable old party known to infamy as the Sar Torrevieja, the 'King of the Sorcerers'. This malevolent old portent, whose gray and crafty face was often seen in the Rue M. le Prince during the life of Mlle. de Tartas had, it seems, fully expected to enjoy her small wealth after her death; and when it appeared that she had left him only the contents of the gloomy old house in the Quartier Latin, giving the house itself and all else of which she died possessed to her nephew in America, the Sar proceeded to remove everything from the place, and then to curse it elaborately and comprehensively, together with all those who should ever dwell therein.

Whereupon he disappeared.

This final episode was the last word I received from Eugene, but I knew the number of the house, 252 Rue M. le Prince. So, after a day or two given to a first cursory survey of Paris, I started across the Seine to find Eugene and compel him to do the honors of the city.

Everyone who knows the Latin Quarter knows the Rue M. le Prince, running up the hill towards the Garden of the Luxembourg. It is full of queer houses and odd corners – or was in '86, – and certainly No. 252 was, when I found it, quite as queer as any. It was nothing but a doorway, a black arch of old stone between and under two new houses painted yellow. The effect of this bit of seventeenth-century masonry, with its dirty old doors, and rusty broken lantern sticking gaunt and grim out over the narrow sidewalk, was, in its frame of fresh plaster, sinister in the extreme.

I wondered if I had made a mistake in the number; it was quite evident that no one lived behind those cobwebs. I went into the doorway of one of the new hotels and interviewed the concierge.

No, M. d'Ardeche did not live there, though to be sure he owned the mansion; he himself resided in Meudon, in the country house of the late Mlle. de Tartas. Would Monsieur like the number and the street?

Monsieur would like them extremely, so I took the card that the concierge wrote for me, and forthwith started for the river, in order that I might take a steamboat for Meudon. By one of those coincidences which happen so often, being quite inexplicable, I had not gone twenty paces down the street before I ran directly into the arms of Eugene d'Ardeche. In three minutes we were sitting in the queer little garden of the Chien Bleu, drinking vermouth and absinthe, and talking it all over.

"You do not live in your aunt's house?" I said at last, interrogatively.

"No, but if this sort of thing keeps on I shall have to. I like Meudon much better, and the house is perfect, all furnished, and nothing in it newer than the last century. You must come out with me tonight and see it. I have got a jolly room fixed up for my Buddha. But there is something wrong with this house opposite. I can't keep a tenant in it – not four days. I have had three, all within six months, but the stories have gone around and a man would as soon think of hiring the Cour des Comptes to live in as No. 252. It is notorious. The fact is, it is haunted the worst way."

I laughed and ordered more vermouth.

"That is all right. It is haunted all the same, or enough to keep it empty, and the funny part is that no one knows *how* it is haunted. Nothing is ever seen, nothing heard. As far as I can find out, people just have the horrors there, and have them so bad they have to go to the hospital afterwards. I have one ex-tenant in the Bicêtre now. So the house stands empty, and as it covers considerable ground and is taxed for a lot, I don't know what to do about it. I think I'll either give it to that child of sin, Torrevieja, or else go and live in it myself. I shouldn't mind the ghosts, I am sure."

"Did you ever stay there?"

"No, but I have always intended to, and in fact I came up here today to see a couple of rake-hell fellows I know, Fargeau and Duchesne, doctors in the Clinical Hospital beyond here, up by the Parc Mont Souris. They promised that they would spend the night with me some time in my aunt's house – which is called around here, you must know, 'la Bouche d'Enfer' – and I thought perhaps they would make it this week, if they can get off duty. Come up with me while I see them, and then we can go across the river to Véfour's and have some luncheon, you can get your things at the Chatham, and we will go out to Meudon, where of course you will spend the night with me."

The plan suited me perfectly, so we went up to the hospital, found Fargeau, who declared that he and Duchesne were ready for anything, the nearer the real 'bouche d'enfer' the better; that the following Thursday they would both be off duty for the night, and that on that day they would join in an attempt to outwit the devil and clear up the mystery of No. 252.

"Does M. l'Américain go with us?" asked Fargeau.

"Why of course," I replied, "I intend to go, and you must not refuse me, d'Ardeche; I decline to be put off. Here is a chance for you to do the honors of your city in a manner which is faultless. Show me a real live ghost, and I will forgive Paris for having lost the Jardin Mabille."

So it was settled.

Later we went down to Meudon and ate dinner in the terrace room of the villa, which was all that d'Ardeche had said, and more, so utterly was its atmosphere that of the seventeenth century. At dinner Eugene told me more about his late aunt, and the queer goings on in the old house.

Mlle. Blaye lived, it seems, all alone, except for one female servant of her own age; a severe, taciturn creature, with massive Breton features and a Breton tongue, whenever she vouchsafed to use it. No one ever was seen to enter the door of No. 252 except Jeanne the servant and the

Sar Torrevieja, the latter coming constantly from none knew whither, and always entering, *never leaving*. Indeed, the neighbors, who for eleven years had watched the old sorcerer sidle crabwise up to the bell almost every day, declared vociferously that *never* had he been seen to leave the house. Once, when they decided to keep absolute guard, the watcher, none other than Maître Garceau of the Chien Bleu, after keeping his eyes fixed on the door from ten o'clock one morning when the Sar arrived until four in the afternoon, during which time the door was unopened (he knew this, for had he not gummed a ten-centime stamp over the joint and was not the stamp unbroken) nearly fell down when the sinister figure of Torrevieja slid wickedly by him with a dry "Pardon, Monsieur!" and disappeared again through the black doorway.

This was curious, for No. 252 was entirely surrounded by houses, its only windows opening on a courtyard into which no eye could look from the hotels of the Rue M. le Prince and the Rue de l'Ecole, and the mystery was one of the choice possessions of the Latin Quarter.

Once a year the austerity of the place was broken, and the denizens of the whole quarter stood open-mouthed watching many carriages drive up to No. 252, many of them private, not a few with crests on the door panels, from all of them descending veiled female figures and men with coat collars turned up. Then followed curious sounds of music from within, and those whose houses joined the blank walls of No. 252 became for the moment popular, for by placing the ear against the wall strange music could distinctly be heard, and the sound of monotonous chanting voices now and then. By dawn the last guest would have departed, and for another year the hotel of Mlle. de Tartas was ominously silent.

Eugene declared that he believed it was a celebration of 'Walpurgisnacht', and certainly appearances favored such a fancy.

"A queer thing about the whole affair is," he said, "the fact that everyone in the street swears that about a month ago, while I was out in Concarneau for a visit, the music and voices were heard again, just as when my revered aunt was in the flesh. The house was perfectly empty, as I tell you, so it is quite possible that the good people were enjoying an hallucination."

I must acknowledge that these stories did not reassure me; in fact, as Thursday came near, I began to regret a little my determination to spend the night in the house. I was too vain to back down, however, and the perfect coolness of the two doctors, who ran down Tuesday to Meudon to make a few arrangements, caused me to swear that I would die of fright before I would flinch. I suppose I believed more or less in ghosts, I am sure now that I am older I believe in them, there are in fact few things I can *not* believe. Two or three inexplicable things had happened to me, and, although this was before my adventure with Rendel in Paestum, I had a strong predisposition to believe some things that I could not explain, wherein I was out of sympathy with the age.

Well, to come to the memorable night of the twelfth of June, we had made our preparations, and after depositing a big bag inside the doors of No. 252, went across to the Chien Bleu, where Fargeau and Duchesne turned up promptly, and we sat down to the best dinner Père Garceau could create.

I remember I hardly felt that the conversation was in good taste. It began with various stories of Indian fakirs and Oriental jugglery, matters in which Eugene was curiously well read, swerved to the horrors of the great Sepoy mutiny, and thus to reminiscences of the dissecting-room. By this time we had drunk more or less, and Duchesne launched into a photographic and Zolaesque account of the only time (as he said) when he was possessed of the panic of fear; namely, one night many years ago, when he was locked by accident into the dissecting-room of the Loucine, together with several cadavers of a rather unpleasant nature. I ventured to protest mildly against the choice of subjects, the result being a perfect carnival of horrors, so that when we finally drank our last *crème de cacao* and started for 'la Bouche d'Enfer', my nerves were in a somewhat rocky condition.

It was just ten o'clock when we came into the street. A hot dead wind drifted in great puffs through the city, and ragged masses of vapor swept the purple sky; an unsavory night altogether, one of those nights of hopeless lassitude when one feels, if one is at home, like doing nothing but drink mint juleps and smoke cigarettes.

Eugene opened the creaking door, and tried to light one of the lanterns; but the gusty wind blew out every match, and we finally had to close the outer doors before we could get a light. At last we had all the lanterns going, and I began to look around curiously. We were in a long, vaulted passage, partly carriageway, partly footpath, perfectly bare but for the street refuse which had drifted in with eddying winds. Beyond lay the courtyard, a curious place rendered more curious still by the fitful moonlight and the flashing of four dark lanterns. The place had evidently been once a most noble palace. Opposite rose the oldest portion, a three-story wall of the time of Francis I., with a great wisteria vine covering half. The wings on either side were more modern, seventeenth century, and ugly, while towards the street was nothing but a flat unbroken wall.

The great bare court, littered with bits of paper blown in by the wind, fragments of packing cases, and straw, mysterious with flashing lights and flaunting shadows, while low masses of torn vapor drifted overhead, hiding, then revealing the stars, and all in absolute silence, not even the sounds of the streets entering this prison-like place, was weird and uncanny in the extreme. I must confess that already I began to feel a slight disposition towards the horrors, but with that curious inconsequence which so often happens in the case of those who are deliberately growing scared, I could think of nothing more reassuring than those delicious verses of Lewis Carroll's:

> *"Just the place for a Snark! I have said it twice,*
> *That alone should encourage the crew.*
> *Just the place for a Snark! I have said it thrice,*
> *What I tell you three times is true"*

which kept repeating themselves over and over in my brain with feverish insistence.

Even the medical students had stopped their chaffing, and were studying the surroundings gravely.

"There is one thing certain," said Fargeau, "*anything* might have happened here without the slightest chance of discovery. Did ever you see such a perfect place for lawlessness?"

"And *anything* might happen here now, with the same certainty of impunity," continued Duchesne, lighting his pipe, the snap of the match making us all start. "D'Ardeche, your lamented relative was certainly well fixed; she had full scope here for her traditional experiments in demonology."

"Curse me if I don't believe that those same traditions were more or less founded on fact," said Eugene. "I never saw this court under these conditions before, but I could believe anything now. What's that!"

"Nothing but a door slamming," said Duchesne, loudly.

"Well, I wish doors wouldn't slam in houses that have been empty eleven months."

"It is irritating," and Duchesne slipped his arm through mine; "but we must take things as they come. Remember we have to deal not only with the spectral lumber left here by your scarlet aunt, but as well with the supererogatory curse of that hell-cat Torrevieja. Come on! Let's get inside before the hour arrives for the sheeted dead to squeak and gibber in these lonely halls. Light your pipes, your tobacco is a sure protection against 'your whoreson dead bodies'; light up and move on."

We opened the hall door and entered a vaulted stone vestibule, full of dust, and cobwebby.

"There is nothing on this floor," said Eugene, "except servants' rooms and offices, and I don't believe there is anything wrong with them. I never heard that there was, anyway. Let's go upstairs."

So far as we could see, the house was apparently perfectly uninteresting inside, all eighteenth-century work, the façade of the main building being, with the vestibule, the only portion of the Francis I work.

"The place was burned during the Terror," said Eugene, "for my great-uncle, from whom Mlle. de Tartas inherited it, was a good and true Royalist; he went to Spain after the Revolution, and did not come back until the accession of Charles X, when he restored the house, and then died, enormously old. This explains why it is all so new."

The old Spanish sorcerer to whom Mlle. de Tartas had left her personal property had done his work thoroughly. The house was absolutely empty, even the wardrobes and bookcases built in had been carried away; we went through room after room, finding all absolutely dismantled, only the windows and doors with their casings, the parquet floors, and the florid Renaissance mantels remaining.

"I feel better," remarked Fargeau. "The house may be haunted, but it don't look it, certainly; it is the most respectable place imaginable."

"Just you wait," replied Eugene. "These are only the state apartments, which my aunt seldom used, except, perhaps, on her annual 'Walpurgisnacht'. Come up stairs and I will show you a better *mise en scène*."

On this floor, the rooms fronting the court, the sleeping-rooms, were quite small – ("They are the bad rooms all the same," said Eugene) – four of them, all just as ordinary in appearance as those below. A corridor ran behind them connecting with the wing corridor, and from this opened a door, unlike any of the other doors in that it was covered with green baize, somewhat moth-eaten. Eugene selected a key from the bunch he carried, unlocked the door, and with some difficulty forced it to swing inward; it was as heavy as the door of a safe.

"We are now," he said, "on the very threshold of hell itself; these rooms in here were my scarlet aunt's unholy of unholies. I never let them with the rest of the house, but keep them as a curiosity. I only wish Torrevieja had kept out; as it was, he looted them, as he did the rest of the house, and nothing is left but the walls and ceiling and floor. They are something, however, and may suggest what the former condition must have been. Tremble and enter."

The first apartment was a kind of anteroom, a cube of perhaps twenty feet each way, without windows, and with no doors except that by which we entered and another to the right. Walls, floor, and ceiling were covered with a black lacquer, brilliantly polished, that flashed the light of our lanterns in a thousand intricate reflections. It was like the inside of an enormous Japanese box, and about as empty. From this we passed to another room, and here we nearly dropped our lanterns. The room was circular, thirty feet or so in diameter, covered by a hemispherical dome; walls and ceiling were dark blue, spotted with gold stars; and reaching from floor to floor across the dome stretched a colossal figure in red lacquer of a nude woman kneeling, her legs reaching out along the floor on either side, her head touching the lintel of the door through which we had entered, her arms forming its sides, with the fore arms extended and stretching along the walls until they met the long feet. The most astounding, misshapen, absolutely terrifying thing, I think, I ever saw. From the navel hung a great white object, like the traditional roe's egg of the Arabian Nights. The floor was of red lacquer, and in it was inlaid a pentagram the size of the room, made of wide strips of brass. In the centre of this pentagram was a circular disk of black stone, slightly saucer-shaped, with a small outlet in the middle.

The effect of the room was simply crushing, with this gigantic red figure crouched over it all, the staring eyes fixed on one, no matter what his position. None of us spoke, so oppressive was the whole thing.

The third room was like the first in dimensions, but instead of being black it was entirely sheathed with plates of brass, walls, ceiling, and floor – tarnished now, and turning green, but still brilliant under the lantern light. In the middle stood an oblong altar of porphyry, its longer dimensions on the axis of the suite of rooms, and at one end, opposite the range of doors, a pedestal of black basalt.

This was all. Three rooms, stranger than these, even in their emptiness, it would be hard to imagine. In Egypt, in India, they would not be entirely out of place, but here in Paris, in a commonplace *hôtel*, in the Rue M. le Prince, they were incredible.

We retraced our steps, Eugene closed the iron door with its baize covering, and we went into one of the front chambers and sat down, looking at each other.

"Nice party, your aunt," said Fargeau. "Nice old party, with amiable tastes; I am glad we are not to spend the night in *those* rooms."

"What do you suppose she did there?" inquired Duchesne. "I know more or less about black art, but that series of rooms is too much for me."

"My impression is," said d'Ardeche, "that the brazen room was a kind of sanctuary containing some image or other on the basalt base, while the stone in front was really an altar – what the nature of the sacrifice might be I don't even guess. The round room may have been used for invocations and incantations. The pentagram looks like it. Anyway it is all just about as queer and *fin de siècle* as I can well imagine. Look here, it is nearly twelve, let's dispose of ourselves, if we are going to hunt this thing down."

The four chambers on this floor of the old house were those said to be haunted, the wings being quite innocent, and, so far as we knew, the floors below. It was arranged that we should each occupy a room, leaving the doors open with the lights burning, and at the slightest cry or knock we were all to rush at once to the room from which the warning sound might come. There was no communication between the rooms to be sure, but, as the doors all opened into the corridor, every sound was plainly audible.

The last room fell to me, and I looked it over carefully.

It seemed innocent enough, a commonplace, square, rather lofty Parisian sleeping-room, finished in wood painted white, with a small marble mantel, a dusty floor of inlaid maple and cherry, walls hung with an ordinary French paper, apparently quite new, and two deeply embrasured windows looking out on the court.

I opened the swinging sash with some trouble, and sat down in the window seat with my lantern beside me trained on the only door, which gave on the corridor.

The wind had gone down, and it was very still without – still and hot. The masses of luminous vapor were gathering thickly overhead, no longer urged by the gusty wind. The great masses of rank wisteria leaves, with here and there a second blossoming of purple flowers, hung dead over the window in the sluggish air. Across the roofs I could hear the sound of a belated *fiacre* in the streets below. I filled my pipe again and waited.

For a time the voices of the men in the other rooms were a companionship, and at first I shouted to them now and then, but my voice echoed rather unpleasantly through the long corridors, and had a suggestive way of reverberating around the left wing beside me, and coming out at a broken window at its extremity like the voice of another man. I soon gave up my attempts at conversation, and devoted myself to the task of keeping awake.

It was not easy; why did I eat that lettuce salad at Père Garceau's? I should have known better. It was making me irresistibly sleepy, and wakefulness was absolutely necessary. It was certainly gratifying to know that I could sleep, that my courage was by me to that extent, but in the interests of science I must keep awake. But almost never, it seemed, had sleep looked so desirable. Half a hundred times, nearly, I would doze for an instant, only to awake with a start, and find my pipe gone out. Nor did the exertion of relighting it pull me together. I struck my match mechanically, and with the first puff dropped off again. It was most vexing. I got up and walked around the room. It was most annoying. My cramped position had almost put both my legs to sleep. I could hardly stand. I felt numb, as though with cold. There was no longer any sound from the other rooms, nor from without. I sank down in my window seat. How dark it was growing! I turned up the lantern. That pipe again, how obstinately it kept going out! And my last match was gone. The lantern, too, was *that* going out? I lifted my hand to turn it up again. It felt like lead, and fell beside me.

Then I awoke – absolutely. I remembered the story of 'The Haunters and the Haunted.' *This* was the Horror. I tried to rise, to cry out. My body was like lead, my tongue was paralyzed. I could hardly move my eyes. And the light was going out. There was no question about that. Darker and darker yet; little by little the pattern of the paper was swallowed up in the advancing night. A prickling numbness gathered in every nerve, my right arm slipped without feeling from my lap to my side, and I could not raise it – it swung helpless. A thin, keen humming began in my head, like the cicadas on a hillside in September. The darkness was coming fast.

Yes, this was it. Something was subjecting me, body and mind, to slow paralysis. Physically I was already dead. If I could only hold my mind, my consciousness, I might still be safe, but could I? Could I resist the mad horror of this silence, the deepening dark, the creeping numbness? I knew that, like the man in the ghost story, my only safety lay here.

It had come at last. My body was dead, I could no longer move my eyes. They were fixed in that last look on the place where the door had been, now only a deepening of the dark.

Utter night: the last flicker of the lantern was gone. I sat and waited; my mind was still keen, but how long would it last? There was a limit even to the endurance of the utter panic of fear.

Then the end began. In the velvet blackness came two white eyes, milky, opalescent, small, far away – awful eyes, like a dead dream. More beautiful than I can describe, the flakes of white flame moving from the perimeter inward, disappearing in the centre, like a never ending flow of opal water into a circular tunnel. I could not have moved my eyes had I possessed the power: they devoured the fearful, beautiful things that grew slowly, slowly larger, fixed on me, advancing, growing more beautiful, the white flakes of light sweeping more swiftly into the blazing vortices, the awful fascination deepening in its insane intensity as the white, vibrating eyes grew nearer, larger.

Like a hideous and implacable engine of death the eyes of the unknown Horror swelled and expanded until they were close before me, enormous, terrible, and I felt a slow, cold, wet breath propelled with mechanical regularity against my face, enveloping me in its fetid mist, in its charnel-house deadliness.

With ordinary fear goes always a physical terror, but with me in the presence of this unspeakable Thing was only the utter and awful terror of the mind, the mad fear of a prolonged and ghostly nightmare. Again and again I tried to shriek, to make some noise, but physically I was utterly dead. I could only feel myself go mad with the terror of hideous death. The eyes were close on me – their movement so swift that they seemed to be but palpitating flames, the dead breath was around me like the depths of the deepest sea.

Suddenly a wet, icy mouth, like that of a dead cuttle-fish, shapeless, jelly-like, fell over mine. The horror began slowly to draw my life from me, but, as enormous and shuddering folds of palpitating jelly swept sinuously around me, my will came back, my body awoke with the reaction of final fear, and I closed with the nameless death that enfolded me.

What was it that I was fighting? My arms sunk through the unresisting mass that was turning me to ice. Moment by moment new folds of cold jelly swept round me, crushing me with the force of Titans. I fought to wrest my mouth from this awful Thing that sealed it, but, if ever I succeeded and caught a single breath, the wet, sucking mass closed over my face again before I could cry out. I think I fought for hours, desperately, insanely, in a silence that was more hideous than any sound – fought until I felt final death at hand, until the memory of all my life rushed over me like a flood, until I no longer had strength to wrench my face from that hellish succubus, until with a last mechanical struggle I fell and yielded to death.

* * *

Then I heard a voice say, "If he is dead, I can never forgive myself; I was to blame."

Another replied, "He is not dead, I know we can save him if only we reach the hospital in time. Drive like hell, *cocher*! Twenty francs for you, if you get there in three minutes."

Then there was night again, and nothingness, until I suddenly awoke and stared around. I lay in a hospital ward, very white and sunny, some yellow *fleurs-de-lis* stood beside the head of the pallet, and a tall sister of mercy sat by my side.

To tell the story in a few words, I was in the Hôtel Dieu, where the men had taken me that fearful night of the twelfth of June. I asked for Fargeau or Duchesne, and by and by the latter came, and sitting beside the bed told me all that I did not know.

It seems that they had sat, each in his room, hour after hour, hearing nothing, very much bored, and disappointed. Soon after two o'clock Fargeau, who was in the next room, called to me to ask if I was awake. I gave no reply, and, after shouting once or twice, he took his lantern and came to investigate. The door was locked on the inside! He instantly called d'Ardeche and Duchesne, and together they hurled themselves against the door. It resisted. Within they could hear irregular footsteps dashing here and there, with heavy breathing. Although frozen with terror, they fought to destroy the door and finally succeeded by using a great slab of marble that formed the shelf of the mantel in Fargeau's room. As the door crashed in, they were suddenly hurled back against the walls of the corridor, as though by an explosion, the lanterns were extinguished, and they found themselves in utter silence and darkness.

As soon as they recovered from the shock, they leaped into the room and fell over my body in the middle of the floor. They lighted one of the lanterns, and saw the strangest sight that can be imagined. The floor and walls to the height of about six feet were running with something that seemed like stagnant water, thick, glutinous, sickening. As for me, I was drenched with the same cursed liquid. The odor of musk was nauseating. They dragged me away, stripped off my clothing, wrapped me in their coats, and hurried to the hospital, thinking me perhaps dead. Soon after sunrise d'Ardeche left the hospital, being assured that I was in a fair way to recovery, with time, and with Fargeau went up to examine by daylight the traces of the adventure that was so nearly fatal. They were too late. Fire engines were coming down the street as they passed the Académie. A neighbor rushed up to d'Ardeche: "O Monsieur! What misfortune, yet what fortune! It is true *la Bouche d'Enfer* – I beg pardon, the residence of the lamented Mlle. de Tartas – was burned, but not wholly, only the ancient building. The wings were saved, and for that great credit is due the brave firemen. Monsieur will remember them, no doubt."

It was quite true. Whether a forgotten lantern, overturned in the excitement, had done the work, or whether the origin of the fire was more supernatural, it was certain that 'the Mouth of Hell' was no more. A last engine was pumping slowly as d'Ardeche came up; half a dozen limp, and one distended, hose stretched through the *porte cochère*, and within only the façade of Francis I. remained, draped still with the black stems of the wisteria. Beyond lay a great vacancy, where thin smoke was rising slowly. Every floor was gone, and the strange halls of Mlle. Blaye de Tartas were only a memory.

With d'Ardeche I visited the place last year, but in the stead of the ancient walls was then only a new and ordinary building, fresh and respectable; yet the wonderful stories of the old *Bouche d'Enfer* still lingered in the quarter, and will hold there, I do not doubt, until the Day of Judgment.

'To Let'

B.M. Croker

SOME YEARS AGO, when I was a slim young spin, I came out to India to live with my brother Tom: he and I were members of a large and somewhat impecunious family, and I do not think my mother was sorry to have one of her four grown-up daughters thus taken off her hands. Tom's wife, Aggie, had been at school with my eldest sister; we had known and liked her all our lives.

She was quite one of ourselves, and as she and the children were at home when Tom's letter was received, and his offer accepted, she helped me to choose my slender outfit with judgement, zeal, and taste; endowed me with several pretty additions to my wardrobe; superintended the fitting of my gowns and the trying on of my hats, with most sympathetic interest, and finally escorted me out to Lucknow, under her own wing, and installed me in the only spare room in her comfortable bungalow in Dilkongha.

My sister-in-law is a pretty little brunette, rather pale, with dark hair, brilliant black eyes, a resolute mouth and a bright, intelligent expression. She is orderly, trim and feverishly energetic, and seems to live every moment of her life. Her children, her wardrobe, her house, her servants, and last, not least, her husband, are all models in their way; and yet she has plenty of time for tennis and dancing, and talking and walking. She is, undoubtedly, a remarkably talented little creature, and especially prides herself on her nerve and her power of will, or will power. I suppose they are the same thing? And I am sure they are all the same to Tom, who worships the sole of her small slipper. Strictly between ourselves she is the ruling member of the family, and turns her lord and master round her little finger. Tom is big and fair, of course, the opposite to his wife, quiet, rather easy-going and inclined to be indolent, but Aggie rouses him up, and pushes him to the front, and keeps him there. She knows all about his department, his prospects of promotion, his prospects of furlough, of getting acting appointments, and so on, even better than he does himself. The chief of Tom's department – have I said that Tom is in the Irritation Office? – has placed it solemnly on record that he considers little Mrs. Shandon a surprisingly clever woman. The two children, Bob and Tor, are merry, oppressively active monkeys, aged three and five years respectively. As for myself I am tall and fair, and I wish I could add pretty; but this is a true story. My eyes are blue, my teeth are white, my hair is red – alas, a blazing red; and I was, at this period, nineteen years of age; and now I think I have given a sufficient outline of the whole family.

We arrived at Lucknow in November, when the cold weather is delightful, and everything was delightful to me. The bustle and life of a great Indian station, the novelty of my surroundings, the early morning rides, picnics down the river, and dances at the 'Chutter Munzil' made me look upon Lucknow as a paradise on earth; and in this light I still regarded it, until a great change came over the temperature, and the month of April introduced me to red-hot winds, sleepless nights, and the intolerable 'brain fever' bird. Aggie had made up her mind definitely on one subject: we were not to go away to the hills until the rains. Tom could only get two months' leave (July and August), and she did not intend to leave him to grill on the plains alone. As for herself and the children – not to speak of me – we had all come out from home so recently we did not require a change. The trip to Europe had made a vast hole in the family stocking, and she wished to economise; and who can economise with two establishments in full swing? Tell me this, ye Anglo-Indian matrons. With a large, cool bungalow, plenty of punkhas, khuskhus tatties, ice, and a thermantidote, surely we could manage to brave May and June – at any rate the attempt was made. Gradually the hills drained Lucknow week by week; family after family packed up, warned us of our folly in remaining on the plains, offered to look for houses for us, and left by the night mail. By the middle of May, the place was figuratively empty. Nothing can be more dreary than a large station in the hot weather, unless it is an equally forsaken hill station in the depths of winter, when the mountains are covered with snow: the mall no longer resounds with gay voices and the tramp of Jampanies, but is visited by bears and panthers, and the houses are closed, and, as it were, put to bed in straw! As for Lucknow in the summer, it was a melancholy spot; the public gardens were deserted, the chairs at the Chutter Munzil stood empty, the very bands had gone to the hills! The shops were shut, the baked white roads, no longer thronged with carriages and bamboo carts, gave ample room to the humble ekka, or a Dhobie's meagre donkey shuffling along in the dust.

Of course we were not the only people remaining in the place, grumbling at the heat and dust and life in general; but there can be no sociability with the thermometer above 100 in the shade.

Through the long, long Indian day we sat and gasped, in darkened rooms, and consumed quantities of 'Nimbo pegs', i.e. limes and soda water, and listened to the fierce hot winds roaring along the road and driving the roasted leaves before it; and in the evening, when the sun had set, we went for a melancholy drive through the Wingfield Park, or round by Martiniere College, and met our friends at the library and compared sensations and thermometers. The season was exceptionally bad, but people say that every year, and presently Bobby and Tor began to fade: their little white faces and listless eyes appealed to Aggie as Tom's anxious expostulations had never done. "Yes, they must go to the hills with me." But this idea I repudiated at once; I refused to undertake the responsibility – I, who could scarcely speak a word to the servants – who had no experience! Then Bobbie had a bad go of fever – intermittent fever: the beginning of the end to his alarmed mother; the end being represented by a large gravestone! She now became as firmly determined to go as she had previously been resolved to stay; but it was so late in the season to take a house. Alas, alas, for the beautiful tempting advertisements in the Pioneer, which we had seen and scorned! Aggie wrote to a friend in a certain hill station, called for this occasion only 'Kantia', and Tom wired to a house agent, who triumphantly replied by letter that there was not one unlet bungalow on his books. This missive threw us into the depths of despair; there seemed no alternative but a hill hotel, and the usual quarters that await the last comers, and the proverbial welcome for children and dogs (we had only four); but the next day brought us good news from Aggie's friend Mrs. Chalmers.

> Dear Mrs. Shandon – she said – I received your letter, and went at once to Cursitjee, the agent. Every hole and corner up here seems full, and he had not a single house to let. Today I had a note from him, saying that Briarwood is vacant; the people who took it are not coming up, they have gone to Naini Tal. You are in luck. I have just been out to see the house, and have secured it for you. It is a mile and a half from the club, but I know that you and your sister are capital walkers. I envy you. Such a charming place – two sitting-rooms, four bedrooms,

four bathrooms, a hall, servants' go-downs, stabling, and a splendid view from a very pretty garden, and only Rs. 800 for the season!

Why, I am paving Rs. 1,000 for a very inferior house, with scarcely a stick of furniture and no view. I feel so proud of myself, and I am longing to show you my treasure trove. Telegraph when you start, and I shall have a milk man in waiting and fires in all the rooms.

Yours sincerely, Edith Chalmers

We now looked upon Mrs. Chalmers as our best and dearest friend, and began to get under way at once. A long Journey in India is a serious business when the party comprises two ladies, two children, two ayahs and five other servants, three fox terriers, a mongoose and a Persian cat – all these animals going to the hills for the benefit of their health – not to speak of a ton of luggage, including crockery and lamps, a cottage piano, a goat and a pony. Aggie and I, the children, one ayah, two terriers, the cat and mongoose, our bedding and pillows, the tiffin basket and ice basket, were all stowed into one compartment, and I must confess that the journey was truly miserable. The heat was stifling, despite the water tatties. One of the terriers had a violent dispute with the cat, and the cat had a difference with the mongoose, and Bob and Tor had a pitched battle more than once. I actually wished myself back in Lucknow. I was most truly thankful to wake one morning to find myself under the shadow of the Himalayas – not a mighty, snow-clad range of everlasting hills, but merely the spurs – the moderate slopes, covered with scrub and loose shale and jungle, and deceitful little trickling watercourses. We sent the servants on ahead, whilst we rested at the Dak bungalow near the railway station, and then followed them at our leisure. We accomplished the ascent in dandies – open kind of boxes, half box half chair, carried on the shoulders of four men. This was an entirely novel sensation to me, and at first an agreeable one, so long as the slopes were moderate and the paths wide; but the higher we went, the narrower became the path, the steeper the naked precipice; and as my coolies would walk at the extreme edge, with the utmost indifference to my frantic appeals to "Bector! Bector!" – and would change poles at the most agonizing corners – my feelings were very mixed, especially when droves of loose pack ponies came thundering down hill, with no respect for the rights of the road. Late at night we passed through Kantia, and arrived at Briarwood far too weary to be critical. Fires were blazing, supper was prepared, and we dispatched it in haste, and most thankfully went to bed and slept soundly, as anyone would do who had spent thirty-six hours in a crowded compartment and ten in a cramped wooden case.

The next morning, rested and invigorated, we set out on a tour of inspection; and it is almost worthwhile to undergo a certain amount of baking on the sweltering heat of the plains, in order to enjoy those deep first draughts of cool hill air, instead of a stifling, dust-laden atmosphere, and to appreciate the green valleys and blue hills by force of contrast to the far-stretching, eye-smarting, white glaring roads that intersect the burnt-up plains – roads and plains that even the pariah abandons, salamander though he be!

To our delight and surprise, Mrs. Chalmers had by no means overdrawn the advantages of our new abode. The bungalow is as solidly built of stone, two storeyed, and ample in size. It stood on a kind of shelf, cut out of the hillside, and was surrounded by a pretty flower garden, full of roses, fuchsias, carnations. The high road passed the gate, from which the avenue descended direct to the entrance door, which was at the end of the house, and from whence ran a long passage. Off this passage three rooms opened to the right, all looking south, and all looking into a deep, delightful, flagged verandah. The stairs were very steep.

At the head of them, the passage and rooms were repeated. There were small nooks, and dressing-rooms, and convenient out-houses, and plenty of good water; but the glory of Briarwood was undoubtedly its verandah: it was fully twelve feet wide, roofed with zinc, and overhung a precipice of a thousand feet – not a startlingly sheer khud, but a tolerably straight descent of grey-blue shale rocks and low jungle. From it there was a glorious view, across a valley, far away, to the snowy range. It opened at one end into the avenue, and was not inclosed; but at the side next the precipice there was a stout wooden railing, with netting at the bottom, for the safety of too enterprising dogs or children. A charming spot, despite its rather bold situation; and as Aggie and I sat in it, surveying the scenery and inhaling the pure hill air, and watching Bob and Tor tearing up and down playing horses, we said to one another that "the verandah alone was worth half the rent".

"It's absurdly cheap," exclaimed my sister-in-law complacently. "I wish you saw the hovel I had, at Simla, for the same rent. I wonder if it is feverish, or badly drained, or what?"

"Perhaps it has a ghost," I suggested facetiously; and at such an absurd idea we both went into peals of laughter.

At this moment Mrs. Chalmers appeared, brisk, rosy, and breathlessly benevolent, having walked over from Kantia.

"So you have found it," she said as we shook hands. "I said nothing about this delicious verandah! I thought I would keep it as a surprise. I did not say a word too much for Briarwood, did I?"

"Not half enough," we returned rapturously; and presently we went in a body, armed with a list from the agent, and proceeded to go over the house and take stock of its contents.

"It's not a bit like a hill furnished house," boasted Mrs. Chalmers, with a glow of pride, as she looked round the drawing-room; "carpets, curtains, solid, very solid chairs, and Berlin wool worked screens, a card-table, and any quantity of pictures."

"Yes, don't they look like family portraits?" I suggested, as we gazed at them. There was one of an officer in faded water colours, another of his wife, two of a previous generation in oils and amply gilded frames, two sketches of an English country house, and some framed photographs, groups of grinning cricketers or wedding guests. All the rooms were well, almost handsomely, furnished in an old-fashioned style. There was no scarcity of wardrobes, looking-glasses, or even armchairs, in the bedrooms, and the pantry was fitted out – a most singular circumstance – with a large supply of handsome glass and china, lamps, old moderators, coffee and tea pots, plated side dishes and candlesticks, cooking utensils and spoons and forks, wine coasters, and a cake-basket.

These articles were all let with the house, much to our amazement, provided we were responsible for the same. The china was Spode, the plate old family heirlooms, with a crest – a winged horse – on everything, down to the very mustard spoons.

"The people who own this house must be lunatics," remarked Aggie as she peered round the pantry; "fancy hiring out one's best family plate and good old china! And I saw some ancient music books in the drawing-room, and there is a side saddle in the bottle khana."

"My dear, the people who owned this house are dead," explained Mrs. Chalmers. "I heard all about them last evening from Mrs. Starkey."

"Oh, is she up there?" exclaimed Aggie somewhat fretfully.

"Yes, her husband is cantonment magistrate. This house belonged to an old retired colonel and his wife. They and his niece lived here. These were all their belongings. They died within a short time of one another, and the old man left a queer will, to say that the house was to remain precisely as they left it for twenty years, and at the end of that time it was to be sold and all the property dispersed. Mrs. Starkey says she is sure that he never intended it to be let, but the heir-at-law insists on that, and is furious at the terms of the will."

"Well, it is a very good thing for us," remarked Aggie; "we are as comfortable here as if we were in our own house: there is a stove in the kitchen; there are nice boxes for firewood in every room, clocks, real hair mattresses – in short, it is as you said, a treasure trove."

We set to work to modernise the drawing-room with phoolkaries, Madras muslin curtains, photograph screens and frames, and such like portable articles. We placed the piano across a corner, arranged flowers in some handsome Dresden china vases, and entirely altered and improved the character of the room. When Aggie had dispatched a most glowing description of our new quarters to Tom, and we had had tiffin, we set off to walk into Kantia to put our names down at the library and to enquire for letters at the post office. Aggie met a good many acquaintances – who does not who has lived five years in India in the same district? Among them Mrs. Starkey, an elderly lady with a prominent nose and goggle eyes, who greeted her loudly across the reading-room table in this agreeable fashion:

"And so you have come up after all, Mrs. Shandon. Someone told me that you meant to remain below, but I knew you never could be so wicked as to keep your poor little children in that heat."

Then coming round and dropping into a chair beside her she said, "And I suppose this young lady is your sister-in-law?"

Mrs. Starkey eyed me critically, evidently appraising my chances in the great marriage market.

She herself had settled her own two daughters most satisfactorily, and had now nothing to do but interest herself in these people's affairs.

"Yes," acquiesced Aggie, "Miss Shandon – Mrs. Starkey."

"And so you have taken Briarwood?"

"Yes, we have been most lucky to get it."

"I hope you will think so at the end of three months," observed Mrs. Starkey with a significant pursing of her lips. "Mrs. Chalmers is a stranger up here, or she would not have been in such a hurry to jump at it."

"Why, what is the matter with it?" enquired Aggie. "It is well built, well furnished, well situated, and very cheap."

"That's just it – suspiciously cheap. Why, my dear Mrs. Shandon, if there was not something against it, it would let for two hundred rupees a month."

"And what is against it?"

"It's haunted! There you have the reason in two words."

"Is that all? I was afraid it was the drains. I don't believe in ghosts and haunted houses. What are we supposed to see?"

"Nothing," retorted Mrs. Starkey, who seemed a good deal nettled at our smiling incredulity. "Nothing!" with an exasperating laugh.

"No, but you will make up for it in hearing. Not now – you are all right for the next six weeks – but after the monsoon breaks I give you a week at Briarwood. No one would stand it longer, and indeed you might as well bespeak your rooms at Cooper's Hotel now. There is always a rush up here in July by the two month's leave people, and you will be poked into some wretched go-down."

Aggie laughed rather a careless ironical little laugh and said, "Thank you, Mrs. Starkey; but I think we will stay on where we are; at any rate for the present."

"Of course it will be as you please. What do you think of the verandah?" she enquired with a curious smile.

"I think, as I was saying to Susan, that it is worth half the rent of the house."

"And in my opinion the house is worth double rent without it," and with this enigmatic remark she rose and sailed away.

"Horrid old frump," exclaimed Aggie as we walked home in the starlight. "She is jealous and angry that she did not get Briarwood herself – I know her so well. She is always hinting and repeating stories about the nicest people – always decrying your prettiest dress or your best servant." We soon forgot all about Mrs. Starkey and her dismal prophecy, being too gay and too busy to give her, or it, a thought. We had so many engagements – tennis parties and tournaments, picnics, concerts, dances and little dinners. We ourselves gave occasional afternoon teas in the verandah, using the best Spode cups and saucers and the old silver cake-basket, and were warmly complimented on our good fortune in securing such a charming house and garden. One day the children discovered to their great joy that the old chowkidar belonging to the bungalow possessed an African grey parrot – a rare bird indeed in India; he had a battered Europe cage, doubtless a remnant of better days, and swung on his ring, looking up at us enquiringly out of his impudent little black eyes.

The parrot had been the property of the former inmates of Briarwood, and as it was a long-lived creature, had survived its master and mistress, and was boarded out with the chowkidar, at one rupee per month.

The chowkidar willingly carried the cage into the verandah, where the bird seemed perfectly at home.

We got a little table for its cage, and the children were delighted with him, as he swung to and fro, with a bit of cake in his wrinkled claw.

Presently be startled us all by suddenly calling "Lucy", in a voice that was as distinct as if it had come from a human throat, "Pretty Lucy – Lu—cy."

"That must have been the niece," said Aggie. "I expect she was the original of that picture over the chimney-piece in your room; she looks like a Lucy."

It was a large framed half-length photograph of a very pretty girl, in a white dress, with gigantic open sleeves. The ancient parrot talked incessantly now that he had been restored to society; he whistled for the dogs, and brought them flying to his summons, to his great satisfaction and their equally great indignation. He called "Qui hye" so naturally, in a lady's shrill soprano, or a gruff male bellow, that I have no doubt our servants would have liked to have wrung his neck. He coughed and expectorated like an old gentleman, and whined like a puppy, and mewed like a cat, and I am sorry to add, sometimes swore like a trooper; but his most constant cry was, "Lucy, where are you, pretty Lucy – Lucy – Lu—cy?"

Aggie and I went to various picnics, but to that given by the Chalmers (in honour of Mr. Chalmers's brother Charlie, a captain in a Gurkha regiment, just come up to Kantia on leave) Aggie was unavoidably absent. Tor had a little touch of fever, and she did not like to leave him; but I went under my hostess's care, and expected to enjoy myself immensely. Alas! On that self-same afternoon the long expected monsoon broke, and we were nearly drowned! We rode to the selected spot, five miles from Kantia, laughing and chattering, indifferent to the big blue-black clouds that came slowly, but surely, sailing up from below; it was a way they had had for days and nothing had come of it. We spread the tablecloth, boiled the kettle, unpacked the hampers, in spite of sharp gusts of wind and warning rumbling thunder. Just as we had commenced to reap the reward of our exertions, there fell a few huge drops, followed by a vivid flash, and then a tremendous crash of thunder, like a whole park of artillery, that seemed to shake the mountains, and after this the deluge. In less than a minute we were soaked through; we hastily gathered up the tablecloth by its four ends, gave it to the coolies and fled. It was all

I could do to stand against the wind; only for Captain Chalmers I believe I would have been blown away; as it was I lost my hat, it was whirled into space. Mrs. Chalmers lost her boa, and Mrs. Starkey, not merely her bonnet, but some portion of her hair. We were truly in a wretched plight, the water streaming down our faces and squelching in our boots; the little trickling mountain rivulets were now like racing seas of turbid water; the lightning was almost blinding; the trees rocked dangerously and lashed one another with their quivering branches. I had never been out in such a storm before, and I hope I never may again. We reached Kantia more dead than alive, and Mrs. Chalmers sent an express to Aggie, and kept me till the next day. After raining as it only can rain in the Himalayas, the weather cleared, the sun shone, and I rode home in borrowed plumes, full of my adventures and in the highest spirits. I found Aggie sitting over the fire in the drawing-room, looking ghastly white: that was nothing uncommon; but terribly depressed, which was most unusual. "I am afraid you have neuralgia?" I said as I kissed her; she nodded and made no reply.

"How is Tor?" I enquired as I drew a chair up to the fire, "Better – quite well."

"Any news – any letter?"

"Not a word – not a line."

"Has anything happened to Pip" – Pip was a fox terrier, renowned for having the shortest tail and being the most impertinent dog in Lucknow – "or the mongoose?"

"No, you silly girl! Why do you ask such questions?"

"I was afraid something was amiss; you seem rather down on your luck." Aggie shrugged her shoulders and then said:

"What put such an absurd idea into your head? Tell me all about the picnic," and she began to talk rapidly and to ask me various questions; but I observed that once she had set me going – no difficult task – her attention flagged, her eyes wandered from my face to the fire. She was not listening to half I said, and my most thrilling descriptions were utterly lost on this indifferent, abstracted little creature! I noticed from this time that she had become strangely nervous for her.

She invited herself to the share of half my bed; she was restless, distrait, and even irritable; and when I was asked out to spend the day, dispensed with my company with an alacrity that was by no means flattering. Formerly, of an evening she used to herd the children home at sundown, and tear me away from the delights of the reading-room at seven o'clock; now she hung about the library until almost the last moment, until it was time to put out the lamps, and kept the children with her, making transparent pretexts for their company. Often we did not arrive at home till half-past eight o'clock. I made no objections to these late hours, neither did Charlie Chalmers, who often walked back with us and remained to dinner. I was amazed to notice that Aggie seemed delighted to have his company, for she had always expressed a rooted aversion to what she called 'tame young men', and here was this new acquaintance dining with us at least thrice a week! About a month after the picnic we had a spell of dreadful weather – thunderstorms accompanied by torrents. One pouring afternoon, Aggie and I were sitting over the drawing-room fire, whilst the rain came fizzing down among the logs and ran in rivers off the roof and out of the spouts. There had been no going out that day, and we were feeling rather flat and dull, as we sat in a kind of ghostly twilight, with all outdoor objects swallowed up in mist, listening to the violent battering of the rain on the zinc verandah, and the storm which was growling round the hills. "Oh, for a visitor!" I exclaimed; "but no one but a fish or a lunatic would be out on such an evening."

"No one, indeed," echoed Aggie in a melancholy tone. "We may as well draw the curtains and have in the lamp and tea to cheer us up."

She had scarcely finished speaking when I heard the brisk trot of a horse along the road. It stopped at the gate and came rapidly down our avenue. I heard the wet gravel crunching under his hoofs and – yes – a man's cheery whistle. My heart jumped, and I half rose from my chair. It must be Charlie Chalmers braving the elements to see me! Such, I must confess, was my incredible vanity! He did not stop at the front door as usual, but rode straight into the verandah, which afforded ample room and shelter for half-a-dozen mounted men.

"Aggie," I said eagerly, "do you hear? It must be—"

I paused – my tongue silenced by the awful pallor of her face and the expression of her eyes as she sat with her little hands clutching the arms of her chair, and her whole figure bent forward in an attitude of listening – an attitude of terror.

"What is it, Aggie?" I said, "Are you ill?"

As I spoke the horse's hoofs made a loud clattering noise on the stone-paved verandah outside and a man's voice – a young man's eager voice – called, "Lucy".

Instantly a chair near the writing table was pushed back and someone went quickly to the window – a French one – and bungled for a moment with the fastening – I always had a difficulty with that window myself. Aggie and I were within the bright circle of the firelight, but the rest of the room was dim and outside the streaming grey sky was spasmodically illuminated by occasional vivid flashes that lit up the surrounding hills as if it were daylight. The trampling of impatient hoofs and the rattling of a door handle were the only sounds that were audible for a few breathless seconds; but during those seconds Pip, bristling like a porcupine and trembling violently in every joint, had sprung off my lap and crawled abjectly under Aggie's chair, seemingly in a transport of fear. The door was opened audibly, and a cold, icy blast swept in, that seemed to freeze my very heart and made me shiver from head to foot. At this moment there came with a sinister blue glare the most vivid flash of lightning I ever saw. It lit up the whole room, which was empty save for ourselves, and was instantly followed by a clap of thunder that caused my knees to knock together and that terrified me and filled me with horror. It evidently terrified the horse too; there was a violent plunge, a clattering of hoofs on the stones, a sudden loud crash of smashing timber, a woman's long, loud, piercing shriek, which stopped the very beating of my heart, and then a frenzied struggle in the cruel, crumbling, treacherous shale, the rattle of loose stones and the hollow roar of something sliding down the precipice.

I rushed to the door and tore it open, with that awful despairing cry still ringing in my ears. The verandah was empty; there was not a soul to be seen or a sound to be heard, save the rain on the roof.

"Aggie," I screamed, "come here! Someone has gone over the verandah and down the khud! You heard him."

"Yes," she said, following me out; "but come in – come in."

"I believe it was Charlie Chalmers" – shaking her as I spoke. "He has been killed – killed – killed! And you stand and do nothing. Send people! Let us go ourselves! Bearer! Ayah! Khidmatgar!" I cried, raising my voice.

"Hush! It was not Charlie Chalmers," she said, vainly endeavouring to draw me into the drawing-room. "Come in – come in."

"No, no!" – pushing her away and wringing my hands. "How cruel you are! How inhuman! There is a path. Let us go at once – at once!"

"You need not trouble yourself, Susan." she interrupted; "and you need not cry and tremble – they will bring him up. What you heard was supernatural; it was not real."

"No – no – no! It was all real. Oh! That scream is in my ears still."

"I will convince you," said Aggie, taking my hand as she spoke. "Feel all along the verandah. Are the railings broken?"

I did as she bade me. No, though it was wet and clammy, the railing was intact.

"Where is the broken place?" she asked.

Where, indeed?

"Now," she continued, "since you will not come in, look over, and you will see something more presently."

Shivering with fear and cold, drifting rain, I gazed down as she bade me, and there far below I saw lights moving rapidly to and fro, evidently in search of something. After a little delay they congregated in one place. There was a low, booming murmur – they had found him – and presently they commenced to ascend the hill, with the 'hum-hum' of coolies carrying a burden.

Nearer and nearer the lights and sounds came up to the very brink of the khud, past the end of the verandah. Many steps and many torches – faint blue torches held by invisible hands – invisible but heavy-footed bearers carried their burden slowly upstairs and along the passage, and deposited it with a dump in Aggie's bedroom! As we stood clasped in one another's arms and shaking all over, the steps descended, the ghostly lights passed up the avenue and disappeared in the gathering darkness. The repetition of the tragedy was over for that day.

"Have you heard it before?" I asked with chattering teeth, as I bolted the drawing-room window.

"Yes, the evening of the picnic and twice since. That is the reason I have always tried to stay out till late and to keep you out. I was hoping and praying you might never hear it. It always happens just before dark. I am afraid you have thought me very queer of late. I have told no end of stories to keep you and the children from harm – I have—"

"I think you have been very kind," I interrupted. "Oh, Aggie, shall you ever get that crash and that awful cry out of your head?"

"Never!" hastily lighting the candles as she spoke.

"Is there anything more?" I asked tremulously.

"Yes; sometimes at night the most terrible weeping and sobbing in my bedroom," and she shuddered at the mere recollection.

"Do the servants know?" I asked anxiously.

"The ayah Mumà has heard it, and the khànsàmàh says his mother is sick and he must go, and the bearer wants to attend his brother's wedding. They will all leave."

"I suppose most people know too?" I suggested dejectedly.

"Yes, don't you remember Mrs. Starkey's warnings and her saying that without the verandah the house was worth double rent? We understand that dark speech of hers now, and we have not come to Cooper's Hotel yet."

"No, not yet. I wish we had. I wonder what Tom will say? He will be here in another fortnight. Oh, I wish he was here now."

In spite of our heart-shaking experience, we managed to eat and drink and sleep, yea, to play tennis – somewhat solemnly, it is true – and go to the club, where we remained to the very last moment; needless to mention that I now entered into Aggie's manoeuvre con amore. Mrs. Starkey evidently divined the reason of our loitering in Kantia, and said in her most truculent manner, as she squared up to us:

"You keep your children out very late, Mrs. Shandon."

"Yes, but we like to have them with us," rejoined Aggie in a meek apologetic voice.

"Then why don't you go home earlier?"

"Because it is so stupid and lonely," was the mendacious answer.

"Lonely is not the word I should use. I wonder if you are as wise as your neighbours now? Come now, Mrs. Shandon."

"About what?" said Aggie with ill-feigned innocence.

"About Briarwood. Haven't you heard it yet? The ghastly precipice and horse affair?"

"Yes, I suppose we may as well confess that we have."

"Humph! You are a brave couple to stay on. The Tombs tried it last year for three weeks. The Paxtons took it the year before, and then sub-let it, not that they believed in ghosts – oh, dear no," and she laughed ironically.

"And what is the story?" I enquired eagerly.

"Well the story is this. An old retired officer and his wife and their pretty niece lived at Briarwood a good many years ago. The girl was engaged to be married to a fine young fellow in the Guides. The day before the wedding what you know of happened, and has happened every monsoon ever since. The poor girl went out of her mind and destroyed herself, and the old colonel and his wife did not long survive her. The house is uninhabitable in the monsoon, and there seems nothing for it but to auction off the furniture and pull it down; it will always be the same as long as it stands. Take my advice and come into Cooper's Hotel. I believe you can have that small set of rooms at the back. The sitting-room smokes, but beggars can't be choosers."

"That will only be our very last resource," said Aggie hotly.

"It's not very grand, I grant you, but any port in a storm."

Tom arrived, was doubly welcome, and was charmed with Briarwood. Chaffed us unmercifully and derided our fears until he himself had a similar experience, and he heard the phantom horse plunging in the verandah and that wild, unearthly and utterly appalling shriek. No, he could not laugh that away, and seeing that we had now a mortal abhorrence of the place, that the children had be kept abroad in the damp till long after dark, that Aggie was a mere hollow-eyed spectre, and that we had scarcely a servant left, that – in short, one day we packed up precipitately and fled in a body to Cooper's Hotel. But we did not basely endeavour to sub-let, nor advertise Briarwood as 'a delightfully situated pucka built house, containing all the requirements of a gentleman's family'. No, no. Tom bore the loss of the rent and – a more difficult feat – Aggie bore Mrs. Starkey's insufferable, "I told you so".

Aggie was at Kantia again last season. She walked out early one morning to see our former abode. The chowkidar and parrot are still in possession, and are likely to remain the sole tenants on the premises. The parrot suns and dusts his ancient feathers in the empty verandah, which re-echoes with his cry of "Lucy, where are you, pretty Lucy?" The chowkidar inhabits a secluded go-down at the back, where he passes most of the day in sleeping, or smoking the soothing 'huka'. The place has a forlorn, uncared-for appearance now. The flowers are nearly all gone; the paint has peeled off the doors and windows; the avenue is grass-grown. Briarwood appears to have resigned itself to emptiness, neglect and decay, although outside the gate there still hangs a battered board on which, if you look very closely you can decipher the words 'To Let'.

Number Ninety

B.M. Croker

FOR A PERIOD extending over some years, a notice appeared periodically in various daily papers. It read:

> *"To let furnished, for a term of years, at a very low rental, a large old-fashioned family residence, comprising eleven bed-rooms, four reception rooms, dressing-rooms, two staircases, complete servants' offices, ample accommodation for a Gentleman's establishment, including six-stall stable, coach-house, etc."*

This advertisement referred to number ninety.

Occasionally you saw it running for a week or a fortnight at a stretch, as if it were resolved to force itself into consideration by sheer persistency. Sometimes for months I looked for it in vain. Other folk might possibly fancy that the effort of the house agent had been crowned at last with success – that it was let, and no longer in the market.

I knew better. I knew that it would never, never find a tenant. I knew that it was passed on as a hopeless case, from house-agent to house-agent. I knew that it would never be occupied, save by rats – and, more than this, I knew the reason why!

I will not say in what square, street, or road number ninety may be found, nor will I divulge to human being its precise and exact locality, but this I'm prepared to state, that it is positively in existence, is in Charleston, and is still empty.

Twenty years ago, this very Christmas, I was down from New York visiting my friend John Hollyoak, a civil engineer from Charleston. We were guests at a little dinner party in the neighborhood of the South Battery. Conversation became very brisk as the champagne circulated, and many topics were started, discussed, and dismissed.

We talked on an extraordinary variety of subjects.

I distinctly recollect a long argument on mushrooms – mushrooms, murders, racing, cholera; from cholera we came to sudden death, from sudden death to churchyards, and from churchyards, it was naturally but a step to ghosts.

John Hollyoak, who was the most vehement, the most incredulous, the most jocular, and the most derisive of the anti-ghost faction, brought matters to a climax by declaring that nothing would give him greater pleasure than to pass a night in a haunted house – and the worse its character, the better he would be pleased!

His challenge was instantly taken up by our somewhat ruffled host, who warmly assured him that his wishes could be easily satisfied, and that he would be accommodated with a night's lodging in a haunted house within twenty-four hours – in fact, in a house of such a desperate reputation, that even the adjoining mansions stood vacant.

He then proceeded to give a brief outline of the history of number ninety. It had once been the residence of a well-known county family, but what evil events had happened therein tradition did not relate.

On the death of the last owner – a diabolical-looking aged person, much resembling the typical wizard – it had passed into the hands of a kinsman, resident abroad, who had no wish to return to Charleston, and who desired his agents to let it, if they could – a most significant condition!

Year by year went by, and still this 'Highly desirable family mansion' could find no tenant, although the rent was reduced, and reduced, and again reduced, to almost zero!

The most ghastly whispers were afloat – the most terrible experiences were actually proclaimed on the housetops!

No tenant would remain, even gratis; and for the last ten years, this 'handsome, desirable town family residence' had been the abode of rats by day, and something else by night – so said the neighbours.

Of course it was the very thing for John, and he snatched up the gauntlet on the spot. He scoffed at its evil repute, and solemnly promised to rehabilitate its character within a week.

I was charged by our host to serve as a witness – to verify that John Hollyoak did indeed spend the night at number ninety. The next night at ten o'clock, I found myself standing with John on the steps of the notorious abode; but I was not going to remain; the carriage that brought us was to take me back to my respectable chambers.

This ill-fated house was large, solemn-looking, and gloomy. A heavy portico frowned down on neighbouring barefaced hall-doors. The elderly caretaker was prudently awaiting us outside with a key, which said key he turned in the lock, and admitted us into a great echoing hall, black as night, saying as he did so: "My missus has made the bed, and stoked up a good fire in the first front, Sir. Your things is all laid out, and I hope you'll have a comfortable night, Sir."

"No, Sir! Thank you, Sir! Excuse me, I'll not come in! Goodnight!" and with the words still on his lips, he clattered down the steps with most indecent haste, and vanished.

"And of course you will not come in either?" said John. "It is not in the bond, and I prefer to face them alone!" and he laughed contemptuously, a laugh that had a curious echo, it struck me at the time. A laugh strangely repeated, with an unpleasant mocking emphasis. 'Call for me, alive or dead, at eight o'clock tomorrow morning!' he added, pushing me forcibly out into the porch, and closing the door with a heavy, reverberating clang, that sounded half-way down the street.

I did call for him the next morning as desired, with the caretaker, who stared at John's commonplace, self-possessed appearance, with an expression of respectful astonishment.

"So it was all humbug, of course," I said, as he took my arm, and we set off for our club.

"You shall have the whole story whenever we have had something to eat," he replied somewhat impatiently. "It will keep till after breakfast – I'm famishing!"

I remarked that he looked unusually grave as we chatted over our broiled fish and omelette, and that occasionally his attention seemed wandering, to say the least. The moment he had brought out his cigar case and lit up he turned to me and said:

"I see you are just quivering to know my experience, and I won't keep you in suspense any longer. In four words – I have seen them!"

I merely looked at him with widely parted mouth and staring interrogative eyes.

I believe I had best endeavor to give the narrative without comment, and in John Hollyoak's own way. This is, as well as I can recollect, his experience word for word:

"I proceeded upstairs, after I had shut you out, lighting my way by a match, and found the front room easily, as the door was ajar, and it was lit up by a roaring and most cheerful-looking fire, and two wax candles. It was a comfortable apartment, furnished with old-fashioned chairs and tables, and the traditional four-poster bed. There were numerous doors, which proved to be cupboards; and when I had executed a rigorous search in each of these closets and locked them, and investigated the bed above and beneath, sounded the walls, and bolted the door, I sat down before the fire, lit a cigar, opened a book, and felt that I was going to be master of the situation, and most thoroughly and comfortably 'at home'. My novel proved absorbing. I read on greedily, chapter after chapter, and so interested was I, and amused – for it was a lively book – that I positively lost sight of my whereabouts, and fancied myself reading in my own chamber! There was not a sound. The coals dropping from the grate occasionally broke the silence, till a neighboring church-clock slowly boomed twelve! 'The hour!' I said to myself, with a laugh, as I gave the fire a rousing poke, and commenced a new chapter; but ere I had read three pages I had occasion to pause and listen. What was that distinct sound now coming nearer and nearer? 'Rats, of course,' said Common-sense – 'it was just the house for vermin.' Then a longish silence. Again a stir, sounds approaching, as if apparently caused by many feet passing down the corridor – high-heeled shoes, the sweeping switch of silken trains! Of course it was all imagination, I assured myself – or rats! Rats were capable of making such curious improbable noises!

"Then another silence. No sound but cinders and the ticking of my watch, which I had laid upon the table."

"I resumed my book, rather ashamed, and a little indignant with myself for having neglected it, and calmly dismissed my late interruption as 'rats – nothing but rats.'"

"I had been reading and smoking for some time in a placid and highly incredulous frame of mind, when I was somewhat rudely startled by a loud single knock at my room door. I took no notice of it, but merely laid down my novel and sat tight. Another knock more imperious this time – after a moment's mental deliberation I arose, armed myself with the poker, prepared to brain any number of rats, and threw the door open with a violent swing that strained its very hinges, and beheld, to my amazement, a tall powdered footman in a laced scarlet uniform, who, making a formal inclination of his head, astonished me still further by saying:

"'Dinner is ready!'"

"'I'm not coming!'" I replied, without a moment's hesitation, and thereupon I slammed the door in his face, locked it, and resumed my seat, also my book; but reading was a farce; my ears were aching for the next sound.

"It came soon – rapid steps running up the stairs, and again a single knock. I went over to the door, and once more discovered the tall butler, who repeated, with a studied courtesy:

"'Dinner is ready, and the company are waiting.'"

"'I told you I was not coming. Be off, and be hanged!' I cried again, shutting the door violently.

"This time I did not make even a pretence at reading. I merely sat and waited for the next move.

"I had not long to sit. In ten minutes I heard a third loud summons. I rose, went to the door, and tore it open. There, as I expected, was the servant again, with his parrot speech:

"'Dinner is ready, the company are waiting, and the master says you must come!'

"'All right, then, I'll come,' I replied, wearied by reason of his importunity, and feeling suddenly fired with a desire to see the end of the adventure.

"He accordingly led the way downstairs, and I followed him, noting as I went the gold buttons on his coat, also that the hall and passages were now brilliantly illuminated by glowing candles, and hung with living green, the crisp leaves of holly, mistletoe and ivy reflecting back the light. There were several uniformed servants passing to and fro, and from the dining room, there issued a buzz of tongues, loud volleys of laughter, many hilarious voices, and a clatter of knives and forks. I was not left much time for speculation, as in another second I found myself inside the door, and my escort announced me in a loud voice as 'Mr. Hollyoak'.

"I could hardly credit my senses, as I looked round and saw about two dozen people, dressed in a fashion of the 18th century, seated at the table, set for a sumptuous Christmas dinner, and lighted up by a blaze of wax candles in massive candelabra.

"A swarthy elderly gentleman, who presided at the head of the board, rose deliberately as I entered. He was dressed in a crimson coat, braided with silver. He wore a white wig, had the most piercing black eyes I ever encountered, made me the finest bow I ever received in all my life, and with a polite wave of his hand, indicated my seat – a vacant chair between two powdered and embroided beauties, with overflowing white shoulders and necks sparkling with diamonds.

"At first I was fully convinced that the whole affair was a superbly matured practical joke. Everything looked so real, so truly flesh and blood, so complete in every detail; but I gazed around in vain for one familiar face.

"I saw young, old, and elderly, handsome and the reverse. On all faces there was a similar expression – reckless, hardened defiance, and something else that made me shudder, but that I could not classify or define.

"Were they a secret community? Burglars or counterfeiters? But no; in one rapid glance I noticed that they belonged exclusively to the upper stratum of society – bygone society. The jabber of talking had momentarily ceased, and the host, imperiously hammering the table with a knife-handle, said in a singularly harsh grating voice:

"'Ladies and gentlemen, permit me to give you a toast! Our guest!' looking straight at me with his glittering coal-black eyes.

"Every glass was immediately raised. Twenty faces were turned towards mine, when, happily, a sudden impulse seized me. I sprang to my feet and said:

"'Ladies and gentlemen, I beg to thank you for your kind hospitality, but before I accept it, allow me to say grace!'

"I did not wait for permission, but hurriedly repeated a Latin benediction. Ere the last syllable was uttered, in an instant there was a violent crash, an uproar, a sound of running, Of screams, groans and curses, and then utter darkness.

"I found myself standing alone by a big mahogany table which I could just dimly discern by the aid of a street-lamp that threw its meagre rays into the great empty dining-room from two deep and narrow windows.

"I must confess that I felt my nerves a little shaken by this instantaneous change from light to darkness – from a crowd of gay and noisy companions, to utter solitude and silence. I stood for a moment trying to recover my mental balance. I rubbed my eyes hard to assure myself that I was wide awake, and then I placed this very cigar-case in the middle of the table, as a sign and token that I had been downstairs – which cigar-case I found exactly where I left it this morning – and then went and groped my way into the hall and regained my room.

"I met with no obstacle en route. I saw no one, but as I closed and double-locked my door I distinctly heard a low laugh outside the keyhole – a sort of suppressed, malicious titter, that made me furious.

"I opened the door at once. There was nothing to be seen. I waited and listened – dead silence. I then undressed and went to bed, resolved that a whole army of butlers would fail to allure me once more to that Christmas feast. I was determined not to lose my night's rest – ghosts or no ghosts.

"Just as I was dozing off I remember hearing the neighbouring clock chime two. It was the last sound I was aware of, the house was now as silent as a vault. My fire burnt away cheerfully. I was no longer in the least degree inclined for reading, and I fell fast asleep and slept soundly till I heard the cabs and milk-carts beginning their morning career.

"I then rose, dressed at my leisure, and found you, my good, faithful friend, awaiting me, rather anxiously, on the hall-door steps.

"I have not done with that house yet. I'm determined to find out who these people are, and where they come from. I shall steep there again tonight, along with my bulldog; and you will see that I shall have news for you tomorrow morning – if I am still alive to tell the tale," he added with a laugh.

In vain I would have dissuaded him. I protested, argued, and implored. I declared that rashness was not courage; that he had seen enough; that I, who had seen nothing, and only listened to his experiences, was convinced that number ninety was a house to be avoided.

I might just as well have talked to my umbrella! So, once more, I reluctantly accompanied him to his previous night's lodging. Once more I saw him swallowed up inside the gloomy, forbidding-looking, re-echoing hall.

I then went home in an unusually anxious, semi-excited, nervous state of mind. I lay wide awake, tumbling and tossing hour after hour, a prey to the most foolish ideas – ideas I would have laughed to scorn in daylight.

More than once I was certain that I heard John Hollyoak distractedly calling me; and I sat up in bed and listened intently. Of course it was fancy, for the instant I did so, there was no sound.

At the first gleam of winter dawn, I rose, dressed, and swallowed a cup of good strong coffee to clear my brain from the misty notions it had harboured during the night. And then I invested myself in my warmest topcoat, and set off for number ninety. Early as it was – it was but half-past seven – I found the caretaker was before me, pacing the pavement, his face drawn with a melancholy expression.

I was not disposed to wait for eight o'clock. I was too uneasy, and too impatient for further particulars of the Christmas dinner-party. So I rang with all my might, and knocked with all my strength.

No sound within – no answer! But John was always a heavy steeper. I was resolved to arouse him all the same, and knocked and rang, and rang and knocked, incessantly for fully ten minutes.

I then stooped down and applied my eye to the keyhole; I looked steadily into the aperture, till I became accustomed to the darkness, and then it seemed to me that another eye – a very strange, fiery eye – was glaring into mine from the other side of the door!

I removed my eye and applied my mouth instead, and shouted with all the power of my lungs: "John! John Hollyoak!"

How his name echoed and re-echoed up through that dark and empty house! "He must hear that," I said to myself as I pressed my ear closely against the lock, and listened with throbbing suspense.

The echo of 'Hollyoak' had hardly died away when I swear that I distinctly heard a low, sniggering, mocking laugh – that was my only answer – that; and a vast unresponsive silence.

I was now quite desperate. I shook the door frantically, with all my strength. I broke the bell; in short, my behaviour was such that it excited the curiosity of a police officer, who crossed the road to know, "What was up?"

"I want to get in!" I panted, breathless with my exertions.

"You'd better stay where you are!" said the police officer; "the outside of this house is the best of it! There are terrible stories…"

"But there is a gentleman inside it!" I interrupted impatiently. "He slept there last night, and I can't wake him. He has the key!"

"Oh, you can't wake him!" returned the police officer gravely. "Then we must get a locksmith!"

But already the thoughtful caretaker had procured one; and already a considerable and curious crowd surrounded the steps.

After five minutes of maddening delay, the great heavy door was opened and swung slowly back, and I instantly rushed in, followed less frantically by the police officer and the caretaker.

I had not far to seek John Hollyoak! He and his dog were lying at the foot of the stairs, both stone dead!

The Patient in Room 96

H.B. Diaz

IMOGENE BEASLEY, the patient in Room 96, secreted herself in a thicket of brambles and waited with a veil of spider silk clinging to her hair. A cricket chirruped, just once, and was answered by the pip of some unseen rodent within the weeds.

No one came for her.

They wouldn't even know she was missing for another hour, when Dr. Thomas would walk into her empty room to give her those yellow pills in the tiny paper cup. She had no more use for antipsychotics than a sparrow did a birdcage.

Imogene Beasley was not insane.

Only once the sun dragged emaciated shadows out of the thorns did she emerge from her hiding place. Imogene knew that in the middle of these woods, quite alone among the pin oaks and the pines, stood Harwood House. From the barred window of her room, she had spent many an evening gazing at its roof, a tiny speck of mottled grey in a blanket of foliage. As the months languished away, the inhabitants that she imagined became as real to her as Dr. Thomas or Nurse Elaine, the many rooms as vivid as her own. She dreamed of velvet curtains and polished silver candlesticks, of lavish parties for people with expensive cars and beautiful dresses. The children, a boy and a girl of about twelve, would fish in the stream that cut a jagged scar into the otherwise unmarred covering of trees. She was certain that they would offer her sanctuary.

Imogene gathered her hospital gown into her fist and splashed through the stream, bare feet aching with cold. She carried on through the current until she reached the bank, and then hoisted herself up. Tiny slugs clung to her fingers and she wiped them on her gown.

It was there, right where she knew it would be. A recent rainstorm had washed out the drive, leaving deep wounds in the gravel. She skirted these as she approached, happy to breathe in the freshness of the air, happier still that it bore no lingering scent of astringent or urine. The wind brushed away a curtain of willow branches so she could pass.

The house slept soundly beneath a blanket of wild ivy, nestled in darkness. No parties had been held here for a long, long time, but the house seemed to prefer it this way. The eves sagged slightly, as a man's shoulders might after a long sigh, and all of the windows peeked at her from behind splintering shutters.

Imogene knew even before her fingers touched the doorknob that she belonged to Harwood House, and now it would belong to her, too. The door opened at her touch, welcoming her with the gentle creaking of its rusted hinges. No one greeted her when she stepped through the threshold. It appeared as though the family she'd imagined had abandoned the place, but surely they would not abandon *her*, not after all this time. No, surely not.

"Colleen? Andrew?" she called aloud, for those were her names for the children, but only the echo of her own voice replied, reverberating off of the vaulted ceiling and shimmering along the crystal chandelier. Cobwebs blurred its sparkle, and although time had tarnished the silver, Imogene still found it magnificent. How could anyone have left this place?

The door closed gently behind her. Imogene did not consider whose hand had done it, only that, for the first time in many years, she did not feel alone.

The armchairs and sofas in the parlor hunched beneath their white sheets like hibernating beasts. She watched them, waiting for one of them to breathe, but they remained in deep slumber. Her bare feet disturbed layers of dust as she continued to the staircase.

The tiny feet that followed behind left no marks at all.

She traced her fingers along the banister, eyes drawn to the gilt-framed mirror at the top of the stairs. Imogene had not seen her face for so long that she could not recall her own features. Occasionally, she'd seen a warped version of her reflection on the surface of a steel instrument or in the glass of a rain-pattered window, but these were only glimpses from a moving train.

Her heart began to race as she reached the top of the staircase. She didn't immediately look in the mirror. No, she wanted to see it all at once this time, not just a glimpse. When she at last lifted her eyes to it, she saw the crystal chandelier. She saw the banister and the paper that hung in strips from the walls, but she did not see herself.

Imogene had no reflection at all.

As she stood dumbfounded before the vacant mirror, she felt a child's hand slip into her own. This felt vaguely comforting; he did not appear in the mirror either, so there must be something wrong with it. But, when she looked down to smile at him, he had gone, leaving only a smear of blood in her palm. When her fingerprint appeared on the glass, she could not remember touching it.

The bloody splotch stretched into a line that soon became a letter, and then another. In moments, they covered every inch of the mirror.

IMOGENE

IMOGENE

IMOGENE

She stumbled backward, and then she was falling. Her hands grasped for purchase. Bones cracked on groaning stairs.

Gravity had its way with her. In a crumpled heap at the bottom of the stairs, Imogene thought at first that she must be dead. She knew she should feel pain, but she felt only a gentle vibrating sensation, like the ringing of a church bell. Then, at the edge of vision already darkened by unconsciousness, Imogene saw a young boy.

"Help me," she whispered, unable to summon strength enough to cry out.

"*Help me*," the boy repeated, but he sounded far away. He shuffled toward her, quickly and with an expression full of anguish. His small face bore a wound so hideous that Imogene screamed. The sound tore from her throat, echoing in the cavernous space and returning to her somehow corrupted. It sounded sickly and shriveled and she covered her ears.

"You're not real," she murmured. He *couldn't* be. The left side of the child's face had been cleaved, as if by an ax, and it hung from his pale skull on tattered bands of flesh and tendon. He smiled down at her, his remaining eye crinkling around the edges. She shut her eyes tight, shrinking away from it. The boy would not leave. She could hear the blood dripping, dripping, dripping, onto the marble beside her face.

"*You're not real*," the boy sang.

"I am, I am!" she cried, but when she opened her eyes, the boy was gone. The wound on her forehead dripped blood into a dark puddle on the floor. It trickled into her eyes when she sat, staining the house scarlet. The staircase seemed impossibly long now, the mirror miles away, but its surface appeared clean from her vantage point beneath it. Imogene saw neither her name nor her face in the glass.

Welcoming the pain that throbbed inside her skull, she rose and shuffled into the parlor to find a place to rest. Portraits of an unknown family hung on the walls, their frames bowed and discolored with time. None of the people here resembled those she had imagined, except for the girl. Imogene approached the painting slowly. Eyes the color of the sea met hers, and something inside her fell quiet. She knew this girl, knew the hook of her nose and the widow's peek of her hairline. Imogene touched the wound on her scalp.

She leaned toward the nameplate beneath the portrait, squinting at the lettering.

No. There must be some mistake.

She backed away. From her perch in the tower, Imogene had believed she would be welcomed here, but stern faces accused her at every turn, their gazes hard beneath cracked paint. She looked away, ashamed. Maybe she'd been wrong about this house all along.

Growing wearier by the moment, Imogene found a sofa with clawed feet. She tugged at the dusty sheet to reveal a floral cushion beneath. Little black lilies wound a lazy pattern through fabric the powdery color of a moth's wing.

How beautiful, she thought. She grasped the sheet with both hands and flung it aside.

Imogene screamed. The boy sat before her on the cushion, cross-legged and clutching a sheet of newspaper in his little hand.

"Who are you?" she asked once she had recovered her senses.

"*Who are you?*"

"I'm," she started, but she could not answer. Imogene covered him again, but the fabric settled onto the sofa as if there were nothing beneath at all. The newspaper fluttered out onto the floor. She picked it up and read the headline, her fingers leaving blood on the page: LOCAL BOY SLAUGHTERED BY DERANGED SISTER: TOWN OUTRAGED AT INSANITY PLEA.

The photograph of the suspect gave Imogene pause. It was the girl in the portrait on the wall, if only a withered husk of her. Sunken cheeks and cracked lips lent her the appearance of one on the verge of death, but there was something of Imogene's mother in the large eyes and wispy blonde hair...

Thump, thump, thump.

A knock on the wall, behind the portraits. The family patriarch, a man with jaundiced skin and a beard that seemed alive even in acrylic, stared down at her from his place above the fireplace mantel, his gaze so malevolent that she ran from the room. One of the portraits crashed to the floor, the frame splintering against the marble. She did not need to turn back to know which of the paintings had been cast out.

She had been cast out.

"*Who are you?*" the boy called after her.

Thump, thump, thump.

"It's not real," she said to herself in a small voice.

Imogene wished she were back in her room, tucked safely beneath the scratchy sheets, little yellow pills in the white cup beside her bed. Yes, that was it. She would just go back. Dr. Thomas must be worried about her.

She flew to the grand front door, but the knob would not turn. It rattled in her hand. Footsteps sounded from the parlor, growing nearer every moment. Imogene could not bring herself to turn around. She pounded on the door until her hands ached, tears streaming down her face.

And then, all at once, the door opened and she fell into Dr. Thomas's arms.

"I'm sorry, I'm sorry," she cried, clutching his white coat.

"We thought you might have come here," he said, but she didn't understand what he meant. The doctor pulled her away and lifted her chin with his finger as if she were made of paper. "Time to go, Imogene."

Dr. Thomas led her away, and the door shut gently behind them. Imogene felt the house inside of her even as it fell away into the forest. She felt its rats gnawing inside her ears, felt its cobwebs inside her lungs and its crystal chandelier shimmering behind her eyes. She belonged to it, after all. She always had.

Imogene Beasley, the patient in Room 96, was not insane.

As she swallowed the yellow pills in the white paper cup, the spirits of Harwood House settled back into the shadows, and waited for her to come home.

A Handful of Dust

Tom English

ALL HIS LIFE old man Brumstead had lived in fear. As a child he had been terrified of the dark, and his overindulgent mother had allowed him to sleep with the light on in his room until he was a senior at Dinsmore High School, back in 1956.

When he was fourteen, three of his 'friends' locked him up in a rotting tool shed behind Grady's Feed Store. It was typical of the pranks Mill Hurst boys were constantly pulling on each other. They stood by the door smoking cigarettes and repeating dirty jokes they'd heard in the locker room, all the while looking about nervously, as poor Brumstead, crouching amid a clutter of hanging harnesses, castoff tractor parts, busted barrels and hay forks, first yelled obscenities, then pleaded for mercy, then started screaming like a frightened girl.

By the time his hysterical cries finally got to them, and his friends dragged his limp, sweat-drenched body from the cluttered shed, Brumstead was sobbing uncontrollably. He'd been locked in that cramped shack for just a few minutes, but a fear of confined spaces stayed with him for the rest of his life.

Brunstead was afraid of heights and crowds, speaking in public and the opposite sex; running out of gas in the middle of nowhere, and being audited by the IRS. He once even told me that the drone of a Hoover vacuum cleaner gave him nightmares. Perhaps some of his fears were silly and unfounded. Obviously, others were not.

* * *

"But there was one thing in particular he feared, which affected him more than all the others," I said. "Something caused by an extremely unpleasant experience he had the year his mother died. One of those stupid and unlikely things you often hear about but can never imagine happening to you."

I paused in my story just long enough to brush away an annoying little insect buzzing about my ear. The room was stuffy, the air musty with the smell of old fabric and mildew. I leaned forward in the overstuffed wingchair and scanned the room where Brumstead had died late one Friday night nearly two months ago.

The old man had managed to dial 911 before going into respiratory arrest, but the fire department was located on the other side of the county and manned totally by volunteers. They had arrived too late to do anything but find Brumstead's dead body slumped against the front door. The coroner wrote the old man's death off as the result of a weakened physical condition: Brumstead had had a bout of flu a couple weeks before, and at seventy-seven he just seemed worn out.

Worn out, I imagined, from too many years spent dreading one thing or another.

My twelve-year-old daughter sat across from me, wide-eyed with anticipation.

"What happened?" Beth asked, eager for me to finish the story of Brumstead's neuroses.

I stood up and walked to the window. Chuck Harper's kids were playing in the yard across the street. "Old man Brumstead had an accident," I continued, but then stopped again while I struggled to raise the window. The thing had been nailed shut – like all the other windows in the house.

When I was a teenager, Brumstead's airtight house had been one of the many peculiar things that fascinated me about the old man. When other kids had begun to shun his place, I became a frequent visitor; while other kids were mocking him, I was lending a respectful, sympathetic ear to all his fearful woes.

"Dad!" Beth whined. Like most kids, she loved a good story, and the weirder the better.

"It happened just outside this two-story farmhouse. Brumstead inherited the place when his mother died, in 1977."

"And now it's ours," Beth said in childish awe.

"Yes," I said slowly.

Evidently, the old man hadn't had anyone else to leave it to. So he left it the skinny kid who used to come by and drink the weak beer Brumstead brewed in his cellar. And listen to the horror stories of all the old man's fears.

I swiped at the buzzing sound near my ear again, and continued: "Forty years ago, this house sat in the middle of a field – this was all farm land. After the accident, Brumstead began selling off the surrounding land. At first, a few homes were built. Then Hurst Street was extended through.

"Then this housing development sprang up," I said, gesturing to the row of almost uniform houses across the street. "Brumstead had always loved the farm…nature…walking through the fields. But after the accident he didn't care about any of that. He was glad to see other people living nearby – relieved to see fields give way to asphalt, and trees to street lights."

"But *why*?" Beth asked impatiently. "What happened?"

"Shortly after the death of his mother, Brumstead went for a walk through a section of field that had lain fallow for two years and was now overgrown with thick weeds. This would have been behind the house," I added, "but still in plain view of it.

"He had been devastated by his mother's death. Brumstead was almost forty years old at the time, and he had still been living with her when she died. He couldn't remember a time when she hadn't been there for him. She'd been his shelter from the dangers of the world; and hers had been the voice that calmed all his fears.

"Wondering if he could ever live without his mother, Brumstead wandered across the field, lost in his thoughts, scuffing his feet over the dry crust. Never before in his life had he felt so alone. Never before had he been so overwhelmed with doubt, so sick with uncertainty. As he walked along he could feel the brittle ground crumbling beneath his shoes; and he gave no thought at all when a small section of the crust gave a bit more than usual, collapsing and caving in an inch or so, accompanied by an unsettling crunch.

"He took several more languorous paces through the rising cloud of dust he'd kicked up before looking down at his feet. They were covered with something black and yellow; something moving – something creeping up his trouser legs.

"A rush of horror surged through his chest. He felt several bursts of pain on his legs, which felt like they were on fire. He slapped at his trousers, stomping and shaking his feet to dislodge the angry mass swarming up his body. Out of the corner of his eye, he could see the dust cloud about his feet thicken, blacken – and quickly rise. He lurched backward, then sideways, his arms flailing violently as he ineffectually grabbed first at one, then another, stab of searing pain. He screamed like he'd never heard himself scream before, stopping just long enough to slap mercilessly at his own face and head, both of which felt like they were burning up.

"When he ran, at first blindly, mindlessly, the seething cloud moved with him, enveloping him – hundreds of winged furies seeking vengeance for their destroyed nest in the dry earth, and each one of them gifted with the ability to sting again and again and again. When at last – after an eternity of mere seconds – a voice inside Brumstead screamed 'Get inside!' and he ran toward the promised safety of the house, the boiling mass chased him.

"With every yard he covered, the number of aggressors dropped and the swarm thinned. But when Brumstead reached the back porch and slammed the screened door shut, there were still several crawling through his hair and clinging to his blue denim.

"His face was a red swollen mask of pain, his body barely better. He managed to drive himself to a doctor who practiced out of his home four or five miles from here."

Beth was starting to feel the itch of some imagined intruder creeping across the back of her neck, her legs, her scalp. As I was soon to learn, she had a particular aversion to crawling insects. "What happened then?" she asked, drawing the collar of her shirt up tight around her neck and shuddered.

"Brumstead was lucky. Some people have severe reactions to the venom of yellow jackets. Even one or two stings can trigger an allergic reaction that can swell the throat shut. Brumstead was *one* of those people. But he made it to the doctor in time.

"When he got there, he was in severe pain, and he could barely breathe. He passed out on the doctor's front porch, and Kearney had to drag him inside."

I sat down again, on an old trunk tucked in a corner of the room. Beth had moved to the overstuffed wingchair, and was sitting with her bare feet on the edge of the cushion, hugging her knees to her chest.

"Which couldn't have been an easy task," I said. "I think Dr. Kearney was around seventy at the time – still making house calls, still x-raying broken bones on an old machine in the backroom of his two-story duplex.

"Anyway, as soon as he got Brumstead stabilized, the doctor phoned Drury County Rescue to send over an ambulance, and had the poor man transported to the hospital. I think Brumstead stayed there a couple nights or so. Kearney told him, later, that if he'd delayed getting there, even a few minutes, he might have died. He also told Brumstead to avoid getting stung again, because his body was now 'sensitized' to the venom. Another dose could perhaps be fatal.

"Needless to say, Brumstead didn't need a new phobia to worry about. But he got one anyway. He stopped going for walks, started staying indoors. Other than driving to the courthouse, where he worked as a clerk, or to Haskin's Food-Mart, the old man hardly strayed from this house.

"He read up on yellow jackets: their life-cycle, their habits, their diet. He learned far more than he needed to know; too much for his own peace of mind. Like honeybees, yellow jackets are communal insects. When their nest is disturbed, or even threatened, they attack as a well-coordinated army to defend the hive. But honeybees die after stinging once. Their stingers break off and become embedded in the flesh. Yellow jackets were not cursed with such a limitation. They're capable of repeatedly stinging an enemy, with no harm to themselves.

"And swatting one of them only incites their fury: a smashed yellow jacket releases a scent that alerts the other members of the communal nest. Sensing that one of their numbers has been killed, the others will attack with a vengeance. But that was an extremely painful experience Brumstead didn't need to learn from a book.

"Again, a little bit of knowledge is a dangerous thing. As Brumstead mulled over the facts, and licked his wounds, he grew increasingly fearful of being stung again. Initially, he kept all the windows shut – no matter how stuffy the house got. But ultimately, he *nailed* them shut."

"I'm glad he had AC," Beth said, scratching hard at her scalp. "Do you think there's any still around here?"

"I doubt it. A few days after being released from the hospital, he paid Mike Fenton's sons to destroy the nest in the backyard. Yellow jackets are supposed to be least active at night, so the two boys waited till dusk, after most of the hive had flown back to the nest. They crept up to a respectful distance of the nest and one of them threw a pail of kerosene on it. The other one flicked a match at it. And then they both ran like mad.

"The kerosene burned long and hot. By the light of the flames rising from the dust, the boys could see dark shapes flying into the heart of the inferno. It was the stragglers returning to the nest – driven by instinct to try and save the hive. Flying to their death.

"Standing at the kitchen window, Brumstead watched the glow of the burning nest until the last ember had disappeared against the blackness of night. Years later, he continued to recount the whole affair, each time rubbing his hands together somewhat fiendishly – peculiarly comforted that vengeance had been served."

I finished my tale in an appropriately solemn tone, but unlike other occasions when Beth would clap and ask for another story, she was unusually quiet. I watched her head tilt slowly back as her eyes rose to the corner above my head.

"Dad," she said in a low, *anxious* voice, "There's one in here!"

I stood and looked around. There was nothing flying about the room but Beth's overworked imagination. She loved a good scare, and my stories – even the more ghoulish ones – rarely caused her even a moment of unease. But perhaps this time, owing to the truth of Brumstead's story, I'd gone too far.

"We don't have to worry about yellow jackets in *this* house, Beth. All the windows are shut. And nothing flew in when we had the door open." I threw my arm around her and squeezed her tightly. Outside, the late summer day had faded, and flashes of heat lightning illuminated the darkening eastern sky.

"We had a long drive today. I bet you're tired," I said, and she nodded in agreement. "Enough excitement for one day. Why don't you go upstairs and get ready for bed. I'll come up in a bit and tuck you in."

She nodded again.

"Tomorrow we'll go treasure hunting. There's tons of neat junk in this old house."

She smiled, scratching her sides and neck. "Maybe I'll find some old skeleton keys for my collection," she said.

"Probably so. We'll go into town and get some pancakes first."

"Yes!"

"Go brush your teeth." I said.

"And Beth," I added before she left the room, "We don't need to tell mom about this story." She nodded in agreement.

I went to the window and studied the heads of the large nails driven into the sides of the frame. It wasn't going to be easy removing them. But it needed to be done soon. Old houses were firetraps and the idea of not being able to raise a single window wasn't exactly comforting.

The whole place would need repainting before I could put it on the market, and I had serious doubts the electrical wiring was up to code. I'd have to climb into the attic tomorrow and take a look at it. Joan would be driving down in a few days, and she'd help me clean the place out. Still, the amount of work involved....

I caught myself. How often do we dream of someone putting us in their will, let alone leaving us everything? It wasn't fair to treat this unexpected blessing from Brumstead as though it were a curse. So I quietly thanked him for my windfall, and then began to wonder if the old man had feared banks as much as he'd feared just about everything else. Was he one of those eccentrics who'd hidden money behind a wall or under the floorboards? What treasures would I find for *my* collection?

I sat musing over this fanciful notion, and over Brumstead's cloistered way of life. He'd lived alone in this old house for close to four decades – with only his fears to occupy him. Not the healthy fear that keeps us from doing stupid things; not the entertaining scare you get from a rollercoaster ride or a really good horror movie; but the kind of fear that has the power to cripple and choke the life out of a man; a genuine and palpable fear.

I yawned and checked my watch. It was a little past ten, and starting to rain. I could hear the soft clatter of the rain striking the house's tin roof, accompanied by occasional rumblings of distant thunder. I switched off the light and headed upstairs. When I reached the landing, I stopped at the first room, where Beth was staying, and gently turned the knob.

Her room was impenetrably dark. I had unthinkingly put her in a room at the back of the house, sheltered from the streetlights. The faint glow of a lamp in the corner of the landing did little to banish the darkness in her room. Neither was there a single shaft of moonlight in the storm-blackened sky.

I stood in the doorway, waiting for my eyes to adjust to the darkness, trying to perceive Beth's shape upon the bed. I stepped softly into the room and was swallowed up in its darkness. If Beth were asleep, I didn't want to awaken her, but I felt a foolish need to reassure myself of her presence in the room. I moved carefully across the room, feeling my way blindly, one hand gently searching for her sleeping form.

I felt something, like a feather, sweep lightly past my nose, my ear – got the impression of frantic movement in the room, of something not quite right in the thick, stale air.

I fumbled for the lamp on the night table, then switched it on. For a moment I thought the sudden brightness that flooded the room had me seeing spots before my eyes – spots that circled, dipped, shot past my head. The whole room was crawling with yellow jackets.

There were dozens swarming about Beth's bed, perhaps hundreds more seething across the walls and clinging to the ceiling above her. The surface of the night table was completely covered over with them, the lampshade crawling with them, the water glass bristling with their winged bodies. I have never had a fear of yellow jackets, knowing that they attack only when provoked; but the sheer multitude of their numbers – forced upon me without warning – combined with some natural revulsion at seeing the things clinging to every available surface and object, sent a rush of utter panic through me.

I lurched back, knocking something from the night table, and stirred up a cloud of moving bodies. Beth sprang up in her bed. She was disorientated from being jarred awake. She squinted at me, puzzled, and rubbed her eyes. Before I could think or speak – before I could warn her and lessen the shock – she saw them. She screamed repeatedly, her legs kicking violently at the sheets.

"Beth!" I said hoarsely, "Be still! They're swarming, not attacking."

Almost as if stimulated by the intensity of her horror, the numbers of black and yellow bodies swarming about the room increased significantly. As the cloud of flying insects swirled around us, moving as a single, intelligent entity, I saw one of them alight on Beth's arm. She flinched in revulsion.

"No, Beth!" I screamed, as her hand arced across her face, and she slapped at the spot, crushing the tiny insect beneath her palm.

I cringed at the sight, like a soldier who's had a grenade tossed at his feet, and knows it's too late to do anything but wait for the explosion.

Nothing happened. Nothing changed.

And then they were on her.

I jerked the sheet over her head, and swept her from the bed. She was screaming and writhing in agony. I wrapped the flapping edges of the sheet about her twisting form and bundled her from the room, slamming the door shut behind me.

* * *

Pacing outside the double doors marked EMERGENCY, I kept wondering: Why hadn't *I* been stung. There had been hundreds of them, and I had been at the heart of their fury.

When the doors parted, I hurried to intercept Dr. Sam Travis as he walked out. "How is she?" I asked.

"Her breathing is no longer constricted. She's resting now."

Sam and I had attended Pratt University together, and I was glad he was on duty. He studied me for a moment, then said, "Let's get some coffee."

It sounded more like a command than an invitation. I followed him into the staff lounge. "Grab a chair," he said, pointing to a table at the back of the room. He poured two cups, then sat down across from me. "Rob," he said, hesitating long enough to sip his coffee, "what the hell are you trying to pull here?"

It took a moment for the implication of his question to sink in. "What are you talking about?"

"You bring your daughter in with all the symptoms of envenomation. Yet there's not a mark on her."

"Are you kidding?" I said. "She was *covered* with swollen stings when I brought her in."

"Yeah, I know she was." He stared at the Styrofoam cup in his hand. "They're gone now; there's no trace of wasp stings."

"How.... Is that normal?"

He shook his head and leaned back in his chair.

"Sam," I said, "do you believe in the power of suggestion?"

"Why? What's that got to do with anything?"

"Beth went to bed tonight thinking about yellow jackets," I said. "We drove down today to work on the farmhouse I inherited from Ray Brumstead. Did you know him?"

"No. But I remember you talking about him. He was phobic."

"Phobic is putting it mildly. He was scared to death of just about everything."

"What's your point, Rob?"

"Brumstead stepped on a ground nest of yellow jackets, years ago, and had to be hospitalized. It was something that changed his life. He sold his fields, stopped going for walks. And he had all the windows in the house nailed shut. I wanted Beth to know why, so I told her the whole story – in all its macabre splendor, unfortunately."

I stood and started pacing about the table. "Could the power of suggestion – hearing the details, seeing the windows nailed shut, being in the very house where it happened – trigger her imagination?"

"You think she conjured up a swarm of wasps out of her head. Got stung," he said, "and her initial symptoms were all psychosomatic?"

"Imagination is a powerful force, Sam."

"Interesting. But that would take *some* imagination." He put his cup down, and leaned back in his chair. "And you saw them, too. Were you seeing the phantoms of a child's overworked imagination?"

"Yeah, I know," I said, realizing how ridiculous the whole thing sounded once it was verbalized. "But Beth *had* seen something that wasn't there: earlier, before bed, right after hearing the story. She said there was a yellow jacket buzzing about my head. I *didn't* see it."

I leaned on the table, and stared at his smug expression. "How else can you explain why *I* wasn't stung?"

"That's what I'm trying to find out," he said. He drummed his index finger against his empty cup. "It's possible. Emotional stress can induce a variety of illnesses, including allergic reaction. There *are* precedents of psychosomatic injury in individuals who too closely identify with a particular situation or person. The wounds in the hands of stigmatics, for instance, may somehow be mentally induced by a close identification with the crucified Christ."

He shook his head. "But this would go way beyond anything I've ever read about psycho-physiological disorders. There's so much we don't understand about the power of the mind – the power of human emotion."

He pushed himself up from his chair. "But you saw it, too." He tossed the Styrofoam cup at the trashcan, but missed it. "This sounds more like a case of mass hysteria," he said. "In fact, the whole thing sounds like the weird stuff you used to write for the college journal."

"That was fiction," I said brusquely, "meant to entertain. I'm talking about my daughter now."

"Whose care you've entrusted to me. That's why we're having this conversation." He glanced at his watch. "It's an interesting theory, Rob, but if I were you, I'd call an exterminator – pronto. Old houses can harbor a lot of things. You could have a nest in the attic or behind a wall. They probably have a way to get inside, a crack or hole somewhere."

"Yeah," I nodded.

"Mack Loomis is an exterminator. Call *him*."

"*Slack* Mack? The guy who quit high school? Haven't seen him in ages."

"Yeah, well, he bummed around for awhile, but I stopped thumbing my nose at him several years ago. He owns his own company now, and he probably makes more money than I do."

"I guess this will give me a chance to see him, again," I said. "Can I take Beth home now?"

"I want to keep her for observation, at least overnight. Besides," he said, "if that house *has* triggered some emotional problems, she shouldn't go back there. And if you *do* have a wasp infestation, she shouldn't be there. Her body's now sensitized to the venom. Another sting, even one, could cause a severe allergic reaction."

I thanked Sam for his time and care, and then hustled upstairs to Beth's room. She was sleeping peacefully. The night-duty nurse reassured me that she would be checking on Beth throughout the night, and that the best thing for me to do was go home and get some rest.

I got back to the Brumstead place a little past midnight, and walked about the empty house, examining the walls, ceiling and floors till almost one in the morning.

Nothing. No cracks, no holes, no hidden passages leading to secret rooms.

I fell asleep with my clothes on, and woke up early with the sun blasting through a curtain-less window. At eight o'clock sharp, I called Loomis Pest Control. When Mack heard it was me, he said he'd come out personally, and less than an hour later he pulled into the gravel driveway.

Mack had gained a great deal of weight since high school – probably from lounging in the air-conditioned office where he dispatched his crew of 'hard-working professionals'. As he clambered up the stepladder he'd placed under the attic door, it wobbled and groaned under his not insignificant mass; and I started wondering if he'd even be able to fit through the narrow opening in the ceiling.

"Yeah, buddy-boy," he bellowed, squirming through the opening. "Business has been good. Mind handing me that flashlight?"

I passed the light to him, and he took another step up the ladder, wedging himself up to the waist. "You gotta dusty attic, buddy-boy," he said, shining the light into one corner of the roof beams. "Yessir, old and dusty. But if you got bugs up here – and I'm sure ya do – your old buddy Mack's gonna fix you up. Yessiree," he said, slowly twisting in the attic doorway as the beam of his flashlight stripped the darkness from each succeeding rafter. "You bastards can forget about Raid, 'cause there's a *new* sheriff in town. Nope. When I find you, you're in for a helluva lot more than a little raid – this is gonna be a full-scale *Mack Attack*."

He had almost completed a half-circle turn in the too-tight opening when his flashlight clattered to the floor. "Shit!" he yelled in a husky voice, and I heard the thud of his elbows against the doorframe as he yanked his upper torso from the attic. The stepladder rocked from side to side, and he almost kicked it over as he stumbled down the rungs, skipping the last two and landing heavily on the floor.

"Outside!" he said, pushing me out the door and onto the landing. "Go, go, go!" he yelled, urging me downstairs. He cleared the front door, leapt from the porch, and ran to the street.

I walked to the sidewalk, where he stood bent over, his hands resting on his thighs, his chest heaving as he gasped for breath. "You okay?" I asked.

He looked up and nodded, then straightened and walked slowly to the van at the end of the driveway. He pulled the rear doors open and sat down on the back of the truck. "Buddy-boy," he said, still breathing hard and wiping sweat from his reddened face, "you gotta big wasp nest up there."

"Yeah, well, isn't that what you're here for?"

"Listen, smartass, I've been doing this for over twelve years. I've gone into barns and silos and rotted-out warehouses, and I've never seen anything like what you got up there!"

He sat there at the back of the van, staring at the ground around his feet, while he caught his breath. "I'm sorry, Rob," he said finally, wiping his face on his sleeve. "I started out in this business because I needed the cash and I couldn't find anything else. But I *do not* like insects, Rob, I hate 'em!" He rubbed the back of his neck. "Maybe that's where my success comes from – I love killing 'em. It's a passion, you understand. But when I run across a bad infestation…." His voice trailed off as he scanned the roofline of the old farmhouse.

"Rob," he said, still looking up, "you got a nest up there the size of…Hell, it takes up two-thirds of the attic space." He looked me in the eye. "It must be home to thousands."

I finally convinced Mack to come back inside with me. He cautiously followed me back upstairs, no doubt motivated more by shame than courage, and then steadied the ladder as I climbed into the attic to see for myself.

I was glad he had prepared me for what I saw.

The beam of the flashlight moved across foot after foot, yard after yard, of dark grey, paper-like shell. The nest stretched from the attic floor to the highest point in the rafters, from the back of the house to the front; and it extended at least half the length of the hipped roof.

It looked like a bloated cocoon, anchored to the heavy beams by a muddy substance the same sickly grey color as the outer shell. Half of the end facing me was honeycombed with thousands of dark holes – tiny tunnels extending deep into the heart of the nest.

I eased myself into the attic and knelt on a joist a few feet from the swollen mass. "What's this thing made of," I called down to Mack.

"Uh, cellulose," he said. "It's pretty much just regurgitated paper. They make it out of plant debris. Old trash, wood shavings...and dust."

"It looks empty," I said.

A couple minutes later, Mack slowly put his head through the attic door. "There's a lot of stuff I may not know, but I *do* know about this," he said. "This thing has all the signs of being an active nest."

"Come on, Mack. There's no sign of them."

"You wanna see 'em?" he said hatefully. "Go rap on it with the flashlight – just gimme a chance to clear out first."

"No, I don't," I said in a wave of anger. "But I do need to know. My daughter was stung last night, repeatedly, by...something I can't explain."

"Well there you have it," he said, pointing to the grey mass.

"But where are they *now*?"

"They probably all left the nest to scavenge. They feed on garbage, you know. Me, I'm glad they're not here. We better clear out too, before some of 'em fly back to the nest."

"Mack. I need to know if I've got a problem with wasps or if last night I was seeing something that wasn't there."

"Something that wasn't there? Are you crazy? Look at the size of this monster. You're lucky to be alive!"

"There's nothing here but an empty shell. What evidence do you have that this thing's inhabited?"

"Evidence?" Mack cried. "There's your evidence!"

"I can see the nest," I said hotly, "That doesn't mean the house is infested with yellow jackets."

"For God's sake, Rob, come on out. Let's shut the door. Do you hafta personally see everything before you believe it. Hell, didn't you ever go to Sunday school? Why can't you trust my judgment? I've been at this for years. I'm telling you the nest is active. Have a little faith in me, will ya?"

"Faith?" I said.

"Yeah, some things you just hafta take on faith."

I stared at the empty grey cocoon rising up before me, but my mind was somewhere else, searching through a jumble of memories for something I'd forgotten – something someone once told me. I felt an urgency to remember it. But *what* was it?

"Hold the ladder," I said, crawling from the attic.

"Now you're talking, buddy-boy," Mack said. "You need to decide what you're gonna do about this thing quick."

"Any suggestions?"

"We can saturate the thing with enough chemical to kill anything that returns to it for weeks. But you'll hafta leave the house. Give the fumes time to clear."

I nodded.

"That's the easy part. I wasn't sure if you noticed, but the damn thing runs down inside the walls. There's probably not a void space in the whole house that's not plugged with paper. And with the old copper wire running behind these walls, you have the potential for one hell of an electrical fire."

"Can it be removed?" I asked.

"If you have enough money you can do anything," Mack said. "But is it worth it?" He shrugged. "You definitely need to have someone pull the stuff outta the attic. But I doubt you can get to the crap behind the walls – not without tearing them out."

I told Mack I needed time to think about it. He said he'd enjoyed seeing me again, despite the circumstances, then warned me not to put off having the nest treated. I watched him back the van out of the drive, and speed away – back to his air-conditioned office, probably.

Then I drove to the hospital to visit Beth. She was sore and a bit sluggish from all the antihistamines, but otherwise she seemed in good spirits. To her delight, I promised her we'd go to the beach before summer vacation was over, and that she could spend the whole day treasure hunting with her metal detector.

I also promised her she'd never have to go inside the old Brumstead house again. I could read the relief in her young eyes.

I walked down to the cafeteria and bought her a chocolate milkshake. When I got back to her room she was sitting up, watching television. I gave her a kiss, then left her happily sipping the shake and watching *Jeopardy*.

Heading back to the farmhouse, I kept replaying the events of the last couple days: that monstrosity in the attic; the terrifying scene in Beth's room; what Dr. Sam Travis had said about the power of human emotion; and the words Mack had bellowed at me through that narrow opening in the ceiling.

I thought about the wretchedness of Brumstead's existence in that lonely old house; how fear had been the old man's constant companion; how it had dominated his thoughts and haunted his dreams.

Suddenly the whole thing started to make sense.

I stopped at City Hall to pick up the permits I would need. I was sent from one office to the next, and spent four hours filling out forms. It hadn't hurt being something of a celebrity: the Mill Hurst boy who'd made it in the big city, and had returned to rub elbows with the folks he'd grown up with.

But by the time I had filed my last form it was too late to do anything but hire the work crew. I scheduled one to start promptly at 7:30 in the morning, then drove back to the Brumstead house.

I phoned Joan. She wouldn't have to drive down after all. Then I packed up Beth's and my things, and loaded up the SUV.

I didn't sleep that night. I sat in Brumstead's over-stuffed wingchair, staring at the walls, a constant stream of words and pictures swirling like flying insects through my brain. In fact, I was still pondering them when I heard the sound of a bulldozer cranking. I stepped from the house, gently closed the door behind me, and walked out to the street.

I stood on the sidewalk with the demolition crew, and watched as the bulldozer raised its blade and approached the house. Twenty minutes later, accompanied by a symphony of cracklings, crunches and hand-clapping, the old farmhouse splintered and collapsed upon itself.

Through the swirling dust, I saw the grey form of the nest protruding through the pile of broken boards and bits of insulation. The demolition crew walked around the ruins, pointing at the cracked shell and swearing in angry tones, but no one ventured near it. No one touched it.

When I was a boy I used to walk to the old Mill Hurst Baptist Church every week to attend Sunday school. Pastor Barnes taught me many interesting things, but the one I remember now – triggered by the impatient words of an old friend – had to do with faith.

Faith, the pastor had taught us kids, was the evidence of things we cannot see; it was the substance of things we hope for. He also told us that fear was the opposite of faith, and that dread held almost as much power as hope.

I thought about the power of raw human emotions. All his life, Brumstead had lived in fear. Fear had shaped his habits. Fear had forged his destiny. Fear and dust and the dread of something that otherwise might never have happened.

Was the grey nest lying amidst these ruins a physical manifestation of everything Brumstead had dreaded? Was this monstrosity the *material* substance of all his fears?

There were no signs of activity about the nest. No stirrings of life from within. Nothing to indicate this was an active hive. At least, nothing in the natural realm.

I left the site for several hours – to visit Beth – and to take care of one last thing. But a little before five, I returned to the pile of rubble that had defined Brumstead's life; to the hideous cocoon reposing beneath the old man's broken dreams.

At 5:30 p.m. a pumper-truck from the local fire department arrived, without fanfare, and I was joined on the sidewalk by Steve Gaston, yet another friend from my youth. He had brought two other men with him, and after a few minutes of quietly conversing, the trio set fire to the pile of rubble.

We watched the flames as they licked and consumed the grey shell. It was the final episode in the long history of a lonely, frightened old man. His terrible legacy would soon return to a handful of dust.

The pile burned hot for three hours. We sat together on the truck, watching the flames, reminiscing as though we were simply gathered around the fireplace at Tall Timber Lodge.

Then, just before dusk, a black, swirling plume rose up from the flames. But it wasn't smoke.

It moved off into the darkening eastern sky, sweeping low over the rooftops of the houses across the street, until it disappeared into the blackness on the horizon.

We had all seen it. But not one of us commented.

The House at the Top of the Hill

John Everson

THE HOUSE at the top of the hill was haunted. Everyone in town knew it. Everybody said so. But, boys being boys, and a dare being a dare, that naturally didn't keep Tommy and Bret from climbing its steps on a cold, darkening afternoon in October.

October 31, to be exact. When else would you dare your friend to put both feet inside the threshold of a haunted house?

* * *

It had started earlier that day in the cafeteria.

"Chicken," Bret had accused, and he wasn't talking about the mystery meat hidden in the disturbingly garish orange Halloween sauce. He was taunting Tommy.

"Not," Tommy quailed, looking around the lunchroom to see who might be listening.

"Are too. Balk, balk balk," Bret continued, raising his voice. "You're a big chicken, afraid of the boogie man."

Some of the other kids were starting to lean in towards their table, and Tommy could hear conversations all around them dying out, as his classmates tried to hear what was going on.

"I'm *not* chicken," Tommy said. "I'll do it under one condition."

"What's that?"

"You've got to do it too."

Bret bit his lip and looked about to back out. But then he nodded.

"Deal."

* * *

And so now they climbed, step by creaking wooden step up the long grey stairs that led from the cracked cement sidewalk up the brown dead hill to the tall grey doors of the haunted house. The doors that seemed to reach up and up into the very rafters of the high thin roof, which seemed to lean and pitch and grasp at the darkening clouds themselves.

Bret sneezed as the cold October wind gusted by, moving the dead weeds in a swishing hiss all around them.

"We could go back," Tommy said. "If you're getting a cold."

Bret wiped his nose with a sleeve. "Chicken?"

"Never mind."

The two boys continued their ascent, 23 steps in all, and at last stood, breathing heavy and chilled from more than simple cold, at the weathered door of the haunted house.

"Well, go ahead," Bret announced. His voice seemed to catch, just a bit. "I dared *you*. I'll go with you, but you've got to go first."

The windows to the left of the door, looking into what had once been a living room, were shattered, and Tommy could see the shredded yellowed curtains swaying in the growing October wind. A storm was blowing in.

"What if it's locked?" he said, stalling.

"What if it's not?" Bret countered.

Tommy reached up and turned the tarnished brass knob.

It wasn't.

Locked, that is.

The door opened with a long, slow, high-pitched creak.

"Well, that should have woke the dead," Bret tried to joke. Tommy didn't laugh.

The door leaned against the inside wall, letting the fading light of the afternoon stretch across the dust-covered wooden floor inside. Tommy could see a stairway leading up just in front of the door, and the tickle of whispering shadows created by the blowing curtains moved across the walls of the room just to their right.

"Well?" Brett said after a moment. "You going in, or are we going to stand here and look at the door all night? Come on, before someone sees us."

At that, on the street below, a car went motoring by. Tommy could hear a Beatles song fading in the background. "Get back, get back, get back to where you once belonged…"

He lifted his right foot, closed his eyes, and stepped inside.

* * *

The house was old, one of the oldest structures in town. Some said it had been built by pilgrims. As long as Tommy could remember, nobody had lived in it. Inside, he could smell mildew and dust, and his feet echoed hollowly on the bare wooden floor. It felt colder inside than it had out. Bret sneezed again, behind him. *He* was still outside.

"Well," Tommy hissed. "I'm in, what about you?"

His friend finally followed him through the open door, and the two boys stood in the dingy front room of the haunted house.

"Doesn't seem very haunted to me," Bret announced bravely. He kept his voice low, however.

Tommy nodded. After all the buildup, the empty room almost seemed a let-down. He didn't feel anything here but neglect.

"Let's look around," Bret said.

They walked through the front room, every step telegraphing itself throughout the house with the clomping echoes of abandoned space. The kitchen was in the back, a small, depressing room. The floor was dirty linoleum that once might have been white, but now looked orange with age. A small steel-rimmed table leaned crookedly against a wall peppered with nail holes, their nails and hangings long removed. One white shellacked cabinet door hung open, and Tommy could make out the bright orange and yellow mottles of sunny flowered shelf paper inside. There were gaps in the cabinetry and blackened spots on the floor there where a refrigerator and stove once stood. One globe from a five-armed light fixture lay shattered on the floor.

"Come on," Bret said, and they stepped back from the kitchen to walk down a dark hallway.

There were three empty bedrooms at its end, and the boys peered quickly into each. The bare windows leered back at them like laughing mouths. There were shadows and holes on the walls where people once had hung their shelves and pictures and posters and more.

All gone.

They passed a door on the way back to the front room, and Bret stopped them.

"Open it," he said.

"Why?"

"See what it is."

Tommy shook his head. "Not part of the deal. Come on, it's getting dark outside. Pretty soon we won't be able to see anything in here."

Bret sneezed again. "Chicken."

"Won't work this time," Tommy said and started back to the front room.

Bret reached out and opened the door himself. Tommy stopped when he heard the creak.

"Halllooooo," Bret called out, his voice echoing weirdly. "Ghosts, where are you? Come out, come out wherever you are…"

Tommy felt his heart stop.

It was one thing to sneak inside a haunted house. It was another to tempt the haunts, if there were any.

"This must be where he killed them," Bret whispered.

"Huh?"

Bret was pointing into the blackness beyond the door. The smell of mildew and decay – the smell of age – had increased.

"Downstairs. They say the father took his kids down into the cellar, tied them up and chopped their heads off, one by one. Then he went upstairs and hung himself. That's why they say you can hear kids crying sometimes late at night. And you can hear the creaking of a body dangling from a rope."

"Why would he do that?" Tommy said.

"His wife ran off with another guy and he freaked out."

"Where'd you hear that?"

"Everybody knows," Bret said. "Where've you been?"

"I just heard it was haunted," Tommy said.

"Yeah, well, get tuned in. Wanna go down?"

"Yeah sure, after you."

Bret closed the door and the two boys started back to the front room. But then, Tommy put his hand on Bret's shoulder and stopped him.

"Shhh. Did you hear that?" he whispered.

The curtains rippled across the room, but it was getting harder to see them in the gathering gloom of a blustery Halloween night.

"What?" Bret hissed.

"Something creaked upstairs."

"Just the wind," Bret said. "Cut it out."

But then he heard it too. It came from just above them, in the room beyond the ceiling.

Creak, cronk, creak, cronk.

A steady push and pull rhythm. Rope sawing board.

"Still think it's the wind?"

Creak, cronk, creak, cronk.

"Does it matter? Let's get out of here before the whole house caves in."

Thump.

The creaking stopped.

Clomp.

Bret and Tommy started towards the door, but before they reached it, Bret held up a hand. He put a finger in front of his lips and pointed, up, in the direction of the stairs leading to the second floor.

Thud.

Tommy listened. A new creaking had begun, but this one sounded more like the creak of feet on boards. Like the creak of someone walking.

Clomp.

Like the creak of one stair after the other, slowly being trodden down.

Thud.

And they had to pass in front of the stairs in order to get out.

Clomp, thud. Clomp, thud.

How many stairs were there? Tommy wondered.

"Come on," Bret hissed, and the two boys started towards the door again, but just as they reached the foyer, the owner of the feet stepped into view.

"Can I help you boys?"

His voice was molasses and nails, dark and sharp. His face was long, and pallid, his nose a crooked hook, his lips like two thin worms come to nestle atop an endless chin. He wore a black jacket that hung low, past his thighs, and pants that hung in folds and wrinkles atop dull, dark shoes. Graveyard shoes.

Brett screamed, and dove beneath the man's arm, making for the door. It was still open, and he hit the stoop in a roll, calling out "Come on, Tommy, come on!"

Tommy sprang to follow, but it was too late. The man flung the door shut with a crack, and stood before it, arms folded. Face drawn.

Tommy noticed that while the man's complexion seemed pale overall, his neck was ringed with an angry red and purple bruise.

"Not so fast," the man said. "Why are you in my house?"

"I'm sorry," Tommy stammered. "We were…we were…just…looking around. We didn't mean any harm."

"Nobody ever does, do they?" he said. "Come, sit down with me a minute before you go. We'll talk. I so rarely get visitors anymore."

Tommy backed away from the man, thinking that there was no place to sit but the floor. But when he turned slightly, trying to keep the man in view as he stepped back into the front room, he sucked in a quick breath.

The dusty, empty, wind-tattered room was now full of furniture. Its floor shone in a deep mahogany gleam and a Chinese rug covered its center. The man gestured to a deep red velvet couch.

"Sit."

Tommy hunched his backside up to the edge of the couch, and pushed backwards, not really believing that anything would be there to support him. The room had been empty a minute ago. He'd walked through the spot where the couch now was.

But the couch felt solid, and he tried to relax into its fuzzy embrace.

His heart was pounding and in his head he cursed the name of Bret over and over and over again.

The man paced the center of the rug and put the fingers of each hand together lightly, as if praying. Then he touched one skeletal finger to the white dome of his forehead and said "they say I'm crazy, don't they?"

"I want to go home," Tommy answered.

"Yes," the man said. "We all want to go home, don't we? But sometimes, we go where we don't belong, we get just a little too far, take just one too many steps…and we can never go home again, eh?"

"Please?" Tommy said. "I promise I won't bother you again."

"And maybe I won't let you go unless you promise that you *will* bother me again," the man said. He chuckled then, a low, creaking sound, like the settling of a house. Or the sound of a man on a noose, swinging slowly in the breeze.

Tommy looked behind him, and saw that the curtains were no longer moving. The curtains were no longer stained and tattered. They were brilliant white, and reflected the colored shadows of the tiffany lamp in the corner. It was rose and orange and emerald, and stretched to ragged points where dragonflies struggled to fly out of the glass and away from its edges. Trying but always trapped in the ornamental glass. Trapped in this room, like Tommy was now.

The man stepped closer and Tommy shrunk back into the couch that couldn't exist.

"Three chances," the man said. "Three chances to go home. If you miss them all, you stay here with me. Here is your first."

The man held up three hairs between his fingers. Two dark. One light.

"Choose the long one, and you must seek your exit upstairs. The short one, downstairs. The middle one…and you can walk out the door right there."

He stood in front of Tommy and held out his hand.

"Choose."

Tommy sucked in his breath. Which hair meant home? And which meant the cellar? In his head he began to chant "eenie, meanie, minie moe…"

"That one," he said, pointing to the blonde one on the right.

The man separated the blonde hair out and nodded. His nose seemed to touch his lips as he bent down to show Tommy the other two. The one Tommy had picked was the longest.

"Upstairs," the man said. "Your first chance takes you upstairs. Don't mind the mess, I haven't cleaned much since my wife's been gone."

Tommy didn't move.

The man pointed. "Go now. Or stay with me here forever."

Tommy slipped off the couch, and walked to the door. When he looked back, the man was gone.

He stood between the door and the stairs and saw his chance. Grabbing the knob, he twisted it hard to the right and pulled.

The knob came off the door and lay cold and useless in his hands.

"Nooo," Tommy cried and stomped his foot. Tears were starting to trickle down the left side of his face.

"Upstairs," came the voice of the long, thin man from out of nowhere.

Dropping the knob, Tommy started up the stairs. They creaked and groaned under his weight, but at last he reached the top landing. There was light here from the room at the end of the hall. He walked toward it, heart beating in his chest like a jackhammer.

He stepped into the lighted room and gasped.

In the corner was a dark chest of drawers, and in the far side, a wide bed with a pink, lacy comforter. In the center of the room, hanging on a rope from the bronze-based light fixture, was the man.

"Hello again," the ghost said, eyes bugging madly as he swayed from the rope around his neck slowly, to and fro. The creak of his passage echoed through the room.

"If you'd gone the other way, you could have slipped out the back window and down the trellis to meet your friend. But instead, you came right to me. Not so good at hide and seek, I bet. Ready to take your second chance?"

Tommy nodded.

"Good. This time, let's try a little riddle. If you guess the answer, you will be allowed to leave. If you don't, you must go to the basement for your third and final chance. 'What always moves at the same speed, but no matter how hard you try, you can never get ahead or behind it?'"

Tommy thought. Cars moved at different speeds, and so did buses. But you could get around them.

"A train?" he guessed.

The ghost's head shook slowly, the purple bruises on its neck twisting like angry veins. "Time," the dead man answered. "And now, it's *time* for you to head downstairs."

The ghost choked a little, and a thick discolored tongue poked through his lips.

"All the way downstairs."

Tommy turned away and went back down the stairs to the front door. He stood for a moment, wondering if there was some way to pry it open without a knob, when he heard the voice from behind him.

"Allllll the way...."

He walked through the front room and down the hall, stopping at the door Bret had found. It was already open. The stairs were lit from the glow of a bare bulb.

He put a foot on the first step and froze as it creaked.

"Allllll the way down..."

He was crying now, crying hard and free. He didn't want to go downstairs, he hadn't wanted to come inside a haunted house. He didn't want to die here. What if he chose wrong the third time? What then?

"Allllll the way," the voice echoed again.

Shutting his eyes to force out the tears, Tommy grasped the handrail and stepped down again and again and again.

The basement had a cement floor, painted grey. A washer and dryer stood against one wall, the tin flues and box and coils of an ancient furnace took up another. When Tommy walked to the center of the open room, he saw the reason that the man was swinging from a rope upstairs.

Planted in a row across the center of the floor were the heads of three boys. Their eyes were open, and blue. One had blonde hair, the other two dark. They were young. And bodiless. Their necks bled streams of ghost blood across the cement.

"Hi" said the blonde one. "Playing with dad, are you?"

"If he asks you anything about squirrels, he hates 'em," said one of the brunettes.

"Have you seen my ma?" asked the third. "My neck hurts."

The stairs behind him creaked.

"And now for our third and final challenge," the gravelly voice said. "Remember, if you miss this one, you get to stay here and keep the boys and me company."

The man walked away from the stairs to stand behind the heads of his three sons. In his hand, he now held a long, wood-handled axe. The steel of its blade was spattered with red and rust.

"One of these boys knows where the key to the back door is. You'll need it if you're going to leave here. Listen to the right head, and you leave here with *your* head still on your shoulders. Pick the wrong one, and you'll join my boys."

Tommy looked at the dark-haired third head and asked, "Do you know where the back door key is?"

The boy stared blankly at the wall behind him. "Ma will come. She's probably just upstairs. Would you get her?"

He looked at the other brunette. "Do you know where the key is?"

"Squirrels," the boy said. "My dad hates squirrels. You don't have a squirrel do you?"

"Enough," the man growled. "Quit stalling. Choose the head that knows where the key is."

"How can I be sure any of them know where the key is?" Tommy asked. "They don't even know where *they* are."

"Because one of them has it in his pocket," the man smiled.

"They don't have bodies!" Tommy said.

"Sure they do. They're just laying over there." The man pointed to a far corner of the basement, where what looked like a bundle of old bound-up rags or laundry was piled. Tommy saw now that it wasn't rags, but feet and arms piled in the corner.

He stared again at the boys, and wondered which to pick. The only one that seemed to have any sense was the blonde boy. And just as he thought that, the boy winked at him.

"I choose…" Tommy began and raised his finger to point at the boy with the blonde hair.

But just as he did so, the blonde boy widened his eyes and crinkled his brow. Then with a twitch of his eye and a squint, he seemed to indicate the squirrel boy to his left.

"That one," Tommy said, pointing at the squirrel-obsessed kid.

"Dad loves to play games," the blonde boy said again, and then faded out of sight.

The ghost's wicked grin slipped away. His haggard face sagged, as his blackened fingernails clenched.

"Looks like you've won," he said grudgingly. "This time. Don't be a stranger, now. And don't forget the key." Then he vanished as well.

Suddenly, the bulb went dark, and Tommy was trapped in the basement in pitch blackness. Laughter sounded from somewhere above in the house.

Tommy almost ran back towards the stairs, but then stopped. The bodies had been over there, in the far corner. And the man had said he'd need the key that had been in the clothes of one of them. Did that mean when the bodies went away, the key would still be there?

Tommy crawled in the direction of the 'rags' he'd seen a moment ago, and stopped when he felt the cold hard concrete of a wall before him. Then he moved his hands back and forth across the floor, hoping to slip across a cold piece of metal.

He'd almost given up hope when his fingers nudged something across the floor that went *ting*.

In seconds, he'd found it again. And then he scrambled back towards the stairs, where the tiniest bit of light was still leaking down from upstairs. Grabbing the wood banister with both hands he launched himself up and clambered up the wooden steps till he got to the hallway. Then he stood, and felt along the wall as he stepped towards what he hoped was the kitchen.

It was. There was the front room, curtains swaying drunkenly in the broken window breeze. Through there, that blackened threshold, was the kitchen, and a back door. The house was silent. And empty again.

He took the step, and heard the crunch of glass beneath his feet.

Then his hand was on the door, and he fumbled the key into the padlock that held the door closed from the inside. It clicked open, and he turned the knob.

From upstairs he heard a steady *creak, cronk, creak, cronk*.

From somewhere outside, he heard his name. "Tommy?"

The door came open with a screeching complaint.

He pushed past the screen door and stumbled down a stand of concrete stairs to find himself in the overgrown backyard of the haunted house.

A harvest moon shone a bloody orange over the yard as he looked back at the tall, slanted structure. The windows stayed black.

Tommy ran around through the tall weeds and found his friend in the front of the house, tears streaming down his face.

"Tommy" he cried once again, staring at the tilted shutters but not daring to go inside again.

"I'm here." Tommy said, and fell to the ground at Bret's feet.

"Are you ok? I thought you were never going to get out."

"Do I look like I've seen a ghost?" Tommy said.

"I saw him too," Bret said.

"Yeah, but I met his kids."

"Whoa," Bret said. "Better you than me. I think I've seen just about enough up here."

"Yeah, me too," Tommy said, fingering the key in his pocket. He looked up at the second story window where he knew the ghost of a man was even now swaying from a ghostly rope. Was there just the hint of a shadow moving to and fro up there now?

Bret started down the twenty-three stairs to the sidewalk. Moving fast.

"Feel like Trick-or-Treating?" he called over his shoulder, aiming himself at a band of short witches and devils and ghosts parading down the sidewalk just ahead.

Tommy hurried to follow.

An Account of Some Strange Disturbances in Aungier Street

Joseph Sheridan Le Fanu

IT IS NOT worth telling, this story of mine – at least, not worth writing. Told, indeed, as I have sometimes been called upon to tell it, to a circle of intelligent and eager faces, lighted up by a good after-dinner fire on a winter's evening, with a cold wind rising and wailing outside, and all snug and cosy within, it has gone off – though I say it, who should not – indifferent well. But it is a venture to do as you would have me. Pen, ink, and paper are cold vehicles for the marvellous, and a 'reader' decidedly a more critical animal than a 'listener'. If, however, you can induce your friends to read it after nightfall, and when the fireside talk has run for a while on thrilling tales of shapeless terror; in short, if you will secure me the *mollia tempora fandi*, I will go to my work, and say my say, with better heart. Well, then, these conditions presupposed, I shall waste no more words, but tell you simply how it all happened.

My cousin (Tom Ludlow) and I studied medicine together. I think he would have succeeded, had he stuck to the profession; but he preferred the Church, poor fellow, and died early, a sacrifice to contagion, contracted in the noble discharge of his duties. For my present purpose, I say enough of his character when I mention that he was of a sedate but frank and cheerful nature; very exact in his observance of truth, and not by any means like myself – of an excitable or nervous temperament.

My Uncle Ludlow – Tom's father – while we were attending lectures, purchased three or four old houses in Aungier Street, one of which was unoccupied. *He* resided in the country, and Tom proposed that we should take up our abode in the untenanted house, so long as it should continue unlet; a move which would accomplish the double end of settling us nearer alike to our lecture-rooms and to our amusements, and of relieving us from the weekly charge of rent for our lodgings.

Our furniture was very scant – our whole equipage remarkably modest and primitive; and, in short, our arrangements pretty nearly as simple as those of a bivouac. Our new plan was, therefore, executed almost as soon as conceived. The front drawing-room was our sitting-room. I had the bedroom over it, and Tom the back bedroom on the same floor, which nothing could have induced me to occupy.

The house, to begin with, was a very old one. It had been, I believe, newly fronted about fifty years before; but with this exception, it had nothing modern about it. The agent who bought it and looked into the titles for my uncle, told me that it was sold, along with much other forfeited property, at Chichester House, I think, in 1702; and had belonged to Sir Thomas Hacket, who was Lord Mayor of Dublin in James II.'s time. How old it was *then*, I can't say; but, at all events, it had seen years and changes enough to have contracted all that mysterious and saddened air, at once exciting and depressing, which belongs to most old mansions.

There had been very little done in the way of modernising details; and, perhaps, it was better so; for there was something queer and by-gone in the very walls and ceilings – in the shape of doors and windows – in the odd diagonal site of the chimney-pieces – in the beams and ponderous cornices – not to mention the singular solidity of all the woodwork, from the banisters to the window-frames, which hopelessly defied disguise, and would have emphatically proclaimed their antiquity through any conceivable amount of modern finery and varnish.

An effort had, indeed, been made, to the extent of papering the drawing-rooms; but somehow, the paper looked raw and out of keeping; and the old woman, who kept a little dirt-pie of a shop in the lane, and whose daughter – a girl of two and fifty – was our solitary handmaid, coming in at sunrise, and chastely receding again as soon as she had made all ready for tea in our state apartment – this woman, I say, remembered it, when old Judge Horrocks (who, having earned the reputation of a particularly 'hanging judge', ended by hanging himself, as the coroner's jury found, under an impulse of 'temporary insanity', with a child's skipping-rope, over the massive old bannisters) resided there, entertaining good company, with fine venison and rare old port. In those halcyon days, the drawing-rooms were hung with gilded leather, and, I dare say, cut a good figure, for they were really spacious rooms.

The bedrooms were wainscoted, but the front one was not gloomy; and in it the cosiness of antiquity quite overcame its sombre associations. But the back bedroom, with its two queerly-placed melancholy windows, staring vacantly at the foot of the bed, and with the shadowy recess to be found in most old houses in Dublin, like a large ghostly closet, which, from congeniality of temperament, had amalgamated with the bedchamber, and dissolved the partition. At night-time, this 'alcove' – as our 'maid' was wont to call it – had, in my eyes, a specially sinister and suggestive character. Tom's distant and solitary candle glimmered vainly into its darkness. *There* it was always overlooking him – always itself impenetrable. But this was only part of the effect. The whole room was, I can't tell how, repulsive to me. There was, I suppose, in its proportions and features, a latent discord – a certain mysterious and indescribable relation, which jarred indistinctly upon some secret sense of the fitting and the safe, and raised indefinable suspicions and apprehensions of the imagination. On the whole, as I began by saying, nothing could have induced me to pass a night alone in it.

I had never pretended to conceal from poor Tom my superstitious weakness; and he, on the other hand, most unaffectedly ridiculed my tremors. The sceptic was, however, destined to receive a lesson, as you shall hear.

We had not been very long in occupation of our respective dormitories, when I began to complain of uneasy nights and disturbed sleep. I was, I suppose, the more impatient under this annoyance, as I was usually a sound sleeper, and by no means prone to nightmares. It was now, however, my destiny, instead of enjoying my customary repose, every night to 'sup full of horrors'. After a preliminary course of disagreeable and frightful dreams, my troubles took a definite form, and the same vision, without an appreciable variation in a single detail, visited me at least (on an average) every second night in the week.

Now, this dream, nightmare, or infernal illusion – which you please – of which I was the miserable sport, was on this wise:

I saw, or thought I saw, with the most abominable distinctness, although at the time in profound darkness, every article of furniture and accidental arrangement of the chamber in which I lay. This, as you know, is incidental to ordinary nightmare. Well, while in this clairvoyant condition, which seemed but the lighting up of the theatre in which was to be exhibited the monotonous tableau of horror, which made my nights insupportable, my attention invariably became, I know not why, fixed upon the windows opposite the foot of my bed; and, uniformly with the same effect, a sense of dreadful anticipation always took slow but sure possession of me. I became somehow conscious of a sort of horrid but undefined preparation going forward in some unknown quarter, and by some unknown agency, for my torment; and, after an interval, which always seemed to me of the same length, a picture suddenly flew up to the window, where it remained fixed, as if by an electrical attraction, and my discipline of horror then commenced, to last perhaps for hours. The picture thus mysteriously glued to the window-panes was the portrait of an old man, in a crimson flowered silk dressing gown, the folds of which I could now describe, with a countenance embodying a strange mixture of intellect, sensuality, and power, but withal sinister and full of malignant omen. His nose was hooked, like the beak of a vulture; his eyes large, grey, and prominent, and lighted up with a more than mortal cruelty and coldness. These features were surmounted by a crimson velvet cap, the hair that peeped from under which was white with age, while the eyebrows retained their original blackness. Well I remember every line, hue, and shadow of that stony countenance, and well I may! The gaze of this hellish visage was fixed upon me, and mine returned it with the inexplicable fascination of nightmare, for what appeared to me to be hours of agony. At last –

The cock he crew, away then flew

the fiend who had enslaved me through the awful watches of the night; and, harassed and nervous, I rose to the duties of the day.

I had – I can't say exactly why, but it may have been from the exquisite anguish and profound impressions of unearthly horror, with which this strange phantasmagoria was associated – an insurmountable antipathy to describing the exact nature of my nightly troubles to my friend and comrade. Generally, however, I told him that I was haunted by abominable dreams; and, true to the imputed materialism of medicine, we put our heads together to dispel my horrors, not by exorcism, but by a tonic.

I will do this tonic justice, and frankly admit that the accursed portrait began to intermit its visits under its influence. What of that? Was this singular apparition – as full of character as of terror – therefore the creature of my fancy, or the invention of my poor stomach? Was it, in short, *subjective* (to borrow the technical slang of the day) and not the palpable aggression and intrusion of an external agent? That, good friend, as we will both admit, by no means follows. The evil spirit, who enthralled my senses in the shape of that portrait, may have been just as near me, just as energetic, just as malignant, though I saw him not. What means the whole moral code of revealed religion regarding the due keeping of our own bodies, soberness, temperance, etc.? Here is an obvious connection between the material and the invisible; the healthy tone of the system, and its unimpaired energy, may, for aught we can tell, guard us against influences which would otherwise render life itself terrific. The mesmerist and the electro-biologist will fail upon an average with nine patients out of ten – so may the evil spirit. Special conditions of the corporeal system are indispensable to the production of certain spiritual phenomena. The operation succeeds sometimes – sometimes fails – that is all.

I found afterwards that my would-be sceptical companion had his troubles too. But of these I knew nothing yet. One night, for a wonder, I was sleeping soundly, when I was roused by a step on the lobby outside my room, followed by the loud clang of what turned out to be a large brass candlestick, flung with all his force by poor Tom Ludlow over the banisters, and rattling with a rebound down the second flight of stairs; and almost concurrently with this, Tom burst open my door, and bounced into my room backwards, in a state of extraordinary agitation.

I had jumped out of bed and clutched him by the arm before I had any distinct idea of my own whereabouts. There we were – in our shirts – standing before the open door – staring through the great old banister opposite, at the lobby window, through which the sickly light of a clouded moon was gleaming.

"What's the matter, Tom? What's the matter with you? What the devil's the matter with you, Tom?" I demanded, shaking him with nervous impatience.

He took a long breath before he answered me, and then it was not very coherently.

"It's nothing, nothing at all – did I speak? – what did I say? – where's the candle, Richard? It's dark; I – I had a candle!"

"Yes, dark enough," I said; "but what's the matter? – what *is* it? – why don't you speak, Tom? – have you lost your wits? – what is the matter?"

"The matter? – oh, it is all over. It must have been a dream – nothing at all but a dream – don't you think so? It could not be anything more than a dream."

"Of *course*" said I, feeling uncommonly nervous, "it *was* a dream."

"I thought," he said, "there was a man in my room, and – and I jumped out of bed; and – and – where's the candle?"

"In your room, most likely," I said, "shall I go and bring it?"

"No; stay here – don't go; it's no matter – don't, I tell you; it was all a dream. Bolt the door, Dick; I'll stay here with you – I feel nervous. So, Dick, like a good fellow, light your candle and open the window – I am in a *shocking state*."

I did as he asked me, and robing himself like Granuaile in one of my blankets, he seated himself close beside my bed.

Everybody knows how contagious is fear of all sorts, but more especially that particular kind of fear under which poor Tom was at that moment labouring. I would not have heard, nor I believe would he have recapitulated, just at that moment, for half the world, the details of the hideous vision which had so unmanned him.

"Don't mind telling me anything about your nonsensical dream, Tom," said I, affecting contempt, really in a panic; "let us talk about something else; but it is quite plain that this dirty old house disagrees with us both, and hang me if I stay here any longer, to be pestered with indigestion and – and – bad nights, so we may as well look out for lodgings – don't you think so? – at once."

Tom agreed, and, after an interval, said –

"I have been thinking, Richard, that it is a long time since I saw my father, and I have made up my mind to go down tomorrow and return in a day or two, and you can take rooms for us in the meantime."

I fancied that this resolution, obviously the result of the vision which had so profoundly scared him, would probably vanish next morning with the damps and shadows of night. But I was mistaken. Off went Tom at peep of day to the country, having agreed that so soon as I had secured suitable lodgings, I was to recall him by letter from his visit to my Uncle Ludlow.

Now, anxious as I was to change my quarters, it so happened, owing to a series of petty procrastinations and accidents, that nearly a week elapsed before my bargain was made and my letter of recall on the wing to Tom; and, in the meantime, a trifling adventure or two had occurred to your humble servant, which, absurd as they now appear, diminished by distance, did certainly at the time serve to whet my appetite for change considerably.

A night or two after the departure of my comrade, I was sitting by my bedroom fire, the door locked, and the ingredients of a tumbler of hot whisky-punch upon the crazy spider-table; for as the best mode of keeping the

> *Black spirits and white,*
> *Blue spirits and grey,*

with which I was environed, at bay, I had adopted the practice recommended by the wisdom of my ancestors, and 'kept my spirits up by pouring spirits down'. I had thrown aside my volume of Anatomy, and was treating myself by way of a tonic, preparatory to my punch and bed, to half-a-dozen pages of the *Spectator*, when I heard a step on the flight of stairs descending from the attics. It was two o'clock, and the streets were as silent as a churchyard – the sounds were therefore, perfectly distinct. There was a slow, heavy tread, characterised by the emphasis and deliberation of age, descending by the narrow staircase from above; and, what made the sound more singular, it was plain that the feet which produced it were perfectly bare, measuring the descent with something between a pound and a flop, very ugly to hear.

I knew quite well that my attendant had gone away many hours before, and that nobody but myself had any business in the house. It was quite plain also that the person who was coming downstairs had no intention whatever of concealing his movements; but, on the contrary, appeared disposed to make even more noise, and proceed more deliberately than was at all necessary. When the step reached the foot of the stairs outside my room, it seemed to stop; and I expected every moment to see my door open spontaneously, and give admission to the original of my detested portrait. I was, however, relieved in a few seconds by hearing the descent renewed, just in the same manner, upon the staircase leading down to the drawing rooms, and thence, after another pause, down the next flight, and so on to the hall, whence I heard no more.

Now, by the time the sound had ceased, I was wound up, as they say, to a very unpleasant pitch of excitement. I listened, but there was not a stir. I screwed up my courage to a decisive experiment – opened my door, and in a stentorian voice bawled over the banisters, "Who's there?"

There was no answer but the ringing of my own voice through the empty old house – no renewal of the movement; nothing, in short, to give my unpleasant sensations a definite direction. There is, I think, something most disagreeably disenchanting in the sound of one's own voice under such circumstances, exerted in solitude, and in vain. It redoubled my sense of isolation, and my misgivings increased on perceiving that the door, which I certainly thought I had left open, was closed behind me; in a vague alarm, lest my retreat should be cut off, I got again into my room as quickly as I could, where I remained in a state of imaginary blockade, and very uncomfortable indeed, till morning.

Next night brought no return of my barefooted fellow-lodger; but the night following, being in my bed, and in the dark – somewhere, I suppose, about the same hour as before, I distinctly heard the old fellow again descending from the garrets.

This time I had had my punch, and the *morale* of the garrison was consequently excellent. I jumped out of bed, clutched the poker as I passed the expiring fire, and in a moment was upon the lobby. The sound had ceased by this time – the dark and chill were discouraging; and, guess my horror, when I saw, or thought I saw, a black monster, whether in the shape of a man or a bear I could not say, standing, with its back to the wall, on the lobby, facing me, with a pair of great greenish eyes shining dimly out. Now, I must be frank, and confess that the cupboard which displayed our plates and cups stood just there, though at the moment I did not recollect it. At the same time I must honestly say, that making every allowance for an excited imagination, I never could satisfy myself that I was made the dupe of my own fancy in this matter; for this apparition, after one or two shiftings of shape, as if in the act of incipient transformation, began, as it seemed on second thoughts, to advance upon me in its original form. From an instinct of terror rather than of courage, I hurled the poker, with all my force, at its head; and to the music of a horrid crash made my way into my room, and double-locked the door. Then, in a minute more, I heard the horrid bare feet walk down the stairs, till the sound ceased in the hall, as on the former occasion.

If the apparition of the night before was an ocular delusion of my fancy sporting with the dark outlines of our cupboard, and if its horrid eyes were nothing but a pair of inverted teacups, I had, at all events, the satisfaction of having launched the poker with admirable effect, and in true 'fancy' phrase, 'knocked its two daylights into one', as the commingled fragments of my tea-service testified. I did my best to gather comfort and courage from these evidences; but it would not do. And then what could I say of those horrid bare feet, and the regular *tramp, tramp, tramp*, which measured the distance of the entire staircase through the solitude of my haunted dwelling, and at an hour when no good influence was stirring? Confound it! The whole affair was abominable. I was out of spirits, and dreaded the approach of night.

It came, ushered ominously in with a thunder-storm and dull torrents of depressing rain. Earlier than usual the streets grew silent; and by twelve o'clock nothing but the comfortless pattering of the rain was to be heard.

I made myself as snug as I could. I lighted *two* candles instead of one. I forswore bed, and held myself in readiness for a sally, candle in hand; for, *coûte qui coûte*, I was resolved to *see* the being, if visible at all, who troubled the nightly stillness of my mansion. I was fidgetty and nervous and tried in vain to interest myself with my books. I walked up and down my room, whistling in turn martial and hilarious music, and listening ever and anon for the dreaded noise. I sat down and stared at the square label on the solemn and reserved-looking black bottle, until 'FLANAGAN & CO'S BEST OLD MALT WHISKY' grew into a sort of subdued accompaniment to all the fantastic and horrible speculations which chased one another through my brain.

Silence, meanwhile, grew more silent, and darkness darker. I listened in vain for the rumble of a vehicle, or the dull clamour of a distant row. There was nothing but the sound of a rising wind, which had succeeded the thunder-storm that had travelled over the Dublin mountains quite out of hearing. In the middle of this great city I began to feel myself alone with nature, and Heaven knows what beside. My courage was ebbing. Punch, however, which makes beasts of so many, made a man of me again – just in time to hear with tolerable nerve and firmness the lumpy, flabby, naked feet deliberately descending the stairs again.

I took a candle, not without a tremour. As I crossed the floor I tried to extemporise a prayer, but stopped short to listen, and never finished it. The steps continued. I confess I hesitated for some seconds at the door before I took heart of grace and opened it. When I peeped out the lobby was perfectly empty – there was no monster standing on the staircase; and as the detested sound ceased, I was reassured enough to venture forward nearly to the banisters. Horror of horrors! Within a stair or two beneath the spot where I stood the unearthly tread smote the floor. My eye caught something in motion; it was about the size of Goliah's foot – it was grey, heavy, and flapped with a dead weight from one step to another. As I am alive, it was the most monstrous grey rat I ever beheld or imagined.

Shakespeare says – 'Some men there are cannot abide a gaping pig, and some that are mad if they behold a cat.' I went well-nigh out of my wits when I beheld this *rat*; for, laugh at me as you may, it fixed upon me, I thought, a perfectly human expression of malice; and, as it shuffled about and looked up into my face almost from between my feet, I saw, I could swear it – I felt it then, and know it now, the infernal gaze and the accursed countenance of my old friend in the portrait, transfused into the visage of the bloated vermin before me.

I bounced into my room again with a feeling of loathing and horror I cannot describe, and locked and bolted my door as if a lion had been at the other side. D—n him or *it*; curse the portrait and its original! I felt in my soul that the rat – yes, the *rat*, the RAT I had just seen, was that evil being in masquerade, and rambling through the house upon some infernal night lark.

Next morning I was early trudging through the miry streets; and, among other transactions, posted a peremptory note recalling Tom. On my return, however, I found a note from my absent 'chum', announcing his intended return next day. I was doubly rejoiced at this, because I had succeeded in getting rooms; and because the change of scene and return of my comrade were rendered specially pleasant by the last night's half ridiculous half horrible adventure.

I slept extemporaneously in my new quarters in Digges' Street that night, and next morning returned for breakfast to the haunted mansion, where I was certain Tom would call immediately on his arrival.

I was quite right – he came; and almost his first question referred to the primary object of our change of residence.

"Thank God," he said with genuine fervour, on hearing that all was arranged. "On *your* account I am delighted. As to myself, I assure you that no earthly consideration could have induced me ever again to pass a night in this disastrous old house."

"Confound the house!" I ejaculated, with a genuine mixture of fear and detestation, "we have not had a pleasant hour since we came to live here"; and so I went on, and related incidentally my adventure with the plethoric old rat.

"Well, if that were *all*," said my cousin, affecting to make light of the matter, "I don't think I should have minded it very much."

"Ay, but its eye – its countenance, my dear Tom," urged I; "if you had seen *that*, you would have felt it might be *anything* but what it seemed."

"I inclined to think the best conjuror in such a case would be an able-bodied cat," he said, with a provoking chuckle.

"But let us hear your own adventure," I said tartly.

At this challenge he looked uneasily round him. I had poked up a very unpleasant recollection.

"You shall hear it, Dick; I'll tell it to you," he said. "Begad, sir, I should feel quite queer, though, telling it *here*, though we are too strong a body for ghosts to meddle with just now."

Though he spoke this like a joke, I think it was serious calculation. Our Hebe was in a corner of the room, packing our cracked delft tea and dinner-services in a basket. She soon suspended operations, and with mouth and eyes wide open became an absorbed listener. Tom's experiences were told nearly in these words:

"I saw it three times, Dick – three distinct times; and I am perfectly certain it meant me some infernal harm. I was, I say, in danger – in *extreme* danger; for, if nothing else had happened, my reason would most certainly have failed me, unless I had escaped so soon. Thank God. I *did* escape.

"The first night of this hateful disturbance, I was lying in the attitude of sleep, in that lumbering old bed. I hate to think of it. I was really wide awake, though I had put out my candle, and was lying as quietly as if I had been asleep; and although accidentally restless, my thoughts were running in a cheerful and agreeable channel.

"I think it must have been two o'clock at least when I thought I heard a sound in that – that odious dark recess at the far end of the bedroom. It was as if someone was drawing a piece of cord slowly along the floor, lifting it up, and dropping it softly down again in coils. I sat up once or twice in my bed, but could see nothing, so I concluded it must be mice in the wainscot. I felt no emotion graver than curiosity, and after a few minutes ceased to observe it.

"While lying in this state, strange to say; without at first a suspicion of anything supernatural, on a sudden I saw an old man, rather stout and square, in a sort of roan-red dressing gown, and with a black cap on his head, moving stiffly and slowly in a diagonal direction, from the recess, across the floor of the bedroom, passing my bed at the foot, and entering the lumber-closet at the left. He had something under his arm; his head hung a little at one side; and, merciful God! when I saw his face."

Tom stopped for a while, and then said –

"That awful countenance, which living or dying I never can forget, disclosed what he was. Without turning to the right or left, he passed beside me, and entered the closet by the bed's head.

"While this fearful and indescribable type of death and guilt was passing, I felt that I had no more power to speak or stir than if I had been myself a corpse. For hours after it had disappeared, I was too terrified and weak to move. As soon as daylight came, I took courage, and examined the room, and especially the course which the frightful intruder had seemed to take, but there was not a vestige to indicate anybody's having passed there; no sign of any disturbing agency visible among the lumber that strewed the floor of the closet.

"I now began to recover a little. I was fagged and exhausted, and at last, overpowered by a feverish sleep. I came down late; and finding you out of spirits, on account of your dreams about the portrait, whose *original* I am now certain disclosed himself to me, I did not care to talk about the infernal vision. In fact, I was trying to persuade myself that the whole thing was an illusion, and I did not like to revive in their intensity the hated impressions of the past night – or to risk the constancy of my scepticism, by recounting the tale of my sufferings.

"It required some nerve, I can tell you, to go to my haunted chamber next night, and lie down quietly in the same bed," continued Tom. "I did so with a degree of trepidation, which, I am not ashamed to say, a very little matter would have sufficed to stimulate to downright panic. This night, however, passed off quietly enough, as also the next; and so too did two or three more. I grew more confident, and began to fancy that I believed in the theories of spectral illusions, with which I had at first vainly tried to impose upon my convictions.

"The apparition had been, indeed, altogether anomalous. It had crossed the room without any recognition of my presence: I had not disturbed *it*, and *it* had no mission to *me*. What, then, was the imaginable use of its crossing the room in a visible shape at all? Of course it might have *been* in the closet instead of *going* there, as easily as it introduced itself into the recess without entering the chamber in a shape discernible by the senses. Besides, how the deuce *had* I seen it? It was a dark night; I had no candle; there was no fire; and yet I saw it as distinctly, in colouring and outline, as ever I beheld human form! A cataleptic dream would explain it all; and I was determined that a dream it should be.

"One of the most remarkable phenomena connected with the practice of mendacity is the vast number of deliberate lies we tell ourselves, whom, of all persons, we can least expect to deceive. In all this, I need hardly tell you, Dick, I was simply lying to myself, and did not believe one word of the wretched humbug. Yet I went on, as men will do, like persevering charlatans and impostors, who tire people into credulity by the mere force of reiteration; so I hoped to win myself over at last to a comfortable scepticism about the ghost.

"He had not appeared a second time – that certainly was a comfort; and what, after all, did I care for him, and his queer old toggery and strange looks? Not a fig! I was nothing the worse for having seen him, and a good story the better. So I tumbled into bed, put out my candle, and, cheered by a loud drunken quarrel in the back lane, went fast asleep.

"From this deep slumber I awoke with a start. I knew I had had a horrible dream; but what it was I could not remember. My heart was thumping furiously; I felt bewildered and feverish; I sat up in the bed and looked about the room. A broad flood of moonlight came in through the curtainless window; everything was as I had last seen it; and though the domestic squabble in the back lane was, unhappily for me, allayed, I yet could hear a pleasant fellow singing, on his way home, the then popular comic ditty called, 'Murphy Delany.' Taking advantage of this diversion I lay down again, with my face towards the fireplace, and closing my eyes, did my best to think of nothing else but the song, which was every moment growing fainter in the distance:

> "'Twas Murphy Delany, so funny and frisky,
> Stept into a shebeen shop to get his skin full;
> He reeled out again pretty well lined with whiskey,
> As fresh as a shamrock, as blind as a bull.

"The singer, whose condition I dare say resembled that of his hero, was soon too far off to regale my ears any more; and as his music died away, I myself sank into a doze, neither sound nor refreshing. Somehow the song had got into my head, and I went meandering on through the adventures of my respectable fellow-countryman, who, on emerging from the 'shebeen shop', fell into a river, from which he was fished up to be 'sat upon' by a coroner's jury, who having learned from a 'horse-doctor' that he was 'dead as a doornail, so there was an end,' returned their verdict accordingly, just as he returned to his senses, when an angry altercation and a pitched battle between the body and the coroner winds up the lay with due spirit and pleasantry.

"Through this ballad I continued with a weary monotony to plod, down to the very last line, and then *da capo*, and so on, in my uncomfortable half-sleep, for how long, I can't conjecture. I found myself at last, however, muttering, '*dead* as a doornail, so there was an end'; and something like another voice within me, seemed to say, very faintly, but sharply, 'dead! dead! *dead*! and may the Lord have mercy on your soul!' and instantaneously I was wide awake, and staring right before me from the pillow.

"Now – will you believe it, Dick? – I saw the same accursed figure standing full front, and gazing at me with its stony and fiendish countenance, not two yards from the bedside."

Tom stopped here, and wiped the perspiration from his face. I felt very queer. The girl was as pale as Tom; and, assembled as we were in the very scene of these adventures, we were all, I dare say, equally grateful for the clear daylight and the resuming bustle out of doors.

"For about three seconds only I saw it plainly; then it grew indistinct; but, for a long time, there was something like a column of dark vapour where it had been standing, between me and the wall; and I felt sure that he was still there. After a good while, this appearance went too. I took my clothes downstairs to the hall, and dressed there, with the door half open; then went out into the street, and walked about the town till morning, when I came back, in a miserable state of nervousness and exhaustion. I was such a fool, Dick, as to be ashamed to tell you how I came to be so upset. I thought you would laugh at me; especially as I had always talked philosophy, and treated *your* ghosts with contempt. I concluded you would give me no quarter; and so kept my tale of horror to myself.

"Now, Dick, you will hardly believe me, when I assure you, that for many nights after this last experience, I did not go to my room at all. I used to sit up for a while in the drawing-room after you had gone up to your bed; and then steal down softly to the hall-door, let myself out, and sit in the 'Robin Hood' tavern until the last guest went off; and then I got through the night like a sentry, pacing the streets till morning.

"For more than a week I never slept in bed. I sometimes had a snooze on a form in the 'Robin Hood', and sometimes a nap in a chair during the day; but regular sleep I had absolutely none.

"I was quite resolved that we should get into another house; but I could not bring myself to tell you the reason, and I somehow put it off from day to day, although my life was, during every hour of this procrastination, rendered as miserable as that of a felon with the constables on his track. I was growing absolutely ill from this wretched mode of life.

"One afternoon I determined to enjoy an hour's sleep upon your bed. I hated mine; so that I had never, except in a stealthy visit every day to unmake it, lest Martha should discover the secret of my nightly absence, entered the ill-omened chamber.

"As ill-luck would have it, you had locked your bedroom, and taken away the key. I went into my own to unsettle the bedclothes, as usual, and give the bed the appearance of having been slept in. Now, a variety of circumstances concurred to bring about the dreadful scene through which I was that night to pass. In the first place, I was literally overpowered with fatigue, and longing for sleep; in the next place, the effect of this extreme exhaustion upon my nerves resembled that of a narcotic, and rendered me less susceptible than, perhaps, I should in any other condition have been, of the exciting fears which had become habitual to me. Then again, a little bit of the window was open, a pleasant freshness pervaded the room, and, to crown all, the cheerful sun of day was making the room quite pleasant. What was to prevent my enjoying an hour's nap *here*? The whole air was resonant with the cheerful hum of life, and the broad matter-of-fact light of day filled every corner of the room.

"I yielded – stifling my qualms – to the almost overpowering temptation; and merely throwing off my coat, and loosening my cravat, I lay down, limiting myself to *half*-an-hour's doze in the unwonted enjoyment of a feather bed, a coverlet, and a bolster.

"It was horribly insidious; and the demon, no doubt, marked my infatuated preparations. Dolt that I was, I fancied, with mind and body worn out for want of sleep, and an arrear of a full week's rest to my credit, that such measure as *half*-an-hour's sleep, in such a situation, was possible. My sleep was death-like, long, and dreamless.

"Without a start or fearful sensation of any kind, I waked gently, but completely. It was, as you have good reason to remember, long past midnight – I believe, about two o'clock. When sleep has been deep and long enough to satisfy nature thoroughly, one often wakens in this way, suddenly, tranquilly, and completely.

"There was a figure seated in that lumbering, old sofa-chair, near the fireplace. Its back was rather towards me, but I could not be mistaken; it turned slowly round, and, merciful heavens! There was the stony face, with its infernal lineaments of malignity and despair, gloating on me. There was now no doubt as to its consciousness of my presence, and the hellish malice with which it was animated, for it arose, and drew close to the bedside. There was a rope about its neck, and the other end, coiled up, it held stiffly in its hand.

"My good angel nerved me for this horrible crisis. I remained for some seconds transfixed by the gaze of this tremendous phantom. He came close to the bed, and appeared on the point of mounting upon it. The next instant I was upon the floor at the far side, and in a moment more was, I don't know how, upon the lobby.

"But the spell was not yet broken; the valley of the shadow of death was not yet traversed. The abhorred phantom was before me there; it was standing near the banisters, stooping a little, and with one end of the rope round its own neck, was poising a noose at the other, as if to throw over mine; and while engaged in this baleful pantomime, it wore a smile so sensual, so unspeakably dreadful, that my senses were nearly overpowered. I saw and remember nothing more, until I found myself in your room.

"I had a wonderful escape, Dick – there is no disputing *that* – an escape for which, while I live, I shall bless the mercy of heaven. No one can conceive or imagine what it is for flesh and blood to stand in the presence of such a thing, but one who has had the terrific experience. Dick, Dick, a shadow has passed over me – a chill has crossed my blood and marrow, and I will never be the same again – never, Dick – never!"

Our handmaid, a mature girl of two-and-fifty, as I have said, stayed her hand, as Tom's story proceeded, and by little and little drew near to us, with open mouth, and her brows contracted over her little, beady black eyes, till stealing a glance over her shoulder now and then, she established herself close behind us. During the relation, she had made various earnest comments, in an undertone; but these and her ejaculations, for the sake of brevity and simplicity, I have omitted in my narration.

"It's often I heard tell of it," she now said, "but I never believed it rightly till now – though, indeed, why should not I? Does not my mother, down there in the lane, know quare stories, God bless us, beyant telling about it? But you ought not to have slept in the back bedroom. She was loath to let me be going in and out of that room even in the daytime, let alone for any Christian to spend the night in it; for sure she says it was his own bedroom."

"*Whose* own bedroom?" we asked, in a breath.

"Why, *his* – the ould Judge's – Judge Horrock's, to be sure, God rest his sowl"; and she looked fearfully round.

"Amen!" I muttered. "But did he die there?"

"Die there! No, not quite *there*," she said. "Shure, was not it over the banisters he hung himself, the ould sinner, God be merciful to us all? And was not it in the alcove they found the handles of the skipping-rope cut off, and the knife where he was settling the cord, God bless us, to hang himself with? It was his housekeeper's daughter owned the rope, my mother often told me, and the child never throve after, and used to be starting up out of her sleep, and screeching in the night time, wid dhrames and frights that cum an her; and they said how it was the speerit of the ould Judge that was tormentin' her; and she used to be roaring and yelling out to hould back the big ould fellow with the crooked neck; and then she'd screech 'Oh, the master! The master! He's stampin' at me, and beckoning to me! Mother, darling, don't let me go!' And so the poor crathure died at last, and the docthers said it was wather on the brain, for it was all they could say."

"How long ago was all this?" I asked.

"Oh, then, how would I know?" she answered. "But it must be a wondherful long time ago, for the housekeeper was an ould woman, with a pipe in her mouth, and not a tooth left, and better nor eighty years ould when my mother was first married; and they said she was a rale buxom, fine-dressed woman when the ould Judge come to his end; an', indeed, my mother's not far from eighty years ould herself this day; and what made it worse for the unnatural ould villain, God rest his soul, to frighten the little girl out of the world the way he did, was what was mostly thought and believed by everyone. My mother says how the poor little crathure was his own child; for he was by all accounts an ould villain every way, an' the hangin'est judge that ever was known in Ireland's ground."

"From what you said about the danger of sleeping in that bedroom," said I, "I suppose there were stories about the ghost having appeared there to others."

"Well, there was things said – quare things, surely," she answered, as it seemed, with some reluctance. "And why would not there? Sure was it not up in that same room he slept for more than twenty years? And was it not in the *alcove* he got the rope ready that done his own business at last, the way he done many a betther man's in his lifetime? And was not the body lying in the same bed after death, and put in the coffin there, too, and carried out to his grave from it in Pether's churchyard, after the coroner was done? But there was quare stories – my mother has them all – about how one Nicholas Spaight got into trouble on the head of it."

"And what did they say of this Nicholas Spaight?" I asked.

"Oh, for that matther, it's soon told," she answered.

And she certainly did relate a very strange story, which so piqued my curiosity, that I took occasion to visit the ancient lady, her mother, from whom I learned many very curious particulars. Indeed, I am tempted to tell the tale, but my fingers are weary, and I must defer it. But if you wish to hear it another time, I shall do my best.

When we had heard the strange tale I have *not* told you, we put one or two further questions to her about the alleged spectral visitations, to which the house had, ever since the death of the wicked old Judge, been subjected.

"No one ever had luck in it," she told us. "There was always cross accidents, sudden deaths, and short times in it. The first that tuck, it was a family – I forget their name – but at any rate there was two young ladies and their papa. He was about sixty, and a stout healthy gentleman as you'd wish to see at that age. Well, he slept in that unlucky back bedroom; and, God between us an' harm! Sure enough he was found dead one morning, half out of the bed, with his head as black as a sloe, and swelled like a puddin', hanging down near the floor. It was a fit, they said. He was as dead as a mackerel, and so *he* could not say what it was; but the ould people was all sure that it was nothing at all but the ould Judge, God bless us! That frightened him out of his senses and his life together.

"Some time after there was a rich old maiden lady took the house. I don't know which room *she* slept in, but she lived alone; and at any rate, one morning, the servants going down early to their work, found her sitting on the passage-stairs, shivering and talkin' to herself, quite mad; and never a word more could any of *them* or her friends get from her ever afterwards but, 'Don't ask me to go, for I promised to wait for him.' They never made out from her who it was she meant by *him*, but of course those that knew all about the ould house were at no loss for the meaning of all that happened to her.

"Then afterwards, when the house was let out in lodgings, there was Micky Byrne that took the same room, with his wife and three little children; and sure I heard Mrs. Byrne myself telling how the children used to be lifted up in the bed at night, she could not see by what mains; and how they were starting and screeching every hour, just all as one as the housekeeper's little girl that died, till at last one night poor Micky had a dhrop in him, the way he used now and again; and what do you think in the middle of the night he thought he heard a noise on the stairs, and being in liquor, nothing less id do him but out he must go himself to see what was wrong. Well, after that, all she ever heard of him was himself sayin', 'Oh, God!' and a tumble that shook the very house; and there, sure enough, he was lying on the lower stairs, under the lobby, with his neck smashed double undher him, where he was flung over the banisters."

Then the handmaiden added –

"I'll go down to the lane, and send up Joe Gavvey to pack up the rest of the taythings, and bring all the things across to your new lodgings."

And so we all sallied out together, each of us breathing more freely, I have no doubt, as we crossed that ill-omened threshold for the last time.

Now, I may add thus much, in compliance with the immemorial usage of the realm of fiction, which sees the hero not only through his adventures, but fairly out of the world. You must have perceived that what the flesh, blood, and bone hero of romance proper is to the regular compounder of fiction, this old house of brick, wood, and mortar is to the humble recorder of this true tale. I, therefore, relate, as in duty bound, the catastrophe which ultimately befell it, which was simply this – that about two years subsequently to my story it was taken by a quack doctor, who called himself Baron Duhlstoerf, and filled the parlour windows with bottles of indescribable horrors preserved in brandy, and the newspapers with the usual grandiloquent and mendacious advertisements. This gentleman among his virtues did not reckon sobriety, and one night, being overcome with much wine, he set fire to his bed curtains, partially burned himself, and totally consumed the house. It was afterwards rebuilt, and for a time an undertaker established himself in the premises.

I have now told you my own and Tom's adventures, together with some valuable collateral particulars; and having acquitted myself of my engagement, I wish you a very good night, and pleasant dreams.

Haunting Christmas

Marina Favila

This story was inspired by my sister, Linda Rae Favila, who once lived in a haunted house, and who, for many years, read to me every night and long into the night.

AT FIRST they were only irritated, the ghosts of Manorville Manor, seven souls haunting the house they died in, or wandered by, in the process of dying, some restless, some pining, as ghosts are wont to be, but mostly content to call the manor home. And that makes sense. For who knows what awaits us after death, the where or why or how of it? But here, in this beautiful old barn of a house, with its old-fashioned gabled roof and tall cathedral ceilings, its imposing stone fireplace and hanging chandelier, with the tiny frosted bulbs the shape of tiny frosted flames, and one large window, set at the top of a spiral staircase, where the ghosts could float up and turn round and look out at the town they were born in, twinkling black and gold at night or washed pale grey at dawn – life could be worse they all knew.

Then she moved in.

Up until now they'd had a fine time, or a good enough time, for they were dead, after all, but before her, why, before her there'd been plenty to do, and they'd done it all and they'd done it well. The house was a veritable gold mine for ghosts. The attic wailed liked a banshee, drafty and cold, and easy to manipulate. A quick turnabout by one or two ghosts could create a mini cyclone within seconds, rattling the attic windows and shoving around old trunks of clothes and hatboxes and hat racks and stacks of *National Geographics*, left long ago by previous frightened owners. And the stairs in the front and the stairs in the back squeaked horribly; and the spirits, especially the young ones, could play those stairs like a violin. Ghostie-music, little Devin called it, when he first squeaked out 'The Water is Wide' in mid-July, when the boards were dry and weak. He'd learned the old song right before catching a cold and dying of influenza in 1899; and his parents, two earnest do-gooders, who ran the Down on Your Luck Soup Kitchen for the town's down on their luck, were so devastated by the loss of their fat-cheeked Devvy, they packed up and moved away within weeks of the little boy's death, leaving him inconsolable. Those wheezing, whining, wood-turned tunes, drawn out from the manor's creaking stairs, did much to distract the young spirit.

So you see, up until then, the manor boasted a sterling reputation, for the living and the dead. There'd even been talk of a listing in the Northeast Haunted House Registry. Especially after Prof. Hautboy, the eldest spirit in human years, had organized the ghosts into performance sections: bumps in the night, staircase interludes, whirlwinds and cold spots, and flashing lights – a specialty of the house on Halloween night, when Manorville Manor lit up like a Star Wars laser show, shooting red and blue across the sky. And those spritely inhabitants might have gone on forever, flashing their lights and moving their trunks and moaning in the dark, had the girl moved into another old house and not their lovely manor.

But that girl, that *girl*, that slip of a girl, with her college sweatshirt and skinny blue jeans. She'd arrived last spring on a warm afternoon, unloading a trunk full of antique mirrors and faux fur rugs. She'd not even bothered to check out the attic before signing the lease. Even the realtor seemed shocked that the girl knew nothing of the house's legendary past. Or perhaps she didn't care. Her smile was as wide as the Mississippi, and her pearl-pink cheeks flushed English rose at the thought she could be so lucky to live here, in this castle-like home, with its bad heat and faulty wires and creaky floor and leaky roof and that terribly romantic staircase, with its wrought iron railing twirling round and round and up and out, to the large picture window set so high you could see the whole town and the river beyond, its dark waters lit by sun and by star, or just slow-moving under slate-grey clouds. She knew life could be worse. So she signed on the dotted line. Alone, she signed, no mother or father beside her, not even a great aunt Lil or Uncle Joe. And the realtor placed the key in her hand, and rushed out the door, leaving the ghosts amazed at her presumption.

Not much past twenty, maybe not that – tall and thin, with the gangly stance of a newborn foal, all knees and elbows in constant motion. Hanging her curtains, stocking her fridge, pirouetting in the hall in front of the mirror, her honey-blonde hair gave a melodic bounce around her heart-shaped face. Something there, too, in her eyes, an open edge, a rawness that perplexed the ghosts. For every so often she'd abruptly stop whatever she was doing, cooking or singing or banister-hopping, and stare into space for minutes on end.

But still, to think the house would welcome her and her knick-knacks and her multiple cans of turquoise paint – preposterous! And for someone so alert to every detail of the house, how could she be so oblivious to their presence? That's what rattled the ghosts. For no matter how hard they rapped or knocked or thumped or flickered the lights, she never gave them the time of day, not a backward glance or a second look or a shiver or shock or a nervous tick – nothing.

"Youse think we didn't exist!" Mrs. Spartini exclaimed, after the first few days. She was particularly perturbed, for the house was originally hers, built by a doting banker for his Ten Cents a Dance bride. He'd stolen Mabeleen from 'The Orange Peel' speakeasy, just before midnight on New Year's Eve, and the former dancehall hostess took pride in reminding the ghosts that *she* was the original mistress of the manor, and still ordered them about to knock on the door with a menacing rap or streak the old walls with their skeletal hands. "I'se been doin' this for over a century," she huffed, "and I don't take kindly to being ignored in me own home!"

"There, there," Prof. Hautboy soothed her. He was by far the most educated of the ghosts, with a PhD in musicology. "She's young. I saw it in many of my students," and they all nodded, if ghosts can nod, that is. Even the Farmer Boy twins shimmered in agreement, two oafish white shadows, blustery and pale, with a touch of aquamarine swirling around. They'd never said a word, nor left each other's side, these past forty years.

"Yes, yes," the professor continued, "she's inattentive, with her iPod and smartphone glued to her ear. But she'll come around."

And they promised each other to give her a month, and took bets that such youthful self-centeredness would wear thin after two or three weeks. Give her time to lug in her Goodwill sofa and flea market lamps, and that god-awful basket of marbleized eggs to clutter the fireplace mantel. They'd even endured her initial cleaning. The fumes alone should have driven them out, but they knew, they just knew, once she settled down, they would have her attention, then send her packing to some sterile apartment in the suburbs!

But that was nearly nine months ago. She'd arrived in April, a gorgeous yellowy month, which turned bright green in early May and emerald-green the next. But those glorious colors faded fast to sage and gold by summer's end, then golded themselves to a ruby fall and fell to the ground with a silent crunch, quilting the earth in cranberry, copper, marigold, mustard, and rust. Three weeks later, all was ice, the air wet-weighted with the promise of snow. But by Christmas Eve the ghosts were no closer to making their presence known. Huddled together for warmth in the attic, they took stock of their situation.

Professor Hautboy called the meeting to order. "Quiet down, quiet down," he started, as he always did, with the only joke he knew: "We don't want to wake the dead!" And he laughed to himself, as he always did, alone.

"But it's ridiculous," rushed in Ravensby, a tattooed punk, triple-pierced and pacing, who'd been hit by a speeding car outside the house two years passing. Still relatively new to the manor, he was young and feisty, though death had admittedly slowed him down. "We've tried it all. Just last week I knocked down every single one of her piles of clean laundry – towels, wash cloths, two sets of sheets, eight pairs of athletic socks, all piled high on her four-poster bed and not a second glance at the mess I'd made!"

"Me too," piped Petunia Sweeney, who turned ninety-nine this month, if you counted the years from her birth not her death. She was the last one to die in the house, surrounded by her children and children's children, who held her hand and patted her cheek, though they'd already sold everything in the house, save the bed where she lay dying.

"I hid her keys in the refrigerator – *my* refrigerator, under the moldy lettuce in the vegetable bin." Petunia fingered remembered pearls, with the air of a duchess who'd suddenly found the maid in her brocade gown. "She looked for them alright, but when she found them in the fridge she merely laughed – laughed! As if I'd done it wrong!"

"She's a mess," Prof. Hautboy sighed. "A terrible housekeeper and unobservant to the max. How can we compete with that? Even the old chairs-on-the-table trick, just administered last month, which took quite a bit of energy ("and coordination," Ravensby added) – a fiasco!" For when the girl came home that night ("too late for a young lady," Petunia sneered) she slammed the door in a fury, blasted her stereo, and jumped round the room till the chairs came crashing down. Then she wove her way to the bedroom, without a backward glance at the dining room wreckage.

"She just can't hear us," Devvy said quietly, "but I might like her if she could." Ravensby rustled himself closer to the forlorn little spirit, by far his favorite in the house.

"A terrible problem," Hautboy concluded. And he slid the finger that didn't exist up the nose that didn't exist to push up the memory of thick glasses falling down his long face. "We must find a way to communicate with our, ahem, guest."

* * *

From the balustrade Devin watched the young girl decorate for Christmas. He had been sent by the other ghosts to guard the new mistress of the house, as if the spirit could effect much of anything at his young age – a ghostly glimmer, perhaps, aided by moonlight, or a lukewarm coolness, for cold was not in his nature. But he liked her, and they knew it, and thought it best for him not to be in their war room as they set their plans in motion.

Devvy was just as glad. The girl was particularly happy tonight, and he liked to watch her then, for her eyes glistened when she was joyful, and she hummed under her breath and sometimes burst into song at the top of her lungs. Tonight was something special to see. She was decorating the house for the holidays, in multi-colored garlands and shimmering icicles. A fire burned in the fireplace, and the mantelpiece was dressed with a delicate crèche: jewel-type stones set in the camel's saddle, and the three kings' crowns were painted in gold. Cutout stars wrapped in shiny foil dangled from a coat rack, and a huge fir wreath hung on the dining room wall with a large red satiny bow. The table was decorated with clips of holly and giant pinecones dusted with glitter. And everywhere – candles! Fifty, more, in wine bottles, jelly jars, tiny votive cups, and one large brass candelabrum, just tarnished enough to look expensive.

But Devvy's favorite was the Christmas tree, a tall blue spruce set up by the window and dressed up fine with red glass balls and candy canes, and a treasure trove of miniature antique toys: rocking horses, pogo sticks, dollies with golden hair and tiny blinkable eyes. Strands and strands of warm yellow lights seemingly floated on prickly branches. *There must be hundreds*, he thought, blinking on and off to the music box tunes of 'Greensleeves' and 'O Christmas Tree'.

Devvy was entranced as he watched the girl climb a rickety ladder to place a five-point star at the top of the tree. When a knock on the door startled them both, the ladder swayed as the girl jumped in surprise. Without thinking, the little ghost rushed to steady the ladder. Pushing himself hard into the wood, till the white oak pinched his very essence, Devvy steadied the ladder, while the girl traipsed down the steps with a lilting laugh at her luck and agility. Thank goodness the other ghosts were still in the attic, else there'd be hell to pay.

The open door let in gusts of wet darkness, but it was swallowed up by the warmth of the candlelit house and the greater warmth of its beaming mistress. The girl's voice hit a high-pitched squeal. There, before her, a dowdy woman in a dark blue coat, a peek of nurse's scrubs beneath, and at her side, a small thing, with a heart-shaped face and honey-brown hair, cramped in a tiny wheelchair. When the girl stepped back, Devvy gasped, for he thought he saw himself, such a wasted creature there, mostly skin and bones, and hollowed-out eyes, darkly and deeply creased. The boy looked nine, maybe ten, and… ghost-like, Devvy thought, for his skin was near translucent, and his eyes glazed over like he wasn't there. The spirit shivered in response, until he saw the boy look up from his chair. Seeing the girl towering above him, he smiled the same wide-as-a-river smile as her own.

With a deep bow, which made the boy giggle, the girl ushered in her visitors, closing the door with a definitive push, as if shutting out all that is bad or indecent in the world. She took over the woman's duties, wheeling her charge to a sofa covered with pillows and a large knitted quilt, kelly green, white, and tangerine, a zigzag pattern with scraggly tassels and many a snag in the yarn. When the girl and the woman pushed the couch closer to the fireplace, the light and the heat brought a healthy flush to the young boy's face.

Then all was a flurry in the house. And the flurry was the girl. Like a humming bird, here, there at once, she leapt and twirled around the room: stoking the fire; plumping the pillows; wheeling in an old-time tray, with mix-matched teacups of cocoa and cream; passing around a platter of cookies, shortbread Santas and chocolate reindeers, one with a raspberry nose. *How wonderful to be here*, Devvy thought to himself, for he felt he too was part of the eating and sipping and singing and pillow-plumping and belly-laughing, for everything seemed funny, now, to the three living inhabitants of Manorville Manor. Even the woman had begun to unwind, as she dipped a second Santa into her cocoa. Devin hoped the ghosts in the attic would take a long time with their evening preparations.

* * *

"Settled!" Hautboy concluded. "We'll wait until the clock strikes twelve, or rather, till I make that clock chime twelve booming clangs, and that in itself should get her attention, for the grandfather clock is a hundred years old and hasn't chimed for fifty.

"Then I'll sweep in," said Ravensby, slicking back the air where his hair used to be, "and do my cyclone thing, picking up anything I can in my wake: cups, saucers, tinkling spoons, knick-knacks – books! She's always leaving them scattered about. The fluttering pages in my little whirlwind will make a fine rat-a-tat-tat, adding to the confusion. If I move fast enough, perhaps I can even raise a chair!"

"Now, now," Prof. Hautboy advised, "we don't want to *kill* her." And he tried to look stern, though his transparent expression conveyed very little. Still, he wanted his tone forbidding, for he worried about the Farmer twins, hearts of gold, those boys, and silent as the grave, but easily stirred to their old roughhouse ways.

"We'll take care of the window," Mrs. Spartini interjected, for she wanted to make sure that everyone knew she was really in charge. "A frosty peel! Inside, of course, for the window's been rusty-eyed shut for years. But if we steam the inside, we can write some dastardly message for her to read. Petunia, dear, what might be fearful for you?

"Anything!" Even at ninety-nine, the ghost's voice went up in a girlish lilt at the sheer pleasure of being asked. "Something about the night, I suppose, for I was always afraid of the dark. I…"

"And the twins?" Ravensby rushed in, worried they'd never escape Petunia's lengthy riff on the dark.

"Lights!" Hautboy responded. "Multi-colored!" The whitish shadows glowed in response, for they loved shooting red and blue across the room, whether they had an audience or not.

"And if that doesn't work?" Petunia whined.

Even in death, Prof. Hautboy was a teacher and a good one, and he responded with authority: "It *will* work. Never fear, Petunia! And if it doesn't – we'll wrap that horrid afghan so tight about her tiny frame that when we finally let her go, she'll run from the house and never return to Manorville Manor!" And the ghosts all shimmered in approval.

But as they floated out to take their places, at the hearth, by the tree, hovering near the window, they paused, for the girl was reading now, to a young boy on the couch, while the older woman faded in and out of sleep in an overstuffed chair. And the girl was reading with enthusiasm and dramatic gestures, about some ghost of Christmas past and a singing child on crutches. Hautboy signaled the spirits to wait. They wouldn't have started even if he hadn't, for they knew, as he knew, what was coming.

* * *

At first Devvy kept his distance, hidden in the branches of the spruced-up spruce. But it had been so many years since someone had read to him, and before long he was pressed up next to the fireplace, then folded around the ottoman, close to the sofa with the ugly quilt, not so close to touch the humans, though he could feel their warmth. And with the cookie crumbs lavishly dotting the floor, and the teacups emptied of cocoa and cream, he saw the girl reach beneath an embroidered cushion to retrieve an old blue book.

It was dusty, cracked, bound in leather, with pages edged in gold. She presented it to the boy like some precious treasure befitting the Magi, and pointed at the illustrations and the lavish scrolled print. Then she jumped from the couch and began to read. Both boy and ghost were transported as she skipped around the room and motioned with her hands and acted all the parts. With the lighted tree sparkling behind her like the backdrop of some Christmas play, the girl became Scrooge, counting his money, and timid Bob Cratchet, cowering before him, and

Tiny Tim, leaning on crutches, but singing in a high sweet voice. Even the joyful nephew with his blasted 'Merry Christmas' brought a tear to the woman's eye, before she fell back to sleep. And though Devin was a ghost himself, he trembled when Marley arrived, with a raspy voice like a rusty nail, floating in air on the living room stairs and clanging his voluminous chains.

But then the boy began to cough, then cough in earnest, great sobbing, hacking coughs, and the girl swept down from her staircase perch and cuddled him up on the sofa. She pulled the raggedy afghan round them, tucked it in tight, on the left and the right, so snug they might have been bound together. And she plodded on, reading aloud, but Devin could tell, as anyone could, that all her attention was on the boy. For even when she raised her voice or pointed to the air when a new ghost appeared, her other hand felt for the young boy's neck and brushed back the hair from his hot flushed face.

And she read for an hour, maybe two, of Ebenezer's life and his love and his money, and though each new ghost prompted Devin to shiver, the boy lay still, so still, in fact, he seemed asleep. And it was then Devin noticed they were not alone, but joined by the ghosts, around the room, still and staring at the boy in the girl's arms. For the ghosts could see, though she could not, the outlines of the boy beginning to blur, like the edges of a photo no longer in focus or the fresh white smear of a dab of paint, titanium white on a dark oil canvas.

And the girl read faster, flipping through pages with furious intent, playing each part with commitment and verve, but the boy was no longer listening...he's rising, trying to shake his body loose. Impatient, his movement, like a pupa shedding its skin, he pushes himself away from himself and from his sister too, oblivious to who she is, even to her loving attention as she turns each page and adjusts the blanket that holds them together. He is no longer who he was, nor does he care for her. He thinks only of ridding himself of this great weight. And though the ghosts have taken this journey themselves, they are transfixed by his ascent, for he does not see them. He does not acknowledge they even exist. He simply rises, past the lighted tree and the fireplace and the spiral staircase, learning how to swim in that great sea of air.

And a light seems to grow inside him, and now he is all titanium white, brilliant and bright-edged. And the ghosts can see right through him; and the lights from the candles and the lights from the tree flicker behind him, and it looks for a moment as if the Milky Way has descended into the room and revolves around them. And the boy's form is some low constellation or gossamer angel descended to earth – but an angel that feels nothing human, and so he is both like the ghosts and nothing like the ghosts, for they have always felt human, and they have always felt tied to this world.

A huge gust of wind opens the window that hasn't been open for years and years, and the boy, looking now like a shiny piece of foil, acts like a magnet to the other ghosts, who also feel the need to rise. And they rise: Petunia and Ravensby, into the air, like helium balloons let loose in the wind. And Mrs. Spartini, waving to the house, like some grand dame in a local parade. And the Farmer Boy twins, still hand in hand, like a pale green fog, frosting the window inside out. Even Prof. Hautboy joins in, waving an imaginary conductor's baton, as if he is leading an orchestra again, pointing to each ghost to play their part. "Two notes up. Now jump the octave! Jump!" He laughs to himself, alone.

But Devvy sees none of this, for all his attention is on the girl. And she is crying, cradling the boy in her arms, while the older woman talks on the phone. From far below Devin can hear Ravensby calling, calling him *now*, and Prof. Hautboy taps the air and motions for him to follow. When Devvy looks up, he sees Mrs. Spartini floating out the window, in a great twisty movement reminiscent of her Orange Peel days; and Petunia joins her, no longer afraid of the dark, but sparkling like a slow-shooting star in the heavens, or a snowflake welcomed by a sky full of glitter. And that sky full of glitter is suddenly covered by a gauzy white cloud with aqua-green swirls, following the boy out the window as well.

Red and blue lights sweep through the house. Not as bright as the dazzle the Farmer Boys planned, but a whirling pattern around the room. A high-pitched wail shaking the walls deafens the calls for Devin to follow. And all is a flurry: rushing and moaning, doors that are opening, closing, and slamming, a table with wheels wheeling round the room, and strangers in uniform shaking their heads. Coats and boots grabbed, gloves by the door, in minutes it's dark, and the whole house is empty of all of the living and all of the dying. Crowding the window, three shadows remain.

* * *

When the girl returns, it is late, and she enters the house alone. She walks like she's been sleeping. Her face holds no expression. She shrugs off her coat in the middle of the room, letting it drop to the floor. Then she climbs the spiral staircase in a slow, measured gait. And she pays no mind to the snow on the steps, blown in from the open window. Nor does she notice the ice on the railing; her hands are just as cold.

She reaches the top of the stairs without stopping. She leans out the window and waits. The clock strikes one and the clock strikes two, and the air grows cold and colder. And every minute of every hour she's searching the town below, from house to house, and street to street, all lit by the muted glow of streetlamps covered deep in snow. Then she raises her face to the sky. She searches its depth with a long, long look, as if she might seriously count the stars or the snowflakes falling around her. And she seems to be listening to something or nothing. Even the wind is silent.

Then she leans out further and extends her hands, into the night and into the snow, her palms face up, her forehead wrinkled, as she squints into the darkness.

And now she's on tiptoe, leaning forward, her bare arms raised to a cloud-laced sky. And she waits and she waits, as the clock strikes three, and she listens. She's listening.

She'll fall if she's not careful, Devin thinks from far below. "She'll fall if she's not careful," he repeats into the air.

"We must grab her attention!" Hautboy commands. "Ravensby, Devin, begin! "

The chandelier creaks as it slowly turns, and the frosted bulbs charge a ruby red, and the lights on the tree blink faster now, its music box tempo increasing as well. And far in the corner, the grandfather clock begins to chime with a booming clang, as a whirlwind rises in the middle of the room, filled with objects of the evening's bliss: teacups, saucers, silver spoons, a platter dotted with cookie crumbs; cut-out stars covered in foil, each one boasting a flickering train of multi-colored candle flames; marbleized eggs and clips of holly and pine cones dusted with silver glitter; and books, books, a vortex of books, flying like starlings around the room, their pages a clattering, thunderous flutter. Even the ottoman knocks on the floor, as if trying to jump to the whirlwind above.

And the girl whips around, amazed at the sight. The house is alive and dances before her. She gasps as a teacup twirls within reach, then a trio of spoons tap together like bells; and with so many candles and jelly jar lights, it looks like the Milky Way now has returned, made up of objects from daily life. And the girl starts to laugh. She laughs in surprise. Doubles over and laughs. She laughs so hard that tears overflow her pearl-pink cheeks and heart-shaped face. Laughing so hard she loses control; and shaking with laughter, she feels herself slip on the snow-laden stairs. Slipping and falling, backwards she's reeling, with only the night and the wide-open window to catch her as she falls.

And then such a rush rushing inside her, a hard-air push. It's almost warm. Wedged in tight it holds her steady, just for a moment, on the edge of the sill, where she sees – she swears, still swears to this day – that she sees the old quilt with its zigzag design and gnarly strings, rising in earnest and billowing out like a tall ship's sail that sails on high, through the air and into her arms.

It wraps her up twice and pulls her in fast, and she slides down the railing, around and around, down to the floor where she's dropped on the sofa in one magnificent plop. And be it fatigue or the ice-edged cold or the wet night air or the warmth of the quilt, or the whirling images of a house come alive that she can't take in and she can't deny, the girl falls asleep as soon as her head hits the plumped up pillow of her Goodwill couch, wrapped up tight in a ragtag throw, with a ghost pressed up to her heart.

* * *

On Christmas Day, the gabled roof of Manorville Manor is sagging, from the snow and the cold and the wind and the rain and the decades it's been standing. But a girl can be seen at the window there, on the second floor, or so it seems, enveloped in an afghan quilt of green and white and tangerine, with a delicate teacup in her hand, from which she slowly sips. And the sun through the window must feel warm, for a lovely glow surrounds her there, the softest cloud of peach and gold, almost a mist that clings and swirls as she stands by the window, one hand up, as if to touch the sun. Some trick, too, of the afternoon light casts three shadows against the wall, making her look both small and bright and strangely not alone. She looks out the window at the town she was born in, washed pearl-white by the glittering snow. And she stares at the river as it circles her home, slow-moving and slate-grey.

House Hunting

Shannon Fay

NOBODY paid much attention to the birdhouse until it bit Mr. Easton's finger. The birdhouse had appeared a week earlier hanging from a tree in the subdivision's communal green space. None of the residents in Cedar Heights knew where it had come from, but as it added a woodsy charm to their otherwise staid suburban block they left it alone.

And then Mr. Easton took it upon himself to put some birdseed in it. The only opening the little box had was a small, round hole near the front. Mr. Easton poured as much birdseed as he could into the hole. He then made the mistake of sticking his finger in to push the contents in deeper. A second later he dropped the bag of seed and lurched back. He didn't scream until he saw his finger hanging by a thread of skin.

Mindy Park was playing a one-person game of badminton in her front yard when it happened. Her parents, Dr. and Dr. Park, were also in the front yard, debating the merits of a stone walkway. The debate was put aside when the Parks heard Mr. Easton's screams.

The two adult Parks rushed over. She had a doctorate in physics, he had one in chemistry. Despite the fact that neither of their degrees were medical in nature, this did not stop the Parks from stepping forward whenever a maître d', airline pilot or supermarket manager asked if there was a doctor in the house. Usually people were more than a little miffed when it was revealed that the Parks couldn't actually, say, perform the Heimlich manoeuvre on the choking man, or help the passenger having a heart attack in economy class, or deliver a baby in aisle three. But what the Parks lacked in actual first aid training they made up with their calm and commanding presence.

"Peter, keep pressing it, we have to staunch the bleeding," Dr. Park said. The other Dr. Park already had his cell phone out and was talking to a 911 dispatcher.

Mindy came over to the green space to see what was going on. Like most children, Mindy had a morbid streak a mile long, but as there was rarely anything gruesome or exciting in Cedar Heights she didn't often get to indulge it. Her mother saw her just standing there, and hating to see her daughter idle, she reached into her pocket and took out a five.

"Mindy, go to the corner store and buy a bag of ice. We'll need it for Mr. Easton's finger. And get me a Coke Zero while you're there."

While Mindy was loath to go and miss anything exciting, she was also pleased to be given what seemed to be an important task. She took the five and ran down to the corner store.

The only people in the store when Mindy arrived were the teenaged store clerk and a grizzled man in a ripped coat.

Mindy had heard her parents and their friends refer to the man as a 'homeless bum', which had struck Mindy as an inaccurate assessment. All the kids in the neighbourhood knew the man wasn't homeless. 'Homeless' meant you slept on the street at night, wrapped in newspaper. This man slept in a white van parked behind the corner store.

Much like the birdhouse, no one knew where the man had come from, only that he had suddenly appeared a few weeks earlier, going through dumpsters and collecting plastic bottles. Unlike the birdhouse he did not bring any 'woodsy charm' to the neighbourhood. Most of the residents of the subdivision wished that he would just move along to the nearest city. Cities, in their opinion, were the natural habitat of the homeless.

The man was standing at his usual place by the copier machine. Over the machine hung a bulletin board. The bulletin board was there to advertize community events, but since there were never any it was instead filled with missing children posters. Some of the posters were even older than Mindy.

She watched as the man looked around. He then reached out and grabbed one of the sheets off the board. The paper made a dry crinkling noise as he shoved it in his pocket.

Mindy remembered that Mr. Easton was probably still screaming and losing blood. She ran to the freezer and lugged a giant bag of ice to the counter.

She put down the ice on the counter with a large *huff.* The store clerk, Luke, was writing a text message and didn't look up.

"*Come on!*" Mindy said, jumping up and down in the front of the counter. "I've got to bring the ice back before Mr. Easton's finger falls off!"

That made both Luke and the van man look over.

"What?" Luke said in his thick teenage drawl.

"The birdhouse on my street bit Mr. Easton's finger off!" Mindy said, still jumping up and down. "There's blood *allllllll* over the green space! It was coming out of his hand like a water fountain! And his finger was just hanging there, like this."

Mindy waved her hand around, making it look like a floppy blur in the air.

Luke shrugged and rang the ice through. Mindy grabbed the bag off the counter and ran as fast as she could back to the scene of the crime, ice water dripping out of the bag and onto her clothes as her feet pounded the pavement.

She arrived just in time to see Mr. Easton being helped into an ambulance. Dr. and Dr. Park were standing in the green space along with several of their neighbours. A few meters away from the group the birdhouse swayed gently. A bit of blood dripped from the hole in the front.

Mindy realized as the ambulance sped away that she had missed all the excitement and that the ice was now destined for mundane tasks like filling ice coolers or cooling drinks. She sighed and went over to where the adults were talking.

Aside from the Parks, there were also the Pratts and Mrs. Henderson. All of them were looking at the birdhouse the same way they had looked at the Henderson's garage door when Mr. Henderson had painted it purple. It was a look of distaste and fear.

"*This* is exactly why the home owners association doesn't allow birdhouses," Mr. Pratt said. "It encourages vermin to move into the neighbourhood, like whatever creature attacked Peter."

"I called animal control," Dr. Park said, putting his cell phone in his pocket. "They said they'll be here within the hour."

"It'll be gone within the hour," a rough voice said.

The group turned to see the homeless man standing on the edge of the green space.

"Excuse me, but this is a matter that concerns *residents,*" said Mrs. Henderson. After the purple door incident she was desperate to earn points with her neighbors.

"That birdy house has just gotten its first taste of human flesh," the man said. "You think it will be happy with birds and squirrels after *that*? Once they move up the food chain, they never go back."

"Look, we don't know what kind of creature is living in there, but whatever it is we're going to let animal control deal with it," Dr. Park, the chemist, said.

"That's right," Mr. Pratt said, nodding. "I'm not insured for wild animal attacks."

"Yer not dealing with an animal," the man growled. "Yer dealing with the embodiment of an ancient and primordial evil."

No one spoke for a moment.

"Well," Mr. Pratt said. "I'm pretty sure my insurance doesn't cover *that* either."

The man growled again.

"I'm telling ya," he said. "You should take care of this now, while it's still a nipper. Cut it down and destroy it before it's too late."

"I think it's best if we left this to the professionals," Dr. Park said. "No offence."

The man snorted and ambled away. The Pratts shook their heads and headed inside. Mrs. Henderson went back to painting her garage door beige. Dr. Park, upon hearing that Mindy had forgotten her Coke Zero, went down to the store, while the other Dr. Park went back to contemplating the pros and cons of a stone walkway.

Mindy went back to playing on the front lawn, but now and then she would glance over at the birdhouse. It seemed to be watching her, the perfectly round hole a single eye that never blinked.

About half an hour later Mindy saw the animal control truck pull up to the curb. Two men wearing white overalls got out of the vehicle. Mindy ran up to them, eager to point out the blood-thirsty birdhouse. But when Mindy looked over at the cluster of trees, there was nothing there. The birdhouse was gone.

* * *

When Mindy found the homeless man he was packing several garbage bags of plastic bottles into the back of his van. When he saw Mindy he slammed the doors shut, though not before she caught a glance inside. The walls were plastered with missing children posters.

"Whattya want?" the man growled.

"How did you know the birdhouse would disappear?" Mindy asked.

The man leaned back and sat on the bumper.

"It's gone, eh? Well, let me tell you girlie, it didn't disappear. It *escaped*." The man patted his pockets and looked at Mindy. "You got any smokes?"

"No. I'm *nine*," Mindy said. The man grunted.

"How did you know the birdhouse would try and escape? Why don't you think it's just an animal living inside of it that bit Mr. Easton's finger?" Mindy persisted.

The man was staring intently at the ground, his gaze sweeping over the pavement like a wave. His scrutiny was rewarded when he spied a half-smoked cigarette butt. He scooped it up and brought it to his lips, lighting it with a flickering lighter.

"I've seen enough to know that evil don't always look the way we think evil should look. More often it looks as warm and inviting as mom's apple pie." He let out a puff of smoke and looked at Mindy. "You probably still think that monsters only live in your closet, don't ya?"

"No," Mindy said. The man grinned.

"Good. Because there aren't any in there. Demons, monsters, creatures of the night, whatever you want to call 'em, they don't look like they do in the movies."

Mindy waited for the man to say more but all he did was take another drag on his cigarette.

"What do they look like?" Mindy asked when she couldn't wait anymore. The man gave her a sideways glance before taking another drag. When he spoke his voice came out in a puff of white smoke.

"Buildings."

"Buildings?" Mindy said.

"Yeah, buildings," the man said. "What better way to catch your prey? This way they don't even have to hunt down humans. They sit and wait for people to come to *them*. And when they have someone in their grasp: *crunch*. Supper time." He dropped the cigarette onto the pavement and ground it out with his foot. "I've seen all types: offices, bus shelters, port-a-potties." The man grimaced. "Now *that's* a nasty way to go."

"Are you serious?" Mindy said.

"Of course I'm serious!" The man said, straightening up. He banged the side of his home. "Why do you think I live in a *van*?"

Mindy could think of lots of reasons, but she knew that none of them were the answer he was looking for.

"It's not stationary," the man explained. "Demons can't impersonate moving objects. Vans, cars, trains and RVs are all safe. Buildings aren't."

"You're crazy," Mindy said, backing up. The man smiled, lips stretching back across his nicotine-stained teeth.

"Maybe I am, but I'm right about *this*. Think about that next time you're lying awake in your bed. Maybe those rumblings you hear aren't from the boogeyman in your closet. Maybe they're coming from the belly of the beast itself."

Mindy turned to go and even started to run before she stopped. She turned back slowly, the gravel on the pavement making a crunching sound under her sneakers.

"Hey," she said. "Those kids in the posters you have. Do you think…do you think the birdhouse ate them?"

The man shook his head. "Nah, too small. All demons start out tiny and grow over time. When they're nippers they usually just go for small mammals, working their way up to humans. Never saw any as small as a birdhouse though. That's new."

"Oh," Mindy said, relieved.

"But there *is* something out there," the man said. "Some demon's made its home here in Cedar Heights. But whatever it is, it's bigger and smarter than that birdy house."

"How do you know?" Mindy asked.

"Every couple of years a kid disappears," the man said. "I'd bet ya dollars to donuts that some demon made a meal out of 'em."

"I haven't heard about any kids disappearing," Mindy said.

The man raised his eyebrows.

"That's 'cause it hasn't struck in a while. Like I said, it's *smart*. It knows that if it kills too often people will get wise to it. If I'm right it's been awhile since it last ate. You better watch yourself, missy. Whatever it is, it's due for a *snack*."

The man snapped his jaws and grinned. This time Mindy ran.

* * *

The next day Bobby Pratt, the Pratt's 13-year-old son, found the Henderson's cat ripped to pieces.

The adults were quick to convene and argue over whether there was anything in the home owners' code about burying pets in backyards. With her heart hammering in her chest Mindy pushed through the tall people to look at the cat. She took one glance at the mangled feline and sprinted down to the corner store.

"Muffles was torn apart!" Mindy said as soon as she was through the door.

Luke looked up from his phone.

"What?"

"I wasn't talking to you," Mindy said, scanning the store. "Where's the guy who lives in the van?"

"I think he said something about the liquor store—"

Mindy ran out. The closest liquor store was at the West End Mall, which was quite a walk away when your legs weren't all that long. Luckily, Mindy had only covered half the distance before she met the man coming back from the store. He was pushing a shopping cart filled with recyclables and a bottle of whiskey.

"You were right," Mindy said. "You were right!"

"Whoa there missy," the man said, talking loudly to be heard over the cart's squeaky wheels. "What are you so fired-up about?"

"The Henderson's cat, Bobby found it, it was torn apart," Mindy said between gasps of breath. "The birdhouse did it, I'm sure of it. You were right."

"How do ya know it wasn't just some dog that did in the kitty cat?" the man asked.

"I saw the body," Mindy said. "It was covered in bird seed."

The man's mouth tightened.

"You're the only one who knows about this stuff," Mindy says. "You've got to help me get rid of it. I'm the smallest kid on my street. I don't want it to eat me."

The man sighed.

"Please!" Mindy said. The man stopped, cutting the cart's squeaking short. He looked at Mindy with fierce eyes.

"Look, missy, why do you think I wander from place to place, never putting down roots or getting a real job?"

"Uh…" Mindy said, once again not willing to voice her thoughts on the subject.

"It's because for the last fifteen years I've been criss-crossing the country, hunting down these monsters. It is my life goal, my sworn duty, the reason I was put here on this Earth. So, yeah, I'll help ya."

For a second the man seemed to lose the ever-present layer of grime that clung to him. He seemed strong and invincible, more like a statue than a human being.

"Really?" Mindy said. "You'll help me?"

"Yes, I will," the man said. He started pushing the cart again. "For twenty bucks."

* * *

Later that night Mindy snuck out of the house, guinea pig cage in one hand and a twenty dollar bill in the other. She met the man in her backyard. In his hands he had a BB gun and a bottle of whiskey.

"Here's your money," Mindy said, holding out the bill. "Though I don't know why you wanted me to bring Jelly Bean."

Jelly Bean made a snorting noise as Mindy lifted up her cage. The man put down the bottle so he could pocket the money. He then took the cage and set it down in the middle of the yard. Mindy looked back and forth between him and Jelly Bean, her eyes growing wider with each pass.

"What? No! We can't just leave her there!"

"We need something to lure the demon in," the man said. "You want to sit out there, snorting and squealing? 'Cause I'm sure the monster would just as soon like some little girl meat."

Mindy looked down and shook her head.

"Fine. Let's get in position."

'Getting in position' meant crawling under the backyard picnic table. Mindy and the man laid there on their bellies, watching Jelly Bean's cage. The man held his BB gun like a commando, eyes scanning the darkness of the backyard. The longer they waited the more Mindy became aware of the man's smell. It was a sickly, sweaty smell that made her eyes water.

"How much longer is it going to take?' Mindy asked.

"That depends on the demon," the man said.

"Yeah, but when will it show up?"

"It might not even show at all tonight," the man said. "We just got to wait and see."

"How can it even move?" Mindy asked. "I mean, it's a *birdhouse*."

"No, it's a *demon* pretending to be a birdhouse," the man said. "Ya gotta remember that."

Mindy sighed. The man glanced her way before looking back out at the yard.

"Let me tell you a story about a man named Jerald Hampton," the man said. "Jerald worked at a call center. Have you ever worked at a call center, uh…"

"My name is Mindy," Mindy said. "And I'm too young to have ever worked anywhere."

"Oh," the man said. "Well, call centres are kind of like factory farms for human beings. The people who work there are all crammed right next to each other, so close your elbows are pinned to your sides. And everyone there has a phone in front of them, and they're all talking on the phones, calling strangers and trying to sell them coupon books or vacation packages or gift cards. And everyone on the other end of the phone hates you. You know they hate you because they tell you they hate you before they hang up, but all you can do is swallow down your remaining pride and dial the next number because you get paid by the sale, not by the hour."

Half of the man's ramblings had gone right over Mindy's head, but she nodded solemnly.

"Jerald worked at a call centre six days a week. One day it dawned on Jerald that he was going to die there. He realized that the building was slowly sucking the life out of him, and that one day he'd just slump over onto his phone, dead. He looked around and saw that it was the same for most of his co-workers. So Jerald decided to do something about it. That night, after everyone had gone home, Jerald came back with several gallons of gasoline and burned the place down."

Mindy whistled.

"And this Jerald guy was you, right?" Mindy asked. The man glared at her.

"What? No, I'm not Jerald Hampton! Why the hell would I talk about myself in third person?" the man said. "Last I heard that crazy bastard was *still* under psychiatric evaluation."

The man sighed and looked back out at the cage. "But I knew Jerry, and when I heard his story it opened my eyes to how the world really works. That call centre wasn't just a regular building. It was a demon, an old and crafty one. It had figured out that it didn't *need* to kill people outright to live off of them. It could just suck a little bit out of them every day, letting them go home at the end of their shift because it *knew* they would be back."

For a moment there was silence.

"Do you like it here, Mindy? Living here in Cedar Heights?" the man asked.

Mindy shrugged. "It's all right."

"Let me give you some advice: get out of here the first chance you get."

Mindy looked at him, scrunching her nose up against his smell. She was about to ask him what he was talking about when there was a noise at the far end of the yard.

Something poked out of the hedge. It looked like a stick. A second later it was joined by another stick, the knots bending like joints. And then the birdhouse itself emerged.

It had eight legs, all of them sticks that ended in sharpened points. The birdhouse moved spiderlike across the grass towards the cage.

"Shoot it!" Mindy whispered. The man shook his head.

"Not yet. Too far."

Mindy heard Jelly Bean shriek at the birdhouse's approach.

"Screw this," Mindy said. She reached over and grabbed the BB gun.

"HEY!" The man shouted. Mindy yanked on the gun, not realising her hand was on the trigger. The gun made a soft *ping!* noise and Jelly Bean squealed.

Mindy looked over to see blood seeping out of a hole on the guinea pig's flank. The birdhouse had frozen at the sound of the gunshot, but now it ran forward towards the cage.

"*JELLY BEAN!*" Mindy yelled. She scrambled out from under the picnic table. She felt the man's hand brush her ankle but she was already out and running towards the birdhouse and the wounded rodent.

Mindy's father often left out gardening tools, a habit that annoyed the other Dr. Park to no end. At that moment Mindy however was very thankful for her father's absent-mindedness. She grabbed a shovel and swung it at the creature.

It connected with the side of the birdhouse, making a loud CRACK that reverberated through the handle and up Mindy's arm. The monster appeared dazed for a moment, and then it stabbed a sharpened point through Mindy's foot.

The tip went through the top of her sneakers, into her foot, and out the other side. Mindy dropped the shovel. She opened her mouth to scream but nothing came out. Mindy was in severe pain, but she was also confused. She had always thought that you could tell how badly someone was hurt by how much they yelled and cried. And yet here she was, in more pain than she had ever been in in her short life, and she couldn't even breathe.

Then the monster drew out its talon and somehow that unlocked all the pain inside of her. Mindy howled.

Her cry was interrupted by the *ping!* of the BB gun. The birdhouse jerked back from Mindy, wobbling from the impact.

Mindy looked over to see the man walking forward, re-loading. The monster turned towards him, crouching down to spring. Jelly Bean lay still in her cage.

"Mindy, run!" the man said. Mindy got to her feet and dashed deeper into the backyard. When she hit the hedge she kept going, ignoring the spider webs that wrapped around her as she pushed through the foliage. When she emerged on the other side she grabbed at the ground with both hands, shaking.

After a few seconds Mindy pushed herself up into a sitting position and looked around. She was in the Hendersons' backyard. Their house was dark and quiet. Off to the side sat their shed. It was hard to tell in the dark, but Mindy knew it was painted the same eggplant shade that Mr. Henderson had used to paint their garage door.

Mindy wondered if the van man was okay. She gulped and listened. She thought she heard voices coming from the direction of the Pratts' house. Somewhere someone's dog was barking. But she didn't hear anything from her own backyard.

Mindy got to her feet and froze when she heard a twig snap.

The birdhouse pushed through the hedge and stepped into the Hendersons' yard. It no longer looked cute or woodsy or charming. It had dried blood around the bird hole in the front, making it look like both a wound and a gaping maw. One side of the little house had a dent where Mindy had hit it with the shovel, the other side had a bullet hole. Each of its eight legs was dipped in blood.

Mindy staggered back, wincing as she put weight on her injured foot. The creature stepped towards her. It raised one of its legs up like a stinger, the tip level with Mindy's heart.

Both Mindy and the creature jumped when the shed door flew open. In that split second the birdhouse seemed to forget all about Mindy. It turned and scrambled towards the hedge. Mindy watched, stunned, as a water hose flew out from the dark doorway of the shed. It wrapped around the birdhouse. The birdhouse tried to dig its claws into the ground, but that didn't stop the shed from reeling it in. Mindy watched as the tips of the creature's limbs sowed rows in the Henderson's yard.

When it got to the doorway the birdhouse splayed its legs, grabbing on to the doorframe to keep from being pulled into the bigger monster's belly. But then one of its legs snapped off and that was the end of it. The birdhouse disappeared inside and the shed door slammed shut.

Mindy fell to her knees and let out a shaking breath. Her foot throbbed, sending pulses of pain throughout her entire body.

Mindy jerked back at the sound of the shed door banging open once more.

GET UP! she yelled inside her head. With a grunt she pushed herself to her feet. She had just made it when the hose wrapped around her waist. It yanked and she fell onto her back, feet in the air. The hose started to reel her in, pulling her towards the darkness of the purple shed.

"No! Nooo!" Mindy yelled. The hose squeezed tight, cutting off Mindy's breath. She clutched at the ground but all she managed to do was pull out patches of grass. She tried pulling at the hose encircling her waist but it was too tight.

Ping! A BB hit one of the shed's windows. Dimly Mindy heard the sound of glass shattering, but she was more concerned with the fact that the hose had loosened its grip on her. She squirmed and managed to slip out of its hold.

"Mindy, get over here!" the man yelled. He had scratches all over his face and his jacket hung in pieces around him. He had put down the BB gun and was busy stuffing what looked like a sock in the mouth of the whiskey bottle. Mindy ran over to stand next to him. She watched as he took out his lighter and held it up to the sock.

"Hurry, hurry," she said, her voice hoarse. From the shed there was a harsh rumbling sound, like a hundred blades moving against each other.

Finally the lighter worked and the sock caught fire. The man hefted up the bottle and lobbed it through the window he had shot out a minute earlier.

The shed went up in a ball of flame, the purple paint illuminated by the rush of fire. For a second Mindy was sure she could hear something screaming, but it was cut short by a second explosion.

"Probably a gas-powered lawn mower," the man said, with the air of someone who has seen a lot of explosions. "Anyway, let's get the hell out of here."

* * *

Mindy and the man watched from atop a jungle gym as the emergency vehicles pulled into the neighbourhood.

"There are ambulances there," the man said. "You should go and have a doctor look at your foot."

"What about you?" Mindy asked.

The man shrugged. "I'll be all right."

Mindy dropped down, letting out a soft 'Ah!' when her feet touched ground. She stood there for a moment.

"After I left, did you see if Jelly Bean was…if she was…"

The man cleared his throat.

"Ya know it was the funniest thing," he said. "While I was fighting the demon, your little rodent managed to get out of her cage and run off. The little thing's probably already putting together her own little guinea pig clan out there in the wild. Next time you see her, she will be queen of the wild guinea pigs and—"

"You don't have to lie to me," Mindy said. "I get it. She died."

The man sighed. He climbed down and stood by Mindy.

"Well missy, just remember it could have been a lot worse," he said. "Anyway, I better get going."

"What? You're leaving?" Mindy asked.

"Yep. My rule is to leave town as soon as the monster's defeated. Or when my parking fines get too high. Whichever comes first."

"Oh," Mindy said. "Well, thanks for saving my life."

"No problem, just making sure you got your twenty dollars worth," the man said. He held out his hand, and after a moment's hesitation, Mindy shook it.

"Goodbye Mindy," the man said. "Maybe someday we'll meet again."

"I doubt it," Mindy said.

The man nodded. "Yeah, probably not. Bye."

And with that the man disappeared into the darkness. Mindy meanwhile headed towards the light, limping as she made her way towards the glow of the fire and the roar of the sirens. Halfway there she stopped. The houses of her neighborhood loomed ahead in the smoke and flames.

Her heart suddenly felt caged in and confined, its frantic beats too big for her tiny chest. Her house looked the same way as it always did but as Mindy looked at it she couldn't shake the feeling that it was looking *back*. And not just it, but every other building on her block. She remembered the grinding noise the shed had made. She heard it now, echoed and magnified in her head.

Up until that point Mindy had been focused solely on surviving. Only now did the larger implications behind the van man's words hit her. How could she know which buildings were safe? How could she tell if her school, or a friend's house, *or even her own home*, wasn't a demon in disguise?

She fell to her knees just as her parents ran over. When Dr. Park picked her up Mindy thrashed in his arms, terrified that he was going to bring her inside. She only relaxed when she saw that he was carrying her to an ambulance. She let out a deep breath and clung to her father. Moving vehicles were safe, she knew. Ambulances, RVs, cars, and buses were all safe. Houses weren't.

The Vacant Lot

Mary E. Wilkins Freeman

WHEN IT BECAME generally known in Townsend Centre that the Townsends were going to move to the city, there was great excitement and dismay. For the Townsends to move was about equivalent to the town's moving. The Townsend ancestors had founded the village a hundred years ago. The first Townsend had kept a wayside hostelry for man and beast, known as the 'Sign of the Leopard'. The sign-board, on which the leopard was painted a bright blue, was still extant, and prominently so, being nailed over the present Townsend's front door. This Townsend, by name David, kept the village store. There had been no tavern since the railroad was built through Townsend Centre in his father's day. Therefore the family, being ousted by the march of progress from their chosen employment, took up with a general country store as being the next thing to a country tavern, the principal difference consisting in the fact that all the guests were transients, never requiring bedchambers, securing their rest on the tops of sugar and flour barrels and codfish boxes, and their refreshment from stray nibblings at the stock in trade, to the profitless deplenishment of raisins and loaf sugar and crackers and cheese.

The flitting of the Townsends from the home of their ancestors was due to a sudden access of wealth from the death of a relative and the desire of Mrs. Townsend to secure better advantages for her son George, sixteen years old, in the way of education, and for her daughter Adrianna, ten years older, better matrimonial opportunities. However, this last inducement for leaving Townsend Centre was not openly stated, only ingeniously surmised by the neighbors.

"Sarah Townsend don't think there's anybody in Townsend Centre fit for her Adrianna to marry, and so she's goin' to take her to Boston to see if she can't pick up somebody there," they said. Then they wondered what Abel Lyons would do. He had been a humble suitor for Adrianna for years, but her mother had not approved, and Adrianna, who was dutiful, had repulsed him delicately and rather sadly. He was the only lover whom she had ever had, and she felt sorry and grateful; she was a plain, awkward girl, and had a patient recognition of the fact.

But her mother was ambitious, more so than her father, who was rather pugnaciously satisfied with what he had, and not easily disposed to change. However, he yielded to his wife and consented to sell out his business and purchase a house in Boston and move there.

David Townsend was curiously unlike the line of ancestors from whom he had come. He had either retrograded or advanced, as one might look at it. His moral character was certainly better, but he had not the fiery spirit and eager grasp at advantage which had distinguished them. Indeed, the old Townsends, though prominent and respected as men of property and influence, had reputations not above suspicions. There was more than one dark whisper regarding them handed down from mother to son in the village, and especially was this true of the first Townsend, he who built the tavern bearing the Sign of the Blue Leopard. His portrait, a hideous effort of contemporary art, hung in the garret of David Townsend's home. There was many a tale of wild roistering, if no worse, in that old roadhouse, and high stakes, and quarreling in cups, and blows, and money gotten in evil fashion, and the matter hushed up with a high hand for inquirers by the imperious Townsends who terrorized everybody. David Townsend terrorized nobody. He had gotten his little competence from his store by honest methods – the exchanging of sterling goods and true weights for country produce and country shillings. He was sober and reliable, with intense self-respect and a decided talent for the management of money. It was principally for this reason that he took great delight in his sudden wealth by legacy. He had thereby greater opportunities for the exercise of his native shrewdness in a bargain. This he evinced in his purchase of a house in Boston.

One day in spring the old Townsend house was shut up, the Blue Leopard was taken carefully down from his lair over the front door, the family chattels were loaded on the train, and the Townsends departed. It was a sad and eventful day for Townsend Centre. A man from Barre had rented the store – David had decided at the last not to sell – and the old familiars congregated in melancholy fashion and talked over the situation. An enormous pride over their departed townsman became evident. They paraded him, flaunting him like a banner in the eyes of the new man. "David is awful smart," they said; "there won't nobody get the better of him in the city if he has lived in Townsend Centre all his life. He's got his eyes open. Know what he paid for his house in Boston? Well, sir, that house cost twenty-five thousand dollars, and David he bought it for five. Yes, sir, he did."

"Must have been some out about it," remarked the new man, scowling over his counter. He was beginning to feel his disparaging situation.

"Not an out, sir. David he made sure on't. Catch him gettin' bit. Everythin' was in apple-pie order, hot an' cold water and all, and in one of the best locations of the city – real high-up street. David he said the rent in that street was never under a thousand. Yes, sir, David he got a bargain – five thousand dollars for a twenty-five-thousand-dollar house."

"Some out about it!" growled the new man over the counter.

However, as his fellow townsmen and allies stated, there seemed to be no doubt about the desirableness of the city house which David Townsend had purchased and the fact that he had secured it for an absurdly low price. The whole family were at first suspicious. It was ascertained that the house had cost a round sum only a few years ago; it was in perfect repair; nothing whatever was amiss with plumbing, furnace, anything. There was not even a soap factory within smelling distance, as Mrs. Townsend had vaguely surmised. She was sure that she had heard of houses being undesirable for such reasons, but there was no soap factory. They all sniffed and peeked; when the first rainfall came they looked at the ceiling, confidently expecting to see dark spots where the leaks had commenced, but there were none. They were forced to confess that their suspicions were allayed, that the house was perfect, even overshadowed with the mystery of a lower price than it was worth. That, however, was an additional perfection in the opinion of the Townsends, who had their share of New England thrift. They had lived just one month in their new house, and were happy, although at times somewhat lonely from missing the society of Townsend Centre, when the trouble began. The Townsends, although they lived in a fine house in a genteel, almost fashionable, part of the city, were true to their antecedents and kept, as they had been accustomed, only one maid. She was the daughter of a farmer on the outskirts of their native village, was middle-aged, and had lived with them for the last ten years. One pleasant Monday morning she rose early and did the family washing before breakfast, which had been prepared by Mrs. Townsend and Adrianna, as was their habit on washing-days. The family were seated at the breakfast table in their basement dining-room, and this maid, whose name was Cordelia, was hanging out the clothes in the vacant lot. This vacant lot seemed a valuable one, being on a corner. It was rather singular that it had not been built upon. The Townsends had wondered at it and agreed that they would have preferred their own house to be there. They had, however, utilized it as far as possible with their innocent, rural disregard of property rights in unoccupied land.

"We might just as well hang out our washing in that vacant lot," Mrs. Townsend had told Cordelia the first Monday of their stay in the house. "Our little yard ain't half big enough for all our clothes, and it is sunnier there, too."

So Cordelia had hung out the wash there for four Mondays, and this was the fifth. The breakfast was about half finished – they had reached the buckwheat cakes – when this maid came rushing into the dining-room and stood regarding them, speechless, with a countenance indicative of the utmost horror. She was deadly pale. Her hands, sodden with soapsuds, hung twitching at her sides in the folds of her calico gown; her very hair, which was light and sparse, seemed to bristle with fear. All the Townsends turned and looked at her. David and George rose with a half-defined idea of burglars.

"Cordelia Battles, what is the matter?" cried Mrs. Townsend. Adrianna gasped for breath and turned as white as the maid. "What is the matter?" repeated Mrs. Townsend, but the maid was unable to speak. Mrs. Townsend, who could be peremptory, sprang up, ran to the frightened woman and shook her violently. "Cordelia Battles, you speak," said she, "and not stand there staring that way, as if you were struck dumb! What is the matter with you?"

Then Cordelia spoke in a fainting voice.

"There's – somebody else – hanging out clothes – in the vacant lot," she gasped, and clutched at a chair for support.

"Who?" cried Mrs. Townsend, rousing to indignation, for already she had assumed a proprietorship in the vacant lot. "Is it the folks in the next house? I'd like to know what right they have! We are next to that vacant lot."

"I – dunno – who it is," gasped Cordelia.

"Why, we've seen that girl next door go to mass every morning," said Mrs. Townsend. "She's got a fiery red head. Seems as if you might know her by this time, Cordelia."

"It ain't that girl," gasped Cordelia. Then she added in a horror-stricken voice, "I couldn't see who 'twas."

They all stared.

"Why couldn't you see?" demanded her mistress. "Are you struck blind?"

"No, ma'am."

"Then why couldn't you see?"

"All I could see –" Cordelia hesitated, with an expression of the utmost horror.

"Go on," said Mrs. Townsend, impatiently.

"All I could see was the shadow of somebody, very slim, hanging out the clothes, and—"

"What?"

"I could see the shadows of the things flappin' on their line."

"You couldn't see the clothes?"

"Only the shadow on the ground."

"What kind of clothes were they?"

"Queer," replied Cordelia, with a shudder.

"If I didn't know you so well, I should think you had been drinking," said Mrs. Townsend. "Now, Cordelia Battles, I'm going out in that vacant lot and see myself what you're talking about."

"I can't go," gasped the woman.

With that Mrs. Townsend and all the others, except Adrianna, who remained to tremble with the maid, sallied forth into the vacant lot. They had to go out the area gate into the street to reach it. It was nothing unusual in the way of vacant lots. One large poplar tree, the relic of the old forest which had once flourished there, twinkled in one corner; for the rest, it was overgrown with coarse weeds and a few dusty flowers. The Townsends stood just inside the rude board fence which divided the lot from the street and stared with wonder and horror, for Cordelia had told the truth. They all saw what she had described – the shadow of an exceedingly slim woman moving along the ground with up-stretched arms, the shadows of strange, nondescript garments flapping from a shadowy line, but when they looked up for the substance of the shadows nothing was to be seen except the clear, blue October air.

"My goodness!" gasped Mrs. Townsend. Her face assumed a strange gathering of wrath in the midst of her terror. Suddenly she made a determined move forward, although her husband strove to hold her back.

"You let me be," said she. She moved forward. Then she recoiled and gave a loud shriek. "The wet sheet flapped in my face," she cried. "Take me away, take me away!" Then she fainted. Between them they got her back to the house. "It was awful," she moaned when she came to herself, with the family all around her where she lay on the dining-room floor. "Oh, David, what do you suppose it is?"

"Nothing at all," replied David Townsend stoutly. He was remarkable for courage and staunch belief in actualities. He was now denying to himself that he had seen anything unusual.

"Oh, there was," moaned his wife.

"I saw something," said George, in a sullen, boyish bass.

The maid sobbed convulsively and so did Adrianna for sympathy.

"We won't talk any about it," said David. "Here, Jane, you drink this hot tea – it will do you good; and Cordelia, you hang out the clothes in our own yard. George, you go and put up the line for her."

"The line is out there," said George, with a jerk of his shoulder.

"Are you afraid?"

"No, I ain't," replied the boy resentfully, and went out with a pale face.

After that Cordelia hung the Townsend wash in the yard of their own house, standing always with her back to the vacant lot. As for David Townsend, he spent a good deal of his time in the lot watching the shadows, but he came to no explanation, although he strove to satisfy himself with many.

"I guess the shadows come from the smoke from our chimneys, or else the poplar tree," he said.

"Why do the shadows come on Monday mornings, and no other?" demanded his wife.

David was silent.

Very soon new mysteries arose. One day Cordelia rang the dinner-bell at their usual dinner hour, the same as in Townsend Centre, high noon, and the family assembled. With amazement Adrianna looked at the dishes on the table.

"Why, that's queer!" she said.

"What's queer?" asked her mother.

Cordelia stopped short as she was about setting a tumbler of water beside a plate, and the water slopped over.

"Why," said Adrianna, her face paling, "I – thought there was boiled dinner. I – smelt cabbage cooking."

"I knew there would something else come up," gasped Cordelia, leaning hard on the back of Adrianna's chair.

"What do you mean?" asked Mrs. Townsend sharply, but her own face began to assume the shocked pallor which it was so easy nowadays for all their faces to assume at the merest suggestion of anything out of the common.

"I smelt cabbage cooking all the morning up in my room," Adrianna said faintly, "and here's codfish and potatoes for dinner."

The Townsends all looked at one another. David rose with an exclamation and rushed out of the room. The others waited tremblingly. When he came back his face was lowering.

"What did you—" Mrs. Townsend asked hesitatingly.

"There's some smell of cabbage out there," he admitted reluctantly. Then he looked at her with a challenge. "It comes from the next house," he said. "Blows over our house."

"Our house is higher."

"I don't care; you can never account for such things."

"Cordelia," said Mrs. Townsend, "you go over to the next house and you ask if they've got cabbage for dinner."

Cordelia switched out of the room, her mouth set hard. She came back promptly.

"Says they never have cabbage," she announced with gloomy triumph and a conclusive glance at Mr. Townsend. "Their girl was real sassy."

"Oh, father, let's move away; let's sell the house," cried Adrianna in a panic-stricken tone.

"If you think I'm going to sell a house that I got as cheap as this one because we smell cabbage in a vacant lot, you're mistaken," replied David firmly.

"It isn't the cabbage alone," said Mrs. Townsend.

"And a few shadows," added David. "I am tired of such nonsense. I thought you had more sense, Jane."

"One of the boys at school asked me if we lived in the house next to the vacant lot on Wells Street and whistled when I said 'Yes'," remarked George.

"Let him whistle," said Mr. Townsend.

After a few hours the family, stimulated by Mr. Townsend's calm, common sense, agreed that it was exceedingly foolish to be disturbed by a mysterious odor of cabbage. They even laughed at themselves.

"I suppose we have got so nervous over those shadows hanging out clothes that we notice every little thing," conceded Mrs. Townsend.

"You will find out some day that that is no more to be regarded than the cabbage," said her husband.

"You can't account for that wet sheet hitting my face," said Mrs. Townsend, doubtfully.

"You imagined it."

"I *felt* it."

That afternoon things went on as usual in the household until nearly four o'clock. Adrianna went downtown to do some shopping. Mrs. Townsend sat sewing beside the bay window in her room, which was a front one in the third story. George had not got home. Mr. Townsend was writing a letter in the library. Cordelia was busy in the basement; the twilight, which was coming earlier and earlier every night, was beginning to gather, when suddenly there was a loud crash which shook the house from its foundations. Even the dishes on the sideboard rattled, and the glasses rang like bells. The pictures on the walls of Mrs. Townsend's room swung out from the walls. But that was not all: every looking-glass in the house cracked simultaneously – as nearly as they could judge – from top to bottom, then shivered into fragments over the floors. Mrs. Townsend was too frightened to scream. She sat huddled in her chair, gasping for breath, her eyes, rolling from side to side in incredulous terror, turned toward the street. She saw a great black group of people crossing it just in front of the vacant lot. There was something inexpressibly strange and gloomy about this moving group; there was an effect of sweeping, wavings and foldings of sable draperies and gleams of deadly white faces; then they passed. She twisted her head to see, and they disappeared in the vacant lot. Mr. Townsend came hurrying into the room; he was pale, and looked at once angry and alarmed.

"Did you fall?" he asked inconsequently, as if his wife, who was small, could have produced such a manifestation by a fall.

"Oh, David, what is it?" whispered Mrs. Townsend.

"Darned if I know!" said David.

"Don't swear. It's too awful. Oh, see the looking-glass, David!"

"I see it. The one over the library mantel is broken, too."

"Oh, it is a sign of death!"

Cordelia's feet were heard as she staggered on the stairs. She almost fell into the room. She reeled over to Mr. Townsend and clutched his arm. He cast a sidewise glance, half furious, half commiserating at her.

"Well, what is it all about?" he asked.

"I don't know. What is it? Oh, what is it? The looking-glass in the kitchen is broken. All over the floor. Oh, oh! What is it?"

"I don't know any more than you do. I didn't do it."

"Lookin'-glasses broken is a sign of death in the house," said Cordelia. "If it's me, I hope I'm ready; but I'd rather die than be so scared as I've been lately."

Mr. Townsend shook himself loose and eyed the two trembling women with gathering resolution.

"Now, look here, both of you," he said. "This is nonsense. You'll die sure enough of fright if you keep on this way. I was a fool myself to be startled. Everything it is is an earthquake."

"Oh, David!" gasped his wife, not much reassured.

"It is nothing but an earthquake," persisted Mr. Townsend. "It acted just like that. Things always are broken on the walls, and the middle of the room isn't affected. I've read about it."

Suddenly Mrs. Townsend gave a loud shriek and pointed.

"How do you account for that," she cried, "if it's an earthquake? Oh, oh, oh!"

She was on the verge of hysterics. Her husband held her firmly by the arm as his eyes followed the direction of her rigid pointing finger. Cordelia looked also, her eyes seeming converged to a bright point of fear. On the floor in front of the broken looking-glass lay a mass of black stuff in a grewsome long ridge.

"It's something you dropped there," almost shouted Mr. Townsend.

"It ain't. Oh!"

Mr. Townsend dropped his wife's arm and took one stride toward the object. It was a very long crape veil. He lifted it, and it floated out from his arm as if imbued with electricity.

"It's yours," he said to his wife.

"Oh, David, I never had one. You know, oh, you know I – shouldn't – unless you died. How came it there?"

"I'm darned if I know," said David, regarding it. He was deadly pale, but still resentful rather than afraid.

"Don't hold it; don't!"

"I'd like to know what in thunder all this means?" said David. He gave the thing an angry toss and it fell on the floor in exactly the same long heap as before.

Cordelia began to weep with racking sobs. Mrs. Townsend reached out and caught her husband's hand, clutching it hard with ice-cold fingers.

"What's got into this house, anyhow?" he growled.

"You'll have to sell it. Oh, David, we can't live here."

"As for my selling a house I paid only five thousand for when it's worth twenty-five, for any such nonsense as this, I won't!"

David gave one stride toward the black veil, but it rose from the floor and moved away before him across the room at exactly the same height as if suspended from a woman's head. He pursued it, clutching vainly, all around the room, then he swung himself on his heel with an exclamation and the thing fell to the floor again in the long heap. Then were heard hurrying feet on the stairs and Adrianna burst into the room. She ran straight to her father and clutched his arm; she tried to speak, but she chattered unintelligibly; her face was blue. Her father shook her violently.

"Adrianna, do have more sense!" he cried.

"Oh, David, how can you talk so?" sobbed her mother.

"I can't help it. I'm mad!" said he with emphasis. "What has got into this house and you all, anyhow?"

"What is it, Adrianna, poor child," asked her mother. "Only look what has happened here."

"It's an earthquake," said her father staunchly; "nothing to be afraid of."

"How do you account for *that*?" said Mrs. Townsend in an awful voice, pointing to the veil.

Adrianna did not look – she was too engrossed with her own terrors. She began to speak in a breathless voice.

"I – was – coming – by the vacant lot," she panted, "and – I– I– had my new hat in a paper bag and – a parcel of blue ribbon, and – I saw a crowd, an awful – oh! A whole crowd of people with white faces, as if – they were dressed all in black."

"Where are they now?"

"I don't know. Oh!" Adrianna sank gasping feebly into a chair.

"Get her some water, David," sobbed her mother.

David rushed with an impatient exclamation out of the room and returned with a glass of water which he held to his daughter's lips.

"Here, drink this!" he said roughly.

"Oh, David, how can you speak so?" sobbed his wife.

"I can't help it. I'm mad clean through," said David.

Then there was a hard bound upstairs, and George entered. He was very white, but he grinned at them with an appearance of unconcern.

"Hullo!" he said in a shaking voice, which he tried to control. "What on earth's to pay in that vacant lot now?"

"Well, what is it?" demanded his father.

"Oh, nothing, only – well, there are lights over it exactly as if there was a house there, just about where the windows would be. It looked as if you could walk right in, but when you look close there are those old dried-up weeds rattling away on the ground the same as ever. I looked at it and couldn't believe my eyes. A woman saw it, too. She came along just as I did. She gave one look, then she screeched and ran. I waited for someone else, but nobody came."

Mr. Townsend rushed out of the room.

"I daresay it'll be gone when he gets there," began George, then he stared round the room. "What's to pay here?" he cried.

"Oh, George, the whole house shook all at once, and all the looking-glasses broke," wailed his mother, and Adrianna and Cordelia joined.

George whistled with pale lips. Then Mr. Townsend entered.

"Well," asked George, "see anything?"

"I don't want to talk," said his father. "I've stood just about enough."

"We've got to sell out and go back to Townsend Centre," cried his wife in a wild voice. "Oh, David, say you'll go back."

"I won't go back for any such nonsense as this, and sell a twenty-five thousand dollar house for five thousand," said he firmly.

But that very night his resolution was shaken. The whole family watched together in the dining-room. They were all afraid to go to bed – that is, all except possibly Mr. Townsend. Mrs. Townsend declared firmly that she for one would leave that awful house and go back to Townsend Centre whether he came or not, unless they all stayed together and watched, and Mr. Townsend yielded. They chose the dining room for the reason that it was nearer the street should they wish to make their egress hurriedly, and they took up their station around the dining table on which Cordelia had placed a luncheon.

"It looks exactly as if we were watching with a corpse," she said in a horror-stricken whisper.

"Hold your tongue if you can't talk sense," said Mr. Townsend.

The dining room was very large, finished in oak, with a dark blue paper above the wainscotting. The old sign of the tavern, the Blue Leopard, hung over the mantel-shelf. Mr. Townsend had insisted on hanging it there. He had a curious pride in it. The family sat together until after midnight and nothing unusual happened. Mrs. Townsend began to nod; Mr. Townsend read the paper ostentatiously. Adrianna and Cordelia stared with roving eyes about the room, then at each other as if comparing notes on terror. George had a book which he studied furtively. All at once Adrianna gave a startled exclamation and Cordelia echoed her. George whistled faintly. Mrs. Townsend awoke with a start and Mr. Townsend's paper rattled to the floor.

"Look!" gasped Adrianna.

The sign of the Blue Leopard over the shelf glowed as if a lantern hung over it. The radiance was thrown from above. It grew brighter and brighter as they watched. The Blue Leopard seemed to crouch and spring with life. Then the door into the front hall opened – the outer door, which had been carefully locked. It squeaked and they all recognized it. They sat staring. Mr. Townsend was as transfixed as the rest. They heard the outer door shut, then the door into the room swung open and slowly that awful black group of people which they had seen in the afternoon entered. The Townsends with one accord rose and huddled together in a far corner; they all held to each other and stared. The people, their faces gleaming with a whiteness of death, their black robes waving and folding, crossed the room. They were a trifle above mortal height, or seemed so to the terrified eyes which saw them. They reached the mantel-shelf where the sign-board hung, then a black-draped long arm was seen to rise and make a motion, as if plying a knocker. Then the whole company passed out of sight, as if through the wall, and the room was as before. Mrs. Townsend was shaking in a nervous chill, Adrianna was almost fainting, Cordelia was in hysterics. David Townsend stood glaring in a curious way at the sign of the Blue Leopard. George stared at him with a look of horror. There was something in his father's face which made him forget everything else. At last he touched his arm timidly.

"Father," he whispered.

David turned and regarded him with a look of rage and fury, then his face cleared; he passed his hand over his forehead.

"Good Lord! What *did* come to me?" he muttered.

"You looked like that awful picture of old Tom Townsend in the garret in Townsend Centre, father," whimpered the boy, shuddering.

"Should think I might look like 'most any old cuss after such darned work as this," growled David, but his face was white. "Go and pour out some hot tea for your mother," he ordered the boy sharply. He himself shook Cordelia violently. "Stop such actions!" he shouted in her ears, and shook her again. "Ain't you a church member?" he demanded; "What be you afraid of? You ain't done nothin' wrong, have ye?"

Then Cordelia quoted Scripture in a burst of sobs and laughter.

"Behold, I was shapen in iniquity; and in sin did my mother conceive me," she cried out. "If I ain't done wrong, mebbe them that's come before me did, and when the Evil One and the Powers of Darkness is abroad I'm liable, I'm liable!" Then she laughed loud and long and shrill.

"If you don't hush up," said David, but still with that white terror and horror on his own face, "I'll bundle you out in that vacant lot whether or no. I mean it."

Then Cordelia was quiet, after one wild roll of her eyes at him. The colour was returning to Adrianna's cheeks; her mother was drinking hot tea in spasmodic gulps.

"It's after midnight," she gasped, "and I don't believe they'll come again tonight. Do you, David?"

"No, I don't," said David conclusively.

"Oh, David, we mustn't stay another night in this awful house."

"We won't. Tomorrow we'll pack off bag and baggage to Townsend Centre, if it takes all the fire department to move us," said David.

Adrianna smiled in the midst of her terror. She thought of Abel Lyons.

The next day Mr. Townsend went to the real estate agent who had sold him the house.

"It's no use," he said, "I can't stand it. Sell the house for what you can get. I'll give it away rather than keep it."

Then he added a few strong words as to his opinion of parties who sold him such an establishment. But the agent pleaded innocent for the most part.

"I'll own I suspected something wrong when the owner, who pledged me to secrecy as to his name, told me to sell that place for what I could get, and did not limit me. I had never heard anything, but I began to suspect something was wrong. Then I made a few inquiries and found out that there was a rumour in the neighborhood that there was something out of the usual about that vacant lot. I had wondered myself why it wasn't built upon. There was a story about it's being undertaken once, and the contract made, and the contractor dying; then another man took it and one of the workmen was killed on his way to dig the cellar, and the others struck. I didn't pay much attention to it. I never believed much in that sort of thing anyhow, and then, too, I couldn't find out that there had ever been anything wrong about the house itself, except as the people who had lived there were said to have seen and heard queer things in the vacant lot, so I thought you might be able to get along, especially as you didn't look like a man who was timid, and the house was such a bargain as I never handled before. But this you tell me is beyond belief."

"Do you know the names of the people who formerly owned the vacant lot?" asked Mr. Townsend.

"I don't know for certain," replied the agent, "for the original owners flourished long before your or my day, but I do know that the lot goes by the name of the old Gaston lot. What's the matter? Are you ill?"

"No; it is nothing," replied Mr. Townsend. "Get what you can for the house; perhaps another family might not be as troubled as we have been."

"I hope you are not going to leave the city?" said the agent, urbanely.

"I am going back to Townsend Centre as fast as steam can carry me after we get packed up and out of that cursed house," replied Mr. David Townsend.

He did not tell the agent nor any of his family what had caused him to start when told the name of the former owners of the lot. He remembered all at once the story of a ghastly murder which had taken place in the Blue Leopard. The victim's name was Gaston and the murderer had never been discovered.

The Bones of Home

Adele Gardner

CROOKED ROADS veered together in the quiet country night. A murderous bend in the road opened on a Cape Cod shrouded by trees.

Leaving her coffee in the car, Kirsten took Paul's hand and followed their realtor inside, over wood floors as smooth as a mirror. The paneling smelled like the house Kirsten's grandfather had built. "Look at that stove!"

"Popcorn!" Paul said, lifting the lid of the potbellied, black woodstove. The floor dipped beneath it. Dark shelves formed the far wall. Beyond them, a heavy door revealed rooms beyond.

The small, square dining room held blond shelves nestling under the windows. Realtor Anne walked ahead, turning on lights, while Paul disappeared around the corner. "Slow down!" Kirsten called. The dining room shone cheery yellow against night-black windows.

Kirsten followed the flow of the house to the kitchen. Over the counter, a square hole bored through the foot-thick wall to reveal another hallway. Paul chuckled, "It just keeps going and going!"

Beyond another door, a set of shallow, slanted stairs rose to a railed balcony. The smell of varnish and the rubber riser brought back Grandma's house.

"This is crazy!" She scampered up, laughing. Her hand slid up the polished rail. At the landing, low shelves hugged the angle where wall met slanted ceiling, a room that begged for games and toys. For a moment, she could almost see Grandma's rocking chair on that oval rag rug and her young brothers sitting at a low table, poring over children's magazines as the three of them waited for Grandma's funeral.

Down the hall, she found a crooked little room. The ceiling stooped so low, meeting the walls at shoulder height, that there was only room to stand along a narrow groove at the center. Built-in shelves jutted in sudden, cluttered spaces and ragged heights. The room twisted in three directions. Under a pitch-black window, the folded end seemed to cradle the shape of a missing bed, with a faint, dark streak at knee-height. She thought of the weary daybed where she'd slept at Grandma's, the mattress soggy with years, the springs singing every time she moved. Grandma had loved her house so much she'd refused to leave, until they found her on the kitchen floor, blood pouring from her mouth.

Paul put a warm hand on her shoulder. "Isn't it wonderful?" His voice was warm and rich.

Hers trembled. "It's a house to go mad in!"

Kirsten hurried through the other two rooms, brighter and larger than the first. Plush blue carpet, built-in shelves. The ceilings met walls in slopes, not edges sharp as a knife. "Come back downstairs!" she shouted.

Their feet clattered behind her. In the lower hallway, Kirsten exclaimed, "Look at all these doors!" She closed them; Paul joined in. A crazy shape emerged, a box built of doors, with only shared lintels to separate them. A nonagon, nine doors all told – kitchen, closets, downstairs bedrooms, dining room, living room, bathroom, stairs – a hidden oval in the heart of the house, doors branching out like spider arms. One bedroom bore a mirror. "There should be a mirror on every door," Kirsten said. "Like a funhouse."

"Perfect for your Halloween parties," Paul agreed.

"Listen," said Kirsten. Not even the hum of the refrigerator penetrated the heavy doors. And yet she felt the ghostly whispers of laughter from the children who must have played here, colors darting past the mirror, socks and striped shirts and bare knees and suspenders.

"They must have loved it here," she murmured. "So many places to hide."

"We're going to love it here," Paul said.

Feeling dizzy, she told Anne, "We made a pact to sleep on any decision."

"That's wise," Anne said warmly.

As Paul got behind the wheel, he quipped, "Two things every writer's got to have: the obligatory writer's cat, and an interesting house."

* * *

Two writers, setting up house together: Paul taught during the day and she worked at the theater by night. In the pale light of early morning, the old house breathed contentment, peaceful sounds as though the old family were still moving about quietly upstairs, trying not to wake them.

Kirsten sipped dark roast and set up her manuscript credenza, slots separating stories to submit from receipts and new publications. But she couldn't write. She walked in the woods behind the house, her little black cat Lucy running on a leash through cracking leaves and snapping twigs. Back home, she raided old notebooks for ideas, going through three cups of joe as she tried to stimulate a story. At last she went upstairs to unpack in the slow, sweet quiet.

Dust sifted through the air, as peaceful as snow. She smiled as she heard children calling up the street as they walked home from school. She arranged her childhood books along the shelves at the landing and set up her mother's dollhouse. Looking over the rail, she saw the bob of a golden head disappear around the corner. The door at the base of the stairs swung closed.

She laughed at herself, afraid. The sound blended with the laughter of the children outside. She looked out the window. Branches, her neighbor's attic window. No sidewalks. The street was empty.

Kirsten backed up into the crooked room, closing the door to block the muffled sound. Dust prickled her lungs. In the silence, loneliness pressed down on her like the weight of that angled ceiling. Behind her, she could hear labored breathing.

* * *

When Paul got back from teaching, he cooked an Italian dinner. He talked and joked, his baritone throaty and low. He poured more wine. And said, quite calmly, "You know, I haven't been able to write a word since we moved in here. Have you?"

Fear fluttered in her like moths. "No. Have you noticed anything strange about the house?"

"There aren't any real attics. The most frightening space of the house has been converted into rooms. Where will I get my inspiration?" he teased. "I think it's time for a writing duel. How about we let the house whisper to us? We'll lock ourselves in separate rooms and see what walks out." He leaned toward her on his elbows, intense. "At night when I lie awake, I hear the wind sighing in the eaves, moaning over the roof. Like the house is telling me stories."

"Okay," she said slowly. "When?"

"How about now? We've got some time to settle in before the witching hour."

"What if we can't stay awake?"

"We've got plenty of coffee. Pick the room that calls to you. I've got dibs on that tiny room upstairs!"

"The crooked room?" Coldness slipped down her back.

"What, you want it for yourself?" His smile hid an edge. "I thought the Florida room was your favorite."

He rose and gave her a long kiss. After a moment of stiffness, she melted into him.

"I really need to get working," he murmured into her hair. "Maybe afterwards..."

She sighed and turned away so he wouldn't see her disappointment. They were both so busy all the time. Paul flew up the stairs, the spare coffee maker under one arm, long legs carrying him swiftly out of sight.

Kirsten set out three cups of black coffee, so she'd have no excuse to leave. As she stared at the blank page, she felt crushed by the weight of the house above. She sipped and hunched over the table.

To her right, the folding doors rattled. The doors parted in the center and her little black cat padded in.

With a grateful laugh, Kirsten patted her lap. Lucy jumped up, lifting her paw to the page. "My little writer's cat," Kirsten murmured. She picked up the pen and put one word after another, not reading them, sipping black coffee and focusing on the Halloween cat who wove daintily among the office supplies.

As night deepened, Kirsten felt her mind opening up under the influence of all that coffee, like rats in their mazes whose spatial memory increased demonstrably with the aid of the bean. She propped her head on one wrist, letting the smell of the coffee mix with the smell of the old house as the words flowed through her, detaching her brain as she watched her hand scrawl, curling around the pen. Her brain expanded; she felt herself floating to fill the house, all those empty rooms above. Paul, contained within one, like a gnarled piece of the house itself.

Her hand finally stopped, jabbing the page with one last period. She flipped excitedly to the first page. 'The Bones of Home'. The story startled her. Their names – but these people didn't act anything like her and Paul. Her skin crawled. She crumpled the pages and fed them to the stove.

Paul seemed to be having more success. She knew better than to disturb him. But he had to teach tomorrow. At 5 a.m., she knocked and called his name. A delicious aroma floated into the hall. She heard the perk of a coffeemaker and a furious scratching like rats in the walls.

"Paul!" She pounded the door. Silence. She turned the cold, crystal knob.

White walls shone bright under one burning light. The roof slanted sharply down. Paul sprawled beneath it, his chest pressed flat to the floor, his limbs folded at awkward angles. In the cold, he huddled there with his clothes off, locked in a grotesque posture, as though broken bones poked out.

The walls swam in her vision, crooked and crazy. Not enough space to stand. The high point of the ceiling was a spike in her heart.

While she watched, Paul crawled under the sheer black window. Kirsten shuddered and forced herself to walk through the solid wall of cold. Sharp, white angles narrowed – the room was closing down on her. The cold poured in the cracks of the window.

He sat with his back to the wall, knees drawn up while his eyes went roving, roving, as though he were watching things she couldn't see. In rigid knuckles he clutched a fat, ragged sheaf of paper written thickly on both sides, words inscribed with such force that they bowed and punctured the pages. Broken pens and an overturned coffee cup littered the floor.

"Paul, are you all right?"

His cheeks were slack, the skin beneath his eyes dark, as though he'd been scared badly, and he now sat drained and calm on the other side. "I felt something shifting inside, like blocks moving around to solve a puzzle. A maze inside my head. I had to get it down just right. I couldn't tell what was happening until I started to write, and then it all fell into place." He unfolded to his lank, lean height. Wobbling in place, he thrust the pages at her. Then he walked past her down the stairs.

She caught him at the landing, steadying him as he hesitated, his foot shaking over the abyss. He looked at her and smiled. "Earlobes are funny things," he said. "Earlobes, earlobes, earlobes," he repeated, and laughed. Her skin crawled. "Joints and fingers. What freakish things. Why don't feet fold on either side? They just flap now. They don't make sense. No house could stand on two feet."

She tucked him into bed. And then, because she could do nothing else, she hunkered down to read his work. Soon she could not move, except to turn a page. Paul's sheets covered her knees. She was afraid to touch them.

At last, rose spilled through the curtains. Paul slept, curled like a baby. He twitched; a flailing arm struck her. He gave a sharp cry, tossing his head, his mouth distended horribly, the corners reaching his chin. He moaned, his vocal chords loose and rattling.

"Paul, wake up!"

He panted, staring into her, his eyes huge, as though he saw through to the architecture beneath her skin.

"I – I'm a murderer," he said.

"You were having a nightmare!"

"That was no dream," he said, his voice low, full of despair. "It was real, Kay, I swear. I held the knife. My hands were covered in blood!"

The look in his eyes terrified her.

* * *

After that night, Paul did all his writing in the crooked room, "Up where I keep my spells," he joked. When he first came down, he'd look out the corners of his eyes at things, as though something wasn't quite right. He frequently reached out a hand for balance.

She scarcely saw him. He kept the coffee maker up there and used the standing-room-only second-floor toilet the size of a linen closet. After they ate lunch together, he retreated to the crooked room for the night. She'd get back from the theater to find him still immured.

She lay awake, feeling like a sick child waiting for the night to end. She couldn't stop listening for the creak of Paul's feet coming down the stairs. But even with his warmth beside her, it was no better. He'd curl quickly on his side, without even a perfunctory kiss, as though he didn't want to touch her. And while he slept, Paul cried out as if he were being murdered; but then out slipped a groan of pleasure, and he would grin in his sleep, a sickening, skeletal smile.

Despite the oddness of their nights, they went about their morning routine as usual, reading the newspaper, eating scrambled eggs and English muffins. Talking about the craft.

Paul said, "Every night I end up in someone else's head. We kill, and I write the story. It's always someone close – someone's mother, sister, or little kid."

"You're spending too much time up there, thinking about horror."

"I'm telling you, they aren't dreams." He showed her the morning paper.

Her face fell. "Your – story."

"My dream. Down to the last severed finger."

"It's a coincidence."

"God, I hope not. It was horrible."

Her scalp prickled. Fear of him washed over her. She said quickly, "So you were attuned to him in some way. Writing in a frenzy like that. All writers touch something true."

"No. I killed that old woman. He would never have done it on his own. He lacked the guts."

"Murders happen all the time!"

"And nobody thinks about how the murderers feel! Think what it must be like to wake up and discover that your hands are covered with blood. That you tortured your own brother. And I get away with it – I wake up! The poor sap whose body I've stolen is stuck with a murder he doesn't know why he committed."

"Paul, you're scaring me."

"Kirsten," he said, gripping her wrists, "I wasn't a writer – not really – before I set foot in this house. I was a dilettante. I spent years polishing a single story, until it shone so much no one could bear to look at it."

He took her upstairs to his locked file cabinet, savagely pulled open the drawers to show her, then stalked away. She ran her fingers through the folders, noticing the dates. All these stories had been written since they'd moved in; all of them had printouts of email acceptance letters clipped to the front, obscuring the first words. Each was brilliant – a perfect, bloody gem.

She flipped through page after page, wanting desperately to reach the end. Masterworks, but so hideous. *Is this his true soul?* No – she remembered what he had been. She turned to the shelves to find the small press magazines.

As if by black magic, that small selection had swelled to fill three shelves, magazines and anthologies and printouts from e-zines. In some of the earlier stories, she now saw little twinges of horror that yawned between the cracks – a moment's glitch, a bump in the road – how odd those moments were.

Paul, gentle Paul, whose horror stories had always been too literary to be shocking, had blossomed at last into these scarlet blotches. And in each new tale, the house crept in, bits and pieces – a room here, a wall there, transported whole and real enough to feel the rough grain of the paint, cool as lead against her hand.

That night, they went to bed later than usual, as though Paul were avoiding the issue. He shuffled a pile of student essays. Normally he stayed at the college however late it took, so he could leave his work behind. "Since when do you carry those out of the office?" she asked.

"Since I'm afraid to read anything more interesting before going to sleep."

"What will you write, if you're afraid of your own genre?"

"What I've always written. I can't very well stop. They love me out there. Besides, do you know what happens when I stop? These leaking images build up in my head like blood pooling in a dead limb. My head starts to feel swollen. Sodden. Ready to explode."

"Can I help take your mind off it?" She already knew the answer. They hadn't made love since they'd moved in.

He gave a ragged sigh. "No."

"Why not?" she whispered.

"Kay, it's like I'm remembering things only the house knows. There's something here I have to uncover, deep inside. I can feel it poking through my chest."

She stared at him. He stared back, his face pinched. He looked bewildered. She brushed the raven curls back from his forehead. Kissed him. They slept.

He woke her in the middle of night. She fumbled groggily for reason, trying to comfort him, cuddling close to hold him still. He kicked hard, and she grunted in pain; he kneed her in the stomach, clawed at her arms. Then the twitching stopped, and he looked at her with wide, frightened eyes.

He cleared his throat. "You need to sleep in the guest room tonight."

"It's okay, baby – you were dreaming, that's all."

He grabbed her wrist. "Get out of here, Kay," he said in a strangled voice. His eyes – maniacal – murderous –

She fled.

* * *

Kirsten sipped her morning coffee. She could feel the house pressing on her, the rooms going on and on, flattening her mind, her emotions.

With Halloween around the corner, she fixed a mirror to each door in the oval center. She hung vampires and ghouls. Skeletons jumped on strings like Dürer's dance of death. Tiny plastic pumpkins lined the windows. She brought out her mother's noisemakers, metallic and cold, their orange painted with owls and witches. She swung one, the sharp metal tooth roaring. The sound brought back her first Halloween, when she'd come downstairs to find a demon in the dining room. At her fright, her father had peeled off the mask.

As she prepared the decorations, she heard faint noises in the walls. Was something listening? She crouched in the crooked room, where the waist-high closet yawned on darkness. She closed her eyes, hand out to touch the wall. "Please, let my husband go!"

The house answered with a chuckle as dry as Grandma's. Kirsten tasted the papery, wrinkled cheek she'd been afraid to kiss before Grandma died.

On Halloween morning, fog settled between the trees. Kirsten fixed candied apples and pumpkin pie, bowls of spaghetti brains and olive eyes. She dressed as a black cat. Paul had chosen a skeleton costume, its glowing white bones painted with the precision of an anatomist. He looked so worn and drawn, his eyes black with lack of sleep, jittery with the caffeine that held him up like a puppet master.

"Don't you think it's odd that we decorate with dead things?" he mused. "Husks of corn, fallen leaves, carved pumpkins, skeletons."

"Most of those things have a hidden life, sleeping inside," she said, to comfort him.

He cursed as he yanked the skeleton suit over his head. Then he took a nap, lying ready in his bones.

The neighborhood children showed up right on time. She led them into the living room amid black balloons and orange streamers, where they tossed beanbag pumpkins and skeleton dice and bobbed for apples. Kirsten draped Lucy around her neck like a stole, the cat warm and purring, her little paws dangling on either side. Her own feet light as a kitten's, Kirsten floated through the rooms.

The party was a great success. Blindfolded children fished in a bowl of slimed olives for dead men's eyeballs, rummaged a head of lettuce for a desiccated brain, and fingered the spaghetti slime of entrails – the soft anatomy that would rot soonest, leaving only the bones. Those bones stepped out from behind a curtain, gaunt and tall: Paul held out the prize to a child who turned and ran. The skeleton laughed – a hollow sound.

Kirsten sent them off on a Halloween hide-'n'-seek. The children ran hither and yon, laughing, jumping out to scare, racing to the sanctuary at the center. In the mirrors, small legs looked cold and blue in antique cuffed shorts and suspenders. Buster Browns adorned small necks. The faint echo of saddle shoes ghosted over the floorboards. Mirrored, giggling, antique children with goose-pimpled, outstretched arms ran from modern-day masked gnomes, red devils, green sea monsters, caped villains, and lovely princesses. They all flowed by so fast, like a swirl of leaves, the live children mingling with the reflected dead.

"Children," Kirsten called. She opened the door to the stairs. The mini-monsters hovered at the bottom, looking up at windows hung with skeletons and ghosts glowing in the dark. They climbed to find their prizes.

Paul joined her at the foot of the stairs, his bones shining. He didn't need the mask. His face was wasted, ashen, the angular hollows of his eyes shadowed like the sockets of a skull. Grinning, his glowing bones followed them through the dusk. Children screamed down the stairs, the front door slamming behind them.

Paul came downstairs, his hand brushing the rail, his face deathly white.

"Is something wrong?"

He put a hand on his stomach. "I think I'm getting an ulcer. Maybe it's all that coffee. I'm going to lie down."

* * *

A musty smell rose within the house as rain drummed on the roof. Kirsten stood on one side of the locked bedroom door.

Paul's weak voice barely penetrated the wood. "Those murders. I know what caused them."

Halloween's euphoria vanished, leaving her to face the fear she'd held at bay. "What?"

"I'm not ready," he groaned, sounding wretched.

"Paul, what's wrong?" She laid her ear against the wood. "Paul – please! I love you!"

"Don't come in," he cried – the moan of the man echoing with the high, frightened plea of a boy. He grunted, panting. "I'm afraid—"

She felt the house shifting in her head, a sinister architecture whose space she could taste like coffee. She rammed the door with her shoulder. The old lock popped loose. She tumbled in.

Paul lay in bed, covers pulled to his armpits, hands laced tight on his chest as though holding himself together. The bedside lamp cast crooked shadows, a bright orange halo on the ceiling above it. He stared at it, the whites of his eyes shining.

Then Paul cried out and arched his back like a woman in labor. The sheet slipped from his naked chest. He closed his eyes, his face rigid and straining over his bones.

Screaming, Paul fell back as his skin split from sternum to groin. Glands and organs shone red as cherries. Bended joints and knees and folded elbows crouched close inside. The soft, malleable cartilage unfolded.

And climbed out.

Thick and hard, an angular form stepped free, draped in a haze of blood. It gleamed pearly white as it sloughed off the red shell.

Paul's features flopped back on the bed, lifeless as a mask.

What had lain hidden stalked out the door, shifting into whatever shape the house desired.

The Old Nurse's Story

Elizabeth Gaskell

YOU KNOW, my dears, that your mother was an orphan, and an only child; and I dare say you have heard that your grandfather was a clergyman up in Westmoreland, where I come from. I was just a girl in the village school, when, one day, your grandmother came in to ask the mistress if there was any scholar there who would do for a nurse-maid; and mighty proud I was, I can tell ye, when the mistress called me up, and spoke to my being a good girl at my needle, and a steady, honest girl, and one whose parents were very respectable, though they might be poor. I thought I should like nothing better than to serve the pretty young lady, who was blushing as deep as I was, as she spoke of the coming baby, and what I should have to do with it. However, I see you don't care so much for this part of my story, as for what you think is to come, so I'll tell you at once. I was engaged and settled at the parsonage before Miss Rosamond (that was the baby, who is now your mother) was born. To be sure, I had little enough to do with her when she came, for she was never out of her mother's arms, and slept by her all night long; and proud enough was I sometimes when missis trusted her to me. There never was such a baby before or since, though you've all of you been fine enough in your turns; but for sweet, winning ways, you've none of you come up to your mother. She took after her mother, who was a real lady born; a Miss Furnivall, a grand-daughter of Lord Furnivall's, in Northumberland. I believe she had neither brother nor sister, and had been brought up in my lord's family till she had married your grandfather, who was just a curate, son to a shopkeeper in Carlisle – but a clever, fine gentleman as ever was – and one who was a right-down hard worker in his parish, which was very wide, and scattered all abroad over the Westmoreland Fells. When your mother, little Miss Rosamond, was about four or five years old, both her parents died in a fortnight – one after the other. Ah! That was a sad time. My pretty young mistress and me was looking for another baby, when my master came home from one of his long rides, wet and tired, and took the fever he died of; and then she never held up her head again, but just lived to see her dead baby, and have it laid on her breast, before she sighed away her life. My mistress had asked me, on her death-bed, never to leave Miss Rosamond; but if she had never spoken a word, I would have gone with the little child to the end of the world.

The next thing, and before we had well stilled our sobs, the executors and guardians came to settle the affairs. They were my poor young mistress's own cousin, Lord Furnivall, and Mr. Esthwaite, my master's brother, a shopkeeper in Manchester; not so well-to-do then as he was afterwards, and with a large family rising about him. Well! I don't know if it were their settling, or because of a letter my mistress wrote on her death-bed to her cousin, my lord; but somehow it was settled that Miss Rosamond and me were to go to Furnivall Manor House, in Northumberland; and my lord spoke as if it had been her mother's wish that she should live with his family, and as if he had no objections, for that one or two more or less could make no difference in so grand a household. So, though that was not the way in which I should have wished the coming of my bright and pretty pet to have been looked at – who was like a sunbeam in any family, be it never so grand – I was well pleased that all the folks in the Dale should stare and admire, when they heard I was going to be young lady's maid at my Lord Furnivall's at Furnivall Manor.

But I made a mistake in thinking we were to go and live where my lord did. It turned out that the family had left Furnivall Manor House fifty years or more. I could not hear that my poor young mistress had ever been there, though she had been brought up in the family; and I was sorry for that, for I should have liked Miss Rosamond's youth to have passed where her mother's had been.

My lord's gentleman, from whom I asked as many questions as I durst, said that the Manor House was at the foot of the Cumberland Fells, and a very grand place; that an old Miss Furnivall, a great-aunt of my lord's, lived there, with only a few servants; but that it was a very healthy place, and my lord had thought that it would suit Miss Rosamond very well for a few years, and that her being there might perhaps amuse his old aunt.

I was bidden by my lord to have Miss Rosamond's things ready by a certain day. He was a stern, proud man, as they say all the Lords Furnivall were; and he never spoke a word more than was necessary. Folk did say he had loved my young mistress; but that, because she knew that his father would object, she would never listen to him, and married Mr. Esthwaite; but I don't know. He never married, at any rate. But he never took much notice of Miss Rosamond; which I thought he might have done if he had cared for her dead mother. He sent his gentleman with us to the Manor House, telling him to join him at Newcastle that same evening; so there was no great length of time for him to make us known to all the strangers before he, too, shook us off; and we were left, two lonely young things (I was not eighteen) in the great old Manor House. It seems like yesterday that we drove there. We had left our own dear parsonage very early, and we had both cried as if our hearts would break, though we were travelling in my lord's carriage, which I thought so much of once. And now it was long past noon on a September day, and we stopped to change horses for the last time at a little smoky town, all full of colliers and miners. Miss Rosamond had fallen asleep, but Mr. Henry told me to waken her, that she might see the park and the Manor House as we drove up. I thought it rather a pity; but I did what he bade me, for fear he should complain of me to my lord. We had left all signs of a town, or even a village, and were then inside the gates of a large wild park – not like the parks here in the south, but with rocks, and the noise of running water, and gnarled thorn-trees, and old oaks, all white and peeled with age.

The road went up about two miles, and then we saw a great and stately house, with many trees close around it, so close that in some places their branches dragged against the walls when the wind blew, and some hung broken down; for no one seemed to take much charge of the place; to lop the wood, or to keep the moss-covered carriage-way in order. Only in front of the house all was clear. The great oval drive was without a weed; and neither tree nor creeper was allowed to grow over the long, many-windowed front; at both sides of which a wing projected, which were each the ends of other side fronts; for the house, although it was so desolate, was even grander than I expected. Behind it rose the Fells, which seemed unenclosed and bare enough; and on the left hand of the house, as you stood facing it, was a little, old-fashioned flower-garden, as I found out afterwards. A door opened out upon it from the west front; it had been scooped out of the thick, dark wood for some old Lady Furnivall; but the branches of the great forest-trees had grown and overshadowed it again, and there were very few flowers that would live there at that time.

When we drove up to the great front entrance, and went into the hall, I thought we should be lost – it was so large, and vast, and grand. There was a chandelier all of bronze, hung down from the middle of the ceiling; and I had never seen one before, and looked at it all in amaze. Then, at one end of the hall, was a great fireplace, as large as the sides of the houses in my country, with massy andirons and dogs to hold the wood; and by it were heavy, old-fashioned sofas. At the opposite end of the hall, to the left as you went in – on the western side – was an organ built into the wall, and so large that it filled up the best part of that end. Beyond it, on the same side, was a door; and opposite, on each side of the fireplace, were also doors leading to the east front; but those I never went through as long as I stayed in the house, so I can't tell you what lay beyond.

The afternoon was closing in, and the hall, which had no fire lighted in it, looked dark and gloomy; but we did not stay there a moment. The old servant, who had opened the door for us, bowed to Mr. Henry, and took us in through the door at the further side of the great organ, and led us through several smaller halls and passages into the west drawing-room, where he said that Miss Furnivall was sitting. Poor little Miss Rosamond held very tight to me, as if she were scared and lost in that great place; and as for myself, I was not much better. The west drawing-room was very cheerful-looking, with a warm fire in it, and plenty of good, comfortable furniture about. Miss Furnivall was an old lady not far from eighty, I should think, but I do not know. She was thin and tall, and had a face as full of fine wrinkles as if they had been drawn all over it with a needle's point. Her eyes were very watchful, to make up, I suppose, for her being so deaf as to be obliged to use a trumpet. Sitting with her, working at the same great piece of tapestry, was Mrs. Stark, her maid and companion, and almost as old as she was. She had lived with Miss Furnivall ever since they both were young, and now she seemed more like a friend than a servant; she looked so cold, and grey, and stony, as if she had never loved or cared for anyone; and I don't suppose she did care for anyone, except her mistress; and, owing to the great deafness of the latter, Mrs. Stark treated her very much as if she were a child. Mr. Henry gave some message from my lord, and then he bowed goodbye to us all – taking no notice of my sweet little Miss Rosamond's outstretched hand – and left us standing there, being looked at by the two old ladies through their spectacles.

I was right glad when they rung for the old footman who had shown us in at first, and told him to take us to our rooms. So we went out of that great drawing-room, and into another sitting-room, and out of that, and then up a great flight of stairs, and along a broad gallery – which was something like a library, having books all down one side, and windows and writing tables all down the other – till we came to our rooms, which I was not sorry to hear were just over the kitchens; for I began to think I should be lost in that wilderness of a house. There was an old nursery, that had been used for all the little lords and ladies long ago, with a pleasant fire burning in the grate, and the kettle boiling on the hob, and tea-things spread out on the table; and out of that room was the night-nursery, with a little crib for Miss Rosamond close to my bed. And old James called up Dorothy, his wife, to bid us welcome; and both he and she were so hospitable and kind, that by-and-by Miss Rosamond and me felt quite at home; and by the time tea was over, she was sitting on Dorothy's knee, and chattering away as fast as her little tongue could go. I soon found out that Dorothy was from Westmoreland, and that bound her and me together, as it were; and I would never wish to meet with kinder people than were old James and his wife. James had lived pretty nearly all his life in my lord's family, and thought there was no one so grand as they. He even looked down a little on his wife; because, till he had married her, she had never lived in any but a farmer's household. But he was very fond of her, as well he might be. They had one servant under them, to do all the rough work. Agnes they called her; and she and me, and James and Dorothy, with Miss Furnivall and Mrs. Stark, made up the family; always remembering my sweet little Miss Rosamond! I used to wonder what they had done before she came, they thought so much of her now. Kitchen and drawing-room, it was all the same. The hard, sad Miss Furnivall, and the cold Mrs. Stark, looked pleased when she came fluttering in like a bird, playing and pranking hither and thither, with a continual murmur, and pretty prattle of gladness. I am sure, they were sorry many a time when she flitted away into the kitchen, though they were too proud to ask her to stay with them, and were a little surprised at her taste; though to be sure, as Mrs. Stark said, it was not to be wondered at, remembering what stock her father had come of. The great, old rambling house was a famous place for little Miss Rosamond. She made expeditions all over it, with me at her heels: all, except the east wing, which was never opened, and whither we never thought of going. But in the western and northern part was many a pleasant room; full of things that were curiosities to us, though they might not have been to people who had seen more. The windows were darkened by the sweeping boughs of the trees, and the ivy which had overgrown them; but, in the green gloom, we could manage to see old china jars and carved ivory boxes, and great heavy books, and, above all, the old pictures!

Once, I remember, my darling would have Dorothy go with us to tell us who they all were; for they were all portraits of some of my lord's family, though Dorothy could not tell us the names of every one. We had gone through most of the rooms, when we came to the old state drawing room over the hall, and there was a picture of Miss Furnivall; or, as she was called in those days, Miss Grace, for she was the younger sister. Such a beauty she must have been! But with such a set, proud look, and such scorn looking out of her handsome eyes, with her eyebrows just a little raised, as if she wondered how anyone could have the impertinence to look at her, and her lip curled at us, as we stood there gazing. She had a dress on, the like of which I had never seen before, but it was all the fashion when she was young: a hat of some soft white stuff like beaver, pulled a little over her brows, and a beautiful plume of feathers sweeping round it on one side; and her gown of blue satin was open in front to a quilted white stomacher.

"Well, to be sure!" said I, when I had gazed my fill. "Flesh is grass, they do say; but who would have thought that Miss Furnivall had been such an out-and-out beauty, to see her now?"

"Yes," said Dorothy. "Folks change sadly. But if what my master's father used to say was true, Miss Furnivall, the elder sister, was handsomer than Miss Grace. Her picture is here somewhere; but, if I show it you, you must never let on, even to James, that you have seen it. Can the little lady hold her tongue, think you?" asked she.

I was not so sure, for she was such a little sweet, bold, open-spoken child, so I set her to hide herself; and then I helped Dorothy to turn a great picture, that leaned with its face towards the wall, and was not hung up as the others were. To be sure, it beat Miss Grace for beauty; and I think, for scornful pride, too, though in that matter it might be hard to choose. I could have looked at it an hour but Dorothy seemed half frightened at having shown it to me, and hurried it back again, and bade me run and find Miss Rosamond, for that there were some ugly places about the house, where she should like ill for the child to go. I was a brave, high-spirited girl, and thought little of what the old woman said, for I liked hide-and-seek as well as any child in the parish; so off I ran to find my little one.

As winter drew on, and the days grew shorter, I was sometimes almost certain that I heard a noise as if someone was playing on the great organ in the hall. I did not hear it every evening; but, certainly, I did very often, usually when I was sitting with Miss Rosamond, after I had put her to bed, and keeping quite still and silent in the bedroom. Then I used to hear it booming and swelling away in the distance. The first night, when I went down to my supper, I asked Dorothy who had been playing music, and James said very shortly that I was a gowk to take the wind soughing among the trees for music; but I saw Dorothy look at him very fearfully, and Bessy, the kitchen maid, said something beneath her breath, and went quite white. I saw they did not like my question, so I held my peace till I was with Dorothy alone, when I knew I could get a good deal out of her. So, the next day, I watched my time, and I coaxed and asked her who it was that played the organ; for I knew that it was the organ and not the wind well enough, for all I had kept silence before James. But Dorothy had had her lesson, I'll warrant, and never a word could I get from her. So then I tried Bessy, though I had always held my head rather above her, as I was evened to James and Dorothy, and she was little better than their servant. So she said I must never, never tell; and if ever told, I was never to say she had told me; but it was a very strange noise, and she had heard it many a time, but most of all on winter nights, and before storms; and folks did say it was the old lord playing on the great organ in the hall, just as he used to do when he was alive; but who the old lord was, or why he played, and why he played on stormy winter evenings in particular, she either could not or would not tell me. Well! I told you I had a brave heart; and I thought it was rather pleasant to have that grand music rolling about the house, let who would be the player; for now it rose above the great gusts of wind, and wailed and triumphed just like a living creature, and then it fell to a softness most complete, only it was always music, and tunes, so it was nonsense to call it the wind. I thought at first, that it might be Miss Furnivall who played, unknown to Bessy; but one day, when I was in the hall by myself, I opened the organ and peeped all about it and around it, as I had done to the organ in Crosthwaite Church once before, and I saw it was all broken and destroyed inside, though it looked so brave and fine; and then, though it was noon-day, my flesh began to creep a little, and I shut it up, and run away pretty quickly to my own bright nursery; and I did not like hearing the music for some time after that, any more than James and Dorothy did. All this time Miss Rosamond was making herself more and more beloved. The old ladies liked her to dine with them at their early dinner. James stood behind Miss Furnivall's chair, and I behind Miss Rosamond's all in state; and, after dinner, she would play about in a corner of the great drawing room as still as any mouse, while Miss Furnivall slept, and I had my dinner in the kitchen. But she was glad enough to come to me in the nursery afterwards; for, as she said Miss Furnivall was so sad, and Mrs. Stark so dull; but she and I were merry enough; and, by-and-by, I got not to care for that weird rolling music, which did one no harm, if we did not know where it came from.

That winter was very cold. In the middle of October the frosts began, and lasted many, many weeks. I remember one day, at dinner, Miss Furnivall lifted up her sad, heavy eyes, and said to Mrs. Stark, "I am afraid we shall have a terrible winter," in a strange kind of meaning way. But Mrs. Stark pretended not to hear, and talked very loud of something else. My little lady and I did not care for the frost; not we! As long as it was dry, we climbed up the steep brows behind the house, and went up on the Fells which were bleak and bare enough, and there we ran races in the fresh, sharp air; and once we came down by a new path, that took us past the two old gnarled holly-trees, which grew about halfway down by the east side of the house. But the days grew shorter and shorter, and the old lord, if it was he, played away, more and more stormily and sadly, on the great organ. One Sunday afternoon – it must have been towards the end of November – I asked Dorothy to take charge of little missy when she came out of the drawing room, after Miss Furnivall had had her nap; for it was too cold to take her with me to church, and yet I wanted to go, and Dorothy was glad enough to promise and was so fond of the child, that all seemed well; and Bessy and I set off very briskly, though the sky hung heavy and black over the white earth, as if the night had never fully gone away, and the air, though still, was very biting.

"We shall have a fall of snow," said Bessy to me. And sure enough, even while we were in church, it came down thick, in great large flakes – so thick, it almost darkened the windows. It had stopped snowing before we came out, but it lay soft, thick, and deep beneath our feet, as we tramped home. Before we got to the hall, the moon rose, and I think it was lighter then – what with the moon, and what with the white dazzling snow – than it had been when we went to church, between two and three o'clock. I have not told you that Miss Furnivall and Mrs. Stark never went to church; they used to read the prayers together, in their quiet, gloomy way; they seemed to feel the Sunday very long without their tapestry work to be busy at. So when I went to Dorothy in the kitchen, to fetch Miss Rosamond and take her upstairs with me, I did not much wonder when the old woman told me that the ladies had kept the child with them, and that she had never come to the kitchen, as I had bidden her, when she was tired of behaving pretty in the drawing-room. So I took off my things and went to find her, and bring her to her supper in the nursery. But when I went into the best drawing-room, there sat the two old ladies, very still and quiet, dropping out a word now and then, but looking as if nothing so bright and merry as Miss Rosamond had ever been near them. Still I thought she might be hiding from me; it was one of her pretty ways – and that she had persuaded them to look as if they knew nothing about her; so I went softly peeping under this sofa and behind that chair, making believe I was sadly frightened at not finding her.

"What's the matter, Hester?" said Mrs. Stark sharply. I don't know if Miss Furnivall had seen me for, as I told you, she was very deaf, and she sat quite still, idly staring into the fire, with her hopeless face. "I'm only looking for my little Rosy Posy," replied I, still thinking that the child was there, and near me, though I could not see her.

"Miss Rosamond is not here," said Mrs. Stark. "She went away, more than an hour ago, to find Dorothy." And she, too, turned and went on looking into the fire.

My heart sank at this, and I began to wish I had never left my darling. I went back to Dorothy and told her. James was gone out for the day, but she, and me, and Bessy took lights, and went up into the nursery first; and then we roamed over the great, large house, calling and entreating Miss Rosamond to come out of her hiding place, and not frighten us to death in that way. But there was no answer; no sound.

"Oh!" said I, at last, "Can she have got into the east wing and hidden there?"

But Dorothy said it was not possible, for that she herself had never been in there; that the doors were always locked, and my lord's steward had the keys, she believed; at any rate, neither she nor James had ever seen them: so I said I would go back, and see if, after all, she was not hidden in the drawing room, unknown to the old ladies; and if I found her there, I said, I would whip her well for the fright she had given me; but I never meant to do it. Well, I went back to the west drawing room, and I told Mrs. Stark we could not find her anywhere, and asked for leave to look all about the furniture there, for I thought now that she might have fallen asleep in some warm, hidden corner; but no! We looked – Miss Furnivall got up and looked, trembling all over – and she was nowhere there; then we set off again, everyone in the house, and looked in all the places we had searched before, but we could not find her. Miss Furnivall shivered and shook so much, that Mrs. Stark took her back into the warm drawing room; but not before they had made me promise to bring her to them when she was found. Well-a-day! I began to think she never would be found, when I bethought me to look into the great front court, all covered with snow. I was upstairs when I looked out; but, it was such clear moonlight, I could see, quite plain, two little footprints, which might be traced from the hall door and round the corner of the east wing. I don't know how I got down, but I tugged open the great stiff hall door, and, throwing the skirt of my gown over my head for a cloak, I ran out. I turned the east corner, and there a black shadow fell on the snow but when I came again into the moonlight, there were the little footmarks going up – up to the Fells. It was bitter cold; so cold, that the air almost took the skin off my face as I ran; but I ran on, crying to think how my poor little darling must be perished and frightened. I was within sight of the holly trees, when I saw a shepherd coming down the hill, bearing something in his arms wrapped in his maud. He shouted to me, and asked me if I had lost a bairn; and, when I could not speak for crying, he bore towards me, and I saw my wee bairnie, lying still, and white, and stiff in his arms, as if she had been dead. He told me he had been up the Fells to gather in his sheep, before the deep cold of night came on, and that under the holly trees (black marks on the hillside, where no other bush was for miles around) he had found my little lady – my lamb – my queen – my darling – stiff and cold in the terrible sleep which is frost-begotten. Oh! The joy and the tears of having her in my arms once again for I would not let him carry her; but took her, maud and all, into my own arms, and held her near my own warm neck and heart, and felt the life stealing slowly back again into her little gentle limbs. But she was still insensible when we reached the hall, and I had no breath for speech. We went in by the kitchen door.

"Bring the warming pan," said I; and I carried her upstairs, and began undressing her by the nursery fire, which Bessy had kept up. I called my little lammie all the sweet and playful names I could think of – even while my eyes were blinded by my tears; and at last, oh! at length she opened her large blue eyes. Then I put her into her warm bed, and sent Dorothy down to tell Miss Furnivall that all was well; and I made up my mind to sit by my darling's bedside the live-long night. She fell away into a soft sleep as soon as her pretty head had touched the pillow, and I watched by her till morning light; when she wakened up bright and clear – or so I thought at first – and, my dears, so I think now.

She said that she had fancied that she should like to go to Dorothy, for that both the old ladies were asleep, and it was very dull in the drawing room; and that, as she was going through the west lobby, she saw the snow through the high window falling – falling – soft and steady; but she wanted to see it lying pretty and white on the ground; so she made her way into the great hall: and then, going to the window, she saw it bright and soft upon the drive; but while she stood there, she saw a little girl, not so old as she was, "but so pretty," said my darling; "and this little girl beckoned to me to come out; and oh, she was so pretty and so sweet, I could not choose but go." And then this other little girl had taken her by the hand, and side by side the two had gone round the east corner.

"Now you are a naughty little girl, and telling stories," said I. "What would your good mamma, that is in heaven, and never told a story in her life, say to her little Rosamond, if she heard her – and I dare say she does – telling stories!"

"Indeed, Hester," sobbed out my child, "I'm telling you true. Indeed I am."

"Don't tell me!" said I, very stern. "I tracked you by your foot-marks through the snow; there were only yours to be seen: and if you had had a little girl to go hand-in-hand with you up the hill, don't you think the footprints would have gone along with yours?"

"I can't help it, dear, dear Hester," said she, crying, "if they did not; I never looked at her feet, but she held my hand fast and tight in her little one, and it was very, very cold. She took me up the Fell-path, up to the holly trees; and there I saw a lady weeping and crying; but when she saw me, she hushed her weeping, and smiled very proud and grand, and took me on her knee, and began to lull me to sleep, and that's all, Hester – but that is true; and my dear mamma knows it is," said she, crying. So I thought the child was in a fever, and pretended to believe her, as she went over her story – over and over again, and always the same. At last Dorothy knocked at the door with Miss Rosamond's breakfast; and she told me the old ladies were down in the eating parlour, and that they wanted to speak to me. They had both been into the night-nursery the evening before, but it was after Miss Rosamond was asleep; so they had only looked at her – not asked me any questions.

"I shall catch it," thought I to myself, as I went along the north gallery. "And yet," I thought, taking courage, "it was in their charge I left her; and it's they that's to blame for letting her steal away unknown and unwatched." So I went in boldly, and told my story. I told it all to Miss Furnivall, shouting it close to her ear; but when I came to the mention of the other little girl out in the snow, coaxing and tempting her out, and wiling her up to the grand and beautiful lady by the holly tree, she threw her arms up – her old and withered arms – and cried aloud, "Oh! Heaven forgive! Have mercy!"

Mrs. Stark took hold of her; roughly enough, I thought; but she was past Mrs. Stark's management, and spoke to me, in a kind of wild warning and authority.

"Hester! Keep her from that child! It will lure her to her death! That evil child! Tell her it is a wicked, naughty child." Then, Mrs. Stark hurried me out of the room; where, indeed, I was glad enough to go; but Miss Furnivall kept shrieking out, "Oh, have mercy! Wilt Thou never forgive! It is many a long year ago—"

I was very uneasy in my mind after that. I durst never leave Miss Rosamond, night or day, for fear lest she might slip off again, after some fancy or other; and all the more, because I thought I could make out that Miss Furnivall was crazy, from their odd ways about her; and I was afraid lest something of the same kind (which might be in the family, you know) hung over my darling. And the great frost never ceased all this time; and, whenever it was a more stormy night than usual, between the gusts, and through the wind we heard the old lord playing on the great organ. But, old lord, or not, wherever Miss Rosamond went, there I followed; for my love for her, pretty, helpless orphan, was stronger than my fear for the grand and terrible sound. Besides, it rested with me to keep her cheerful and merry, as beseemed her age. So we played together, and wandered together, here and there, and everywhere; for I never dared to lose sight of her again in that large and rambling house. And so it happened, that one afternoon, not long before Christmas day, we were playing together on the billiard-table in the great hall (not that we knew the right way of playing, but she liked to roll the smooth ivory balls with her pretty hands, and I liked to do whatever she did); and, by-and-by, without our noticing it, it grew dusk indoors, though it was still light in the open air, and I was thinking of taking her back into the nursery, when, all of a sudden, she cried out –

"Look, Hester! Look! There is my poor little girl out in the snow!"

I turned towards the long narrow windows, and there, sure enough, I saw a little girl, less than my Miss Rosamond – dressed all unfit to be out-of-doors such a bitter night – crying, and beating against the window panes, as if she wanted to be let in. She seemed to sob and wail, till Miss Rosamond could bear it no longer, and was flying to the door to open it, when, all of a sudden, and close upon us, the great organ pealed out so loud and thundering, it fairly made me tremble; and all the more, when I remembered me that, even in the stillness of that dead-cold weather, I had heard no sound of little battering hands upon the window-glass, although the phantom child had seemed to put forth all its force; and, although I had seen it wail and cry, no faintest touch of sound had fallen upon my ears. Whether I remembered all this at the very moment, I do not know; the great organ sound had so stunned me into terror; but this I know, I caught up Miss Rosamond before she got the hall door opened, and clutched her, and carried her away, kicking and screaming, into the large, bright kitchen, where Dorothy and Agnes were busy with their mince-pies.

"What is the matter with my sweet one?" cried Dorothy, as I bore in Miss Rosamond, who was sobbing as if her heart would break.

"She won't let me open the door for my little girl to come in; and she'll die if she is out on the Fells all night. Cruel, naughty Hester," she said, slapping me; but she might have struck harder, for I had seen a look of ghastly terror on Dorothy's face, which made my very blood run cold.

"Shut the back-kitchen door fast, and bolt it well," said she to Agues. She said no more; she gave me raisins and almonds to quiet Miss Rosamond; but she sobbed about the little girl in the snow, and would not touch any of the good things. I was thankful when she cried herself to sleep in bed. Then I stole down to the kitchen, and told Dorothy I had made up my mind. I would carry my darling back to my father's house in Applethwaite; where, if we lived humbly, we lived at peace. I said I had been frightened enough with the old lord's organ-playing; but now that I had seen for myself this little moaning child, all decked out as no child in the neighbourhood could be, beating and battering to get in, yet always without any sound or noise – with the dark wound on its right shoulder; and that Miss Rosamond had known it again for the phantom that had nearly lured her to death (which Dorothy knew was true); I would stand it no longer.

I saw Dorothy change colour once or twice. When I had done, she told me she did not think I could take Miss Rosamond with me, for that she was my lord's ward, and I had no right over her; and she asked me would I leave the child that I was so fond of just for sounds and sights that could do me no harm; and that they had all had to get used to in their turns? I was all in a hot, trembling passion; and I said it was very well for her to talk, that knew what these sights and noises betokened, and that had, perhaps, had something to do with the spectre child while it was alive. And I taunted her so, that she told me all she knew at last; and then I wished I had never been told, for it only made me more afraid than ever.

She said she had heard the tale from old neighbours that were alive when she was first married; when folks used to come to the hall sometimes, before it had got such a bad name on the country side: it might not be true, or it might, what she had been told.

The old lord was Miss Furnivall's father – Miss Grace, as Dorothy called her, for Miss Maude was the elder, and Miss Furnivall by lights. The old lord was eaten up with pride. Such a proud man was never seen or heard of; and his daughters were like him. No one was good enough to wed them, although they had choice enough; for they were the great beauties of their day, as I had seen by their portraits, where they hung in the state drawing-room. But, as the old saying is, 'Pride will have a fall'; and these two haughty beauties fell in love with the same man, and he no better than a foreign musician, whom their father had down from London to play music with him at the Manor House. For, above all things, next to his pride, the old lord loved music. He could play on nearly every instrument that ever was heard of; and it was a strange thing it did not soften him; but he was a fierce, dour old man, and had broken his poor wife's heart with his cruelty, they said. He was mad after music, and would pay any money for it. So he got this foreigner to come; who made such beautiful music, that they said the very birds on the trees stopped their singing to listen. And, by degrees, this foreign gentleman got such a hold over the old lord, that nothing would serve him but that he must come every year; and it was he that had the great organ brought from Holland, and built up in the hall, where it stood now. He taught the old lord to play on it; but many and many a time, when Lord Furnivall was thinking of nothing but his fine organ, and his finer music, the dark foreigner was walking abroad in the woods, with one of the young ladies: now Miss Maude, and then Miss Grace.

Miss Maude won the day and carried off the prize, such as it was; and he and she were married, all unknown to anyone; and, before he made his next yearly visit, she had been confined of a little girl at a farmhouse on the Moors, while her father and Miss Grace thought she was away at Doncaster Races. But though she was a wife and a mother, she was not a bit softened, but as haughty and as passionate as ever; and perhaps more so, for she was jealous of Miss Grace, to whom her foreign husband paid a deal of court – by way of blinding her – as he told his wife. But Miss Grace triumphed over Miss Maude, and Miss Maude grew fiercer and fiercer, both with her husband and with her sister; and the former – who could easily shake off what was disagreeable, and hide himself in foreign countries – went away a month before his usual time that summer, and half-threatened that he would never come back again. Meanwhile, the little girl was left at the farmhouse, and her mother used to have her horse saddled and gallop wildly over the hills to see her once every week, at the very least; for where she loved she loved, and where she hated she hated. And the old lord went on playing – playing on his organ; and the servants thought the sweet music he made had soothed down his awful temper, of which (Dorothy said) some terrible tales could be told. He grew infirm too, and had to walk with a crutch; and his son – that was the present Lord Furnivall's father – was with the army in America, and the other son at sea; so Miss Maude had it pretty much her own way, and she and Miss Grace grew colder and bitterer to each other every day; till at last they hardly ever spoke, except when the old lord was by. The foreign musician came again the next summer, but it was for the last time; for they led him such a life with their jealousy and their passions, that he grew weary, and went away, and never was heard of again. And Miss Maude, who had always meant to have her marriage acknowledged when her father should be dead, was left now a deserted wife, whom nobody knew to have been married, with a child that she dared not own, although she loved it to distraction; living with a father whom she feared, and a sister whom she hated. When the next summer passed over, and the dark foreigner never came, both Miss Maude and Miss Grace grew gloomy and sad; they had a haggard look about them, though they looked handsome as ever. But, by-and-by, Miss Maude brightened; for her father grew more and more infirm, and more than ever carried away by his music, and she and Miss Grace lived almost entirely apart, having separate rooms, the one on the west side, Miss Maude on the east – those very rooms which were now shut up. So she thought she might have her little girl with her, and no one need ever know except those who dared not speak about it, and were bound to believe that it was, as she said, a cottager's child she had taken a fancy to. All this, Dorothy said, was pretty well known; but what came afterwards no one knew, except Miss Grace and Mrs. Stark, who was even then her maid, and much more of a friend to her than ever her sister had been. But the servants supposed, from words that were dropped, that Miss Maude had triumphed over Miss Grace, and told her that all the time the dark foreigner had been mocking her with pretended love – he was her own husband. The colour left Miss Grace's cheek and lips that very day forever, and she was heard to say many a time that sooner or later she would have her revenge; and Mrs. Stark was forever spying about the east rooms.

One fearful night, just after the New Year had come in, when the snow was lying thick and deep; and the flakes were still falling – fast enough to blind anyone who might be out and abroad – there was a great and violent noise heard, and the old lord's voice above all, cursing and swearing awfully, and the cries of a little child, and the proud defiance of a fierce woman, and the sound of a blow, and a dead stillness, and moans and wailings, dying away on the hillside! Then the old lord summoned all his servants, and told them, with terrible oaths, and words more terrible, that his daughter had disgraced herself, and that he had turned her out of doors – her, and her child – and that if ever they gave her help, or food, or shelter, he prayed that they might never enter heaven. And, all the while, Miss Grace stood by him, white and still as any stone; and, when he had ended, she heaved a great sigh, as much as to say her work was done, and her end was accomplished. But the old lord never touched his organ again, and died within the year; and no wonder I for, on the morrow of that wild and fearful night, the shepherds, coming down the Fell side, found Miss Maude sitting, all crazy and smiling, under the holly trees, nursing a dead child, with a terrible mark on its right shoulder. "But that was not what killed it," said Dorothy: "it was the frost and the cold. Every wild creature was in its hole, and every beast in its fold, while the child and its mother were turned out to wander on the Fells! And now you know all! And I wonder if you are less frightened now?"

I was more frightened than ever; but I said I was not. I wished Miss Rosamond and myself well out of that dreadful house forever; but I would not leave her, and I dared not take her away. But oh, how I watched her, and guarded her! We bolted the doors, and shut the window-shutters fast, an hour or more before dark, rather than leave them open five minutes too late. But my little lady still heard the weird child crying and mourning; and not all we could do or say could keep her from wanting to go to her, and let her in from the cruel wind and snow. All this time I kept away from Miss Furnivall and Mrs. Stark, as much as ever I could; for I feared them – I knew no good could be about them, with their grey, hard faces, and their dreamy eyes, looking back into the ghastly years that were gone. But, even in my fear, I had a kind of pity for Miss Furnivall, at least. Those gone down to the pit can hardly have a more hopeless look than that which was ever on her face. At last I even got so sorry for her – who never said a word but what was quite forced from her – that I prayed for her; and I taught Miss Rosamond to pray for one who had done a deadly sin; but often, when she came to those words, she would listen, and start up from her knees, and say, "I hear my little girl plaining and crying, very sad – oh, let her in, or she will die!"

One night – just after New Year's Day had come at last, and the long winter had taken a turn, as I hoped – I heard the west drawing-room bell ring three times, which was the signal for me. I would not leave Miss Rosamond alone, for all she was asleep – for the old lord had been playing wilder than ever – and I feared lest my darling should waken to hear the spectre child; see her I knew she could not. I had fastened the windows too well for that. So I took her out of her bed, and wrapped her up in such outer clothes as were most handy, and carried her down to the drawing room, where the old ladies sat at their tapestry work as usual. They looked up when I came in, and Mrs. Stark asked, quite astounded, "Why did I bring Miss Rosamond there, out of her warm bed?" I had begun to whisper, "Because I was afraid of her being tempted out while I was away, by the wild child in the snow," when she stopped me short (with a glance at Miss Furnivall), and said Miss Furnivall wanted me to undo some work she had done wrong, and which neither of them could see to unpick. So I laid my pretty dear on the sofa, and sat down on a stool by them, and hardened my heart against them, as I heard the wind rising and howling.

Miss Rosamond slept on sound, for all the wind blew so; and Miss Furnivall said never a word, nor looked round when the gusts shook the windows. All at once she started up to her full height, and put up one hand, as if to bid us listen.

"I hear voices!" said she. "I hear terrible screams – I hear my father's voice!"

Just at that moment my darling wakened with a sudden start: "My little girl is crying, oh, how she is crying!" and she tried to get up and go to her, but she got her feet entangled in the blanket, and I caught her up; for my flesh had begun to creep at these noises, which they heard while we could catch no sound. In a minute or two the noises came, and gathered fast, and filled our ears; we, too, heard voices and screams, and no longer heard the winter's wind that raged abroad. Mrs. Stark looked at me, and I at her, but we dared not speak. Suddenly Miss Furnivall went towards the door, out into the ante-room, through the west lobby, and opened the door into the great hall. Mrs. Stark followed, and I durst not be left, though my heart almost stopped beating for fear. I wrapped my darling tight in my arms, and went out with them. In the hall the screams were louder than ever; they seemed to come from the east wing – nearer and nearer – close on the other side of the locked-up doors – close behind them. Then I noticed that the great bronze chandelier seemed all alight, though the hall was dim, and that a fire was blazing in the vast hearth-place, though it gave no heat; and I shuddered up with terror, and folded my darling closer to me. But as I did so the east door shook, and she, suddenly struggling to get free from me, cried, "Hester! I must go. My little girl is there, I hear her; she is coming! Hester, I must go!"

I held her tight with all my strength; with a set will, I held her. If I had died, my hands would have grasped her still, I was so resolved in my mind. Miss Furnivall stood listening, and paid no regard to my darling, who had got down to the ground, and whom I, upon my knees now, was holding with both my arms clasped round her neck; she still striving and crying to get free.

All at once, the east door gave way with a thundering crash, as if torn open in a violent passion, and there came into that broad and mysterious light, the figure of a tall old man, with grey hair and gleaming eyes. He drove before him, with many a relentless gesture of abhorrence, a stern and beautiful woman, with a little child clinging to her dress.

"O Hester! Hester!" cried Miss Rosamond; "It's the lady! The lady below the hollytrees; and my little girl is with her. Hester! Hester! Let me go to her; they are drawing me to them. I feel them – I feel them. I must go!"

Again she was almost convulsed by her efforts to get away; but I held her tighter and tighter, till I feared I should do her a hurt; but rather that than let her go towards those terrible phantoms. They passed along towards the great hall door, where the winds howled and ravened for their prey; but before they reached that, the lady turned; and I could see that she defied the old man with a fierce and proud defiance; but then she quailed – and then she threw up her arms wildly and piteously to save her child – her little child – from a blow from his uplifted crutch.

And Miss Rosamond was torn as by a power stronger than mine, and writhed in my arms, and sobbed (for by this time the poor darling was growing faint).

"They want me to go with them on to the Fells – they are drawing me to them. Oh, my little girl! I would come, but cruel, wicked Hester holds me very tight." But when she saw the uplifted crutch, she swooned away, and I thanked God for it. Just at this moment – when the tall old man, his hair streaming as in the blast of a furnace, was going to strike the little shrinking child – Miss Furnivall, the old woman by my side, cried out, "O father! Father! Spare the little innocent child!" But just then I saw – we all saw – another phantom shape itself, and grow clear out of the blue and misty light that filled the hall; we had not seen her till now, for it was another lady who stood by the old man, with a look of relentless hate and triumphant scorn. That figure was very beautiful to look upon, with a soft, white hat drawn down over the proud brows, and a red and curling lip. It was dressed in an open robe of blue satin. I had seen that figure before. It was the likeness of Miss Furnivall in her youth; and the terrible phantoms moved on, regardless of old Miss Furnivall's wild entreaty – and the uplifted crutch fell on the right shoulder of the little child, and the younger sister looked on, stony, and deadly serene. But at that moment, the dim lights, and the fire that gave no heat, went out of themselves, and Miss Furnivall lay at our feet stricken down by the palsy – death-stricken.

Yes! She was carried to her bed that night never to rise again. She lay with her face to the wall, muttering low, but muttering always: "Alas! Alas! What is done in youth can never be undone in age! What is done in youth can never be undone in age!"

The Giant Wistaria

Charlotte Perkins Gilman

"MEDDLE NOT with my new vine, child! See! Thou hast already broken the tender shoot! Never needle or distaff for thee, and yet thou wilt not be quiet!"

The nervous fingers wavered, clutched at a small carnelian cross that hung from her neck, then fell despairingly.

"Give me my child, mother, and then I will be quiet!"

"Hush! Hush! Thou fool – someone might be near! See – there is thy father coming, even now! Get in quickly!"

She raised her eyes to her mother's face, weary eyes that yet had a flickering, uncertain blaze in their shaded depths.

"Art thou a mother and hast no pity on me, a mother? Give me my child!"

Her voice rose in a strange, low cry, broken by her father's hand upon her mouth.

"Shameless!" said he, with set teeth. "Get to thy chamber, and be not seen again tonight, or I will have thee bound!"

She went at that, and a hard-faced serving woman followed, and presently returned, bringing a key to her mistress.

"Is all well with her – and the child also?"

"She is quiet, Mistress Dwining, well for the night, be sure. The child fretteth endlessly, but save for that it thriveth with me."

The parents were left alone together on the high square porch with its great pillars, and the rising moon began to make faint shadows of the young vine leaves that shot up luxuriantly around them: moving shadows, like little stretching fingers, on the broad and heavy planks of the oaken floor.

"It groweth well, this vine thou broughtest me in the ship, my husband."

"Aye," he broke in bitterly, "and so doth the shame I brought thee! Had I known of it I would sooner have had the ship founder beneath us, and have seen our child cleanly drowned, than live to this end!"

"Thou art very hard, Samuel, art thou not afeard for her life? She grieveth sore for the child, aye, and for the green fields to walk in!"

"Nay," said he grimly, "I fear not. She hath lost already what is more than life; and she shall have air enough soon. Tomorrow the ship is ready, and we return to England. None knoweth of our stain here, not one, and if the town hath a child unaccounted for to rear in decent ways – why, it is not the first, even here. It will be well enough cared for! And truly we have matter for thankfulness, that her cousin is yet willing to marry her."

"Has thou told him?"

"Aye! Thinkest thou I would cast shame into another man's house, unknowing it? He hath always desired her, but she would none of him, the stubborn! She hath small choice now!"

"Will he be kind, Samuel? Can he—"

"Kind? What call'st thou it to take such as she to wife? Kind! How many men would take her, an' she had double the fortune? And being of the family already, he is glad to hide the blot forever."

"An' if she would not? He is but a coarse fellow, and she ever shunned him."

"Art thou mad, woman? She weddeth him ere we sail tomorrow, or she stayeth ever in that chamber. The girl is not so sheer a fool! He maketh an honest woman of her, and saveth our house from open shame. What other hope for her than a new life to cover the old? Let her have an honest child, an' she so longeth for one!"

He strode heavily across the porch, till the loose planks creaked again, strode back and forth, with his arms folded and his brows fiercely knit above his iron mouth.

Overhead the shadows flickered mockingly across a white face among the leaves, with eyes of wasted fire.

* * *

"O, George, what a house! What a lovely house! I am sure it's haunted! Let us get that house to live in this summer! We will have Kate and Jack and Susy and Jim of course, and a splendid time of it!"

Young husbands are indulgent, but still they have to recognize facts.

"My dear, the house may not be to rent: and it may also not be habitable."

"There is surely somebody in it. I am going to inquire!"

The great central gate was rusted off its hinges, and the long drive had trees in it, but a little footpath showed signs of steady usage, and up that Mrs. Jenny went, followed by her obedient George. The front windows of the old mansion were blank, but in a wing at the back they found white curtains and open doors. Outside, in the clear May sunshine, a woman was washing. She was polite and friendly, and evidently glad of visitors in that lonely place. She "guessed it could be rented – didn't know." The heirs were in Europe, but "there was a lawyer in New York had the lettin' of it."

There had been folks there years ago, but not in her time. She and her husband had the rent of their part for taking care of the place. "Not that they took much care on't either, but keepin' robbers out." It was furnished throughout, old-fashioned enough, but good; and "if they took it she could do the work for 'em herself, she guessed – if he was willin'!"

Never was a crazy scheme more easily arranged. George knew that lawyer in New York; the rent was not alarming; and the nearness to a rising sea-shore resort made it a still pleasanter place to spend the summer.

Kate and Jack and Susy and Jim cheerfully accepted, and the June moon found them all sitting on the high front porch.

They had explored the house from top to bottom, from the great room in the garret, with nothing in it but a rickety cradle, to the well in the cellar without a curb and with a rusty chain going down to unknown blackness below. They had explored the grounds, once beautiful with rare trees and shrubs, but now a gloomy wilderness of tangled shade.

The old lilacs and laburnums, the spirea and syringa, nodded against the second-story windows. What garden plants survived were great ragged bushes or great shapeless beds. A huge wistaria vine covered the whole front of the house. The trunk, it was too large to call a stem, rose at the corner of the porch by the high steps, and had once climbed its pillars; but now the pillars were wrenched from their places and held rigid and helpless by the tightly wound and knotted arms.

It fenced in all the upper story of the porch with a knitted wall of stem and leaf; it ran along the eaves, holding up the gutter that had once supported it; it shaded every window with heavy green; and the drooping, fragrant blossoms made a waving sheet of purple from roof to ground…"Did you ever see such a wistaria!" cried ecstatic Mrs. Jenny. "It is worth the rent just to sit under such a vine – a fig tree beside it would be sheer superfluity and wicked extravagance!"

"Jenny makes much of her wistaria," said George, "because she's so disappointed about the ghosts. She made up her mind at first sight to have ghosts in the house, and she can't find even a ghost story!"

"No," Jenny assented mournfully; "I pumped poor Mrs. Pepperill for three days, but could get nothing out of her. But I'm convinced there is a story, if we could only find it. You need not tell me that a house like this, with a garden like this, and a cellar like this, isn't haunted!"

"I agree with you," said Jack. Jack was a reporter on a New York daily, and engaged to Mrs. Jenny's pretty sister. "And if we don't find a real ghost, you may be very sure I shall make one. It's too good an opportunity to lose!"

The pretty sister, who sat next him, resented. "You shan't do anything of the sort, Jack! This is a real ghostly place, and I won't have you make fun of it! Look at that group of trees out there in the long grass – it looks for all the world like a crouching, hunted figure!"

"It looks to me like a woman picking huckleberries," said Jim, who was married to George's pretty sister.

"Be still, Jim!" said that fair young woman. "I believe in Jenny's ghost as much as she does. Such a place! Just look at this great wistaria trunk crawling up by the steps here! It looks for all the world like a writhing body – cringing – beseeching!"

"Yes," answered the subdued Jim, "it does, Susy. See its waist – about two yards of it, and twisted at that! A waste of good material!"

"Don't be so horrid, boys! Go off and smoke somewhere if you can't be congenial!"

"We can! We will! We'll be as ghostly as you please." And forthwith they began to see bloodstains and crouching figures so plentifully that the most delightful shivers multiplied, and the fair enthusiasts started for bed, declaring they should never sleep a wink.

"We shall all surely dream," cried Mrs. Jenny, "and we must all tell our dreams in the morning!"

"There's another thing certain," said George, catching Susy as she tripped over a loose plank; "and that is that you frisky creatures must use the side door till I get this Eiffel tower of a portico fixed, or we shall have some fresh ghosts on our hands! We found a plank here that yawns like a trapdoor – big enough to swallow you – and I believe the bottom of the thing is in China!"

The next morning found them all alive, and eating a substantial New England breakfast, to the accompaniment of saws and hammers on the porch, where carpenters of quite miraculous promptness were tearing things to pieces generally.

"It's got to come down mostly," they had said. "These timbers are clean rotted through, what ain't pulled out o' line by this great creeper. That's about all that holds the thing up."

There was clear reason in what they said, and with a caution from anxious Mrs. Jenny not to hurt the wistaria, they were left to demolish and repair at leisure.

"How about ghosts?" asked Jack after a fourth griddle cake. "I had one, and it's taken away my appetite!"

Mrs. Jenny gave a little shriek and dropped her knife and fork.

"Oh, so had I! I had the most awful – well, not dream exactly, but feeling. I had forgotten all about it!"

"Must have been awful," said Jack, taking another cake. "Do tell us about the feeling. My ghost will wait."

"It makes me creep to think of it even now," she said. "I woke up, all at once, with that dreadful feeling as if something were going to happen, you know! I was wide awake, and hearing every little sound for miles around, it seemed to me. There are so many strange little noises in the country for all it is so still. Millions of crickets and things outside, and all kinds of rustles in the trees! There wasn't much wind, and the moonlight came through in my three great windows in three white squares on the black old floor, and those fingery wistaria leaves we were talking of last night just seemed to crawl all over them. And – O, girls, you know that dreadful well in the cellar?"

A most gratifying impression was made by this, and Jenny proceeded cheerfully:

"Well, while it was so horridly still, and I lay there trying not to wake George, I heard as plainly as if it were right in the room, that old chain down there rattle and creak over the stones!"

"Bravo!" cried Jack. "That's fine! I'll put it in the Sunday edition!"

"Be still!" said Kate. "What was it, Jenny? Did you really see anything?"

"No, I didn't, I'm sorry to say. But just then I didn't want to. I woke George, and made such a fuss that he gave me bromide, and said he'd go and look, and that's the last I thought of it till Jack reminded me – the bromide worked so well."

"Now, Jack, give us yours," said Jim. "Maybe, it will dovetail in somehow. Thirsty ghost, I imagine; maybe they had prohibition here even then!"

Jack folded his napkin, and leaned back in his most impressive manner.

"It was striking twelve by the great hall clock—" he began.

"There isn't any hall clock!"

"O hush, Jim, you spoil the current! It was just one o'clock then, by my old-fashioned repeater."

"Waterbury! Never mind what time it was!"

"Well, honestly, I woke up sharp, like our beloved hostess, and tried to go to sleep again, but couldn't. I experienced all those moonlight and grasshopper sensations, just like Jenny, and was wondering what could have been the matter with the supper, when in came my ghost, and I knew it was all a dream! It was a female ghost, and I imagine she was young and handsome, but all those crouching, hunted figures of last evening ran riot in my brain, and this poor creature looked just like them. She was all wrapped up in a shawl, and had a big bundle under her arm – dear me, I am spoiling the story! With the air and gait of one in frantic haste and terror, the muffled figure glided to a dark old bureau, and seemed taking things from the drawers. As she turned, the moonlight shone full on a little red cross that hung from her neck by a thin gold chain – I saw it glitter as she crept noiselessly from the room! That's all."

"O Jack, don't be so horrid! Did you really? Is that all! What do you think it was?"

"I am not horrid by nature, only professionally. I really did. That was all. And I am fully convinced it was the genuine, legitimate ghost of an eloping chambermaid with kleptomania!"

"You are too bad, Jack!" cried Jenny. "You take all the horror out of it. There isn't a 'creep' left among us."

"It's no time for creeps at nine-thirty a.m., with sunlight and carpenters outside! However, if you can't wait till twilight for your creeps, I think I can furnish one or two," said George. "I went down the cellar after Jenny's ghost!"

There was a delighted chorus of female voices, and Jenny cast upon her lord a glance of genuine gratitude.

"It's all very well to lie in bed and see ghosts, or hear them," he went on. "But the young householder suspecteth burglars, even though as a medical man he knoweth nerves, and after Jenny dropped off I started on a voyage of discovery. I never will again, I promise you!"

"Why, what was it?"

"Oh, George!"

"I got a candle—"

"Good mark for the burglars," murmured Jack.

"And went all over the house, gradually working down to the cellar and the well."

"Well?" said Jack.

"Now you can laugh; but that cellar is no joke by daylight, and a candle there at night is about as inspiring as a lightning-bug in the Mammoth Cave. I went along with the light, trying not to fall into the well prematurely; got to it all at once; held the light down and then I saw, right under my feet – (I nearly fell over her, or walked through her, perhaps) – a woman, hunched up under a shawl! She had hold of the chain, and the candle shone on her hands – white, thin hands – on a little red cross that hung from her neck – ride Jack! I'm no believer in ghosts, and I firmly object to unknown parties in the house at night; so I spoke to her rather fiercely. She didn't seem to notice that, and I reached down to take hold of her – then I came upstairs!"

"What for?"

"What happened?"

"What was the matter?"

"Well, nothing happened. Only she wasn't there! May have been indigestion, of course, but as a physician I don't advise anyone to court indigestion alone at midnight in a cellar!"

"This is the most interesting and peripatetic and evasive ghost I ever heard of!" said Jack. "It's my belief she has no end of silver tankards, and jewels galore, at the bottom of that well, and I move we go and see!"

"To the bottom of the well, Jack?"

"To the bottom of the mystery. Come on!"

There was unanimous assent, and the fresh cambrics and pretty boots were gallantly escorted below by gentlemen whose jokes were so frequent that many of them were a little forced.

The deep old cellar was so dark that they had to bring lights, and the well so gloomy in its blackness that the ladies recoiled.

"That well is enough to scare even a ghost. It's my opinion you'd better let well enough alone?" quoth Jim.

"Truth lies hid in a well, and we must get her out," said George. "Bear a hand with the chain?"

Jim pulled away on the chain, George turned the creaking windlass, and Jack was chorus.

"A wet sheet for this ghost, if not a flowing sea," said he. "Seems to be hard work raising spirits! I suppose he kicked the bucket when he went down!"

As the chain lightened and shortened there grew a strained silence among them; and when at length the bucket appeared, rising slowly through the dark water, there was an eager, half-reluctant peering, and a natural drawing back. They poked the gloomy contents. "Only water."

"Nothing but mud."

"Something—"

They emptied the bucket up on the dark earth, and then the girls all went out into the air, into the bright warm sunshine in front of the house, where was the sound of saw and hammer, and the smell of new wood. There was nothing said until the men joined them, and then Jenny timidly asked:

"How old should you think it was, George?"

"All of a century," he answered. "That water is a preservative – lime in it. Oh! – you mean? – Not more than a month: a very little baby!" There was another silence at this, broken by a cry from the workmen. They had removed the floor and the side walls of the old porch, so that the sunshine poured down to the dark stones of the cellar bottom. And there, in the strangling grasp of the roots of the great wistaria, lay the bones of a woman, from whose neck still hung a tiny scarlet cross on a thin chain of gold.

The Furnished Room

O. Henry

RESTLESS, SHIFTING, FUGACIOUS as time itself is a certain vast bulk of the population of the red brick district of the lower West Side. Homeless, they have a hundred homes. They flit from furnished room to furnished room, transients forever – transients in abode, transients in heart and mind. They sing 'Home, Sweet Home' in ragtime; they carry their *lares et penates* in a bandbox; their vine is entwined about a picture hat; a rubber plant is their fig tree.

Hence the houses of this district, having had a thousand dwellers, should have a thousand tales to tell, mostly dull ones, no doubt; but it would be strange if there could not be found a ghost or two in the wake of all these vagrant guests.

One evening after dark a young man prowled among these crumbling red mansions, ringing their bells. At the twelfth he rested his lean hand baggage upon the step and wiped the dust from his hatband and forehead. The bell sounded faint and far away in some remote, hollow depths.

To the door of this, the twelfth house whose bell he had rung, came a housekeeper who made him think of an unwholesome, surfeited worm that had eaten its nut to a hollow shell and now sought to fill the vacancy with edible lodgers.

He asked if there was a room to let.

"Come in," said the housekeeper. Her voice came from her throat; her throat seemed lined with fur. "I have the third floor back, vacant since a week back. Should you wish to look at it?"

The young man followed her up the stairs. A faint light from no particular source mitigated the shadows of the halls. They trod noiselessly upon a stair carpet that its own loom would have forsworn. It seemed to have become vegetable; to have degenerated in that rank, sunless air to lush lichen or spreading moss that grew in patches to the staircase and was viscid under the foot like organic matter. At each turn of the stairs were vacant niches in the wall. Perhaps plants had once been set within them. If so they had died in that foul and tainted air. It may be that statues of the saints had stood there, but it was not difficult to conceive that imps and devils had dragged them forth in the darkness and down to the unholy depths of some furnished pit below.

"This is the room," said the housekeeper, from her furry throat. "It's a nice room. It ain't often vacant. I had some most elegant people in it last summer – no trouble at all, and paid in advance to the minute. The water's at the end of the hall. Sprowls and Mooney kept it three months. They done a vaudeville sketch. Miss B'retta Sprowls – you may have heard of her – oh, that was just the stage names – right there over the dresser is where the marriage certificate hung, framed. The gas is here, and you see there is plenty of closet room. It's a room everybody likes. It never stays idle long."

"Do you have many theatrical people rooming here?" asked the young man.

"They comes and goes. A good proportion of my lodgers is connected with the theatres. Yes, sir, this is the theatrical district. Actor people never stays long anywhere. I get my share. Yes, they comes and they goes."

He engaged the room, paying for a week in advance. He was tired, he said, and would take possession at once. He counted out the money. The room had been made ready, she said, even to towels and water. As the housekeeper moved away he put, for the thousandth time, the question that he carried at the end of his tongue.

"A young girl – Miss Vashner – Miss Eloise Vashner – do you remember such a one among your lodgers? She would be singing on the stage, most likely. A fair girl, of medium height and slender, with reddish, gold hair and a dark mole near her left eyebrow."

"No, I don't remember the name. Them stage people has names they change as often as their rooms. They comes and they goes. No, I don't call that one to mind."

No. Always no. Five months of ceaseless interrogation and the inevitable negative. So much time spent by day in questioning managers, agents, schools and choruses; by night among the audiences of theatres from all-star casts down to music halls so low that he dreaded to find what he most hoped for. He who had loved her best had tried to find her. He was sure that since her disappearance from home this great, water-girt city held her somewhere, but it was like a monstrous quicksand, shifting its particles constantly, with no foundation, its upper granules of today buried tomorrow in ooze and slime.

The furnished room received its latest guest with a first glow of pseudo-hospitality, a hectic, haggard, perfunctory welcome like the specious smile of a demirep. The sophistical comfort came in reflected gleams from the decayed furniture, the ragged brocade upholstery of a couch and two chairs, a foot-wide cheap pier glass between the two windows, from one or two gilt picture frames and a brass bedstead in a corner.

The guest reclined, inert, upon a chair, while the room, confused in speech as though it were an apartment in Babel, tried to discourse to him of its divers tenantry.

A polychromatic rug like some brilliant-flowered rectangular, tropical islet lay surrounded by a billowy sea of soiled matting. Upon the gay-papered wall were those pictures that pursue the homeless one from house to house – The Huguenot Lovers, The First Quarrel, The Wedding Breakfast, Psyche at the Fountain. The mantel's chastely severe outline was ingloriously veiled behind some pert drapery drawn rakishly askew like the sashes of the Amazonian ballet. Upon it was some desolate flotsam cast aside by the room's marooned when a lucky sail had borne them to a fresh port – a trifling vase or two, pictures of actresses, a medicine bottle, some stray cards out of a deck.

One by one, as the characters of a cryptograph become explicit, the little signs left by the furnished room's procession of guests developed a significance. The threadbare space in the rug in front of the dresser told that lovely woman had marched in the throng. Tiny finger prints on the wall spoke of little prisoners trying to feel their way to sun and air. A splattered stain, raying like the shadow of a bursting bomb, witnessed where a hurled glass or bottle had splintered with its contents against the wall. Across the pier glass had been scrawled with a diamond in staggering letters the name "Marie." It seemed that the succession of dwellers in the furnished room had turned in fury – perhaps tempted beyond forbearance by its garish coldness – and wreaked upon it their passions. The furniture was chipped and bruised; the couch, distorted by bursting springs, seemed a horrible monster that had been slain during the stress of some grotesque convulsion. Some more potent upheaval had cloven a great slice from the marble mantel. Each plank in the floor owned its particular cant and shriek as from a separate and individual agony. It seemed incredible that all this malice and injury had been wrought upon the room by those who had called it for a time their home; and yet it may have been the cheated home instinct surviving blindly, the resentful rage at false household gods that had kindled their wrath. A hut that is our own we can sweep and adorn and cherish.

The young tenant in the chair allowed these thoughts to file, soft-shod, through his mind, while there drifted into the room furnished sounds and furnished scents. He heard in one room a tittering and incontinent, slack laughter; in others the monologue of a scold, the rattling of dice, a lullaby, and one crying dully; above him a banjo tinkled with spirit. Doors banged somewhere; the elevated trains roared intermittently; a cat yowled miserably upon a back fence. And he breathed the breath of the house – a dank savour rather than a smell – a cold, musty effluvium as from underground vaults mingled with the reeking exhalations of linoleum and mildewed and rotten woodwork.

Then, suddenly, as he rested there, the room was filled with the strong, sweet odor of mignonette. It came as upon a single buffet of wind with such sureness and fragrance and emphasis that it almost seemed a living visitant. And the man cried aloud: "What, dear?" as if he had been called, and sprang up and faced about. The rich odor clung to him and wrapped him around. He reached out his arms for it, all his senses for the time confused and commingled. How could one be peremptorily called by an odour? Surely it must have been a sound. But, was it not the sound that had touched, that had caressed him?

"She has been in this room," he cried, and he sprang to wrest from it a token, for he knew he would recognize the smallest thing that had belonged to her or that she had touched. This enveloping scent of mignonette, the odor that she had loved and made her own – whence came it?

The room had been but carelessly set in order. Scattered upon the flimsy dresser scarf were half a dozen hairpins – those discreet, indistinguishable friends of womankind, feminine of gender, infinite of mood and uncommunicative of tense. These he ignored, conscious of their triumphant lack of identity. Ransacking the drawers of the dresser he came upon a discarded, tiny, ragged handkerchief. He pressed it to his face. It was racy and insolent with heliotrope; he hurled it to the floor. In another drawer he found odd buttons, a theatre programme, a pawnbroker's card, two lost marshmallows, a book on the divination of dreams. In the last was a woman's black satin hair bow, which halted him, poised between ice and fire. But the black satin hair-bow also is femininity's demure, impersonal, common ornament, and tells no tales.

And then he traversed the room like a hound on the scent, skimming the walls, considering the corners of the bulging matting on his hands and knees, rummaging mantel and tables, the curtains and hangings, the drunken cabinet in the corner, for a visible sign, unable to perceive that she was there beside, around, against, within, above him, clinging to him, wooing him, calling him so poignantly through the finer senses that even his grosser ones became cognisant of the call. Once again he answered loudly: "Yes, dear!" and turned, wild-eyed, to gaze on vacancy, for he could not yet discern form and colour and love and outstretched arms in the odor of mignonette. Oh, God! Whence that odor, and since when have odors had a voice to call? Thus he groped.

He burrowed in crevices and corners, and found corks and cigarettes. These he passed in passive contempt. But once he found in a fold of the matting a half-smoked cigar, and this he ground beneath his heel with a green and trenchant oath. He sifted the room from end to end. He found dreary and ignoble small records of many a peripatetic tenant; but of her whom he sought, and who may have lodged there, and whose spirit seemed to hover there, he found no trace.

And then he thought of the housekeeper.

He ran from the haunted room downstairs and to a door that showed a crack of light. She came out to his knock. He smothered his excitement as best he could.

"Will you tell me, madam," he besought her, "who occupied the room I have before I came?"

"Yes, sir. I can tell you again. 'Twas Sprowls and Mooney, as I said. Miss B'retta Sprowls it was in the theatres, but Missis Mooney she was. My house is well known for respectability. The marriage certificate hung, framed, on a nail over—"

"What kind of a lady was Miss Sprowls – in looks, I mean?"

"Why, black-haired, sir, short, and stout, with a comical face. They left a week ago Tuesday."

"And before they occupied it?"

"Why, there was a single gentleman connected with the draying business. He left owing me a week. Before him was Missis Crowder and her two children, that stayed four months; and back of them was old Mr. Doyle, whose sons paid for him. He kept the room six months. That goes back a year, sir, and further I do not remember."

He thanked her and crept back to his room. The room was dead. The essence that had vivified it was gone. The perfume of mignonette had departed. In its place was the old, stale odor of moldy house furniture, of atmosphere in storage.

The ebbing of his hope drained his faith. He sat staring at the yellow, singing gaslight. Soon he walked to the bed and began to tear the sheets into strips. With the blade of his knife he drove them tightly into every crevice around windows and door. When all was snug and taut he turned out the light, turned the gas full on again and laid himself gratefully upon the bed.

* * *

It was Mrs. McCool's night to go with the can for beer. So she fetched it and sat with Mrs. Purdy in one of those subterranean retreats where housekeepers foregather and the worm dieth seldom.

"I rented out my third floor, back, this evening," said Mrs. Purdy, across a fine circle of foam. "A young man took it. He went up to bed two hours ago."

"Now, did ye, Mrs. Purdy, ma'am?" said Mrs. McCool, with intense admiration. "You do be a wonder for rentin' rooms of that kind. And did ye tell him, then?" she concluded in a husky whisper, laden with mystery.

"Rooms," said Mrs. Purdy, in her furriest tones, "are furnished for to rent. I did not tell him, Mrs. McCool."

"'Tis right ye are, ma'am; 'tis by renting rooms we kape alive. Ye have the rale sense for business, ma'am. There be many people will rayjict the rentin' of a room if they be tould a suicide has been after dyin' in the bed of it."

"As you say, we has our living to be making," remarked Mrs. Purdy.

"Yis, ma'am; 'tis true. 'Tis just one wake ago this day I helped ye lay out the third floor, back. A pretty slip of a colleen she was to be killin' herself wid the gas – a swate little face she had, Mrs. Purdy, ma'am."

"She'd a-been called handsome, as you say," said Mrs. Purdy, assenting but critical, "but for that mole she had a-growin' by her left eyebrow. Do fill up your glass again, Mrs. McCool."

The Whistling Room

William Hope Hodgson

CARNACKI shook a friendly fist at me as I entered, late. Then he opened the door into the dining room, and ushered the four of us – Jessop, Arkright, Taylor and myself – in to dinner.

We dined well, as usual, and, equally as usual, Carnacki was pretty silent during the meal. At the end, we took our wine and cigars to our usual positions, and Carnacki – having got himself comfortable in his big chair – began without any preliminary:

"I have just got back from Ireland, again," he said. "And I thought you chaps would be interested to hear my news. Besides, I fancy I shall see the thing clearer, after I have told it all out straight. I must tell you this, though, at the beginning – up to the present moment, I have been utterly and completely 'stumped'. I have tumbled upon one of the most peculiar cases of 'haunting' – or devilment of some sort – that I have come against. Now listen.

"I have been spending the last few weeks at Iastrae Castle, about twenty miles northeast of Galway. I got a letter about a month ago from a Mr. Sid K. Tassoc, who it seemed had bought the place lately, and moved in, only to find that he had bought a very peculiar piece of property.

"When I got there, he met me at the station, driving a jaunting car, and drove me up to the castle, which, by the way, he called a 'house shanty'. I found that he was 'pigging it' there with his boy brother and another American, who seemed to be half-servant and half-companion. It seems that all the servants had left the place, in a body, as you might say, and now they were managing among themselves, assisted by some day-help.

"The three of them got together a scratch feed, and Tassoc told me all about the trouble whilst we were at table. It is most extraordinary, and different from anything that I have had to do with; though that Buzzing Case was very queer, too.

"Tassoc began right in the middle of his story. 'We've got a room in this shanty,' he said, 'which has got a most infernal whistling in it; sort of haunting it. The thing starts any time; you never know when, and it goes on until it frightens you. All the servants have gone, as you know. It's not ordinary whistling, and it isn't the wind. Wait till you hear it.'

"'We're all carrying guns,' said the boy; and slapped his coat pocket.

"'As bad as that?' I said; and the older boy nodded. 'It may be soft,' he replied; 'but wait till you've heard it. Sometimes I think it's some infernal thing, and the next moment, I'm just as sure that someone's playing a trick on me.'

"'Why?' I asked. 'What is to be gained?'

"'You mean,' he said, 'that people usually have some good reason for playing tricks as elaborate as this. Well, I'll tell you. There's a lady in this province, by the name of Miss Donnehue, who's going to be my wife, this day two months. She's more beautiful than they make them, and so far as I can see, I've just stuck my head into an Irish hornet's nest. There's about a score of hot young Irishmen been courting her these two years gone, and now that I'm come along and cut them out, they feel raw against me. Do you begin to understand the possibilities?'

"'Yes,' I said. 'Perhaps I do in a vague sort of way; but I don't see how all this affects the room?'

"'Like this,' he said. 'When I'd fixed it up with Miss Donnehue, I looked out for a place, and bought this little house shanty. Afterward, I told her – one evening during dinner, that I'd decided to tie up here. And then she asked me whether I wasn't afraid of the whistling room. I told her it must have been thrown in gratis, as I'd heard nothing about it. There were some of her men friends present, and I saw a smile go 'round. I found out, after a bit of questioning, that several people have bought this place during the last twenty-odd years. And it was always on the market again, after a trial.

"'Well, the chaps started to bait me a bit, and offered to take bets after dinner that I'd not stay six months in the place. I looked once or twice to Miss Donnehue, so as to be sure I was 'getting the note' of the talkee-talkee; but I could see that she didn't take it as a joke, at all. Partly, I think, because there was a bit of a sneer in the way the men were tackling me, and partly because she really believes there is something in this yarn of the Whistling Room.

"'However, after dinner, I did what I could to even things up with the others. I nailed all their bets, and screwed them down hard and safe. I guess some of them are going to be hard hit, unless I lose; which I don't mean to. Well, there you have practically the whole yarn.'

"'Not quite,' I told him. 'All that I know, is that you have bought a castle with a room in it that is in some way 'queer', and that you've been doing some betting. Also, I know that your servants have got frightened and run away. Tell me something about the whistling?'

"'Oh, that!' said Tassoc; 'that started the second night we were in. I'd had a good look 'round the room, in the daytime, as you can understand; for the talk up at Arlestrae – Miss Donnehue's place – had made me wonder a bit. But it seems just as usual as some of the other rooms in the old wing, only perhaps a bit more lonesome. But that may be only because of the talk about it, you know.

"'The whistling started about ten o'clock, on the second night, as I said. Tom and I were in the library, when we heard an awfully queer whistling, coming along the East Corridor – the room is in the East Wing, you know.

"'That's that blessed ghost!' I said to Tom, and we collared the lamps off the table, and went up to have a look. I tell you, even as we dug along the corridor, it took me a bit in the throat, it was so beastly queer. It was a sort of tune, in a way; but more as if a devil or some rotten thing were laughing at you, and going to get 'round at your back. That's how it makes you feel.

"'When we got to the door, we didn't wait; but rushed it open; and then I tell you the sound of the thing fairly hit me in the face. Tom said he got it the same way – sort of felt stunned and bewildered. We looked all 'round, and soon got so nervous, we just cleared out, and I locked the door.

"'We came down here, and had a stiff peg each. Then we got fit again, and began to think we'd been nicely had. So we took sticks, and went out into the grounds, thinking after all it must be some of these confounded Irishmen working the ghost-trick on us. But there was not a leg stirring.

"'We went back into the house, and walked over it, and then paid another visit to the room. But we simply couldn't stand it. We fairly ran out, and locked the door again. I don't know how to put it into words; but I had a feeling of being up against something that was rottenly dangerous. You know! We've carried our guns ever since.

"'Of course, we had a real turn out of the room next day, and the whole house place; and we even hunted 'round the grounds; but there was nothing queer. And now I don't know what to think; except that the sensible part of me tells me that it's some plan of these Wild Irishmen to try to take a rise out of me.'

"'Done anything since?' I asked him.

"'Yes,' he said – 'watched outside of the door of the room at nights, and chased 'round the grounds, and sounded the walls and floor of the room. We've done everything we could think of; and it's beginning to get on our nerves; so we sent for you.'

"By this, we had finished eating. As we rose from the table, Tassoc suddenly called out: 'Ssh! Hark!'

"We were instantly silent, listening. Then I heard it, an extraordinary hooning whistle, monstrous and inhuman, coming from far away through corridors to my right.

"'By G—d!' said Tassoc; 'and it's scarcely dark yet! Collar those candles, both of you, and come along.'

"In a few moments, we were all out of the door and racing up the stairs. Tassoc turned into a long corridor, and we followed, shielding our candles as we ran. The sound seemed to fill all the passage as we drew near, until I had the feeling that the whole air throbbed under the power of some wanton Immense Force – a sense of an actual taint, as you might say, of monstrosity all about us.

"Tassoc unlocked the door; then, giving it a push with his foot, jumped back, and drew his revolver. As the door flew open, the sound beat out at us, with an effect impossible to explain to one who has not heard it – with a certain, horrible personal note in it; as if in there in the darkness you could picture the room rocking and creaking in a mad, vile glee to its own filthy piping and whistling and hooning. To stand there and listen, was to be stunned by Realisation. It was as if someone showed you the mouth of a vast pit suddenly, and said: That's Hell. And you knew that they had spoken the truth. Do you get it, even a little bit?

"I stepped back a pace into the room, and held the candle over my head, and looked quickly 'round. Tassoc and his brother joined me, and the man came up at the back, and we all held our candles high. I was deafened with the shrill, piping hoon of the whistling; and then, clear in my ear, something seemed to be saying to me: 'Get out of here – quick! Quick! Quick!'

"As you chaps know, I never neglect that sort of thing. Sometimes it may be nothing but nerves; but as you will remember, it was just such a warning that saved me in the 'Grey Dog' Case, and in the 'Yellow Finger' Experiments; as well as other times. Well, I turned sharp 'round to the others: 'Out!' I said. 'For God's sake, *out* quick.' And in an instant I had them into the passage.

"There came an extraordinary yelling scream into the hideous whistling, and then, like a clap of thunder, an utter silence. I slammed the door, and locked it. Then, taking the key, I looked 'round at the others. They were pretty white, and I imagine I must have looked that way too. And there we stood a moment, silent.

"'Come down out of this, and have some whisky,' said Tassoc, at last, in a voice he tried to make ordinary; and he led the way. I was the back man, and I know we all kept looking over our shoulders. When we got downstairs, Tassoc passed the bottle 'round. He took a drink, himself, and slapped his glass down on to the table. Then sat down with a thud.

"'That's a lovely thing to have in the house with you, isn't it!' he said. And directly afterward: 'What on earth made you hustle us all out like that, Carnacki?'

"'Something seemed to be telling me to get out, quick,' I said. 'Sounds a bit silly, superstitious, I know; but when you are meddling with this sort of thing, you've got to take notice of queer fancies, and risk being laughed at.'

"I told him then about the 'Grey Dog' business, and he nodded a lot to that. 'Of course,' I said, 'this may be nothing more than those would-be rivals of yours playing some funny game; but, personally, though I'm going to keep an open mind, I feel that there is something beastly and dangerous about this thing.'

"We talked for a while longer, and then Tassoc suggested billiards, which we played in a pretty half-hearted fashion, and all the time cocking an ear to the door, as you might say, for sounds; but none came, and later, after coffee, he suggested early bed, and a thorough overhaul of the room on the morrow.

"My bedroom was in the newer part of the castle, and the door opened into the picture gallery. At the East end of the gallery was the entrance to the corridor of the East Wing; this was shut off from the gallery by two old and heavy oak doors, which looked rather odd and quaint beside the more modern doors of the various rooms.

"When I reached my room, I did not go to bed; but began to unpack my instrument trunk, of which I had retained the key. I intended to take one or two preliminary steps at once, in my investigation of the extraordinary whistling.

"Presently, when the castle had settled into quietness, I slipped out of my room, and across to the entrance of the great corridor. I opened one of the low, squat doors, and threw the beam of my pocket searchlight down the passage. It was empty, and I went through the doorway, and pushed-to the oak behind me. Then along the great passageway, throwing my light before and behind, and keeping my revolver handy.

"I had hung a 'protection belt' of garlic 'round my neck, and the smell of it seemed to fill the corridor and give me assurance; for, as you all know, it is a wonderful 'protection' against the more usual Aeiirii forms of semi-materialisation, by which I supposed the whistling might be produced; though, at that period of my investigation, I was quite prepared to find it due to some perfectly natural cause; for it is astonishing the enormous number of cases that prove to have nothing abnormal in them.

"In addition to wearing the necklet, I had plugged my ears loosely with garlic, and as I did not intend to stay more than a few minutes in the room, I hoped to be safe.

"When I reached the door, and put my hand into my pocket for the key, I had a sudden feeling of sickening funk. But I was not going to back out, if I could help it. I unlocked the door and turned the handle. Then I gave the door a sharp push with my foot, as Tassoc had done, and drew my revolver, though I did not expect to have any use for it, really.

"I shone the searchlight all 'round the room, and then stepped inside, with a disgustingly horrible feeling of walking slap into a waiting Danger. I stood a few seconds, waiting, and nothing happened, and the empty room showed bare from corner to corner. And then, you know, I realised that the room was full of an abominable silence; can you understand that? A sort of purposeful silence, just as sickening as any of the filthy noises the Things have power to make. Do you remember what I told you about that 'Silent Garden' business? Well, this room had just that same *malevolent* silence – the beastly quietness of a thing that is looking at you and not seeable itself, and thinks that it has got you. Oh, I recognised it instantly, and I whipped the top off my lantern, so as to have light over the *whole* room.

"Then I set-to, working like fury, and keeping my glance all about me. I sealed the two windows with lengths of human hair, right across, and sealed them at every frame. As I worked, a queer, scarcely perceptible tenseness stole into the air of the place, and the silence seemed, if you can understand me, to grow more solid. I knew then that I had no business there without 'full protection'; for I was practically certain that this was no mere Aeiirii development; but one of the worst forms, as the Saiitii; like that 'Grunting Man' case – you know.

"I finished the window, and hurried over to the great fireplace. This is a huge affair, and has a queer gallows-iron, I think they are called, projecting from the back of the arch. I sealed the opening with seven human hairs – the seventh crossing the six others.

"Then, just as I was making an end, a low, mocking whistle grew in the room. A cold, nervous pricking went up my spine, and 'round my forehead from the back. The hideous sound filled all the room with an extraordinary, grotesque parody of human whistling, too gigantic to be human – as if something gargantuan and monstrous made the sounds softly. As I stood there a last moment, pressing down the final seal, I had no doubt but that I had come across one of those rare and horrible cases of the *Inanimate* reproducing the functions of the *Animate*, I made a grab for my lamp, and went quickly to the door, looking over my shoulder, and listening for the thing that I expected. It came, just as I got my hand upon the handle – a squeal of incredible, malevolent anger, piercing through the low hooning of the whistling. I dashed out, slamming the door and locking it. I leant a little against the opposite wall of the corridor, feeling rather funny; for it had been a narrow squeak…. 'Theyr be noe sayfetie to be gained bye gayrds of holiness when the monyster hath pow'r to speak throe woode and stoene.' So runs the passage in the Sigsand MS., and I proved it in that 'Nodding Door' business. There is no protection against this particular form of monster, except, possibly, for a fractional period of time; for it can reproduce itself in, or take to its purpose, the very protective material which you may use, and has the power to *'forme* wythine the pentycle'; though not immediately. There is, of course, the possibility of the Unknown Last Line of the Saaamaaa Ritual being uttered; but it is too uncertain to count upon, and the danger is too hideous; and even then it has no power to protect for more than 'maybee fyve beats of the harte', as the Sigsand has it.

"Inside of the room, there was now a constant, meditative, hooning whistling; but presently this ceased, and the silence seemed worse; for there is such a sense of hidden mischief in a silence.

"After a little, I sealed the door with crossed hairs, and then cleared off down the great passage, and so to bed.

"For a long time I lay awake; but managed eventually to get some sleep. Yet, about two o'clock I was waked by the hooning whistling of the room coming to me, even through the closed doors. The sound was tremendous, and seemed to beat through the whole house with a presiding sense of terror. As if (I remember thinking) some monstrous giant had been holding mad carnival with itself at the end of that great passage.

"I got up and sat on the edge of the bed, wondering whether to go along and have a look at the seal; and suddenly there came a thump on my door, and Tassoc walked in, with his dressing gown over his pajamas.

"'I thought it would have waked you, so I came along to have a talk,' he said. '*I* can't sleep. Beautiful! Isn't it!'

"'Extraordinary!' I said, and tossed him my case.

"He lit a cigarette, and we sat and talked for about an hour; and all the time that noise went on, down at the end of the big corridor.

"Suddenly, Tassoc stood up:

"'Let's take our guns, and go and examine the brute,' he said, and turned toward the door.

"'No!' I said. 'By Jove – *no!* I can't say anything definite, yet; but I believe that room is about as dangerous as it well can be.'

"'Haunted – *really* haunted?' he asked, keenly and without any of his frequent banter.

"I told him, of course, that I could not say a definite *yes* or *no* to such a question; but that I hoped to be able to make a statement, soon. Then I gave him a little lecture on the False Re-Materialisation of the Animate-Force through the Inanimate-Inert. He began then to see the particular way in the room might be dangerous, if it were really the subject of a manifestation.

"About an hour later, the whistling ceased quite suddenly, and Tassoc went off again to bed. I went back to mine, also, and eventually got another spell of sleep.

"In the morning, I went along to the room. I found the seals on the door intact. Then I went in. The window seals and the hair were all right; but the seventh hair across the great fireplace was broken. This set me thinking. I knew that it might, very possibly, have snapped, through my having tensioned it too highly; but then, again, it might have been broken by something else. Yet, it was scarcely possible that a man, for instance, could have passed between the six unbroken hairs; for no one would ever have noticed them, entering the room that way, you see; but just walked through them, ignorant of their very existence.

"I removed the other hairs, and the seals. Then I looked up the chimney. It went up straight, and I could see blue sky at the top. It was a big, open flue, and free from any suggestion of hiding places, or corners. Yet, of course, I did not trust to any such casual examination, and after breakfast, I put on my overalls, and climbed to the very top, sounding all the way; but I found nothing.

"Then I came down, and went over the whole of the room – floor, ceiling, and walls, mapping them out in six-inch squares, and sounding with both hammer and probe. But there was nothing abnormal.

"Afterward, I made a three-weeks search of the whole castle, in the same thorough way; but found nothing. I went even further, then; for at night, when the whistling commenced, I made a microphone test. You see, if the whistling were mechanically produced, this test would have made evident to me the working of the machinery, if there were any such concealed within the walls. It certainly was an up-to-date method of examination, as you must allow.

"Of course, I did not think that any of Tassoc's rivals had fixed up any mechanical contrivance; but I thought it just possible that there had been some such thing for producing the whistling, made away back in the years, perhaps with the intention of giving the room a reputation that would ensure its being free of inquisitive folk. You see what I mean? Well, of course, it was just possible, if this were the case, that someone knew the secret of the machinery, and was utilising the knowledge to play this devil of a prank on Tassoc. The microphone test of the walls would certainly have made this known to me, as I have said; but there was nothing of the sort in the castle; so that I had practically no doubt at all now, but that it was a genuine case of what is popularly termed 'haunting'.

"All this time, every night, and sometimes most of each night, the hooning whistling of the Room was intolerable. It was as if an intelligence there knew that steps were being taken against it, and piped and hooned in a sort of mad, mocking contempt. I tell you, it was as extraordinary as it was horrible. Time after time, I went along – tiptoeing noiselessly on stockinged feet – to the sealed door (for I always kept the Room sealed). I went at all hours of the night, and often the whistling, inside, would seem to change to a brutally malignant note, as though the half-animate monster saw me plainly through the shut door. And all the time the shrieking, hooning whistling would fill the whole corridor, so that I used to feel a precious lonely chap, messing about there with one of Hell's mysteries.

"And every morning, I would enter the room, and examine the different hairs and seals. You see, after the first week, I had stretched parallel hairs all along the walls of the room, and along the ceiling; but over the floor, which was of polished stone, I had set out little, colourless wafers, tacky-side uppermost. Each wafer was numbered, and they were arranged after a definite plan, so that I should be able to trace the exact movements of any living thing that went across the floor.

"You will see that no material being or creature could possibly have entered that room, without leaving many signs to tell me about it. But nothing was ever disturbed, and I began to think that I should have to risk an attempt to stay the night in the room, in the Electric Pentacle.

Yet, mind you, I knew that it would be a crazy thing to do; but I was getting stumped, and ready to do anything.

"Once, about midnight, I did break the seal on the door, and have a quick look in; but, I tell you, the whole Room gave one mad yell, and seemed to come toward me in a great belly of shadows, as if the walls had bellied in toward me. Of course, that must have been fancy. Anyway, the yell was sufficient, and I slammed the door, and locked it, feeling a bit weak down my spine. You know the feeling.

"And then, when I had got to that state of readiness for anything, I made something of a discovery. It was about one in the morning, and I was walking slowly 'round the castle, keeping in the soft grass. I had come under the shadow of the East Front, and far above me, I could hear the vile, hooning whistle of the Room, up in the darkness of the unlit wing. Then, suddenly, a little in front of me, I heard a man's voice, speaking low, but evidently in glee:

"'By George! You Chaps; but I wouldn't care to bring a wife home in that!' it said, in the tone of the cultured Irish.

"Someone started to reply; but there came a sharp exclamation, and then a rush, and I heard footsteps running in all directions. Evidently, the men had spotted me.

"For a few seconds, I stood there, feeling an awful ass. After all, *they* were at the bottom of the haunting! Do you see what a big fool it made me seem? I had no doubt but that they were some of Tassoc's rivals; and here I had been feeling in every bone that I had hit a real, bad, genuine Case! And then, you know, there came the memory of hundreds of details, that made me just as much in doubt again. Anyway, whether it was natural, or ab-natural, there was a great deal yet to be cleared up.

"I told Tassoc, next morning, what I had discovered, and through the whole of every night, for five nights, we kept a close watch 'round the East Wing; but there was never a sign of anyone prowling about; and all the time, almost from evening to dawn, that grotesque whistling would hoon incredibly, far above us in the darkness.

"On the morning after the fifth night, I received a wire from here, which brought me home by the next boat. I explained to Tassoc that I was simply bound to come away for a few days; but told him to keep up the watch 'round the castle. One thing I was very careful to do, and that was to make him absolutely promise never to go into the Room, between sunset and sunrise. I made it clear to him that we knew nothing definite yet, one way or the other; and if the room were what I had first thought it to be, it might be a lot better for him to die first, than enter it after dark.

"When I got here, and had finished my business, I thought you chaps would be interested; and also I wanted to get it all spread out clear in my mind; so I rung you up. I am going over again tomorrow, and when I get back, I ought to have something pretty extraordinary to tell you. By the way, there is a curious thing I forgot to tell you. I tried to get a phonographic record of the whistling; but it simply produced no impression on the wax at all. That is one of the things that has made me feel queer, I can tell you. Another extraordinary thing is that the microphone will not magnify the sound – will not even transmit it; seems to take no account of it, and acts as if it were nonexistent. I am absolutely and utterly stumped, up to the present. I am a wee bit curious to see whether any of your dear clever heads can make daylight of it. *I* cannot – not yet."

He rose to his feet.

"Goodnight, all," he said, and began to usher us out abruptly, but without offence, into the night.

A fortnight later, he dropped each of us a card, and you can imagine that I was not late this time. When we arrived, Carnacki took us straight into dinner, and when we had finished, and all made ourselves comfortable, he began again, where he had left off:

"Now just listen quietly; for I have got something pretty queer to tell you. I got back late at night, and I had to walk up to the castle, as I had not warned them that I was coming. It was bright moonlight; so that the walk was rather a pleasure, than otherwise. When I got there, the whole place was in darkness, and I thought I would take a walk 'round outside, to see whether Tassoc or his brother was keeping watch. But I could not find them anywhere, and concluded that they had got tired of it, and gone off to bed.

"As I returned across the front of the East Wing, I caught the hooning whistling of the Room, coming down strangely through the stillness of the night. It had a queer note in it, I remember – low and constant, queerly meditative. I looked up at the window, bright in the moonlight, and got a sudden thought to bring a ladder from the stable yard, and try to get a look into the Room, through the window.

"With this notion, I hunted 'round at the back of the castle, among the straggle of offices, and presently found a long, fairly light ladder; though it was heavy enough for one, goodness knows! And I thought at first that I should never get it reared. I managed at last, and let the ends rest very quietly against the wall, a little below the sill of the larger window. Then, going silently, I went up the ladder. Presently, I had my face above the sill and was looking in alone with the moonlight.

"Of course, the queer whistling sounded louder up there; but it still conveyed that peculiar sense of something whistling quietly to itself – can you understand? Though, for all the meditative lowness of the note, the horrible, gargantuan quality was distinct – a mighty parody of the human, as if I stood there and listened to the whistling from the lips of a monster with a man's soul.

"And then, you know, I saw something. The floor in the middle of the huge, empty room, was puckered upward in the centre into a strange soft-looking mound, parted at the top into an ever-changing hole, that pulsated to that great, gentle hooning. At times, as I watched, I saw the heaving of the indented mound, gap across with a queer, inward suction, as with the drawing of an enormous breath; then the thing would dilate and pout once more to the incredible melody. And suddenly, as I stared, dumb, it came to me that the thing was living. I was looking at two enormous, blackened lips, blistered and brutal, there in the pale moonlight....

"Abruptly, they bulged out to a vast, pouting mound of force and sound, stiffened and swollen, and hugely massive and clean-cut in the moon-beams. And a great sweat lay heavy on the vast upper-lip. In the same moment of time, the whistling had burst into a mad screaming note, that seemed to stun me, even where I stood, outside of the window. And then, the following moment, I was staring blankly at the solid, undisturbed floor of the room – smooth, polished stone flooring, from wall to wall; and there was an absolute silence.

"You can picture me staring into the quiet Room, and knowing what I knew. I felt like a sick, frightened kid, and wanted to slide *quietly* down the ladder, and run away. But in that very instant, I heard Tassoc's voice calling to me from within the Room, for help, *help*. My God! But I got such an awful dazed feeling; and I had a vague, bewildered notion that, after all, it was the Irishmen who had got him in there, and were taking it out of him. And then the call came again, and I burst the window, and jumped in to help him. I had a confused idea that the call had come from within the shadow of the great fireplace, and I raced across to it; but there was no one there.

"'Tassoc!' I shouted, and my voice went empty-sounding 'round the great apartment; and then, in a flash, *I knew that Tassoc had never called*. I whirled 'round, sick with fear, toward the window, and as I did so, a frightful, exultant whistling scream burst through the Room. On my left, the end wall had bellied in toward me, in a pair of gargantuan lips, black and utterly monstrous, to within a yard of my face. I fumbled for a mad instant at my revolver; not for *it*, but myself; for the danger was a thousand times worse than death. And then, suddenly, the Unknown Last Line of the Saaamaaa Ritual was whispered quite audibly in the room. Instantly, the thing happened that I have known once before. There came a sense as of dust falling continually and monotonously, and I knew that my life hung uncertain and suspended for a flash, in a brief, reeling vertigo of unseeable things. Then *that* ended, and I knew that I might live. My soul and body blended again, and life and power came to me. I dashed furiously at the window, and hurled myself out head-foremost; for I can tell you that I had stopped being afraid of death. I crashed down on to the ladder, and slithered, grabbing and grabbing; and so came some way or other alive to the bottom. And there I sat in the soft, wet grass, with the moonlight all about me; and far above, through the broken window of the Room, there was a low whistling.

"That is the chief of it. I was not hurt, and I went 'round to the front, and knocked Tassoc up. When they let me in, we had a long yarn, over some good whisky – for I was shaken to pieces – and I explained things as much as I could, I told Tassoc that the room would have to come down, and every fragment of it burned in a blast-furnace, erected within a pentacle. He nodded. There was nothing to say. Then I went to bed.

"We turned a small army on to the work, and within ten days, that lovely thing had gone up in smoke, and what was left was calcined, and clean.

"It was when the workmen were stripping the paneling, that I got hold of a sound notion of the beginnings of that beastly development. Over the great fireplace, after the great oak panels had been torn down, I found that there was let into the masonry a scrollwork of stone, with on it an old inscription, in ancient Celtic, that here in this room was burned Dian Tiansay, Jester of King Alzof, who made the Song of Foolishness upon King Ernore of the Seventh Castle.

"When I got the translation clear, I gave it to Tassoc. He was tremendously excited; for he knew the old tale, and took me down to the library to look at an old parchment that gave the story in detail. Afterward, I found that the incident was well known about the countryside; but always regarded more as a legend than as history. And no one seemed ever to have dreamt that the old East Wing of Iastrae Castle was the remains of the ancient Seventh Castle.

"From the old parchment, I gathered that there had been a pretty dirty job done, away back in the years. It seems that King Alzof and King Ernore had been enemies by birthright, as you might say truly; but that nothing more than a little raiding had occurred on either side for years, until Dian Tiansay made the Song of Foolishness upon King Ernore, and sang it before King Alzof; and so greatly was it appreciated that King Alzof gave the jester one of his ladies, to wife.

"Presently, all the people of the land had come to know the song, and so it came at last to King Ernore, who was so angered that he made war upon his old enemy, and took and burned him and his castle; but Dian Tiansay, the jester, he brought with him to his own place, and having torn his tongue out because of the song which he had made and sung, he imprisoned him in the Room in the East Wing (which was evidently used for unpleasant purposes), and the jester's wife he kept for himself, having a fancy for her prettiness.

"But one night, Dian Tiansay's wife was not to be found, and in the morning they discovered her lying dead in her husband's arms, and he sitting, whistling the Song of Foolishness, for he had no longer the power to sing it.

"Then they roasted Dian Tiansay, in the great fireplace – probably from that selfsame 'galley-iron' which I have already mentioned. And until he died, Dian Tiansay ceased not to whistle the Song of Foolishness, which he could no longer sing. But afterward, 'in that room' there was often heard at night the sound of something whistling; and there 'grew a power in that room', so that none dared to sleep in it. And presently, it would seem, the King went to another castle; for the whistling troubled him.

"There you have it all. Of course, that is only a rough rendering of the translation of the parchment. But it sounds extraordinarily quaint. Don't you think so?"

"Yes," I said, answering for the lot. "But how did the thing grow to such a tremendous manifestation?"

"One of those cases of continuity of thought producing a positive action upon the immediate surrounding material," replied Carnacki. "The development must have been going forward through centuries, to have produced such a monstrosity. It was a true instance of Saiitii manifestation, which I can best explain by likening it to a living spiritual fungus, which involves the very structure of the aether-fiber itself, and, of course, in so doing, acquires an essential control over the 'material substance' involved in it. It is impossible to make it plainer in a few words."

"What broke the seventh hair?" asked Taylor.

But Carnacki did not know. He thought it was probably nothing but being too severely tensioned. He also explained that they found out that the men who had run away had not been up to mischief; but had come over secretly, merely to hear the whistling, which, indeed, had suddenly become the talk of the whole countryside.

"One other thing," said Arkright, "have you any idea what governs the use of the Unknown Last Line of the Saaamaaa Ritual? I know, of course, that it was used by the Ab-human Priests in the Incantation of Raaaee; but what used it on your behalf, and what made it?"

"You had better read Harzan's Monograph, and my Addenda to it, on Astral and Astral Co-ordination and Interference," said Carnacki. "It is an extraordinary subject, and I can only say here that the human vibration may not be insulated from the astral (as is always believed to be the case, in interferences by the Ab-human), without immediate action being taken by those Forces which govern the spinning of the outer circle. In other words, it is being proved, time after time, that there is some inscrutable Protective Force constantly intervening between the human soul (not the body, mind you) and the Outer Monstrosities. Am I clear?"

"Yes, I think so," I replied. "And you believe that the Room had become the material expression of the ancient Jester – that his soul, rotten with hatred, had bred into a monster – eh?" I asked.

"Yes," said Carnacki, nodding, "I think you've put my thought rather neatly. It is a queer coincidence that Miss Donnehue is supposed to be descended (so I have heard since) from the same King Ernore. It makes one think some curious thoughts, doesn't it? The marriage coming on, and the Room waking to fresh life. If she had gone into that room, ever...eh? *It* had waited a long time. Sins of the fathers. Yes, I've thought of that. They're to be married next week, and I am to be best man, which is a thing I hate. And he won his bets, rather! Just think, *if* ever she had gone into that room. Pretty horrible, eh?"

He nodded his head, grimly, and we four nodded back. Then he rose and took us collectively to the door, and presently thrust us forth in friendly fashion on the Embankment and into the fresh night air.

"Goodnight," we all called back, and went to our various homes. If she had, eh? If she had? That is what I kept thinking.

The Toll-House

W.W. Jacobs

"IT'S ALL NONSENSE," said Jack Barnes. "Of course people have died in the house; people die in every house. As for the noises – wind in the chimney and rats in the wainscot are very convincing to a nervous man. Give me another cup of tea, Meagle."

"Lester and White are first," said Meagle, who was presiding at the tea-table of the Three Feathers Inn. "You've had two."

Lester and White finished their cups with irritating slowness, pausing between sips to sniff the aroma, and to discover the sex and dates of arrival of the 'strangers' which floated in some numbers in the beverage. Mr. Meagle served them to the brim, and then, turning to the grimly expectant Mr. Barnes, blandly requested him to ring for hot water.

"We'll try and keep your nerves in their present healthy condition," he remarked. "For my part I have a sort of half-and-half belief in the supernatural."

"All sensible people have," said Lester. "An aunt of mine saw a ghost once."

White nodded.

"I had an uncle that saw one," he said.

"It always is somebody else that sees them," said Barnes.

"Well, there is a house," said Meagle, "a large house at an absurdly low rent, and nobody will take it. It has taken toll of at least one life of every family that has lived there – however short the time – and since it has stood empty caretaker after caretaker has died there. The last caretaker died fifteen years ago."

"Exactly," said Barnes. "Long enough ago for legends to accumulate."

"I'll bet you a sovereign you won't spend the night there alone, for all your talk," said White, suddenly.

"And I," said Lester.

"No," said Barnes slowly. "I don't believe in ghosts nor in any supernatural things whatever; all the same I admit that I should not care to pass a night there alone."

"But why not?" inquired White.

"Wind in the chimney," said Meagle with a grin.

"Rats in the wainscot," chimed in Lester. "As you like," said Barnes, colouring.

"Suppose we all go," said Meagle. "Start after supper, and get there about eleven. We have been walking for ten days now without an adventure – except Barnes's discovery that ditchwater smells longest. It will be a novelty, at any rate, and, if we break the spell by all surviving, the grateful owner ought to come down handsome."

"Let's see what the landlord has to say about it first," said Lester. "There is no fun in passing a night in an ordinary empty house. Let us make sure that it is haunted."

He rang the bell, and, sending for the landlord, appealed to him in the name of our common humanity not to let them waste a night watching in a house in which spectres and hobgoblins had no part. The reply was more than reassuring, and the landlord, after describing with considerable art the exact appearance of a head which had been seen hanging out of a window in the moonlight, wound up with a polite but urgent request that they would settle his bill before they went.

"It's all very well for you young gentlemen to have your fun," he said indulgently; "but supposing as how you are all found dead in the morning, what about me? It ain't called the Toll-House for nothing, you know."

"Who died there last?" inquired Barnes, with an air of polite derision.

"A tramp," was the reply. "He went there for the sake of half a crown, and they found him next morning hanging from the balusters, dead."

"Suicide," said Barnes. "Unsound mind."

The landlord nodded. "That's what the jury brought it in," he said slowly; "but his mind was sound enough when he went in there. I'd known him, off and on, for years. I'm a poor man, but I wouldn't spend the night in that house for a hundred pounds."

He repeated this remark as they started on their expedition a few hours later. They left as the inn was closing for the night; bolts shot noisily behind them, and, as the regular customers trudged slowly homewards, they set off at a brisk pace in the direction of the house. Most of the cottages were already in darkness, and lights in others went out as they passed.

"It seems rather hard that we have got to lose a night's rest in order to convince Barnes of the existence of ghosts," said White.

"It's in a good cause," said Meagle. "A most worthy object; and something seems to tell me that we shall succeed. You didn't forget the candles, Lester?"

"I have brought two," was the reply; "all the old man could spare."

There was but little moon, and the night was cloudy. The road between high hedges was dark, and in one place, where it ran through a wood, so black that they twice stumbled in the uneven ground at the side of it.

"Fancy leaving our comfortable beds for this!" said White again. "Let me see; this desirable residential sepulchre lies to the right, doesn't it?"

"Farther on," said Meagle.

They walked on for some time in silence, broken only by White's tribute to the softness, the cleanliness, and the comfort of the bed which was receding farther and farther into the distance. Under Meagle's guidance they turned oft at last to the right, and, after a walk of a quarter of a mile, saw the gates of the house before them.

The lodge was almost hidden by overgrown shrubs and the drive was choked with rank growths. Meagle leading, they pushed through it until the dark pile of the house loomed above them.

"There is a window at the back where we can get in, so the landlord says," said Lester, as they stood before the hall door.

"Window?" said Meagle. "Nonsense. Let's do the thing properly. Where's the knocker?"

He felt for it in the darkness and gave a thundering rat-tat-tat at the door.

"Don't play the fool," said Barnes crossly.

"Ghostly servants are all asleep," said Meagle gravely, "but I'll wake them up before I've done with them. It's scandalous keeping us out here in the dark."

He plied the knocker again, and the noise volleyed in the emptiness beyond. Then with a sudden exclamation he put out his hands and stumbled forward.

"Why, it was open all the time," he said, with an odd catch in his voice. "Come on."

"I don't believe it was open," said Lester, hanging back. "Somebody is playing us a trick."

"Nonsense," said Meagle sharply. "Give me a candle. Thanks. Who's got a match?"

Barnes produced a box and struck one, and Meagle, shielding the candle with his hand, led the way forward to the foot of the stairs. "Shut the door, somebody," he said, "there's too much draught."

"It is shut," said White, glancing behind him.

Meagle fingered his chin. "Who shut it?" he inquired, looking from one to the other. "Who came in last?"

"I did," said Lester, "but I don't remember shutting it – perhaps I did, though."

Meagle, about to speak, thought better of it, and, still carefully guarding the flame, began to explore the house, with the others close behind. Shadows danced on the walls and lurked in the corners as they proceeded. At the end of the passage they found a second staircase, and ascending it slowly gained the first floor.

"Careful!" said Meagle, as they gained the landing.

He held the candle forward and showed where the balusters had broken away. Then he peered curiously into the void beneath.

"This is where the tramp hanged himself, I suppose," he said thoughtfully.

"You've got an unwholesome mind," said White, as they walked on. "This place is qutie creepy enough without your remembering that. Now let's find a comfortable room and have a little nip of whiskey apiece and a pipe. How will this do?"

He opened a door at the end of the passage and revealed a small square room. Meagle led the way with the candle, and, first melting a drop or two of tallow, stuck it on the mantelpiece. The others seated themselves on the floor and watched pleasantly as White drew from his pocket a small bottle of whiskey and a tin cup.

"H'm! I've forgotten the water," he exclaimed. "I'll soon get some," said Meagle.

He tugged violently at the bell-handle, and the rusty jangling of a bell sounded from a distant kitchen. He rang again.

"Don't play the fool," said Barnes roughly.

Meagle laughed. "I only wanted to convince you," he said kindly. "There ought to be, at any rate, one ghost in the servants' hall."

Barnes held up his hand for silence.

"Yes?" said Meagle with a grin at the other two. "Is anybody coming?"

"Suppose we drop this game and go back," said Barnes suddenly. "I don't believe in spirits, but nerves are outside anybody's command. You may laugh as you like, but it really seemed to me that I heard a door open below and steps on the stairs."

His voice was drowned in a roar of laughter.

"He is coming round," said Meagle with a smirk. "By the time I have done with him he will be a confirmed believer. Well, who will go and get some water? Will you, Barnes?"

"No," was the reply.

"If there is any it might not be safe to drink after all these years," said Lester. "We must do without it."

Meagle nodded, and taking a seat on the floor held out his hand for the cup. Pipes were lit and the clean, wholesome smell of tobacco filled the room. White produced a pack of cards; talk and laughter rang through the room and died away reluctantly in distant corridors.

"Empty rooms always delude me into the belief that I possess a deep voice," said Meagle. "Tomorrow—"

He started up with a smothered exclamation as the light went out suddenly and something struck him on the head. The others sprang to their feet. Then Meagle laughed.

"It's the candle," he exclaimed. "I didn't stick it enough."

Barnes struck a match and relighting the candle stuck it on the mantelpiece, and sitting down took up his cards again.

"What was I going to say?" said Meagle. "Oh, I know; tomorrow I—"

"Listen!" said White, laying his hand on the other's sleeve. "Upon my word I really thought I heard a laugh."

"Look here!" said Barnes. "What do you say to going back? I've had enough of this. I keep fancying that I hear things too; sounds of something moving about in the passage outside. I know it's only fancy, but it's uncomfortable."

"You go if you want to," said Meagle, "and we will play dummy. Or you might ask the tramp to take your hand for you, as you go downstairs."

Barnes shivered and exclaimed angrily. He got up and, walking to the half-closed door, listened.

"Go outside," said Meagle, winking at the other two. "I'll dare you to go down to the hall door and back by yourself."

Barnes came back and, bending forward, lit his pipe at the candle.

"I am nervous but rational," he said, blowing out a thin cloud of smoke. "My nerves tell me that there is something prowling up and down the long passage outside; my reason tells me that it is all nonsense. Where are my cards?"

He sat down again, and taking up his hand, looked through it carefully and led.

"Your play, White," he said after a pause. White made no sign.

"Why, he is asleep," said Meagle. "Wake up, old man. Wake up and play."

Lester, who was sitting next to him, took the sleeping man by the arm and shook him, gently at first and then with some roughness; but White, with his back against the wall and his head bowed, made no sign. Meagle bawled in his ear and then turned a puzzled face to the others.

"He sleeps like the dead," he said, grimacing. "Well, there are still three of us to keep each other company."

"Yes," said Lester, nodding. "Unless—Good Lord! Suppose—"

He broke off and eyed them trembling.

"Suppose what?" inquired Meagle.

"Nothing," stammered Lester. "Let's wake him. Try him again. *White! White!*"

"It's no good," said Meagle seriously; "there's something wrong about that sleep."

"That's what I meant," said Lester; "and if he goes to sleep like that, why shouldn't—"

Meagle sprang to his feet. "Nonsense," he said roughly. "He's tired out; that's all. Still, let's take him up and clear out. You take his legs and Barnes will lead the way with the candle. Yes? Who's that?"

He looked up quickly towards the door. "Thought I heard somebody tap," he said with a shamefaced laugh. "Now, Lester, up with him. One, two— Lester! Lester!"

He sprang forward too late; Lester, with his face buried in his arms, had rolled over on the floor fast asleep, and his utmost efforts failed to awaken him.

"He – is – asleep," he stammered. "'Asleep!"

Barnes, who had taken the candle from the mantelpiece, stood peering at the sleepers in silence and dropping tallow over the floor.

"We must get out of this," said Meagle. "Quick!" Barnes hesitated. "We can't leave them here—" he began.

"We must," said Meagle in strident tones. "If you go to sleep I shall go—Quick! Come."

He seized the other by the arm and strove to drag him to the door. Barnes shook him off, and putting the candle back on the mantelpiece, tried again to arouse the sleepers.

"It's no good," he said at last, and, turning from them, watched Meagle. "Don't you go to sleep," he said anxiously.

Meagle shook his head, and they stood for some time in uneasy silence. "May as well shut the door," said Barnes at last.

He crossed over and closed it gently. Then at a scuffling noise behind him he turned and saw Meagle in a heap on the hearthstone.

With a sharp catch in his breath he stood motionless. Inside the room the candle, fluttering in the draught, showed dimly the grotesque attitudes of the sleepers. Beyond the door there seemed to his over-wrought imagination a strange and stealthy unrest. He tried to whistle, but his lips were parched, and in a mechanical fashion he stooped, and began to pick up the cards which littered the floor.

He stopped once or twice and stood with bent head listening. The unrest outside seemed to increase; a loud creaking sounded from the stairs.

"Who is there?" he cried loudly.

The creaking ceased. He crossed to the door and flinging it open, strode out into the corridor. As he walked his fears left him suddenly.

"Come on!" he cried with a low laugh. "All of you! All of you! Show your faces – your infernal ugly faces! Don't skulk!"

He laughed again and walked on; and the heap in the fireplace put out his head tortoise fashion and listened in horror to the retreating footsteps. Not until they had become inaudible in the distance did the listeners' features relax.

"Good Lord, Lester, we've driven him mad," he said in a frightened whisper. "We must go after him."

There was no reply. Meagle sprung to his feet. "Do you hear?" he cried. "Stop your fooling now; this is serious. White! Lester! Do you hear?"

He bent and surveyed them in angry bewilderment. "All right," he said in a trembling voice. "You won't frighten me, you know."

He turned away and walked with exaggerated carelessness in the direction of the door. He even went outside and peeped through the crack, but the sleepers did not stir. He glanced into the blackness behind, and then came hastily into the room again.

He stood for a few seconds regarding them. The stillness in the house was horrible; he could not even hear them breathe. With a sudden resolution he snatched the candle from the mantelpiece and held the flame to White's finger. Then as he reeled back stupefied the footsteps again became audible.

He stood with the candle in his shaking hand listening. He heard them ascending the farther staircase, but they stopped suddenly as he went to the door. He walked a little way along the passage, and they went scurrying down the stairs and then at a jog-trot along the corridor below. He went back to the main staircase, and they ceased again.

For a time he hung over the balusters, listening and trying to pierce the blackness below; then slowly, step by step, he made his way downstairs, and, holding the candle above his head, peered about him.

"Barnes!" he called. "Where are you?" Shaking with fright, he made his way along the passage, and summoning up all his courage pushed open doors and gazed fearfully into empty rooms. Then, quite suddenly, he heard the footsteps in front of him.

He followed slowly for fear of extinguishing the candle, until they led him at last into a vast bare kitchen with damp walls and a broken floor. In front of him a door leading into an inside room had just closed. He ran towards it and flung it open, and a cold air blew out the candle. He stood aghast.

"Barnes!" he cried again. "Don't be afraid! It is I – Meagle!"

There was no answer. He stood gazing into the darkness, and all the time the idea of something close at hand watching was upon him. Then suddenly the steps broke out overhead again.

He drew back hastily, and passing through the kitchen groped his way along the narrow passages. He could now see better in the darkness, and finding himself at last at the foot of the staircase began to ascend it noiselessly. He reached the landing just in time to see a figure disappear round the angle of a wall. Still careful to make no noise, he followed the sound of the steps until they led him to the top floor, and he cornered the chase at the end of a short passage.

"Barnes!" he whispered. "Barnes!"

Something stirred in the darkness. A small circular window at the end of the passage just softened the blackness and revealed the dim outlines of a motionless figure. Meagle, in place of advancing, stood almost as still as a sudden horrible doubt took possession of him. With his eyes fixed on the shape in front he fell back slowly and, as it advanced upon him, burst into a terrible cry.

"Barnes! For God's sake! Is it you?"

The echoes of his voice left the air quivering, but the figure before him paid no heed. For a moment he tried to brace his courage up to endure its approach, then with a smothered cry he turned and fled.

The passages wound like a maze, and he threaded them blindly in a vain search for the stairs. If he could get down and open the hall door—

He caught his breath in a sob; the steps had begun again. At a lumbering trot they clattered up and down the bare passages, in and out, up and down, as though in search of him. He stood appalled, and then as they drew near entered a small room and stood behind the door as they rushed by. He came out and ran swiftly and noiselessly in the other direction, and in a moment the steps were after him. He found the long corridor and raced along it at top speed. The stairs he knew were at the end, and with the steps close behind he descended them in blind haste. The steps gained on him, and he shrank to the side to let them pass, still continuing his headlong flight. Then suddenly he seemed to slip off the earth into space.

Lester awoke in the morning to find the sunshine streaming into the room, and White sitting up and regarding with some perplexity a badly blistered finger.

"Where are the others?" inquired Lester. "Gone, I suppose," said White. "We must have been asleep."

Lester arose, and stretching his stiffened limbs, dusted his clothes with his hands, and went out into the corridor. White followed. At the noise of their approach a figure which had been lying asleep at the other end sat up and revealed the face of Barnes. "Why, I've been asleep," he said in surprise. "I don't remember coming here. How did I get here?"

"Nice place to come for a nap," said Lester, severely, as he pointed to the gap in the balusters. "Look there! Another yard and where would you have been?"

He walked carelessly to the edge and looked over. In response to his startled cry the others drew near, and all three stood gazing at the dead man below.

Number 13

M.R. James

AMONG THE TOWNS of Jutland, Viborg justly holds a high place. It is the seat of a bishopric; it has a handsome but almost entirely new cathedral, a charming garden, a lake of great beauty, and many storks. Near it is Hald, accounted one of the prettiest things in Denmark; and hard by is Finderup, where Marsk Stig murdered King Erik Clipping on St. Cecilia's Day, in the year 1286. Fifty-six blows of square-headed iron maces were traced on Erik's skull when his tomb was opened in the seventeenth century. But I am not writing a guide-book.

There are good hotels in Viborg – Preisler's and the Phoenix are all that can be desired. But my cousin, whose experiences I have to tell you now, went to the Golden Lion the first time that he visited Viborg. He has not been there since, and the following pages will perhaps explain the reason of his abstention.

The Golden Lion is one of the very few houses in the town that were not destroyed in the great fire of 1726, which practically demolished the cathedral, the Sognekirke, the Raadhuus, and so much else that was old and interesting. It is a great red-brick house – that is, the front is of brick, with corbie steps on the gables and a text over the door; but the courtyard into which the omnibus drives is of black and white wood and plaster.

The sun was declining in the heavens when my cousin walked up to the door, and the light smote full upon the imposing façade of the house. He was delighted with the old-fashioned aspect of the place, and promised himself a thoroughly satisfactory and amusing stay in an inn so typical of old Jutland.

It was not business in the ordinary sense of the word that had brought Mr. Anderson to Viborg. He was engaged upon some researches into the Church history of Denmark, and it had come to his knowledge that in the Kigsarkiv of Viborg there were papers, saved from the fire, relating to the last days of Roman Catholicism in the country. He proposed, therefore, to spend a considerable time – perhaps as much as a fortnight or three weeks – in examining and copying these, and he hoped that the Golden Lion would be able to give him a room of sufficient size to serve alike as a bedroom and a study. His wishes were explained to the landlord, and, after a certain amount of thought, the latter suggested that perhaps it might be the best way for the gentleman to look at one or two of the larger rooms and pick one for himself. It seemed a good idea.

The top floor was soon rejected as entailing too much getting upstairs after the day's work; the second floor contained no room of exactly the dimensions required; but on the first floor there was a choice of two or three rooms which would, so far as size went, suit admirably.

The landlord was strongly in favour of Number 17, but Mr. Anderson pointed out that its windows commanded only the blank wall of the next house, and that it would be very dark in the afternoon. Either Number 12 or Number 14 would be better, for both of them looked on the street, and the bright evening light and the pretty view would more than compensate him for the additional amount of noise.

Eventually Number 12 was selected. Like its neighbours, it had three windows, all on one side of the room; it was fairly high and unusually long. There was, of course, no fireplace, but the stove was handsome and rather old – a cast-iron erection, on the side of which was a representation of Abraham sacrificing Isaac, and the inscription, '1 Bog Mose, Cap. 22', above. Nothing else in the room was remarkable; the only interesting picture was an old coloured print of the town, date about 1820.

Suppertime was approaching, but when Anderson, refreshed by the ordinary ablutions, descended the staircase, there were still a few minutes before the bell rang. He devoted them to examining the list of his fellow-lodgers. As is usual in Denmark, their names were displayed on a large blackboard, divided into columns and lines, the numbers of the rooms being painted in at the beginning of each line. The list was not exciting. There was an advocate, or Sagförer, a German, and some bagmen from Copenhagen. The one and only point which suggested any food for thought was the absence of any Number 13 from the tale of the rooms, and even this was a thing which Anderson had already noticed half a dozen times in his experience of Danish hotels. He could not help wondering whether the objection to that particular number, common as it is, was so widespread and so strong as to make it difficult to let a room so ticketed, and he resolved to ask the landlord if he and his colleagues in the profession had actually met with many clients who refused to be accommodated in the thirteenth room.

He had nothing to tell me (I am giving the story as I heard it from him) about what passed at supper, and the evening, which was spent in unpacking and arranging his clothes, books, and papers, was not more eventful. Towards eleven o'clock he resolved to go to bed, but with him, as with a good many other people nowadays, an almost necessary preliminary to bed, if he meant to sleep, was the reading of a few pages of print, and he now remembered that the particular book which he had been reading in the train, and which alone would satisfy him at that present moment, was in the pocket of his great-coat, then hanging on a peg outside the dining-room.

To run down and secure it was the work of a moment, and, as the passages were by no means dark, it was not difficult for him to find his way back to his own door. So, at least, he thought; but when he arrived there, and turned the handle, the door entirely refused to open, and he caught the sound of a hasty movement towards it from within. He had tried the wrong door, of course. Was his own room to the right or to the left? He glanced at the number: it was 13. His room would be on the left; and so it was. And not before he had been in bed for some minutes, had read his wonted three or four pages of his book, blown out his light, and turned over to go to sleep, did it occur to him that, whereas on the blackboard of the hotel there had been no Number 13, there was undoubtedly a room numbered 13 in the hotel. He felt rather sorry he had not chosen it for his own. Perhaps he might have done the landlord a little service by occupying it, and given him the chance of saying that a well-born English gentleman had lived in it for three weeks and liked it very much. But probably it was used as a servant's room or something of the kind. After all, it was most likely not so large or good a room as his own. And he looked drowsily about the room, which was fairly perceptible in the half-light from the street-lamp. It was a curious effect, he thought. Rooms usually look larger in a dim light than a full one, but this seemed to have contracted in length and grown proportionately higher. Well, well! Sleep was more important than these vague ruminations – and to sleep he went.

On the day after his arrival Anderson attacked the Rigsarkiv of Viborg. He was, as one might expect in Denmark, kindly received, and access to all that he wished to see was made as easy for him as possible. The documents laid before him were far more numerous and interesting than he had at all anticipated. Besides official papers, there was a large bundle of correspondence relating to Bishop Jörgen Friis, the last Roman Catholic who held the see, and in these there cropped up many amusing and what are called 'intimate' details of private life and individual character. There was much talk of a house owned by the Bishop, but not inhabited by him, in the town. Its tenant was apparently somewhat of a scandal and a stumbling-block to the reforming party. He was a disgrace, they wrote, to the city; he practised secret and wicked arts, and had sold his soul to the enemy. It was of a piece with the gross corruption and superstition of the Babylonish Church that such a viper and blood-sucking *Troldmand* should be patronised and harboured by the Bishop. The Bishop met these reproaches boldly; he protested his own abhorrence of all such things as secret arts, and required his antagonists to bring the matter before the proper court – of course, the spiritual court – and sift it to the bottom. No one could be more ready and willing than himself to condemn Mag. Nicolas Francken if the evidence showed him to have been guilty of any of the crimes informally alleged against him.

Anderson had not time to do more than glance at the next letter of the Protestant leader, Rasmus Nielsen, before the record office was closed for the day, but he gathered its general tenor, which was to the effect that Christian men were now no longer bound by the decisions of Bishops of Rome, and that the Bishop's Court was not, and could not be, a fit or competent tribunal to judge so grave and weighty a cause.

On leaving the office, Mr. Anderson was accompanied by the old gentleman who presided over it, and, as they walked, the conversation very naturally turned to the papers of which I have just been speaking.

Herr Scavenius, the Archivist of Viborg, though very well informed as to the general run of the documents under his charge, was not a specialist in those of the Reformation period. He was much interested in what Anderson had to tell him about them. He looked forward with great pleasure, he said, to seeing the publication in which Mr. Anderson spoke of embodying their contents. "This house of the Bishop Friis," he added, "it is a great puzzle to me where it can have stood. I have studied carefully the topography of old Viborg, but it is most unlucky – of the old terrier of, the Bishop's property which was made in 1560, and of which we have the greater part in the Arkiv, just the piece which had the list of the town property is missing. Never mind. Perhaps I shall some day succeed to find him."

After taking some exercise – I forget exactly how or where – Anderson went back to the Golden Lion, his supper, his game of patience, and his bed. On the way to his room it occurred to him that he had forgotten to talk to the landlord about the omission of Number 13 from the hotel board, and also that he might as well make sure that Number 13 did actually exist before he made any reference to the matter.

The decision was not difficult to arrive at. There was the door with its number as plain as could be, and work of some kind was evidently going on inside it, for as he neared the door he could hear footsteps and voices, or a voice, within. During the few seconds in which he halted to make sure of the number, the footsteps ceased, seemingly very near the door, and he was a little startled at hearing a quick hissing breathing as of a person in strong excitement. He went on to his own room, and again he was surprised to find how much smaller it seemed now than it had when he selected it. It was a slight disappointment, but only slight. If he found it really not large enough, he could very easily shift to another. In the meantime he wanted something – as far as I remember it was a pocket-handkerchief – out of his portmanteau, which had been placed by the porter on a very inadequate trestle or stool against the wall at the furthest end of the room from his bed. Here was a very curious thing: the portmanteau was not to be seen. It had been moved by officious servants; doubtless the contents had been put in the wardrobe. No, none of them were there. This was vexatious. The idea of a theft he dismissed at once. Such things rarely happen in Denmark, but some piece of stupidity had certainly been performed (which is not so uncommon), and the *stuepige* must be severely spoken to. Whatever it was that he wanted, it was not so necessary to his comfort that he could not wait till the morning for it, and he therefore settled not to ring the bell and disturb the servants. He went to the window – the right-hand window it was – and looked out on the quiet street. There was a tall building opposite, with large spaces of dead wall; no passers by; a dark night; and very little to be seen of any kind.

The light was behind him, and he could see his own shadow clearly cast on the wall opposite. Also the shadow of the bearded man in Number 11 on the left, who passed to and fro in shirtsleeves once or twice, and was seen first brushing his hair, and later on in a nightgown. Also the shadow of the occupant of Number 13 on the right. This might be more interesting. Number 13 was, like himself, leaning on his elbows on the windowsill looking out into the street. He seemed to be a tall thin man – or was it by any chance a woman? – at least, it was someone who covered his or her head with some kind of drapery before going to bed, and, he thought, must be possessed of a red lamp-shade – and the lamp must be flickering very much. There was a distinct playing up and down of a dull red light on the opposite wall. He craned out a little to see if he could make any more of the figure, but beyond a fold of some light, perhaps white, material on the windowsill he could see nothing.

Now came a distant step in the street, and its approach seemed to recall Number 13 to a sense of his exposed position, for very swiftly and suddenly he swept aside from the window, and his red light went out. Anderson, who had been smoking a cigarette, laid the end of it on the windowsill and went to bed.

Next morning he was woken by the *stuepige* with hot water, etc. He roused himself, and after thinking out the correct Danish words, said as distinctly as he could:

"You must not move my portmanteau. Where is it?"

As is not uncommon, the maid laughed, and went away without making any distinct answer.

Anderson, rather irritated, sat up in bed, intending to call her back, but he remained sitting up, staring straight in front of him. There was his portmanteau on its trestle, exactly where he had seen the porter put it when he first arrived. This was a rude shock for a man who prided himself on his accuracy of observation. How it could possibly have escaped him the night before he did not pretend to understand; at any rate, there it was now.

The daylight showed more than the portmanteau; it let the true proportions of the room with its three windows appear, and satisfied its tenant that his choice after all had not been a bad one. When he was almost dressed he walked to the middle one of the three windows to look out at the weather. Another shock awaited him. Strangely unobservant he must have been last night. He could have sworn ten times over that he had been smoking at the right-hand window the last thing before he went to bed, and here was his cigarette-end on the sill of the middle window.

He started to go down to breakfast. Rather late, but Number 13 was later: here were his boots still outside his door – a gentleman's boots. So then Number 13 was a man, not a woman. Just then he caught sight of the number on the door. It was 14. He thought he must have passed Number 13 without noticing it. Three stupid mistakes in twelve hours were too much for a methodical, accurate-minded man, so he turned back to make sure. The next number to 14 was number 12, his own room. There was no Number 13 at all.

After some minutes devoted to a careful consideration of everything he had had to eat and drink during the last twenty-four hours, Anderson decided to give the question up. If his eyes or his brain were giving way he would have plenty of opportunities for ascertaining that fact;

if not, then he was evidently being treated to a very interesting experience. In either case the development of events would certainly be worth watching.

During the day he continued his examination of the episcopal correspondence which I have already summarised. To his disappointment, it was incomplete. Only one other letter could be found which referred to the affair of Mag. Nicolas Francken. It was from the Bishop Jörgen Friis to Rasmus Nielsen. He said:

> *Although we are not in the least degree inclined to assent to your judgment concerning our court, and shall be prepared if need be to withstand you to the uttermost in that behalf, yet forasmuch as our trusty and well-beloved Mag. Nicolas Francken, against whom you have dared to allege certain false and malicious charges, hath been suddenly removed from among us, it is apparent that the question for this term falls. But forasmuch as you further allege that the Apostle and Evangelist St. John in his heavenly Apocalypse describes the Holy Roman Church under the guise and symbol of the Scarlet Woman, be it known to you,' etc.*

Search as he would, Anderson could find no sequel to this letter nor any clue to the cause or manner of the 'removal' of the *casus belli*. He could only suppose that Francken had died suddenly; and as there were only two days between the date of Nielsen's last letter – when Francken was evidently still in being – and that of the Bishop's letter, the death must have been completely unexpected.

In the afternoon he paid a short visit to Hald, and took his tea at Baekkelund; nor could he notice, though he was in a somewhat nervous frame of mind, that there was any indication of such a failure of eye or brain as his experiences of the morning had led him to fear.

At supper he found himself next to the landlord.

"What," he asked him, after some indifferent conversation, "is the reason why in most of the hotels one visits in this country the number thirteen is left out of the list of rooms? I see you have none here."

The landlord seemed amused.

"To think that you should have noticed a thing like that! I've thought about it once or twice myself, to tell the truth. An educated man, I've said, has no business with these superstitious notions. I was brought up myself here in the high school of Viborg, and our old master was always a man to set his face against anything of that kind. He's been dead now this many years – a fine upstanding man he was, and ready with his hands as well as his head. I recollect us boys, one snowy day—"

Here he plunged into reminiscence.

"Then you don't think there is any particular objection to having a Number 13?" said Anderson.

"Ah! To be sure. Well, you understand, I was brought up to the business by my poor old father. He kept an hotel in Aarhuus first, and then, when we were born, he moved to Viborg here, which was his native place, and had the Phoenix here until he died. That was in 1876. Then I started business in Silkeborg, and only the year before last I moved into this house."

Then followed more details as to the state of the house and business when first taken over.

"And when you came here, was there a Number 13?"

"No, no. I was going to tell you about that. You see, in a place like this, the commercial class – the travellers – are what we have to provide for in general. And put them in Number 13? Why, they'd as soon sleep in the street, or sooner. As far as I'm concerned myself, it wouldn't make a penny difference to me what the number of my room was, and so I've often said to them; but they stick to it that it brings them bad luck. Quantities of stories they have among them of men that have slept in a Number 13 and never been the same again, or lost their best customers, or – one thing and another," said the landlord, after searching for a more graphic phrase.

"Then, what do you use your Number 13 for?" said Anderson, conscious as he said the words of a curious anxiety quite disproportionate to the importance of the question.

"My Number 13? Why, don't I tell you that there isn't such a thing in the house? I thought you might have noticed that. If there was it would be next door to your own room."

"Well, yes; only I happened to think – that is, I fancied last night that I had seen a door numbered thirteen in that passage; and, really, I am almost certain I must have been right, for I saw it the night before as well."

Of course, Herr Kristensen laughed this notion to scorn, as Anderson had expected, and emphasised with much iteration the fact that no Number 13 existed or had existed before him in that hotel.

Anderson was in some ways relieved by his certainty, but still puzzled, and he began to think that the best way to make sure whether he had indeed been subject to an illusion or not was to invite the landlord to his room to smoke a cigar later on in the evening. Some photographs of English towns which he had with him formed a sufficiently good excuse.

Herr Kristensen was flattered by the invitation, and most willingly accepted it. At about ten o'clock he was to make his appearance, but before that Anderson had some letters to write, and retired for the purpose of writing them. He almost blushed to himself at confessing it, but he could not deny that it was the fact that he was becoming quite nervous about the question of the existence of Number 13; so much so that he approached his room by way of Number 11, in order that he might not be obliged to pass the door, or the place where the door ought to be. He looked quickly and suspiciously about the room when he entered it, but there was nothing, beyond that indefinable air of being smaller than usual, to warrant any misgivings. There was no question of the presence or absence of his portmanteau tonight. He had himself emptied it of its contents and lodged it under his bed. With a certain effort he dismissed the thought of Number 13 from his mind, and sat down to his writing.

His neighbours were quiet enough. Occasionally a door opened in the passage and pair of boots was thrown out, or a bagman walked past humming to himself, and outside, from time to time a cart thundered over the atrocious cobblestones, or a quick step hurried along the flags.

Anderson finished his letters, ordered whisky and soda, and then went to the window and studied the dead wall opposite and the shadows upon it.

As far as he could remember, Number 14 had been occupied by the lawyer, a staid man, who said little at meals, being generally engaged in studying a small bundle of papers beside his plate. Apparently, however, he was in the habit of giving vent to his animal spirits when alone. Why else should he be dancing? The shadow from the next room evidently showed that he was. Again and again his thin form crossed the window, his arms waved, and a gaunt leg was kicked up with surprising agility. He seemed to be barefooted, and the floor must be well laid, for no sound betrayed his movements. Sagförer Herr Anders Jensen, dancing at ten o'clock at night in a hotel bedroom, seemed a fitting subject for a historical painting in the grand style; and Anderson's thoughts, like those of Emily in the 'Mysteries of Udolpho', began to 'arrange themselves in the following lines':

When I return to my hotel.
At ten o'clock p.m.,

> *The waiters think I am unwell;*
> *I do not care for them.*
> *But when I've locked my chamber door,*
> *And put my boots outside.*
> *I dance all night upon the floor.*
> *And even if my neighbours swore,*
> *I go on dancing all the more.*
> *For I'm acquainted with the law.*
> *And in despite of all their jaw.*
> *Their protests I deride.'*

Had not the landlord at this moment knocked at the door, it is probable that quite a long poem might have been laid before the reader. To judge from his look of surprise when he found himself in the room, Herr Kristensen was struck, as Anderson had been, by something unusual in its aspect. But he made no remark. Anderson's photographs interested him mightily, and formed the text of many autobiographical discourses. Nor is it quite clear how the conversation could have been diverted into the desired channel of Number 13, had not the lawyer at this moment begun to sing, and to sing in a manner which could leave no doubt in anyone's mind that he was either exceedingly drunk or raving mad. It was a high, thin voice that they heard, and it seemed dry, as if from long disuse. Of words or tune there was no question. It went sailing up to a surprising height, and was carried down with a despairing moan as of a winter wind in a hollow chimney, or an organ whose wind fails suddenly. It was a really horrible sound, and Anderson felt that if he had been alone he must have fled for refuge and society to some neighbour bagman's room.

The landlord sat open-mouthed.

"I don't understand it" he said at last, wiping his forehead. "It is dreadful. I have heard it once before, but I made sure it was a cat."

"Is he mad?" said Anderson.

"He must be; and what a sad thing! Such a good customer, too, and so successful in his business, by what I hear, and a young family to bring up."

Just then came an impatient knock at the door, and the knocker entered, without waiting to be asked. It was the lawyer, in deshabille and very rough-haired; and very angry he looked.

"I beg pardon, sir," he said, "but I should be much obliged if you would kindly desist—"

Here he stopped, for it was evident that neither of the persons before him was responsible for the disturbance; and after a moment's lull it swelled forth again more wildly than before.

"But what in the name of Heaven does it mean?" broke out the lawyer. "Where is it? Who is it? Am I going out of my mind?"

"Surely, Herr Jensen, it comes from your room next door? Isn't there a cat or something stuck in the chimney?"

This was the best that occurred to Anderson to say, and he realised its futility as he spoke; but anything was better than to stand and listen to that horrible voice, and look at the broad, white face of the landlord, all perspiring and quivering as he clutched the arms of his chair.

"Impossible," said the lawyer, "impossible. There is no chimney. I came here because I was convinced the noise was going on here. It was certainly in the next room to mine."

"Was there no door between yours and mine?" said Anderson eagerly.

"No, sir," said Herr Jensen, rather sharply. "At least, not this morning."

"Ah!" said Anderson. "Nor tonight?"

"I am not sure," said the lawyer with some hesitation.

Suddenly the crying or singing voice in the next room died away, and the singer was heard seemingly to laugh to himself in a crooning manner. The three men actually shivered at the sound. Then there was a silence.

"Come," said the lawyer, "what have you to say, Herr Kristensen? What does this mean?"

"Good Heaven!" said Kristensen. "How should I tell! I know no more than you, gentlemen. I pray I may never hear such a noise again."

"So do I," said Herr Jensen, and he added something under his breath. Anderson thought it sounded like the last words of the Psalter, 'omnis spirittis laudet Dominum' but he could not be sure.

"But we must do something," said Anderson – "the three of us. Shall we go and investigate in the next room?"

"But that is Herr Jensen's room," wailed the landlord. "It is no use; he has come from there himself."

"I am not so sure" said Jensen. "I think this gentleman is right: we must go and see."

The only weapons of defence that could be mustered on the spot were a stick and umbrella. The expedition went out into the passage, not without quakings. There was a deadly quiet outside, but a light shone from under the next door. Anderson and Jensen approached it. The latter turned the handle, and gave a sudden vigorous push. No use. The door stood fast.

"Herr Kristensen," said Jensen, "will you go and fetch the strongest servant you have in the place? We must see this through."

The landlord nodded, and hurried off, glad to be away from the scene of action. Jensen and Anderson remained outside looking at the door.

"It *is* Number 13, you see," said the latter.

"Yes; there is your door, and there is mine," said Jensen.

"My room has three windows in the daytime," said Anderson, with difficulty suppressing a nervous laugh.

"By George, so has mine!" said the lawyer, turning and looking at Anderson. His back was now to the door. In that moment the door opened, and an arm came out and clawed at his shoulder. It was clad in ragged, yellowish linen, and the bare skin, where it could be seen, had long gray hair upon it.

Anderson was just in time to pull Jensen out of its reach with a cry of disgust and fright, when the door shut again, and a low laugh was heard.

Jensen had seen nothing, but when Anderson hurriedly told him what a risk he had run, he fell into a great state of agitation, and suggested that they should retire from the enterprise and lock themselves up in one or other of their rooms.

However, while he was developing this plan, the landlord and two able-bodied men arrived on the scene, all looking rather serious and alarmed. Jensen met them with a torrent of description and explanation, which did not at all tend to encourage them for the fray.

The men dropped the crowbars they brought, and said flatly that they were going to risk their throats in that devil's den. The landlord was miserably nervous and decided, conscious that if the danger were faced his hotel was ruined, and very loath to face it himself. Luckily Anderson hit upon a way of rallying the demoralised force.

"Is this," he said, "the Danish courage I heard so much of? It isn't a German in there and if it was, we are five to one."

The two servants and Jensen were stung into action by this, and made a dash at the door.

"Stop!" said Anderson. "Don't lose your heads. You stay out here with the light, landlord, and one of you two men break the door, and don't go in when it gives way."

The men nodded, and the younger stepped forward, raised his crowbar, and dealt a tremendous blow on the upper panel. The result was not in the least what any of them anticipated. There was no cracking or rending of wood – only a dull sound, as if the solid wall had been struck. The man dropped his tool with a shout, and began rubbing his elbow. His cry drew their eyes upon him for a moment; then Anderson looked at the door again. It was gone; the plaster wall of the passage stared him in the face, with a considerable gash in it where the crowbar had struck it. Number 13 had passed out of existence.

For a brief space they stood perfectly still, gazing at the blank wall. An early cock in the yard beneath was heard to crow; and as Anderson glanced in the direction of the sound, he saw through the window at the end of the long passage that the eastern sky was paling to the dawn.

* * *

"Perhaps," said the landlord, with hesitation, "you gentlemen would like another room for tonight – a double-bedded one?"

Neither Jensen nor Anderson was averse to the suggestion. They felt inclined to hunt in couples after their late experience. It was found convenient, when each of them went to his room to collect the articles he wanted for the night, that the other should go with him and hold the candle. They noticed that both Number 12 and Number 14 had *three* windows.

Next morning the same party re-assembled in Number 12. The landlord was naturally anxious to avoid engaging outside help, and yet it was imperative that the mystery attaching to that part of the house should be cleared up. Accordingly the two servants had been induced to take upon them the function of carpenters. The furniture was cleared away, and, at the cost of a good many irretrievably damaged planks, that portion of the floor was taken up which lay nearest to Number 14.

You will naturally suppose that a skeleton – say that of Mag. Nicolas Francken – was discovered. That was not so. What they did find lying between the beams which supported the flooring was a small copper box. In it was a neatly-folded vellum document, with about twenty lines of writing. Both Anderson and Jensen (who proved to be something of a palaeographer) were much excited by this discovery, which promised to afford the key to these extraordinary phenomena.

* * *

I possess a copy of an astrological work which I have never read. It has, by way of frontispiece, a woodcut by Hans Sebald Beham, representing a number of sages seated round a table. This detail may enable connoisseurs to identify the book. I cannot myself recollect its title, and it is not at this moment within reach; but the fly-leaves of it are covered with writing, and, during the ten years in which I have owned the volume, I have not been able to determine which way up this writing ought to be read, much less in what language it is. Not dissimilar was the position of Anderson and Jensen after the protracted examination to which they submitted the document in the copper box.

After two days' contemplation of it, Jensen, who was the bolder spirit of the two, hazarded the conjecture that the language was either Latin or Old Danish.

Anderson ventured upon no surmises, and was very willing to surrender the box and the parchment to the Historical Society of Viborg to be placed in their museum.

I had the whole story from him a few months later, as we sat in a wood near Upsala, after a visit to the library there, where we – or, rather, I – had laughed over the contract by which Daniel Salthenius (in later life Professor of Hebrew at Königsberg) sold himself to Satan. Anderson was not really amused.

"Young idiot!" he said, meaning Salthenius, who was only an undergraduate when he committed that indiscretion, "How did he know what company he was courting?"

And when I suggested the usual considerations he only grunted. That same afternoon he told me what you have read; but he refused to draw any inferences from it, and to assent to any that I drew for him.

The Residence at Whitminster

M.R. James

DR. ASHTON – Thomas Ashton, Doctor of Divinity – sat in his study, habited in a dressing gown, and with a silk cap on his shaven head – his wig being for the time taken off and placed on its block on a side table. He was a man of some fifty-five years, strongly made, of a sanguine complexion, an angry eye, and a long upper lip. Face and eye were lighted up at the moment when I picture him by the level ray of an afternoon sun that shone in upon him through a tall sash window, giving on the west. The room into which it shone was also tall, lined with book-cases, and, where the wall showed between them, panelled. On the table near the doctor's elbow was a green cloth, and upon it what he would have called a silver standish – a tray with inkstands – quill pens, a calf-bound book or two, some papers, a church-warden pipe and brass tobacco-box, a flask cased in plaited straw, and a liqueur glass. The year was 1730, the month December, the hour somewhat past three in the afternoon.

I have described in these lines pretty much all that a superficial observer would have noted when he looked into the room. What met Dr. Ashton's eye when he looked out of it, sitting in his leather armchair? Little more than the tops of the shrubs and fruit trees of his garden could be seen from that point, but the red-brick wall of it was visible in almost all the length of its western side. In the middle of that was a gate – a double gate of rather elaborate iron scroll-work, which allowed something of a view beyond. Through it he could see that the ground sloped away almost at once to a bottom, along which a stream must run, and rose steeply from it on the other side, up to a field that was park-like in character, and thickly studded with oaks, now, of course, leafless. They did not stand so thick together but that some glimpse of sky and horizon could be seen between their stems. The sky was now golden and the horizon, a horizon of distant woods, it seemed, was purple.

But all that Dr. Ashton could find to say, after contemplating this prospect for many minutes, was: "Abominable!"

A listener would have been aware, immediately upon this, of the sound of footsteps coming somewhat hurriedly in the direction of the study: by the resonance he could have told that they were traversing a much larger room. Dr. Ashton turned round in his chair as the door opened, and looked expectant. The incomer was a lady – a stout lady in the dress of the time: though I have made some attempt at indicating the doctor's costume, I will not enterprise that of his wife – for it was Mrs. Ashton who now entered. She had an anxious, even a sorely distracted, look, and it was in a very disturbed voice that she almost whispered to Dr. Ashton, putting her head close to his, "He's in a very sad way, love, worse, I'm afraid."

"Tt—tt, is he really?" and he leaned back and looked in her face. She nodded. Two solemn bells, high up, and not far away, rang out the half-hour at this moment. Mrs. Ashton started. "Oh, do you think you can give order that the minster clock be stopped chiming tonight? 'Tis just over his chamber, and will keep him from sleeping, and to sleep is the only chance for him, that's certain."

"Why, to be sure, if there were need, real need, it could be done, but not upon any light occasion. This Frank, now, do you assure me that his recovery stands upon it?" said Dr. Ashton: his voice was loud and rather hard. "I do verily believe it," said his wife. "Then, if it must be, bid Molly run across to Simpkins and say on my authority that he is to stop the clock chimes at sunset: and – yes – she is after that to say to my lord Saul that I wish to see him presently in this room." Mrs. Ashton hurried off.

Before any other visitor enters, it will be well to explain the situation.

Dr. Ashton was the holder, among other preferments, of a prebend in the rich collegiate church of Whitminster, one of the foundations which, though not a cathedral, survived Dissolution and Reformation, and retained its constitution and endowments for a hundred years after the time of which I write. The great church, the residences of the dean and the two prebendaries, the choir and its appurtenances, were all intact and in working order. A dean who flourished soon after 1500 had been a great builder, and had erected a spacious quadrangle of red brick adjoining the church for the residence of the officials. Some of these persons were no longer required: their offices had dwindled down to mere titles, borne by clergy or lawyers in the town and neighbourhood; and so the houses that had been meant to accommodate eight or ten people were now shared among three – the dean and the two prebendaries. Dr. Ashton's included what had been the common parlour and the dining-hall of the whole body. It occupied a whole side of the court, and at one end had a private door into the minster. The other end, as we have seen, looked out over the country.

So much for the house. As for the inmates, Dr. Ashton was a wealthy man and childless, and he had adopted, or rather undertaken to bring up, the orphan son of his wife's sister. Frank Sydall was the lad's name: he had been a good many months in the house. Then one day came a letter from an Irish peer, the Earl of Kildonan (who had known Dr. Ashton at college), putting it to the doctor whether he would consider taking into his family the Viscount Saul, the Earl's heir, and acting in some sort as his tutor. Lord Kildonan was shortly to take up a post in the Lisbon Embassy, and the boy was unfit to make the voyage: "not that he is sickly," the Earl wrote, "though you'll find him whimsical, or of late I've thought him so, and to confirm this, 'twas only today his old nurse came expressly to tell me he was possess'd: but let that pass; I'll warrant you can find a spell to make all straight. Your arm was stout enough in old days, and I give you plenary authority to use it as you see fit. The truth is, he has here no boys of his age or quality to consort with, and is given to moping about in our raths and graveyards: and he brings home romances that fright my servants out of their wits. So there are you and your lady fore-warned." It was perhaps with half an eye open to the possibility of an Irish bishopric (at which another sentence in the Earl's letter seemed to hint) that Dr. Ashton accepted the charge of my Lord Viscount Saul and of the 200 guineas a year that were to come with him.

So he came, one night in September. When he got out of the chaise that brought him, he went first and spoke to the postboy and gave him some money, and patted the neck of his horse. Whether he made some movement that scared it or not, there was very nearly a nasty accident, for the beast started violently, and the postilion being unready was thrown and lost his fee, as he found afterwards, and the chaise lost some paint on the gateposts, and the wheel went over the man's foot who was taking out the baggage. When Lord Saul came up the steps into the light of the lamp in the porch to be greeted by Dr. Ashton, he was seen to be a thin youth of, say, sixteen years old, with straight black hair and the pale colouring that is common to such a figure. He took the accident and commotion calmly enough, and expressed a proper anxiety for the people who had been, or might have been, hurt: his voice was smooth and pleasant, and without any trace, curiously, of an Irish brogue.

Frank Sydall was a younger boy, perhaps of eleven or twelve, but Lord Saul did not for that reject his company. Frank was able to teach him various games he had not known in Ireland, and he was apt at learning them; apt, too, at his books, though he had had little or no regular teaching at home. It was not long before he was making a shift to puzzle out the inscriptions on the tombs in the minster, and he would often put a question to the doctor about the old books in the library that required some thought to answer. It is to be supposed that he made himself very agreeable to the servants, for within ten days of his coming they were almost falling over each other in their efforts to oblige him. At the same time, Mrs. Ashton was rather put to it to find new maidservants; for there were several changes, and some of the families in the town from which she had been accustomed to draw seemed to have no one available. She was forced to go farther afield than was usual.

These generalities I gather from the doctor's notes in his diary and from letters. They are generalities, and we should like, in view of what has to be told, something sharper and more detailed. We get it in entries which begin late in the year, and, I think, were posted up all together after the final incident; but they cover so few days in all that there is no need to doubt that the writer could remember the course of things accurately.

On a Friday morning it was that a fox, or perhaps a cat, made away with Mrs. Ashton's most prized black cockerel, a bird without a single white feather on its body. Her husband had told her often enough that it would make a suitable sacrifice to Aesculapius; that had discomfited her much, and now she would hardly be consoled. The boys looked everywhere for traces of it: Lord Saul brought in a few feathers, which seemed to have been partially burnt on the garden rubbish heap. It was on the same day that Dr. Ashton, looking out of an upper window, saw the two boys playing in the corner of the garden at a game he did not understand. Frank was looking earnestly at something in the palm of his hand. Saul stood behind him and seemed to be listening. After some minutes he very gently laid his hand on Frank's head, and almost instantly thereupon, Frank suddenly dropped whatever it was that he was holding, clapped his hands to his eyes, and sank down on the grass. Saul, whose face expressed great anger, hastily picked the object up, of which it could only be seen that it was glittering, put it in his pocket, and turned away, leaving Frank huddled up on the grass. Dr. Ashton rapped on the window to attract their attention, and Saul looked up as if in alarm, and then springing to Frank, pulled him up by the arm and led him away. When they came in to dinner, Saul explained that they had been acting a part of the tragedy of Radamistus, in which the heroine reads the future fate of her father's kingdom by means of a glass ball held in her hand, and is overcome by the terrible events she has seen. During this explanation Frank said nothing, only looked rather bewilderedly at Saul. He must, Mrs. Ashton thought, have contracted a chill from the wet of the grass, for that evening he was certainly feverish and disordered; and the disorder was of the mind as well as the body, for he seemed to have something he wished to say to Mrs. Ashton, only a press of household affairs prevented her from paying attention to him; and when she went, according to her habit, to see that the light in the boys' chamber had been taken away, and to bid them good night, he seemed to be sleeping, though his face was unnaturally flushed, to her thinking: Lord Saul, however, was pale and quiet, and smiling in his slumber.

Next morning it happened that Dr. Ashton was occupied in church and other business, and unable to take the boys' lessons. He therefore set them tasks to be written and brought to him. Three times, if not oftener, Frank knocked at the study door, and each time the doctor chanced to be engaged with some visitor, and sent the boy off rather roughly, which he later regretted. Two clergymen were at dinner this day, and both remarked – being fathers of families – that the lad seemed sickening for a fever, in which they were too near the truth, and it had been better if he had been put to bed forthwith: for a couple of hours later in the afternoon he came running into the house, crying out in a way that was really terrifying, and rushing to Mrs. Ashton, clung about her, begging her to protect him, and saying, "Keep them off! Keep them off!" without intermission. And it was now evident that some sickness had taken strong hold of him. He was therefore got to bed in another chamber from that in which he commonly lay, and the physician brought to him: who pronounced the disorder to be grave and affecting the lad's brain, and prognosticated a fatal end to it if strict quiet were not observed, and those sedative remedies used which he should prescribe.

We are now come by another way to the point we had reached before. The minster clock has been stopped from striking, and Lord Saul is on the threshold of the study.

"What account can you give of this poor lad's state?" was Dr. Ashton's first question.

"Why, sir, little more than you know already, I fancy. I must blame myself, though, for giving him a fright yesterday when we were acting that silly play you saw. I fear I made him take it more to heart than I meant."

"How so?"

"Well, by telling him foolish tales I had picked up in Ireland of what we call the second sight."

"*Second* sight! What kind of sight might that be?"

"Why, you know our ignorant people pretend that some are able to foresee what is to come – sometimes in a glass, or in the air, maybe, and at Kildonan we had an old woman that pretended to such a power. And I dare say I coloured the matter more highly than I should: but I never dreamed Frank would take it so near as he did."

"You were wrong, my lord, very wrong, in meddling with such superstitious matters at all, and you should have considered whose house you were in, and how little becoming such actions are to my character and person or to your own: but pray how came it that you, acting, as you say, a play, should fall upon anything that could so alarm Frank?"

"That is what I can hardly tell, sir: he passed all in a moment from rant about battles and lovers and Cleodora and Antigenes to something I could not follow at all, and then dropped down as you saw."

"Yes: was that at the moment when you laid your hand on the top of his head?" Lord Saul gave a quick look at his questioner – quick and spiteful – and for the first time seemed unready with an answer. "About that time it may have been," he said. "I have tried to recollect myself, but I am not sure. There was, at any rate, no significance in what I did then."

"Ah!" said Dr. Ashton, "Well, my lord, I should do wrong were I not to tell you that this fright of my poor nephew may have very ill consequences to him. The doctor speaks very despondingly of his state." Lord Saul pressed his hands together and looked earnestly upon Dr. Ashton. "I am willing to believe you had no bad intention, as assuredly you could have no reason to bear the poor boy malice: but I cannot wholly free you from blame in the affair." As he spoke, the hurrying steps were heard again, and Mrs. Ashton came quickly into the room, carrying a candle, for the evening had by this time closed in. She was greatly agitated. "O come!" she cried, "Come directly. I'm sure he is going."

"Going? Frank? Is it possible? Already?" With some such incoherent words the doctor caught up a book of prayers from the table and ran out after his wife. Lord Saul stopped for a moment where he was. Molly, the maid, saw him bend over and put both hands to his face. If it were the last words she had to speak, she said afterwards, he was striving to keep back a fit of laughing. Then he went out softly, following the others.

Mrs. Ashton was sadly right in her forecast. I have no inclination to imagine the last scene in detail. What Dr. Ashton records is, or may be taken to be, important to the story. They asked Frank if he would like to see his companion, Lord Saul, once again. The boy was quite collected, it appears, in these moments. "No," he said, "I do not want to see him; but you should tell him I am afraid he will be very cold."

"What do you mean, my dear?" said Mrs. Ashton.

"Only that," said Frank; "but say to him besides that I am free of them now, but he should take care. And I am sorry about your black cockerel, Aunt Ashton; but he said we must use it so, if we were to see all that could be seen."

Not many minutes after, he was gone. Both the Ashtons were grieved, she naturally most; but the doctor, though not an emotional man, felt the pathos of the early death: and, besides, there was the growing suspicion that all had not been told him by Saul, and that there was something here which was out of his beaten track. When he left the chamber of death, it was to walk across the quadrangle of the residence to the sexton's house. A passing bell, the greatest of the minster bells, must be rung, a grave must be dug in the minster yard, and there was now no need to silence the chiming of the minster clock. As he came slowly back in the dark, he thought he must see Lord Saul again. That matter of the black cockerel – trifling as it might seem – would have to be cleared up. It might be merely a fancy of the sick boy, but if not, was there not a witch trial he had read, in which some grim little rite of sacrifice had played a part? Yes, he must see Saul.

I rather guess these thoughts of his than find written authority for them. That there was another interview is certain: certain also that Saul would (or, as he said, could) throw no light on Frank's words: though the message, or some part of it, appeared to affect him horribly. But there is no record of the talk in detail. It is only said that Saul sat all that evening in the study, and when he bid goodnight, which he did most reluctantly, asked for the doctor's prayers.

The month of January was near its end when Lord Kildonan, in the Embassy at Lisbon, received a letter that for once gravely disturbed that vain man and neglectful father. Saul was dead. The scene at Frank's burial had been very distressing. The day was awful in blackness and wind: the bearers, staggering blindly along under the flapping black pall, found it a hard job, when they emerged from the porch of the minster, to make their way to the grave. Mrs. Ashton was in her room – women did not then go to their kinsfolk's funerals – but Saul was there, draped in the mourning cloak of the time, and his face was white and fixed as that of one dead, except when, as was noticed three or four times, he suddenly turned his head to the left and looked over his shoulder. It was then alive with a terrible expression of listening fear. No one saw him go away: and no one could find him that evening. All night the gale buffeted the high windows of the church, and howled over the upland and roared through the woodland. It was useless to search in the open: no voice of shouting or cry for help could possibly be heard. All that Dr. Ashton could do was to warn the people about the college, and the town constables, and to sit up, on the alert for any news, and this he did. News came early next morning, brought by the sexton, whose business it was to open the church for early prayers at seven, and who sent the maid rushing upstairs with wild eyes and flying hair to summon her master. The two men dashed across to the south door of the minster, there to find Lord Saul clinging desperately to the great ring of the door, his head sunk between his shoulders, his stockings in rags, his shoes gone, his legs torn and bloody.

This was what had to be told to Lord Kildonan, and this really ends the first part of the story. The tomb of Frank Sydall and of the Lord Viscount Saul, only child and heir to William Earl of Kildonan, is one: a stone altar tomb in Whitminster churchyard.

Dr. Ashton lived on for over thirty years in his prebendal house, I do not know how quietly, but without visible disturbance. His successor preferred a house he already owned in the town, and left that of the senior prebendary vacant. Between them these two men saw the eighteenth century out and the nineteenth in; for Mr. Hindes, the successor of Ashton, became prebendary at nine-and-twenty and died at nine-and-eighty. So that it was not till 1823 or 1824 that anyone succeeded to the post who intended to make the house his home. The man who did so was Dr. Henry Oldys, whose name may be known to some of my readers as that of the author of a row of volumes labelled *Oldys's Works*, which occupy a place that must be honoured, since it is so rarely touched, upon the shelves of many a substantial library.

Dr. Oldys, his niece, and his servants took some months to transfer furniture and books from his Dorsetshire parsonage to the quadrangle of Whitminster, and to get everything into place. But eventually the work was done, and the house (which, though untenanted, had always been kept sound and weather-tight) woke up, and like Monte Cristo's mansion at Auteuil, lived, sang, and bloomed once more. On a certain morning in June it looked especially fair, as Dr. Oldys strolled in his garden before breakfast and gazed over the red roof at the minster tower with its four gold vanes, backed by a very blue sky, and very white little clouds.

"Mary," he said, as he seated himself at the breakfast table and laid down something hard and shiny on the cloth, "here's a find which the boy made just now. You'll be sharper than I if you can guess what it's meant for." It was a round and perfectly smooth tablet – as much as an inch thick – of what seemed clear glass. "It is rather attractive, at all events," said Mary: she was a fair woman, with light hair and large eyes, rather a devotee of literature.

"Yes," said her uncle, "I thought you'd be pleased with it. I presume it came from the house: it turned up in the rubbish-heap in the corner."

"I'm not sure that I do like it, after all," said Mary, some minutes later.

"Why in the world not, my dear?"

"I don't know, I'm sure. Perhaps it's only fancy."

"Yes, only fancy and romance, of course. What's that book, now – the name of that book, I mean, that you had your head in all yesterday?"

"*The Talisman*, Uncle. Oh, if this should turn out to be a talisman, how enchanting it would be!"

"Yes, *The Talisman*: ah, well, you're welcome to it, whatever it is: I must be off about my business. Is all well in the house? Does it suit you? Any complaints from the servants' hall?"

"No, indeed, nothing could be more charming. The only *soupçon* of a complaint besides the lock of the linen closet, which I told you of, is that Mrs. Maple says she cannot get rid of the sawflies out of that room you pass through at the other end of the hall. By the way, are you sure you like your bedroom? It is a long way off from anyone else, you know."

"Like it? To be sure I do; the farther off from you, my dear, the better. There, don't think it necessary to beat me; accept my apologies. But what are sawflies? Will they eat my coats? If not, they may have the room to themselves for what I care. We are not likely to be using it."

"No, of course not. Well, what she calls sawflies are those reddish things like a daddy-long-legs, but smaller, and there are a great many of them perching about that room, certainly. I don't like them, but I don't fancy they are mischievous."

"There seem to be several things you don't like this fine morning," said her uncle, as he closed the door. Miss Oldys remained in her chair looking at the tablet, which she was holding in the palm of her hand. The smile that had been on her face faded slowly from it and gave place to an expression of curiosity and almost strained attention. Her reverie was broken by the entrance of Mrs. Maple, and her invariable opening, "Oh, Miss, could I speak to you a minute?"

A letter from Miss Oldys to a friend in Lichfield, begun a day or two before, is the next source for this story. It is not devoid of traces of the influence of that leader of female thought in her day, Miss Anna Seward, known to some as the Swan of Lichfield.

> *My sweetest Emily will be rejoiced to hear that we are at length – my beloved uncle and myself – settled in the house that now calls us master – nay, master and mistress – as in past ages it has called so many others. Here we taste a mingling of modern elegance and hoary antiquity, such as has never ere now graced life for either of us. The town, small as it is, affords us some reflection, pale indeed, but veritable, of the sweets of polite intercourse: the adjacent country numbers amid the occupants of its scattered mansions some whose polish is annually refreshed by contact with metropolitan splendour, and others whose robust and homely geniality is, at times,*

and by way of contrast, not less cheering and acceptable. Tired of the parlours and drawing rooms of our friends, we have ready to hand a refuge from the clash of wits or the small talk of the day amid the solemn beauties of our venerable minster, whose silver chimes daily 'knoll us to prayer', and in the shady walks of whose tranquil graveyard we muse with softened heart, and ever and anon with moistened eye, upon the memorials of the young, the beautiful, the aged, the wise, and the good.

Here there is an abrupt break both in the writing and the style.

But my dearest Emily, I can no longer write with the care which you deserve, and in which we both take pleasure. What I have to tell you is wholly foreign to what has gone before. This morning my uncle brought in to breakfast an object which had been found in the garden; it was a glass or crystal tablet of this shape (a little sketch is given), which he handed to me, and which, after he left the room, remained on the table by me. I gazed at it, I know not why, for some minutes, till called away by the day's duties; and you will smile incredulously when I say that I seemed to myself to begin to descry reflected in it objects and scenes which were not in the room where I was. You will not, however, think it strange that after such an experience I took the first opportunity to seclude myself in my room with what I now half believed to be a talisman of mickle might. I was not disappointed. I assure you, Emily, by that memory which is dearest to both of us, that what I went through this afternoon transcends the limits of what I had before deemed credible. In brief, what I saw, seated in my bedroom, in the broad daylight of summer, and looking into the crystal depth of that small round tablet, was this. First, a prospect, strange to me, of an enclosure of rough and hillocky grass, with a grey stone ruin in the midst, and a wall of rough stones about it. In this stood an old, and very ugly, woman in a red cloak and ragged skirt, talking to a boy dressed in the fashion of maybe a hundred years ago. She put something which glittered into his hand, and he something into hers, which I saw to be money, for a single coin fell from her trembling hand into the grass. The scene passed: I should have remarked, by the way, that on the rough walls of the enclosure I could distinguish bones, and even a skull, lying in a disorderly fashion. Next, I was looking upon two boys; one the figure of the former vision, the other younger. They were in a plot of garden, walled round, and this garden, in spite of the difference in arrangement, and the small size of the trees, I could clearly recognise as being that upon which I now look from my window. The boys were engaged in some curious play, it seemed. Something was smouldering on the ground. The elder placed his hands upon it, and then raised them in what I took to be an attitude of prayer: and I saw, and started at seeing, that on them were deep stains of blood. The sky above was overcast. The same boy now turned his face towards the wall of the garden, and beckoned with both his raised hands, and as he did so I was conscious that some moving objects were becoming visible over the top of the wall – whether heads or other parts of some animal or human forms I could not tell. Upon the instant the elder boy turned sharply, seized the arm of the younger (who all this time had been poring over what lay on the ground), and both hurried off. I then saw blood upon the grass, a little pile of bricks, and what I thought were black feathers scattered about. That scene closed, and the next was so dark that perhaps the full meaning of it escaped me. But what I seemed to see was a form, at first crouching low among trees or bushes that were being threshed by a violent wind, then running very swiftly, and constantly turning a pale face to look behind him, as if he feared a pursuer: and, indeed, pursuers were following hard after him. Their shapes were but dimly seen, their number – three or four, perhaps – only guessed. I suppose they were on the whole more like dogs than anything else, but dogs such as we have seen they assuredly were not. Could I have closed my eyes to this horror, I would have done so at once, but I was helpless. The last I saw was the victim darting beneath an arch and clutching at some object to which he clung: and those that were pursuing him overtook him, and I seemed to hear the echo of a cry of despair. It may be that I became unconscious: certainly I had the sensation of awaking to the light of day after an interval of darkness. Such, in literal truth, Emily, was my vision – I can call it by no other name – of this afternoon. Tell me, have I not been the unwilling witness of some episode of a tragedy connected with this very house?

The letter is continued next day.

The tale of yesterday was not completed when I laid down my pen. I said nothing of my experiences to my uncle – you know, yourself, how little his robust common sense would be prepared to allow of them, and how in his eyes the specific remedy would be a black draught or a glass of port. After a silent evening, then – silent, not sullen – I retired to rest. Judge of my terror, when, not yet in bed, I heard what I can only describe as a distant bellow, and knew it for my uncle's voice, though never in my hearing so exerted before. His sleeping-room is at the farther extremity of this large house, and to gain access to it one must traverse an antique hall some eighty feet long, a lofty panelled chamber, and two unoccupied bedrooms. In the second of these – a room almost devoid of furniture – I found him, in the dark, his candle lying smashed on the floor. As I ran in, bearing a light, he clasped me in arms that trembled for the first time since I have known him, thanked God, and hurried me out of the room. He would say nothing of what had alarmed him. 'Tomorrow, tomorrow,' was all I could get from him. A bed was hastily improvised for him in the room next to my own. I doubt if his night was more restful than mine. I could only get to sleep in the small hours, when daylight was already strong, and then my dreams were of the grimmest – particularly one which stamped itself on my brain, and which I must set down on the chance of dispersing the impression it has made. It was that I came up to my room with a heavy foreboding of evil oppressing me, and went with a hesitation and reluctance I could not explain to my chest of drawers. I opened the top drawer, in which was nothing but ribbons and handkerchiefs, and then the second, where was as little to alarm, and then, O heavens, the third and last: and there was a mass of linen neatly folded: upon which, as I looked with a curiosity that began to be tinged with horror, I perceived a movement in it, and a pink hand was thrust out of the folds and began to grope feebly in the air. I could bear it no more, and rushed from the room, clapping the door after me, and strove with all my force to lock it. But the key would not turn in the wards, and from within the room came a sound of rustling and bumping, drawing nearer and nearer to the door. Why I did not flee down the stairs I know not. I continued grasping the handle, and mercifully, as the door was plucked from my hand with an irresistible force, I awoke. You may not think this very alarming, but I assure you it was so to me.

At breakfast today my uncle was very uncommunicative, and I think ashamed of the fright he had given us; but afterwards he inquired of me whether Mr. Spearman was still in town, adding that he thought that was a young man who had some sense left in his head. I think you know, my dear Emily, that I am not inclined to disagree with him there, and also that I was not unlikely to be able to answer his question. To Mr. Spearman he accordingly went, and I have not seen him since. I must send this strange budget of news to you now, or it may have to wait over more than one post.

The reader will not be far out if he guesses that Miss Mary and Mr. Spearman made a match of it not very long after this month of June. Mr. Spearman was a young spark, who had a good property in the neighbourhood of Whitminster, and not unfrequently about this time spent a few days at the 'King's Head', ostensibly on business. But he must have had some leisure, for his diary is copious, especially for the days of which I am telling the story. It is probable to me that he wrote this episode as fully as he could at the bidding of Miss Mary:

"Uncle Oldys (how I hope I may have the right to call him so before long!) called this morning. After throwing out a good many short remarks on indifferent topics, he said, 'I wish, Spearman, you'd listen to an odd story and keep a close tongue about it just for a bit, till I get more light on it.' 'To be sure,' said I, 'you may count on me.' 'I don't know what to make of it,' he said. 'You know my bedroom. It is well away from everyone else's, and I pass through the great hall and two or three other rooms to get to it.' 'Is it at the end next the minster, then?' I asked. 'Yes, it is: well, now, yesterday morning my Mary told me that the room next before it was infested with some sort of fly that the housekeeper couldn't get rid of. That may be the explanation, or it may not. What do you think?' 'Why,' said I, 'you've not yet told me what has to be explained.' 'True enough, I don't believe I have; but by the by, what are these sawflies? What's the size of them?' I began to wonder if he was touched in the head. 'What I call a sawfly,' I said very patiently, 'is a red animal, like a daddy-long-legs, but not so big, perhaps an inch long, perhaps less. It is very hard in the body, and to me' – I was going to say 'particularly offensive,' but he broke in, 'Come, come; an inch or less. That won't do.' 'I can only tell you,' I said, 'what I know. Would it not be better if you told me from first to last what it is that has puzzled you, and then I may be able to give you some kind of an opinion.' He gazed at me meditatively. 'Perhaps it would,' he said. 'I told Mary only today that I thought you had some vestiges of sense in your head.' (I bowed my acknowledgments.) 'The thing is, I've an odd kind of shyness about talking of it. Nothing of the sort has happened to me before. Well, about eleven o'clock last night, or after, I took my candle and set out for my room. I had a book in my other hand – I always read something for a few minutes before I drop off to sleep. A dangerous habit: I don't recommend it: but *I* know how to manage my light and my bed curtains. Now then, first, as I stepped out of my study into the great hall that's next to it, and shut the door, my candle went out. I supposed I had clapped the door behind me too quick, and made a draught, and I was annoyed, for I'd no tinderbox nearer than my bedroom. But I knew my way well enough, and went on. The next thing was that my book was struck out of my hand in the dark: if I said twitched out of my hand it would better express the sensation. It fell on the floor. I picked it up, and went on, more annoyed than before, and a little startled. But as you know, that hall has many windows without curtains, and in summer nights like these it's easy to see not only where the furniture is, but whether there's anyone or anything moving: and there was no one – nothing of the kind. So on I went through the hall and through the audit chamber next to it, which also has big windows, and then into the bedrooms which lead to my own, where the curtains were drawn, and I had to go slower because of steps here and there. It was in the second of those rooms that I nearly got my *quietus*. The moment I opened the door of it I felt there was something wrong. I thought twice, I confess, whether I shouldn't turn back and find another way there is to my room rather than go through that one. Then I was ashamed of myself, and thought what people call better of it, though I don't know about 'better' in this case. If I was to describe my experience exactly, I should say this: there was a dry, light, rustling sound all over the room as I went in, and then (you remember it was perfectly dark) something seemed to rush at me, and there was – I don't know how to put it – a sensation of long thin arms, or legs, or feelers, all about my face, and neck, and body. Very little strength in them, there seemed to be, but, Spearman, I don't think I was ever more horrified or disgusted in all my life, that I remember: and it does take something to put me out. I roared out as loud as I could, and flung away my candle at random, and, knowing I was near the window, I tore at the curtain and somehow let in enough light to be able to see something waving which I knew was an insect's leg, by the shape of it: but, Lord, what a size! Why, the beast must have been as tall as I am. And now you tell me sawflies are an inch long or less. What do you make of it, Spearman?'

'"For goodness' sake finish your story first,' I said. 'I never heard anything like it.' 'Oh,' said he, 'there's no more to tell. Mary ran in with a light, and there was nothing there. I didn't tell her what was the matter. I changed my room for last night, and I expect for good.' 'Have you searched this odd room of yours?' I said. 'What do you keep in it?' 'We don't use it,' he answered. 'There's an old press there, and some little other furniture.' 'And in the press?' said I. 'I don't know; I never saw it opened, but I do know that it's locked.' 'Well, I should have it looked into, and, if you had time, I own to having some curiosity to see the place myself.' 'I didn't exactly like to ask you, but that's rather what I hoped you'd say. Name your time and I'll take you there.' 'No time like the present,' I said at once, for I saw he would never settle down to anything while this affair was in suspense. He got up with great alacrity, and looked at me, I am tempted to think, with marked approval. 'Come along,' was all he said, however; and was pretty silent all the way to his house. My Mary (as he calls her in public, and I in private) was summoned, and we proceeded to the room. The Doctor had gone so far as to tell her that he had had something of a fright there last night, of what nature he had not yet divulged; but now he pointed out and described, very briefly, the incidents of his progress. When we were near the important spot, he pulled up, and allowed me to pass on. 'There's the room,' he said. 'Go in, Spearman, and tell us what you find.' Whatever I might have felt at midnight, noonday I was sure would keep back anything sinister, and I flung the door open with an air and stepped in. It was a well-lighted room, with its large window on the right, though not, I thought, a very airy one. The principal piece of furniture was the gaunt old press of dark wood. There was, too, a four-post bedstead, a mere skeleton which could hide nothing, and there was a chest of drawers. On the windowsill and the floor near it were the dead bodies of many hundred sawflies, and one torpid one which I had some satisfaction in killing. I tried the door of the press, but could not open it: the drawers, too, were locked. Somewhere, I was conscious, there was a faint rustling sound, but I could not locate it, and when I made my report to those outside, I said nothing of it. But, I said, clearly the next thing was to see what was in those locked receptacles. Uncle Oldys turned to Mary. 'Mrs. Maple,' he said, and Mary ran off – no one, I am sure, steps like her – and soon came back at a soberer pace, with an elderly lady of discreet aspect.

'"Have you the keys of these things, Mrs. Maple?' said Uncle Oldys. His simple words let loose a torrent (not violent, but copious) of speech: had she been a shade or two higher in the social scale, Mrs. Maple might have stood as the model for Miss Bates.

'"Oh, Doctor, and Miss, and you too, sir,' she said, acknowledging my presence with a bend, 'them keys! Who was that again that come when first we took over things in this house – a gentleman in business it was, and I gave him his luncheon in the small parlour on account of us not having everything as we should like to see it in the large one – chicken, and apple-pie, and a glass of madeira – dear, dear, you'll say I'm running on, Miss Mary; but I only mention it to bring back my recollection; and there it comes – Gardner, just the same as it did last week with the artichokes and the text of the sermon. Now that Mr. Gardner, every key I got from him were labelled to itself, and each and every one was a key of some door or another in this house, and sometimes two; and when I say door, my meaning is door of a room, not like such a press as this is. Yes, Miss Mary, I know full well, and I'm just making it clear to your uncle and you too, sir. But now there *was* a box which this same gentleman he give over into my charge, and thinking no harm after he was gone I took the liberty, knowing it was your uncle's property, to rattle it: and unless I'm most surprisingly deceived, in that box there was keys, but what keys, that, Doctor, is known Elsewhere, for open the box, no that I would not do.'

"I wondered that Uncle Oldys remained as quiet as he did under this address. Mary, I knew, was amused by it, and he probably had been taught by experience that it was useless to break in upon it. At any rate he did not, but merely said at the end, 'Have you that box handy, Mrs. Maple? If so, you might bring it here.' Mrs. Maple pointed her finger at him, either in accusation or in gloomy triumph. 'There,' she said, 'was I to choose out the very words out of your mouth, Doctor, them would be the ones. And if I've took it to my own rebuke one half a dozen times, it's been nearer fifty. Laid awake I have in my bed, sat down in my chair I have, the same you and Miss Mary gave me the day I was twenty year in your service, and no person could desire a better – yes, Miss Mary, but it *is* the truth, and well we know who it is would have it different if he could. 'All very well,' says I to myself, 'but pray, when the Doctor calls you to account for that box, what are you going to say?' No, Doctor, if you was some masters I've heard of and I was some servants I could name, I should have an easy task before me, but things being, humanly speaking, what they are, the one course open to me is just to say to you that without Miss Mary comes to my room and helps me to my recollection, which her wits *may* manage what's slipped beyond mine, no such box as that, small though it be, will cross your eyes this many a day to come.'

"'Why, dear Mrs. Maple, why didn't you tell me before that you wanted me to help you to find it?' said my Mary. 'No, never mind telling me why it was: let us come at once and look for it.' They hastened off together. I could hear Mrs. Maple beginning an explanation which, I doubt not, lasted into the farthest recesses of the housekeeper's department. Uncle Oldys and I were left alone. 'A valuable servant,' he said, nodding towards the door. 'Nothing goes wrong under her: the speeches are seldom over three minutes.' 'How will Miss Oldys manage to make her remember about the box?' I asked.

"'Mary? Oh, she'll make her sit down and ask her about her aunt's last illness, or who gave her the china dog on the mantelpiece – something quite off the point. Then, as Maple says, one thing brings up another, and the right one will come round sooner than you could suppose. There! I believe I hear them coming back already.'

"It was indeed so, and Mrs. Maple was hurrying on ahead of Mary with the box in her outstretched hand, and a beaming face. 'What was it,' she cried as she drew near, 'what was it as I said, before ever I come out of Dorsetshire to this place? Not that I'm a Dorset woman myself, nor had need to be. 'Safe bind, safe find', and there it was in the place where I'd put it – what? – two months back, I dare say.' She handed it to Uncle Oldys, and he and I examined it with some interest, so that I ceased to pay attention to Mrs. Ann Maple for the moment, though I know that she went on to expound exactly where the box had been, and in what way Mary had helped to refresh her memory on the subject.

"It was an oldish box, tied with pink tape and sealed, and on the lid was pasted a label inscribed in old ink, 'The Senior Prebendary's House, Whitminster'. On being opened it was found to contain two keys of moderate size, and a paper, on which, in the same hand as the label, was 'Keys of the Press and Box of Drawers standing in the disused Chamber'. Also this: 'The Effects in this Press and Box are held by me, and to be held by my successors in the Residence, in trust for the noble Family of Kildonan, if claim be made by any survivor of it. I having made all the Enquiry possible to myself am of the opinion that that noble House is wholly extinct: the last Earl having been, as is notorious, cast away at sea, and his only Child and Heire deceas'd in my House (the Papers as to which melancholy Casualty were by me repos'd in the same Press in this year of our Lord 1753, 21 March). I am further of opinion that unless grave discomfort arise, such persons, not being of the Family of Kildonan, as shall become possess'd of these keys, will be well advised to leave matters as they are: which opinion I do not express without weighty and sufficient reason; and am Happy to have my Judgment confirm'd by the other Members of this College and Church who are conversant with the Events referr'd to in this Paper. Tho. Ashton, *S.T.P.*, *Praeb. senr.* Will. Blake, *S.T.P.*, *Decanus.* Hen. Goodman, *S.T.B.*, *Praeb. junr.*'

"'Ah!' said Uncle Oldys, 'grave discomfort! So he thought there might be something. I suspect it was that young man,' he went on, pointing with the key to the line about the 'only Child and Heire.' 'Eh, Mary? The viscounty of Kildonan was Saul.' 'How *do* you know that, Uncle?' said Mary. 'Oh, why not? It's all in Debrett – two little fat books. But I meant the tomb by the lime walk. He's there. What's the story, I wonder? Do you know it, Mrs. Maple? And, by the way, look at your sawflies by the window there.'

"Mrs. Maple, thus confronted with two subjects at once, was a little put to it to do justice to both. It was no doubt rash in Uncle Oldys to give her the opportunity. I could only guess that he had some slight hesitation about using the key he held in his hand.

"'Oh them flies, how bad they was, Doctor and Miss, this three or four days: and you, too, sir, you wouldn't guess, none of you! And how they come, too! First we took the room in hand, the shutters was up, and had been, I dare say, years upon years, and not a fly to be seen. Then we got the shutter bars down with a deal of trouble and left it so for the day, and next day I sent Susan in with the broom to sweep about, and not two minutes hadn't passed when out she come into the hall like a blind thing, and we had regular to beat them off her. Why, her cap and her hair, you couldn't see the colour of it, I do assure you, and all clustering round her eyes, too. Fortunate enough she's not a girl with fancies, else if it had been me, why only the tickling of the nasty things would have drove me out of my wits. And now there they lay like so many dead things. Well, they was lively enough on the Monday, and now here's Thursday, is it, or no, Friday. Only to come near the door and you'd hear them pattering up against it, and once you opened it, dash at you, they would, as if they'd eat you. I couldn't help thinking to myself, 'If you was bats, where should we be this night?' Nor you can't cresh 'em, not like a usual kind of a fly. Well, there's something to be thankful for, if we could but learn by it. And then this tomb, too,' she said, hastening on to her second point to elude any chance of interruption, 'of them two poor young lads. I say poor, and yet when I recollect myself, I was at tea with Mrs. Simpkins, the sexton's wife, before you come, Doctor and Miss Mary, and that's a family has been in the place, what? I dare say a hundred years in that very house, and could put their hand on any tomb or yet grave in all the yard and give you name and age. And his account of that young man, Mr. Simpkins's I mean to say – *well!*" She compressed her lips and nodded several times. 'Tell us, Mrs. Maple,' said Mary. 'Go on,' said Uncle Oldys. 'What about him?' said I. 'Never was such a thing seen in this place, not since Queen Mary's times and the Pope and all,' said Mrs. Maple. 'Why, do you know he lived in this very house, him and them that was with him, and for all I can tell in this identical room' (she shifted her feet uneasily on the floor). 'Who was with him? Do you mean the people of the house?' said Uncle Oldys suspiciously. 'Not to call people, Doctor, dear no,' was the answer; 'more what he brought with him from Ireland, I believe it was. No, the people in the house was the last to hear anything of his goings-on. But in the town not a family but knew how he stopped out at night: and them that was with him, why, they were such as would strip the skin from the child in its grave; and a withered heart makes an ugly thin ghost, says Mr. Simpkins. But they turned on him at the last, he says, and there's the mark still to be seen on the minster door where they run him down. And that's no more than the truth, for I got him to show it to myself, and that's what he said. A lord he was, with a Bible name of a wicked king, whatever his god-fathers could have been thinking of.' 'Saul was the name,' said Uncle Oldys. 'To be sure it was Saul, Doctor, and thank you; and now isn't it King Saul that we read of raising up the dead ghost that was slumbering in its tomb till he disturbed it, and isn't that a strange thing, this young lord to have such a name, and Mr. Simpkins's grandfather to see him out of his window of a dark night going about from one grave to another in the yard with a candle, and them that was with him following through the grass at his heels: and one night him to come right up to old Mr. Simpkins's window that gives on the yard and press his face up against it to find out if there was anyone in the room that could see him: and only just time there was for old Mr. Simpkins to drop down like, quiet, just under the window and hold his breath, and not stir till he heard him stepping away again, and this rustling-like in the grass after him as he went, and then when he looked out of his window in the morning there was treadings in the grass and a dead man's bone. Oh, he was a cruel child for certain, but he had to pay in the end, and after.' 'After?' said Uncle Oldys, with a frown. 'Oh yes, Doctor, night after night in old Mr. Simpkins's time, and his son, that's our Mr. Simpkins's father, yes, and our own Mr. Simpkins too. Up against that same window, particular when they've had a fire of a chilly evening, with his face right on the panes, and his hands fluttering out, and his mouth open and shut, open and shut, for a minute or more, and then gone off in the dark yard. But open the window at such times, no, that they dare not do, though they could find it in their heart to pity the poor thing, that pinched up with the cold, and seemingly fading away to a nothink as the years passed on. Well, indeed, I believe it is no more than the truth what our Mr. Simpkins says on his own grandfather's word, 'A withered heart makes an ugly thin ghost.'' 'I dare say,' said Uncle Oldys suddenly: so suddenly that Mrs. Maple stopped short. 'Thank you. Come away, all of you.' 'Why, *Uncle*,' said Mary, 'are you not going to open the press after all?' Uncle Oldys blushed, actually blushed. 'My dear,' he said, 'you are at liberty to call me a coward, or applaud me as a prudent man, whichever you please. But I am neither going to open that press nor that chest of drawers myself, nor am I going to hand over the keys to you or to any other person. Mrs. Maple, will you kindly see about getting a man or two to move those pieces of furniture into the garret?' 'And when they do it, Mrs. Maple,' said Mary, who seemed to me – I did not then know why – more relieved than disappointed by her uncle's decision, 'I have something that I want put with the rest; only quite a small packet.'

"We left that curious room not unwillingly, I think. Uncle Oldys's orders were carried out that same day. And so," concludes Mr. Spearman, "Whitminster has a Bluebeard's chamber, and, I am rather inclined to suspect, a Jack-in-the-box, awaiting some future occupant of the residence of the senior prebendary."

They

Rudyard Kipling

ONE VIEW called me to another; one hilltop to its fellow, half across the county, and since I could answer at no more trouble than the snapping forward of a lever, I let the country flow under my wheels. The orchid-studded flats of the East gave way to the thyme, ilex, and grey grass of the Downs; these again to the rich cornland and fig-trees of the lower coast, where you carry the beat of the tide on your left hand for fifteen level miles; and when at last I turned inland through a huddle of rounded hills and woods I had run myself clean out of my known marks. Beyond that precise hamlet which stands godmother to the capital of the United States, I found hidden villages where bees, the only things awake, boomed in eighty-foot lindens that overhung grey Norman churches; miraculous brooks diving under stone bridges built for heavier traffic than would ever vex them again; tithe barns larger than their churches, and an old smithy that cried out aloud how it had once been a hall of the Knights of the Temple. Gipsies I found on a common where the gorse, bracken, and heath fought it out together up a mile of Roman road; and a little farther on I disturbed a red fox rolling dog-fashion in the naked sunlight.

As the wooded hills closed about me I stood up in the car to take the bearings of that great Down whose ringed head is a landmark for fifty miles across the low countries. I judged that the lie of the country would bring me across some westward running road that went to his feet, but I did not allow for the confusing veils of the woods. A quick turn plunged me first into a green cutting brimful of liquid sunshine, next into a gloomy tunnel where last year's dead leaves whispered and scuffled about my tyres. The strong hazel stuff meeting overhead had not been cut for a couple of generations at least, nor had any axe helped the moss-cankered oak and beech to spring above them. Here the road changed frankly into a carpeted ride on whose brown velvet spent primrose-clumps showed like jade, and a few sickly, white-stalked bluebells nodded together. As the slope favoured I shut off the power and slid over the whirled leaves, expecting every moment to meet a keeper; but I only heard a jay, far off, arguing against the silence under the twilight of the trees.

Still the track descended. I was on the point of reversing and working my way back on the second speed ere I ended in some swamp, when I saw sunshine through the tangle ahead and lifted the brake.

It was down again at once. As the light beat across my face my fore-wheels took the turf of a great still lawn from which sprang horsemen ten feet high with levelled lances, monstrous peacocks, and sleek round-headed maids of honour – blue, black, and glistening – all of clipped yew. Across the lawn – the marshalled woods besieged it on three sides – stood an ancient house of lichened and weather-worn stone, with mullioned windows and roofs of rose-red tile. It was flanked by semi-circular walls, also rose-red, that closed the lawn on the fourth side, and at their feet a box hedge grew man-high. There were doves on the roof about the slim brick chimneys, and I caught a glimpse of an octagonal dove-house behind the screening wall.

Here, then, I stayed; a horseman's green spear laid at my breast; held by the exceeding beauty of that jewel in that setting.

"If I am not packed off for a trespasser, or if this knight does not ride a wallop at me," thought I, "Shakespeare and Queen Elizabeth at least must come out of that half-open garden door and ask me to tea."

A child appeared at an upper window, and I thought the little thing waved a friendly hand. But it was to call a companion, for presently another bright head showed. Then I heard a laugh among the yew-peacocks, and turning to make sure (till then I had been watching the house only) I saw the silver of a fountain behind a hedge thrown up against the sun. The doves on the roof cooed to the cooing water; but between the two notes I caught the utterly happy chuckle of a child absorbed in some light mischief.

The garden door – heavy oak sunk deep in the thickness of the wall – opened further: a woman in a big garden hat set her foot slowly on the time-hollowed stone step and as slowly walked across the turf. I was forming some apology when she lifted up her head and I saw that she was blind.

"I heard you," she said. "Isn't that a motor car?"

"I'm afraid I've made a mistake in my road. I should have turned off up above – I never dreamed—" I began.

"But I'm very glad. Fancy a motor car coming into the garden! It will be such a treat—" She turned and made as though looking about her. "You – you haven't seen anyone have you – perhaps?"

"No one to speak to, but the children seemed interested at a distance."

"Which?"

"I saw a couple up at the window just now, and I think I heard a little chap in the grounds."

"Oh, lucky you!" she cried, and her face brightened. "I hear them, of course, but that's all. You've seen them and heard them?"

"Yes," I answered. "And if I know anything of children one of them's having a beautiful time by the fountain yonder. Escaped, I should imagine."

"You're fond of children?"

I gave her one or two reasons why I did not altogether hate them.

"Of course, of course," she said. "Then you understand. Then you won't think it foolish if I ask you to take your car through the gardens, once or twice – quite slowly. I'm sure they'd like to see it. They see so little, poor things. One tries to make their life pleasant, but—" she threw out her hands towards the woods. "We're so out of the world here."

"That will be splendid," I said. "But I can't cut up your grass."

She faced to the right. "Wait a minute," she said. "We're at the South gate, aren't we? Behind those peacocks there's a flagged path. We call it the Peacock's Walk. You can't see it from here, they tell me, but if you squeeze along by the edge of the wood you can turn at the first peacock and get on to the flags."

It was sacrilege to wake that dreaming house-front with the clatter of machinery, but I swung the car to clear the turf, brushed along the edge of the wood and turned in on the broad stone path where the fountain-basin lay like one star-sapphire.

"May I come too?" she cried. "No, please don't help me. They'll like it better if they see me."

She felt her way lightly to the front of the car, and with one foot on the step she called: "Children, oh, children! Look and see what's going to happen!"

The voice would have drawn lost souls from the Pit, for the yearning that underlay its sweetness, and I was not surprised to hear an answering shout behind the yews. It must have been the child by the fountain, but he fled at our approach, leaving a little toy boat in the water. I saw the glint of his blue blouse among the still horsemen.

Very disposedly we paraded the length of the walk and at her request backed again. This time the child had got the better of his panic, but stood far off and doubting.

"The little fellow's watching us," I said. "I wonder if he'd like a ride."

"They're very shy still. Very shy. But, oh, lucky you to be able to see them! Let's listen."

I stopped the machine at once, and the humid stillness, heavy with the scent of box, cloaked us deep. Shears I could hear where some gardener was clipping; a mumble of bees and broken voices that might have been the doves.

"Oh, unkind!" she said wearily.

"Perhaps they're only shy of the motor. The little maid at the window looks tremendously interested."

"Yes?" She raised her head. "It was wrong of me to say that. They are really fond of me. It's the only thing that makes life worth living – when they're fond of you, isn't it? I daren't think what the place would be without them. By the way, is it beautiful?"

"I think it is the most beautiful place I have ever seen."

"So they all tell me. I can feel it, of course, but that isn't quite the same thing."

"Then have you never—?" I began, but stopped abashed.

"Not since I can remember. It happened when I was only a few months old, they tell me. And yet I must remember something, else how could I dream about colours. I see light in my dreams, and colours, but I never see *them*. I only hear them just as I do when I'm awake."

"It's difficult to see faces in dreams. Some people can, but most of us haven't the gift," I went on, looking up at the window where the child stood all but hidden.

"I've heard that too," she said. "And they tell me that one never sees a dead person's face in a dream. Is that true?"

"I believe it is – now I come to think of it."

"But how is it with yourself – yourself?" The blind eyes turned towards me.

"I have never seen the faces of my dead in any dream," I answered.

"Then it must be as bad as being blind."

The sun had dipped behind the woods and the long shades were possessing the insolent horsemen one by one. I saw the light die from off the top of a glossy-leaved lance and all the brave hard green turn to soft black. The house, accepting another day at end, as it had accepted a hundred thousand gone, seemed to settle deeper into its rest among the shadows.

"Have you ever wanted to?" she said after the silence.

"Very much sometimes," I replied. The child had left the window as the shadows closed upon it.

"Ah! So've I, but I don't suppose it's allowed.... Where d'you live?"

"Quite the other side of the county – sixty miles and more, and I must be going back. I've come without my big lamp."

"But it's not dark yet. I can feel it."

"I'm afraid it will be by the time I get home. Could you lend me someone to set me on my road at first? I've utterly lost myself."

"I'll send Madden with you to the cross-roads. We are so out of the world, I don't wonder you were lost! I'll guide you round to the front of the house; but you will go slowly, won't you, till you're out of the grounds? It isn't foolish, do you think?"

"I promise you I'll go like this," I said, and let the car start herself down the flagged path.

We skirted the left wing of the house, whose elaborately cast lead guttering alone was worth a day's journey; passed under a great rose-grown gate in the red wall, and so round to the high front of the house which in beauty and stateliness as much excelled the back as that all others I had seen.

"Is it so very beautiful?" she said wistfully when she heard my raptures. "And you like the lead figures too? There's the old azalea garden behind. They say that this place must have been made for children. Will you help me out, please? I should like to come with you as far as the cross-roads, but I mustn't leave them. Is that you, Madden? I want you to show this gentleman the way to the cross-roads. He has lost his way but – he has seen them."

A butler appeared noiselessly at the miracle of old oak that must be called the front door, and slipped aside to put on his hat. She stood looking at me with open blue eyes in which no sight lay, and I saw for the first time that she was beautiful.

"Remember," she said quietly, "if you are fond of them you will come again," and disappeared within the house.

The butler in the car said nothing till we were nearly at the lodge gates, where catching a glimpse of a blue blouse in a shrubbery I swerved amply lest the devil that leads little boys to play should drag me into child-murder.

"Excuse me," he asked of a sudden, "but why did you do that, Sir?"

"The child yonder."

"Our young gentleman in blue?"

"Of course."

"He runs about a good deal. Did you see him by the fountain, Sir?"

"Oh, yes, several times. Do we turn here?"

"Yes, Sir. And did you 'appen to see them upstairs too?"

"At the upper window? Yes."

"Was that before the mistress come out to speak to you, Sir?"

"A little before that. Why d'you want to know?"

He paused a little. "Only to make sure that – that they had seen the car, Sir, because with children running about, though I'm sure you're driving particularly careful, there might be an accident. That was all, Sir. Here are the crossroads. You can't miss your way from now on. Thank you, Sir, but that isn't *our* custom, not with—"

"I beg your pardon," I said, and thrust away the British silver.

"Oh, it's quite right with the rest of 'em as a rule. Goodbye, Sir."

He retired into the armour-plated conning tower of his caste and walked away. Evidently a butler solicitous for the honour of his house, and interested, probably through a maid, in the nursery.

Once beyond the signposts at the crossroads I looked back, but the crumpled hills interlaced so jealously that I could not see where the house had lain. When I asked its name at a cottage along the road, the fat woman who sold sweetmeats there gave me to understand that people with motor cars had small right to live – much less to "go about talking like carriage folk." They were not a pleasant-mannered community.

When I retraced my route on the map that evening I was little wiser. Hawkin's Old Farm appeared to be the survey title of the place, and the old County Gazetteer, generally so ample, did not allude to it. The big house of those parts was Hodnington Hall, Georgian with early Victorian embellishments, as an atrocious steel engraving attested. I carried my difficulty to a neighbour – a deep-rooted tree of that soil – and he gave me a name of a family which conveyed no meaning.

A month or so later – I went again, or it may have been that my car took the road of her own volition. She over-ran the fruitless Downs, threaded every turn of the maze of lanes below the hills, drew through the high-walled woods, impenetrable in their full leaf, came out at the crossroads where the butler had left me, and a little further on developed an internal trouble which forced me to turn her in on a grass way-waste that cut into a summer-silent hazel wood. So far as I could make sure by the sun and a six-inch Ordnance map, this should be the road flank of that wood which I had first explored from the heights above. I made a mighty serious business of my repairs and a glittering shop of my repair kit, spanners, pump, and the like, which I spread out orderly upon a rug. It was a trap to catch all childhood, for on such a day, I argued, the children would not be far off. When I paused in my work I listened, but the wood was so full of the noises of summer (though the birds had mated) that I could not at first distinguish these from the tread of small cautious feet stealing across the dead leaves. I rang my bell in an alluring manner, but the feet fled, and I repented, for to a child a sudden noise is very real terror. I must have been at work half an hour when I heard in the wood the voice of the blind woman crying: "Children, oh children, where are you?" and the stillness made slow to close on the perfection of that cry. She came towards me, half feeling her way between the tree boles, and though a child it seemed clung to her skirt, it swerved into the leafage like a rabbit as she drew nearer.

"Is that you?" she said, "from the other side of the county?"

"Yes, it's me from the other side of the county."

"Then why didn't you come through the upper woods? They were there just now."

"They were here a few minutes ago. I expect they knew my car had broken down, and came to see the fun."

"Nothing serious, I hope? How do cars break down?"

"In fifty different ways. Only mine has chosen the fifty first."

She laughed merrily at the tiny joke, cooed with delicious laughter, and pushed her hat back.

"Let me hear," she said.

"Wait a moment," I cried, "and I'll get you a cushion."

She set her foot on the rug all covered with spare parts, and stooped above it eagerly. "What delightful things!" The hands through which she saw glanced in the chequered sunlight. "A box here – another box! Why you've arranged them like a playing shop!"

"I confess now that I put it out to attract them. I don't need half those things really."

"How nice of you! I heard your bell in the upper wood. You say they were here before that?"

"I'm sure of it. Why are they so shy? That little fellow in blue who was with you just now ought to have got over his fright. He's been watching me like a Red Indian."

"It must have been your bell," she said. "I heard one of them go past me in trouble when I was coming down. They're shy – so shy even with me." She turned her face over her shoulder and cried again: "Children! Oh, children! Look and see!"

"They must have gone off together on their own affairs," I suggested, for there was a murmur behind us of lowered voices broken by the sudden squeaking giggles of childhood. I returned to my tinkerings and she leaned forward, her chin on her hand, listening interestedly.

"How many are they?" I said at last. The work was finished, but I saw no reason to go.

Her forehead puckered a little in thought. "I don't quite know," she said simply. "Sometimes more – sometimes less. They come and stay with me because I love them, you see."

"That must be very jolly," I said, replacing a drawer, and as I spoke I heard the inanity of my answer.

"You – you aren't laughing at me," she cried. "I – I haven't any of my own. I never married. People laugh at me sometimes about them because – because—"

"Because they're savages," I returned. "It's nothing to fret for. That sort laugh at everything that isn't in their own fat lives."

"I don't know. How should I? I only don't like being laughed at about *them*. It hurts; and when one can't see…I don't want to seem silly," her chin quivered like a child's as she spoke, "but we blindies have only one skin, I think. Everything outside hits straight at our souls. It's different with you. You've such good defences in your eyes – looking out – before anyone can really pain you in your soul. People forget that with us."

I was silent reviewing that inexhaustible matter – the more than inherited (since it is also carefully taught) brutality of the Christian peoples, beside which the mere heathendom of the West Coast nigger is clean and restrained. It led me a long distance into myself.

"Don't do that!" she said of a sudden, putting her hands before her eyes.

"What?"

She made a gesture with her hand.

"That! It's – it's all purple and black. Don't! That colour hurts."

"But, how in the world do you know about colours?" I exclaimed, for here was a revelation indeed.

"Colours as colours?" she asked.

"No. *Those* Colours which you saw just now."

"You know as well as I do," she laughed, "else you wouldn't have asked that question. They aren't in the world at all. They're in *you* – when you went so angry."

"D'you mean a dull purplish patch, like port wine mixed with ink?" I said.

"I've never seen ink or port wine, but the colours aren't mixed. They are separate – all separate."

"Do you mean black streaks and jags across the purple?"

She nodded. "Yes – if they are like this," and zigzagged her finger again, "but it's more red than purple – that bad colour."

"And what are the colours at the top of the – whatever you see?"

Slowly she leaned forward and traced on the rug the figure of the Egg itself.

"I see them so," she said, pointing with a grass stem, "white, green, yellow, red, purple, and when people are angry or bad, black across the red – as you were just now."

"Who told you anything about it – in the beginning?" I demanded.

"About the colours? No one. I used to ask what colours were when I was little – in table covers and curtains and carpets, you see – because some colours hurt me and some made me happy. People told me; and when I got older that was how I saw people." Again she traced the outline of the Egg which it is given to very few of us to see.

"All by yourself?" I repeated.

"All by myself. There wasn't anyone else. I only found out afterwards that other people did not see the Colours."

She leaned against the tree hole plaiting and unplaiting chance-plucked grass stems. The children in the wood had drawn nearer. I could see them with the tail of my eye frolicking like squirrels.

"Now I am sure you will never laugh at me," she went on after a long silence. "Nor at *them*."

"Goodness! No!" I cried, jolted out of my train of thought. "A man who laughs at a child – unless the child is laughing too – is a heathen!"

"I didn't mean that of course. You'd never laugh *at* children, but I thought – I used to think – that perhaps you might laugh about *them*. So now I beg your pardon…. What are you going to laugh at?"

I had made no sound, but she knew.

"At the notion of your begging my pardon. If you had done your duty as a pillar of the state and a landed proprietress you ought to have summoned me for trespass when I barged through your woods the other day. It was disgraceful of me – inexcusable."

She looked at me, her head against the tree trunk – long and steadfastly – this woman who could see the naked soul.

"How curious," she half whispered. "How very curious."

"Why, what have I done?"

"You don't understand…and yet you understood about the Colours. Don't you understand?"

She spoke with a passion that nothing had justified, and I faced her bewilderedly as she rose. The children had gathered themselves in a roundel behind a bramble bush. One sleek head bent over something smaller, and the set of the little shoulders told me that fingers were on lips. They, too, had some child's tremendous secret. I alone was hopelessly astray there in the broad sunlight.

"No," I said, and shook my head as though the dead eyes could note. "Whatever it is, I don't understand yet. Perhaps I shall later – if you'll let me come again."

"You will come again," she answered. "You will surely come again and walk in the wood."

"Perhaps the children will know me well enough by that time to let me play with them – as a favour. You know what children are like."

"It isn't a matter of favour but of right," she replied, and while I wondered what she meant, a dishevelled woman plunged round the bend of the road, loose-haired, purple, almost lowing with agony as she ran. It was my rude, fat friend of the sweetmeat shop. The blind woman heard and stepped forward. "What is it, Mrs. Madehurst?" she asked.

The woman flung her apron over her head and literally grovelled in the dust, crying that her grandchild was sick to death, that the local doctor was away fishing, that Jenny the mother was at her wits' end, and so forth, with repetitions and bellowings.

"Where's the next nearest doctor?" I asked between paroxysms.

"Madden will tell you. Go round to the house and take him with you. I'll attend to this. Be quick!" She half-supported the fat woman into the shade. In two minutes I was blowing all the horns of Jericho under the front of the House Beautiful, and Madden, in the pantry, rose to the crisis like a butler and a man.

A quarter of an hour at illegal speeds caught us a doctor five miles away. Within the half-hour we had decanted him, much interested in motors, at the door of the sweetmeat shop, and drew up the road to await the verdict.

"Useful things cars," said Madden, all man and no butler. "If I'd had one when mine took sick she wouldn't have died."

"How was it?" I asked.

"Croup. Mrs. Madden was away. No one knew what to do. I drove eight miles in a tax cart for the doctor. She was choked when we came back. This car 'd ha' saved her. She'd have been close on ten now."

"I'm sorry," I said. "I thought you were rather fond of children from what you told me going to the crossroads the other day."

"Have you seen 'em again, Sir – this mornin'?"

"Yes, but they're well broke to cars. I couldn't get any of them within twenty yards of it."

He looked at me carefully as a scout considers a stranger – not as a menial should lift his eyes to his divinely appointed superior.

"I wonder why," he said just above the breath that he drew.

We waited on. A light wind from the sea wandered up and down the long lines of the woods, and the wayside grasses, whitened already with summer dust, rose and bowed in sallow waves.

A woman, wiping the suds off her arms, came out of the cottage next to the sweetmeat shop.

"I've be'n listenin' in de back-yard," she said cheerily. "He says Arthur's unaccountable bad. Did ye hear him shruck just now? Unaccountable bad. I reckon t'will come Jenny's turn to walk in de wood nex' week along, Mr. Madden."

"Excuse me, Sir, but your lap-robe is slipping," said Madden deferentially. The woman started, dropped a curtsey, and hurried away.

"What does she mean by 'walking in the wood'?" I asked.

"It must be some saying they use hereabouts. I'm from Norfolk myself," said Madden. "They're an independent lot in this county. She took you for a chauffeur, Sir."

I saw the Doctor come out of the cottage followed by a draggle-tailed wench who clung to his arm as though he could make treaty for her with Death. "Dat sort," she wailed – "dey're just as much to us dat has 'em as if dey was lawful born. Just as much – just as much! An' God he'd be just as pleased if you saved 'un, Doctor. Don't take it from me. Miss Florence will tell ye de very same. Don't leave 'im, Doctor!"

"I know. I know," said the man, "but he'll be quiet for a while now. We'll get the nurse and the medicine as fast as we can." He signalled me to come forward with the car, and I strove not to be privy to what followed; but I saw the girl's face, blotched and frozen with grief, and I felt the hand without a ring clutching at my knees when we moved away.

The Doctor was a man of some humour, for I remember he claimed my car under the Oath of Aesculapius, and used it and me without mercy. First we convoyed Mrs. Madehurst and the blind woman to wait by the sick bed till the nurse should come. Next we invaded a neat county town for prescriptions (the Doctor said the trouble was cerebro-spinal meningitis), and when the County Institute, banked and flanked with scared market cattle, reported itself out of nurses for the moment we literally flung ourselves loose upon the county. We conferred with the owners of great houses – magnates at the ends of overarching avenues whose big-boned womenfolk strode away from their tea-tables to listen to the imperious Doctor. At last a white-haired lady sitting under a cedar of Lebanon and surrounded by a court of magnificent Borzois – all hostile to motors – gave the Doctor, who received them as from a princess, written orders which we bore many miles at top speed, through a park, to a French nunnery, where we took over in exchange a pallid-faced and trembling Sister. She knelt at the bottom of the tonneau telling her beads without pause till, by short cuts of the Doctor's invention, we had her to the sweetmeat shop once more. It was a long afternoon crowded with mad episodes that rose and dissolved like the dust of our wheels; cross-sections of remote and incomprehensible lives through which we raced at right angles; and I went home in the dusk, wearied out, to dream of the clashing horns of cattle; round-eyed nuns walking in a garden of graves; pleasant tea-parties beneath shaded trees; the carbolic-scented, grey-painted corridors of the County Institute; the steps of shy children in the wood, and the hands that clung to my knees as the motor began to move.

* * *

I had intended to return in a day or two, but it pleased Fate to hold me from that side of the county, on many pretexts, till the elder and the wild rose had fruited. There came at last a brilliant day, swept clear from the south-west, that brought the hills within hand's reach – a day of unstable airs and high filmy clouds. Through no merit of my own I was free, and set the car for the third time on that known road. As I reached the crest of the Downs I felt the soft air change, saw it glaze under the sun; and, looking down at the sea, in that instant beheld the blue of the Channel turn through polished silver and dulled steel to dingy pewter. A laden collier hugging the coast steered outward for deeper water and, across copper-coloured haze, I saw sails rise one by one on the anchored fishing-fleet. In a deep dene behind me an eddy of sudden wind drummed through sheltered oaks, and spun aloft the first day sample of autumn leaves. When I reached the beach road the sea-fog fumed over the brickfields, and the tide was telling all the groins of the gale beyond Ushant. In less than an hour summer England vanished in chill grey. We were again the shut island of the North, all the ships of the world bellowing at our perilous gates; and between their outcries ran the piping of bewildered gulls. My cap dripped moisture, the folds of the rug held it in pools or sluiced it away in runnels, and the salt-rime stuck to my lips.

Inland the smell of autumn loaded the thickened fog among the trees, and the drip became a continuous shower. Yet the late flowers – mallow of the wayside, scabious of the field, and dahlia of the garden – showed gay in the mist, and beyond the sea's breath there was little sign of decay in the leaf. Yet in the villages the house doors were all open, and bare-legged, bare-headed children sat at ease on the damp doorsteps to shout 'pip-pip' at the stranger.

I made bold to call at the sweetmeat shop, where Mrs. Madehurst met me with a fat woman's hospitable tears. Jenny's child, she said, had died two days after the nun had come. It was, she felt, best out of the way, even though insurance offices, for reasons which she did not pretend to follow, would not willingly insure such stray lives. "Not but what Jenny didn't tend to Arthur as though he'd come all proper at de end of de first year – like Jenny herself." Thanks to Miss Florence, the child had been buried with a pomp which, in Mrs. Madehurst's opinion, more than covered the small irregularity of its birth. She described the coffin, within and without, the glass hearse, and the evergreen lining of the grave.

"But how's the mother?" I asked.

"Jenny? Oh, she'll get over it. I've felt dat way with one or two o' my own. She'll get over. She's walkin' in de wood now."

"In this weather?"

Mrs. Madehurst looked at me with narrowed eyes across the counter.

"I dunno but it opens de 'eart like. Yes, it opens de 'eart. Dat's where losin' and bearin' comes so alike in de long run, we do say."

Now the wisdom of the old wives is greater than that of all the Fathers, and this last oracle sent me thinking so extendedly as I went up the road, that I nearly ran over a woman and a child at the wooded corner by the lodge gates of the House Beautiful.

"Awful weather!" I cried, as I slowed dead for the turn.

"Not so bad," she answered placidly out of the fog. "Mine's used to 'un. You'll find yours indoors, I reckon."

Indoors, Madden received me with professional courtesy, and kind inquiries for the health of the motor, which he would put under cover.

I waited in a still, nut-brown hall, pleasant with late flowers and warmed with a delicious wood fire – a place of good influence and great peace. (Men and women may sometimes, after great effort, achieve a creditable lie; but the house, which is their temple, cannot say anything save the truth of those who have lived in it.) A child's cart and a doll lay on the black-and-white floor, where a rug had been kicked back. I felt that the children had only just hurried away – to hide themselves, most like – in the many turns of the great adzed staircase that climbed statelily out of the hall, or to crouch at gaze behind the lions and roses of the carven gallery above. Then I heard her voice above me, singing as the blind sing – from the soul:

> *In the pleasant orchard-closes.*
> *And all my early summer came back at the call.*
> *In the pleasant orchard-closes,*
> *God bless all our gains say we –*
> *But may God bless all our losses,*
> *Better suits with our degree,*
> She dropped the marring fifth line, and repeated –
> *Better suits with our degree!*

I saw her lean over the gallery, her linked hands white as pearl against the oak.

"Is that you – from the other side of the county?" she called.

"Yes, me – from the other side of the county," I answered laughing.

"What a long time before you had to come here again." She ran down the stairs, one hand lightly touching the broad rail. "It's two months and four days. Summer's gone!"

"I meant to come before, but Fate prevented."

"I knew it. Please do something to that fire. They won't let me play with it, but I can feel it's behaving badly. Hit it!"

I looked on either side of the deep fireplace, and found but a half-charred hedge-stake with which I punched a black log into flame.

"It never goes out, day or night," she said, as though explaining. "In case anyone comes in with cold toes, you see."

"It's even lovelier inside than it was out," I murmured. The red light poured itself along the age-polished dusky panels till the Tudor roses and lions of the gallery took colour and motion. An old eagle-topped convex mirror gathered the picture into its mysterious heart, distorting afresh the distorted shadows, and curving the gallery lines into the curves of a ship. The day was shutting down in half a gale as the fog turned to stringy scud. Through the uncurtained mullions of the broad window I could see valiant horsemen of the lawn rear and recover against the wind that taunted them with legions of dead leaves. "Yes, it must be beautiful," she said. "Would you like to go over it? There's still light enough upstairs."

I followed her up the unflinching, wagon-wide staircase to the gallery whence opened the thin fluted Elizabethan doors.

"Feel how they put the latch low down for the sake of the children." She swung a light door inward.

"By the way, where are they?" I asked. "I haven't even heard them today."

She did not answer at once. Then, "I can only hear them," she replied softly. "This is one of their rooms – everything ready, you see."

She pointed into a heavily-timbered room. There were little low gate tables and children's chairs. A doll's house, its hooked front half open, faced a great dappled rocking-horse, from whose padded saddle it was but a child's scramble to the broad window-seat overlooking the lawn. A toy gun lay in a corner beside a gilt wooden cannon.

"Surely they've only just gone," I whispered. In the failing light a door creaked cautiously. I heard the rustle of a frock and the patter of feet – quick feet through a room beyond.

"I heard that," she cried triumphantly. "Did you? Children, O children, where are you?"

The voice filled the walls that held it lovingly to the last perfect note, but there came no answering shout such as I had heard in the garden. We hurried on from room to oak-floored room; up a step here, down three steps there; among a maze of passages; always mocked by our quarry. One might as well have tried to work an unstopped warren with a single ferret. There were bolt-holes innumerable – recesses in walls, embrasures of deep slitten windows now darkened, whence they could start up behind us; and abandoned fireplaces, six feet deep in the masonry, as well as the tangle of communicating doors. Above all, they had the twilight for their helper in our game. I had caught one or two joyous chuckles of evasion, and once or twice had seen the silhouette of a child's frock against some darkening window at the end of a passage; but we returned empty-handed to the gallery, just as a middle-aged woman was setting a lamp in its niche.

"No, I haven't seen her either this evening, Miss Florence," I heard her say, "but that Turpin he says he wants to see you about his shed."

"Oh, Mr. Turpin must want to see me very badly. Tell him to come to the hall, Mrs. Madden."

I looked down into the hall whose only light was the dulled fire, and deep in the shadow I saw them at last. They must have slipped down while we were in the passages, and now thought themselves perfectly hidden behind an old gilt leather screen. By child's law, my fruitless chase was as good as an introduction, but since I had taken so much trouble I resolved to force them to come forward later by the simple trick, which children detest, of pretending not to notice them. They lay close, in a little huddle, no more than shadows except when a quick flame betrayed an outline.

"And now we'll have some tea," she said. "I believe I ought to have offered it you at first, but one doesn't arrive at manners somehow when one lives alone and is considered – h'm – peculiar." Then with very pretty scorn, "would you like a lamp to see to eat by?"

"The firelight's much pleasanter, I think." We descended into that delicious gloom and Madden brought tea.

I took my chair in the direction of the screen ready to surprise or be surprised as the game should go, and at her permission, since a hearth is always sacred, bent forward to play with the fire.

"Where do you get these beautiful short faggots from?" I asked idly. "Why, they are tallies!"

"Of course," she said. "As I can't read or write I'm driven back on the early English tally for my accounts. Give me one and I'll tell you what it meant."

I passed her an unburned hazel-tally, about a foot long, and she ran her thumb down the nicks.

"This is the milk-record for the home farm for the month of April last year, in gallons," said she. "I don't know what I should have done without tallies. An old forester of mine taught me the system. It's out of date now for everyone else; but my tenants respect it. One of them's coming now to see me. Oh, it doesn't matter. He has no business here out of office hours. He's a greedy, ignorant man – very greedy or – he wouldn't come here after dark."

"Have you much land then?"

"Only a couple of hundred acres in hand, thank goodness. The other six hundred are nearly all let to folk who knew my folk before me, but this Turpin is quite a new man – and a highway robber."

"But are you sure I sha'n't be—?"

"Certainly not. You have the right. He hasn't any children."

"Ah, the children!" I said, and slid my low chair back till it nearly touched the screen that hid them. "I wonder whether they'll come out for me."

There was a murmur of voices – Madden's and a deeper note – at the low, dark side door, and a ginger-headed, canvas-gaitered giant of the unmistakable tenant farmer type stumbled or was pushed in.

"Come to the fire, Mr. Turpin," she said.

"If – if you please, Miss, I'll – I'll be quite as well by the door." He clung to the latch as he spoke like a frightened child. Of a sudden I realised that he was in the grip of some almost overpowering fear.

"Well?"

"About that new shed for the young stock – that was all. These first autumn storms settin' in... but I'll come again, Miss." His teeth did not chatter much more than the door latch.

"I think not," she answered levelly. "The new shed – m'm. What did my agent write you on the 15th?"

"I – fancied p'raps that if I came to see you – ma – man to man like, Miss. But—"

His eyes rolled into every corner of the room wide with horror. He half opened the door through which he had entered, but I noticed it shut again – from without and firmly.

"He wrote what I told him," she went on. "You are overstocked already. Dunnett's Farm never carried more than fifty bullocks – even in Mr. Wright's time. And _he_ used cake. You've sixty-seven and you don't cake. You've broken the lease in that respect. You're dragging the heart out of the farm."

"I'm – I'm getting some minerals – superphosphates – next week. I've as good as ordered a truck-load already. I'll go down to the station tomorrow about 'em. Then I can come and see you man to man like, Miss, in the daylight.... That gentleman's not going away, is he?" He almost shrieked.

I had only slid the chair a little further back, reaching behind me to tap on the leather of the screen, but he jumped like a rat.

"No. Please attend to me, Mr. Turpin." She turned in her chair and faced him with his back to the door. It was an old and sordid little piece of scheming that she forced from him – his plea for the new cowshed at his landlady's expense, that he might with the covered manure pay his next year's rent out of the valuation after, as she made clear, he had bled the enriched pastures to the bone. I could not but admire the intensity of his greed, when I saw him out-facing for its sake whatever terror it was that ran wet on his forehead.

I ceased to tap the leather – was, indeed, calculating the cost of the shed – when I felt my relaxed hand taken and turned softly between the soft hands of a child. So at last I had triumphed. In a moment I would turn and acquaint myself with those quick-footed wanderers....

The little brushing kiss fell in the centre of my palm – as a gift on which the fingers were, once, expected to close: as the all faithful half-reproachful signal of a waiting child not used to neglect even when grown-ups were busiest – a fragment of the mute code devised very long ago.

Then I knew. And it was as though I had known from the first day when I looked across the lawn at the high window.

I heard the door shut. The woman turned to me in silence, and I felt that she knew.

What time passed after this I cannot say. I was roused by the fall of a log, and mechanically rose to put it back. Then I returned to my place in the chair very close to the screen.

"Now you understand," she whispered, across the packed shadows.

"Yes, I understand – now. Thank you."

"I – I only hear them." She bowed her head in her hands. "I have no right, you know – no other right. I have neither borne nor lost – neither borne nor lost!"

"Be very glad then," said I, for my soul was torn open within me.

"Forgive me!"

She was still, and I went back to my sorrow and my joy.

"It was because I loved them so," she said at last, brokenly. "*That* was why it was, even from the first – even before I knew that they – they were all I should ever have. And I loved them so!"

She stretched out her arms to the shadows and the shadows within the shadow.

"They came because I loved them – because I needed them. I – I must have made them come. Was that wrong, think you?"

"No – no."

"I – I grant you that the toys and – and all that sort of thing were nonsense, but – but I used to so hate empty rooms myself when I was little." She pointed to the gallery. "And the passages all empty…. And how could I ever bear the garden door shut? Suppose—"

"Don't! For pity's sake, don't!" I cried. The twilight had brought a cold rain with gusty squalls that plucked at the leaded windows.

"And the same thing with keeping the fire in all night. *I* don't think it so foolish – do you?"

I looked at the broad brick hearth, saw, through tears I believe, that there was no unpassable iron on or near it, and bowed my head.

"I did all that and lots of other things – just to make believe. Then they came. I heard them, but I didn't know that they were not mine by right till Mrs. Madden told me—"

"The butler's wife? What?"

"One of them – I heard – she saw. And knew. Hers! *Not* for me. I didn't know at first. Perhaps I was jealous. Afterwards, I began to understand that it was only because I loved them, not because—. Oh, you *must* bear or lose," she said piteously. "There is no other way – and yet they love me. They must! Don't they?"

There was no sound in the room except the lapping voices of the fire, but we two listened intently, and she at least took comfort from what she heard. She recovered herself and half rose. I sat still in my chair by the screen.

"Don't think me a wretch to whine about myself like this, but – but I'm all in the dark, you know, and *you* can see."

In truth I could see, and my vision confirmed me in my resolve, though that was like the very parting of spirit and flesh. Yet a little longer I would stay since it was the last time.

"You think it is wrong, then?" she cried sharply, though I had said nothing.

"Not for you. A thousand times no. For you it is right…. I am grateful to you beyond words. For me it would be wrong. For me only…"

"Why?" she said, but passed her hand before her face as she had done at our second meeting in the wood. "Oh, I see," she went on simply as a child. "For you it would be wrong." Then with a little indrawn laugh, "and, d'you remember, I called you lucky – once – at first. You who must never come here again!"

She left me to sit a little longer by the screen, and I heard the sound of her feet die out along the gallery above.

The Woman out of the Attic

Gwendolyn Kiste

HERE'S what you know for sure: you won't survive the film. There's no chance a woman like you will live to see the end credits. Heck, you might not make it through the opening credits.

But even if you're dead before the very first frame, that doesn't mean you're gone. There are other ways of being in the picture. You could, for instance, linger like a ghost, there and not there. A whisper in the heroine's ear, a dull ache in the brooding hero's heart.

But it's important that you remember: this isn't your story. None of this – not the man or the glory or the happy ending – belongs to you.

Please don't forget. Or the film will have to remind you.

* * *

Fade in.

You blink into existence and wonder where you are. *Who* you are. This could be many different places, and you could be many different people.

For instance, if the audience is in the mood for propriety and corsets, this could be England in the nineteenth century, and you're the wife tucked away in an attic, forgotten like a yellowed family photo album or a box of moth-eaten winter clothes.

Or this could be mid-century after the war with you as a bright-eyed, wanton socialite, or maybe it's modern-day and you're a lonely career girl who isn't eager to be ignored. After all, there's never a lack of women who misbehave in a world desperate to correct them for it.

You blink again, and regain your bearings. This time, your role is simple. This time, you're already dead.

Your husband isn't your husband anymore, and you're haunting his mansion where he's got a new woman at his side, a dewy, ruddy-cheeked bride. She might have a name. She probably won't. Or if she does, he'll never use it. Instead, he calls her what she means to him.

Beloved. Wife. Mine.

For what it's worth, she knows your name. As she wanders the long corridors alone, your name brands itself on her tongue, though she never speaks it aloud. That, of course, won't stop her from speaking *about* you.

"I hear she was very beautiful," his bride whispers, and the staff members on the estate nod and hurry about their business.

This is what you've come to expect. Your beauty is the one thing everyone remembers about you. It was all you had to offer. You were never a nice girl. You laughed too loudly. You stayed out until dawn. You enjoyed sex, and sometimes not with your husband. If his new bride wants to do better than you, she should be a good little wife and stop with the questions now.

But perhaps she isn't as docile as they think. The bride keeps asking, and everyone keeps pretending they don't know what she's talking about. Especially her new husband.

"Do you grow roses on the grounds?" she asks him at dinner, and he bristles on instinct.

"Absolutely not," he says with a snuff, and doesn't elaborate, doesn't tell her how he hacked down your dozen rosebushes the day after your funeral, his palms blistered and his face burnt and twisted in the sun.

At the other end of the long table, his bride blushes and regards her plate of sirloin and wilted asparagus. "That's strange," she says. "I swear I smell them everywhere I go here."

At this, he slams down his wine glass, the jagged shards shattering across the scarlet tablecloth. He storms off without another word, and with dinner abruptly over, she sneaks off to the study, where she cries alone at a blackened hearth.

You ripple through the walls after her. You aren't a very good ghost. A ghost would haunt this young girl, terrify her in this moment of grief. All you want to do is comfort her, though you don't know how.

As you watch her in the lamplight glow, she reminds you of someone. The gap between her teeth, the way her hair falls over her eyes. You barely remember who you are, but somehow, you remember her.

Films can play tricks on you. They can cast the same person in two roles, or reincarnate someone just for kicks, just to drive the knife in deeper.

You do your best to avoid her, to avoid remembering, but she senses you in the house. She's the only one who seems to know you're still here. When he retires to bed in his separate room each night, she whispers to the high-up cornices on the ceiling.

"What do you want?" she asks, her voice sweet as candy floss, but trembling too. "I'll give you anything. Anything except him."

You try to tell her you don't want him and that she shouldn't want him either, but you're dead, and nobody listens to the dead.

As she sleeps, you smooth her hair, and you hum her a lullaby to help her through a nightmare. In the darkness, she calls out his name, not yours. As though he's the one here to comfort her.

Then she returns to dreaming. You pretend you can still dream too.

* * *

On a lonely winter morning, you stumble upon her in the wardrobe that was once yours. It's filled with her satin gowns purchased in expensive boutiques on the Champs-Elysees. You know because those are the same places he took you on your honeymoon.

She runs her fingers along the tailored seams. "I don't belong here," she says.

At first, you think she's talking to herself. Until you realize she's speaking to you. His bride is having a conversation with a ghost.

You part your lips to respond, but no sounds comes out.

* * *

Flashback.
In every version of the film, one thing is a constant. You always ask yourself the same question: *How did I die this time?*

Maybe it was in an accident. That's if you're lucky. More than likely, your end was something much more sinister. A coarse hand around your neck, a dollop of rat poison in your afternoon high tea. So long as you got what was coming to you.

It's a lesson every girl learns early. Strange women, disobedient women, never claw their way to a happy ending. They put their heads in ovens or stones in their pockets. They swallow lye. They wrap a rope around their throats instead of waiting for a hand to come along and do the job for them.

Or they take the hard way out like you did. They marry a man who everyone loves and wait until the day he no longer loves them.

The film will be halfway over before he makes his confession to his bride. The midpoint is the perfect time for a Byronic man to spew his secrets to a woman who shouldn't have to listen. But you always listen. Because until he speaks it aloud, you aren't completely certain how you died. Film after film, you always have your suspicions, but until he names it, you can't be sure.

"She was so beautiful," he says, reminding the audience again of your worth.

His gaze is set on some faraway point, and his bride huddles next to him in the bedroom or the boathouse or the bathtub where you died.

"But after we married," he says, "she changed."

You could play a game of bingo with the words that inevitably follow.

Spoiled. Lying. Lascivious.

"She had unchaste desires," he whispers, and says no more about it, because to him, this is your greatest sin, the one too terrible to mention aloud. A woman who doesn't swoon at her handsome husband, who swoons at someone else instead. Another woman's husband perhaps. Or another woman.

"I didn't mean to hurt her," he says, and spends more time describing what he did to you than who you were. His brow knit, he insists you coerced him into hurting you. How it was all your fault.

You wonder if he's ever stopped to think how a woman should never be able to goad her husband into murdering her.

"I'm sorry," he says, his words and heart hollow, and his bride watches him, tears glistening in her earnest eyes. She must be crying for him, but you pretend she's weeping for you. For how he owns your narrative, and shapes it like clay in his hands.

At this point, you wish you could rewind the film and try again. You would take this new information about your death, and you would try to live. It wouldn't matter, though. The film would always turn out the same way. That's because you're the same. You won't get a happy ending.

The film has taught you that much.

* * *

Jump cut.

Now his bride knows about you. He thinks, his chest puffing out like a peacock, that she'll feel for him. That she'll understand him and what he's done. That he has her in the palm of his hand forever.

But as the winter days wear into spring, she isn't so worried about him anymore. It's you she can't stop thinking about. Each afternoon, while he's out, she gazes at your faded portrait strung above the staircase. A flicker of memory passes across her face. You want to call to her, to tell her you remember too, but the moment is quickly gone.

Still, the two of you have plenty of time to get to know each other. Her husband's always away on some obscure errand.

"What does he do when he's gone?" she asks you, and though you could tell her all about his dubious business dealings, she doesn't really want to talk about him.

She wants to talk to you. Sitting cross-legged on the lawn, she leans back next to the air you occupy and smiles. She tells you her secrets. She tells you her name. You spend every day together, listening to the sea if it's nearby in this version, or listening to the wind if you're landlocked. Or maybe just listening to each other, her body nestled in the dirt where your rosebushes used to grow.

"What are you doing out there in the muck?" her husband asks when he returns home early, but she only shrugs.

"He's a fool," she whispers to you in the dark that night, and giggles. You're desperate to giggle back, to share something as intimate as joy with her, but you lost your voice when he stole it from you.

She turns over in bed to sleep, and your invisible hand lingers over her.

"I love you," you want to say, but the white noise of your existence rattles in the empty walls, fading like an echo into the night.

* * *

Deleted scene.
There are no moments in the film from your point of view. This isn't your story, remember. But if you could get only one scene, this is what you'd choose: the day you met her.

It might have happened at a boarding school or a Beverly Hills high school or in the forest behind the church where you skipped out early on Sunday school. It doesn't matter the era or the place. She was always there, and you always recognized her.

It was behind a line of rosebushes where she sneaked off to smoke, so the headmistress or pastor wouldn't see her. You stumbled upon her there, and she grinned at you, a tiny impish gap between her front teeth.

"Hello," she said, and you blushed and smiled back at her.

After that, you met there regularly. Every day if you could, you saw her, and every moment, you thought of her. The two of you in the grass, giggling, her hair falling over her eyes.

"We don't have to stay here," she said, and you wished that were true. You wished you could run or fly or vanish together.

But you couldn't, especially once your parents found out about her. They kept you apart, locking you in your room, letting you out only for school and sometimes not even then. They told you what you wanted was wrong, and because you were tired and afraid and worn down, you believed them. You spent every moment for the rest of your very short life hating yourself for it, but you believed them.

So when a man with a fortune and a mansion and no love in his heart proposed to you, you had no reason to decline. No reason except her.

You asked her to meet you in front of the rosebushes at midnight. She brought her satchel, and this twisted a blade in your guts. She thought the two of you were running away together. It was what you both wanted, but what you couldn't have. Not in this version anyhow.

You shook your head, not looking at her. "I'm sorry."

You told her goodbye, and then you left to tell him yes.

As you walked away, you didn't turn back.

Afterward, no one ever mentioned what happened to her, and you never asked. But it was easy to guess. A razor, a rope, an accident. You already knew how it ended for women like you.

You tried not to think of any of that. Instead, you put on white lace and a string of vintage pearls tighter than a noose, and you took the longest walk of your life down that aisle.

At the altar, he lifted your veil, and you kissed his lips, but all you could taste were roses.

* * *

Dissolve.

Back to the house you haunt. Back to being dead.

It's a humid afternoon, spring rain pattering against the stained glass windows, and his bride wanders down a hallway and hums a little tune to herself.

From inside his study where he hunches over a mountain of useless papers, he hears her, and with his eyes dark, he charges into the hallway and takes hold of her arm.

"Where did you learn that song?" he demands, tightening his grasp until she cries out.

She yanks herself free. "I don't remember."

That's because she never learned it, not on purpose. It's the lullaby you sing to her in her sleep. That means she can hear you, even if she doesn't realize it. This strikes an ember of hope in your heart. Just because you're a ghost doesn't mean you have to give up.

Besides, what you want is so simple: to exist. To not be erased the way the film intends. You aren't asking that much, but in a world like this, you're asking for everything. You're demanding the basic plot be rearranged in your favor.

But that's what you want, and that's what you have to fight for.

* * *

Close-up.

There's a box of matches on the mantle. Later, they'll say it was faulty wiring or a drip candle that didn't go out the way it should have. They won't know it's your hand that reaches through the in-between and strikes the flame into existence.

(These familial estates always burn to the ground, don't they? Secrets must make for the best kindling.)

You wait until she's outside on a walk around the grounds, and he's in his study, but it does no good. He escapes the smoky hallways anyhow, and they reunite in front of the crumbling house. As you stare out the window through the fire, he loops his arms around her, as if to remind you: *she's mine, forever and always.* She can't be yours. Love can never be yours.

She sobs silently into his chest, not looking at you, not able to do anything except cry out.

You want to cry out too, but the flames draw closer and melt what little remains of you. As the world cascades to black, you watch your former husband and you burn and you hate him with every cinder left sparking inside you, until there's nothing left of you at all.

* * *

Fade out.

Try again.

* * *

Fade in.

The film starts over. The era might be different this time, and the mansion might be in the Art Deco style rather than the Queen Anne, but the fundamental thing remains: you're dead from the get-go. It's pointless to think you could change that, so you creep up into the ceiling and leave her to celebrate what ought to be her wedded bliss.

But she doesn't want to be alone with him anymore. She wants to be with you. She remembers the before, gauzy as a dream. Bits and pieces, out of focus, just enough to make her want to know more.

"Where are you?" she whispers to the walls, her fingers gliding along the plaster, as though she's searching for a heartbeat.

Your heartbeat. You wish she could find it.

Her husband leaves the house less often now, especially once he notices her spending more time looking for you than at the dinner table or in the four-poster bed with him.

"You have your duty," he tells her, and this chills you to the bones you no longer have.

The fire starts earlier in the film this round, and you aren't the one to light the match. You couldn't light it if you tried. Your spectral hands are numb suddenly, and you don't know why.

As the mansion burns to the ground at midnight, she watches helplessly from the front lawn, tears streaking her rouged cheeks. In the final frame, you stare out from the window and wish she could see you, but her eyes stare blindly through you, and because she can do nothing else, she shudders and turns away.

* * *

Fade out.

Back into the darkness. Why can't you just find a way to survive?

* * *

Fade in.

In the garden where your roses used to grow, you meet her again, as if for the first time. You're still a ghost, and she's still a newlywed, but it feels different somehow. Like maybe this time, she's yours, and you're hers.

"I can almost remember it all," she says to you. "Both of us here before. Do you remember too?"

If only you could smile and tell her that all ghosts can do is remember.

She misses his birthday supper that night, and his anger flares at her, the way it used to flare at you.

"I won't tolerate this behavior," he says, and you both know what he means. He sees how she converses openly with you, waiting and listening day and night for you, the phantom hanging over the film.

He watches her through narrowed eyes, his fists clenched, and all you want is to protect her. You want to do *something*, but you're so strangely tired now. Too tired even to smooth the cowlick from her hair after the gaslight goes out. It seems the more she remembers about you, the weaker you become. Another trick of the film to ensure it gets its way.

In the last reel, he grins and lights the match when no one's looking. But even as the wallpaper peels away like flesh, she doesn't run with him. She stays in the house searching for you until all the servants come for her, coughing and clawing and pulling her to safety.

She screams, as they drag her out the front door. "Where are you?" she calls out, and you only wish you knew

* * *

Fade out.
You're fading too. Even the dead have a shelf life, and someone might say you've done pretty well for yourself. A hundred run-throughs of this film at least. And anyhow, you're a ghost, and ghosts don't get happy endings. The same as women like you. Stop expecting anything else.

But this film keeps playing, keeps looping.

* * *

Try again. Try one last time.

* * *

Fade in.
You can barely speak, barely move this time. There are no respites in the garden, no giggles in the bedroom. You're thinner than mist and less substantial.

"Please," she whispers. "Don't leave me."

You wish you could stay, but the final scene comes so early this time. His hand that lights the match. A blaze you can't escape. They haul her to safety, and in front of the burning estate, he pulls her into him with a rough hand.

She recoils and turns back to the house, back to you. The flames move into you and through you, and the end credits are drawing nearer. This is almost over, probably for the last time. Weeping, she gazes up at your window. You expect nothing to happen, just like nothing's happened before, but an electric look passes between you, and you're sure of it: she sees you.

And she remembers everything.

The meeting among the roses, the engagement that shouldn't have been, all the incarnations of the film that came before.

You think she hates you for abandoning her, to condemning the two of you to this fate. You're wrong. She stares at the smoldering mansion, and with her eyes wild and unafraid, she calls out to you.

This is the first time she's said your name, and at once, something in you shifts. The weight of the past and a thousand lives lost whirlpool within you, and you're no longer without form. As the heat closes in on you, you don't dissolve. You become the fire. Your body is whole again but different: more powerful, and surging through the halls you've haunted, devouring everything in your path.

She sees you there in the flames, peering out all the windows, turning the beautiful gowns he bought her on their Parisian honeymoon to ash. She should be afraid. She should run with the rest.

But she doesn't. She walks to you instead.

Her husband, the man the two of you have shared, glowers on the lawn, his heart cold as the hand he placed around your neck. This isn't how his story is supposed to end. Jaw set, he starts back toward the house, ready to admonish her, to strike her, to drag her back to him by her hair, but the flames rise – you rise – and knock him backward.

Not her, though. She keeps coming.

He's frozen there in the grass, choking on the smoke, watching her go. He would scream her name if he remembered it, but she's merely his wife, his missus, the second incarnation of you.

You aren't the same as him. You know her name, and over the roar of the fire, you speak it to her. You repeat that name until she smiles and you're sure she hears you.

She's on the front stairs now, on the precipice of you. Without hesitating, she swings open the door to what's left of the mansion, and the two of you are truly alone for the first time.

"Hello," you say, as she crosses the threshold, and her hand reaches out for you. The heat of your new body should melt the flesh from her bones, but the flames don't sear her skin. Instead, she moves into you, and all at once, she becomes the fire too.

Together, you keep burning, and you don't stop, not when her husband and the staff come with their buckets of well water, or when they bring in a whole village with firehoses and hand-powered pumps. There are more extras here than this film could ever afford.

They're too late. The opulent floors of the house collapse beneath you, and even once the mansion's fallen, you keep going. Burning on with no kindling except yourself. All the while, her husband stands there, watching the film he thought belonged to him dissolve to nothing at his feet. The last turret of his estate crumbles, and he screams out again, your name this time, but it's for nothing. The extras have retreated in defeat, and no one's left to hear him now.

The last of the Technicolor film stock unspools, but you don't fade to black this time. Wrapped up as one, you and his bride-no-more laugh together, and as your flames rise to the sky, the scent of roses fills the air.

Drydown, 1973

Bill Kte'pi

TESS DIED on Easter, which meant two days every year that were the 'anniversary' of her death. The first Easter without her, the first Easter that *started* without her, was a full three weeks after the anniversary of her death, and it was bullshit. It was a bullshit Easter capping off weeks and weeks of bullshit Easter candy on display every time he went to the store, a bullshit Easter he avoided by retreating to the barn, with its clutter of hoarder crates and old smells.

George and Tess had moved to Tennessee because they could afford the land. They'd lived in cities dense with colleges and coffee shops on three coasts, but when they were ready to turn the part-time fascination of perfume blending into a full-time business, the only way they could take the plunge was somewhere with cheaper real estate and a lower cost of living. The farmhouse was an hour from Nashville, and closer to an M&M plant where chocolates were panned by the millions.

A two-person boutique perfume house. It was the kind of plan that convinced you that, yeah, this could work, this could be great, living in a farmhouse with some dogs and maybe raise some chickens and every morning after coffee on the porch – because they had a porch now! with a porch swing! – they'd walk past the old well to their workshop in the barn, and that would be work for eight or nine hours a day. Lunch on the porch or maybe they'd put a table in that little loft that overlooked the barn interior. Most of their scents, apart from goofy themed scents they did when a new Harry Potter movie came out or whatever, were drawn from their personal mythology, a mythology that sometimes threatened to overtake them, a story that had slipped away from their telling.

Winnipesaukee, 1987 was the smell of Banana Boat tanning lotion, lake water, Jolly Rancher candies, L.A. Looks hair gel, and hot baking sand. Tess and George had each spent the summer of 1987 at Lake Winnipesaukee, years before they knew each other or even lived in the same state, and part of the serial they told each other about themselves was about the near misses they had that summer – sitting at separate tables at Hart's Turkey Farm for dinner, one going up Rattlesnake Mountain while the other was coming down, one playing Skee-Ball while the other played Spy Hunter.

Josephine, 1914 was cinnamon and fresh bread and violets, named for Tess's grandmother. The one thing Tess always made was pie crust. It was something she had made with her grandmother at the holidays, a ritual requiring ice water, frozen butter grated like parmesan, a specific brand of flour. After Tess died, George got up one morning, one of those mornings when you wake up and somehow you've forgotten, you've forgotten that she isn't just out of town or not in the room but she's gone, and he got the special flour out that had been sitting in the cabinet all that time, measured it and tossed a spoonful away for luck and grated in the butter and it wasn't until he had rolled it out that he realized he had watched her enough times that he knew, now. He knew how to make Tess's pie crust, knew how to make pie without her. He didn't crumple to his knees or shriek with anguish or anything so outward as that, but he didn't answer the phone for a week, and the pie sat uneaten in the microwave until finally he gave it to the dogs.

Without Tess there was no core line. Most of the business's revenue now came from licensing the scents for use in soaps, air fresheners, candles. Loyal fans – perfume fandom was a thing, a huge thing – kept putting in their orders for *Korean Restaurant, 2005* or *Wedding Day, 2001*, but what drove them was the discovery of the new.

The last scent they'd worked on was *Polaroid, 1981*. It was a tribute to another bit of their shared lives lived apart, the coincidence they had both received a Polaroid camera for Christmas in 1981. By itself, big deal. It was the aggregation of coincidences that made each one matter so much. That their mothers and fathers had the same middle names, that their colleges had the same school colors (pretty much), that they each had a grandfather born in a different Milan, neither of them in Italy. Sometimes, sometimes this story was too important to them: their biggest dumb fight was over the vintage wedding ring he bought, because Tess was horrified, horrified at the thought of wearing a stranger's ring, of repeating some other woman's marriage.

Oh we have things in common too, their couples friends would tell them: we were both good at math in high school but not in college, we both love those Grasshopper cookies, neither of us had seen *The Godfather* when we met.

Not the same thing!

Not the same at all!

The barn was going to be their workshop, but they'd kept putting off the remodeling, kept saying we'll really dig in and get it done after this next batch ships. You can get a small business loan to remodel the barn, you know, George's father told them. We'd be willing to help out, Tess's mother said. Yes, but. But that meant adding to the amount of money they needed to make every month. It meant a bigger chance of failure.

They were going to work it out eventually. They were going to get it done. He kept thinking about that on that bullshit Easter after she died, looking across the dusty beams of light from the high windows. They'd bought a shop vac to deal with some of the accumulated dust, but there were still great gusts of it lying in wait in the nooks and crannies of all the damn stuff that had been stored there by generations of previous owners. George tried to remember how long ago they had talked about clearing everything out completely so they could power wash it.

Well, it wasn't supposed to rain this week, so he may as well. He set to work carrying everything outside. Anything metal was rusted out. There were boxes of plates and glassware wrapped in newspapers from the 1950s, 60s, 70s, other boxes full of old clothes that would probably never not smell like the barn. After a couple hours, he had made a bit of a dent but had to take a breather because the dust was so thick it had coated his hands and neck and was making him sneeze. God, how much of that dust was just old animal shit?

When he came back outside after washing his hands and face, taking an Allegra, and grabbing a bottle of beer, he saw that one of the boxes he had stacked outside was falling open at the bottom now, the cardboard too soggy to stand up to being moved. One of the milk crates had extra room in it, so he started unpacking the ruptured box and putting everything on top of the crate. T-shirts with iron-ons of bubbly print: Groovy, Gnarly, Keep On Truckin. Brochures for Vacation Bible School. Two thick smoky glass ashtrays. Several carefully wrapped McDonald's coffee mugs. A Polaroid camera.

He smiled when he saw the camera. It was the same general kind he'd had as a kid, the kind that folded. When he didn't have film – which was a lot of the time – he used to just sit there with it, slowly collapsing it back into its flat rectangle and then opening it back up. This was – Lord, he was getting old – what he missed about cameras now that you took all your photos on your phone. That constant reminder of the mechanical processes going on.

George aimed it at the open door of the barn and clicked the button, to see if there was still film in it, see if it still worked. The photo squelched out, and he put the camera down on the milk crate as he shook the photo a few times to speed it up. As it fanned him, the air seemed cleaner, brighter, that mustiness disappearing for an instant.

The image started to come into focus. The camera was working, at least. And he must have gotten more done than he realized, because from what he could see of the barn's interior, the boxes were all gone –

No, it was more than that. As it finished developing, he realized it was more than that. In the photo, the barn didn't have any boxes at all. It was furnished, the windows were completely different, it was well-lit. Was this – it must have been an old photo stuck in the camera somehow. An image of what the barn had looked like once.

He picked the camera back up, took a photo of the house from where he stood, and sat there letting the sweat dry on the back of his neck as the developing chemicals dried on the second photo. That one came out fine. So yeah, the first one was probably a photo that had already been taken and got stuck in the camera somehow.

George put the beer down, stepped into the barn, and took another photo of the interior. You could barely tell he had touched the boxes; between boxes and old farm equipment, the clutter still took up maybe a quarter of the main room and most of the milking room. As the third photograph developed, though, detail and color emerging from that queasy grey, none of that clutter was evident. Instead he saw a better angle of what he'd seen in the first photo: a clean furnished room, with a few crates, sure, but crates stacked purposefully to the side of one of two desks. There was a long work table with perfumery equipment, including amber glass jars labeled in what he was pretty sure was Tess's handwriting.

It was the workshop they'd intended, and at one side, mostly off camera, was a leg. He turned toward where it would have been in the real workshop, took another photo.

This is ridiculous, he told himself while the fourth photograph developed. I am stressed out and maybe I had more beer than I realized, and I'm having some kind of stupid waking dream, widowers probably have this happen all the time.

The leg in the photograph belonged to Tess, Tess as she'd looked before she got sick, Tess standing next to one of the desks with a cell phone to her ear, looking at a binder on the desk in front of her. The binder and her hand were a little blurry, like the photo had caught them in motion.

George clicked the button and took a fifth photo. The Polaroid made that frustrating noise it makes when it's out of film. He caught himself about to throw the camera, and stopped.

It was Easter Sunday in small town Tennessee, and even if somehow someone somewhere had old Polaroid film – one of the antique stores down the interstate? that eBay store? – they wouldn't be open today. The only thing to do was to sleep this off, to sleep this off and... see what things looked like in the morning.

He took a couple sleeping pills and a couple beers. He lay on the pullout bed downstairs looking at the camera sitting on the coffee table, the photos laid out chronologically next to it, and fell asleep swearing he could smell not that Polaroid film smell but a whiff of pomegranate, of cedar, of opoponax and clove – Tess's signature perfume, the one she only blended in small amounts for herself so no one else would smell like her.

* * *

Morning was not reassuring. The photographs still looked the same, still showed the same remodeled barn, the same living Tess. He had a few voicemails. Easter plans he wasn't sure he had officially canceled, and people who were reminded of Tess the same way he had been. He didn't listen to them: he could see the names and times and guess well enough what they said.

There were three cardboard boxes nearest to where he thought that one had been, but none of them yielded any film, and seemed of a completely different vintage: old glass bottles, a few books and magazines from the 1930s. He radiated out from there and then circled back to rummage through wooden and plastic crates just in case, but there seemed no order to where things went. Probably these boxes had been moved around before. Or the house had been emptied out after some previous owner had died after a long residence.

The next boxes, then.

The next.

Mickey Mouse phone, a handheld electronic toy called Merlin, tablecloths, marbles and jacks, shoeboxes of matchboxes, Lincoln Logs, a whole box just of potholders with different kinds of birds on them, another with jar after jar of fruit preserves and pickled vegetables, the hand-written labels long since flaked off and sitting at the bottom of the box.

The light was rusty and losing when he finally found two cartridges wrapped in cloth handkerchiefs. They weren't marked but they sure as hell looked like Polaroid film to him. He hadn't even been conscious of the fact that all through the day he had kept the camera near him, but the next thing he knew he was slotting the cartridge into it, muscle memory reminding him where it went, going through the motions as easily and mindlessly as walking the dog on a Duncan Yo-Yo, which he now had four of.

George took a photo. He took a photo. He took a photo.

How many photos did a cartridge of old Polaroid film have, anyway? He couldn't remember but thought it was less than a dozen anyway, a lot less than on a roll of film for what you would've called back then a regular camera. He laid the photos out in front of him, watching them develop, watching a complete view of the barn he'd sat himself in come into focus. The barn he saw was the workshop just as they'd always imagined it, more or less, with new or refinished walls, good lighting, a vent on the ceiling that must've meant they'd put in heat or central air.

There was no one working there. There was no Tess. The binder had been closed and put away, though he could see some of the papers on one of the desks, the names of a handful of online perfume boutiques and what looked like notes on a scent, though he couldn't make out the writing, just recognized the format they used for development.

But there was more than that. When he took his mask off to scratch where it rubbed his face, there was a scent. There was sillage, what people in The Trade and the nerds who followed them online called the trail of fragrance, the smell of the air someone wearing it has just walked through. It was coming off the photos, it was the air that had wafted to him as he shook them dry. Or he was imagining it. Or imagining every part of this. Real or imagined it was there and he recognized it as his work, his and Tess's. Not a scent they had made; the kind of scent they would. Ozone and geosmin (the earthiness of beets, the crowns of raindrops in dirt), tree bark, and – chocolate? Chocolate. From the M&M plant.

It was the smell of their home after a rainstorm. Had it rained their first night? Hadn't it? Or when they came to visit the property before buying it? Hadn't it then? He closed his eyes and inhaled but the smell was gone now, all he could smell now was the dust tickling his nose, the dirt rustled awake.

What had they done in the house?

What was different there?

Not different, but—

Not 'there', but—

He took a photo. He took a photo. He – don't waste them.

The porch, the kitchen. The kitchen was different mainly because – well, he hadn't been the best at housekeeping in the last year. He thought everything in the photo of the kitchen looked the same apart from the cleanliness – looked the way his, their, kitchen could look, just not the way it currently looked.

When the photo of the porch developed, he immediately stumbled back outside and held it up, held it against the real thing. The empty porch swing they'd bought at that place by the strip mall with the Cook Out. The porch swing that wasn't empty in the photo, but filled with Tess and George sitting next to each other, a table pulled over to hold the takeout containers from Shake Shack ("not that Shake Shack"). She probably had a butterscotch shake and a pimento cheese. He could see the paperboat corner of what might have been a half-finished order of corn nuggets.

Neither of them were looking at him. Goddamn it, he needed them to – he took a photo.

He used the first photo of the porch swing to gauge where to take the next one from, and watched them materialize as he shook it dry, smelled that faint trail of pomegranate and the animalic note of dry-distilled Kenyan opoponax. She looked healthy. She looked happy. She looked almost exactly like she had two years ago, three years ago. Maybe her hair was different. The way the light hit and the things Polaroids did to color, it was hard to say. He was crying and breathless before he noticed that George, Polaroid George, was looking

right at him.

Not a cute 'can you believe this character?' Jim from The Office look.

Not that.

* * *

George didn't know how many photos were in the pack, so he left it at that for now. He had to. He'd used five photos up. For all he knew that was the whole cartridge. It probably wasn't, but what if. What if.

He tried to take a photograph in the middle of the night and got nothing but black, wasting another photo. They were sleeping too. They had put their lights out long before he did. Would it have made a difference if he had a flash?

He stayed up late looking through their own things, the boxes in the attic, the boxes in closets. Did he still have his old Polaroid? He was pretty sure his parents had sold it in a yard sale when he was in high school. If he'd had any film left for it, would he have kept it? Surely they would have sold it too. Did Tess have hers? Did he, that is, now have hers? Without thinking of it, he called her parents. They were two hours behind Central, but Jesus, he was still calling them at what was nearly midnight their—

"I know," her mother said without hello. "I know, George. I know, I miss her too. I've been thinking about her all month."

"I'm never not thinking about her," he said, and he had never really known, deep down, that he would be the kind of person who would ever say that about another person.

"It's late there," she said.

"Couldn't sleep. How you two doing?"

"You know."

He did. If anyone could understand what it was to be without Tess, it would be her parents. Was he – should he tell them? He could always just send them the Polaroids. He could just pretend they were older photos. What would he tell them if he told them?

"Do you remember if Tess kept her old Polaroid camera?" he asked.

"Polaroid camera?"

"Sorry," he said. "That's kind of out of the blue. I just – I don't know. I think about random things. They get under my skin."

"It was that way when my sister died," she said. "But which camera?"

"We have that scent we were working on, you know, the Polaroid one, and we talked about how we both got Polaroids for Christmas when we were kids. Just one of those coincidences. You know our coincidences."

"I'm sorry, honey. I just don't remember a camera."

"But she – she said you gave her a camera for Christmas? In 1981?"

"She said we did? We never could have gotten her something that expensive. Who would get a gift that expensive for an eight year old?" There was that implied criticism of his own parents that sometimes came out; there had been a few years when he'd had the shit spoiled out of him for what seemed no reason and later turned out to be consolation over a miscarriage he didn't know about and the divorce it eventually, cruelly, brought about.

"Are you positive? Maybe it was a used camera?" But he thought he knew the answer.

He hadn't been to Winnipesaukee in 1987, is the thing. Oh, he went to Lake Winnipesaukee before that, but his parents stopped taking him not long after the divorce, and the friend he had told Tess he spent that summer with was someone who only brought him up to the lake for the Fourth of July, and he was pretty sure that had been the previous year anyway. But it – it fit, for them both to have been there. It was so close to true. They had both been to the lake as kids, long before they knew each other. It was a near miss. It just wasn't exactly, per se, the near miss he told her it was.

And maybe she didn't get a Polaroid either.

Maybe purple and teal wasn't exactly the same as purple and green.

It was thinking about this, after getting off the phone and apologizing again, that let him finally get to sleep, a hurt and bonebruised sleep.

* * *

There were ten photographs in a pack.

He found this out because he took four more photos and after that the Polaroid would only give up an empty click. Four photos and Tess was only in one of them. One of the dogs was in one of the others, sitting on the sofa with his tongue hanging out and his paw on a toy George didn't recognize, but the other two were just empty fucking rooms. A little more lived-in than their real-world counterparts, but same furniture, same lighting. That was one thing that struck him. The light coming through the living room window, the shadow of the curtain and the chain of the porch swing, it was exactly the same in the photograph as with his bare eyes, it fell in the same place. The photos he was taking, they were – whatever they were, they were *at the same time*, which shouldn't mean anything but seemed to mean so much. He could have already figured this out, of course. He could have taken photos of clocks. He could have Gone Into Town and taken photos of newspaper displays. He could have been scientific about the whole fucking business.

The one she was in, Polaroid George was in it too: they were in the kitchen, he had had the sense to take a photo in the kitchen around dinner time, figuring they would be there then. They were motion blurs, fuzzy at the edges, features smeared into watercolor. Recognizable – Polaroid George seemed slimmer than he was, despite the camera putting on ten pounds – but impossible to tell anything about their mood or demeanor.

He knew she was in it before it had even finished developing, because of the air coming off it as he shook the picture, because of that pomegranate, that opoponax. Good perfume didn't smell the same on a person as it did in the bottle or sprayed in the air. Good perfume was all about the drydown, the specific way it smelled on you after it had settled on your skin. He wasn't smelling Tess's scent the way the half-empty bottle of it next to the bathroom sink smelled, that he had sprayed on his pillows from time to time. He was smelling the smell of her, close up, the smell of her hair mid-morning, the smell of her neck before bed.

He waited the week. He made himself do that much. He tried all of the film he'd bought online, and none of it would fit the camera. One type was too small, the other too wide. By that point he suspected as much. Of course the film would be special. How could he pretend it was an ordinary camera, something he could just load with ordinary film? He had one cartridge of film left and it was probably the last. He had spent the week, while waiting for the eBay shipments to arrive, ransacking the rest of the clutter in the barn, leaving it worse than when he'd started, and found no more film, no more cameras, not even a tape recorder. He had one cartridge of film, ten photos.

What George had to do was plan how to use those ten. Keep from wasting them. He wasn't sure what that meant, exactly, except that Tess had to be in all of them. That's all he was sure of.

Taking photos at night was no good. The sunlight was the same in the day, yes, but turning on a light here didn't mean a light would be on in the Polaroid, which meant he could get more photos of dark rooms. He had to take them during the day, and plan them so that he could be reasonably sure Tess would be there when he took them.

He started waking up early in the morning in order to go up to the bedroom and take a photo in the mid-spring light before she got out of bed. The alarm clock was still upstairs so he used his phone, setting it for early enough that he could have a cup of coffee and decide if he wanted to do it or not, and some mornings he didn't, he went back to sleep or he left the house and walked the fields, saving that photo for another day, another time.

But other mornings he finished his coffee, put the mug in the dishwasher, took the camera out of the cabinet where he had been putting it so no one who stopped by to chat or something could see it, and walked upstairs and around the corner, standing by the dresser where she put her jewelry every night and where some of it was still sitting. When the light was enough, he took a photo of the bedroom, focusing on the head of the bed. In some of the shots the mirror on the other wall should have shown his reflection, but didn't.

In the first of these, they were in bed together, Tess and Polaroid George, sound asleep. She was facing away from camera. He was on his back and tilted towards camera, mouth a little open. There was something about the body language he didn't like. Was it just seeing himself, 'himself', asleep in a photograph? That couldn't help conjure heebie-jeebies, making you think about being watched in your sleep.

In the second, Tess was a motion blur – getting out of bed? shifting position? – but somehow even through the smear, he recognized that groggy first thing in the morning look on her face, the one that wasn't captured in any of the photographs he had of her on his phone or the desktop or the sparse album they'd kept of 'real pictures'. He was so fixated on it that he didn't even notice right away that Polaroid George was laying on his side in the photo, facing camera, one hand propping his head up while the other reached for her, hand as blurry as she was.

He kept thinking about what he would do if he had more film. If he could open the camera up and hack it to use different film or turn it into a digital camera somehow. Not that he could do that, but maybe he could learn to do it online, or find someone who could do it. He could rig it to take a photo every morning on a timer, or a dozen photos in a row, a flipbook of Tess getting out of bed, still healthy, still fine. He could rig it for video, for sound, he could hear her voice, hoarse in the morning, the "good morning, honey", the in-jokes, the silly things they said to make each other laugh. These are the possibilities you think of, right? These are the paths you wander. Trying to stretch that golden hour. Trying to bottle it.

In one of the photos, Polaroid George's head was snapping toward camera so quickly that he looked like he was trying to shake his face off the way a dog shakes rain, the body language of someone startled by a sound. Was he seeing the world as it could have been, as it was somewhere else? Cancer starts with one mutated cell, right? What if it never started? What if it zigged instead of zagged?

He varied the exact time he took the photos, which meant sometimes he wasted one – an empty bed, or both of them still asleep – but he wasn't sure what he was looking for anyway. He would stop—

He'd stop before he used up all the photos. He'd save some. It was hard to say what for.

In one of the photos, Tess was standing by the window, drinking coffee and looking at something out of frame. Polaroid George was on top of the bed covers, crawling towards the photo, one leg stretched back behind him, a hand reaching forward like he was in the midst of leaping forward to cover the lens with his open palm. George thought about that photo a lot, kept coming back to it as he shuffled through his growing Polaroid album.

In the seventh photo, Polaroid George wasn't in the room, and Tess looked – unhealthy, but not like when she'd been sick. Her hair was flat and dull and not in a way that could easily be chalked up to sleep or film. Her skin was shiny and pale. She was sitting up in bed, body facing camera but face tilted away from it, holding out her palm, and the writing on it, the black marker.

I SEE YOU.

He knew he only had three photos left, but he wanted to take another before Polaroid George came back to the bedroom or Tess left it, so the seventh had barely finished developing, sitting on the bed in front of him, when he took another, focused more closely on the space where Tess was sat.

Beneath the paleness she looked bruised all over, her veins shockingly blue even in the offcolor of Polaroid film, and there were red marks around her nails as though she had been picking at them. She was in the same pose, her hand lowered now, and he followed her gaze to the open notepad on her bedside table, where she'd written, *he isn't*. Isn't what? "He isn't you"? He isn't real? He isn't kind? There was a false start of ink like she had been interrupted before she could finish writing.

He could smell stale coffee coming off the photo, and their *Blackout, 2004* scented body lotion aerated by the hot water of the off-camera shower, and closed his eyes, inhaling that warm woody honey smell of Tess's perfume, and he couldn't help himself, as soon as the scent was gone he took another photo. The more he thought about only having two photos left, the more frantic he was to take the next one, the harder it was to imagine saving it. Now Tess was holding the bed covers up to her face and a blur of motion was in the air over the bed, something shaped like George but faster, longer, as though as the shutter had opened he had flung himself through the air towards the mattress.

George forced himself out of the room, forced himself to close the door behind him, holding the camera tight against his chest, looking at the shower, which he didn't think he had used in several days, and then back at the bedroom door. He stood there for a long time broken up over the next few weeks and years to come, time interrupted by his own sleep and by checking and double-checking the barn and by searching the internet for a special kind of film, time split into pieces by talking to her parents and his parents and her friends and their friends and doing and saying all the things you do and say to signal I'm getting better, but all of that seemed to be happening in another frame while here he stood in front of a bedroom that had become strange, while he stood until eventually he took a final photo, just to smell her one more time.

The Rats in the Walls

H.P. Lovecraft

ON 16 JULY 1923, I moved into Exham Priory after the last workman had finished his labours. The restoration had been a stupendous task, for little had remained of the deserted pile but a shell-like ruin; yet because it had been the seat of my ancestors, I let no expense deter me. The place had not been inhabited since the reign of James the First, when a tragedy of intensely hideous, though largely unexplained, nature had struck down the master, five of his children, and several servants; and driven forth under a cloud of suspicion and terror the third son, my lineal progenitor and the only survivor of the abhorred line.

With this sole heir denounced as a murderer, the estate had reverted to the crown, nor had the accused man made any attempt to exculpate himself or regain his property. Shaken by some horror greater than that of conscience or the law, and expressing only a frantic wish to exclude the ancient edifice from his sight and memory, Walter de la Poer, eleventh Baron Exham, fled to Virginia and there founded the family which by the next century had become known as Delapore.

Exham Priory had remained untenanted, though later allotted to the estates of the Norrys family and much studied because of its peculiarly composite architecture; an architecture involving Gothic towers resting on a Saxon or Romanesque substructure, whose foundation in turn was of a still earlier order or blend of orders – Roman, and even Druidic or native Cymric, if legends speak truly. This foundation was a very singular thing, being merged on one side with the solid limestone of the precipice from whose brink the priory overlooked a desolate valley three miles west of the village of Anchester.

Architects and antiquarians loved to examine this strange relic of forgotten centuries, but the country folk hated it. They had hated it hundreds of years before, when my ancestors lived there, and they hated it now, with the moss and mould of abandonment on it. I had not been a day in Anchester before I knew I came of an accursed house. And this week workmen have blown up Exham Priory, and are busy obliterating the traces of its foundations. The bare statistics of my ancestry I had always known, together with the fact that my first American forebear had come to the colonies under a strange cloud. Of details, however, I had been kept wholly ignorant through the policy of reticence always maintained by the Delapores. Unlike our planter neighbours, we seldom boasted of crusading ancestors or other mediaeval and Renaissance heroes; nor was any kind of tradition handed down except what may have been recorded in the sealed envelope left before the Civil War by every squire to his eldest son for posthumous opening. The glories we cherished were those achieved since the migration; the glories of a proud and honourable, if somewhat reserved and unsocial Virginia line.

During the war our fortunes were extinguished and our whole existence changed by the burning of Carfax, our home on the banks of the James. My grandfather, advanced in years, had perished in that incendiary outrage, and with him the envelope that had bound us all to the past. I can recall that fire today as I saw it then at the age of seven, with the federal soldiers shouting, the women screaming, and the negroes howling and praying. My father was in the army, defending Richmond, and after many formalities my mother and I were passed through the lines to join him.

When the war ended we all moved north, whence my mother had come; and I grew to manhood, middle age, and ultimate wealth as a stolid Yankee. Neither my father nor I ever knew what our hereditary envelope had contained, and as I merged into the greyness of Massachusetts business life I lost all interest in the mysteries which evidently lurked far back in my family tree. Had I suspected their nature, how gladly I would have left Exham Priory to its moss, bats and cobwebs!

My father died in 1904, but without any message to leave to me, or to my only child, Alfred, a motherless boy of ten. It was this boy who reversed the order of family information, for although I could give him only jesting conjectures about the past, he wrote me of some very interesting ancestral legends when the late war took him to England in 1917 as an aviation officer. Apparently the Delapores had a colourful and perhaps sinister history, for a friend of my son's, Capt. Edward Norrys of the Royal Flying Corps, dwelt near the family seat at Anchester and related some peasant superstitions which few novelists could equal for wildness and incredibility. Norrys himself, of course, did not take them so seriously; but they amused my son and made good material for his letters to me. It was this legendry which definitely turned my attention to my transatlantic heritage, and made me resolve to purchase and restore the family seat which Norrys showed to Alfred in its picturesque desertion, and offered to get for him at a surprisingly reasonable figure, since his own uncle was the present owner.

I bought Exham Priory in 1918, but was almost immediately distracted from my plans of restoration by the return of my son as a maimed invalid. During the two years that he lived I thought of nothing but his care, having even placed my business under the direction of partners.

In 1921, as I found myself bereaved and aimless, a retired manufacturer no longer young, I resolved to divert my remaining years with my new possession. Visiting Anchester in December, I was entertained by Capt. Norrys, a plump, amiable young man who had thought much of my son, and secured his assistance in gathering plans and anecdotes to guide in the coming restoration. Exham Priory itself I saw without emotion, a jumble of tottering mediaeval ruins covered with lichens and honeycombed with rooks' nests, perched perilously upon a precipice, and denuded of floors or other interior features save the stone walls of the separate towers.

As I gradually recovered the image of the edifice as it had been when my ancestors left it over three centuries before, I began to hire workmen for the reconstruction. In every case I was forced to go outside the immediate locality, for the Anchester villagers had an almost unbelievable fear and hatred of the place. The sentiment was so great that it was sometimes communicated to the outside labourers, causing numerous desertions; whilst its scope appeared to include both the priory and its ancient family.

My son had told me that he was somewhat avoided during his visits because he was a de la Poer, and I now found myself subtly ostracized for a like reason until I convinced the peasants how little I knew of my heritage. Even then they sullenly disliked me, so that I had to collect most of the village traditions through the mediation of Norrys. What the people could not forgive, perhaps, was that I had come to restore a symbol so abhorrent to them; for, rationally or not, they viewed Exham Priory as nothing less than a haunt of fiends and werewolves.

Piecing together the tales which Norrys collected for me, and supplementing them with the accounts of several savants who had studied the ruins, I deduced that Exham Priory stood on the site of a prehistoric temple; a Druidical or ante-Druidical thing which must have been contemporary with Stonehenge. That indescribable rites had been celebrated there, few doubted, and there were unpleasant tales of the transference of these rites into the Cybele worship which the Romans had introduced.

Inscriptions still visible in the sub-cellar bore such unmistakable letters as 'DIV... OPS...MAGNA. MAT...', sign of the Magna Mater whose dark worship was once vainly forbidden to Roman citizens. Anchester had been the camp of the third Augustan legion, as many remains attest, and it was said that the temple of Cybele was splendid and thronged with worshippers who performed nameless ceremonies at the bidding of a Phrygian priest. Tales added that the fall of the old religion did not end the orgies at the temple, but that the priests lived on in the new faith without real change. Likewise was it said that the rites did not vanish with the Roman power, and that certain among the Saxons added to what remained of the temple, and gave it the essential outline it subsequently preserved, making it the centre of a cult feared through half the heptarchy. About 1000 A.D. the place is mentioned in a chronicle as being a substantial stone priory housing a strange and powerful monastic order and surrounded by extensive gardens which needed no walls to exclude a frightened populace. It was never destroyed by the Danes, though after the Norman Conquest it must have declined tremendously, since there was no impediment when Henry the Third granted the site to my ancestor, Gilbert de la Poer, First Baron Exham, in 1261.

Of my family before this date there is no evil report, but something strange must have happened then. In one chronicle there is a reference to a de la Poer as 'cursed of God in 1307', whilst village legendry had nothing but evil and frantic fear to tell of the castle that went up on the foundations of the old temple and priory. The fireside tales were of the most grisly description, all the ghastlier because of their frightened reticence and cloudy evasiveness. They represented my ancestors as a race of hereditary daemons beside whom Gilles de Retz and the Marquis de Sade would seem the veriest tyros, and hinted whisperingly at their responsibility for the occasional disappearances of villagers through several generations.

The worst characters, apparently, were the barons and their direct heirs; at least, most was whispered about these. If of healthier inclinations, it was said, an heir would early and mysteriously die to make way for another more typical scion. There seemed to be an inner cult in the family, presided over by the head of the house, and sometimes closed except to a few members. Temperament rather than ancestry was evidently the basis of this cult, for it was entered by several who married into the family. Lady Margaret Trevor from Cornwall, wife of Godfrey, the second son of the fifth baron, became a favourite bane of children all over the countryside, and the daemon heroine of a particularly horrible old ballad not yet extinct near the Welsh border. Preserved in balladry, too, though not illustrating the same point, is the hideous tale of Lady Mary de la Poer, who shortly after her marriage to the Earl of Shrewsfield was killed by him and his mother, both of the slayers being absolved and blessed by the priest to whom they confessed what they dared not repeat to the world.

These myths and ballads, typical as they were of crude superstition, repelled me greatly. Their persistence, and their application to so long a line of my ancestors, were especially annoying; whilst the imputations of monstrous habits proved unpleasantly reminiscent of the one known scandal of my immediate forebears – the case of my cousin, young Randolph Delapore of Carfax who went among the negroes and became a voodoo priest after he returned from the Mexican War.

I was much less disturbed by the vaguer tales of wails and howlings in the barren, windswept valley beneath the limestone cliff; of the graveyard stenches after the spring rains; of the floundering, squealing white thing on which Sir John Clave's horse had trod one night in a lonely field; and of the servant who had gone mad at what he saw in the priory in the full light of day. These things were hackneyed spectral lore, and I was at that time a pronounced sceptic. The accounts of vanished peasants were less to be dismissed, though not especially significant in view of mediaeval custom. Prying curiosity meant death, and more than one severed head had been publicly shown on the bastions – now effaced – around Exham Priory.

A few of the tales were exceedingly picturesque, and made me wish I had learnt more of the comparative mythology in my youth. There was, for instance, the belief that a legion of bat-winged devils kept witches' sabbath each night at the priory – a legion whose sustenance might explain the disproportionate abundance of coarse vegetables harvested in the vast gardens. And, most vivid of all, there was the dramatic epic of the rats – the scampering army of obscene vermin which had burst forth from the castle three months after the tragedy that doomed it to desertion – the lean, filthy, ravenous army which had swept all before it and devoured fowl, cats, dogs, hogs, sheep, and even two hapless human beings before its fury was spent. Around that unforgettable rodent army a whole separate cycle of myths revolves, for it scattered among the village homes and brought curses and horrors in its train.

Such was the lore that assailed me as I pushed to completion, with an elderly obstinacy, the work of restoring my ancestral home. It must not be imagined for a moment that these tales formed my principal psychological environment. On the other hand, I was constantly praised and encouraged by Capt. Norrys and the antiquarians who surrounded and aided me. When the task was done, over two years after its commencement, I viewed the great rooms, wainscoted walls, vaulted ceilings, mullioned windows, and broad staircases with a pride which fully compensated for the prodigious expense of the restoration.

Every attribute of the Middle Ages was cunningly reproduced and the new parts blended perfectly with the original walls and foundations. The seat of my fathers was complete, and I looked forward to redeeming at last the local fame of the line which ended in me. I could reside here permanently, and prove that a de la Poer (for I had adopted again the original spelling of the name) need not be a fiend. My comfort was perhaps augmented by the fact that, although Exham Priory was mediaevally fitted, its interior was in truth wholly new and free from old vermin and old ghosts alike.

As I have said, I moved in on 16 July 1923. My household consisted of seven servants and nine cats, of which latter species I am particularly fond. My eldest cat, 'Nigger-Man', was seven years old and had come with me from my home in Bolton,

Massachusetts; the others I had accumulated whilst living with Capt. Norrys' family during the restoration of the priory.

For five days our routine proceeded with the utmost placidity, my time being spent mostly in the codification of old family data. I had now obtained some very circumstantial accounts of the final tragedy and flight of Walter de la Poer, which I conceived to be the probable contents of the hereditary paper lost in the fire at Carfax. It appeared that my ancestor was accused with much reason of having killed all the other members of his household, except four servant confederates, in their sleep, about two weeks after a shocking discovery which changed his whole demeanour, but which, except by implication, he disclosed to no one save perhaps the servants who assisted him and afterwards fled beyond reach.

This deliberate slaughter, which included a father, three brothers, and two sisters, was largely condoned by the villagers, and so slackly treated by the law that its perpetrator escaped honoured, unharmed, and undisguised to Virginia; the general whispered sentiment being that he had purged the land of an immemorial curse. What discovery had prompted an act so terrible, I could scarcely even conjecture. Walter de la Poer must have known for years the sinister tales about his family, so that this material could have given him no fresh impulse. Had he, then, witnessed some appalling ancient rite, or stumbled upon some frightful and revealing symbol in the priory or its vicinity? He was reputed to have been a shy, gentle youth in England. In Virginia he seemed not so much hard or bitter as harassed and apprehensive. He was spoken of in the diary of another gentleman adventurer, Francis Harley of Bellview, as a man of unexampled justice, honour, and delicacy.

On 22 July occurred the first incident which, though lightly dismissed at the time, takes on a preternatural significance in relation to later events. It was so simple as to be almost negligible, and could not possibly have been noticed under the circumstances; for it must be recalled that since I was in a building practically fresh and new except for the walls, and surrounded by a well-balanced staff of servitors, apprehension would have been absurd despite the locality.

What I afterward remembered is merely this – that my old black cat, whose moods I know so well, was undoubtedly alert and anxious to an extent wholly out of keeping with his natural character. He roved from room to room, restless and disturbed, and sniffed constantly about the walls which formed part of the Gothic structure. I realise how trite this sounds – like the inevitable dog in the ghost story, which always growls before his master sees the sheeted figure – yet I cannot consistently suppress it.

The following day a servant complained of restlessness among all the cats in the house. He came to me in my study, a lofty west room on the second storey, with groined arches, black oak panelling, and a triple Gothic window overlooking the limestone cliff and desolate valley; and even as he spoke I saw the jetty form of Nigger-Man creeping along the west wall and scratching at the new panels which overlaid the ancient stone.

I told the man that there must be a singular odor or emanation from the old stonework, imperceptible to human senses, but affecting the delicate organs of cats even through the new woodwork. This I truly believed, and when the fellow suggested the presence of mice or rats, I mentioned that there had been no rats there for three hundred years, and that even the field mice of the surrounding country could hardly be found in these high walls, where they had never been known to stray. That afternoon

I called on Capt. Norrys, and he assured me that it would be quite incredible for field mice to infest the priory in such a sudden and unprecedented fashion.

That night, dispensing as usual with a valet, I retired in the west tower chamber which I had chosen as my own, reached from the study by a stone staircase and short gallery – the former partly ancient, the latter entirely restored. This room was circular, very high, and without wainscoting, being hung with arras which I had myself chosen in London.

Seeing that Nigger-Man was with me, I shut the heavy Gothic door and retired by the light of the electric bulbs which so cleverly counterfeited candles, finally switching off the light and sinking on the carved and canopied four-poster, with the venerable cat in his accustomed place across my feet. I did not draw the curtains, but gazed out at the narrow window which I faced. There was a suspicion of aurora in the sky, and the delicate traceries of the window were pleasantly silhouetted.

At some time I must have fallen quietly asleep, for I recall a distinct sense of leaving strange dreams, when the cat started violently from his placid position. I saw him in the faint auroral glow, head strained forward, fore feet on my ankles, and hind feet stretched behind. He was looking intensely at a point on the wall somewhat west of the window, a point which to my eye had nothing to mark it, but toward which all my attention was now directed.

And as I watched, I knew that Nigger-Man was not vainly excited. Whether the arras actually moved I cannot say. I think it did, very slightly. But what I can swear to is that behind it I heard a low, distinct scurrying as of rats or mice. In a moment the cat had jumped bodily on the screening tapestry, bringing the affected section to the floor with his weight, and exposing a damp, ancient wall of stone; patched here and there by the restorers, and devoid of any trace of rodent prowlers.

Nigger-Man raced up and down the floor by this part of the wall, clawing the fallen arras and seemingly trying at times to insert a paw between the wall and the oaken floor. He found nothing, and after a time returned wearily to his place across my feet. I had not moved, but I did not sleep again that night.

In the morning I questioned all the servants, and found that none of them had noticed anything unusual, save that the cook remembered the actions of a cat which had rested on her windowsill. This cat had howled at some unknown hour of the night, awaking the cook in time for her to see him dart purposefully out of the open door down the stairs. I drowsed away the noontime, and in the afternoon called again on Capt. Norrys, who became exceedingly interested in what I told him. The odd incidents – so slight yet so curious – appealed to his sense of the picturesque and elicited from him a number of reminiscenses of local ghostly lore. We were genuinely perplexed at the presence of rats, and Norrys lent me some traps and Paris green, which I had the servants place in strategic localities when I returned.

I retired early, being very sleepy, but was harassed by dreams of the most horrible sort. I seemed to be looking down from an immense height upon a twilit grotto, knee-deep with filth, where a white-bearded daemon swineherd drove about with his staff a flock of fungous, flabby beasts whose appearance filled me with unutterable loathing. Then, as the swineherd paused and nodded over his task, a mighty swarm of rats rained down on the stinking abyss and fell to devouring beasts and man alike.

From this terrific vision I was abruptly awakened by the motions of Nigger-Man, who had been sleeping as usual across my feet. This time I did not have to question the source of his snarls and hisses, and of the fear which made him sink his claws into my ankle, unconscious of their effect; for on every side of the chamber the walls were alive with nauseous sound – the verminous slithering of ravenous, gigantic rats. There was now no aurora to show the state of the arras – the fallen section of which had been replaced – but I was not too frightened to switch on the light.

As the bulbs leapt into radiance I saw a hideous shaking all over the tapestry, causing the somewhat peculiar designs to execute a singular dance of death. This motion disappeared almost at once, and the sound with it. Springing out of bed, I poked at the arras with the long handle of a warming-pan that rested near, and lifted one section to see what lay beneath. There was nothing but the patched stone wall, and even the cat had lost his tense realisation of abnormal presences. When I examined the circular trap that had been placed in the room, I found all of the openings sprung, though no trace remained of what had been caught and had escaped.

Further sleep was out of the question, so lighting a candle, I opened the door and went out in the gallery towards the stairs to my study, Nigger-Man following at my heels. Before we had reached the stone steps, however, the cat darted ahead of me and vanished down the ancient flight. As I descended the stairs myself, I became suddenly aware of sounds in the great room below; sounds of a nature which could not be mistaken.

The oak-panelled walls were alive with rats, scampering and milling whilst Nigger-Man was racing about with the fury of a baffled hunter. Reaching the bottom, I switched on the light, which did not this time cause the noise to subside. The rats continued their riot, stampeding with such force and distinctness that I could finally assign to their motions a definite direction. These creatures, in numbers apparently inexhaustible, were engaged in one stupendous migration from inconceivable heights to some depth conceivably or inconceivably below.

I now heard steps in the corridor, and in another moment two servants pushed open the massive door. They were searching the house for some unknown source of disturbance which had thrown all the cats into a snarling panic and caused them to plunge precipitately down several flights of stairs and squat, yowling, before the closed door to the sub-cellar. I asked them if they had heard the rats, but they replied in the negative. And when I turned to call their attention to the sounds in the panels, I realised that the noise had ceased.

With the two men, I went down to the door of the sub-cellar, but found the cats already dispersed. Later I resolved to explore the crypt below, but for the present I merely made a round of the traps. All were sprung, yet all were tenantless. Satisfying myself that no one had heard the rats save the felines and me, I sat in my study till morning, thinking profoundly and recalling every scrap of legend I had unearthed concerning the building I inhabited. I slept some in the forenoon, leaning back in the one comfortable library chair which my mediaeval plan of furnishing could not banish. Later I telephoned to Capt. Norrys, who came over and helped me explore the sub-cellar.

Absolutely nothing untoward was found, although we could not repress a thrill at the knowledge that this vault was built by Roman hands. Every low arch and massive pillar was Roman – not the debased Romanesque of the bungling Saxons, but the severe and harmonious classicism of the age of the Caesars; indeed, the walls abounded with inscriptions familiar to the antiquarians who had repeatedly explored the place – things like 'P. GETAE. PROP…TEMP…DONA…' and 'L. PRAEG…VS…PONTIFI…ATYS…'

The reference to Atys made me shiver, for I had read Catullus and knew something of the hideous rites of the Eastern god, whose worship was so mixed with that of Cybele. Norrys and I, by the light of lanterns, tried to interpret the odd and nearly effaced designs on certain irregularly rectangular blocks of stone generally held to be altars, but could make nothing of them. We remembered that one pattern, a sort of rayed sun, was held by students to imply a non-Roman origin suggesting that these altars had merely been adopted by the Roman priests from some older and perhaps aboriginal temple on the same site. On one of these blocks were some brown stains which made me wonder. The largest, in the centre of the room, had certain features on the upper surface which indicated its connection with fire – probably burnt offerings.

Such were the sights in that crypt before whose door the cats howled, and where Norrys and I now determined to pass the night. Couches were brought down by the servants, who were told not to mind any nocturnal actions of the cats, and Nigger-Man was admitted as much for help as for companionship. We decided to keep the great oak door – a modern replica with slits for ventilation – tightly closed; and, with this attended to, we retired with lanterns still burning to await whatever might occur.

The vault was very deep in the foundations of the priory, and undoubtedly far down on the face of the beetling limestone cliff overlooking the waste valley. That it had been the goal of the scuffling and unexplainable rats I could not doubt, though why, I could not tell. As we lay there expectantly, I found my vigil occasionally mixed with half-formed dreams from which the uneasy motions of the cat across my feet would rouse me.

These dreams were not wholesome, but horribly like the one I had had the night before. I saw again the twilit grotto, and the swineherd with his unmentionable fungous beasts wallowing in filth, and as I looked at these things they seemed nearer and more distinct – so distinct that I could almost observe their features. Then I did observe the flabby features of one of them – and awakened with such a scream that Nigger-Man started up, whilst Capt. Norrys, who had not slept, laughed considerably. Norrys might have laughed more – or perhaps less – had he known what it was that made me scream. But I did not remember myself till later. Ultimate horror often paralyses memory in a merciful way.

Norrys waked me when the phenomena began. Out of the same frightful dream I was called by his gentle shaking and his urging to listen to the cats. Indeed, there was much to listen to, for beyond the closed door at the head of the stone steps was a veritable nightmare of feline yelling and clawing, whilst Nigger-Man, unmindful of his kindred outside, was running excitedly round the bare stone walls, in which I heard the same babel of scurrying rats that had troubled me the night before.

An acute terror now rose within me, for here were anomalies which nothing normal could well explain. These rats, if not the creatures of a madness which I shared with the cats alone, must be burrowing and sliding in Roman walls I had thought to be solid limestone blocks…unless perhaps the action of water through more than seventeen centuries had eaten winding tunnels which rodent bodies had worn clear and ample …But even so, the spectral horror was no less; for if these were living vermin why did not Norrys hear their disgusting commotion? Why did he urge me to watch Nigger-Man and listen to the cats outside, and why did he guess wildly and vaguely at what could have aroused them?

By the time I had managed to tell him, as rationally as I could, what I thought I was hearing, my ears gave me the last fading impression of scurrying; which had retreated still downward, far underneath this deepest of sub-cellars till it seemed as if the whole cliff below were riddled with questing rats. Norrys was not as sceptical as I had anticipated, but instead seemed profoundly moved. He motioned to me to notice that the cats at the door had ceased their clamour, as if giving up the rats for lost; whilst Nigger-Man had a burst of renewed restlessness, and was clawing frantically around the bottom of the large stone altar in the center of the room, which was nearer Norrys' couch than mine.

My fear of the unknown was at this point very great. Something astounding had occurred, and I saw that Capt. Norrys, a younger, stouter, and presumably more naturally materialistic man, was affected fully as much as myself – perhaps because of his lifelong and intimate familiarity with local legend. We could for the moment do nothing but watch the old black cat as he pawed with decreasing fervour at the base of the altar, occasionally looking up and mewing to me in that persuasive manner which he used when he wished me to perform some favour for him.

Norrys now took a lantern close to the altar and examined the place where Nigger-Man was pawing; silently kneeling and scraping away the lichens of the centuries which joined the massive pre-Roman block to the tessellated floor. He did not find anything, and was about to abandon his efforts when I noticed a trivial circumstance which made me shudder, even though it implied nothing more than I had already imagined.

I told him of it, and we both looked at its almost imperceptible manifestation with the fixedness of fascinated discovery and acknowledgment. It was only this – that the flame of the lantern set down near the altar was slightly but certainly flickering from a draught of air which it had not before received, and which came indubitably from the crevice between floor and altar where Norrys was scraping away the lichens.

We spent the rest of the night in the brilliantly-lighted study, nervously discussing what we should do next. The discovery that some vault deeper than the deepest known masonry of the Romans underlay this accursed pile, some vault unsuspected by the curious antiquarians of three centuries, would have been sufficient to excite us without any background of the sinister. As it was, the fascination became two-fold; and we paused in doubt whether to abandon our search and quit the priory forever in superstitious caution, or to gratify our sense of adventure and brave whatever horrors might await us in the unknown depths.

By morning we had compromised, and decided to go to London to gather a group of archaeologists and scientific men fit to cope with the mystery. It should be mentioned that before leaving the sub-cellar we had vainly tried to move the central altar which we now recognized as the gate to a new pit of nameless fear. What secret would open the gate, wiser men than we would have to find.

During many days in London Capt. Norrys and I presented our facts, conjectures, and legendary anecdotes to five eminent authorities, all men who could be trusted to respect any family disclosures which future explorations might develop. We found most of them little disposed to scoff but, instead, intensely interested and sincerely sympathetic. It is hardly necessary to name them all, but I may say that they included Sir William Brinton, whose excavations in the Troad excited most of the world in their day. As we all took the train for Anchester I felt myself poised on the brink of frightful revelations, a sensation symbolized by the air of mourning among the many Americans at the unexpected death of the President on the other side of the world.

On the evening of 7 August we reached Exham Priory, where the servants assured me that nothing unusual had occurred. The cats, even old Nigger-Man, had been perfectly placid, and not a trap in the house had been sprung. We were to begin exploring on the following day, awaiting which I assigned well-appointed rooms to all my guests.

I myself retired in my own tower chamber, with Nigger-Man across my feet. Sleep came quickly, but hideous dreams assailed me. There was a vision of a Roman feast like that of Trimalchio, with a horror in a covered platter. Then came that damnable, recurrent thing about the swineherd and his filthy drove in the twilit grotto. Yet when I awoke it was full daylight, with normal sounds in the house below. The rats, living or spectral, had not troubled me; and Nigger-Man was still quietly asleep. On going down, I found that the same tranquillity had prevailed elsewhere; a condition which one of the assembled servants – a fellow named Thornton, devoted to the psychic – rather absurdly laid to the fact that I had now been shown the thing which certain forces had wished to show me.

All was now ready, and at 11 a.m. our entire group of seven men, bearing powerful electric searchlights and implements of excavation, went down to the sub-cellar and bolted the door behind us. Nigger-Man was with us, for the investigators found no occasion to despise his excitability, and were indeed anxious that he be present in case of obscure rodent manifestations. We noted the Roman inscriptions and unknown altar designs only briefly, for three of the savants had already seen them, and all knew their characteristics. Prime attention was paid to the momentous central altar, and within an hour Sir William Brinton had caused it to tilt backward, balanced by some unknown species of counterweight.

There now lay revealed such a horror as would have overwhelmed us had we not been prepared. Through a nearly square opening in the tiled floor, sprawling on a flight of stone steps so prodigiously worn that it was little more than an inclined plane at the centre, was a ghastly array of human or semi-human bones. Those which retained their collocation as skeletons showed attitudes of panic fear, and over all were the marks of rodent gnawing. The skulls denoted nothing short of utter idiocy, cretinism, or primitive semi-apedom.

Above the hellishly littered steps arched a descending passage seemingly chiselled from the solid rock, and conducting a current of air. This current was not a sudden and noxious rush as from a closed vault, but a cool breeze with something of freshness in it. We did not pause long, but shiveringly began to clear a passage down the steps. It was then that Sir William, examining the hewn walls, made the odd observation that the passage, according to the direction of the strokes, must have been chiselled from beneath.

I must be very deliberate now, and choose my words. After ploughing down a few steps amidst the gnawed bones we saw that there was light ahead; not any mystic phosphorescence, but a filtered daylight which could not come except from unknown fissures in the cliff that over-looked the waste valley. That such fissures had escaped notice from outside was hardly remarkable, for not only is the valley wholly uninhabited, but the cliff is so high and beetling that only an aeronaut could study its face in detail. A few steps more, and our breaths were literally snatched from us by what we saw; so literally that Thornton, the psychic investigator, actually fainted in the arms of the dazed men who stood behind him. Norrys, his plump face utterly white and flabby, simply cried out inarticulately; whilst I think that what I did was to gasp or hiss, and cover my eyes.

The man behind me – the only one of the party older than I – croaked the hackneyed "My God!" in the most cracked voice I ever heard. Of seven cultivated men, only Sir William Brinton retained his composure, a thing the more to his credit because he led the party and must have seen the sight first.

It was a twilit grotto of enormous height, stretching away farther than any eye could see; a subterraneous world of limitless mystery and horrible suggestion. There were buildings and other architectural remains – in one terrified glance I saw a weird pattern of tumuli, a savage circle of monoliths, a low-domed Roman ruin, a sprawling Saxon pile, and an early English edifice of wood – but all these were dwarfed by the ghoulish spectacle presented by the general surface of the ground. For yards about the steps extended an insane tangle of human bones, or bones at least as human as those on the steps. Like a foamy sea they stretched, some fallen apart, but others wholly or partly articulated as skeletons; these latter invariably in postures of daemoniac frenzy, either fighting off some menace or clutching other forms with cannibal intent.

When Dr. Trask, the anthropologist, stopped to classify the skulls, he found a degraded mixture which utterly baffled him. They were mostly lower than the Piltdown man in the scale of evolution, but in every case definitely human. Many were of higher grade, and a very few were the skulls of supremely and sensitively developed types. All the bones were gnawed, mostly by rats, but somewhat by others of the half-human drove. Mixed with them were many tiny bones of rats – fallen members of the lethal army which closed the ancient epic.

I wonder that any man among us lived and kept his sanity through that hideous day of discovery. Not Hoffman nor Huysmans could conceive a scene more wildly incredible, more frenetically repellent, or more Gothically grotesque than the twilit grotto through which we seven staggered; each stumbling on revelation after revelation, and trying to keep for the nonce from thinking of the events which must have taken place there three hundred, or a thousand, or two thousand or ten thousand years ago. It was the antechamber of hell, and poor Thornton fainted again when Trask told him that some of the skeleton things must have descended as quadrupeds through the last twenty or more generations.

Horror piled on horror as we began to interpret the architectural remains. The quadruped things – with their occasional recruits from the biped class – had been kept in stone pens, out of which they must have broken in their last delirium of hunger or rat-fear. There had been great herds of them, evidently fattened on the coarse vegetables whose remains could be found as a sort of poisonous ensilage at the bottom of the huge stone bins older than Rome. I knew now why my ancestors had had such excessive gardens – would to heaven I could forget! The purpose of the herds I did not have to ask.

Sir William, standing with his searchlight in the Roman ruin, translated aloud the most shocking ritual I have ever known; and told of the diet of the antediluvian cult which the priests of Cybele found and mingled with their own. Norrys, used as he was to the trenches, could not walk straight when he came out of the English building. It was a butcher shop and kitchen – he had expected that – but it was too much to see familiar English implements in such a place, and to read familiar English graffiti there, some as recent as 1610. I could not go in that building – that building whose daemon activities were stopped only by the dagger of my ancestor Walter de la Poer.

What I did venture to enter was the low Saxon building whose oaken door had fallen, and there I found a terrible row of ten stone cells with rusty bars. Three had tenants, all skeletons of high grade, and on the bony forefinger of one I found a seal ring with my own coat-of-arms. Sir William found a vault with far older cells below the Roman chapel, but these cells were empty. Below them was a low crypt with cases of formally arranged bones, some of them bearing terrible parallel inscriptions carved in Latin, Greek, and the tongue of Phrygia.

Meanwhile, Dr. Trask had opened one of the prehistoric tumuli, and brought to light skulls which were slightly more human than a gorilla's, and which bore indescribably ideographic carvings. Through all this horror my cat stalked unperturbed. Once I saw him monstrously perched atop a mountain of bones, and wondered at the secrets that might lie behind his yellow eyes.

Having grasped to some slight degree the frightful revelations of this twilit area – an area so hideously foreshadowed by my recurrent dream – we turned to that apparently boundless depth of midnight cavern where no ray of light from the cliff could penetrate. We shall never know what sightless Stygian worlds yawn beyond the little distance we went, for it was decided that such secrets are not good for mankind. But there was plenty to engross us close at hand, for we had not gone far before the searchlights showed that accursed infinity of pits in which the rats had feasted, and whose sudden lack of replenishment had driven the ravenous rodent army first to turn on the living herds of starving things, and then to burst forth from the priory in that historic orgy of devastation which the peasants will never forget.

God! Those carrion black pits of sawed, picked bones and opened skulls! Those nightmare chasms choked with the pithecanthropoid, Celtic, Roman, and English bones of countless unhallowed centuries! Some of them were full, and none can say how deep they had once been. Others were still bottomless to our searchlights, and peopled by unnamable fancies. What, I thought, of the hapless rats that stumbled into such traps amidst the blackness of their quests in this grisly Tartarus?

Once my foot slipped near a horribly yawning brink, and I had a moment of ecstatic fear. I must have been musing a long time, for I could not see any of the party but plump Capt. Norrys. Then there came a sound from that inky, boundless, farther distance that I thought I knew; and I saw my old black cat dart past me like a winged Egyptian god, straight into the illimitable gulf of the unknown. But I was not far behind, for there was no doubt after another second. It was the eldritch scurrying of those fiend-born rats, always questing for new horrors, and determined to lead me on even unto those grinning caverns of earth's centre where Nyarlathotep, the mad faceless god, howls blindly in the darkness to the piping of two amorphous idiot flute-players.

My searchlight expired, but still I ran. I heard voices, and yowls, and echoes, but above all there gently rose that impious, insidious scurrying; gently rising, rising, as a stiff bloated corpse gently rises above an oily river that flows under the endless onyx bridges to a black, putrid sea.

Something bumped into me – something soft and plump. It must have been the rats; the viscous, gelatinous, ravenous army that feast on the dead and the living.... Why shouldn't rats eat a de la Poer as a de la Poer eats forbidden things? ...The war ate my boy, damn them all...and the Yanks ate Carfax with flames and burnt Grandsire

Delapore and the secret…No, no, I tell you, I am not that daemon swineherd in the twilit grotto! It was not Edward Norrys' fat face on that flabby fungous thing! Who says I am a de la Poer? He lived, but my boy died! …Shall a Norrys hold the land of a de la Poer? …It's voodoo, I tell you…that spotted snake…Curse you, Thornton, I'll teach you to faint at what my family do! …'Sblood, thou stinkard, I'll learn ye how to gust…wolde ye swynke me thilke wys? …Magna Mater! Magna Mater! …Atys…Dia ad aghaidh's ad aodaun…agus bas dunarch ort! Dhonas 's dholas ort, agus leat-sa! …Ungl unl…rrlh…chchch…

This is what they say I said when they found me in the blackness after three hours; found me crouching in the blackness over the plump, half-eaten body of Capt. Norrys, with my own cat leaping and tearing at my throat. Now they have blown up Exham Priory, taken my Nigger-Man away from me, and shut me into this barred room at Hanwell with fearful whispers about my heredity and experience. Thornton is in the next room, but they prevent me from talking to him. They are trying, too, to suppress most of the facts concerning the priory. When I speak of poor Norrys they accuse me of this hideous thing, but they must know that I did not do it. They must know it was the rats; the slithering scurrying rats whose scampering will never let me sleep; the daemon rats that race behind the padding in this room and beckon me down to greater horrors than I have ever known; the rats they can never hear; the rats, the rats in the walls.

The Apparition

Guy de Maupassant

The subject of sequestration of the person came up in speaking of a recent lawsuit, and each of us had a story to tell – a true story, he said. We had been spending the evening together at an old family mansion in the Rue de Grenelle, just a party of intimate friends. The old Marquis de la Tour-Samuel, who was eighty-two, rose, and, leaning his elbow on the mantelpiece, said in his somewhat shaky voice:

"I also know of something strange, so strange that it has haunted me all my life. It is now fifty-six years since the incident occurred, and yet not a month passes that I do not see it again in a dream, so great is the impression of fear it has left on my mind. For ten minutes I experienced such horrible fright that ever since then a sort of constant terror has remained with me. Sudden noises startle me violently, and objects imperfectly distinguished at night inspire me with a mad desire to flee from them. In short, I am afraid of the dark!

"But I would not have acknowledged that before I reached my present age. Now I can say anything. I have never receded before real danger, ladies. It is, therefore, permissible, at eighty-two years of age, not to be brave in presence of imaginary danger.

"That affair so completely upset me, caused me such deep and mysterious and terrible distress, that I never spoke of it to anyone. I will now tell it to you exactly as it happened, without any attempt at explanation.

"In July, 1827, I was stationed at Rouen. One day as I was walking along the quay I met a man whom I thought I recognised without being able to recall exactly who he was. Instinctively I made a movement to stop. The stranger perceived it and at once extended his hand.

"He was a friend to whom I had been deeply attached as a youth. For five years I had not seen him; he seemed to have aged half a century. His hair was quite white and he walked bent over as though completely exhausted. He apparently understood my surprise, and he told me of the misfortune which had shattered his life.

"Having fallen madly in love with a young girl, he had married her, but after a year of more than earthly happiness she died suddenly of an affection of the heart. He left his country home on the very day of her burial and came to his town house in Rouen, where he lived, alone and unhappy, so sad and wretched that he thought constantly of suicide.

"'Since I have found you again in this manner,' he said, 'I will ask you to render me an important service. It is to go and get me out of the desk in my bedroom – our bedroom – some papers of which I have urgent need. I cannot send a servant or a business clerk, as discretion and absolute silence are necessary. As for myself, nothing on earth would induce me to reenter that house. I will give you the key of the room, which I myself locked on leaving, and the key of my desk, also a few words for my gardener, telling him to open the chateau for you. But come and breakfast with me tomorrow and we will arrange all that.'

"I promised to do him the slight favor he asked. It was, for that matter, only a ride which I could make in an hour on horseback, his property being but a few miles distant from Rouen.

"At ten o'clock the following day I breakfasted, tête-à-tête, with my friend, but he scarcely spoke.

"He begged me to pardon him; the thought of the visit I was about to make to that room, the scene of his dead happiness, overcame him, he said. He, indeed, seemed singularly agitated and preoccupied, as though undergoing some mysterious mental struggle.

"At length he explained to me exactly what I had to do. It was very simple. I must take two packages of letters and a roll of papers from the first right-hand drawer of the desk, of which I had the key. He added:

"'I need not beg you to refrain from glancing at them.'

"I was wounded at that remark and told him so somewhat sharply. He stammered:

"'Forgive me, I suffer so,' and tears came to his eyes.

"At about one o'clock I took leave of him to accomplish my mission.

"'The weather was glorious, and I trotted across the fields, listening to the song of the larks and the rhythmical clang of my sword against my boot. Then I entered the forest and walked my horse. Branches of trees caressed my face as I passed, and now and then I caught a leaf with my teeth and chewed it, from sheer gladness of heart at being alive and vigorous on such a radiant day.

"As I approached the chateau I took from my pocket the letter I had for the gardener, and was astonished at finding it sealed. I was so irritated that I was about to turn back without having fulfilled my promise, but reflected that I should thereby display undue susceptibility. My friend in his troubled condition might easily have fastened the envelope without noticing that he did so.

"The manor looked as if it had been abandoned for twenty years. The open gate was falling from its hinges, the walks were overgrown with grass and the flower beds were no longer distinguishable.

"The noise I made by kicking at a shutter brought out an old man from a side door. He seemed stunned with astonishment at seeing me. On receiving my letter, he read it, reread it, turned it over and over, looked me up and down, put the paper in his pocket and finally said:

"'Well, what is it you wish?'

"I replied shortly:

"'You ought to know, since you have just read your master's orders. I wish to enter the chateau.'

"He seemed overcome.

"'Then you are going in – into her room?'

"I began to lose patience.

"'Damn it! Are you presuming to question me?'

"He stammered in confusion:

"'No – sir – but – but it has not been opened since – since the – death. If you will be kind enough to wait five minutes I will go and – and see if—'

"I interrupted him angrily:

"'See here, what do you mean by your tricks?

"'You know very well you cannot enter the room, since here is the key!'

"He no longer objected.

"'Then, sir, I will show you the way.'

"'Show me the staircase and leave me. I'll find my way without you.'

"'But – sir – indeed—'

"This time I lost patience, and pushing him aside, went into the house.

"I first went through the kitchen, then two rooms occupied by this man and his wife. I then crossed a large hall, mounted a staircase and recognised the door described by my friend.

"I easily opened it, and entered the apartment. It was so dark that at first I could distinguish nothing. I stopped short, disagreeably affected by that disagreeable, musty odour of closed, unoccupied rooms. As my eyes slowly became accustomed to the darkness I saw plainly enough a large and disordered bedroom, the bed without sheets but still retaining its mattresses and pillows, on one of which was a deep impression, as though an elbow or a head had recently rested there.

"The chairs all seemed out of place. I noticed that a door, doubtless that of a closet, had remained half open.

"I first went to the window, which I opened to let in the light, but the fastenings of the shutters had grown so rusty that I could not move them. I even tried to break them with my sword, but without success. As I was growing irritated over my useless efforts and could now see fairly well in the semi-darkness, I gave up the hope of getting more light, and went over to the writing desk.

"I seated myself in an armchair and, letting down the lid of the desk, I opened the drawer designated. It was full to the top. I needed but three packages, which I knew how to recognise, and began searching for them.

"I was straining my eyes in the effort to read the superscriptions when I seemed to hear, or, rather, feel, something rustle back of me. I paid no attention, believing that a draught from the window was moving some drapery. But in a minute or so another movement, almost imperceptible, sent a strangely disagreeable little shiver over my skin. It was so stupid to be affected, even slightly, that self-respect prevented my turning around. I had just found the second package I needed and was about to lay my hand on the third when a long and painful sigh, uttered just at my shoulder, made me bound like a madman from my seat and land several feet off. As I jumped I had turned round my hand on the hilt of my sword, and, truly, if I had not felt it at my side I should have taken to my heels like a coward.

"A tall woman dressed in white, stood gazing at me from the back of the chair where I had been sitting an instant before.

"Such a shudder ran through all my limbs that I nearly fell backward. No one who has not experienced it can understand that frightful, unreasoning terror! The mind becomes vague, the heart ceases to beat, the entire body grows as limp as a sponge.

"I do not believe in ghosts, nevertheless I collapsed from a hideous dread of the dead, and I suffered, oh! I suffered in a few moments more than in all the rest of my life from the irresistible terror of the supernatural. If she had not spoken I should have died perhaps. But she spoke, she spoke in a sweet, sad voice that set my nerves vibrating. I dare not say that I became master of myself and recovered my reason. No! I was terrified and scarcely knew what I was doing. But a certain innate pride, a remnant of soldierly instinct, made me, almost in spite of myself, maintain a bold front. She said:

"'Oh, sir, you can render me a great service.'

"I wanted to reply, but it was impossible for me to pronounce a word. Only a vague sound came from my throat. She continued:

"'Will you? You can save me, cure me. I suffer frightfully. I suffer, oh! How I suffer!' and she slowly seated herself in my armchair, still looking at me.

"'Will you?' she said.

"I nodded in assent, my voice still being paralysed.

"Then she held out to me a tortoise-shell comb and murmured:

"'Comb my hair, oh! Comb my hair; that will cure me; it must be combed. Look at my head – how I suffer; and my hair pulls so!'

"Her hair, unbound, very long and very black, it seemed to me, hung over the back of the armchair and touched the floor.

"Why did I promise? Why did I take that comb with a shudder, and why did I hold in my hands her long black hair that gave my skin a frightful cold sensation, as though I were handling snakes? I cannot tell.

"That sensation has remained in my fingers, and I still tremble in recalling it.

"I combed her hair. I handled, I know not how, those icy locks. I twisted, knotted, and unknotted, and braided them. She sighed, bowed her head, seemed happy. Suddenly she said, 'Thank you!' snatched the comb from my hands and fled by the door that I had noticed ajar.

"Left alone, I experienced for several seconds the horrible agitation of one who awakens from a nightmare. At length I regained my senses. I ran to the window and with a mighty effort burst open the shutters, letting a flood of light into the room. Immediately I sprang to the door by which that being had departed. I found it closed and immovable!

"Then the mad desire to flee overcame me like a panic – the panic which soldiers know in battle. I seized the three packets of letters on the open desk, ran from the room, dashed down the stairs four steps at a time, found myself outside, I know not how, and, perceiving my horse a few steps off, leaped into the saddle and galloped away.

"I stopped only when I reached Rouen and alighted at my lodgings. Throwing the reins to my orderly, I fled to my room and shut myself in to reflect. For an hour I anxiously asked myself if I were not the victim of a hallucination. Undoubtedly I had had one of those incomprehensible nervous attacks those exaltations of mind that give rise to visions and are the stronghold of the supernatural. And I was about to believe I had seen a vision, had a hallucination, when, as I approached the window, my eyes fell, by chance, upon my breast. My military cape was covered with long black hairs! One by one, with trembling fingers, I plucked them off and threw them away.

"I then called my orderly. I was too disturbed, too upset to go and see my friend that day, and I also wished to reflect more fully upon what I ought to tell him. I sent him his letters, for which he gave the soldier a receipt. He asked after me most particularly, and, on being told I was ill – had had a sunstroke – appeared exceedingly anxious. Next morning I went to him, determined to tell him the truth. He had gone out the evening before and had not yet returned. I called again during the day; my friend was still absent. After waiting a week longer without news of him, I notified the authorities and a judicial search was instituted. Not the slightest trace of his whereabouts or manner of disappearance was discovered.

"A minute inspection of the abandoned chateau revealed nothing of a suspicious character. There was no indication that a woman had been concealed there.

"After fruitless researches all further efforts were abandoned, and for fifty-six years I have heard nothing; I know no more than before."

Nina

John M. McIlveen

THE TENEMENT was by far the oldest of the abandoned buildings they had considered for renovation. Andrea's boss, Fred Bastian, had made a fortune buying these old dinosaurs around the Boston area for pennies on the dollar, refurbishing them at moderate expense, and then renting the units out for substantial profit, not-quite accurately labeled as luxury properties. A good friend once told Andrea, you can't shine a turd. Good old Fred had done well at proving her friend wrong.

In nearly eight years as an interior designer, Andrea had become very good at recognizing the potential in properties. She could envision the grand foyer hidden in an old decrepit entryway, or the beauty in converting a dilapidated old attic into an open concept loft. Fred Bastian recognized the profitability of Andrea's talent, and capitalized many-fold on it.

Andrea climbed the stairway to the fifth floor, stepping over a riser that had a little too much give, and stood on the top landing, sweeping her flashlight back and forth over the deteriorated carpet. If they did purchase this, an elevator would be indispensable. The building, like most, had potential, but would the renovation costs exceed Fred's spending boundary? She hoped not. The building had a lot of little effects that were appealing, like carved woodwork and moldings, glass doorknobs, and the nifty little built-in cabinets that were so common in the twenties and thirties. The glass doorknobs surprised Andrea, not in that the building had them, but in that they were still present. Glass and bronze doorknobs were usually one of the first things stolen from abandoned properties, collectible as they were.

The hallway stretched nearly two hundred feet in front of her, but the slowly fading flashlight only lit the first forty or so in the boarded-up darkness of the building. Treks like this intimidated Andrea when she first started evaluating older properties, but she found there was never anything her pepper spray couldn't handle. If the pepper spray didn't work, she could always revert to the 9mm Beretta she had tucked in the small of her back. Fortunately, it had never come to that.

She moved down the dusty hallway, stepping lightly, testing for weak spots. A rot-through could mean a fast, ten-foot descent.

The smell of urine, booze, and rotting food that had assaulted her upon entering the building faded considerably after the third floor. The fifth floor only offered the lonely smell of desertion.

Counting doorways – as was her habit, a reference act not unlike Hansel & Gretel's breadcrumb trail – she continued down the corridor, but stopped in front of unit 518. The door was closed, which wasn't unusual, but Andrea could swear she heard singing coming from inside.

She had heard plenty mournful renditions in other abandoned buildings, but they were usually the drunken lamentations of the homeless, inebriated, or any mixture thereof. This was feminine, eerie, and beautiful, unmistakably a child's voice. She moved closer, almost resting her ear on the door while her flashlight played across the floor. The voice was much clearer now, unaccompanied by music and very distinctly live, not a recording or a radio.

Andrea reached out and gently pushed the door. It opened with a click that echoed throughout the fifth floor, betraying the claustrophobic confines of the darkness.

No way, Andrea thought as the door silently swung open on smooth hinges, as if oiled weekly instead of thirty years ignored. The singing was louder, but still sounded distant.

Andrea entered a deserted room, her flashlight falling upon abandoned piping within the ghostly outlines of where kitchen cabinets had hung, jutting from the walls like gnarled branches. She moved forward breaching the corner to a lonely living room, across which stood two doorways, one opened, one closed. From beneath the closed door a band of light emanated, looking as bright as fire in the muted gloom of the old room.

She raised the flashlight and swept the beam over the doorway. Once white, now yellowed with age, the door looked very much like the other doors throughout the building, the only difference being that instead of a clear glass doorknob, this one was an uncommonly rich shade of amber.

Andrea quietly approached the doorway and halted when the singing from within stopped.

"Who's there?" asked a small voice from beyond the door. Light and feminine, guarded, yet unwavering, it was clearly the voice of a child…most likely a girl.

"Hello? My name is Andrea. Are you up here by yourself? Are you okay?"

"Will you play with me?" the voice asked.

What was a little girl doing up here? She must know the dangers of a building this age.

Andrea softly grasped the amber knob and turned. The door opened as easily and as silently as the last. Inside the room was complete transformation. An ornate brass and crystal gas chandelier blazed brilliantly, its dancing flames displaying a bedroom of any girl's dreams. The walls were adorned in lustrous, pink and white silk-cloth wallpaper, feminine, yet exquisite. A dark walnut desk was nestled in one corner of the room and a matching six-drawer dresser centered the opposing wall. A large window bisected the wall to the left of the desk giving view to a crystalline sky. A full bed, lovingly made, centered the room. A pink and white comforter, the lacy skirt and shams matched the curtains and wallpaper perfectly.

Andrea was astonished by the pure innocence of the room, but most of all, the dolls – hundreds of dolls – perfectly propped on the floor, the desk, the bed…on every available surface. White dolls, Black dolls, Asian dolls, Hispanic dolls, they were all here; female, male, young and old. The clothing styles ranged from the roaring twenties to present day, from ascots to FUBU sweatshirts.

"Will you play with me?" the little voice asked again.

Standing at the foot of the bed was a little girl, probably nine years old, dressed in a frilly blue and white ankle-length dress, reminiscent of those worn by most porcelain dolls, or children of the early twentieth century. Her light brown hair fell just over her shoulders in large looping curls, framing a face so pale it seemed to be porcelain, or maybe marble. Her eyes, so dark they almost appeared black, were wide and nearly expressionless. To Andrea, she looked like one of the dolls, like a perfect living doll.

Andrea looked behind her, at the deserted room she had just passed through, lit by the brilliance of the light from the little girl's room. Behind her, her footprints were evident on the dusty floor…only hers.

Everything is wrong here, thought Andrea. The building was abandoned, the utilities long turned off. There should be no lights, especially gas.

"What's your name?" Andrea asked the girl. She wondered if she was trapped here, some sick bastard's prisoner.

No footprints.

"Nina," said the child.

"Are you alone?"

"No," Nina said, never moving, standing perfectly straight. She looked around her room, seeming confused.

"Can you move?" Andrea asked, wary, but concerned. Nina took a hesitant step forward. Behind her came the unmistakable rattling of chain on carpet.

"Oh my god!" said Andrea.

She rushed to the child, knelt, and lifted the hem of Nina's dress, exposing braces on both of Nina's legs. They were not the streamline, modern braces, but the cumbersome contraptions worn by polio victims of decades earlier. The sight was heartrending, but what caused the lump to form in Andrea's chest, and the tears to spring to her eyes, was the shackle with a padlock tethered to Nina's right ankle, connected by a chain to the frame of the heavy iron bed. Nina's leg bore the scars – old scars – of long imprisonment.

"Who did this to you?" Andrea asked, unable to keep her voice from breaking.

"Daddy," said Nina. "Mommy."

Andrea looked back to the doorway, expecting to see the faces of the child's insane parents looking at her.

She needed the key!

"Who has the key, Nina? Where's your family...your parents?"

"Here," said Nina. Again, she looked confused. "They're...somewhere."

Call the police, Andrea thought, and reached into her blazer pocket for her phone.

"Don't worry, sweetie," she assured Nina. "Once the police get here, they'll get those chains off of you."

"Can't," said Nina.

"Of course we can, honey," said Andrea. "You won't have to wear that chain any longer."

"They protect," Nina said.

Andrea felt her rage leap up a dozen pegs. What the hell was the matter with people? Were they some kind of extreme fundamentalists, thinking imprisonment the only way to protect their child?

"Protect you from what?" Andrea barked, astounded.

"Not me," said Nina, and then she repeated, "Will you play with me?"

Andrea started to tap in 911, but Nina's small hand gently closed over the phone.

"Not me," Nina said again. "You."

Andrea looked at the girl and saw a smile spread across her face, but the smile was wrong. *Demented*, Andrea thought, and then thought again, *No...evil.*

Nina stepped toward Andrea, her steps disjointed and jerky under the weight of the braces, and placed her hand on Andrea's head. Fear traced fire up Andrea's spine and a chill wracked her body. She tried to rise and move away, but her sudden fear wouldn't carry her; her legs felt leaden and immovable. Her vision wavered and her stomach clenched.

Somehow, Andrea managed to stand. She stepped back from Nina, towards the door, but Nina – moving impossibly fast – stepped directly in front of her and stared at her eye to eye.

But that wasn't right – couldn't be right – Andrea was a woman, and this girl was hardly four feet tall.

Did she drug me? Andrea wondered as reality warped and the room swayed and tumbled. Suddenly Andrea only saw the hem Nina's frilly blue and white dress. She couldn't move, and when she tried to cry out, it felt as if her throat was solid and immovable.

Andrea felt herself being lifted what seemed a great height. She was placed on the bed, seated with her back on the pink, heart-shaped pillow, a place of honor for the girl's newest toy.

Andrea couldn't turn her head, but through her peripheral, she saw the doll nearest to her, a porcelain doll of a policewoman. She saw a single tear run down the policewoman's cheek.

The Ebony Frame

Edith Nesbit

TO BE RICH is a luxurious sensation, the more so when you have plumbed the depths of hard-up-ness as a Fleet Street hack, a picker-up of unconsidered pars, a reporter, an unappreciated journalist; all callings utterly inconsistent with one's family feeling and one's direct descent from the Dukes of Picardy.

When my Aunt Dorcas died and left me seven hundred a year and a furnished house in Chelsea, I felt that life had nothing left to offer except immediate possession of the legacy. Even Mildred Mayhew, whom I had hitherto regarded as my life's light, became less luminous. I was not engaged to Mildred, but I lodged with her mother, and I sang duets with Mildred and gave her gloves when it would run to it, which was seldom. She was a dear, good girl, and I meant to marry her some day. It is very nice to feel that a good little woman is thinking of you – it helps you in your work – and it is pleasant to know she will say "Yes," when you say, "Will you?"

But my legacy almost put Mildred out of my head, especially as she was staying with friends in the country.

Before the gloss was off my new mourning, I was seated in my aunt's armchair in front of the fire in the drawing room of my own house. My own house! It was grand, but rather lonely. I did think of Mildred just then.

The room was comfortably furnished with rosewood and damask. On the walls hung a few fairly good oil paintings, but the space above the mantelpiece was disfigured by an exceedingly bad print, 'The Trial of Lord William Russell', framed in a dark frame. I got up to look at it. I had visited my aunt with dutiful regularity, but I never remembered seeing this frame before. It was not intended for a print, but for an oil painting. It was of fine ebony, beautifully and curiously carved. I looked at it with growing interest, and when my aunt's housemaid – I had retained her modest staff of servants – came in with the lamp, I asked her how long the print had been there.

"Mistress only bought it two days before she was took ill," she said; "but the frame – she didn't want to buy a new one. So she got this out of the attic. There's lots of curious old things there, sir."

"Had my aunt had this frame long?"

"Oh, yes, sir. It must have come long before I did, and I've been here seven years come Christmas. There was a picture in it. That's upstairs too – but it's that black and ugly it might as well be a chimney-back."

I felt a desire to see this picture. What if it were some priceless old master, in which my aunt's eyes had only seen rubbish?

Directly after breakfast next morning, I paid a visit to the attic.

It was crammed with old furniture enough to stock a curiosity shop. All the house was furnished solidly in the Mid-Victorian style, and in this room everything not in keeping with the drawing room suite ideal was stowed away. Tables of paper-mache and mother-of-pearl, straight-backed chairs with twisted feet and faded needle-work cushions, fire-screens of gilded carving and beaded banners, oak bureaux with brass handles, a little worktable with its faded, moth-eaten, silk flutings hanging in disconsolate shreds; on these, and the dust that covered them, blazed the full daylight as I pulled up the blinds. I promised myself a good time in re-enshrining these household gods in my parlour, and promoting the Victorian suite to the attic. But at present my business was to find the picture as 'black as the chimney back'; and presently, behind a heap of fenders and boxes, I found it.

Jane, the housemaid, identified it at once. I took it downstairs carefully, and examined it. Neither subject nor colour was distinguishable. There was a splodge of a darker tint in the middle, but whether it was figure, or tree, or house, no man could have told. It seemed to be painted on a very thick panel bound with leather. I decided to send it to one of those persons who pour on rotting family portraits the water of eternal youth; but even as I did so, I thought, why not try my own restorative hand at a corner of it.

My bath-sponge soap and nail-brush, vigorously applied for a few seconds, showed me that there was no picture to clean. Bare oak presented itself to my persevering brush. I tried the other side, Jane watching me with indulgent interest. The same result. Then the truth dawned on me. Why was the panel so thick? I tore off the leather binding, and the panel divided and fell to the ground in a cloud of dust. There were two pictures, they had been nailed face to face. I leaned them against the wall, and the next moment I was leaning against it myself.

For one of the pictures was myself, a perfect portrait, no shade of expression or turn of feature wanting. Myself, in the dress men wore when James the First was King. When had this been done? And how, without my knowledge? Was this some whim of my aunt's?

"Lor', sir!" the shrill surprise of Jane at my elbow; "What a lovely photo it is! Was it a fancy ball, sir?"

"Yes," I stammered. "I – I don't think I want anything more now. You can go."

She went; and I turned, still with my heart beating violently, to the other picture. This was a beautiful woman's picture, very beautiful she was. I noted all her beauties, straight nose, low brows, full lips, thin hands, large, deep, luminous eyes. She wore a black velvet gown. It was a three-quarter-length portrait. Her arms rested on a table beside her, and her head on her hands; but her face was turned full forward, and her eyes met those of the spectator bewilderingly. On the table by her were compasses and shining instruments whose uses I did not know, books, a goblet, and a heap of papers and pens. I saw all this afterwards. I believe it was a quarter of an hour before I could turn my eyes from her. I have never seen any other eyes like hers; they appealed, as a child's or a dog's do; they commanded, as might those of an empress.

"Shall I sweep up the dust sir?" Curiosity had brought Jane back. I acceded. I turned from her my portrait. I kept between her and the woman in the black velvet. When I was alone again I tore down 'The Trial of Lord William Russell', and I put the picture of the woman in its strong ebony frame.

Then I wrote to a frame-maker for a frame for my portrait. It had so long lived face-to-face with this beautiful witch that I had not the heart to banish it from her presence; I suppose I am sentimental, if it be sentimental to think such things as that.

The new frame came home, and I hung it opposite the fireplace. An exhaustive search among my aunt's papers showed no explanation of the portrait of myself, no history of the portrait of the woman with the wonderful eyes. I only learned that all the old furniture together had come to my aunt at the death of my great-uncle, the head of the family; and I should have concluded that the resemblance was only a family one, if everyone who came in had not exclaimed at the 'speaking likeness'. I adopted Jane's 'fancy ball' explanation.

And there, one might suppose, the matter of the portraits ended. One might suppose it, that is, if there were not evidently a good deal more written here about it. However, to me then the matter seemed ended.

I went to see Mildred; I invited her and her mother to come and stay with me; I rather avoided glancing at the picture in ebony frame. I could not forget, nor remember without singular emotion, the look in the eyes of that woman when mine first met them. I shrank from meeting that look again.

I reorganised the house somewhat, preparing for Mildred's visit. I brought down much of the old-fashioned furniture, and after a long day of arranging and re-arranging, I sat down before the fire, and lying back in a pleasant languor, I idly raised my eyes to the picture of the woman. I met her dark, deep, hazel eyes, and once more my gaze was held fixed as by strong magic, the kind of fascination that keeps one sometimes staring for whole minutes into one's own eyes in the glass. I gazed into her eyes, and felt my own dilate, pricked with a smart like the smart of tears.

"I wish," I said, "oh, how I wish you were a woman and not a picture! Come down! Ah, come down!"

I laughed at myself as I spoke; but even as I laughed, I held out my arms.

I was not sleepy; I was not drunk. I was as wide awake and as sober as ever was a man in the world. And yet, as I held out my arms, I saw the eyes of the picture dilate, her lips tremble? – if I were to be hanged for saying it, it is true.

Her hands moved slightly; and a sort of flicker of a smile passed over her face.

I sprang to my feet. "This won't do," I said aloud. "Firelight does play strange tricks. I'll have the lamp."

I made for the bell. My hand was on it, when I heard a sound behind me, and turned, the bell still unrung. The fire had burned low and the corners of the room were deeply shadowed; but surely, there, behind the tall worked chair, was something darker than a shadow.

"I must face this out," I said, "or I shall never be able to face myself again." I left the bell, I seized the poker, and battered the dull coals to a blaze. Then I stepped back resolutely, and looked at the picture. The ebony frame was empty! From the shadow of the worked chair came a soft rustle, and out of the shadow the woman of the picture was coming, coming towards me.

I hope I shall never again know a moment of terror as blank and absolute. I could not have moved or spoken to save my life. Either all the known laws of nature were nothing, or I was mad. I stood trembling, but, I am thankful to remember, I stood still, while the black velvet gown swept across the hearthrug towards me.

Next moment a hand touched me, a hand, soft, warm, and human, and a low voice said, "You called me. I am here."

At that touch and that voice, the world seemed to give a sort of bewildering half-turn. I hardly know how to express it, but at once it seemed not awful, not even unusual, for portraits to become flesh, only most natural, most right, most unspeakably fortunate.

I laid my hand on hers. I looked from her to my portrait. I could not see it in the firelight. "We are not strangers," I said.

"Oh, no, not strangers." Those luminous eyes were looking up into mine, those red lips were near me. With a passionate cry, a sense of having recovered life's one great good, that had seemed wholly lost, I clasped her in my arms. She was no ghost, she was a woman, the only woman in the world.

"How long," I said, "how long is it since I lost you?"

She leaned back, hanging her full weight on the hands that were clasped behind my head. "How can I tell how long? There is no time in hell," she answered.

It was not a dream. Ah! No – there are no such dreams. I wish to God there could be. When in dreams do I see her eyes, hear her voice, feel her lips against my cheek, hold her hands to my lips, as I did that night, the supreme night of my life! At first we hardly spoke. It seemed enough: after long grief and pain. To feel the arms of my true love. Round me once again.

It is very difficult to tell my story. There are no words to express the sense of glad reunion, the complete realisation of every hope and dream of a life, that came upon me as I sat with my hand in hers, and looked into her eyes.

How could it have been a dream, when I left her sitting in the straight-backed chair, and went down to the kitchen to tell the maids I should want nothing more, that I was busy, and did not wish to be disturbed; when I fetched wood for the fire with my own hands, and, bringing it in, found her still sitting there, saw the little brown head turn as I entered, saw the love in her dear eyes; when I threw myself at her feet and blessed the day I was born, since life had given me this.

Not a thought of Mildred; all other things in my life were a dream, this, its one splendid reality.

"I am wondering," she said, after a while, when we had made such cheer, each of the other, as true lovers may after long parting, "I am wondering how much you remember of our past?"

"I remember nothing but that I love you, that I have loved you all my life."

"You remember nothing? Really nothing?"

"Only that I am truly yours; that we have both suffered; that, tell me, my mistress dear, all that you remember. Explain it all to me. Make me understand. And yet – no, I don't want to understand. It is enough that we are together."

If it was a dream, why have I never dreamed it again?

She leaned down towards me, her arm lay on my neck, and drew my head till it rested on her shoulder. "I am a ghost, I suppose," she said, laughing softly; and her laughter stirred memories which I just grasped at and just missed. "But you and I know better, don't we? I will tell you everything you have forgotten. We loved each other, ah! No, you have not forgotten that, and when you came back from the wars, we were to be married. Our pictures were painted before you went away. You know I was more learned than women of that day. Dear one, when you were gone, they said I was a witch. They tried me. They said I should be burned. Just because I had looked at the stars and gained more knowledge than other women, they must needs bind me to a stake and let me be eaten by the fire. And you far away!"

Her whole body trembled and shrank. Oh love, what dream would have told me that my kisses would soothe even that memory?

"The night before," she went on, "the devil did come to me. I was innocent before, you know it, don't you? And even then my sin was for you! For you! Because of the exceeding love I bore you! The devil came, and I sold my soul to eternal flame. But I got a good price. I got the right to come back through my picture (if anyone, looking at it, wished for me), as long as my picture stayed in its ebony frame. That frame was not carved by man's hand. I got the right to come back to you, oh, my heart's heart. And another thing I won, which you shall hear anon. They burned me for a witch, they made me suffer hell on earth. Those faces, all crowding round, the crackling wood and the choking smell of the smoke!"

"Oh, love, no more, no more!"

"When my mother sat that night before my picture, she wept and cried, 'Come back, my poor, lost child!' And I went to her with glad leaps of heart. Dear, she shrank from me, she fled, she shrieked and moaned of ghosts. She had our pictures covered from sight, and put again in the ebony frame. She had promised me my picture should stay always there. Ah, through all these years your face was against mine."

She paused.

"But the man you loved?"

"You came home. My picture was gone. They lied to you, and you married another woman; but someday I knew you would walk the world again, and that I should find you."

"The other gain?" I asked.

"The other gain," she said slowly, "I gave my soul for. It is this. If you also will give up your hopes of heaven, I can remain a woman, I can remain in your world! I can be your wife. Oh my dear, after all these years, at last! At last!"

"If I sacrifice my soul," I said slowly, and the words did not seem an imbecility, "if I sacrifice my soul I win you? Why, love, it's a contradiction in terms. You are my soul."

Her eyes looked straight into mine. Whatever might happen, whatever did happen, whatever may happen, our two souls in that moment met and became one.

"Then you choose, you deliberately choose, to give up your hopes of heaven for me, as I gave up mine for you?"

"I will not," I said, "give up my hope of heaven on any terms. Tell me what I must do that you and I may make our heaven here, as now?"

"I will tell you tomorrow," she said. "Be alone here tomorrow night, twelve is ghost's time, isn't it? And then I will come out of the picture, and never go back to it. I shall live with you, and die, and be buried, and there will be an end of me. But we shall live first, my heart's heart."

I laid my head on her knee. A strange drowsiness overcame me. Holding her hand against my cheek, I lost consciousness. When I awoke, the grey November dawn was glimmering, ghost-like, through the uncurtained window. My head was pillowed on my arm, and rested. I raised my head quickly, ah! not on my lady's knee, but on the needle-worked cushion of the straight-backed chair. I sprang to my feet. I was stiff with cold and dazed with dreams, but I turned my eyes on the picture.. There she sat, my lady, my dear love. I held out my arms, but the passionate cry I would have uttered died on my lips. She had said twelve o'clock. Her lightest word was my law. So I only stood in front of the picture, and gazed into those grey-green eyes till tears of passionate happiness filled my own.

·"Oh! My dear, my dear, how shall I pass the hours till I hold you again?"

No thought, then, of my whole life's completion and consummation being a dream.

I staggered up to my room, fell across my bed, and slept heavily and dreamlessly. When I awoke it was high noon. Mildred and her mother were coming to lunch.

I remembered, at one o'clock, Mildred coming and her existence.

Now indeed the dream began.

With a penetrating sense of the futility of any action apart from her, I gave the necessary orders for the reception of my guests. When Mildred and her mother came I received them with cordiality; but my genial phrases all seemed to be someone else's. My voice sounded like an echo; my heart was not there.

Still, the situation was not intolerable, until the hour when afternoon tea was served in the drawing room. Mildred and mother kept the conversational pot boiling with a profusion of genteel commonplaces, and I bore it, as one in sight of heaven can bear mild purgatory. I looked up at my sweetheart in the ebony frame, and I felt that anything which might happen, any irresponsible imbecility, any bathos of boredom, was nothing, if, after all, she came to me again.

And yet, when Mildred, too, looked at the portrait and said: "Doesn't she think a lot of herself? Theatrical character, I suppose? One of your flames, Mr. Devigne?" I had a sickening sense of impotent irritation which became absolute torture when Mildred (how could I ever have admired that chocolate-box barmaid style of prettiness) threw herself into the high-backed chair, covering the needlework with ridiculous flounces, and added, "Silence gives consent! Who is it, Mr. Devigne? Tell us all about her: I am sure she has a story."

Poor little Mildred, sitting there smiling, serene in her confidence that her every word charmed me, sitting there with her rather pinched waist, her rather tight boots, her rather vulgar voice, sitting in the chair where my dear lady had sat when she told me her story! I could not bear it.

"Don't sit there," I said, "it's not comfortable!"

But the girl would not be warned. With a laugh that set every nerve in my body vibrating with annoyance, she said, "Oh, dear! Mustn't I even sit in the same chair as your black-velvet woman?"

I looked at the chair in the picture. It was the same, and in her chair Mildred was sitting. Then a horrible sense of the reality of Mildred came upon me, was all this a reality after all? But for fortunate chance, might Mildred have occupied, not only her chair, but her place in my life? I rose.

"I hope you won't think me very rude," I said, "but I am obliged to go out."

I forget what appointment I alleged. The lie came readily enough.

I faced Mildred's pouts with the hope that she and her mother would not wait dinner for me. I fled. In another minute I was safe, alone, under the chill, cloudy, autumn sky – free to think, think, think of my dear lady.

I walked for hours along streets and squares; I lived over and over again every look, word and hand-touch, every kiss; I was completely, unspeakably happy.

Mildred was utterly forgotten; my lady of the ebony frame filled my heart, and soul, and spirit.

As I heard eleven boom through the fog, I turned and went home.

When I got to my street, I found a crowd surging through it, a strong red, light filling the air. A house was on fire. Mine!

I elbowed my way through the crowd.

The picture of my lady, that, at least, I could save.

As I sprang up the steps, I saw, as in a dream, yes, all this was really dream-like, I saw Mildred leaning out of the first-floor window, wringing her hands.

"Come back, sir," cried a fireman; "we'll get the young lady out right enough."

But my lady? The stairs were crackling, smoking, and as hot as hell. I went up to the room where her picture was. Strange to say, I only felt that the picture was a thing we should like to look on through the long, glad, wedded life that was to be ours. I never thought of it as being one with her.

As I reached the first floor I felt arms about my neck. The smoke was too thick for me to distinguish features.

"Save me," a voice whispered. I clasped a figure in my arms and bore it with a strange disease, down the shaking stairs and out into safety. It was Mildred. I knew that directly I clasped her.

"Stand back," cried the crowd.

"Everyone's safe," cried a fireman.

The flames leaped from every window. The sky grew redder and redder. I sprang from the hands that would have held me. I leaped up the steps. I crawled up the stairs. Suddenly the whole horror came to me. "As long as my picture remains in the ebony frame." What if picture and frame perished together?

I fought with the fire and with my own choking inability to fight with it. I pushed on. I must save my picture. I reached the drawing room.

As I sprang in, I saw my lady, I swear it, through the smoke and the flames, hold out her arms to me, to me, who came too late to save her, and to save my own life's joy. I never saw her again.

Before I could reach her, or cry out to her, I felt the floor yield beneath my feet, and I fell into the flames below.

How did they save me? What does that matter? They saved me somehow, curse them. Every stick of my aunt's furniture was destroyed. My friends pointed out that, as the furniture was heavily insured, the carelessness of a nightly-studious housemaid had done me no harm.

No harm!

That was how I won and lost my only love.

I deny, with all my soul in the denial, that it was a dream. There are no such dreams. Dreams of longing and pain there are in plenty; but dreams of complete, of unspeakable happiness – ah, no – it is the rest of life that is the dream.

But, if I think that, why have I married Mildred and grown stout, and dull, and prosperous?

I tell you, it is all this that is the dream; my dear lady only is the reality. And what does it matter what one does in a dream?

creak!

Kurt Newton

THE HOUSE needed work. Plaster, paint, polish, a light bulb here, a new fitting there. It was a beautiful old Victorian, emphasis on was, emphasis on old. But Janey Lavinsky knew what she wanted, and there was nothing her husband, Michael, was going to say to talk her out of it.

"Mommy, is this our new house?"

Janey looked at their six-year-old daughter, Jessica, and then at her husband, who simply shrugged his shoulders. "I guess it is, Honey," Michael answered for her.

Janey put her arms around Michael and kissed him on the lips.

"Let's go sign some papers," she said.

* * *

From high above, the attic windows stared down upon the family of three as they got into their car and drove off. Behind the windows, surrounded by age and dust and silence, something creaked.

* * *

Moving day.

Janey and Michael enlisted help from their friends with bribes of pizza and beer. It was a long day filled with activity and laughter and only a few broken items. Jessica played ring-around-the-boxes and hide-and-go-seek with Eve, another little girl stranded with nothing to do but watch the grown-ups shuffle in and out of the big house. When it was Jessica's turn to hide, she ran upstairs, leaving her newfound friend with her face against the refrigerator door counting.

The staircase was wide and winding and by the time Jessica reached the top she was nearly out of breath. The upstairs carpet swallowed her footsteps. She passed by first one door, then another. She remembered these rooms from when her mom and dad first looked at the house with the realtor lady. Jessica kept walking until she reached the end of the hall. At the end was a narrow door that led to another staircase, that led to the attic.

"*...nine, ten, here I come, ready or not!*" came her friend's voice from below. Jessica heard tiny shoes running up the hardwood stairs after her. Jessica opened the narrow door and stepped inside. The door shut behind her.

"*I'm gonna find you...*"

Jessica stepped up onto the first step of the staircase, her heart pounding in her chest. She felt invisible, as if she were in a closet.

"*It's only a matter of time, Jessie...I'm getting warmer...I can hear you breathing...*"

Jessica didn't really believe Eve could hear her but she wasn't taking any chances. She began to back up the narrow stairs, careful not to make any sounds. When she reached the top, she couldn't believe what she saw.

The attic was huge. And dusty. And dark.

The floorboards seemed to go on forever. There were windows in the shapes of half-moons, like sleepy eyes, dust- and cobweb-covered. Daylight struggled through them. There were thick posts like telephone poles that ran from floor to ceiling. Wide beams ran cross-wise overhead.

It was neat. And a little bit scary.

"I'm gonna find you…" Eve called, but she sounded less confident, now.

creak

What was that? Jessica's inner voice whispered. She turned her head in the direction of the noise.

In the middle of the room sat a large wooden chest with gold hinges. It looked like a big toy box. Jessica took two steps toward it.

creak

Maybe it was her own feet making the noise. The floor was old, and old things made strange noises. But she could swear it was coming from the box.

"C'mon Jessie…no fair…" Her friend was tiring of the game. Eve's voice trailed farther and farther away.

creak

There was something special about this place, thought Jessica, and something really special about that box.

She walked over to the chest and stood before it. She waited. Her heartbeat was all she heard. Then—

creak

She smiled. Then she reached down to lift the lid.

* * *

Downstairs, Janey saw Eve sitting on the sofa, her arms laced across her chest.

"Where's Jess?" she asked the girl.

"I don't know."

"Where do you think she went?"

"She's upstairs, I think, hiding. I couldn't find her. She doesn't play fair."

"Upstairs, huh?"

Janey put what she had in her hands down onto the floor. She didn't like Jessica running up and down the staircase, it was too dangerous.

When she reached the top of the stairs, Janey called for her daughter.

There was no answer.

She checked every room, every closet, looked under every bed. She even checked behind the dressers. After all, a six-year-old could squeeze herself into quite a small space.

"Jess, stop playing now and answer me!"

Not a sound.

Maybe she wasn't up here, thought Janey. Maybe Eve was mistaken and Jessica was sitting inside one of the kitchen cupboards waiting to be found.

Janey was about to head downstairs when her ears pinned back.

creak

The sound came from the end of the hall.

But the only thing at the end of the hall was the door leading up to the attic. That door was locked. Off limits. She and Mike had agreed, the stairs were too steep, the potential for danger too great for their curious daughter.

But Janey needed to be sure. She walked to the end of the hall and sure enough, the door's ornate, hundred-year-old knob rattled in her hand but did not turn.

Relieved, Janey headed for the stairwell—

creak

—and stopped. She knew the house was old, she knew creaks in old houses were as common as aches and pains in the bones of the elderly. She also knew her daughter. Call it mother's intuition, but Janey couldn't shake the feeling that something was wrong.

She reached into her back pocket. Maybe the attic door had been left unlocked. Maybe Jess went up the narrow stairs and the door closed behind her – and locked.

But why wouldn't she answer? Why isn't she kicking and screaming and crying to be let out?

Janey began to panic. She couldn't find the key the realtor had given her. It was an old skeleton key, like the ones found at flea markets. A simple, stupid thing to open a simple, stupid lock.

"Jessica!" Janey pounded on the attic door. "Jessica, are you up there?"

She tried the knob again, and to her surprise it turned in her palm. The door opened.

She rushed up the narrow stairway. "Jess?" Her voice sounded shrill and weak in the still, lifeless air.

She saw the chest in the middle of the room and her throat constricted. Tears filled the corners of her eyes. As she walked toward the chest, she remembered the plans she and Jim had for this room: a study for him, an arts and crafts studio for herself, a play room for Jessica, a nursery for the new baby, if and when that time came…

Janey crouched in front of the old chest and slowly lifted its lid…and their lives changed.

Downstairs, Janey's scream was heard by everyone.

* * *

After the investigation, Janey and Mike were told to move on with their lives. It was an accident.

Their friends stopped by to check in on them now and then to see how they were coping, to provide an open ear or a shoulder to cry on. But eventually the silence of the Levinsky household became too depressive and everyone just stayed away.

Janey blamed herself for not keeping an eye on her only child. Michael blamed himself for not recognizing the old chest as a hazard. And when they tired of bearing the weight of the guilt themselves, they set it down and blamed each other.

It was an accident.

Babies drown in bathtubs filled with six inches of water.

It was an accident.

Kids are backed over by their parent's cars while playing in the driveway.

It was an accident.

Children crawl into things they can't get out of and suffocate. An empty freezer. An old wooden chest. It's never easy to understand, but it's a part of life, and for whatever reason these things happen.

Four months after the death of her daughter, Janey Levinsky stopped trying to convince herself that these things just happen when she finally made the trip back upstairs to the attic. Her return wasn't prompted by the idea that it would be therapeutically healing, or because she was struck with a sudden sentimental yearning – although Oprah told her that she must and will eventually do these things. No, Janey found herself scaling the steep, narrow attic staircase because in the silence of the afternoon – a silence she occupied all-too-often since her husband went back to work and left her to her unpredictable tears and her daily medication – she heard footsteps. Running playfully. Followed by laughter. Coming from the attic.

Janey cautiously peered up over the top step and into the open space beyond. She expected to see Jessica as she last remembered her, dressed in her little blue jumper, a smile as bright as the sun, getting ready to make another mad dash to go hide from Eve.

But Jessica wasn't there. In place of the previous emptiness, the attic now hosted Michael's computer desk, a bookshelf, a small refrigerator and a recliner. A large braided rug covered the plank flooring in the middle of the room. Michael had also moved his weight bench up here. The old wooden chest was now a coffee table, only instead of coffee cups it was crowned with empty beer bottles.

It looked like a bachelor's apartment, thought Janey. Perhaps that's how Michael felt. After all, she was hardly there for him, locked up in her own one-room world of guilt and grief. And when she did come out, the distance between them was, most times, too difficult to bridge.

She walked over to the chest. A sense of déjà vu washed through her.

She crouched down and ran her fingers along the chest's edges. She caressed its smooth wooden surface and the cold metal corner reinforcements. She cleared the top of empty bottles and lifted the lid.

Her daughter lay inside, her face tinged with blue, her eyes closed as if she were sleeping.

Janey looked away as tears flooded her eyes. When she looked back, Jessie was sitting upright, her face still blue. She had a smile from ear to ear.

"You found me, Mommy. Now it's your turn to hide!" Her daughter giggled.

Janey felt her daughter's breath upon her face. It smelled of fish and sour milk. Janey fell backward and crawled for the stairwell, her heart racing in her chest. Janey didn't look back as she fled the attic, but she could hear the creak of little girl bones chasing after her.

* * *

"I saw her, Michael. She's up there."

Michael had come home to find Janey locked in their bedroom. Michael held her as they sat on the bed together.

"Janey, listen to yourself. You must be having a reaction to your medication. I'm calling Dr. Hemmingson."

She pulled away. "No! I saw her. Her face was blue." Janey's eyes grew as wide as Easter eggs. "We have to help her, Michael."

"No, Janey, our Jessica is at St. Columba cemetery. We buried her, remember? She's in the ground. Now please, stop this."

"It hid her soul. Hide and go seek. Now it wants us to play. Don't you see?" Janey's eyes looked toward the ceiling.

"You want to ruin it all, don't you? You're not satisfied that our Jessie's gone, you have to throw it all away?" Michael grabbed her by the shoulders. "I'm here, Janey. It's just us now. We can try again. We can have more children."

She stared at him. "But she isn't gone. She's up there, Michael. Don't you believe me?"

"I believe you need some professional help."

"You don't believe me." Janey looked away, a veil of disillusionment descending over her features. Maybe she didn't see what she had seen. Or heard what she had heard. Maybe this was all a dream that she would soon wake up from.

"Janey, listen to me."

"I'm tired, Michael. Can we do this some other time?" She lowered herself onto her pillow.

Her husband sat in silence. "I love you, Janey," he said finally, "but I won't sit by and watch you destroy yourself, and our marriage in the process."

He got up then and walked out. When he closed the door behind him, Janey closed her eyes and drifted off to sleep.

* * *

Michael sat in his recliner, two beers emptied, a third ready to join the first two. His nerves were calm now, settled into a comfortable bath of ennui. Outside, the night pressed against the attic windows. The house was still.

Michael liked it up here. It was high and away from everything else. It was almost as if he were floating above the world and all its problems. Michael didn't believe in evil spirits. The old chest beneath his feet was just an old chest. And if Jessica's spirit were trapped inside of it, the result couldn't be anything but beautiful and sweet. Because that was the kind of child she was.

So when he heard the floor creak and saw his daughter standing in the corner hand-in-hand with a young woman, he was more surprised than shocked, more intrigued than fearful. Jessica was smiling. The woman was also smiling. The woman was beautiful. She wore a long flowing gown, white as window curtains and just as sheer.

As they walked toward him, Michael didn't think it strange that he could see the shadows of furniture behind them – through them. All he could think about was the way his life used to be, when Janey was Janey and Jessica was there to leap into his arms when he walked through the front door after a long day's work. The way he wished it could be again.

His daughter led the woman over to where he was seated, almost as if to introduce her to him. The woman proceeded to push the recliner back.

creak

Michael closed his eyes as the woman pressed her lips against his. He felt a strange sensation and realized he couldn't breathe. His eyes flew open and what was staring at him was hideous.

The woman's skin clung to her face in dry leathery strips. Grey strands of hair sprouted from her bony skull. Her eyes were black pools of nothingness. Her lips crawled with tiny movements.

Jessica giggled at her side, her face now a pale blue.

Michael couldn't move. All he could feel was the life escaping him as if something had stuck a spigot into his heart and had opened it up full.

* * *

Janey entered a fitful dream. Her body struggled to pull her awake, but inside her sleeping consciousness she was an unwilling spectator to a domestic squabble.

The man was shouting. "I married you so you could bear me children. Not babies born without a breath of life in them!"

"But we can try again," the woman replied, sobbing.

The house was the same, only newer. Beautiful hardwood furniture surrounded them, cherry and mahogany. Lace doilies sat beneath crystal lamps which sat atop marble end-tables. Patterned wallpaper adorned the walls. A large Persian rug lay perfectly on the floor. The man was dressed in a fine suit, the woman in a beautiful flowing gown. Each bore hairstyles that hadn't been worn in over a hundred years.

The woman clutched at her husband's arm. "I love you. Won't you hold me?"

"Love?" the husband looked at her with disdain. "I hold the livelihoods of two thousand families in my hands, and I can't even have a family of my own. Do you know how that makes me feel? It's a disgrace." He turned away from her. "Leave me, now."

"But Phillip."

"Get out!"

The woman ran from the room in tears. She rushed upstairs.

Janey followed her.

At first, the woman entered the bedroom. She looked around desperately. Finally, she stared at herself in the mirror. Janey could also see herself in the mirror standing behind the woman. The woman rushed passed her and out into the hallway, and up to the attic.

The attic was stacked with moving crates. Some had fallen and excelsior had spilled out onto the floor. Amid the jumble of items sat the chest. It was new and shined a golden honey brown. The woman kneeled before it and opened its lid. Inside were linens, small knitted clothing, a silver baby's rattle, a music box. It was a hope chest created in anticipation of the arrival of a newborn.

The woman closed the chest. Tears stained her cheekbones. She set about unraveling some wire used to secure one of the crates. She stood the chest up on end and climbed on top of it. She looped the wire up over the top attic beam and wrapped the two ends around her neck and twisted it tightly.

Janey watched in horror as the woman then kicked the chest out from under her and fell with a sudden jerk, the wire sinking deep into her throat, cutting off her airway. The last image Janey saw before she woke was the woman's eyes staring hopelessly into space, her face turning a light shade of blue.

* * *

Janey rushed up the attic stairs. "Michael!" she yelled. She reached the top step—

"Michael, we have to get out here."

—and stood in disbelief.

Michael was fully reclined, his neck was bent, mouth open, his face a now familiar cyanotic hue. He was absolutely still.

Janey numbly walked over to him. She wanted to cry but tears no longer seemed to hold much meaning. "Now you believe me," she said as she reached out and caressed his face.

Janey turned.

creak

The old wooden chest sat at her husband's feet. It was touching him. It shouldn't be touching him, she thought and shoved the chest away.

She heard a giggle. Her heart sank. What if Jessica was still inside? She reached down and lifted the lid.

The chest was empty.

creak

Another giggle, this time accompanied by a grown woman's laughter.

Janey looked up. Her daughter was standing just three feet away. Standing beside her was the woman from the dream.

creak

They looked the same as the day they both died. Then they changed, their faces transforming into the hideous death masks they presently wore.

Janey stepped back in horror—

—into the arms of her husband, who picked her up and forcibly placed her in the open chest and shut the lid tight.

* * *

The young couple stood on the front lawn of the old Victorian and admired its stateliness. The woman turned to her husband. "Are you sure we can afford this?"

"Not a problem," her husband said. "I've got it all figured out."

"Did you figure in junior here?" She pointed to her stomach, which bulged beneath her dress.

"He or she will be in diapers and formula up to his or her kneecaps," he said.

"That's not very deep."

"You know what I mean."

They gazed at the old home.

"Why do you think it sat empty for so long?"

"Probate probably. But whatever the reason, it's a steal."

They turned to each other and decided with a kiss.

"Let's go tell the realtor the good news."

* * *

From high above, the attic windows stared down upon the expectant couple as they got into their car and drove away. Behind the windows, surrounded by age and dust and silence, something creaked.

The Burned House

Vincent O'Sullivan

ONE NIGHT at the end of dinner, the last time I crossed the Atlantic, somebody in our group remarked that we were just passing over the spot where the Lusitania had gone down. Whether this was the case or not, the thought of it was enough to make us rather grave, and we dropped into some more or less serious discussion about the emotions of men and women who see all hope gone, and realize that they are going to sink with the vessel. From that the talk wandered to the fate of the drowned: was not theirs, after all, a fortunate end? Somebody related details from the narratives of those who had been all but drowned in the accidents of the war. A Scotch lady inquired fancifully if the ghosts of those who are lost at sea ever appear above the waters and come aboard ships. Would there be danger of seeing one when the light was turned out in her cabin? This put an end to all seriousness, and most of us laughed. But a little tight-faced man from Fall River, bleak and iron-gray, who had been listening attentively, did not laugh. The lady noticed his decorum and appealed to him for support.

"You are like me – you believe in ghosts?" she asked lightly. He hesitated, thinking it over.

"In ghosts?" he repeated slowly.

"N-no; I don't know as I do. I've never had any personal experience that way. I've never seen the ghost of anyone I knew. Has anybody here?"

No one replied. Instead, most of us laughed again, a little uneasily, perhaps.

"Well, I guess not," resumed the man from Fall River. "All the same, strange-enough things happen in life, even if you cut out ghosts, that you can't clear up by laughing. You laugh till you've had some experience big enough to shock you, and then you don't laugh anymore. It's like being thrown out of a car—"

At this moment there was a blast on the whistle, and everybody rushed up on deck. As it turned out, we had only entered into a belt of fog. On the upper deck I fell in again with the New-Englander, smoking a cigar and walking up and down. We took a few turns together, and he referred to the conversation at dinner. Our laughter evidently rankled in his mind.

"So many damn' strange things happen in life that you can't account for," he protested. "You go on laughing at faith-healing and at dreams and this and that, and then something comes along that you just can't explain. You have got to throw up your hands and allow that it doesn't answer to any tests our experience has provided us with. Now, I guess I'm as matter of fact a man as any of those folks down there. I'm in the outfitting business. My favorite author is Ingersoll; whenever I go on a journey like this I carry one of his books. If you read Ingersoll and think Ingersoll year in, year out, you don't have much use for wool-gathering. But once I had an experience which I had to conclude was out of the ordinary. Whether other people believe it or not, or whether they think they can explain it, don't matter; it happened to me, and I could no more doubt it than I could doubt having had a tooth pulled after the dentist had done it. I only wish Ingersoll was still alive; I'd like to put it up to him. If you will sit down here with me in this corner out of the wind, I'll tell you how it was.

"Some years ago I had to be for several months in New York. I was before the courts; it does not signify now what for, and it is all forgotten by this time. But it was a long and worrying case, and it aged me by twenty years. Well, sir, all through the trial, in that grimy court-room, I kept thinking and thinking of a fresh little place I knew in the Vermont hills; and I helped to get through the hours by thinking that if things went well with me I'd go there at once. And so it was that on the very next morning after I was acquitted I stepped on the cars at the Grand Central station.

"It was the early fall; the days were closing in, and it was night and cold when I arrived. The village was very dark and deserted; they don't go out much after dark in those parts, anyhow, and the keen mountain wind was enough to quell any lingering desire. The hotel was not one of those modern places called inns from sentiment in America, which are equipped and upholstered like the great city hotels; it was one of the real old-fashioned New England taverns, about as uncomfortable places as there are on earth, where the idea is to show the traveler that traveling is a penitential state, and that morally and physically the best place for him is home.

"The landlord brought me a kind of supper, with his hat on and a pipe in his mouth. The room was chilly; but when I asked for a fire, he said he guessed he couldn't go out to the wood-pile till morning. There was nothing else to do when I had eaten my supper but to go outside, both to get the smell of the lamp out of my nose and to warm myself by a short walk.

"As I did not know the country well, I did not mean to go far. But although it was an overcast night, with a high north-east wind and an occasional flurry of rain, the moon was up, and even concealed by clouds as it was, it yet lit the night with a kind of twilight gray, not vivid, like the open moonlight, but good enough to see some distance. On account of this I pro-longed my stroll, and kept walking on and on till I was a considerable way from the village, and in a region as lonely as anywhere in the State. Great trees and shrubs bordered the road, and niany feet below was a mountain stream. What with the passion of the wind pouring through the high trees and the shout of the water racing among the boulders, it seemed to me sometimes like the noise of a crowd of people, and two or three times I turned to see if a crowd might be out after me, well as I knew that no crowd could be there. Sometimes the branches of the trees became so thick that I was walking as if in a black pit, unable to see my hand close to my face. Then, coming out from the tunnel of branches, I would step once more into a gray clearness which opened the road and surrounding country a good way on all sides.

"I suppose it might be some three quarters of an hour I had been walking when I came to a fork of the road. One branch ran downward, getting almost on a level with the bed of the torrent. The other mounted in a steep hill, and this, after a little idle debating, I decided to follow. After I had climbed for more than half a mile, thinking that if I should happen to lose track of one of the landmarks I should be very badly lost, the path – for it was now no more than that – curved, and I came out on a broad plateau. There, to my astonishment, I saw a house. It was a good-sized wooden house, three stories high, with a piazza round two sides of it, and from the elevation on which it stood it commanded a far stretch of country. There were a few great trees at a little distance from the house, and behind it, a stone's-throw away, was a clump of bushes. Still, it looked lonely and stark, offering its four sides unprotected to the winds. For all that, I was very glad to see it. 'It does not matter now,' I thought, 'whether I have lost my way or not. The house people will set me right.'

"But when I came up to it, I found that it was, to all appearance, uninhabited. The shutters were closed on all the windows; there was not a spark of light anywhere. There was something about it, something sinister and barren, that gave me the kind of shiver you have at the door of a room where you know that a dead man lies inside, or if you get thinking hard about dropping over the rail into that black waste of waters out there. This feeling, you know, isn't altogether unpleasant; you relish all the better your present security. It was the same with me standing before that house. I was not really scared. I was alone up here, miles from any kind of help, at the mercy of whoever might be lurking behind the shutters of that sullen house; but I felt that by all the chances I was perfectly alone and safe. My sensation of the uncanny was due to the effect on the nerves produced by wild scenery and the unexpected sight of a house in such a very lonely situation. Thus I reasoned, and instead of following the road farther, I walked over the grass till I came to a stone wall perhaps two hundred and fifty yards in front of the house, and rested my arms on it, looking forth at the scene.

"On the crests of the hills far away a strange light lingered, like the first touch of dawn in the sky on a rainy morning or the last glimpse of twilight before night comes. Between me and the hills was a wide stretch of open country. On my right hand was an apple-orchard, and I observed that a stile had been made in the wall of piled stones to enable the house people to go back and forth.

"Now, after I had been there leaning on the wall some considerable time, I saw a man coming toward me through the orchard. He was walking with a good, free stride, and as he drew nearer I could see that he was a tall, sinewy fellow between twenty-five and thirty, with a shaven face, wearing the slouch-hat of that country, a dark woolen shirt, and high boots. When he reached the stile and began climbing over it, I bade him goodnight in neighborly fashion. He made no reply, but he looked me straight in the face, and the look gave me a qualm. Not that it was an evil face, mind you – it was a handsome, serious face – but it was ravaged by some terrible passion: stealth was on it, ruthlessness, and a deadly resolution, and at the same time such a look as a man driven by some uncontrollable power might throw on surrounding things, asking for comprehension and mercy. It was impossible for me to resent his churlishness, his thoughts were so certainly elsewhere. I doubt if he even saw me.

"He could not have gone by more than a quarter of a minute when I turned to look after him. He had disappeared. The plateau lay bare before me, and it seemed impossible that even if he had sprinted like an athlete he could have got inside the house in so little time. But I have always made it a rule to attribute what I cannot understand to natural causes that I have failed to observe. I said to myself that no doubt the man had gone back into the orchard by some other opening in the wall lower down, or there might be some flaw in my vision owing to the uncertain and distorting light.

"But even as I continued to look toward the house, leaning my back now against the wall, I noticed that there were lights springing up in the windows behind the shutters. They were flickering lights, now bright, now dim, and had a ruddy glow like firelight. Before I had looked long, I became convinced that it was indeed firelight: the house was on fire. Black smoke began to pour from the roof; the red sparks flew in the wind. Then at a window above the roof of the piazza the shutters were thrown open, and I heard a woman shriek. I ran toward the house as hard as I could, and when I drew near I could see her plainly.

"She was a young woman; her hair fell in disorder over her white nightgown. She stretched out her bare arms, screaming. I saw a man come behind and seize her. But they were caught in a trap. The flames were licking round the windows, and the smoke was killing them. Even now the part of the house where they stood was caving in.

"Appalled by this horrible tragedy, which had thus suddenly risen before me, I made my way still nearer the house, thinking that if the two could struggle to the side of the house not bounded by the piazza they might jump, and I might break the fall. I was shouting this at them; I was right up close to the fire; and then I was struck by – I noticed for the first time an astonishing thing – the flames had no heat in them!

"I was standing near enough to the fire to be singed by it, and yet I felt no heat. The sparks were flying about my head; some fell on my hands, and they did not burn. And now I perceived that although the smoke was rolling in columns, I was not choked by the smoke, and that there had been no smell of smoke since the fire broke out. Neither was there any glare against the sky.

"As I stood there stupefied, wondering how these things could be, the whole house was swept by a very tornado of flame, and crashed down in a red ruin.

"Stricken to the heart by this abominable catastrophe, I made my way uncertainly down the hill, shouting for help. As I came to a little wooden bridge spanning the torrent, just beyond where the roads forked, I saw what appeared to be a rope in loose coils lying there. I saw that part of it was fastened to the railing of the bridge and hung outside, and I looked over. There was a man's body swinging by the neck between the road and the stream. I leaned over still farther, and then I recognized him as the man I had seen coming out of the orchard. His hat had fallen off, and the toes of his boots just touched the water.

"It seemed hardly possible, and yet it was certain. That was the man, and he was hanging there. I scrambled down at the side of the bridge, and put out my hand to seize the body, so that I might lift it up and relieve the weight on the rope. I succeeded in clutching hold of his loose shirt, and for a second I thought that it had come away in my hand. Then I found that my hand had closed on nothing; I had clutched nothing but air. And yet the figure swung by the neck before my eyes!

"I was suffocated with such horror that I feared for a moment I must lose consciousness. The next minute I was running and stumbling along that dark road in mortal anxiety, my one idea being to rouse the town and bring men to the bridge. That, I say, was my intention; but the fact is that when I came at last in sight of the village, I slowed down instinctively and began to reflect. After all, I was unknown there; I had just gone through a disagreeable trial in New York, and rural people were notoriously given to groundless suspicion. I had had enough of the law and of arrests without sufficient evidence. The wisest thing would be to drop a hint or two before the landlord and judge by his demeanor whether to proceed.

"I found him sitting where I had left him, smoking, in his shirt-sleeves, with his hat on.

"'Well,' he said slowly, 'I didn't know where the gosh-blamed blazes you had got to. Been to see the folks?'

"I told him I had been taking a walk. I went on to mention casually the fork in the road, the hill, and the plateau.

"'And who lives in that house,' I asked with a good show of indifference, 'on top of the hill?'

"He stared.

"'House? There ain't no house up there,' he said positively. 'Old Joe Snedker, who owns the land, says he's going to build a house up there for his son to live in when he gets married; but he ain't begun yet, and some folks reckon he never will.'

"'I feel sure I saw a house,' I protested feebly. But I was thinking – no heat in the fire, no substance in the body. I had not the courage to dispute.

"The landlord looked at me not unkindly. 'You seem sort of sick,' he remarked. 'Guess you been doin' too much down in the city. What you want is to go to bed.'"

The man from Fall River paused, and for a moment we sat silent, listening to the pant of the machinery, the thrumming of the wind in the wire stays, and the lash of the sea. Some voices were singing on the deck below. I considered him with the shade of contemptuous superiority we feel, as a rule, toward those who tell us their dreams or what some fortune-teller has predicted.

"Hallucinations," I said at last, with reassuring indulgence. "Trick of the vision, toxic ophthalmia. After the long strain of your trial your nerves were shattered."

"That's what I thought myself," he replied shortly, "especially after I had been out to the plateau the next morning and saw no sign that a house had ever stood there."

"And no corpse at the bridge?" I said, and laughed.

"And no corpse at the bridge."

He tried to get a light for another cigar. This took him some little time, and when at last he managed it, he got out of his chair and stood looking down at me.

"Now listen here. I told you that the thing happened several years ago. I'd got almost to forget it; if you can only persuade yourself that a thing is a freak of imagination, it pretty soon gets dim inside your head. Delusions have no staying power once it is realized that they are delusions. Whenever it did come back to me I used to think how near I had once been to going out of my mind. That was all.

"Well, last year I went up to that village again from Boston. I went to the same hotel and found the same landlord. He remembered me at once as 'The feller who come up from the city and thought he see a house. I believe you had the jimjams,' he said.

"We laughed, and the landlord spat.

"'There's been a house there since; though.'

"'Has there?'

"'Why, yes; an' it ha' been as well if there never had been. Old man Snedeker built it for his son, a fine big house with a piazza on two sides. The son, young Joe, got courting Mamie Elting from here around. She'd gone down to work in a store somewhere in Connecticut – darned if I can remember where. New Haven or Danbury, maybe. Well, sir, she used to get carrying on with another young feller 'bout here, Jim Travers, and Jim was sure wild about her; used to save up his quarters to go down State to see her. But she turned him down in the end, and married Joe; I guess because Joe had the house, and the old man's money to expect. Well, poor Jim must ha' gone plumb crazy. What do you think he did? The very first night the new-wed pair spent in that house he burned it down. Burned the two of them in their bed, and he was as nice and quiet a feller as you want to see. He may ha' been full of whisky at the time.'

"'No, he wasn't,' I said.

"The landlord looked surprised.

"'I guess you've heard some about it?'

"'No; go on.'

"'Yes, sir, he burned them in their bed. And then what do you think he did? He hung himself at the little bridge half a mile below. Do you remember where the road divides? Well, it was there. I saw his body hanging there myself the next morning. The toes of his boots were just touching the water.'"

The Library Window

Margaret Oliphant

Chapter One

I WAS NOT aware at first of the many discussions which had gone on about that window. It was almost opposite one of the windows of the large old-fashioned drawing-room of the house in which I spent that summer, which was of so much importance in my life. Our house and the library were on opposite sides of the broad High Street of St Rule's, which is a fine street, wide and ample, and very quiet, as strangers think who come from noisier places; but in a summer evening there is much coming and going, and the stillness is full of sound – the sound of footsteps and pleasant voices, softened by the summer air. There are even exceptional moments when it is noisy: the time of the fair, and on Saturday nights sometimes, and when there are excursion trains. Then even the softest sunny air of the evening will not smooth the harsh tones and the stumbling steps; but at these unlovely moments we shut the windows, and even I, who am so fond of that deep recess where I can take refuge from all that is going on inside, and make myself a spectator of all the varied story out of doors, withdraw from my watch-tower. To tell the truth, there never was very much going on inside. The house belonged to my aunt, to whom (she says, Thank God!) nothing ever happens. I believe that many things have happened to her in her time; but that was all over at the period of which I am speaking, and she was old, and very quiet. Her life went on in a routine never broken. She got up at the same hour every day, and did the same things in the same rotation, day by day the same. She said that this was the greatest support in the world, and that routine is a kind of salvation. It may be so; but it is a very dull salvation, and I used to feel that I would rather have incident, whatever kind of incident it might be. But then at that time I was not old, which makes all the difference. At the time of which I speak the deep recess of the drawing-room window was a great comfort to me. Though she was an old lady (perhaps because she was so old) she was very tolerant, and had a kind of feeling for me. She never said a word, but often gave me a smile when she saw how I had built myself up, with my books and my basket of work. I did very little work, I fear – now and then a few stitches when the spirit moved me, or when I had got well afloat in a dream, and was more tempted to follow it out than to read my book, as sometimes happened. At other times, and if the book were interesting, I used to get through volume after volume sitting there, paying no attention to anybody. And yet I did pay a kind of attention. Aunt Mary's old ladies came in to call, and I heard them talk, though I very seldom listened; but for all that, if they had anything to say that was interesting, it is curious how I found it in my mind afterwards, as if the air had blown it to me. They came and went, and I had the sensation of their old bonnets gliding out and in, and their dresses rustling; and now and then had to jump up and shake hands with someone who knew me, and asked after my papa and mamma. Then Aunt Mary would give me a little smile again, and I slipped back to my window. She never seemed to mind. My mother would not have let me do it, I know. She would have remembered dozens of things there were to do. She would have sent me upstairs to fetch something which I was quite sure she did not want, or downstairs to carry some quite unnecessary message to the housemaid. She liked to keep me running about. Perhaps that was one reason why I was so fond of Aunt Mary's drawing room, and the deep recess of the window, and the curtain that fell half over it, and the broad window-seat where one could collect so many things without being found fault with for untidiness. Whenever we had anything the matter with us in these days, we were sent to St Rule's to get up our strength. And this was my case at the time of which I am going to speak.

Everybody had said, since ever I learned to speak, that I was fantastic and fanciful and dreamy, and all the other words with which a girl who may happen to like poetry, and to be fond of thinking, is so often made uncomfortable. People don't know what they mean when they say fantastic. It sounds like Madge Wildfire or something of that sort. My mother thought I should always be busy, to keep nonsense out of my head. But really I was not at all fond of nonsense. I was rather serious than otherwise. I would have been no trouble to anybody if I had been left to myself. It was only that I had a sort of second-sight, and was conscious of things to which I paid no attention. Even when reading the most interesting book, the things that were being talked about blew in to me; and I heard what the people were saying in the streets as they passed under the window. Aunt Mary always said I could do two or indeed three things at once – both read and listen, and see. I am sure that I did not listen much, and seldom looked out, of set purpose – as some people do who notice what bonnets the ladies in the street have on; but I did hear what I couldn't help hearing, even when I was reading my book, and I did see all sorts of things, though often for a whole half-hour I might never lift my eyes.

This does not explain what I said at the beginning, that there were many discussions about that window. It was, and still is, the last window in the row, of the College Library, which is opposite my aunt's house in the High Street. Yet it is not exactly opposite, but a little to the west, so that I could see it best from the left side of my recess. I took it calmly for granted that it was a window like any other till I first heard the talk about it which was going on in the drawing-room. "Have you never made up your mind, Mrs. Balcarres," said old Mr. Pitmilly, "whether that window opposite is a window or no?" He said Mistress Balcarres – and he was always called Mr. Pitmilly, Morton: which was the name of his place.

"I am never sure of it, to tell the truth," said Aunt Mary, "all these years."

"Bless me!" said one of the old ladies, "and what window may that be?"

Mr. Pitmilly had a way of laughing as he spoke, which did not please me; but it was true that he was not perhaps desirous of pleasing me. He said, "Oh, just the window opposite," with his laugh running through his words; "our friend can never make up her mind about it, though she has been living opposite it since—"

"You need never mind the date," said another; "the Leebrary window! Dear me, what should it be but a window? Up at that height it could not be a door."

"The question is," said my aunt, "if it is a real window with glass in it, or if it is merely painted, or if it once was a window, and has been built up. And the oftener people look at it, the less they are able to say."

"Let me see this window," said old Lady Carnbee, who was very active and strong-minded; and then they all came crowding upon me – three or four old ladies, very eager, and Mr. Pitmilly's white hair appearing over their heads, and my aunt sitting quiet and smiling behind.

"I mind the window very well," said Lady Carnbee; "Ay: and so do more than me. But in its present appearance it is just like any other window; but has not been cleaned, I should say, in the memory of man."

"I see what ye mean," said one of the others. "It is just a very dead thing without any reflection in it; but I've seen as bad before."

"Ay, it's dead enough," said another, "but that's no rule; for these hizzies of women-servants in this ill age—"

"Nay, the women are well enough," said the softest voice of all, which was Aunt Mary's. "I will never let them risk their lives cleaning the outside of mine. And there are no women-servants in the Old Library: there is maybe something more in it than that."

They were all pressing into my recess, pressing upon me, a row of old faces, peering into something they could not understand. I had a sense in my mind how curious it was, the wall of old ladies in their old satin gowns all glazed with age, Lady Carnbee with her lace about her head. Nobody was looking at me or thinking of me; but I felt unconsciously the contrast of my youngness to their oldness, and stared at them as they stared over my head at the Library window. I had given it no attention up to this time. I was more taken up with the old ladies than with the thing they were looking at.

"The framework is all right at least, I can see that, and pented black—"

"And the panes are pented black too. It's no window, Mrs. Balcarres. It has been filled in, in the days of the window duties: you will mind, Leddy Carnbee."

"Mind!" said that oldest lady. "I mind when your mother was marriet, Jeanie: and that's neither the day nor yesterday. But as for the window, it's just a delusion: and that is my opinion of the matter, if you ask me."

"There's a great want of light in that muckle room at the college," said another. "If it was a window, the Leebrary would have more light."

"One thing is clear," said one of the younger ones, "it cannot be a window to see through. It may be filled in or it may be built up, but it is not a window to give light."

"And whoever heard of a window that was not to see through?" Lady Carnbee said. I was fascinated by the look on her face, which was a curious scornful look as of one who knew more than she chose to say: and then my wandering fancy was caught by her hand as she held it up, throwing back the lace that dropped over it. Lady Carnbee's lace was the chief thing about her – heavy black Spanish lace with large flowers. Everything she wore was trimmed with it. A large veil of it hung over her old bonnet. But her hand coming out of this heavy lace was a curious thing to see. She had very long fingers, very taper, which had been much admired in her youth; and her hand was very white, or rather more than white, pale, bleached, and bloodless, with large blue veins standing up upon the back; and she wore some fine rings, among others a big diamond in an ugly old claw setting. They were too big for her, and were wound round and round with yellow silk to make them keep on: and this little cushion of silk, turned brown with long wearing, had twisted round so that it was more conspicuous than the jewels; while the big diamond blazed underneath in the hollow of her hand, like some dangerous thing hiding and sending out darts of light. The hand, which seemed to come almost to a point, with this strange ornament underneath, clutched at my half-terrified imagination. It too seemed to mean far more than was said. I felt as if it might clutch me with sharp claws, and the lurking, dazzling creature bite – with a sting that would go to the heart.

Presently, however, the circle of the old faces broke up, the old ladies returned to their seats, and Mr. Pitmilly, small but very erect, stood up in the midst of them, talking with mild authority like a little oracle among the ladies. Only Lady Carnbee always contradicted the neat, little, old gentleman. She gesticulated, when she talked, like a Frenchwoman, and darted forth that hand of hers with the lace hanging over it, so that I always caught a glimpse of the lurking diamond. I thought she looked like a witch among the comfortable little group which gave such attention to everything Mr. Pitmilly said.

"For my part, it is my opinion there is no window there at all," he said. "It's very like the thing that's called in scientific language an optical illusion. It arises generally, if I may use such a word in the presence of ladies, from a liver that is not just in the perfitt order and balance that organ demands – and then you will see things – a blue dog, I remember, was the thing in one case, and in another—"

"The man has gane gyte," said Lady Carnbee; "I mind the windows in the Auld Leebrary as long as I mind anything. Is the Leebrary itself an optical illusion too?"

"Na, na," and "No, no," said the old ladies; "a blue dogue would be a strange vagary: but the Library we have all kent from our youth," said one. "And I mind when the Assemblies were held there one year when the Town Hall was building," another said.

"It is just a great divert to me," said Aunt Mary: but what was strange was that she paused there, and said in a low tone, "now": and then went on again, "for whoever comes to my house, there are aye discussions about that window. I have never just made up my mind about it myself. Sometimes I think it's a case of these wicked window duties, as you said, Miss Jeanie, when half the windows in our houses were blocked up to save the tax. And then, I think, it may be due to that blank kind of building like the great new buildings on the Earthen Mound in Edinburgh, where the windows are just ornaments. And then whiles I am sure I can see the glass shining when the sun catches it in the afternoon."

"You could so easily satisfy yourself, Mrs. Balcarres, if you were to—"

"Give a laddie a penny to cast a stone, and see what happens," said Lady Carnbee.

"But I am not sure that I have any desire to satisfy myself," Aunt Mary said. And then there was a stir in the room, and I had to come out from my recess and open the door for the old ladies and see them downstairs, as they all went away following one another. Mr. Pitmilly gave his arm to Lady Carnbee, though she was always contradicting him; and so the tea-party dispersed. Aunt Mary came to the head of the stairs with her guests in an old-fashioned gracious way, while I went down with them to see that the maid was ready at the door. When I came back Aunt Mary was still standing in the recess looking out. Returning to my seat she said, with a kind of wistful look, "Well, honey: and what is your opinion?"

"I have no opinion. I was reading my book all the time," I said.

"And so you were, honey, and no' very civil; but all the same I ken well you heard every word we said."

Chapter Two

IT WAS a night in June; dinner was long over, and had it been winter the maids would have been shutting up the house, and my Aunt Mary preparing to go upstairs to her room. But it was still clear daylight, that daylight out of which the sun has been long gone, and which has no longer any rose reflections, but all has sunk into a pearly neutral tint – a light which is daylight yet is not day. We had taken a turn in the garden after dinner, and now we had returned to what we called our usual occupations. My aunt was reading. The English post had come in, and she had got her 'Times', which was her great diversion. The 'Scotsman' was her morning reading, but she liked her 'Times' at night.

As for me, I too was at my usual occupation, which at that time was doing nothing. I had a book as usual, and was absorbed in it: but I was conscious of all that was going on all the same. The people strolled along the broad pavement, making remarks as they passed under the open window which came up into my story or my dream, and sometimes made me laugh. The tone and the faint sing-song, or rather chant, of the accent, which was 'a wee Fifish', was novel to me, and associated with holiday, and pleasant; and sometimes they said to each other something that was amusing, and often something that suggested a whole story; but presently they began to drop off, the footsteps slackened, the voices died away. It was getting late, though the clear soft daylight went on and on. All through the lingering evening, which seemed to consist of interminable hours, long but not weary, drawn out as if the spell of the light and the outdoor life might never end, I had now and then, quite unawares, cast a glance at the mysterious window which my aunt and her friends had discussed, as I felt, though I dared not say it even to myself, rather foolishly. It caught my eye without any intention on my part, as I paused, as it were, to take breath, in the flowing and current of undistinguishable thoughts and things from without and within which carried me along. First it occurred to me, with a little sensation of discovery, how absurd to say it was not a window, a living window, one to see through! Why, then, had they never seen it, these old folk? I saw as I looked up suddenly the faint greyness as of visible space within – a room behind, certainly dim, as it was natural a room should be on the other side of the street – quite indefinite: yet so clear that if someone were to come to the window there would be nothing surprising in it. For certainly there was a feeling of space behind the panes which these old half-blind ladies had disputed about whether they were glass or only fictitious panes marked on the wall. How silly! When eyes that could see could make it out in a minute. It was only a greyness at present, but it was unmistakable, a space that went back into gloom, as every room does when you look into it across a street. There were no curtains to show whether it was inhabited or not; but a room – oh, as distinctly as ever room was! I was pleased with myself, but said nothing, while Aunt Mary rustled her paper, waiting for a favourable moment to announce a discovery which settled her problem at once. Then I was carried away upon the stream again, and forgot the window, till somebody threw unawares a word from the outer world, "I'm goin' hame; it'll soon be dark." Dark! What was the fool thinking of? it never would be dark if one waited out, wandering in the soft air for hours longer; and then my eyes, acquiring easily that new habit, looked across the way again.

Ah, now! Nobody indeed had come to the window; and no light had been lighted, seeing it was still beautiful to read by – a still, clear, colourless light; but the room inside had certainly widened. I could see the grey space and air a little deeper, and a sort of vision, very dim, of a wall, and something against it; something dark, with the blackness that a solid article, however indistinctly seen, takes in the lighter darkness that is only space – a large, black, dark thing coming out into the grey. I looked more intently, and made sure it was a piece of furniture, either a writing table or perhaps a large book-case. No doubt it must be the last, since this was part of the old library. I never visited the old College Library, but I had seen such places before, and I could well imagine it to myself. How curious that for all the time these old people had looked at it, they had never seen this before!

It was more silent now, and my eyes, I suppose, had grown dim with gazing, doing my best to make it out, when suddenly Aunt Mary said, "Will you ring the bell, my dear? I must have my lamp."

"Your lamp?" I cried, "When it is still daylight!" But then I gave another look at my window, and perceived with a start that the light had indeed changed: for now I saw nothing. It was still light, but there was so much change in the light that my room, with the grey space and the large shadowy bookcase, had gone out, and I saw them no more: for even a Scotch night in June, though it looks as if it would never end, does darken at the last. I had almost cried out, but checked myself, and rang the bell for Aunt Mary, and made up my mind I would say nothing till next morning, when to be sure naturally it would be more clear.

Next morning I rather think I forgot all about it – or was busy: or was more idle than usual: the two things meant nearly the same. At all events I thought no more of the window, though I still sat in my own, opposite to it, but occupied with some other fancy. Aunt Mary's visitors came as usual in the afternoon; but their talk was of other things, and for a day or two nothing at all happened to bring back my thoughts into this channel. It might be nearly a week before the subject came back, and once more it was old Lady Carnbee who set me thinking; not that she said anything upon that particular theme. But she was the last of my aunt's afternoon guests to go away, and when she rose to leave she threw up her hands, with those lively gesticulations which so many old Scotch ladies have. "My faith!" said she, "there is that bairn there still like a dream. Is the creature bewitched, Mary Balcarres? And is she bound to sit there by night and by day for the rest of her days? You should mind that there's things about, uncanny for women of our blood."

I was too much startled at first to recognise that it was of me she was speaking. She was like a figure in a picture, with her pale face the colour of ashes, and the big pattern of the Spanish lace hanging half over it, and her hand held up, with the big diamond blazing at me from the inside of her uplifted palm. It was held up in surprise, but it looked as if it were raised in malediction; and the diamond threw out darts of light and glared and twinkled at me. If it had been in its right place it would not have mattered; but there, in the open of the hand! I started up, half in terror, half in wrath. And then the old lady laughed, and her hand dropped. "I've wakened you to life, and broke the spell," she said, nodding her old head at me, while the large black silk flowers of the lace waved and threatened. And she took my arm to go downstairs, laughing and bidding me be steady, and no' tremble and shake like a broken reed. "You should be as steady as a rock at your age. I was like a young tree," she said, leaning so heavily that my willowy girlish frame quivered – "I was a support to virtue, like Pamela, in my time."

"Aunt Mary, Lady Carnbee is a witch!" I cried, when I came back.

"Is that what you think, honey? Well: maybe she once was," said Aunt Mary, whom nothing surprised.

And it was that night once more after dinner, and after the post came in, and the 'Times', that I suddenly saw the Library window again. I had seen it every day and noticed nothing; but tonight, still in a little tumult of mind over Lady Carnbee and her wicked diamond which wished me harm, and her lace which waved threats and warnings at me, I looked across the street, and there I saw quite plainly the room opposite, far more clear than before. I saw dimly that it must be a large room, and that the big piece of furniture against the wall was a writing-desk. That in a moment, when first my eyes rested upon it, was quite clear: a large old-fashioned escritoire, standing out into the room: and I knew by the shape of it that it had a great many pigeon-holes and little drawers in the back, and a large table for writing. There was one just like it in my father's library at home. It was such a surprise to see it all so clearly that I closed my eyes, for the moment almost giddy, wondering how papa's desk could have come here – and then when I reminded myself that this was nonsense, and that there were many such writing tables besides papa's, and looked again – lo! It had all become quite vague and indistinct as it was at first; and I saw nothing but the blank window, of which the old ladies could never be certain whether it was filled up to avoid the window-tax, or whether it had ever been a window at all.

This occupied my mind very much, and yet I did not say anything to Aunt Mary. For one thing, I rarely saw anything at all in the early part of the day; but then that is natural: you can never see into a place from outside, whether it is an empty room or a looking-glass, or people's eyes, or anything else that is mysterious, in the day. It has, I suppose, something to do with the light. But in the evening in June in Scotland – then is the time to see. For it is daylight, yet it is not day, and there is a quality in it which I cannot describe, it is so clear, as if every object was a reflection of itself.

I used to see more and more of the room as the days went on. The large escritoire stood out more and more into the space: with sometimes white glimmering things, which looked like papers, lying on it: and once or twice I was sure I saw a pile of books on the floor close to the writing table, as if they had gilding upon them in broken specks, like old books. It was always about the time when the lads in the street began to call to each other that they were going home, and sometimes a shriller voice would come from one of the doors, bidding somebody to "cry upon the laddies" to come back to their suppers. That was always the time I saw best, though it was close upon the moment when the veil seemed to fall and the clear radiance became less living, and all the sounds died out of the street, and Aunt Mary said in her soft voice, "Honey! Will you ring for the lamp?" She said honey as people say darling: and I think it is a prettier word.

Then finally, while I sat one evening with my book in my hand, looking straight across the street, not distracted by anything, I saw a little movement within. It was not anyone visible – but everybody must know what it is to see the stir in the air, the little disturbanc – you cannot tell what it is, but that it indicates someone there, even though you can see no one. Perhaps it is a shadow making just one flicker in the still place. You may look at an empty room and the furniture in it for hours, and then suddenly there will be the flicker, and you know that something has come into it. It might only be a dog or a cat; it might be, if that were possible, a bird flying across; but it is someone, something living, which is so different, so completely different, in a moment from the things that are not living. It seemed to strike quite through me, and I gave a little cry. Then Aunt Mary stirred a little, and put down the huge newspaper that almost covered her from sight, and said, "What is it, honey?" I cried "Nothing," with a little gasp, quickly, for I did not want to be disturbed just at this moment when somebody was coming! But I suppose she was not satisfied, for she got up and stood behind to see what it was, putting her hand on my shoulder. It was the softest touch in the world, but I could have flung it off angrily: for that moment everything was still again, and the place grew grey and I saw no more.

"Nothing," I repeated, but I was so vexed I could have cried. "I told you it was nothing, Aunt Mary. Don't you believe me, that you come to look – and spoil it all!"

I did not mean of course to say these last words; they were forced out of me. I was so much annoyed to see it all melt away like a dream: for it was no dream, but as real as – as real as – myself or anything I ever saw.

She gave my shoulder a little pat with her hand. "Honey," she said, "were you looking at something? Is't that? Is't that?" "Is it what?" I wanted to say, shaking off her hand, but something in me stopped me: for I said nothing at all, and she went quietly back to her place. I suppose she must have rung the bell herself, for immediately I felt the soft flood of the light behind me, and the evening outside dimmed down, as it did every night, and I saw nothing more.

It was next day, I think, in the afternoon that I spoke. It was brought on by something she said about her fine work. "I get a mist before my eyes," she said; "you will have to learn my old lace stitches, honey – for I soon will not see to draw the threads."

"Oh, I hope you will keep your sight," I cried, without thinking what I was saying. I was then young and very matter-of-fact. I had not found out that one may mean something, yet not half or a hundredth part of what one seems to mean: and even then probably hoping to be contradicted if it is anyhow against one's self.

"My sight!" she said, looking up at me with a look that was almost angry; "There is no question of losing my sight – on the contrary, my eyes are very strong. I may not see to draw fine threads, but I see at a distance as well as ever I did – as well as you do."

"I did not mean any harm, Aunt Mary," I said. "I thought you said – but how can your sight be as good as ever when you are in doubt about that window? I can see into the room as clear as—". My voice wavered, for I had just looked up and across the street, and I could have sworn that there was no window at all, but only a false image of one painted on the wall.

"Ah!" she said, with a little tone of keenness and of surprise: and she half rose up, throwing down her work hastily, as if she meant to come to me: then, perhaps seeing the bewildered look on my face, she paused and hesitated – "Ay, honey!" she said, "have you got so far ben as that?"

What did she mean? Of course I knew all the old Scotch phrases as well as I knew myself; but it is a comfort to take refuge in a little ignorance, and I know I pretended not to understand whenever I was put out. "I don't know what you mean by 'far ben'," I cried out, very impatient. I don't know what might have followed, but someone just then came to call, and she could only give me a look before she went forward, putting out her hand to her visitor. It was a very soft look, but anxious, and as if she did not know what to do: and she shook her head a very little, and I thought, though there was a smile on her face, there was something wet about her eyes. I retired into my recess, and nothing more was said.

But it was very tantalising that it should fluctuate so; for sometimes I saw that room quite plain and clear – quite as clear as I could see papa's library, for example, when I shut my eyes. I compared it naturally to my father's study, because of the shape of the writing table, which, as I tell you, was the same as his. At times I saw the papers on the table quite plain, just as I had seen his papers many a day. And the little pile of books on the floor at the foot – not ranged regularly in order, but put down one above the other, with all their angles going different ways, and a speck of the old gilding shining here and there. And then again at other times I saw nothing, absolutely nothing, and was no better than the old ladies who had peered over my head, drawing their eyelids together, and arguing that the window had been shut up because of the old long-abolished window tax, or else that it had never been a window at all. It annoyed me very much at those dull moments to feel that I too puckered up my eyelids and saw no better than they.

Aunt Mary's old ladies came and went day after day while June went on. I was to go back in July, and I felt that I should be very unwilling indeed to leave until I had quite cleared up – as I was indeed in the way of doing – the mystery of that window which changed so strangely and appeared quite a different thing, not only to different people, but to the same eyes at different times. Of course I said to myself it must simply be an effect of the light. And yet I did not quite like that explanation either, but would have been better pleased to make out to myself that it was some superiority in me which made it so clear to me, if it were only the great superiority of young eyes over old – though that was not quite enough to satisfy me, seeing it was a superiority which I shared with every little lass and lad in the street. I rather wanted, I believe, to think that there was some particular insight in me which gave clearness to my sight – which was a most impertinent assumption, but really did not mean half the harm it seems to mean when it is put down here in black and white. I had several times again, however, seen the room quite plain, and made out that it was a large room, with a great picture in a dim gilded frame hanging on the farther wall, and many other pieces of solid furniture making a blackness here and there, besides the great escritoire against the wall, which had evidently been placed near the window for the sake of the light. One thing became visible to me after another, till I almost thought I should end by being able to read the old lettering on one of the big volumes which projected from the others and caught the light; but this was all preliminary to the great event which happened about Midsummer Day – the day of St John, which was once so much thought of as a festival, but now means nothing at all in Scotland any more than any other of the saints' days: which I shall always think a great pity and loss to Scotland, whatever Aunt Mary may say.

Chapter Three

IT WAS about midsummer, I cannot say exactly to a day when, but near that time, when the great event happened. I had grown very well acquainted by this time with that large dim room. Not only the escritoire, which was very plain to me now, with the papers upon it, and the books at its foot, but the great picture that hung against the farther wall, and various other shadowy pieces of furniture, especially a chair which one evening I saw had been moved into the space before the escritoire – a little change which made my heart beat, for it spoke so distinctly of someone who must have been there, the someone who had already made me start, two or three times before, by some vague shadow of him or thrill of him which made a sort of movement in the silent space: a movement which made me sure that next minute I must see something or hear something which would explain the whole – if it were not that something always happened outside to stop it, at the very moment of its accomplishment. I had no warning this time of movement or shadow. I had been looking into the room very attentively a little while before, and had made out everything almost clearer than ever; and then had bent my attention again on my book, and read a chapter or two at a most exciting period of the story: and consequently had quite left St Rule's, and the High Street, and the College Library, and was really in a South American forest, almost throttled by the flowery creepers, and treading softly lest I should put my foot on a scorpion or a dangerous snake. At this moment something suddenly calling my attention to the outside, I looked across, and then, with a start, sprang up, for I could not contain myself. I don't know what I said, but enough to startle the people in the room, one of whom was old Mr. Pitmilly. They all looked round upon me to ask what was the matter. And when I gave my usual answer of "Nothing", sitting down again shamefaced but very much excited, Mr. Pitmilly got up and came forward, and looked out, apparently to see what was the cause. He saw nothing, for he went back again, and I could hear him telling Aunt Mary not to be alarmed, for Missy had fallen into a doze with the heat, and had startled herself waking up, at which they all laughed: another time I could have killed him for his impertinence, but my mind was too much taken up now to pay any attention. My head was throbbing and my heart beating. I was in such high excitement, however, that to restrain myself completely, to be perfectly silent, was more easy to me then than at any other time of my life. I waited until the old gentleman had taken his seat again, and then I looked back. Yes, there he was! I had not been deceived. I knew then, when I looked across, that this was what I had been looking for all the time – that I had known he was there, and had been waiting for him, every time there was that flicker of movement in the room – him and no one else. And there at last, just as I had expected, he was. I don't know that in reality I ever had expected him, or anyone: but this was what I felt when, suddenly looking into that curious dim room, I saw him there.

He was sitting in the chair, which he must have placed for himself, or which someone else in the dead of night when nobody was looking must have set for him, in front of the escritoire –

with the back of his head towards me, writing. The light fell upon him from the left hand, and therefore upon his shoulders and the side of his head, which, however, was too much turned away to show anything of his face. Oh, how strange that there should be someone staring at him as I was doing, and he never to turn his head, to make a movement! If anyone stood and looked at me, were I in the soundest sleep that ever was, I would wake, I would jump up, I would feel it through everything. But there he sat and never moved. You are not to suppose, though I said the light fell upon him from the left hand, that there was very much light. There never is in a room you are looking into like that across the street; but there was enough to see him by – the outline of his figure dark and solid, seated in the chair, and the fairness of his head visible faintly, a clear spot against the dimness. I saw this outline against the dim gilding of the frame of the large picture which hung on the farther wall.

I sat all the time the visitors were there, in a sort of rapture, gazing at this figure. I knew no reason why I should be so much moved. In an ordinary way, to see a student at an opposite window quietly doing his work might have interested me a little, but certainly it would not have moved me in any such way. It is always interesting to have a glimpse like this of an unknown life – to see so much and yet know so little, and to wonder, perhaps, what the man is doing, and why he never turns his head. One would go to the window – but not too close, lest he should see you and think you were spying upon him – and one would ask, Is he still there? Is he writing, writing always? I wonder what he is writing! And it would be a great amusement: but no more. This was not my feeling at all in the present case. It was a sort of breathless watch, an absorption. I did not feel that I had eyes for anything else, or any room in my mind for another thought. I no longer heard, as I generally did, the stories and the wise remarks (or foolish) of Aunt Mary's old ladies or Mr. Pitmilly. I heard only a murmur behind me, the interchange of voices, one softer, one sharper; but it was not as in the time when I sat reading and heard every word, till the story in my book, and the stories they were telling (what they said almost always shaped into stories), were all mingled into each other, and the hero in the novel became somehow the hero (or more likely heroine) of them all. But I took no notice of what they were saying now. And it was not that there was anything very interesting to look at, except the fact that he was there. He did nothing to keep up the absorption of my thoughts. He moved just so much as a man will do when he is very busily writing, thinking of nothing else. There was a faint turn of his head as he went from one side to another of the page he was writing; but it appeared to be a long long page which never wanted turning. Just a little inclination when he was at the end of the line, outward, and then a little inclination inward when he began the next. That was little enough to keep one gazing. But I suppose it was the gradual course of events leading up to this, the finding out of one thing after another as the eyes got accustomed to the vague light: first the room itself, and then the writing table, and then the other furniture, and last of all the human inhabitant who gave it all meaning. This was all so interesting that it was like a country which one had discovered. And then the extraordinary blindness of the other people who disputed among themselves whether it was a window at all! I did not, I am sure, wish to be disrespectful, and I was very fond of my Aunt Mary, and I liked Mr. Pitmilly well enough, and I was afraid of Lady Carnbee. But yet to think of the – I know I ought not to say stupidity – the blindness of them, the foolishness, the insensibility! Discussing it as if a thing that your eyes could see was a thing to discuss! It would have been unkind to think it was because they were old and their faculties dimmed. It is so sad to think that the faculties grow dim, that such a woman as my Aunt Mary should fail in seeing, or hearing, or feeling, that I would not have dwelt on it for a moment, it would have seemed so cruel! And then such a clever old lady as Lady Carnbee, who could see through a millstone, people said – and Mr. Pitmilly, such an old man of the world. It did indeed bring tears to my eyes to think that all those clever people, solely by reason of being no longer young as I was, should have the simplest things shut out from them; and for all their wisdom and their knowledge be unable to see what a girl like me could see so easily. I was too much grieved for them to dwell upon that thought, and half ashamed, though perhaps half proud too, to be so much better off than they.

All those thoughts flitted through my mind as I sat and gazed across the street. And I felt there was so much going on in that room across the street! He was so absorbed in his writing, never looked up, never paused for a word, never turned round in his chair, or got up and walked about the room as my father did. Papa is a great writer, everybody says: but he would have come to the window and looked out, he would have drummed with his fingers on the pane, he would have watched a fly and helped it over a difficulty, and played with the fringe of the curtain, and done a dozen other nice, pleasant, foolish things, till the next sentence took shape. "My dear, I am waiting for a word," he would say to my mother when she looked at him, with a question why he was so idle, in her eyes; and then he would laugh, and go back again to his writing table. But He over there never stopped at all. It was like a fascination. I could not take my eyes from him and that little scarcely perceptible movement he made, turning his head. I trembled with impatience to see him turn the page, or perhaps throw down his finished sheet on the floor, as somebody looking into a window like me once saw Sir Walter do, sheet after sheet. I should have cried out if this Unknown had done that. I should not have been able to help myself, whoever had been present; and gradually I got into such a state of suspense waiting for it to be done that my head grew hot and my hands cold. And then, just when there was a little movement of his elbow, as if he were about to do this, to be called away by Aunt Mary to see Lady Carnbee to the door! I believe I did not hear her till she had called me three times, and then I stumbled up, all flushed and hot, and nearly crying. When I came out from the recess to give the old lady my arm (Mr. Pitmilly had gone away some time before), she put up her hand and stroked my cheek. "What ails the bairn?" she said; "she's fevered. You must not let her sit her late in the window, Mary Balcarres. You and me know what comes of that." Her old fingers had a strange touch, cold like something not living, and I felt that dreadful diamond sting me on the cheek.

I do not say that this was not just a part of my excitement and suspense; and I know it is enough to make anyone laugh when the excitement was all about an unknown man writing in a room on the other side of the way, and my impatience because he never came to an end of the page. If you think I was not quite as well aware of this as anyone could be! But the worst was that this dreadful old lady felt my heart beating against her arm that was within mine.

"You are just in a dream," she said to me, with her old voice close at my ear as we went downstairs. "I don't know who it is about, but it's bound to be some man that is not worth it. If you were wise you would think of him no more."

"I am thinking of no man!" I said, half crying. "It is very unkind and dreadful of you to say so, Lady Carnbee. I never thought of – any man, in all my life!" I cried in a passion of indignation. The old lady clung tighter to my arm, and pressed it to her, not unkindly.

"Poor little bird," she said, "how it's strugglin' and flutterin'! I'm not saying but what it's more dangerous when it's all for a dream."

She was not at all unkind; but I was very angry and excited, and would scarcely shake that old pale hand which she put out to me from her carriage window when I had helped her in. I was angry with her, and I was afraid of the diamond, which looked up from under her finger as if it saw through and through me; and whether you believe me or not, I am certain that it stung me again – a sharp malignant prick, oh full of meaning! She never wore gloves, but only black lace mittens, through which that horrible diamond gleamed.

I ran upstairs – she had been the last to go and Aunt Mary too had gone to get ready for dinner, for it was late. I hurried to my place, and looked across, with my heart beating more than ever. I made quite sure I should see the finished sheet lying white upon the floor. But what I gazed at was only the dim blank of that window which they said was no window. The light had changed in some wonderful way during that five minutes I had been gone, and there was nothing, nothing, not a reflection, not a glimmer. It looked exactly as they all said, the blank form of a window painted on the wall. It was too much: I sat down in my excitement and cried as if my heart would break. I felt that they had done something to it, that it was not natural, that I could not bear their unkindness – even Aunt Mary. They thought it not good for me! not good for me! and they had done something – even Aunt Mary herself – and that wicked diamond that hid itself in Lady Carnbee's hand. Of course I knew all this was ridiculous as well as you could tell me; but I was exasperated by the disappointment and the sudden stop to all my excited feelings, and I could not bear it. It was more strong than I.

I was late for dinner, and naturally there were some traces in my eyes that I had been crying when I came into the full light in the dining room, where Aunt Mary could look at me at her pleasure, and I could not run away. She said, "Honey, you have been shedding tears. I'm loth, loth that a bairn of your mother's should be made to shed tears in my house."

"I have not been made to shed tears," cried I; and then, to save myself another fit of crying, I burst out laughing and said, "I am afraid of that dreadful diamond on old Lady Carnbee's hand. It bites – I am sure it bites! Aunt Mary, look here."

"You foolish lassie," Aunt Mary said; but she looked at my cheek under the light of the lamp, and then she gave it a little pat with her soft hand. "Go away with you, you silly bairn. There is no bite; but a flushed cheek, my honey, and a wet eye. You must just read out my paper to me after dinner when the post is in: and we'll have no more thinking and no more dreaming for tonight."

"Yes, Aunt Mary," said I. But I knew what would happen; for when she opens up her 'Times', all full of the news of the world, and the speeches and things which she takes an interest in, though I cannot tell why – she forgets. And as I kept very quiet and made not a sound, she forgot tonight what she had said, and the curtain hung a little more over me than usual, and I sat down in my recess as if I had been a hundred miles away. And my heart gave a great jump, as if it would have come out of my breast; for he was there. But not as he had been in the morning – I suppose the light, perhaps, was not good enough to go on with his work without a lamp or candles – for he had turned away from the table and was fronting the window, sitting leaning back in his chair, and turning his head to me. Not to me – he knew nothing about me. I thought he was not looking at anything; but with his face turned my way. My heart was in my mouth: it was so unexpected, so strange! Though why it should have seemed strange I know not, for there was no communication between him and me that it should have moved me; and what could be more natural than that a man, wearied of his work, and feeling the want perhaps of more light, and yet that it was not dark enough to light a lamp, should turn round in his own chair, and rest a little, and think – perhaps of nothing at all? Papa always says he is thinking of nothing at all. He says things blow through his mind as if the doors were open, and he has no responsibility. What sort of things were blowing through this man's mind? Or was he thinking, still thinking, of what he had been writing and going on with it still? The thing that troubled me most was that I could not make out his face. It is very difficult to do so when you see a person only through two windows, your own and his. I wanted very much to recognise him afterwards if I should chance to meet him in the street. If he had only stood up and moved about the room, I should have made out the rest of his figure, and then I should have known him again; or if he had only come to the window (as papa always did), then I should have seen his face clearly enough to have recognised him. But, to be sure, he did not see any need to do anything in order that I might recognise him, for he did not know I existed; and probably if he had known I was watching him, he would have been annoyed and gone away.

But he was as immovable there facing the window as he had been seated at the desk. Sometimes he made a little faint stir with a hand or a foot, and I held my breath, hoping he was about to rise from his chair – but he never did it. And with all the efforts I made I could not be sure of his face. I puckered my eyelids together as old Miss Jeanie did who was shortsighted, and I put my hands on each side of my face to concentrate the light on him: but it was all in vain. Either the face changed as I sat staring, or else it was the light that was not good enough, or I don't know what it was. His hair seemed to me light – certainly there was no dark line about his head, as there would have been had it been very dark – and I saw, where it came across the old gilt frame on the wall behind, that it must be fair: and I am almost sure he had no beard. Indeed I am sure that he had no beard, for the outline of his face was distinct enough; and the daylight was still quite clear out of doors, so that I recognised perfectly a baker's boy who was on the pavement opposite, and whom I should have known again whenever I had met him: as if it was of the least importance to recognise a baker's boy! There was one thing, however, rather curious about this boy. He had been throwing stones at something or somebody. In St Rule's they have a great way of throwing stones at each other, and I suppose there had been a battle. I suppose also that he had one stone in his hand left over from the battle, and his roving eye took in all the incidents of the street to judge where he could throw it with most effect and mischief. But apparently he found nothing worthy of it in the street, for he suddenly turned round with a flick under his leg to show his cleverness, and aimed it straight at the window. I remarked without remarking that it struck with a hard sound and without any breaking of glass, and fell straight down on the pavement. But I took no notice of this even in my mind, so intently was I watching the figure within, which moved not nor took the slightest notice, and remained just as dimly clear, as perfectly seen, yet as indistinguishable, as before. And then the light began to fail a little, not diminishing the prospect within, but making it still less distinct than it had been.

Then I jumped up, feeling Aunt Mary's hand upon my shoulder. "Honey," she said, "I asked you twice to ring the bell; but you did not hear me."

"Oh, Aunt Mary!" I cried in great penitence, but turning again to the window in spite of myself.

"You must come away from there: you must come away from there," she said, almost as if she were angry: and then her soft voice grew softer, and she gave me a kiss: "never mind about the lamp, honey; I have rung myself, and it is coming; but, silly bairn, you must not aye be dreaming – your little head will turn."

All the answer I made, for I could scarcely speak, was to give a little wave with my hand to the window on the other side of the street.

She stood there patting me softly on the shoulder for a whole minute or more, murmuring something that sounded like, "She must go away, she must go away." Then she said, always with her hand soft on my shoulder, "Like a dream when one awaketh." And when I looked again, I saw the blank of an opaque surface and nothing more.

Aunt Mary asked me no more questions. She made me come into the room and sit in the light and read something to her. But I did not know what I was reading, for there suddenly came into my mind and took possession of it, the thud of the stone upon the window, and its descent straight down, as if from some hard substance that threw it off: though I had myself seen it strike upon the glass of the panes across the way.

Chapter Four

I AM afraid I continued in a state of great exaltation and commotion of mind for some time. I used to hurry through the day till the evening came, when I could watch my neighbour through the window opposite. I did not talk much to anyone, and I never said a word about my own questions and wonderings. I wondered who he was, what he was doing, and why he never came till the evening (or very rarely); and I also wondered much to what house the room belonged in which he sat. It seemed to form a portion of the old College Library, as I have often said. The window was one of the line of windows which I understood lighted the large hall; but whether this room belonged to the library itself, or how its occupant gained access to it, I could not tell. I made up my mind that it must open out of the hall, and that the gentleman must be the Librarian or one of his assistants, perhaps kept busy all the day in his official duties, and only able to get to his desk and do his own private work in the evening. One has heard of so many things like that – a man who had to take up some other kind of work for his living, and then when his leisure-time came, gave it all up to something he really loved – some study or some book he was writing. My father himself at one time had been like that. He had been in the Treasury all day, and then in the evening wrote his books, which made him famous. His daughter, however little she might know of other things, could not but know that! But it discouraged me very much when somebody pointed out to me one day in the street an old gentleman who wore a wig and took a great deal of snuff, and said, That's the Librarian of the old College. It gave me a great shock for a moment; but then I remembered that an old gentleman has generally assistants, and that it must be one of them.

Gradually I became quite sure of this. There was another small window above, which twinkled very much when the sun shone, and looked a very kindly bright little window, above that dullness of the other which hid so much. I made up my mind this was the window of his other room, and that these two chambers at the end of the beautiful hall were really beautiful for him to live in, so near all the books, and so retired and quiet, that nobody knew of them. What a fine thing for him! And you could see what use he made of his good fortune as he sat there, so constant at his writing for hours together. Was it a book he was writing, or could it be perhaps Poems? This was a thought which made my heart beat; but I concluded with much regret that it could not be Poems, because no one could possibly write Poems like that, straight off, without pausing for a word or a rhyme. Had they been Poems he must have risen up, he must have paced about the room or come to the window as papa did – not that papa wrote Poems: he always said, "I am not worthy even to speak of such prevailing mysteries," shaking his head – which gave me a wonderful admiration and almost awe of a Poet, who was thus much greater even than papa. But I could not believe that a Poet could have kept still for hours and hours like that. What could it be then? Perhaps it was history; that is a great thing to work at, but you would not perhaps need to move nor to stride up and down, or look out upon the sky and the wonderful light.

He did move now and then, however, though he never came to the window. Sometimes, as I have said, he would turn round in his chair and turn his face towards it, and sit there for a long time musing when the light had begun to fail, and the world was full of that strange day which was night, that light without colour, in which everything was so clearly visible, and there were no shadows. "It was between the night and the day, when the fairy folk have power." This was the after-light of the wonderful, long, long summer evening, the light without shadows. It had a spell in it, and sometimes it made me afraid: and all manner of strange thoughts seemed to come in, and I always felt that if only we had a little more vision in our eyes we might see beautiful folk walking about in it, who were not of our world. I thought most likely he saw them, from the way he sat there looking out: and this made my heart expand with the most curious sensation, as if of pride that, though I could not see, he did, and did not even require to come to the window, as I did, sitting close in the depth of the recess, with my eyes upon him, and almost seeing things through his eyes.

I was so much absorbed in these thoughts and in watching him every evening – for now he never missed an evening, but was always there – that people began to remark that I was looking pale and that I could not be well, for I paid no attention when they talked to me, and did not care to go out, nor to join the other girls for their tennis, nor to do anything that others did; and some said to Aunt Mary that I was quickly losing all the ground I had gained, and that she could never send me back to my mother with a white face like that. Aunt Mary had begun to look at me anxiously for some time before that, and, I am sure, held secret consultations over me, sometimes with the doctor, and sometimes with her old ladies, who thought they knew more about young girls than even the doctors. And I could hear them saying to her that I wanted diversion, that I must be diverted, and that she must take me out more, and give a party, and that when the summer visitors began to come there would perhaps be a ball or two, or Lady Carnbee would get up a picnic. "And there's my young lord coming home," said the old lady whom they called Miss Jeanie, "and I never knew the young lassie yet that would not cock up her bonnet at the sight of a young lord."

But Aunt Mary shook her head. "I would not lippen much to the young lord," she said. "His mother is sore set upon siller for him; and my poor bit honey has no fortune to speak of. No, we must not fly so high as the young lord; but I will gladly take her about the country to see the old castles and towers. It will perhaps rouse her up a little."

"And if that does not answer we must think of something else," the old lady said.

I heard them perhaps that day because they were talking of me, which is always so effective a way of making you hear – for latterly I had not been paying any attention to what they were saying; and I thought to myself how little they knew, and how little I cared about even the old castles and curious houses, having something else in my mind. But just about that time Mr. Pitmilly came in, who was always a friend to me, and, when he heard them talking, he managed to stop them and turn the conversation into another channel. And after a while, when the ladies were gone away, he came up to my recess, and gave a glance right over my head. And then he asked my Aunt Mary if ever she had settled her question about the window opposite, "that you thought was a window sometimes, and then not a window, and many curious things," the old gentleman said.

My Aunt Mary gave me another very wistful look; and then she said, "Indeed, Mr. Pitmilly, we are just where we were, and I am quite as unsettled as ever; and I think my niece she has taken up my views, for I see her many a time looking across and wondering, and I am not clear now what her opinion is."

"My opinion!" I said, "Aunt Mary." I could not help being a little scornful, as one is when one is very young. "I have no opinion. There is not only a window but there is a room, and I could show you" I was going to say, "show you the gentleman who sits and writes in it," but I stopped, not knowing what they might say, and looked from one to another. "I could tell you--all the furniture that is in it," I said. And then I felt something like a flame that went over my face, and that all at once my cheeks were burning. I thought they gave a little glance at each other, but that may have been folly. "There is a great picture, in a big dim frame," I said, feeling a little breathless, "on the wall opposite the window".

"Is there so?" said Mr. Pitmilly, with a little laugh. And he said, "Now I will tell you what we'll do. You know that there is a conversation party, or whatever they call it, in the big room tonight, and it will be all open and lighted up. And it is a handsome room, and two-three things well worth looking at. I will just step along after we have all got our dinner, and take you over to the pairty, madam – Missy and you—"

"Dear me!" said Aunt Mary. "I have not gone to a pairty for more years than I would like to say – and never once to the Library Hall." Then she gave a little shiver, and said quite low, "I could not go there."

"Then you will just begin again tonight, madam," said Mr. Pitmilly, taking no notice of this, "and a proud man will I be leading in Mistress Balcarres that was once the pride of the ball!"

"Ah, once!" said Aunt Mary, with a low little laugh and then a sigh. "And we'll not say how long ago"; and after that she made a pause, looking always at me: and then she said, "I accept your offer, and we'll put on our braws; and I hope you will have no occasion to think shame of us. But why not take your dinner here?"

That was how it was settled, and the old gentleman went away to dress, looking quite pleased. But I came to Aunt Mary as soon as he was gone, and besought her not to make me go. "I like the long bonnie night and the light that lasts so long. And I cannot bear to dress up and go out, wasting it all in a stupid party. I hate parties, Aunt Mary!" I cried, "and I would far rather stay here."

"My honey," she said, taking both my hands, "I know it will maybe be a blow to you, but it's better so."

"How could it be a blow to me?" I cried; "but I would far rather not go."

"You'll just go with me, honey, just this once: it is not often I go out. You will go with me this one night, just this one night, my honey sweet."

I am sure there were tears in Aunt Mary's eyes, and she kissed me between the words. There was nothing more that I could say; but how I grudged the evening! A mere party, a conversazione (when all the College was away, too, and nobody to make conversation!), instead of my enchanted hour at my window and the soft strange light, and the dim face looking out, which kept me wondering and wondering what was he thinking of, what was he looking for, who was he? All one wonder and mystery and question, through the long, long, slowly fading night!

It occurred to me, however, when I was dressing – though I was so sure that he would prefer his solitude to everything – that he might perhaps, it was just possible, be there. And when I thought of that, I took out my white frock though Janet had laid out my blue one – and my little pearl necklace which I had thought was too good to wear. They were not very large pearls, but they were real pearls, and very even and lustrous though they were small; and though I did not think much of my appearance then, there must have been something about me – pale as I was but apt to colour in a moment, with my dress so white, and my pearls so white, and my hair all shadowy perhaps, that was pleasant to look at: for even old Mr. Pitmilly had a strange look in his eyes, as if he was not only pleased but sorry too, perhaps thinking me a creature that would have troubles in this life, though I was so young and knew them not. And when Aunt Mary looked at me, there was a little quiver about her mouth. She herself had on her pretty lace and her white hair very nicely done, and looking her best. As for Mr. Pitmilly, he had a beautiful fine French cambric frill to his shirt, plaited in the most minute plaits, and with a diamond pin in it which sparkled as much as Lady Carnbee's ring; but this was a fine frank kindly stone, that looked you straight in the face and sparkled, with the light dancing in it as if it were pleased to see you, and to be shining on that old gentleman's honest and faithful breast: for he had been one of Aunt Mary's lovers in their early days, and still thought there was nobody like her in the world.

I had got into quite a happy commotion of mind by the time we set out across the street in the soft light of the evening to the Library Hall. Perhaps, after all, I should see him, and see the room which I was so well acquainted with, and find out why he sat there so constantly and never was seen abroad. I thought I might even hear what he was working at, which would be such a pleasant thing to tell papa when I went home. A friend of mine at St Rule's – oh, far, far more busy than you ever were, papa! – and then my father would laugh as he always did, and say he was but an idler and never busy at all.

The room was all light and bright, flowers wherever flowers could be, and the long lines of the books that went along the walls on each side, lighting up wherever there was a line of gilding or an ornament, with a little response. It dazzled me at first all that light: but I was very eager, though I kept very quiet, looking round to see if perhaps in any corner, in the middle of any group, he would be there. I did not expect to see him among the ladies. He would not be with them – he was too studious, too silent: but, perhaps among that circle of grey heads at the upper end of the room – perhaps—

No: I am not sure that it was not half a pleasure to me to make quite sure that there was not one whom I could take for him, who was at all like my vague image of him. No: it was absurd to think that he would be here, amid all that sound of voices, under the glare of that light. I felt a little proud to think that he was in his room as usual, doing his work, or thinking so deeply over it, as when he turned round in his chair with his face to the light.

I was thus getting a little composed and quiet in my mind, for now that the expectation of seeing him was over, though it was a disappointment, it was a satisfaction too – when Mr. Pitmilly came up to me, holding out his arm. "Now," he said, "I am going to take you to see the curiosities." I thought to myself that after I had seen them and spoken to everybody I knew, Aunt Mary would let me go home, so I went very willingly, though I did not care for the curiosities. Something, however, struck me strangely as we walked up the room. It was the air, rather fresh and strong, from an open window at the east end of the hall. How should there be a window there? I hardly saw what it meant for the first moment, but it blew in my face as if there was some meaning in it, and I felt very uneasy without seeing why.

Then there was another thing that startled me. On that side of the wall which was to the street there seemed no windows at all. A long line of bookcases filled it from end to end. I could not see what that meant either, but it confused me. I was altogether confused. I felt as if I was in a strange country, not knowing where I was going, not knowing what I might find out next. If there were no windows on the wall to the street, where was my window? My heart, which had been jumping up and calming down again all this time, gave a great leap at this, as if it would have come out of me – but I did not know what it could mean.

Then we stopped before a glass case, and Mr. Pitmilly showed me some things in it. I could not pay much attention to them. My head was going round and round. I heard his voice going on, and then myself speaking with a queer sound that was hollow in my ears; but I did not know what I was saying or what he was saying. Then he took me to the very end of the room, the east end, saying something that I caught – that I was pale, that the air would do me good. The air was blowing full on me, lifting the lace of my dress, lifting my hair, almost chilly. The window opened into the pale daylight, into the little lane that ran by the end of the building. Mr. Pitmilly went on talking, but I could not make out a word he said. Then I heard my own voice, speaking through it, though I did not seem to be aware that I was speaking. "Where is my window? Where, then, is my window?" I seemed to be saying, and I turned right round, dragging him with me, still holding his arm. As I did this my eye fell upon something at last which I knew. It was a large picture in a broad frame, hanging against the farther wall.

What did it mean? Oh, what did it mean? I turned round again to the open window at the east end, and to the daylight, the strange light without any shadow, that was all round about this lighted hall, holding it like a bubble that would burst, like something that was not real. The real place was the room I knew, in which that picture was hanging, where the writing table was, and where he sat with his face to the light. But where was the light and the window through which it came? I think my senses must have left me. I went up to the picture which I knew, and then I walked straight across the room, always dragging Mr. Pitmilly, whose face was pale, but who did not struggle but allowed me to lead him, straight across to where the window was – where the window was not – where there was no sign of it. "Where is my window? Where is my window?" I said. And all the time I was sure that I was in a dream, and these lights were all some theatrical illusion, and the people talking; and nothing real but the pale, pale, watching, lingering day standing by to wait until that foolish bubble should burst.

"My dear," said Mr. Pitmilly, "my dear! Mind that you are in public. Mind where you are. You must not make an outcry and frighten your Aunt Mary. Come away with me. Come away, my dear young lady! And you'll take a seat for a minute or two and compose yourself; and I'll get you an ice or a little wine." He kept patting my hand, which was on his arm, and looking at me very anxiously. "Bless me! Bless me! I never thought it would have this effect," he said.

But I would not allow him to take me away in that direction. I went to the picture again and looked at it without seeing it: and then I went across the room again, with some kind of wild thought that if I insisted I should find it. "My window – my window!" I said.

There was one of the professors standing there, and he heard me. "The window!" said he. "Ah, you've been taken in with what appears outside. It was put there to be in uniformity with the window on the stair. But it never was a real window. It is just behind that bookcase. Many people are taken in by it," he said.

His voice seemed to sound from somewhere far away, and as if it would go on for ever; and the hall swam in a dazzle of shining and of noises round me; and the daylight through the open window grew greyer, waiting till it should be over, and the bubble burst.

Chapter Five

IT WAS Mr. Pitmilly who took me home; or rather it was I who took him, pushing him on a little in front of me, holding fast by his arm, not waiting for Aunt Mary or anyone. We came out into the daylight again outside, I, without even a cloak or a shawl, with my bare arms, and uncovered head, and the pearls round my neck. There was a rush of the people about, and a baker's boy, that baker's boy, stood right in my way and cried, "Here's a braw ane!" shouting to the others: the words struck me somehow, as his stone had struck the window, without any reason. But I did not mind the people staring, and hurried across the street, with Mr. Pitmilly half a step in advance. The door was open, and Janet standing at it, looking out to see what she could see of the ladies in their grand dresses. She gave a shriek when she saw me hurrying across the street; but I brushed past her, and pushed Mr. Pitmilly up the stairs, and took him breathless to the recess, where I threw myself down on the seat, feeling as if I could not have gone another step farther, and waved my hand across to the window. "There! There!" I cried. Ah! There it was – not that senseless mob – not the theatre and the gas, and the people all in a murmur and clang of talking. Never in all these days had I seen that room so clearly. There was a faint tone of light behind, as if it might have been a reflection from some of those vulgar lights in the hall, and he sat against it, calm, wrapped in his thoughts, with his face turned to the window. Nobody but must have seen him. Janet could have seen him had I called her upstairs. It was like a picture, all the things I knew, and the same attitude, and the atmosphere, full of quietness, not disturbed by anything. I pulled Mr. Pitmilly's arm before I let him go – "You see, you see!" I cried. He gave me the most bewildered look, as if he would have liked to cry. He saw nothing! I was sure of that from his eyes. He was an old man, and there was no vision in him. If I had called up Janet, she would have seen it all. "My dear!" he said. "My dear!" waving his hands in a helpless way. "He has been there all these nights," I cried, "and I thought you could tell me who he was and what he was doing; and that he might have taken me in to that room, and showed me, that I might tell papa. Papa would understand, he would like to hear. Oh, can't you tell me what work he is doing, Mr. Pitmilly? He never lifts his head as long as the light throws a shadow, and then when it is like this he turns round and thinks, and takes a rest!"

Mr. Pitmilly was trembling, whether it was with cold or I know not what. He said, with a shake in his voice, "My dear young lady – my dear—" and then stopped and looked at me as if he were going to cry. "It's peetiful, it's peetiful," he said; and then in another voice, "I am going across there again to bring your Aunt Mary home; do you understand, my poor little thing, I am going to bring her home – you will be better when she is here." I was glad when he went away, as he could not see anything: and I sat alone in the dark which was not dark, but quite clear light--a light like nothing I ever saw. How clear it was in that room! Not glaring like the gas and the voices, but so quiet, everything so visible, as if it were in another world. I heard a little rustle behind me, and there was Janet, standing staring at me with two big eyes wide open. She was only a little older than I was. I called to her, "Janet, come here, come here, and you will see him – come here and see him!" impatient that she should be so shy and keep behind. "Oh, my bonnie young leddy!" she said, and burst out crying. I stamped my foot at her, in my indignation that she would not come, and she fled before me with a rustle and swing of haste, as if she were afraid. None of them, none of them! Not even a girl like myself, with the sight in her eyes, would understand. I turned back again, and held out my hands to him sitting there, who was the only one that knew. "Oh," I said, "say something to me! I don't know who you are, or what you are: but you're lonely and so am I; and I only – feel for you. Say something to me!" I neither hoped that he would hear, nor expected any answer. How could he hear, with the street between us, and his window shut, and all the murmuring of the voices and the people standing about? But for one moment it seemed to me that there was only him and me in the whole world.

But I gasped with my breath, that had almost gone from me, when I saw him move in his chair! He had heard me, though I knew not how. He rose up, and I rose too, speechless, incapable of anything but this mechanical movement. He seemed to draw me as if I were a puppet moved by his will. He came forward to the window, and stood looking across at me. I was sure that he looked at me. At last he had seen me: at last he had found out that somebody, though only a girl, was watching him, looking for him, believing in him. I was in such trouble and commotion of mind and trembling, that I could not keep on my feet, but dropped kneeling on the window-seat, supporting myself against the window, feeling as if my heart were being drawn out of me. I cannot describe his face. It was all dim, yet there was a light on it: I think it must have been a smile; and as closely as I looked at him he looked at me. His hair was fair, and there was a little quiver about his lips. Then he put his hands upon the window to open it. It was stiff and hard to move; but at last he forced it open with a sound that echoed all along the street. I saw that the people heard it, and several looked up. As for me, I put my hands together, leaning with my face against the glass, drawn to him as if I could have gone out of myself, my heart out of my bosom, my eyes out of my head. He opened the window with a noise that was heard from the West Port to the Abbey. Could anyone doubt that?

And then he leaned forward out of the window, looking out. There was not one in the street but must have seen him. He looked at me first, with a little wave of his hand, as if it were a salutation – yet not exactly that either, for I thought he waved me away; and then he looked up and down in the dim shining of the ending day, first to the east, to the old Abbey towers, and then to the west, along the broad line of the street where so many people were coming and going, but so little noise, all like enchanted folk in an enchanted place. I watched him with such a melting heart, with such a deep satisfaction as words could not say; for nobody could tell me now that he was not there – nobody could say I was dreaming any more. I watched him as if I could not breathe – my heart in my throat, my eyes upon him. He looked up and down, and then he looked back to me. I was the first, and I was the last, though it was not for long: he did know, he did see, who it was that had recognised him and sympathised with him all the time. I was in a kind of rapture, yet stupor too; my look went with his look, following it as if I were his shadow; and then suddenly he was gone, and I saw him no more.

I dropped back again upon my seat, seeking something to support me, something to lean upon. He had lifted his hand and waved it once again to me. How he went I cannot tell, nor where he went I cannot tell; but in a moment he was away, and the window standing open, and the room fading into stillness and dimness, yet so clear, with all its space, and the great picture in its gilded frame upon the wall. It gave me no pain to see him go away. My heart was so content, and I was so worn out and satisfied – for what doubt or question could there be about him now? As I was lying back as weak as water, Aunt Mary came in behind me, and flew to me with a little rustle as if she had come on wings, and put her arms round me, and drew my head on to her breast. I had begun to cry a little, with sobs like a child. "You saw him, you saw him!" I said. To lean upon her, and feel her so soft, so kind, gave me a pleasure I cannot describe, and her arms round me, and her voice saying "Honey, my honey!" – as if she were nearly crying too. Lying there I came back to myself, quite sweetly, glad of everything. But I wanted some assurance from them that they had seen him too. I waved my hand to the window that was still standing open, and the room that was stealing away into the faint dark. "This time you saw it all?" I said, getting more eager.

"My honey!" said Aunt Mary, giving me a kiss: and Mr. Pitmilly began to walk about the room with short little steps behind, as if he were out of patience. I sat straight up and put away Aunt Mary's arms. "You cannot be so blind, so blind!" I cried. "Oh, not tonight, at least not tonight!" But neither the one nor the other made any reply. I shook myself quite free, and raised myself up. And there, in the middle of the street, stood the baker's boy like a statue, staring up at the open window, with his mouth open and his face full of wonder – breathless, as if he could not believe what he saw. I darted forward, calling to him, and beckoned him to come to me. "Oh, bring him up! Bring him, bring him to me!" I cried.

Mr. Pitmilly went out directly, and got the boy by the shoulder. He did not want to come. It was strange to see the little old gentleman, with his beautiful frill and his diamond pin, standing out in the street, with his hand upon the boy's shoulder, and the other boys round, all in a little crowd. And presently they came towards the house, the others all following, gaping and wondering. He came in unwilling, almost resisting, looking as if we meant him some harm. "Come away, my laddie, come and speak to the young lady," Mr. Pitmilly was saying. And Aunt Mary took my hands to keep me back. But I would not be kept back.

"Boy," I cried, "you saw it too: you saw it: tell them you saw it! It is that I want, and no more."

He looked at me as they all did, as if he thought I was mad. "What's she wantin' wi' me?" he said; and then, "I did nae harm, even if I did throw a bit stane at it – and it's nae sin to throw a stane.

"You rascal!" said Mr. Pitmilly, giving him a shake; "have you been throwing stones? You'll kill somebody some of these days with your stones." The old gentleman was confused and troubled, for he did not understand what I wanted, nor anything that had happened. And then Aunt Mary, holding my hands and drawing me close to her, spoke. "Laddie," she said, "answer the young lady, like a good lad. There's no intention of finding fault with you. Answer her, my man, and then Janet will give ye your supper before you go."

"Oh speak, speak!" I cried; "Answer them and tell them! You saw that window opened, and the gentleman look out and wave his hand?"

"I saw nae gentleman," he said, with his head down, "except this wee gentleman here."

"Listen, laddie," said Aunt Mary. "I saw ye standing in the middle of the street staring. What were ye looking at?"

"It was naething to make a wark about. It was just yon windy yonder in the library that is nae windy. And it was open as sure's death. You may laugh if you like. Is that a' she's wantin' wi' me?"

"You are telling a pack of lies, laddie," Mr. Pitmilly said.

"I'm tellin' nae lee – -it was standin' open just like ony ither windy. It's as sure's death. I couldna believe it mysel'; but it's true."

"And there it is," I cried, turning round and pointing it out to them with great triumph in my heart. But the light was all grey, it had faded, it had changed. The window was just as it had always been, a sombre break upon the wall.

I was treated like an invalid all that evening, and taken upstairs to bed, and Aunt Mary sat up in my room the whole night through. Whenever I opened my eyes she was always sitting there close to me, watching. And there never was in all my life so strange a night. When I would talk in my excitement, she kissed me and hushed me like a child. "Oh, honey, you are not the only one!" she said. "Oh whisht, whisht, bairn! I should never have let you be there!"

"Aunt Mary, Aunt Mary, you have seen him too?"

"Oh whisht, whisht, honey!" Aunt Mary said: her eyes were shining – there were tears in them. "Oh whisht, whisht! Put it out of your mind, and try to sleep. I will not speak another word," she cried.

But I had my arms round her, and my mouth at her ear. "Who is he there? Tell me that and I will ask no more—"

"Oh honey, rest, and try to sleep! It is just – how can I tell you? – a dream, a dream! Did you not hear what Lady Carnbee said? – the women of our blood—"

"What? What? Aunt Mary, oh Aunt Mary—"

"I canna tell you," she cried in her agitation, "I canna tell you! How can I tell you, when I know just what you know and no more? It is a longing all your life after – it is a looking – for what never comes."

"He will come," I cried. "I shall see him tomorrow – that I know, I know!"

She kissed me and cried over me, her cheek hot and wet like mine. "My honey, try if you can sleep – try if you can sleep: and we'll wait to see what tomorrow brings."

"I have no fear," said I; and then I suppose, though it is strange to think of, I must have fallen asleep--I was so worn-out, and young, and not used to lying in my bed awake. From time to time I opened my eyes, and sometimes jumped up remembering everything: but Aunt Mary was always there to soothe me, and I lay down again in her shelter like a bird in its nest.

But I would not let them keep me in bed next day. I was in a kind of fever, not knowing what I did. The window was quite opaque, without the least glimmer in it, flat and blank like a piece of wood. Never from the first day had I seen it so little like a window. "It cannot be wondered at," I said to myself, "that seeing it like that, and with eyes that are old, not so clear as mine, they should think what they do." And then I smiled to myself to think of the evening and the long light, and whether he would look out again, or only give me a signal with his hand. I decided I would like that best: not that he should take the trouble to come forward and open it again, but just a turn of his head and a wave of his hand. It would be more friendly and show more confidence – not as if I wanted that kind of demonstration every night.

I did not come down in the afternoon, but kept at my own window upstairs alone, till the tea-party should be over. I could hear them making a great talk; and I was sure they were all in the recess staring at the window, and laughing at the silly lassie. Let them laugh! I felt above all that now. At dinner I was very restless, hurrying to get it over; and I think Aunt Mary was restless too. I doubt whether she read her 'Times' when it came; she opened it up so as to shield her, and watched from a corner. And I settled myself in the recess, with my heart full of expectation. I wanted nothing more than to see him writing at his table, and to turn his head and give me a little wave of his hand, just to show that he knew I was there. I sat from half-past seven o'clock to ten o'clock: and the daylight grew softer and softer, till at last it was as if it was shining through a pearl, and not a shadow to be seen. But the window all the time was as black as night, and there was nothing, nothing there.

Well: but other nights it had been like that: he would not be there every night only to please me. There are other things in a man's life, a great learned man like that. I said to myself I was not disappointed. Why should I be disappointed? There had been other nights when he was not there. Aunt Mary watched me, every movement I made, her eyes shining, often wet, with a pity in them that almost made me cry: but I felt as if I were more sorry for her than for myself. And then I flung myself upon her, and asked her, again and again, what it was, and who it was, imploring her to tell me if she knew? And when she had seen him, and what had happened? And what it meant about the women of our blood? She told me that how it was she could not tell, nor when: it was just at the time it had to be; and that we all saw him in our time – "that is," she said, "the ones that are like you and me." What was it that made her and me different from the rest? But she only shook her head and would not tell me. "They say," she said, and then stopped short. "Oh, honey, try and forget all about it – if I had but known you were of that kind! They say – that once there was one that was a Scholar, and liked his books more than any lady's love. Honey, do not look at me like that. To think I should have brought all this on you!"

"He was a Scholar?" I cried.

"And one of us, that must have been a light woman, not like you and me. But maybe it was just in innocence; for who can tell? She waved to him and waved to him to come over: and yon ring was the token: but he would not come. But still she sat at her window and waved and waved – till at last her brothers heard of it, that were stirring men; and then – oh, my honey, let us speak of it no more!"

"They killed him!" I cried, carried away. And then I grasped her with my hands, and gave her a shake, and flung away from her. "You tell me that to throw dust in my eyes – when I saw him only last night: and he as living as I am, and as young!"

"My honey, my honey!" Aunt Mary said.

After that I would not speak to her for a long time; but she kept close to me, never leaving me when she could help it, and always with that pity in her eyes. For the next night it was the same; and the third night. That third night I thought I could not bear it any longer. I would have to do something if only I knew what to do! If it would ever get dark, quite dark, there might be something to be done. I had wild dreams of stealing out of the house and getting a ladder, and mounting up to try if I could not open that window, in the middle of the night – if perhaps I could get the baker's boy to help me; and then my mind got into a whirl, and it was as if I had done it; and I could almost see the boy put the ladder to the window, and hear him cry out that there was nothing there. Oh, how slow it was, the night! And how light it was, and everything so clear no darkness to cover you, no shadow, whether on one side of the street or on the other side! I could not sleep, though I was forced to go to bed. And in the deep midnight, when it is dark in every other place, I slipped very softly downstairs, though there was one board on the landing-place that creaked – and opened the door and stepped out. There was not a soul to be seen, up or down, from the Abbey to the West Port: and the trees stood like ghosts, and the silence was terrible, and everything as clear as day. You don't know what silence is till you find it in the light like that, not morning but night, no sunrising, no shadow, but everything as clear as the day.

It did not make any difference as the slow minutes went on: one o'clock, two o'clock. How strange it was to hear the clocks striking in that dead light when there was nobody to hear them! But it made no difference. The window was quite blank; even the marking of the panes seemed to have melted away. I stole up again after a long time, through the silent house, in the clear light, cold and trembling, with despair in my heart.

I am sure Aunt Mary must have watched and seen me coming back, for after a while I heard faint sounds in the house; and very early, when there had come a little sunshine into the air, she came to my bedside with a cup of tea in her hand; and she, too, was looking like a ghost. "Are you warm, honey – are you comfortable?" she said. "It doesn't matter," said I. I did not feel as if anything mattered; unless if one could get into the dark somewhere – the soft, deep dark that would cover you over and hide you – but I could not tell from what. The dreadful thing was that there was nothing, nothing to look for, nothing to hide from – only the silence and the light.

That day my mother came and took me home. I had not heard she was coming; she arrived quite unexpectedly, and said she had no time to stay, but must start the same evening so as to be in London next day, papa having settled to go abroad. At first I had a wild thought I would not go. But how can a girl say I will not, when her mother has come for her, and there is no reason, no reason in the world, to resist, and no right! I had to go, whatever I might wish or any one might say. Aunt Mary's dear eyes were wet; she went about the house drying them quietly with her handkerchief, but she always said, "It is the best thing for you, honey – the best thing for you!" Oh, how I hated to hear it said that it was the best thing, as if anything mattered, one more than another! The old ladies were all there in the afternoon, Lady Carnbee looking at me from under her black lace, and the diamond lurking, sending out darts from under her finger. She patted me on the shoulder, and told me to be a good bairn. "And never lippen to what you see from the window," she said. "The eye is deceitful as well as the heart." She kept patting me on the shoulder, and I felt again as if that sharp wicked stone stung me. Was that what Aunt Mary meant when she said yon ring was the token? I thought afterwards I saw the mark on my shoulder. You will say why? How can I tell why? If I had known, I should have been contented, and it would not have mattered any more.

I never went back to St Rule's, and for years of my life I never again looked out of a window when any other window was in sight. You ask me did I ever see him again? I cannot tell: the imagination is a great deceiver, as Lady Carnbee said: and if he stayed there so long, only to punish the race that had wronged him, why should I ever have seen him again? For I had received my share. But who can tell what happens in a heart that often, often, and so long as that, comes back to do its errand? If it was he whom I have seen again, the anger is gone from him, and he means good and no longer harm to the house of the woman that loved him. I have seen his face looking at me from a crowd. There was one time when I came home a widow from India, very sad, with my little children: I am certain I saw him there among all the people coming to welcome their friends. There was nobody to welcome me – for I was not expected: and very sad was I, without a face I knew: when all at once I saw him, and he waved his hand to me. My heart leaped up again: I had forgotten who he was, but only that it was a face I knew, and I landed almost cheerfully, thinking here was someone who would help me. But he had disappeared, as he did from the window, with that one wave of his hand.

And again I was reminded of it all when old Lady Carnbee died – an old, old woman – and it was found in her will that she had left me that diamond ring. I am afraid of it still. It is locked up in an old sandal-wood box in the lumber-room in the little old country-house which belongs to me, but where I never live. If anyone would steal it, it would be a relief to my mind. Yet I never knew what Aunt Mary meant when she said, "Yon ring was the token", nor what it could have to do with that strange window in the old College Library of St Rule's.

The Fall of the House of Usher

Edgar Allan Poe

Son coeur est un luth suspendu;
Sitôt qu'on le touche il rèsonne.[1]
Pierre-Jean de Béranger

DURING the whole of a dull, dark, and soundless day in the autumn of the year, when the clouds hung oppressively low in the heavens, I had been passing alone, on horseback, through a singularly dreary tract of country; and at length found myself, as the shades of the evening drew on, within view of the melancholy House of Usher. I know not how it was – but, with the first glimpse of the building, a sense of insufferable gloom pervaded my spirit. I say insufferable; for the feeling was unrelieved by any of that half-pleasurable, because poetic, sentiment, with which the mind usually receives even the sternest natural images of the desolate or terrible. I looked upon the scene before me – upon the mere house, and the simple landscape features of the domain – upon the bleak walls – upon the vacant eye-like windows – upon a few rank sedges – and upon a few white trunks of decayed trees – with an utter depression of soul which I can compare to no earthly sensation more properly than to the after-dream of the reveller upon opium – the bitter lapse into everyday life – the hideous dropping off of the veil. There was an iciness, a sinking, a sickening of the heart – an unredeemed dreariness of thought which no goading of the imagination could torture into aught of the sublime. What was it – I paused to think – what was it that so unnerved me in the contemplation of the House of Usher? It was a mystery all insoluble; nor could I grapple with the shadowy fancies that crowded upon me as I pondered. I was forced to fall back upon the unsatisfactory conclusion, that while, beyond doubt, there are combinations of very simple natural objects which have the power of thus affecting us, still the analysis of this power lies among considerations beyond our depth. It was possible, I reflected, that a mere different arrangement of the particulars of the scene, of the details of the picture, would be sufficient to modify, or perhaps to annihilate its capacity for sorrowful impression; and, acting upon this idea, I reined my horse to the precipitous brink of a black and lurid tarn that lay in unruffled lustre by the dwelling, and gazed down – but with a shudder even more thrilling than before – upon the remodelled and inverted images of the gray sedge, and the ghastly tree-stems, and the vacant and eye-like windows.

Nevertheless, in this mansion of gloom I now proposed to myself a sojourn of some weeks. Its proprietor, Roderick Usher, had been one of my boon companions in boyhood; but many years had elapsed since our last meeting. A letter, however, had lately reached me in a distant part of the country – a letter from him – which, in its wildly importunate nature, had admitted of no other than a personal reply.

The MS. gave evidence of nervous agitation. The writer spoke of acute bodily illness – of a mental disorder which oppressed him – and of an earnest desire to see me, as his best, and indeed his only personal friend, with a view of attempting, by the cheerfulness of my society, some alleviation of his malady. It was the manner in which all this, and much more, was said – it was the apparent *heart* that went with his request – which allowed me no room for hesitation; and I accordingly obeyed forthwith what I still considered a very singular summons.

Although, as boys, we had been even intimate associates, yet I really knew little of my friend. His reserve had been always excessive and habitual. I was aware, however, that his very ancient family had been noted, time out of mind, for a peculiar sensibility of temperament, displaying itself, through long ages, in many works of exalted art, and manifested, of late, in repeated deeds of munificent yet unobtrusive charity, as well as in a passionate devotion to the intricacies, perhaps even more than to the orthodox and easily recognizable beauties, of musical science. I had learned, too, the very remarkable fact, that the stem of the Usher race, all time-honored as it was, had put forth, at no period, any enduring branch; in other words, that the entire family lay in the direct line of descent, and had always, with very trifling and very temporary variation, so lain. It was this deficiency, I considered, while running over in thought the perfect keeping of the character of the premises with the accredited character of the people, and while speculating upon the possible influence which the one, in the long lapse of centuries, might have exercised upon the other – it was this deficiency, perhaps, of collateral issue, and the consequent undeviating transmission, from sire to son, of the patrimony with the name, which had, at length, so identified the two as to merge the original title of the estate in the quaint and equivocal appellation of the 'House of Usher' – an appellation which seemed to include, in the minds of the peasantry who used it, both the family and the family mansion.

I have said that the sole effect of my somewhat childish experiment – that of looking down within the tarn – had been to deepen the first singular impression. There can be no doubt that the consciousness of the rapid increase of my superstition – for why should I not so term it? – served mainly to accelerate the increase itself. Such, I have long known, is the paradoxical law of all sentiments having terror as a basis. And it might have been for this reason only, that, when I again uplifted my eyes to the house itself, from its image in the pool, there grew in my mind a strange fancy – a fancy so ridiculous, indeed, that I but mention it to show the vivid force of the sensations which oppressed me. I had so worked upon my imagination as really to believe that about the whole mansion and domain there hung an atmosphere peculiar to themselves and their immediate vicinity – an atmosphere which had no affinity with the air of heaven, but which had reeked up from the decayed trees, and the gray wall, and the silent tarn – a pestilent and mystic vapor, dull, sluggish, faintly discernible, and leaden-hued.

Shaking off from my spirit what *must* have been a dream, I scanned more narrowly the real aspect of the building. Its principal feature seemed to be that of an excessive antiquity. The discoloration of ages had been great. Minute fungi overspread the whole exterior, hanging in a fine tangled web-work from the eaves. Yet all this was apart from any extraordinary dilapidation. No portion of the masonry had fallen; and there appeared to be a wild inconsistency between its still perfect adaptation of parts, and the crumbling condition of the individual stones. In this there was much that reminded me of the specious totality of old wood-work which has rotted for long years in some neglected vault, with no disturbance from the breath of the external air. Beyond this indication of extensive decay, however, the fabric gave little token of instability. Perhaps the eye of a scrutinizing observer might have discovered a barely perceptible fissure, which, extending from the roof of the building in front, made its way down the wall in a zigzag direction, until it became lost in the sullen waters of the tarn.

Noticing these things, I rode over a short causeway to the house. A servant in waiting took my horse, and I entered the Gothic archway of the hall. A valet, of stealthy step, thence conducted me, in silence, through many dark and intricate passages in my progress to the *studio* of his master. Much that I encountered on the way contributed, I know not how, to heighten the vague sentiments of which I have already spoken. While the objects around me – while the carvings of the ceilings, the sombre tapestries of the walls, the ebon blackness of the floors, and the phantasmagoric armorial trophies which rattled as I strode, were but matters to which, or to such as which, I had been accustomed from my infancy – while I hesitated not to acknowledge how familiar was all this – I still wondered to find how unfamiliar were the fancies which ordinary images were stirring up. On one of the staircases, I met the physician of the family. His countenance, I thought, wore a mingled expression of low cunning and perplexity. He accosted me with trepidation and passed on. The valet now threw open a door and ushered me into the presence of his master.

The room in which I found myself was very large and lofty. The windows were long, narrow, and pointed, and at so vast a distance from the black oaken floor as to be altogether inaccessible from within. Feeble gleams of encrimsoned light made their way through the trellissed panes, and served to render sufficiently distinct the more prominent objects around; the eye, however, struggled in vain to reach the remoter angles of the chamber, or the recesses of the vaulted and fretted ceiling. Dark draperies hung upon the walls. The general furniture was profuse, comfortless, antique, and tattered. Many books and musical instruments lay scattered about, but failed to give any vitality to the scene. I felt that I breathed an atmosphere of sorrow. An air of stern, deep, and irredeemable gloom hung over and pervaded all.

Upon my entrance, Usher arose from a sofa on which he had been lying at full length, and greeted me with a vivacious warmth which had much in it, I at first thought, of an overdone cordiality – of the constrained effort of the *ennuyé*; man of the world. A glance, however, at his countenance, convinced me of his perfect sincerity. We sat down; and for some moments, while he spoke not, I gazed upon him with a feeling half of pity, half of awe. Surely, man had never before so terribly altered, in so brief a period, as had Roderick Usher! It was with difficulty that I could bring myself to admit the identity of the wan being before me with the companion of my early boyhood. Yet the character of his face had been at all times remarkable. A cadaverousness of complexion; an eye large, liquid, and luminous beyond comparison; lips somewhat thin and very pallid, but of a surpassingly beautiful curve; a nose of a delicate Hebrew model, but with a breadth of nostril unusual in similar formations; a finely moulded chin, speaking, in its want of prominence, of a want of moral energy; hair of a more than web-like softness and tenuity; these features, with an inordinate expansion above the regions of the temple, made up altogether a countenance not easily to be forgotten. And now in the mere exaggeration of the prevailing character of these features, and of the expression they were wont to convey, lay so much of change that I doubted to whom I spoke. The now ghastly pallor of the skin, and the now miraculous lustre of the eye, above all things startled and even awed me. The silken hair, too, had been suffered to grow all unheeded, and as, in its wild gossamer texture, it floated rather than fell about the face, I could not, even with effort, connect its Arabesque expression with any idea of simple humanity.

In the manner of my friend I was at once struck with an incoherence – an inconsistency; and I soon found this to arise from a series of feeble and futile struggles to overcome an habitual trepidancy – an excessive nervous agitation. For something of this nature I had indeed been prepared, no less by his letter, than by reminiscences of certain boyish traits, and by conclusions deduced from his peculiar physical conformation and temperament. His action was alternately vivacious and sullen. His voice varied rapidly from a tremulous indecision (when the animal spirits seemed utterly in abeyance) to that species of energetic concision – that abrupt, weighty, unhurried, and hollow-sounding enunciation – that leaden, self-balanced and perfectly modulated guttural utterance, which may be observed in the lost drunkard, or the irreclaimable eater of opium, during the periods of his most intense excitement.

It was thus that he spoke of the object of my visit, of his earnest desire to see me, and of the solace he expected me to afford him. He entered, at some length, into what he conceived to be the nature of his malady. It was, he said, a constitutional and a family evil, and one for which he despaired to find a remedy – a mere nervous affection, he immediately added, which would undoubtedly soon pass off. It displayed itself in a host of unnatural sensations. Some of these, as he detailed them, interested and bewildered me; although, perhaps, the terms, and the general manner of the narration had their weight. He suffered much from a morbid acuteness of the senses; the most insipid food was alone endurable; he could wear only garments of certain texture; the odors of all flowers were oppressive; his eyes were tortured by even a faint light; and there were but peculiar sounds, and these from stringed instruments, which did not inspire him with horror.

To an anomalous species of terror I found him a bounden slave. "I shall perish," said he, "I must perish in this deplorable folly. Thus, thus, and not otherwise, shall I be lost. I dread the events of the future, not in themselves, but in their results. I shudder at the thought of any, even the most trivial, incident, which may operate upon this intolerable agitation of soul. I have, indeed, no abhorrence of danger, except in its absolute effect – in terror. In this unnerved – in this pitiable condition – I feel that the period will sooner or later arrive when I must abandon life and reason together, in some struggle with the grim phantasm, *fear*."

I learned, moreover, at intervals, and through broken and equivocal hints, another singular feature of his mental condition. He was enchained by certain superstitious impressions in regard to the dwelling which he tenanted, and whence, for many years, he had never ventured forth – in regard to an influence whose supposititious force was conveyed in terms too shadowy here to be re-stated – an influence which some peculiarities in the mere form and substance of his family mansion, had, by dint of long sufferance, he said, obtained over his spirit – an effect which the *physique* of the gray walls and turrets, and of the dim tarn into which they all looked down, had, at length, brought about upon the *morale* of his existence.

He admitted, however, although with hesitation, that much of the peculiar gloom which thus afflicted him could be traced to a more natural and far more palpable origin – to the severe and long-continued illness – indeed to the evidently approaching dissolution – of a tenderly beloved sister – his sole companion for long years – his last and only relative on earth. "Her decease," he said, with a bitterness which I can never forget, "would leave him (him the hopeless and the frail) the last of the ancient race of the Ushers." While he spoke, the lady Madeline (for so was she called) passed slowly through a remote portion of the apartment, and, without having noticed my presence, disappeared. I regarded her with an utter astonishment not unmingled with dread – and yet I found it impossible to account for such feelings. A sensation of stupor oppressed me, as my eyes followed her retreating steps. When a door, at length, closed upon her, my glance sought instinctively and eagerly the countenance of the brother – but he had buried his face in his hands, and I could only perceive that a far more than ordinary wanness had overspread the emaciated fingers through which trickled many passionate tears.

The disease of the lady Madeline had long baffled the skill of her physicians. A settled apathy, a gradual wasting away of the person, and frequent although transient affections of a partially cataleptical character, were the unusual diagnosis. Hitherto she had steadily borne up against the pressure of her malady, and had not betaken herself finally to bed; but, on the closing in of the evening of my arrival at the house, she succumbed (as her brother told me at night with inexpressible agitation) to the prostrating power of the destroyer; and I learned that the glimpse I had obtained of her person would thus probably be the last I should obtain – that the lady, at least while living, would be seen by me no more.

For several days ensuing, her name was unmentioned by either Usher or myself: and during this period I was busied in earnest endeavors to alleviate the melancholy of my friend. We painted and read together; or I listened, as if in a dream, to the wild improvisations of his speaking guitar. And thus, as a closer and still closer intimacy admitted me more unreservedly into the recesses of his spirit, the more bitterly did I perceive the futility of all attempt at cheering a mind from which darkness, as if an inherent positive quality, poured forth upon all objects of the moral and physical universe, in one unceasing radiation of gloom.

I shall ever bear about me a memory of the many solemn hours I thus spent alone with the master of the House of Usher. Yet I should fail in any attempt to convey an idea of the exact character of the studies, or of the occupations, in which he involved me, or led me the way. An excited and highly distempered ideality threw a sulphureous lustre over all. His long improvised dirges will ring forever in my ears. Among other things, I hold painfully in mind a certain singular perversion and amplification of the wild air of the last waltz of Von Weber. From the paintings over which his elaborate fancy brooded, and which grew, touch by touch, into vaguenesses at which I shuddered the more thrillingly, because I shuddered knowing not why; – from these paintings (vivid as their images now are before me) I would in vain endeavor to educe more than a small portion which should lie within the compass of merely written words. By the utter simplicity, by the nakedness of his designs, he arrested and overawed attention. If ever mortal painted an idea, that mortal was

Roderick Usher. For me at least – in the circumstances then surrounding me – there arose out of the pure abstractions which the hypochondriac contrived to throw upon his canvas, an intensity of intolerable awe, no shadow of which felt I ever yet in the contemplation of the certainly glowing yet too concrete reveries of Fuseli.

One of the phantasmagoric conceptions of my friend, partaking not so rigidly of the spirit of abstraction, may be shadowed forth, although feebly, in words. A small picture presented the interior of an immensely long and rectangular vault or tunnel, with low walls, smooth, white, and without interruption or device. Certain accessory points of the design served well to convey the idea that this excavation lay at an exceeding depth below the surface of the earth. No outlet was observed in any portion of its vast extent, and no torch, or other artificial source of light was discernible; yet a flood of intense rays rolled throughout, and bathed the whole in a ghastly and inappropriate splendor.

I have just spoken of that morbid condition of the auditory nerve which rendered all music intolerable to the sufferer, with the exception of certain effects of stringed instruments. It was, perhaps, the narrow limits to which he thus confined himself upon the guitar, which gave birth, in great measure, to the fantastic character of his performances. But the fervid *facility* of his *impromptus* could not be so accounted for. They must have been, and were, in the notes, as well as in the words of his wild fantasias (for he not unfrequently accompanied himself with rhymed verbal improvisations), the result of that intense mental collectedness and concentration to which I have previously alluded as observable only in particular moments of the highest artificial excitement. The words of one of these rhapsodies I have easily remembered. I was, perhaps, the more forcibly impressed with it, as he gave it, because, in the under or mystic current of its meaning, I fancied that I perceived, and for the first time, a full consciousness on the part of Usher, of the tottering of his lofty reason upon her throne. The verses, which were entitled 'The Haunted Palace', ran very nearly, if not accurately, thus:

I

In the greenest of our valleys,
By good angels tenanted,
Once a fair and stately palace –
Radiant palace – reared its head.
In the monarch Thought's dominion –
It stood there!
Never seraph spread a pinion
Over fabric half so fair.

II

Banners yellow, glorious, golden,
On its roof did float and flow;
(This – all this – was in the olden
Time long ago)
And every gentle air that dallied,
In that sweet day,
Along the ramparts plumed and pallid,
A winged odor went away.

III

Wanderers in that happy valley
Through two luminous windows saw
Spirits moving musically
To a lute's well-tunéd law,
Round about a throne, where sitting
(Porphyrogene!)
In state his glory well befitting,
The ruler of the realm was seen.

IV

And all with pearl and ruby glowing
Was the fair palace door,
Through which came flowing, flowing, flowing,
And sparkling evermore,
A troop of Echoes whose sweet duty
Was but to sing,
In voices of surpassing beauty,
The wit and wisdom of their king.

V

But evil things, in robes of sorrow,
Assailed the monarch's high estate;
(Ah, let us mourn, for never morrow
Shall dawn upon him, desolate!)
And, round about his home, the glory
That blushed and bloomed
Is but a dim-remembered story
Of the old time entombed.

VI

And travellers now within that valley,
Through the red-litten windows, see
Vast forms that move fantastically
To a discordant melody;
While, like a rapid ghastly river,
Through the pale door,
A hideous throng rush out forever,
And laugh – but smile no more.

I well remember that suggestions arising from this ballad led us into a train of thought wherein there became manifest an opinion of Usher's which I mention not so much on account of its novelty (for other men have thought thus), as on account of the pertinacity with which he maintained it. This opinion, in its general form, was that of the sentience of all vegetable things. But, in his disordered fancy, the idea had assumed a more daring character, and trespassed, under certain conditions, upon the kingdom of inorganization. I lack words to express the full extent, or the earnest *abandon* of his persuasion. The belief, however, was connected (as I have previously hinted) with the gray stones of the home of his forefathers. The conditions of the sentience had been here, he imagined, fulfilled in the method of collocation of these stones – in the order of their arrangement, as well as in that of the many *fungi* which overspread them, and of the decayed trees which stood around – above all, in the long undisturbed endurance of this arrangement, and in its reduplication in the still waters of the tarn. Its evidence – the evidence of the sentience – was to be seen, he said (and I here started as he spoke), in the gradual yet certain condensation of an atmosphere of their own about the waters and the walls. The result was discoverable, he added, in that silent, yet importunate and terrible influence which for centuries had moulded the destinies of his family, and which made *him* what I now saw him – what he was. Such opinions need no comment, and I will make none.

Our books – the books which, for years, had formed no small portion of the mental existence of the invalid – were, as might be supposed, in strict keeping with this character of phantasm. We pored together over such works as the *Ververt et Chartreuse* of Gresset; the *Belphegor* of Machiavelli; the *Heaven and Hell* of Swedenborg; the *Subterranean Voyage of Nicholas Klimm* by Holberg; the *Chiromancy* of Robert Flud, of Jean D'Indaginé, and of De la Chambre; the *Journey into the Blue Distance* of Tieck; and the *City of the Sun* of Campanella. One favorite volume was a small octavo edition of the *Directorium Inquisitorium*, by the Dominican Eymeric de Gironne; and there were passages in Pomponius Mela, about the old African Satyrs and Oegipans, over which Usher would sit dreaming for hours. His chief delight, however, was found in the perusal of an exceedingly rare and curious book in quarto Gothic – the manual of a forgotten church – the *Vigiliae Mortuorum secundum Chorum Ecclesiae Maguntinae*.

I could not help thinking of the wild ritual of this work, and of its probable influence upon the hypochondriac, when, one evening, having informed me abruptly that the lady Madeline was no more, he stated his intention of preserving her corpse for a fortnight (previously to its final interment), in one of the numerous vaults within the main walls of the building. The worldly reason, however, assigned for this singular proceeding, was one which I did not feel at liberty to dispute. The brother had been led to his resolution (so he told me) by consideration of the unusual character of the malady of the deceased, of certain obtrusive and eager inquiries on the part of her medical men, and of the remote and exposed situation of the burial-ground of the family. I will not deny that when I called to mind the sinister countenance of the person whom I met upon the staircase, on the day of my arrival at the house, I had no desire to oppose what I regarded as at best but a harmless, and by no means an unnatural, precaution.

At the request of Usher, I personally aided him in the arrangements for the temporary entombment. The body having been encoffined, we two alone bore it to its rest. The vault in which we placed it (and which had been so long unopened that our torches, half smothered in its oppressive atmosphere, gave us little opportunity for investigation) was small, damp, and entirely without means of admission for light; lying, at great depth, immediately beneath that portion of the building in which was my own sleeping apartment. It had been used, apparently, in remote feudal times, for the worst purposes of a donjon-keep, and, in later days, as a place of deposit for powder, or some other highly combustible substance, as a portion of its floor, and the whole interior of a long archway through which we reached it, were carefully sheathed with copper. The door, of massive iron, had been, also, similarly protected. Its immense weight caused an unusually sharp grating sound, as it moved upon its hinges.

Having deposited our mournful burden upon tressels within this region of horror, we partially turned aside the yet unscrewed lid of the coffin, and looked upon the face of the tenant. A striking similitude between the brother and sister now first arrested my attention; and Usher, divining, perhaps, my thoughts, murmured out some few words from which I learned that the deceased and himself had been twins, and that sympathies of a scarcely intelligible nature had always existed between them. Our glances, however, rested not long upon the dead – for we could not regard her unawed. The disease which had thus entombed the lady in the maturity of youth, had left, as usual in all maladies of a strictly cataleptical character, the mockery of a faint blush upon the bosom and the face, and that suspiciously lingering smile upon the lip which is so terrible in death. We replaced and screwed down the lid, and, having secured the door of iron, made our way, with toil, into the scarcely less gloomy apartments of the upper portion of the house.

And now, some days of bitter grief having elapsed, an observable change came over the features of the mental disorder of my friend. His ordinary manner had vanished. His ordinary occupations were neglected or forgotten. He roamed from chamber to chamber with hurried, unequal, and objectless step. The pallor of his countenance had assumed, if possible, a more ghastly hue – but the luminousness of his eye had utterly gone out. The once occasional huskiness of his tone was heard no more; and a tremulous quaver, as if of extreme terror, habitually characterized his utterance. There were times, indeed, when I thought his unceasingly agitated mind was laboring with some oppressive secret, to divulge which he struggled for the necessary courage. At times, again, I was obliged to resolve all into the mere inexplicable vagaries of madness, for I beheld him gazing upon vacancy for long hours, in an attitude of the profoundest attention, as if listening to some imaginary sound. It was no wonder that his condition terrified – that it infected me. I felt creeping upon me, by slow yet certain degrees, the wild influences of his own fantastic yet impressive superstitions.

It was, especially, upon retiring to bed late in the night of the seventh or eighth day after the placing of the lady Madeline within the donjon, that I experienced the full power of such feelings. Sleep came not near my couch – while the hours waned and waned away. I struggled to reason off the nervousness which had dominion over me. I endeavored to believe that much, if not all of what I felt, was due to the bewildering influence of the gloomy furniture of the room – of the dark and tattered draperies, which, tortured into motion by the breath of a rising tempest, swayed fitfully to and fro upon the walls, and rustled uneasily about the decorations of the bed. But my efforts were fruitless. An irrepressible tremor gradually pervaded my frame; and, at length, there sat upon my very heart an incubus of utterly causeless alarm. Shaking this off with a gasp and a struggle, I uplifted myself upon the pillows, and, peering earnestly within the intense darkness of the chamber, harkened – I know not why, except that an instinctive spirit prompted me – to certain low and indefinite sounds which came, through the pauses of the storm, at long intervals, I knew not whence.

Overpowered by an intense sentiment of horror, unaccountable yet unendurable, I threw on my clothes with haste (for I felt that I should sleep no more during the night), and endeavored to arouse myself from the pitiable condition into which I had fallen, by pacing rapidly to and fro through the apartment.

I had taken but few turns in this manner, when a light step on an adjoining staircase arrested my attention. I presently recognized it as that of Usher. In an instant afterward he rapped, with a gentle touch, at my door, and entered, bearing a lamp. His countenance was, as usual, cadaverously wan – but, moreover, there was a species of mad hilarity in his eyes – an evidently restrained *hysteria* in his whole demeanor. His air appalled me – but anything was preferable to the solitude which I had so long endured, and I even welcomed his presence as a relief.

"And you have not seen it?" he said abruptly, after having stared about him for some moments in silence – "You have not then seen it? – But, stay! you shall." Thus speaking, and having carefully shaded his lamp, he hurried to one of the casements, and threw it freely open to the storm.

The impetuous fury of the entering gust nearly lifted us from our feet. It was, indeed, a tempestuous yet sternly beautiful night, and one wildly singular in its terror and its beauty. A whirlwind had apparently collected its force in our vicinity; for there were frequent and violent alterations in the direction of the wind; and the exceeding density of the clouds (which hung so low as to press upon the turrets of the house) did not prevent our perceiving the life-like velocity with which they flew careering from all points against each other, without passing away into the distance. I say that even their exceeding density did not prevent our perceiving this – yet we had no glimpse of the moon or stars – nor was there any flashing forth of the lightning. But the under surfaces of the huge masses of agitated vapor, as well as all terrestrial objects immediately around us, were glowing in the unnatural light of a faintly luminous and distinctly visible gaseous exhalation which hung about and enshrouded the mansion.

"You must not – you shall not behold this!" said I, shudderingly, to Usher, as I led him, with a gentle violence, from the window to a seat. "These appearances, which bewilder you, are merely electrical phenomena not uncommon – or it may be that they have their ghastly origin in the rank miasma of the tarn. Let us close this casement; the air is chilling and dangerous to your frame. Here is one of your favorite romances. I will read, and you shall listen; and so we will pass away this terrible night together."

The antique volume which I had taken up was the *Mad Trist* of Sir Launcelot Canning; but I had called it a favorite of Usher's more in sad jest than in earnest; for, in truth, there is little in its uncouth and unimaginative prolixity which could have had interest for the lofty and spiritual ideality of my friend. It was, however, the only book immediately at hand; and I indulged a vague hope that the excitement which now agitated the hypochondriac, might find relief (for the history of mental disorder is full of similar anomalies) even in the extremeness of the folly which I should read. Could I have judged, indeed, by the wild overstrained air of vivacity with which he harkened, or apparently harkened, to the words of the tale, I might well have congratulated myself upon the success of my design.

I had arrived at that well-known portion of the story where Ethelred, the hero of the Trist, having sought in vain for peaceable admission into the dwelling of the hermit, proceeds to make good an entrance by force. Here, it will be remembered, the words of the narrative run thus:

> *"And Ethelred, who was by nature of a doughty heart, and who was now mighty withal, on account of the powerfulness of the wine which he had drunken, waited no longer to hold parley with the hermit, who, in sooth, was of an obstinate and maliceful turn, but, feeling the rain upon his shoulders, and fearing the rising of the tempest, uplifted his mace outright, and, with blows, made quickly room in the plankings of the door for his gauntleted hand; and now pulling therewith sturdily, he so cracked, and ripped, and tore all asunder, that the noise of the dry and hollow-sounding wood alarummed and reverberated throughout the forest."*

At the termination of this sentence I started, and for a moment, paused; for it appeared to me (although I at once concluded that my excited fancy had deceived me) – it appeared to me that, from some very remote portion of the mansion, there came, indistinctly, to my ears, what might have been, in its exact similarity of character, the echo (but a stifled and dull one certainly) of the very cracking and ripping sound which Sir Launcelot had so particularly described. It was, beyond doubt, the coincidence alone which had arrested my attention; for, amid the rattling of the sashes of the casements, and the ordinary commingled noises of the still increasing storm, the sound, in itself, had nothing, surely, which should have interested or disturbed me. I continued the story:

> *"But the good champion Ethelred, now entering within the door, was sore enraged and amazed to perceive no signal of the maliceful hermit; but, in the stead thereof, a dragon of a scaly and prodigious demeanor, and of a fiery tongue, which sate in guard before a palace of gold, with a floor of silver; and upon the wall there hung a shield of shining brass with this legend enwritten –*
>
> > *Who entereth herein, a conqueror hath bin;*
> > *Who slayeth the dragon, the shield he shall win;*
>
> *And Ethelred uplifted his mace, and struck upon the head of the dragon, which fell before him, and gave up his pesty breath, with a shriek so horrid and harsh, and withal so piercing, that Ethelred had fain to close his ears with his hands against the dreadful noise of it, the like whereof was never before heard."*

Here again I paused abruptly, and now with a feeling of wild amazement – for there could be no doubt whatever that, in this instance, I did actually hear (although from what direction it proceeded I found it impossible to say) a low and apparently distant, but harsh, protracted, and most unusual screaming or grating sound – the exact counterpart of what my fancy had already conjured up for the dragon's unnatural shriek as described by the romancer.

Oppressed, as I certainly was, upon the occurrence of this second and most extraordinary coincidence, by a thousand conflicting sensations, in which wonder and extreme terror were predominant, I still retained sufficient presence of mind to avoid exciting, by any observation, the sensitive nervousness of my companion. I was by no means certain that he had noticed the sounds in question; although, assuredly, a strange alteration had, during the last few minutes, taken place in his demeanor. From a position fronting my own, he had gradually brought round his chair, so as to sit with his face to the door of the chamber; and thus I could but partially perceive his features, although I saw that his lips trembled as if he were murmuring inaudibly. His head had dropped upon his breast – yet I knew that he was not asleep, from the wide and rigid opening of the eye as I caught a glance of it in profile. The motion of his body, too, was at variance with this idea – for he rocked from side to side with a gentle yet constant and uniform sway. Having rapidly taken notice of all this, I resumed the narrative of Sir Launcelot, which thus proceeded:

"And now, the champion, having escaped from the terrible fury of the dragon, bethinking himself of the brazen shield, and of the breaking up of the enchantment which was upon it, removed the carcass from out of the way before him, and approached valorously over the silver pavement of the castle to where the shield was upon the wall; which in sooth tarried not for his full coming, but fell down at his feet upon the silver floor, with a mighty great and terrible ringing sound."

No sooner had these syllables passed my lips, than – as if a shield of brass had indeed, at the moment, fallen heavily upon a floor of silver – I became aware of a distinct, hollow, metallic, and clangorous, yet apparently muffled reverberation. Completely unnerved, I leaped to my feet; but the measured rocking movement of Usher was undisturbed. I rushed to the chair in which he sat. His eyes were bent fixedly before him, and throughout his whole countenance there reigned a stony rigidity. But, as I placed my hand upon his shoulder, there came a strong shudder over his whole person; a sickly smile quivered about his lips; and I saw that he spoke in a low, hurried, and gibbering murmur, as if unconscious of my presence. Bending closely over him, I at length drank in the hideous import of his words.

"Not hear it? – Yes, I hear it, and have heard it. Long – long – long – many minutes, many hours, many days, have I heard it – yet I dared not – oh, pity me, miserable wretch that I am! – I dared not – I dared not speak! We have put her living in the tomb! Said I not that my senses were acute? I now tell you that I heard her first feeble movements in the hollow coffin. I heard them – many, many days ago – yet I dared not – I dared not speak! And now – tonight – Ethelred – ha! ha! – the breaking of the hermit's door, and the death-cry of the dragon, and the clangor of the shield! – Say, rather, the rending of her coffin, and the grating of the iron hinges of her prison, and her struggles within the coppered archway of the vault! Oh whither shall I fly? Will she not be here anon? Is she not hurry in my haste? Have I not heard her footstep on the stair? Do I not distinguish that heavy and horrible beating of her heart? Madman!" – here he sprang furiously to his feet, and shrieked out his syllables, as if in the effort he were giving up his soul – "Madman! I tell you that she now stands without the door!"

As if in the superhuman energy of his utterance there had been found the potency of a spell – the huge antique pannels to which the speaker pointed, threw slowly back, upon the instant, their ponderous and ebony jaws. It was the work of the rushing gust – but then without those doors there *did* stand the lofty and enshrouded figure of the lady Madeline of Usher. There was blood upon her white robes, and the evidence of some bitter struggle upon every portion of her emaciated frame. For a moment she remained trembling and reeling to and fro upon the threshold – then, with a low moaning cry, fell heavily inward upon the person of her brother, and in her violent and now final death-agonies, bore him to the floor a corpse, and a victim to the terrors he had anticipated.

From that chamber, and from that mansion, I fled aghast. The storm was still abroad in all its wrath as I found myself crossing the old causeway. Suddenly there shot along the path a wild light, and I turned to see whence a gleam so unusual could have issued; for the vast house and its shadows were alone behind me. The radiance was that of the full, setting, and blood-red moon, which now shone vividly through that once barely-discernible fissure, of which I have before spoken as extending from the roof of the building, in a zigzag direction, to the base. While I gazed, this fissure rapidly widened – there came a fierce breath of the whirlwind – the entire orb of the satellite burst at once upon my sight – my brain reeled as I saw the mighty walls rushing asunder – there was a long tumultuous shouting sound like the voice of a thousand waters – and the deep and dank tarn at my feet closed sullenly and silently over the fragments of the *'House of Usher'*.

Footnote for 'The Fall of the House of Usher'

1. 'His/her heart is a poised lute; / as soon as it is touched, it resounds.'

A Pair of Hands
An Old Maid's Ghost-Story

Arthur Quiller-Couch

"YES," SAID MISS LE PETYT, gazing into the deep fireplace and letting her hands and her knitting lie for the moment idle in her lap. "Oh, yes, I have seen a ghost. In fact I have lived in a house with one for quite a long time."

"How you *could*—" began one of my host's daughters; and "*You*, Aunt Emily?" cried the other at the same moment.

Miss Le Petyt, gentle soul, withdrew her eyes from the fireplace and protested with a gay little smile. "Well, my dears, I am not quite the coward you take me for. And, as it happens, mine was the most harmless ghost in the world. In fact"– and here she looked at the fire again – "I was quite sorry to lose her."

"It was a woman, then? Now *I* think," said Miss Blanche, "that female ghosts are the horridest of all. They wear little shoes with high red heels, and go about *tap, tap*, wringing their hands."

"This one wrung her hands, certainly. But I don't know about the high red heels, for I never saw her feet. Perhaps she was like the Queen of Spain, and hadn't any. And as for the hands, it all depends *how* you wring them. There's an elderly shop-walker at Knightsbridge, for instance —"

"Don't be prosy, dear, when you know that we're just dying to hear the story."

Miss Le Petyt turned to me with a small deprecating laugh. "It's such a little one."

"The story, or the ghost?"

"Both."

And this was Miss Le Petyt's story:

"It happened when I lived down in Cornwall, at Tresillack on the south coast. Tresillack was the name of the house, which stood quite alone at the head of a coombe, within sound of the sea but without sight of it; for though the coombe led down to a wide open beach, it wound and twisted half a dozen times on its way, and its overlapping sides closed the view from the house, which was advertised as 'secluded'. I was very poor in those days. Your father and all of us were poor then, as I trust, my dears, you will never be; but I was young enough to be romantic and wise enough to like independence, and this word 'secluded' took my fancy.

"The misfortune was that it had taken the fancy, or just suited the requirements, of several previous tenants. You know, I dare say, the kind of person who rents a secluded house in the country? Well, yes, there are several kinds; but they seem to agree in being odious. No one knows where they come from, though they soon remove all doubt about where they're 'going to', as the children say. 'Shady' is the word, is it not? Well, the previous tenants of Tresillack (from first to last a bewildering series) had been shady with a vengeance.

"I knew nothing of this when I first made application to the landlord, a solid yeoman inhabiting a farm at the foot of the coombe, on a cliff overlooking the beach. To him I presented myself fearlessly as a spinster of decent family and small but assured income, intending a rural life of combined seemliness and economy. He met my advances politely enough, but with an air of suspicion which offended me. I began by disliking him for it: afterwards I set it down as an unpleasant feature in the local character. I was doubly mistaken. Farmer Hosking was slow-witted, but as honest a man as ever stood up against hard times; and a more open and hospitable race than the people on that coast I never wish to meet. It was the caution of a child who had burnt his fingers, not once but many times. Had I known what I afterwards learned of Farmer Hosking's tribulations as landlord of a 'secluded country residence', I should have approached him with the bashfulness proper to my suit and faltered as I undertook to prove the bright exception in a long line of painful experiences. He had bought the Tresillack estate twenty years before – on mortgage, I fancy – because the land adjoined his own and would pay him for tillage. But the house was a nuisance, an incubus; and had been so from the beginning.

"'Well, miss,' he said, 'you're welcome to look over it; a pretty enough place, inside and out. There's no trouble about keys, because I've put in a housekeeper, a widow-woman, and she'll show you round. With your leave I'll step up the coombe so far with you, and put you in your way.' As I thanked him he paused and rubbed his chin. 'There's one thing I must tell you, though. Whoever takes the house must take Mrs. Carkeek along with it.'

"'Mrs. Carkeek?' I echoed dolefully. 'Is that the housekeeper?'

"'Yes: she was wife to my late hind. I'm sorry, miss,' he added, my face telling him no doubt what sort of woman I expected Mrs. Carkeek to be; 'but I had to make it a rule after – after some things that happened. And I dare say you won't find her so bad. Mary Carkeek's a sensible comfortable woman, and knows the place. She was in service there to Squire Kendall when he sold up and went: her first place it was.'

"'I may as well see the house, anyhow,' said I dejectedly. So we started to walk up the coombe. The path, which ran beside a little chattering stream, was narrow for the most part, and Farmer Hosking, with an apology, strode on ahead to beat aside the brambles. But whenever its width allowed us to walk side by side I caught him from time to time stealing a shy inquisitive glance under his rough eyebrows. Courteously though he bore himself, it was clear that he could not sum me up to his satisfaction or bring me square with his notion of a tenant for his 'secluded country residence'.

"I don't know what foolish fancy prompted it, but about halfway up the coombe I stopped short and asked:

"'There are no ghosts, I suppose?'

"It struck me, a moment after I had uttered it, as a supremely silly question; but he took it quite seriously. 'No; I never heard tell of any *ghosts*.' He laid a queer sort of stress on the word. 'There's always been trouble with servants, and maids' tongues will be runnin'. But Mary Carkeek lives up there alone, and she seems comfortable enough.'

"We walked on. By-and-by he pointed with his stick. 'It don't look like a place for ghosts, now, do it?'

"Certainly it did not. Above an untrimmed orchard rose a terrace of turf scattered with thorn-bushes, and above this a terrace of stone, upon which stood the prettiest cottage I had ever seen. It was long and low and thatched; a deep verandah ran from end to end. Clematis, Banksia roses and honeysuckle climbed the posts of this verandah, and big blooms of the Marechal Niel were clustered along its roof, beneath the lattices of the bedroom windows. The house was small enough to be called a cottage, and rare enough in features and in situation to confer distinction on any tenant. It suggested what in those days we should have called 'elegant' living. And I could have clapped my hands for joy.

"My spirits mounted still higher when Mrs. Carkeek opened the door to us. I had looked for a Mrs. Gummidge, and I found a healthy middle-aged woman with a thoughtful but contented face, and a smile which, without a trace of obsequiousness, quite bore out the farmer's description of her. She was a comfortable woman; and while we walked through the rooms together (for Mr. Hosking waited outside) I 'took to' Mrs. Carkeek. Her speech was direct and practical; the rooms, in spite of their faded furniture, were bright and exquisitely clean; and somehow the very atmosphere of the house gave me a sense of well-being, of feeling at home and cared for; yes, *of being loved*. Don't laugh, my dears; for when I've done you may not think this fancy altogether foolish.

"I stepped out into the verandah, and Farmer Hosking pocketed the pruning knife which he had been using on a bush of jasmine.

"'This is better than anything I had dreamed of,' said I.

"'Well, miss, that's not a wise way of beginning a bargain, if you'll excuse me.'

"He took no advantage, however, of my admission; and we struck the bargain as we returned down the coombe to his farm, where the hired chaise waited to convey me back to the market town. I had meant to engage a maid of my own, but now it occurred to me that I might do very well with Mrs. Carkeek. This, too, was settled in the course of the next day or two, and within the week I had moved into my new home.

"I can hardly describe to you the happiness of my first month at Tresillack; because (as I now believe) if I take the reasons which I had for being happy, one by one, there remains over something which I cannot account for. I was moderately young, entirely healthy; I felt myself independent and adventurous; the season was high summer, the weather glorious, the garden in all the pomp of June, yet sufficiently unkempt to keep me busy, give me a sharp appetite for meals, and send me to bed in that drowsy stupor which comes of the odours of earth. I spent the most of my time out of doors, winding up the day's work as a rule with a walk down the cool valley, along the beach and back.

"I soon found that all housework could be safely left to Mrs. Carkeek. She did not talk much; indeed her only fault (a rare one in housekeepers) was that she talked too little, and even when I addressed her seemed at times unable to give me her attention. It was as though her mind strayed off to some small job she had forgotten, and her eyes wore a listening look, as though she waited for the neglected task to speak and remind her. But as a matter of fact she forgot nothing. Indeed, my dears, I was never so well attended to in my life.

"Well, that is what I'm coming to. That, so to say, is just *it*. The woman not only had the rooms swept and dusted, and my meals prepared to the moment. In a hundred odd little ways this orderliness, these preparations, seemed to read my desires. Did I wish the roses renewed in a bowl upon the dining-table, sure enough at the next meal they would be replaced by fresh ones. Mrs. Carkeek (I told myself) must have surprised and interpreted a glance of mine. And yet I could not remember having glanced at the bowl in her presence. And how on earth had she guessed the very roses, the very shapes and colours I had lightly wished for? This is only an instance, you understand. Every day, and from morning to night, I happened on others, each slight enough, but all together bearing witness to a ministering intelligence as subtle as it was untiring.

"I am a light sleeper, as you know, with an uncomfortable knack of waking with the sun and roaming early. No matter how early I rose at Tresillack, Mrs. Carkeek seemed to have prevented me. Finally I had to conclude that she arose and dusted and tidied as soon as she judged me safely a-bed. For once, finding the drawing-room (where I had been sitting late) 'redded up' at four in the morning, and no trace of a plate of raspberries which I had carried thither after dinner and left overnight, I determined to test her, and walked through to the kitchen, calling her by name. I found the kitchen as clean as a pin, and the fire laid, but no trace of Mrs. Carkeek. I walked upstairs and knocked at her door. At the second knock a sleepy voice cried out, and presently the good woman stood before me in her nightgown, looking (I thought) very badly scared.

"'No,' I said, 'it's not a burglar. But I've found out what I wanted, that you do your morning's work over night. But you mustn't wait for me when I choose to sit up. And now go back to your bed like a good soul, whilst I take a run down to the beach.'

"She stood blinking in the dawn. Her face was still white.

"'Oh, miss,' she gasped, 'I made sure you must have seen something!'

"'And so I have,' I answered, 'but it was neither burglars nor ghosts.'

"'Thank God!' I heard her say as she turned her back to me in her grey bedroom – which faced the north. And I took this for a carelessly pious expression and ran downstairs, thinking no more of it.

"A few days later I began to understand.

"The plan of Tresillack house (I must explain) was simplicity itself. To the left of the hall as you entered was the dining room; to the right the drawing-room, with a boudoir beyond. The foot of the stairs faced the front door, and beside it, passing a glazed inner door, you found two others right and left, the left opening on the kitchen, the right on a passage which ran by a store cupboard under the bend of the stairs to a neat pantry with the usual shelves and linen press, and under the window (which faced north) a porcelain basin and brass tap. On the first morning of my tenancy I had visited this pantry and turned the tap; but no water ran. I supposed this to be accidental. Mrs. Carkeek had to wash up glassware and crockery, and no doubt Mrs. Carkeek would complain of any failure in the water supply.

"But the day after my surprise visit (as I called it) I had picked a basketful of roses, and carried them into the pantry as a handy place to arrange them in. I chose a china bowl and went to fill it at the tap. Again the water would not run.

"I called Mrs. Carkeek. 'What is wrong with this tap?' I asked. 'The rest of the house is well enough supplied.'

"'I don't know, miss. I never use it.'

"'But there must be a reason; and you must find it a great nuisance washing up the plate and glasses in the kitchen. Come around to the back with me, and we'll have a look at the cisterns.'

"'The cisterns'll be all right, miss. I assure you I don't find it a trouble.'

"But I was not to be put off. The back of the house stood but ten feet from a wall which was really but a stone face built against the cliff cut away by the architect. Above the cliff rose the kitchen garden, and from its lower path we looked over the wall's parapet upon the cisterns. There were two – a very large one, supplying the kitchen and the bathroom above the kitchen; and a small one, obviously fed by the other, and as obviously leading, by a pipe which I could trace, to the pantry. Now the big cistern stood almost full, and yet the small one, though on a lower level, was empty.

"'It's as plain as daylight,' said I. 'The pipe between the two is choked.' And I clambered on to the parapet.

"'I wouldn't, miss. The pantry tap is only cold water, and no use to me. From the kitchen boiler I gets it hot, you see.'

"'But I want the pantry water for my flowers.' I bent over and groped. 'I thought as much!' said I, as I wrenched out a thick plug of cork and immediately the water began to flow. I turned triumphantly on Mrs. Carkeek, who had grown suddenly red in the face. Her eyes were fixed on the cork in my hand. To keep it more firmly wedged in its place somebody had wrapped it round with a rag of calico print; and, discoloured though the rag was, I seemed to recall the pattern (a lilac sprig). Then, as our eyes met, it occurred to me that only two mornings before Mrs. Carkeek had worn a print gown of that same sprigged pattern.

"I had the presence of mind to hide this very small discovery, sliding over it some quite trivial remark; and presently Mrs. Carkeek regained her composure. But I own I felt disappointed in her. It seemed such a paltry thing to be disingenuous over. She had deliberately acted a fib before me; and why? Merely because she preferred the kitchen to the pantry tap. It was childish. 'But servants are all the same,' I told myself. 'I must take Mrs. Carkeek as she is; and, after all, she is a treasure.'

"On the second night after this, and between eleven and twelve o'clock, I was lying in bed and reading myself sleepy over a novel of Lord Lytton's, when a small sound disturbed me. I listened. The sound was clearly that of water trickling; and I set it down to rain. A shower (I told myself) had filled the water-pipes which drained the roof. Somehow I could not fix the sound. There was a water pipe against the wall just outside my window. I rose and drew up the blind.

"To my astonishment no rain was falling; no rain had fallen. I felt the slate windowsill; some dew had gathered there – no more. There was no wind, no cloud: only a still moon high over the eastern slope of the coombe, the distant plash of waves, and the fragrance of many roses. I went back to bed and listened again. Yes, the trickling sound continued, quite distinct in the silence of the house, not to be confused for a moment with the dull murmur of the beach. After a while it began to grate on my nerves. I caught up my candle, flung my dressing gown about me, and stole softly downstairs.

"Then it was simple. I traced the sound to the pantry. 'Mrs. Carkeek has left the tap running,' said I: and, sure enough, I found it so – a thin trickle steadily running to waste in the porcelain basin. I turned off the tap, went contentedly back to my bed, and slept.

"—for some hours. I opened my eyes in darkness, and at once knew what had awakened me. The tap was running again. Now it had shut easily in my hand, but not so easily that I could believe it had slipped open again of its own accord. 'This is Mrs. Carkeek's doing,' said I; and am afraid I added 'Bother Mrs. Carkeek!'

"Well, there was no help for it: so I struck a light, looked at my watch, saw that the hour was just three o'clock, and descended the stairs again. At the pantry door I paused. I was not afraid – not one little bit. In fact the notion that anything might be wrong had never crossed my mind. But I remember thinking, with my hand on the door, that if Mrs. Carkeek were in the pantry I might happen to give her a severe fright.

"I pushed the door open briskly. Mrs. Carkeek was not there. But something *was* there, by the porcelain basin – something which might have sent me scurrying upstairs two steps at a time, but which as a matter of fact held me to the spot. My heart seemed to stand still – so still! And in the stillness I remember setting down the brass candlestick on a tall nest of drawers beside me.

"Over the porcelain basin and beneath the water trickling from the tap I saw two hands.

"That was all – two small hands, a child's hands. I cannot tell you how they ended.

"No: they were not cut off. I saw them quite distinctly: just a pair of small hands and the wrists, and after that – nothing. They were moving briskly – washing themselves clean. I saw the water trickle and splash over them – not *through* them – but just as it would on real hands. They were the hands of a little girl, too. Oh, yes, I was sure of that at once. Boys and girls wash their hands differently. I can't just tell you what the difference is, but it's unmistakable.

"I saw all this before my candle slipped and fell with a crash. I had set it down without looking – for my eyes were fixed on the basin – and had balanced it on the edge of the nest of drawers. After the crash, in the darkness there, with the water running, I suffered some bad moments. Oddly enough, the thought uppermost with me was that I *must* shut off that tap before escaping. I *had* to. And after a while I picked up all my courage, so to say, between my teeth, and with a little sob thrust out my hand and did it. Then I fled.

"The dawn was close upon me: and as soon as the sky reddened I took my bath, dressed and went downstairs. And there at the pantry door I found Mrs. Carkeek, also dressed, with my candlestick in her hand.

"'Ah!' said I, 'you picked it up.'

"Our eyes met. Clearly Mrs. Carkeek wished me to begin, and I determined at once to have it out with her.

"'And you knew all about it. That's what accounts for your plugging up the cistern.'

"'You saw...?' she began.

"'Yes, yes. And you must tell me all about it – never mind how bad. Is – is it – murder?'

"'Law bless you, miss, whatever put such horrors in your head?'

"'She was washing her hands.'

"'Ah, so she does, poor dear! But – murder! And dear little Miss Margaret, that wouldn't go to hurt a fly!'

"'Miss Margaret?'

"'Eh, she died at seven year. Squire Kendall's only daughter; and that's over twenty year ago. I was her nurse, miss, and I know – diphtheria it was; she took it down in the village.'

"'But how do you know it is Margaret?'

"'Those hands – why, how could I mistake, that used to be her nurse?'

"'But why does she wash them?'

"'Well, miss, being always a dainty child – and the house-work, you see—'

"I took a long breath. 'Do you mean to tell me that all this tidying and dusting—' I broke off. 'Is it *she* who has been taking this care of me?'

"Mrs. Carkeek met my look steadily.

"'Who else, miss?'

"'Poor little soul!'

"'Well now' – Mrs. Carkeek rubbed my candlestick with the edge of her apron – 'I'm so glad you take it like this. For there isn't really nothing to be afraid of – is there?' She eyed me wistfully. 'It's my belief she loves you, miss. But only to think what a time she must have had with the others!'

"'The others?' I echoed.

"'The other tenants, miss: the ones afore you.'

"'Were they bad?'

"'They was awful. Didn't Farmer Hosking tell you? They carried on fearful – one after another, and each one worse than the last.'

"'What was the matter with them? Drink?'

"'Drink, miss, with some of 'em. There was the Major – he used to go mad with it, and run about the coombe in his nightshirt. Oh, scandalous! And his wife drank too – that is, if she ever *was* his wife. Just think of that tender child washing up after their nasty doings!'

"I shivered.

"'But that wasn't the worst, miss – not by a long way. There was a pair here – from the colonies, or so they gave out – with two children, a boy and gel, the eldest scarce six. Poor mites!'

"'Why, what happened?'

"'They beat those children, miss – your blood would boil! – *and* starved, *and* tortured 'em, it's my belief. You could hear their screams, I've been told, away back in the high road, and that's the best part of half a mile. Sometimes they was locked up without food for days together. But it's my belief that little Miss Margaret managed to feed them somehow. Oh, I can see her, creeping to the door and comforting!'

"'But perhaps she never showed herself when these awful people were here, but took to flight until they left.'

"'You didn't never know her, miss. The brave she was! She'd have stood up to lions. She've been here all the while: and only to think what her innocent eyes and ears must have took in! There was another couple—' Mrs. Carkeek sunk her voice.

"'Oh, hush!' said I, 'if I'm to have any peace of mind in this house!'

"'But you won't go, miss? She loves you, I know she do. And think what you might be leaving her to – what sort of tenant might come next. For she can't go. She've been here ever since her father sold the place. He died soon after. You musn't go!'

"Now I had resolved to go, but all of a sudden I felt how mean this resolution was.

"'After all,' said I, 'there's nothing to be afraid of.'

"'That's it, miss; nothing at all. I don't even believe it's so very uncommon. Why, I've heard my mother tell of farmhouses where the rooms were swept every night as regular as clockwork, and the floors sanded, and the pots and pans scoured, and all while the maids slept. They put it down to the piskies; but we know better, miss, and now we've got the secret between us we can lie easy in our beds, and if we hear anything, say 'God bless the child!' and go to sleep.'

"'Mrs. Carkeek,' said I, 'there's only one condition I have to make.'

"'What's that?'

"'Why, that you let me kiss you.'

"'Oh, you dear!' said Mrs. Carkeek as we embraced: and this was as close to familiarity as she allowed herself to go in the whole course of my acquaintance with her.

"I spent three years at Tresillack, and all that while Mrs. Carkeek lived with me and shared the secret. Few women, I dare to say, were ever so completely wrapped around with love as we were during those three years. It ran through my waking life like a song: it smoothed my pillow, touched and made my table comely, in summer lifted the heads of the flowers as I passed, and in winter watched the fire with me and kept it bright.

"'Why did I ever leave Tresillack?' Because one day, at the end of five years, Farmer Hosking brought me word that he had sold the house – or was about to sell it; I forget which. There was no avoiding it, at any rate; the purchaser being a Colonel Kendall, a brother of the old Squire.'

"'A married man?' I asked.

"'Yes, miss; with a family of eight. As pretty children as ever you see, and the mother a good lady. It's the old home to Colonel Kendall.'

"'I see. And that is why you feel bound to sell.'

"'It's a good price, too, that he offers. You mustn't think but I'm sorry enough—'

"'To turn me out? I thank you, Mr. Hosking; but you are doing the right thing.'

"Since Mrs. Carkeek was to stay, the arrangement lacked nothing of absolute perfection – except, perhaps, that it found no room for me.

"'*She* – Margaret – will be happy,' I said; 'with her cousins, you know.'

"'Oh yes, miss, she will be happy, sure enough,' Mrs. Carkeek agreed.

"So when the time came I packed up my boxes, and tried to be cheerful. But on the last morning, when they stood corded in the hall, I sent Mrs. Carkeek upstairs upon some poor excuse, and stepped alone into the pantry.

"'Margaret!' I whispered.

"There was no answer at all. I had scarcely dared to hope for one. Yet I tried again, and, shutting my eyes this time, stretched out both hands and whispered:

"'Margaret!'

"And I will swear to my dying day that two little hands stole and rested – for a moment only – in mine."

Sparrow

M. Regan

I

("Who killed Cock Robin?" "I," said the Sparrow,
"With my bow and arrow, I killed Cock Robin.")

II

I AM ALIVE.

I live in the corners, dusty and dark. I hide behind furnishings, frightened by sunlight. I chase after his shadow, and I pounce on his heels.

His shadow is my favorite place to be. I love it there. I feel safe in the shape of him, warm and surrounded, as if we were embracing. My fingers dig playfully into his ankles, into the tendons and skin and brittle bones that have been cloistered inside his boots.

He cannot see me. He cannot feel me. But a shiver races up his spine, and he knows that I am there.

III

MORNINGS are too bright for silhouettes. In the office, bow windows shine like crystal, their lattices bleached to nihility. I crouch beside his writing desk, watching as he works.

Sometimes, I poke his inkpots. Sometimes, I rustle his mail. Sometimes, I make him smile.

Afternoon performs strange alchemy to the light, turning its watery rays thick and golden. The wash of it gilds the parlor, making baroque furnishings gleam. He takes his tea while I take my nap, lulled by the silvery song of spoons in Wedgewood cups, and when I wake, I find that he has set aside a biscuit or a tiny cake for me, newspaper foregone in favor of watching cream melt and fruit glazing ooze.

I cannot eat what he eats. I cannot eat at all. But it is nice to play pretend.

Evening comes like a hundred thousand ravens, their feathers smothering the sun. Plumage rustles; beady eyes gaze unnoticed from within the downy gloom. He groans and whimpers and sighs atop his feather bed, against another's body, as the moon casts delicate reflections of cage bars across the floor.

("Who saw him die?" "I," said the Fly,
"With my little eye, I saw him die.")

"Is she…here…?" he asks, breathlessly wanton, his bruised lips parted and bright gaze darting. Straining, desperate, he tries to see beyond the veil that hides me from his sight.

I peek from behind the four-poster's curtain. That I am spotted immediately is a surprise to no one.

"She is, Master," the house maid chuckles, affection stitching together the tattered silk of her voice. Monochrome petticoats and pools of ruche froth around her hips. Long hair spills over bare flesh. Violet eyes cut sideways, sharp enough to slice through the atramentous night, inhuman enough to see me for what I am.

For who I am.

"...tell her to leave us."

The maid's lashes flutter, as light as a nested bird's wing.

"You heard him, little one."

A draft urges me into the hall; the corridor stretches long, so I do the same. Tendrils of my consciousness expand freely, drifting outward, and I meld peacefully into the blackness.

IV

I SAY NOTHING. I weigh nothing. I am nothing.

"No, little one. You are *everything*."

The maid's silhouette is as much a comfort to me as her Master's. I wrap around and around her legs, weaving myself through the eyelets of her boots. She pares and peels potatoes while I pout.

"Just a bit longer, dear heart. Just hold out a bit longer."

V

HE SEES ME – metaphorically – as one would a tiny child. He sees me as innocent, as naïve and fragile.

He does not *see* me. He has never seen me, and so is far from correct in his assumptions.

But neither is he wrong.

His body is newly twenty. My essence is now two and one-half. Yet, it seems to me that we are older than we appear – our minds as wicked and ancient as the violet-eyed creature who dubbed herself his maid.

VI

EVERY CHRISTMAS, I am given a doll. They are left for me on the sill of the nursery's window, their miniature legs hooked over the crib bars. Dust motes spin as mobiles would above them; when the sun shines, its rays press warmth into china spines. I learned to tell time off the dials of dangling feet.

Hours pass. Then days, then months, then years. I change. They don't. They sit, angelified by halos of backlight, as I marvel at their beauty.

A window frame of whitewashed wood borders the brunette, the crushed velvet of her bonnet bluer than the sky in summer. Beside her sits a redhead with a braid, her doe eyes wide and filamented and lifeless.

I cannot play with my dolls. I cannot move them, cannot touch them. But I can love them. I can paw at them, and sniff them, and stare. I can *want*.

I *do* want. I want a blonde this year. A blonde with curls. I want her to be pale, to wear pinks and pearls. I want this very badly. I want that want to be known.

The maid laughs when I loop myself around her skirts, begging, nearly getting lost in labyrinthine lace patterns.

"Perhaps," she coos, "if you are good."

VII

BEFORE there were dolls to teach me time, before there were sweets left for my pleasure, before he knew I was there at all, I saw the Master cry.

*("Who'll be chief mourner?" "I," said the Dove,
"I mourn for my love, I'll be chief mourner.")*

He blamed chills on the winter, jostled mail on crosswinds. His inkpot tipped due to his own carelessness, though he swore it'd been placed nowhere near his elbow.

He swore in other ways, too. Walking past me, walking through me, the Master cursed and wandered, stumbling about until he reached the manor's barren garden. He was alone there, sans the birds.

There are always, always birds.

The marble bench that the Master favors was as cold as a grave in February, as white as the snow and the sound of silence; the flowers that had been planted last spring lay withered and dead at his feet.

Branches shivered beside him, shriveled, clawing from the earth like corpse arms. They strained for him. I did, too.

Neither of us could reach.

Don't cry, I tried but could not say. I had no voice, no mouth, no face. He had no shadow in the colorless day, no idea that I was beside him, sobbing, *Please, don't be sad.*

You don't need to be sad.

I am alive.

VIII

SOMETIMES, my biscuit is taken. Sometimes, my cake is eaten. Sometimes, the Lady comes to call, and decorum compels the Master to bow, gracious, and offer what would have been my share.

I do not mind. The Lady fascinates me. She is the closest one can get to sunshine without being burned: golden tresses and rosy cheeks, frills and ruffles and opalescent gossamer. Pinky daintily extended, she sips at Earl Grey and flashes a smile, her teeth the exact same shade of porcelain as her cup.

Her eyes shimmer, and I can tell she loves him.

I like that, too. I touch the instep of her shoe, stroking reverentially to her heel. She does not understand that chilly static tickle, only knows that her foot suddenly, gracelessly jerks.

The Lady apologizes.

He tells her not to worry. Pours her a spot more tea. Asks her once again if she is sure, very sure, that she wishes to be his.

*("Who'll be the parson?" "I," said the Rook,
"With my little book, I'll be the parson.")*

"Yes," the Lady vows. "In every way."

He loves her, too. Obviously he loves her, too.

The wedding is in one week.

IX

I DON'T like it in here.

It's dark. Hot. Wet. Too wet. What are these? I can't move. I don't recognize— I can't move. I can't breathe. I don't like it. He said I would like it. I'm trapped. I can't breathe. I can't breathe. I can'tbreathe. Icantbreathe.Icantbreatheicantbreathe*icantbreathe*—

("Who caught his blood?" "I," said the Fish,
"With my little dish, I caught his blood.")

A snap, a squelch; I burst into the world with a sickening *crack*, like a hatchling escaping its egg. Mist hisses, deafening. The walls are copper-damp where sprayed.

I am riled. Terrified. In a panic, I flee my prison and scramble over to their shadows, quivering as I cling to the maid's leg. She comforts me with a hush.

Then, turning to her Master, she says:

"I told you she would reject it."

X

HE HAD to be told.

About the vertebrae, about the viscera, about the chunks. About the slurry of half-formed organs that his maid had labored over, silent, on that starry night two and one-half years ago.

It had been an agonizing ordeal, even for one like herself. The pain overwhelmed. The horror could drive one mad. Cursing her body for its failures, the maid cried and cried, cradling what fleshy parts could be fished from the mire. She gathered a tendon, an eye, pushed through another contraction, and then— finally—

"There you were, little one."

That's what he was told, and that's what she tells me. I have to be told, too; no one really remembers being born. I don't *want* to remember being born. I coil closer to the maid, shuddering to imagine myself in so many raw lumps, splattered across ruined sheets.

"You were like a doll," the maid continues, her voice as warm as my entrails had been. "Disassembled. Broken beyond repair. But...in being what I am, I had ways to preserve your pieces."

A tender finger traces the edge of a jar, the ridge of its lid, the warped and pickled contours of what floats behind thick glass. The rate of decay is measured; the blanket nest readjusted. The stench of bitter herbs puffs up from the crib, stirring the nursery's stagnant air.

Dust wheels, winks, and falls like stars in the ichorous twilight.

She checks the time on my dolls. Soon, their shadows will disappear.

Soon, I will disappear.

XI

THE MASTER does not see me. He cannot see me. He cannot bear to see me, not as I yet am. He stands outside the nursery door, his hand pressed flat to painted wood, and tells me I am beautiful.

He tells me that he loves me.

He tells me that he'll save me.

("Who'll bear the pall?" "We," said the Wren,
"Both the cock and the hen, we'll bear the pall.")

"Leave everything to me."

XII

I LIKE HER.

The Lady is comely. She smells of gardenias. I orbit her shins, and I wonder if she would like me, too, could she see me. Would she allow me to sit on her lap and try on her jewels? Would she sing *Who Killed Cock Robin* with me, or play hide-and-go-seek?

I doubt it.

XIII

I AM ALIVE.

"Without a body, she'll have no anchor."

Living things die.

"I know."

I am dying.

"Without an anchor, she'll disappear."

I am disintegrating.

"I *know!*"

I am fading.

"There is only one choice."

Help me…

"…I know."

XIV

"IS THE LADY ready to begin her new life?"

Lashes low, the maid smiles at her Master's intended: at her rouged cheeks, her glossed lips, her powdered décolletage. A veil is pinned into her ringlets, as fine as spun sugar or rime. Or cobwebs. Diamonds are stitched into its pleats, glittering like the dust to which we all return.

Blushing with excitement, the Lady beams. Behind her lay the silk of a long train, its drag reminding me of shorn wings.

"I am."

"Well," purrs the maid, "You look beautiful."

("Who'll make the shroud?" "I," said the Beetle,
"With my thread and needle, I'll make the shroud.")

The praise is enough to turn the Lady's flush magenta.

But when the maid opens her preternatural eyes, the one she is looking at is me.

XV

HE ENTERS when she leaves.

Finery suits a man as regal as the Master; he was born for gems and roses and satin. The top hat he wears is as black as his shadow, and I take an immediate shine to it.

It is beautiful. *He* is beautiful – not her, not me. I wonder if he knows that. Does he see? Though he is gazing into the vanity's mirror, his focus is over his shoulder, not his own reflection.

Fingertips settle upon the seatback. Cufflinks make prisms of the light. His expression is troubled, but his eyes are calm; I see them both, see *through* them both, to the soul that tarnishes behind them.

I remember the day that he cried, the day he was told. But maybe he is thinking of the day that he *believed*, for when the Master next speaks, he uses those same words he had with the maid.

("Who'll dig his grave?" "I," said the Owl,
"With my pick and shovel, I'll dig his grave.")

"Everything else be damned."

XVI

WE AWAIT the bride and groom in the townhouse, away from the dangers of consecrated grounds. Being alone proves a different sort of blessing; with no Lady or servants around, the maid can openly play with me, and play she does. I hardly notice the passing of time as it stretches across the floor, and forget my fretfulness completely during hide-and-go-seek and rounds of song.

("Who'll toll the bell?" "I," said the bull,
"Because I can pull, I'll toll the bell.")

Throughout the city, the church bells sound.

XVII

DURING SUPPER, I sit in his lap.

I try not to wriggle. I earnestly try. Wriggling makes me seem impatient, which adds to his guilt; my presumed distress makes it difficult for him to touch his meal.

That isn't my intention. I only want his attention. Unimpressed by my behavior, the maid glares as she fills crystal flutes with champagne, but her disapproval does not faze me. Privacy is a concept I put little stock in.

I spiral contentedly atop his thighs.

The Lady is lovelier than ever in the smoldering candlelight: young and vibrant, skin supple and cheeks glowing. Her wedding had swollen her heart with joy, and that had swollen her bosom, too; she lifts her glass towards her husband and proposes a toast.

"To our happiness. To the happiness of our families. And to the happiness of the family... that we will have together."

Her voice is husky, shy. Enchanting. Alcohol bubbles in glasses and veins. He is nervous as well, but still smiles when he reiterates:

"To family."

XVIII

THE BEDCHAMBER is dark. I can move as I please. Excited, I race on ahead, slipping between ankles and flying over floorboards. I roll atop the coverlet. I spin around the posters, fold into the curtains, bounce atop the mattress.

I turn, and find the Master and the Lady have hesitated in the threshold. Behind them, the maid looms, her brow arched.

"Once upon a time not terribly long ago, outside parties were required to pay witness to a couple's first night together," she comments, her monotone painfully professional. "Comparatively, this shouldn't be nearly as embarrassing, I don't think."

The Master splutters. His flusterment visibly charms his new wife, who relaxes when he grumbles, "You're not helping."

The maid's expression betrays nothing.

"Does my Lord *need* help to...get the job done?"

"No."

The newlyweds enter the room, walking directly towards me.

XIX

THE RIBBONS in her hair hiss when unwoven, almost like flames being snuffed. Curls tumble around slender shoulders, their waves swept away by a hand. This gives her husband better access to the cords that crisscross down her back.

He presses a dry kiss to her nape, his fingers tangling in the knots.

> ("Who'll carry the coffin?" "I," said the Kite,
> "If it's not through the night, I'll carry the coffin.")

A dress and a petticoat fall to the floor. The Lady steps out of them as one would a fairy ring, her toes delicately pointed. Fanciful murmurings – vows and dreams and pretty things that I can only catch parts of – slur together on the tip of her tongue, because he is kissing her, kissing her fiercely, and she is losing oxygen and strength and her train of thought.

They fall back on the eiderdown, twisting like I did. I watch them from the pillows, enthralled by all the ways that she is beautiful, and pliant, and trapped between the Master's thighs, gazing trustingly up at him as he pins her wrists to the blankets.

He returns her smile. Touches his mouth to her forehead.

Whispers, "Now."

XX

THE LADY does not realize something is wrong until she feels me in her trachea, lodged like a lump of undigested food.

Instinctively, she chokes. Keens – surely struggles against her husband, hips jerking and eyes bulging – but his grip remains firm. He is unmoved.

I do not move, either. Not *up*, not *out*. I endure esophageal contractions, wait for painful spasms to subside, then tear my way purposefully *down*, skittering along ribbed muscles as an insect would. Or a parasite.

I am not a parasite.

I tumble into her belly with a splash of acid. For a moment, I sit in that puddle: dazed, trembling, listening to the rhythm of an unseen heart, to the undulating rumble of intestines. Blood rushes through tubers and capillaries.

It is warm here. Pleasant. Familiar? The same.

We are the same. The blood, the bile, the helixing bits. We are compatible.

Family.

My essence uncoils, tentative. Feeling. I feel, and am felt, and am doing the feeling. I can breathe. I can *breathe* – her lungs are mine. I want to *clutch* them, *squeeze—*

No. No, wait. I need them.

Be gentle.

I pet them. They are porous and soft. Like the cushions in the parlor, she is soft all over. And still warm. Soft and warm.

I like her very much.

And so I fill her, slowly, with wisps and vines of Self. I spiral downward to thread through ligaments; I loop upward to coat her bones. Every nerve and artery and lipid is prodded, catalogued, assimilated. I feel so happy – she feels so frightened.

Oh dear.

Her mind resists me. Her soul fights.

But a doll has no need for minds or souls.

XXI

I AM a Covenant.

I am *their* Covenant. I am a vow that bound two into one, born from hatred and desire and corruption and something depraved that twisted into something profound.

I am the soul that a witch sold for power.

I am the lives that a greedy count sacrificed.

I am their spawn, their sins personified, their squandered chance to relearn humanity, to remember that love lets go.

He does not let her go. I do not let her go.

We love – we *love* – and we do not let go.

XXII

HE IS above me.

He is speaking.

He is above me and is speaking and I can *feel* him, I can *hear* him, as I never have before, from specified points of pressure and contact. His hands are no longer bound around her – around *me* – but I can feel where they'd been clutching. My wrists are sore, and my legs are tired. She must have thrashed more than I'd realized.

He speaks again. Words. Language. I know words and language. As did she. She kept her words and language in her brain. Her brain should tell me—

Ah. I ate her brain. I put my knowledge in it instead. Where did I put that knowledge? I rifle and rummage as he speaks a third time. Maybe I can read his lips…? No, I cannot see. Why can't I see?

My eyes are closed.

Oh.

At once, I snap them open. There is little light, for it is still night, but the candle-fire burns with a fierceness I did not expect. My pupils dilate, and the wet film between the balls and the lids replenish themselves as I blink once, twice, three times.

"—yn…?"

His voice echoes out of his chest, unexpectedly deep. Soft. Humans are so *soft*. His face is soft, too, as if seen through hoar; its details are blurry and underdefined. Only when I remember how to utilize my corneas do he and his worries come into focus.

I realize he is saying my name.

"—ryn…?"

He sees *me.*

Though it takes concentrated effort, I pinch the corners of my lips. I lift them. They skim the flesh of his knuckle, tasting soap and sweat, and I am smiling. I am *smiling*. He can see me and he cares and I am *smiling*.

The Master's breath hitches. The gasp of it wedges in his throat, fluttering like a pulse. Like wings.

"Aderyn?" he repeats, fingers unfurling along the curve of my – *my* – face. "Aderyn, is that you?"

Response. Answer. Words. Language. Knowledge. Yes. Yes.

"Yes," I tell him. My own voice resounds in my ears, in my head, in the room. It is loud and reverberating. It is startling, but I am too elated to be alarmed.

I want to make more noises. I want to move my tongue and my limbs. I want to touch. I want to *do*.

I suck down another mouthful of air – it tastes of wax and smoke and makeup and hot skin – and move my arm-elbow-hand jerkily, carefully, to cover his own.

I say again, "Yes, Father."

XXIII

I RECEIVE many compliments.

The Master tells me I am beautiful. The maid tells me she is proud. She joins us sometime later, and we three lay atop the bed, my heart beating so fast I am afraid it will break through my breast. Ribcage shattered, blood everywhere. Another ruined body.

When I speak of these fears, my sires laugh.

"You were brave."

"You did well."

They kiss each other, then kiss me. Different kisses. I like mine better.

I like *being* better.

I feel so much *better*. But though I am no longer sick, the Master says I am.

"My poor cousin," he laments at a gathering, sighing into his wineglass as I nurse a cordial at his side. "Her memories are gone. Victim to a new wife's stress, I expect."

Behind us, the maid feigns remorse. Violet eyes flash. The shock of the pronouncement comes and goes like a draft, the chill it had elicited forgotten within moments.

She is like a different person, the guests say in a hush, hiding behind gloves and ornate fans. Old friends marvel at the change, and family members gawk. They debate my transformation as if I could not hear them before ultimately deciding, *Perhaps this is for the best. The Lady was always a bit…well. How like a doll she is now! Graceful, demure, and poised.*

Concerns are dismissed. The scandal breezes over. A murder of ravens screech outside.

("Who'll sing a psalm?" "I," said the Thrush
"As she sat on a bush, I'll sing a psalm.")

She is not missed.

XXIV

I ALWAYS wanted to sing with her.

Now, I can. I do.

We chant nursery rhymes that harmonize with the church bells, our sweet voice fluting high. Swooping low. Using the window as a mirror, I brush the blonde curls of my favorite doll, the brunette and the redhead watching on in jealousy.

The cradle and its load have vanished. Time is stopped by my shadow.

I am alive.

Beyond frosted glass, a sparrow flits from a dead tree.

XXV

(All the birds of the air fell a-sighing and a-sobbing,
When they heard the bell toll for poor Cock Robin.)

Gretel

Zandra Renwick

GRETEL met Hansel the day her stepmother drove her to Brykerwoods Juvenile Rehabilitation Facility and left her standing in the front hall with no money or phone or anything other than the clothes she wore and two hits of acid hidden in an empty lipstick tube stuffed in her bra.

He was tall and quiet, and thinner even than Gretel. Cigarette burn scars covered one cheek, and he was blind in his left eye from an especially bad night with his father. Gretel thought he was beautiful.

You're beautiful, he told her later that night, after her stepmother had driven away and Brykerwoods orderlies had taken Gretel's leather jacket and the contents of her pockets – but not the lipstick tube they hadn't found in her bra. After she'd found him, like an uncharted territory, or an undiscovered planet, sitting on dirty white linoleum next to a vacant chair in an empty TV room without a television. After she'd had handed him one hit of acid and placed the other under her tongue. *You're beautiful.*

I'm not, she said. *My front teeth jut like fallen tombstones. My nose is the size of a bus and my hair is like strips of rotting bacon and my eyes are small and brown as rabbit turds. You must be tripping.*

And he said, *I am, but that's not why I like you.*

Over the next few days Hansel showed Gretel how not to take the little pleated paper cupful of pills each morning, noon, and evening. Brykerwoods was built on historic land as a private sanatorium for morphine-addicted soldiers after the war; their medications were outdated, their orderlies slow. Mostly, people in charge watched television all day and sucked like hard candies the pills their patients traded them for cigarettes and favors.

The pills were large and hard to swallow, and when Gretel got out of bed at night and pried away the loose segment of baseboard and held her cache of untaken meds in her cupped palms, they glowed like little radioactive pebbles in moonlight filtering past the grating over the high window in her room which never opened.

When the day came – when Gretel and Hansel had saved enough pills between them to trade for the usual unsupervised half hour in the rickety sports equipment shed at the edge of the old battlefield between the massive crumbling sanitorium and the weed-choked soccer field with no nets or chalk lines, just two rusting off-kilter goal frames rising askance from tall dead grass like bleached mammoth bones – when that day came, they poured the pills from their hands onto the desk of the hall orderly like a waterfall of small round stones. He didn't look at them as he stepped from behind the counter and sauntered to the front door, jangling his enormous keyring in counterrhythm to his sucking on one of the pills from his pocket, the pills that tasted like razorblades and deadened Gretel's tongue. No staff member at Brykerwoods had functioning taste buds, and their breath always smelled of bleach.

The orderly led them through the narrow hall, past the ornate grille of the old front door, down the chalky walk and across the field rumored to have seen one of the bloodiest battles of the war. He opened the slatted shed door and they shuffled past him into the small dusty place, one corner decorated with greasy mattress and ragged sheets with the words *Brykerwoods Juvenile Facility* printed across once-starched hems. Gretel closed her eyes and breathed deep, savoring unchemical scents of spiderwebs and old wood.

Thirty minutes, said the hall orderly, tossing a condom in a worn packet to the dirt at their feet. *Thirty minutes, then I come back to get you*, and locked them in from the outside.

Gretel listened to the orderly's keys jingle away. She leaned against Hansel and breathed in cobwebs and the sandalwood scent of his hair, and when she was sure they were completely alone she looked into his face, only barely visible in the dim afternoon light filtering past the cracks between wooden boards of the windowless shed.

Hansel hugged her tight, then gently pushed her behind him and kicked loose rotted boards leaking the most light between planks. They squeezed out the small ragged hole, splinters raking Gretel's back as she shimmied through the rough, narrow gap. She imagined splinters prickling from her flesh like quills.

They ran through breast-high weeds to the trees, leaving behind the raggedy field, the listing shed, the hulking square brick toad of Brykerwoods Juvenile Rehabilitation Facility. He held her hand as they ran, barren trees raking at Gretel's hair and face like zombie fingers, leaving bloody furrows in her cheeks. He caught her arm when she tripped on a root, though her ankle twisted cruelly and she bit her tongue hard against pain. Her side hurt from running, like the sharpened ends of toothbrushes shoved between her ribs, and her breath came short and hard and panting, like a dog's.

When she couldn't run anymore she plunged to her knees in the leaves. The sun had sunk low behind the trees, and though it seemed they should already have crossed the main road a dozen times, they'd seen nothing but forest and dirt and dead scrub. Gretel lay on her back, twigs digging into her spine, her face streaked with hard-caked mud rather than tears and her lungs burning as if drawing fire rather than air.

Hansel lay beside her in the dirt. *You're beautiful*, he murmured in her ear as he stroked her tangled hair and bloody cheeks. *You're beautiful.*

Gretel woke herself with her own violent shivering. Hansel wrapped around her as best he could with his long, thin limbs and bony, large-knuckled hands; but her skin – bared to night air – was covered with cold dew. Her limbs were so icy they burned, and her teeth rattled in her skull as they chattered.

Come, said Hansel, standing, helping her to her feet. *We'll find the road and hitch a ride to somewhere.*

A ride to where? she asked.

He shrugged, looking up at the purpling slivers of dawn sky visible between naked tree branches, and said: *To anywhere.*

They stumbled through the undergrowth in what increasingly felt like circles. Shivers in Gretel's limbs disappeared with the rising sun, replaced with an ache radiating from deep in her bones. Toward the end of the second day, hunger pangs wrenched her stomach and her head felt too large. She no longer thought about where they were going or what they would do; it was enough to concentrate on one shuffling step after another, avoiding gnarls of root and fallen branch and ignoring the jagged pain slicing through her empty stomach as it chewed itself.

After a second night in the cold, her fingers curled into clawlike fists. With great difficulty she scraped small red berries off a stunted bush and shoved them into her mouth. The cramps came a couple hours later, and on the third morning Gretel woke doubled over, retching her body's own juices into the undergrowth. Hansel held back her hair and stroked her arms.

You're beautiful, he told her between heaves. *You're beautiful*.

By midday, Gretel felt well enough to stumble after him like a mindless creature. Her legs felt like broken rubberbands and her head throbbed inside her skull, but he held her hand and led her through the woods. She wanted to simply lie down and wait. She couldn't think past the hammering in her mind to exactly what they'd wait for, so she bit her tongue harder and forced her rubbery legs and leaden feet to follow after him, swallowing the blood in her mouth as if it were sustenance.

A sound like whistling rain made Gretel look up. Directly above, silhouetted against dishwater sky veined with black branches, perched a perfect white bird. It fluttered its wings and hopped from one tree to the next, and they stumbled after it like moths flapping after the flickering light of a moving candle. Gretel ignored the stabbing in her ribcage and the hollow empty feeling of her stomach and the ashes on her tongue. She only dimly sensed Hansel beside her, crashing through dead undergrowth and old leaves. When they reached the clearing she nearly tumbled to the ground at the sudden absence of things over which to trip.

In the middle of the clearing stood a little gingerbread house. Clouds parted overhead. A shaft of perfect yellow light sluiced down to illuminate the glossy cinnamon-candy red of painted trim, the ornate frosted eaves, the sugar-glaze sparkle of beveled glass windows. The white bird trilled once before fluttering directly upward into golden sunlight.

The house looked good enough to eat. Gretel's stomach churned. The sharp tang of bile flooded her mouth as she clutched her stomach and turned to heave again into the brush. When her shudders subsided, she felt Hansel's cool hand on her forehead and the long bony strength of him standing next to her. She drew her hand across her mouth. He tucked her hair behind her ears. Without speaking, he led her through the clearing and up the wide candy-striped steps of the wraparound gingerbread porch to the door.

After his third unanswered knock, he turned the ornate iron of the heavy doorknob, black and slick like licorice. The door – painted thickly and decorated with white garlands like a wedding cake – swung inward, and together they stepped into the warm red and white peppermint old-fashioned kitchen. In one corner hunkered an enormous enamel stove, and in another a broad table heaped high with food.

Who's there?

At the sharp voice Gretel's breath caught in her throat. But when an old woman hobbled in from the hall, Gretel was ashamed: ashamed of the mud from her boots, clumped thickly on the striped kitchen floor; ashamed by the awkward angles of her limbs, which stuck out in all directions; ashamed of her instinctive disgust at the sight of the old woman, who was stooped, and limped, and had two rheumy red puddles for eyes.

The woman smiled vaguely in their direction, and by the questing dip of head and the way she sniffed the air, Gretel could tell she was blind.

You're from that place at the edge of Bryker's Wood, the old woman said. *I smell it on you both, like rotten teeth packed with iodine gauze. You're not the first runaways to make it all the way to my house, poor little things.* She shuffled closer, lifting her hands to their faces. Gretel tried not to flinch at the cold knuckles on her cheeks tracing paths of caked dirt, poking at her lips and the hardened scabs across her cheeks. The scents of opium smoke and dried flowers rose off the stooped shoulders, and something else that made Gretel think of verdigrised pennies.

You sweet little babies feel gaunter than barbed wire, said the woman, her fingers probing the hollows under Hansel's cheekbones, tracing past the line of his jaw downward until her splayed palm pressed against the pulse at the base of his throat. She gestured at the table of food, saying *eat, eat*, and Gretel was ashamed again, this time at the way water flooded her mouth, uncontrollable, as if she were an animal.

But Hansel stepped forward and with dirty hands grabbed fistfuls of cookies and shoved them all into his mouth at once. Crumbs rolled down the front of his filthy shirt to mingle with mud he'd tracked across the candy-striped floor. He slid a butter-slathered pancake from a teetering stack and offered it to Gretel.

They ate until Gretel was afraid she'd throw it all back up, her stomach muscles still sore from the morning's heaving. But the old woman patted her hand and stroked Hansel's hair, and when they couldn't eat any more she led them upstairs to an attic room furnished only with a beautiful white bed, an enormous wardrobe, and a low candlelit table surrounded with cushions. The woman eased herself with a grunt to the pillows, pulling an elaborately carved meerschaum pipe from the folds of her dress. She lit the pipe with the candle, and exhaled a thick haze from the wrinkled hole of her mouth. Smoke streamed into the room and separated to hang low in visible strata which clung together like drowning lovers before breaking apart and swirling away into nothing.

The old woman smiled a witch's smile. She gestured to another pipe – a smaller one of bone – on the table. Hansel tugged his hand from Gretel's with an apologetic smile that made the scars on his face drag his skin into random puckering patterns. He lifted the pipe and reclined, gesturing for Gretel to join him. Up close the cushions weren't comfortable at all, but mushroom slimy and poisonous smelling, with sharper corners than they should've had.

When the witch woman passed the meerschaum pipe, Gretel looked into the red gouges where her eyes should've been, and asked, *Is this opium?*

The witch snorted. *Better; it's my own special blend, cooked up in my cauldron. Besides, this isn't how you smoke opium. Didn't they teach you anything about the soldier's disease at that morphine school?*

Gretel understood she meant Brykerwoods, but the rest of her words meant less than nothing. Her stomach felt heavy, her head light. She reached for the pipe.

The afternoon passed in smoke and silence, though the old woman rose sometime after the pipe went cold and shuffled out, her full skirts leaving swirling patterns in her wake in the hazy air of the room. Hansel lay beside Gretel, stroked her tangled hair and called her beautiful until she fell asleep.

When Gretel woke, it was to a cold empty bed and a hand like a clamp on her arm, shaking. *Wake up, wake up, you worthless creature. You're no better than the last one. I miss the days of battlefield soldiers. No older than you they were, but desperate, and strong. Not lazy and useless like you children of this last century and more.*

The old woman smacked Gretel hard across the face, harder than her stepmother had ever smacked her. A barely-healed wound on her cheek split, and a trickle of warmth ran down her throat. *Hansel!* she cried, flinching from the gnarled hand stronger than it looked, nails sharp and long as talons. *Hansel!*

The woman gestured to the wardrobe, nodding when Gretel moved to open the door. Inside it was lined with bars like a cage, and on the metal floor lay Hansel, eyes closed, chest rising and falling with shallow breaths, his slack fingers curled loosely around the slender bone pipe he'd smoked earlier.

The woman licked her cracked lips. *I can't see your face, little sister,* she said, *but I can taste you in the air like poppy smoke. I was birthed over a century ago from the amputated limbs of 400,000 morphine-addicted soldiers hacking each other's flesh – brother against brother, father against son – to pieces in that field beyond Bryker's Wood. Now, go fetch some wood from out back. We'll stoke the oven, get food into that scarecrow of yours and fatten him up.*

And then the pains started. Pain roiled in Gretel's marrow until the witch brought out the meerschaum pipe and blew smoke in her direction, which she against her will drew deep into her lungs. It filled her mind, making it hazy as the room, until all she could remember was that she couldn't leave Hansel.

And so she drew water from the well. There was no electricity in the gingerbread cottage in the middle of the woods. Gretel spent her days between pains cleaning and cooking, bringing in wood and carrying heaped trays of food to Hansel's cage. The witch was always there, smoke from her pipe as she puffed it smoothing away aches in Gretel's heart and limbs, blanketing her mind in a numbing fog until she almost convinced herself she didn't care what happened to any of them. Almost.

Each day the witch flung open the doors to Hansel's cupboard cage, and each day she'd demand he stick his finger through the bars so she could test it for ripeness. Hansel – with no exercise and nothing to do but eat – was in fact less gaunt than Gretel had ever seen him, but each day at the witch's command he extended the segmented bone stem of his pipe instead of his own finger for the witch to feel and scowl over.

Each night, the witch grumbled about Hansel's skeletal thinness. She'd lie next to Gretel on the big white bed, blow smoke into her face, and smile when she felt the mattress cease to quiver with Gretel's cravings and tremblings. By the second week, the witch began mumbling through her smoke about taking just a limb or two from the boy.

Surely an arm, say, from the elbow down, wouldn't hinder the swelling of his middle, she would mutter, and Gretel would shudder, causing the witch to blow more smoke her direction. By the third week, Gretel had defied the witch's instructions to bring her Hansel's right arm, cutting instead small strips of skin off her own arms, serving them raw to the witch on little salted platters, breathing deep the secondhand smoke from the witch's pipe to keep her legs from collapsing under her. By the fourth week, the witch discovered Gretel's ruse, but rather than becoming angry, she cackled with delight: *Charming you are, my girl, no worthless creature after all. Charming, a good girl, and utterly delicious.*

And so the witch told Gretel to light the fires of the big oven in the kitchen. Gretel moved slowly, her arms and legs where she'd stripped her own flesh to appease the witch's appetite and keep Hansel whole not hurting, exactly – not through the thick haze of pipe smoke which hung around the gingerbread cottage in great white puffy wreaths, sweet and cloying like candied fog – but hindering her movements, slowing her with their lack of elasticity and the eternal burning and ripping and re-ripping of damaged skin.

The witch stumbled over Gretel collapsed on the white kitchen floor. *Oh, little sister,* said the witch. *You've used yourself much more harshly than I have. You've gone too far for my smoke to follow, and now I know how delicious you are, I can't let that happen. Here; I've got a special brew to put all the strength back into you, so you can serve yourself up properly, like a good, obedient girl.*

The witch dug in the folds of her skirt for what Gretel assumed was the meerschaum, but instead pulled out a silver syringe. It was made of antique rippled glass chased with silver, studded with tiny garnets like drops of blood. The witch probed the inside of Gretel's limp arm, looking for a vein but finding only great swaths of ravaged, unhealed wounds in long jagged strips.

Little sister, plunge this into a vein where it'll do you the most good.

Gretel shifted her head feebly, following the witch's movements and gropings at her arm. *I've never done that before*, she said, her voice thin in her throat.

Then what do they teach these days at that morphine school? The witch pantomimed, thrusting an imagined needle into her own vein and pressing the plunger. *One good vein, then a short climb into the lovely warm oven, and you'll never be cold or hurt again. Be a good girl.* She laid the antique tube of glass and silver in Gretel's palm and curled her fingers over the cold cylinder. *Be a good girl; a good, delicious girl.*

Gretel lifted the syringe, heavy and awkward and not like anything she'd felt or seen before, and the witch leaned close, lifting a strand of Gretel's hair to her lips and putting it in her mouth just as Gretel shoved the syringe into the woman's arm and hammered the plunger with her other fist.

The witch didn't cry out, but her body went rigid. Her teeth clamped down on the lock of Gretel's hair, and Gretel dragged herself backward across the candy-striped floor, ignoring the ripping sound and the fresh welling blood from her scalp. She fumbled with numb fingers in the folds of the witch's full skirts, finding hidden pockets containing the carved meerschaum pipe, the small packets of dark brown smoking cake, the single iron key. Leaving all but the key scattered about the taut prone body of the witch, Gretel dragged herself to the stairs. She clawed up one stair, then the next, certain at every moment the witch would rise and fly up behind her, her unnaturally strong claws scrabbling at Gretel's legs like the talons of rabid foxes, her old-penny breath sweet and metallic, her voice as mocking as Gretel's stepmother's: *If only you'd been a good girl, your father and I could've loved you...why can't you just be a good, obedient girl?*

With fingers scraped bloody by her climb, Gretel opened Hansel's cupboard. Twice, the key had slipped from her red-slick fingers and fell to the ground, but on the third try the lock tumbled, and the iron grate swung wide. Hansel pulled himself out and fell immediately to the floor. Clinging together, they rose. Gretel had no strength to stand, but enough to prop up Hansel, and he did the same for her. Reeling, stumbling, they clutched and tugged each other across floor and down stairs. As they skirted the rigid body of the witch Hansel paused to scoop something up.

You'll need this, he said, opening his palm and showing Gretel the small meerschaum pipe and brown cake. *You'll need this for when the pain starts.*

Gretel closed her bloody fingers on the contents of his palm and threw everything into the flames of the open oven. *No.*

He looked into her eyes and said nothing, but finally drew the bone pipe from his pocket and flung it after the rest. It hit the fire with a shower of sparks, which scorched peppermint floor and ignited candyfloss curtains, licking glossy red cinnamon trim. They staggered out the front door and down the wide steps, and at the edge of the clearing Gretel glanced over her shoulder to watch the frosted gingerbread eaves of the little house go up in a whoosh of flame.

They stumbled through night-dark woods, finding the main road in what seemed like minutes. Pains wracked Gretel's body as they crouched to wait for a ride to somewhere by someone, anywhere by anyone, and Hansel cradled her against him, stroking her arms where she'd cut strips from her flesh to save his, her knuckles lacerated where she'd worked to keep him fed, the bloody patch on her scalp where she'd pulled herself from the witch to save him.

You're beautiful, he whispered over and over in her ear as he touched her scars and the sun crested the rim of trees, throwing their silhouettes stark and jagged against the sky. *You're beautiful.*

The Old House in Vauxhall Walk

Charlotte Riddell

Chapter One

"HOUSELESS – homeless – hopeless!"

Many a one who had before him trodden that same street must have uttered the same words – the weary, the desolate, the hungry, the forsaken, the waifs and strays of struggling humanity that are always coming and going, cold, starving and miserable, over the pavements of Lambeth Parish; but it is open to question whether they were ever previously spoken with a more thorough conviction of their truth, or with a feeling of keener self-pity, than by the young man who hurried along Vauxhall Walk one rainy winter's night, with no overcoat on his shoulders and no hat on his head.

A strange sentence for one-and-twenty to give expression to – and it was stranger still to come from the lips of a person who looked like and who was a gentleman. He did not appear either to have sunk very far down in the good graces of Fortune. There was no sign or token which would have induced a passer-by to imagine he had been worsted after a long fight with calamity. His boots were not worn down at the heels or broken at the toes, as many, many boots were which dragged and shuffled and scraped along the pavement. His clothes were good and fashionably cut, and innocent of the rents and patches and tatters that slunk wretchedly by, crouched in doorways, and held out a hand mutely appealing for charity. His face was not pinched with famine or lined with wicked wrinkles, or brutalised by drink and debauchery, and yet he said and thought he was hopeless, and almost in his young despair spoke the words aloud.

It was a bad night to be about with such a feeling in one's heart. The rain was cold, pitiless and increasing. A damp, keen wind blew down the cross streets leading from the river. The fumes of the gas works seemed to fall with the rain. The roadway was muddy; the pavement greasy; the lamps burned dimly; and that dreary district of London looked its very gloomiest and worst.

Certainly not an evening to be abroad without a home to go to, or a sixpence in one's pocket, yet this was the position of the young gentleman who, without a hat, strode along Vauxhall Walk, the rain beating on his unprotected head.

Upon the houses, so large and good – once inhabited by well-to-do citizens, now let out for the most part in floors to weekly tenants – he looked enviously. He would have given much to have had a room, or even part of one. He had been walking for a long time, ever since dark in fact, blind dark falls soon in December. He was tired and cold and hungry, and he saw no prospect save of pacing the streets all night.

As he passed one of the lamps, the light falling on his face revealed handsome young features, a mobile, sensitive mouth, and that particular formation of the eyebrows – not a frown exactly, but a certain draw of the brows – often considered to bespeak genius, but which more surely accompanies an impulsive organisation easily pleased, easily depressed, capable of suffering very keenly or of enjoying fully. In his short life he had not enjoyed much, and he had suffered a good deal. That night, when he walked bareheaded through the rain, affairs had come to a crisis.

So far as he in his despair felt able to see or reason, the best thing he could do was to die. The world did not want him; he would be better out of it.

The door of one of the houses stood open, and he could see in the dimly lighted hall some few articles of furniture waiting to be removed. A van stood beside the curb, and two men were lifting a table into it as he, for a second, paused.

"Ah," he thought, "even those poor people have some place to go to, some shelter provided, while I have not a roof to cover my head, or a shilling to get a night's lodging." And he went on fast, as if memory were spurring him, so fast that a man running after had some trouble to overtake him.

"Master Graham! Master Graham!" this man exclaimed, breathlessly; arid, thus addressed, the young fellow stopped as if he had been shot.

"Who are you that know me?" he asked, facing round.

"I'm William; don't you remember William, Master Graham? And, Lord's sake, sir, what are you doing out a night like this without your hat?"

"I forgot it," was the answer; "and I did not care to go back and fetch it."

'then why don't you buy another, sir? You'll catch your death of cold; and besides, you'll excuse me, sir, but it does look odd."

"I know that," said Master Graham grimly; "but I haven't a halfpenny in the world."

"Have you and the master, then—" began the man, but there he hesitated and stopped.

"Had a quarrel? Yes, and one that will last us our lives," finished the other, with a bitter laugh.

"And where are you going now?"

"Going! Nowhere, except to seek out the softest paving stone, or the shelter of an arch."

"You are joking, sir."

"I don't feel much in a mood for jesting either."

"Will you come back with me, Master Graham? We are just at the last of our moving, but there is a spark of fire still in the grate, and it would be better talking out of this rain. Will you come, sir?"

"Come! Of course I will come," said the young fellow, and, turning, they retraced their steps to the house he had looked into as he passed along.

An old, old house, with long, wide hall, stairs low, easy of ascent, with deep cornices to the ceilings, and oak floorings, and mahogany doors, which still spoke mutely of the wealth and stability of the original owner, who lived before the Tradescants and Ashmoles were thought of, and had been sleeping far longer than they, in St Mary's churchyard, hard by the archbishop's palace.

"Step upstairs, sir," entreated the departing tenant; "it's cold down here, with the door standing wide."

"Had you the whole house, then, William?" asked Graham Coulton, in some surprise.

"The whole of it, and right sorry I, for one, am to leave it; but nothing else would serve my wife. This room, sir," and with a little conscious pride, William, doing the honours of his late residence, asked his guest into a spacious apartment occupying the full width of the house on the first floor.

Tired though he was, the young man could not repress an exclamation of astonishment.

"Why, we have nothing so large as this at home, William," he said.

"It's a fine house," answered William, raking the embers together as he spoke and throwing some wood upon them; "but, like many a good family, it has come down in the world."

There were four windows in the room, shuttered close; they had deep, low seats, suggestive of pleasant days gone by; when, well-curtained and well-cushioned, they formed snug retreats for the children, and sometimes for adults also; there was no furniture left, unless an oaken settle beside the hearth, and a large mirror let into the panelling at the opposite end of the apartment, with a black marble console table beneath it, could be so considered; but the very absence of chairs and tables enabled the magnificent proportions of the chamber to be seen to full advantage, and there was nothing to distract the attention from the ornamented ceiling, the panelled walls, the old-world chimney-piece so quaintly carved, and the fireplace lined with tiles, each one of which contained a picture of some scriptural or allegorical subject.

"Had you been staying on here, William," said Coulton, flinging himself wearily on the settle, "I'd have asked you to let me stop where I am for the night."

"If you can make shift, sir, there is nothing as I am aware of to prevent you stopping," answered the man, fanning the wood into a flame. "I shan't take the key back to the landlord till tomorrow, and this would be better for you than the cold streets at any rate."

"Do you really mean what you say?" asked the other eagerly. "I should be thankful to lie here; I feel dead beat."

"Then stay, Master Graham, and welcome. I'll fetch a basket of coals I was going to put in the van, and make up a good fire, so that you can warm yourself, then I must run round to the other house for a minute or two, but it's not far, and I'll be back as soon as ever I can."

"Thank you, William; you were always good to me," said the young man gratefully. "This is delightful," and he stretched his numbed hands over the blazing wood, and looked round the room with a satisfied smile.

"I did not expect to get into such quarters," he remarked, as his friend in need reappeared, carrying a half-bushel basket full of coals, with which he proceeded to make up a roaring fire. "I am sure the last thing I could have imagined was meeting with anyone I knew in Vauxhall Walk."

"Where were you coming from, Master Graham?" asked William curiously.

"From old Melfield's. I was at his school once, you know, and he has now retired, and is living upon the proceeds of years of robbery in Kennington Oval. I thought, perhaps he would lend me a pound, or offer me a night's lodging, or even a glass of wine; but, oh dear, no. He took the moral tone, and observed he could have nothing to say to a son who defied his father's authority.

He gave me plenty of advice, but nothing else, and showed me out into the rain with a bland courtesy, for which I could have struck him."

William muttered something under his breath which was not a blessing, and added aloud:

"You are better here, sir, I think, at any rate. I'll be back in less than half an hour."

Left to himself, young Coulton took off his coat, and shifting the settle a little, hung it over the end to dry. With his handkerchief he rubbed some of the wet out of his hair; then, perfectly exhausted, he lay down before the fire and, pillowing his head on his arm, fell fast asleep.

He was awakened nearly an hour afterwards by the sound of someone gently stirring the fire and moving quietly about the room. Starting into a sitting posture, he looked around him, bewildered for a moment, and then, recognising his humble friend, said laughingly:

"I had lost myself; I could not imagine where I was."

"I am sorry to see you here, sir," was the reply; "but still this is better than being out of doors. It has come on a nasty night. I brought a rug round with me that, perhaps, you would wrap yourself in."

"I wish, at the same time, you had brought me something to eat," said the young man, laughing.

"Are you hungry, then, sir?" asked William, in a tone of concern.

"Yes; I have had nothing to eat since breakfast. The governor and I commenced rowing the minute we sat down to luncheon, and I rose and left the table. But hunger does not signify; I am dry and warm, and can forget the other matter in sleep."

"And it's too late now to buy anything," soliloquised the man; "the shops are all shut long ago.

"Do you think, sir," he added, brightening, "you could manage some bread and cheese?"

"Do I think – I should call it a perfect feast," answered Graham Coulton. "But never mind about food tonight, William; you have had trouble enough, and to spare, already."

William's only answer was to dart to the door and run downstairs. Presently he reappeared, carrying in one hand bread and cheese wrapped up in paper, and in the other a pewter measure full of beer.

"It's the best I could do, sir," he said apologetically. "I had to beg this from the landlady."

"Here's to her good health!" exclaimed the young fellow gaily, taking a long pull at the tankard. "That tastes better than champagne in my father's house."

"Won't he be uneasy about you?" ventured William, who, having by this time emptied the coals, was now seated on the inverted basket, looking wistfully at the relish with which the son of the former master was eating his bread and cheese.

"No," was the decided answer. "When he hears it pouring cats and dogs he will only hope I am out in the deluge, and say a good drenching will cool my pride."

"I do not think you are right there," remarked the man.

"But I am sure I am. My father always hated me, as he hated my mother."

"Begging your pardon, sir; he was over fond of your mother."

"If you had heard what he said about her today, you might find reason to alter your opinion. He told me I resembled her in mind as well as body; that I was a coward, a simpleton, and a hypocrite."

"He did not mean it, sir."

"He did, every word. He does think I am a coward, because I – I—" And the young fellow broke into a passion of hysterical tears.

"I don't half like leaving you here alone," said William, glancing round the room with a quick trouble in his eyes; "but I have no place fit to ask you to stop, and I am forced to go myself, because I am night watchman, and must be on at twelve o'clock."

"I shall be right enough," was the answer. "Only I mustn't talk any more of my father. Tell me about yourself, William. How did you manage to get such a big house, and why are you leaving it?"

"The landlord put me in charge, sir; and it was my wife's fancy not to like it."

"Why did she not like it?"

"She felt desolate alone with the children at night," answered William, turning away his head; then added, next minute: "Now, sir, if you think I can do no more for you, I had best be off. Time's getting on. I'll look round tomorrow morning."

"Goodnight," said the young fellow, stretching out his hand, which the other took as freely and frankly as it was offered. "What should I have done this evening if I had not chanced to meet you?"

"I don't think there is much chance in the world, Master Graham," was the quiet answer. "I do hope you will rest well, and not be the worse for your wetting."

"No fear of that," was the rejoinder, and the next minute the young man found himself all alone in the Old House in Vauxhall Walk.

Chapter Two

LYING on the settle, with the fire burnt out, and the room in total darkness, Graham Coulton dreamed a curious dream. He thought he awoke from deep slumber to find a log smouldering away upon the hearth, and the mirror at the end of the apartment reflecting fitful gleams of light.

He could not understand how it came to pass that, far away as he was from the glass, he was able to see everything in it; but he resigned himself to the difficulty without astonishment, as people generally do in dreams.

Neither did he feel surprised when he beheld the outline of a female figure seated beside the fire, engaged in picking something out of her lap and dropping it with a despairing gesture.

He heard the mellow sound of gold, and knew she was lifting and dropping sovereigns. He turned a little so as to see the person engaged in such a singular and meaningless manner, and found that, where there had been no chair on the previous night, there was a chair now, on which was seated an old, wrinkled hag, her clothes poor and ragged, a mob cap barely covering her scant white hair, her cheeks sunken, her nose hooked, her fingers more like talons than aught else as they dived down into the heap of gold, portions of which they lifted but to scatter mournfully.

"Oh! My lost life," she moaned, in a voice of the bitterest anguish. "Oh! My lost life – for one day, for one hour of it again!"

Out of the darkness – out of the corner of the room where the shadows lay deepest – out from the gloom abiding near the door – out from the dreary night, with their sodden feet and wet dripping from their heads, came the old men and the young children, the worn women and the weary hearts, whose misery that gold might have relieved, but whose wretchedness it mocked.

Round that miser, who once sat gloating as she now sat lamenting, they crowded – all those pale, sad shapes – the aged of days, the infant of hours, the sobbing outcast, honest poverty, repentant vice; but one low cry proceeded from those pale lips – a cry for help she might have given, but which she withheld.

They closed about her, all together, as they had done singly in life; they prayed, they sobbed, they entreated; with haggard eyes the figure regarded the poor she had repulsed, the children against whose cry she had closed her ears, the old people she had suffered to starve and die for want of what would have been the merest trifle to her; then, with a terrible scream, she raised her lean arms above her head, and sank down – down – the gold scattering as it fell out of her lap, and rolling along the floor, till its gleam was lost in the outer darkness beyond.

Then Graham Coulton awoke in good earnest, with the perspiration oozing from every pore, with a fear and an agony upon him such as he had never before felt in all his existence, and with the sound of the heart-rending cry – "Oh! My lost life" – still ringing in his ears.

Mingled with all, too, there seemed to have been some lesson for him which he had forgotten, that, try as he would, eluded his memory, and which, in the very act of waking, glided away.

He lay for a little thinking about all this, and then, still heavy with sleep, retraced his way into dreamland once more.

It was natural, perhaps, that, mingling with the strange fantasies which follow in the train of night and darkness, the former vision should recur, and the young man ere long found himself toiling through scene after scene wherein the figure of the woman he had seen seated beside a dying fire held principal place.

He saw her walking slowly across the floor munching a dry crust – she who could have purchased all the luxuries wealth can command; on the hearth, contemplating her, stood a man of commanding presence, dressed in the fashion of long ago. In his eyes there was a dark look of anger, on his lips a curling smile of disgust, and somehow, even in his sleep, the dreamer understood it was the ancestor to the descendant he beheld – that the house put to mean uses in which he lay had never so far descended from its high estate, as the woman possessed of so pitiful a soul, contaminated with the most despicable and insidious vice poor humanity knows, for all other vices seem to have connection with the flesh, but the greed of the miser eats into the very soul.

Filthy of person, repulsive to look at, hard of heart as she was, he yet beheld another phantom, which, coming into the room, met her almost on the threshold, taking her by the hand, and pleading, as it seemed, for assistance. He could not hear all that passed, but a word now and then fell upon his ear. Some talk of former days; some mention of a fair young mother – an appeal, as it seemed, to a time when they were tiny brother and sister, and the accursed greed for gold had not divided them. All in vain; the hag only answered him as she had answered the children, and the young girls, and the old people in his former vision. Her heart was as invulnerable to natural affection as it had proved to human sympathy. He begged, as it appeared, for aid to avert some bitter misfortune or terrible disgrace, and adamant might have been found more yielding to his prayer. Then the figure standing on the hearth changed to an angel, which folded its wings mournfully over its face, and the man, with bowed head, slowly left the room.

Even as he did so the scene changed again; it was night once more, and the miser wended her way upstairs. From below, Graham Coulton fancied he watched her toiling wearily from step to step. She had aged strangely since the previous scenes. She moved with difficulty; it seemed the greatest exertion for her to creep from step to step, her skinny hand traversing the balusters with slow and painful deliberateness. Fascinated, the young man's eyes followed the progress of that feeble, decrepit woman. She was solitary in a desolate house, with a deeper blackness than the darkness of night waiting to engulf her.

It seemed to Graham Coulton that after that he lay for a time in a still, dreamless sleep, upon awaking from which he found himself entering a chamber as sordid and unclean in its appointments as the woman of his previous vision had been in her person. The poorest labourer's wife would have gathered more comforts around her than that room contained. A four-poster bedstead without hangings of any kind – a blind drawn up awry – an old carpet covered with dust, and dirt on the floor – a rickety washstand with all the paint worn off it – an ancient mahogany dressing table, and a cracked glass spotted all over – were all the objects he could at first discern, looking at the room through that dim light which oftentimes obtains in dreams.

By degrees, however, he perceived the outline of someone lying huddled on the bed. Drawing nearer, he found it was that of the person whose dreadful presence seemed to pervade the house.

What a terrible sight she looked, with her thin white locks scattered over the pillow, with what were mere remnants of blankets gathered about her shoulders, with her claw-like fingers clutching the clothes, as though even in sleep she was guarding her gold!

An awful and a repulsive spectacle, but not with half the terror in it of that which followed.

Even as the young man looked he heard stealthy footsteps on the stairs. Then he saw first one man and then his fellow steal cautiously into the room. Another second, and the pair stood beside the bed, murder in their eyes.

Graham Coulton tried to shout – tried to move, but the deterrent power which exists in dreams only tied his tongue and paralysed his limbs. He could but hear and look, and what he heard and saw was this: aroused suddenly from sleep, the woman started, only to receive a blow from one of the ruffians, whose fellow followed his lead by plunging a knife into her breast.

Then, with a gurgling scream, she fell back on the bed, and at the same moment, with a cry, Graham Coulton again awoke, to thank heaven it was but an illusion.

Chapter Three

"I HOPE you slept well, sir." It was William, who, coming into the hall with the sunlight of a fine bright morning streaming after him asked this question: "Had you a good night's rest?"

Graham Coulton laughed, and answered:

"Why, faith, I was somewhat in the case of Paddy, 'who could not slape for dhraming'. I slept well enough, I suppose, but whether it was in consequence of the row with my dad, or the hard bed, or the cheese – most likely the bread and cheese so late at night – I dreamt all the night long, the most extraordinary dreams. Some old woman kept cropping up, and I saw her murdered."

"You don't say that, sir?" said William nervously.

"I do, indeed," was the reply. "However, that is all gone and past. I have been down in the kitchen and had a good wash, and I am as fresh as a daisy, and as hungry as a hunter; and, oh, William, can you get me any breakfast?"

"Certainly, Master Graham. I have brought round a kettle, and I will make the water boil immediately. I suppose, sir" – this tentatively – "you'll be going home today?"

"Home!" repeated the young man. "Decidedly not. I'll never go home again till I return with some medal hung to my coat, or a leg or arm cut off. I've thought it all out, William. I'll go and enlist. There's a talk of war; and, living or dead, my father shall have reason to retract his opinion about my being a coward."

"I am sure the admiral never thought you anything of the sort, sir," said William. "Why, you have the pluck of ten!"

"Not before him," answered the young fellow sadly.

"You'll do nothing rash, Master Graham; you won't go 'listing, or aught of that sort, in your anger?"

"If I do not, what is to become of me?" asked the other. "I cannot dig – to beg I am ashamed. Why, but for you, I should not have had a roof over my head last night."

"Not much of a roof, I am afraid, sir."

"Not much of a roof!" repeated the young man. "Why, who could desire a better? What a capital room this is," he went on, looking around the apartment, where William was now kindling a fire; "one might dine twenty people here easily!"

"If you think so well of the place, Master Graham, you might stay here for a while, till you have made up your mind what you are going to do. The landlord won't make any objection, I am very sure."

"Oh! Nonsense; he would want a long rent for a house like this."

"I dare say; if he could get it," was William's significant answer.

"What do you mean? Won't the place let?"

"No, sir. I did not tell you last night, but there was a murder done here, and people are shy of the house ever since."

"A murder! What sort of a murder? Who was murdered?"

"A woman, Master Graham – the landlord's sister; she lived here all alone, and was supposed to have money. Whether she had or not, she was found dead from a stab in her breast, and if there ever was any money, it must have been taken at the same time, for none ever was found in the house from that day to this."

"Was that the reason your wife would not stop here?" asked the young man, leaning against the mantelshelf, and looking thoughtfully down on William.

"Yes, sir. She could not stand it any longer; she got that thin and nervous one would have believed it possible; she never saw anything, but she said she heard footsteps and voices, and then when she walked through the hall, or up the staircase, someone always seemed to be following her. We put the children to sleep in that big room you had last night, and they declared they often saw an old woman sitting by the hearth. Nothing ever came my way," finished William, with a laugh; "I was always ready to go to sleep the minute my head touched the pillow."

"Were not the murderers discovered?" asked Graham Coulton.

"No, sir; the landlord, Miss Tynan's brother, had always lain under the suspicion of it – quite wrongfully, I am very sure – but he will never clear himself now. It was known he came and asked her for help a day or two before the murder, and it was also known he was able within a week or two to weather whatever trouble had been harassing him. Then, you see, the money was never found; and, altogether, people scarce knew what to think."

"Humph!" ejaculated Graham Coulton, and he took a few turns up and down the apartment. "Could I go and see this landlord?"

"Surely, sir, if you had a hat," answered William, with such a serious decorum that the young man burst out laughing.

"That is an obstacle, certainly," he remarked, "and I must make a note do instead. I have a pencil in my pocket, so here goes."

Within half an hour from the dispatch of that note William was back again with a sovereign; the landlord's compliments, and he would be much obliged if Mr. Coulton could 'step round'.

"You'll do nothing rash, sir," entreated William.

"Why, man," answered the young fellow, "one may as well be picked off by a ghost as a bullet. What is there to be afraid of?"

William only shook his head. He did not think his young master was made of the stuff likely to remain alone in a haunted house and solve the mystery it assuredly contained by dint of his own unassisted endeavours. And yet when Graham Coulton came out of the landlord's house he looked more bright and gay than usual, and walked up the Lambeth road to the place where William awaited his return, humming an air as he paced along.

"We have settled the matter," he said. "And now if the dad wants his son for Christmas, it will trouble him to find him."

"Don't say that, Master Graham, don't," entreated the man, with a shiver; "maybe after all it would have been better if you had never happened to chance upon Vauxhall Walk."

"Don't croak, William," answered the young man; "if it was not the best day's work I ever did for myself I'm a Dutchman."

During the whole of that forenoon and afternoon, Graham Coulton searched diligently for the missing treasurc Mr. Tynan assured him had never been discovered. Youth is confident and self-opinionated, and this fresh explorer felt satisfied that, though others had failed, he would be successful. On the second floor he found one door locked, but he did not pay much attention to that at the moment, as he believed if there was anything concealed it was more likely to be found in the lower than the upper part of the house. Late into the evening he pursued his researches in the kitchen and cellars and old-fashioned cupboards, of which the basement had an abundance.

It was nearly eleven, when, engaged in poking about amongst the empty bins of a wine cellar as large as a family vault, he suddenly felt a rush of cold air at his back. Moving, his candle was instantly extinguished, and in the very moment of being left in darkness he saw, standing in the doorway, a woman, resembling her who had haunted his dreams overnight.

He rushed with outstretched hands to seize her, but clutched only air. He relit his candle, and closely examined the basement, shutting off communication with the ground floor ere doing so.

All in vain. Not a trace could he find of living creature – not a window was open – not a door unbolted.

"It is very odd," he thought, as, after securely fastening the door at the top of the staircase, he searched the whole upper portion of the house, with the exception of the one room mentioned.

"I must get the key of that tomorrow," he decided, standing gloomily with his back to the fire and his eyes wandering about the drawing room, where he had once again taken up his abode.

Even as the thought passed through his mind, he saw standing in the open doorway a woman with white dishevelled hair, clad in mean garments, ragged and dirty. She lifted her hand and shook it at him with a menacing gesture, and then, just as he was darting towards her, a wonderful thing occurred.

From behind the great mirror there glided a second female figure, at the sight of which the first turned and fled, littering piercing shrieks as the other followed her from storey to storey.

Sick almost with terror, Graham Coulton watched the dreadful pair as they fled upstairs past the locked room to the top of the house.

It was a few minutes before he recovered his self-possession. When he did so, and searched the upper apartments, he found them totally empty.

That night, ere lying down before the fire, he carefully locked and bolted the drawing-room door; before he did more he drew the heavy settle in front of it, so that if the lock were forced no entrance could be effected without considerable noise.

For some time he lay awake, then dropped into a deep sleep, from which he was awakened suddenly by a noise as if of something scuffling stealthily behind the wainscot. He raised himself on his elbow and listened, and, to his consternation, beheld seated at the opposite side of the hearth the same woman he had seen before in his dreams, lamenting over her gold.

The fire was not quite out, and at that moment shot up a last tongue of flame. By the light, transient as it was, he saw that the figure pressed a ghostly finger to its lips, and by the turn of its head and the attitude of its body seemed to be listening.

He listened also – indeed, he was too much frightened to do aught else; more and more distinct grew the sounds which had aroused him, a stealthy rustling coming nearer and nearer – up and up it seemed, behind the wainscot.

"It is rats," thought the young man, though, indeed, his teeth were almost chattering in his head with fear. But then in a moment he saw what disabused him of that idea – the gleam of a candle or lamp through a crack in the panelling. He tried to rise, he strove to shout – all in vain; and, sinking down, remembered nothing more till he awoke to find the grey light of an early morning stealing through one of the shutters he had left partially unclosed.

For hours after his breakfast, which he scarcely touched, long after William had left him at midday, Graham Coulton, having in the morning made a long and close survey of the house, sat thinking before the fire, then, apparently having made up his mind, he put on the hat he had bought, and went out.

When he returned the evening shadows were darkening down, but the pavements were full of people going marketing, for it was Christmas Eve, and all who had money to spend seemed bent on shopping.

It was terribly dreary inside the old house that night. Through the deserted rooms Graham could feel that ghostly semblance was wandering mournfully. When he turned his back he knew she was flitting from the mirror to the fire, from the fire to the mirror; but he was not afraid of her now – he was far more afraid of another matter he had taken in hand that day.

The horror of the silent house grew and grew upon him. He could hear the beating of his own heart in the dead quietude which reigned from garret to cellar.

At last William came; but the young man said nothing to him of what was in his mind. He talked to him cheerfully and hopefully enough – wondered where his father would think he had got to, and hoped Mr. Tynan might send him some Christmas pudding. Then the man said it was time for him to go, and, when Mr. Coulton went downstairs to the hall-door, remarked the key was not in it.

"No," was the answer, "I took it out today, to oil it."

"It wanted oiling," agreed William, "for it worked terribly stiff." Having uttered which truism he departed.

Very slowly the young man retraced his way to the drawing room, where he only paused to lock the door on the outside; then taking off his boots he went up to the top of the house, where, entering the front attic, he waited patiently in darkness and in silence.

It was a long time, or at least it seemed long to him, before he heard the same sound which had aroused him on the previous night – a stealthy rustling – then a rush of cold air – then cautious footsteps – then the quiet opening of a door below.

It did not take as long in action as it has required to tell. In a moment the young man was out on the landing and had closed a portion of the panelling on the wall which stood open; noiselessly he crept back to the attic window, unlatched it, and sprung a rattle, the sound of which echoed far and near through the deserted streets, then rushing down the stairs, he encountered a man who, darting past him, made for the landing above; but perceiving the way of escape closed, fled down again, to find Graham struggling desperately with his fellow.

"Give him the knife – come along," he said savagely; and next instant Graham felt something like a hot iron through his shoulder, and then heard a thud, as one of the men, tripping in his rapid flight, fell from the top of the stairs to the bottom.

At the same moment there came a crash, as if the house was falling, and faint, sick, and bleeding, young Coulton lay insensible on the threshold of the room where Miss Tynan had been murdered.

When he recovered he was in the dining room, and a doctor was examining his wound.

Near the door a policeman stiffly kept guard. The hall was full of people; all the misery and vagabondism the streets contain at that hour was crowding in to see what had happened.

Through the midst two men were being conveyed to the station house; one, with his head dreadfully injured, on a stretcher, the other handcuffed, uttering frightful imprecations as he went.

After a time the house was cleared of the rabble, the police took possession of it, and Mr. Tynan was sent for.

"What was that dreadful noise?" asked Graham feebly, now seated on the floor, with his back resting against the wall.

"I do not know. Was there a noise?" said Mr. Tynan, humouring his fancy, as he thought.

"Yes, in the drawing room, I think; the key is in my pocket."

Still humouring the wounded lad, Mr. Tynan took the key and ran upstairs.

When he unlocked the door, what a sight met his eyes! The mirror had fallen – it was lying all over the floor shivered into a thousand pieces; the console table had been borne down by its weight, and the marble slab was shattered as well. But this was not what chained his attention.

Hundreds, thousands of gold pieces were scattered about, and an aperture behind the glass contained boxes filled with securities amid deeds amid bonds, the possession of which had cost his sister her life.

* * *

"Well, Graham, and what do you want?" asked Admiral Coulton that evening as his eldest-born appeared before him, looking somewhat pale but otherwise unchanged.

"I want nothing," was the answer, "but to ask your forgiveness. William has told me all the story I never knew before; and, if you let me, I will try to make it up to you for the trouble you have had. I am provided for," went on the young fellow, with a nervous laugh; "I have made my fortune since I left you, and another man's fortune as well."

"I think you are out of your senses," said the Admiral shortly.

"No, sir, I have found them," was the answer; "and I mean to strive and make a better thing of my life than I should ever have done had I not gone to the Old House in Vauxhall Walk."

"Vauxhall Walk! What is the lad talking about?"

"I will tell you, sir, if I may sit down," was Graham Coulton's answer, and then he told his story.

The Great Indoors

Zach Shephard

LINDSEY HELD the bone between thumb and forefinger, admiring it as she drove. It was just a tiny thing: maybe an inch long and slender as a twig, with nicks along its dirty white surface. Probably a piece of a bird, but Lindsey hoped for something more interesting. A badger's toe, maybe? She wondered…

No, it was too late to go back and search for a matching claw; the red summer sky was already fading toward night. And besides, she'd had enough hiking for one day.

Her grandparents' house stood tall on the street corner, a two-story bully intimidating the neighborhood's younger homes. Its blue-gray paint peeled like a healing sunburn, while the roof's sharp silhouette blotted out arriving stars. Lindsey couldn't help but smile – the place was creepy as hell, in the best way possible. Part of her hoped her grandparents would extend their trip by another week.

She pulled into the narrow driveway alongside the house and parked just before the back alley. Four short steps led up to the side door. As Lindsey worked the lock, her phone rang.

"Shit," she muttered, checking the caller ID. Just what she needed: a call from Mom. Part of her wanted to ignore it – to take the bone inside and get right to work on her little project. After all, her horror-art blog – the pseudonymously named *Nightmares by Nalia* – had gone entirely too long without an update, and she hated to disappoint her followers. But if she didn't answer the phone, it would ring throughout the evening. She brought it to her ear.

"Hi, Mom."

"Two hours. That's how long I've been trying to reach you. *Two. Hours.*"

"I was at the park."

"With whom?"

Lindsey cringed. She knew where this was going.

"No one. I went alone."

"Hm."

Silence, as dark as the hall Lindsey stepped into. She busied herself with her boot-strings at the foot of the stairs, not wanting to fill the conversational void.

"What's his name?" her mother asked.

"Mom, there's no guy."

"Well, whoever he is, you'd better not be bringing him back to your grandparents' house. They'd throw a fit if they knew you'd had a boy over."

Lindsey bit back a response. She wasn't seeing anyone. And she probably never *would* until she moved out of her parents' house. Her mother's nosiness had ruined her last relationship.

"I swear," she said, moving down the hall, "I've been by myself this whole time. Just been watching some movies."

"*Movies?*"

Right away, Lindsey recognized her mistake. She cursed her own stupidity as she stepped into the kitchen and flicked on the lights.

"I don't want you watching those horror movies at your grandparents' house. I don't want you watching them *anywhere*. You need to come home."

"Grandma and Grandpa asked me to watch the house."

"They didn't ask you to stay overnight. Water the plants, take in the mail – that's it. You've been gone two days. It's time to come back. We've got church in the morning."

"Mom, I'm twenty-four. If I don't want to go to church, I—"

A brief skittering sound emerged from the hall. It was a quick, muted thing, like fingers drumming carpet. Silence followed.

Lindsey poked her head out of the kitchen. At the end of the dark hall, the side door was open.

"Sorry, Mom – I've gotta go."

"Are you coming home?"

"No, but—"

"Fine. Just remember that Jesus loves you, even if you don't love him."

The call ended. Lindsey set her phone on the counter a little too hard, and placed the bone by its side. She moved into the hall.

"Wonderful," she said, eyeing the opened door. If Mom hadn't been distracting her, she wouldn't have forgotten to close it. Now she'd have to chase out whatever critter had wandered in. The bone would have to wait.

She moved to the door. Anything coming inside could have shot straight up the staircase. She wasn't thrilled about conducting a search.

Outside, a cat meowed.

Lindsey looked out. Across the driveway, standing just outside the neighbor's fence, was a black-and-white cat.

Lindsey smiled with relief. "Oreo," she said. "You're supposed to stay in your own yard, you goof." She descended the steps and approached the cat. "If you're hungry, all you've gotta do is ask. No need to sneak in."

When she got close enough, she realized the cat wasn't looking at her: his gaze was fixed somewhere above and beyond Lindsey's left shoulder. She looked that way, but saw only the darkened house.

"Hey, Oreo. Over here. Hellooo." She snapped her fingers at the cat. He stared intently, ignoring her.

Without warning Oreo tensed up, as if preparing to spring away. His eyes never lost their focus on the upper story of the house.

"Okay, weirdo. I guess you're—"

The cat darted away, a streak of black and white disappearing into the back alley.

Lindsey shook her head. "*Cats.*" She went back inside, being sure to close the door this time.

The bone was a beautiful thing, and Lindsey knew right where to put it. She went to the double-sized living room, with its mismatched furniture chronicling a lifetime of acquisitions: outdated armchairs, antique end-tables, homemade quilts on a soft blue couch. Near the room's back corner a low, wide cabinet displayed Grandma's collection of figurines. Lindsey scooted the pieces to either side, making space. In doing so, she rubbed her arm over a scarred edge of the cabinet. The childhood memory came back with sudden sharpness, like a nail pounded into her skull.

She'd been young – ten, maybe twelve years old. The family was over for Easter, everyone milling about while Grandma and Aunt Roberta worked in the kitchen. Bent over the cabinet, Lindsey's mom pointed out the collection of figurines. She told Lindsey it was okay to touch them, so long as she was careful. Lindsey reached for a wolf in the back, her dress-sleeve knocking over a porcelain angel. It didn't break, but she still let out a quiet "goddamn it!"

The hand struck the back of her head like a comet colliding with Earth. Lindsey jarred forward so violently she lost three teeth against the cabinet's edge. She wailed through a mouth of blood and chipped bone while her mother shouted, asking what she'd just said. Unable to answer, Lindsey earned a hard slap across the cheek.

Grown-up Lindsey blinked hard, shaking the memory from her mind. She placed the bone in the space she'd cleared.

It looked a little lonely on its own, but that could be fixed with a trip to the craft store tomorrow. For the time being, Lindsey spotted a great addition to her display: a carved wooden owl, its body the size of her fist, its wings spread wide. It was one of her grandmother's few figurines she actually liked. Something about its eyes, and the way it looked ready to swoop in for a kill…

She moved the owl over and propped the bone against its belly. That must have been it: it was an *owl's* bone. At least, that's the theme she'd go with. She couldn't wait to finish the dark shrine and post pictures online. But for now, she needed a snack.

Her grandparents had emptied the fridge before leaving, but they usually had some chips lying around. Lindsey opened the glass-paneled door at the back corner of the kitchen, and stepped onto the small landing that led down to the basement. There at the top of the stairs, two tall, lavender doors opened into a pantry.

Except they didn't. The doors hung at an imperfect angle, and had always been prone to sticking together. She pulled on the faux-crystal knobs, but nothing budged. Oh well – she was too tired to put up a fight. Maybe it would be better to just hit the sack. Hunger's easy to ignore when you're sleeping.

Up the main staircase she went, its wooden steps groaning beneath a strip of blue carpet. Lindsey entered her mother's old room, slipped her socks off, and collapsed onto the bed.

Consciousness faded, to be replaced by dreams of bone-charms and feathered fiends.

* * *

The gnawing woke her.

Lindsey squinted at the clock. Four in the morning – too early. She rolled back over and closed her eyes.

Again, the gnawing. This time, Lindsey was awake enough to realize it signaled something unusual. She dragged herself out of bed and flicked on the light, only to find the brightness unbearable. She flicked the switch off and felt her way into the hall.

The sound was soft, like the whispers of careful conspirators. And yet, in the house's silence, it rang clearly.

At the bottom of the stairs Lindsey stepped into something cold and damp; it squished between her toes. She pulled her foot to her nose and sniffed. An earthy scent – mud. She must have tracked it in without realizing.

"Damn it," she muttered, brushing off her foot.

The gnawing stopped.

Lindsey listened. Silence clung to darkened walls, patient as a lurking spider.

One slow step at a time, she traversed the hall. The sound had been coming from the kitchen. She squinted against impending brightness and hit the lights.

The room appeared before her, just as she'd left it: peeling white cupboards, small round table, a shelf full of 'cute' salt & pepper shakers. In the back corner, the glass-paneled door to the basement landing was closed. Beyond that, Lindsey noticed something unusual.

The pantry was open.

One of the lavender doors was just visible through the glass. Lindsey advanced with caution, unable to see into the pantry from that angle; she'd have to go out onto the landing.

Turning the loose doorknob, she pulled.

Something darted out of the pantry and down the stairs.

Lindsey leapt back with a yelp. She shut the glass-paneled door.

What had she seen? A mouse? No – bigger than that. A rat, maybe. Either way, not something she wanted to deal with just then. She'd get some traps while she was out tomorrow.

As she turned to leave, something beyond the landing's window caught her eye: a black-and-white cat, perched atop a recycling bin in the alley, illuminated by a motion-lamp. Oreo spared Lindsey a brief glance, then resumed staring in the direction of her basement windows.

Lindsey shook off a feeling of unease and went back to bed. As she lay in the dark, her ears remained perked against the house's empty silence.

* * *

Morning's light slipped between the blinds like thrown razorblades, cutting bright gashes into the wall. Lindsey rubbed her eyes and checked the clock: 8:26. Much more reasonable.

She headed downstairs. This time, she saw the mud before stepping in it.

It was much worse than she'd realized.

"Damn it, Mom." Lindsey sighed. If she hadn't been distracted by the phone, she probably would've taken her boots off outside. Now she had an awful mess to clean up, from all the pacing she'd evidently done.

Lindsey went to the kitchen and peered through the glass-paneled door. No rats visible. That was something, anyway.

She checked on her bone in the living room. Contemplating the next steps of her shrine made her smile.

She got dressed and left the house. The sunny town seemed strangely quiet, until Lindsey remembered where everyone was: church. She shrugged and went to the Kettle for food, ordering French toast because her mother wasn't there to disapprove of the sugary breakfast. She went overboard with the syrup.

Next stop was the craft store, where Lindsey picked out some black candles, red silk ribbon and fake moss for her shrine. Grinning at her good finds, she went to the hardware shop for rat-traps and headed home.

The moment she stepped inside, her excitement faded. She'd forgotten about the mud.

Lindsey got right to work, scrubbing on her hands and knees. She couldn't believe the mess. It extended the full length of the hall, from side door to kitchen. All because she'd had to endure a typically stressful conversation with Mom.

A few minutes into the process, Lindsey noticed something unusual. On a hunch, she retrieved one of her boots and held its sole next to the muddy prints.

The patterns didn't match.

She looked back at the side door. She'd locked it after talking to Oreo last night, hadn't she?

Hating herself for doing it, Lindsey pulled out her phone. She dialed.

The voice on the other end was short and pointed. "Lindsey."

"Hey, Mom – quick question. Do you know if Uncle Dennis and Aunt Roberta have keys to the house?"

"Missed you at church today."

Lindsey sighed. "I know. Sorry. I just woke up. But really, I need—"

"We passed the Kettle on the way home. Your car needs a wash."

Lindsey pinched the bridge of her nose. *Fuck.*

"I just put fresh sheets on your bed, if you ever want to come back. Hope you're having fun over there."

"Mom, I—"

The call ended. Lindsey cursed again, finished cleaning, and plopped in front of the TV to occupy her mind.

Of course the boot print had been Uncle Dennis's. He always came over to do yard work while the grandparents traveled. He'd probably trimmed the grape-bush while Lindsey was out that morning, and left a print among her mess.

Still, it'd be nice to confirm her suspicions. Too bad she'd have to call Mom to get Uncle Dennis's number.

The campy horror flick wasn't holding Lindsey's attention, so she decided to resume her chores. Off to the kitchen she went, rat-traps in hand.

Beyond the glass-paneled door, the pantry was still open. Of course – why wouldn't it be? Lindsey shook the thought away and stepped onto the landing to the basement stairs.

Inside the pantry, a shredded chip-bag lay on the ground. Lindsey tossed a trap in with it, closed the door and descended to the basement.

The staircase made a stop at the house's back door, then continued to the right. Lindsey reached the small basement, where sunlight struggled to penetrate the dirty, ground-level windows.

She went about setting the traps, placing them beside the freezer, between the laundry machines, and around the miscellaneous clutter. Along the way she came across a long, rectangular tent-bag. She pulled it out and read the label.

"You're about twice as big as *my* tent," she said. "I may just have to borrow—"

"Run, goddamn it! Run!"

It was a man's voice, powerful but desperate, coming from upstairs. There followed a violent crash and a long, pained scream.

Lindsey dropped the tent and ran upstairs. Part of her wanted to stop at the first landing and run out the back door, but she had to know what was going on. No one would break into the house in broad daylight – would they?

She rushed through the kitchen and slowed as she entered the dining room. The living room was visible from there, not being separated by a wall. Suddenly, everything became clear.

She'd left the TV on.

Lindsey exhaled with relief. She turned off the movie, cursing it for giving her a heart attack.

With her chores out of the way, Lindsey could finally have some fun. She gathered her art supplies and went to the bone.

Like a director framing a shot, Lindsey eyed the shrine from every angle. She lined up the slender black candles in arcs running from the owl figurine's wings, their height descending. Patches of fake moss complemented the bone's outdoorsy look, while red silk ribbons woven between the candles gave the whole thing a ritualistic vibe. Lindsey smiled at the idea of cultists meeting in the woods to worship their owl-god's sacred bone.

The day was too bright for spooky pictures, so she figured she'd wait until night, then post everything to her blog. Until then, though, she kept herself busy tidying the house, watching movies, and running errands. After twenty-four years of answering to her mother, it was nice to experience a little independence.

By the time Lindsey returned to her grandparents' place in the evening, the mail had arrived. She scooped it off the floor by the front door's drop-slot and carried it to the dining-room table. Something fell out of the stack.

A driver's license: Randall Erwin Myers, fifty-two years old, dark-skinned, graying hair. A long scratch ran diagonally through the card's lamination.

Lindsey couldn't fathom why someone's license would get mixed up with the mail, but her curiosity was piqued. She pulled out her phone to see what the internet knew about Mr. Myers.

The search results yielded a number of news headlines, each including some variation of the same four words: 'Camper'; 'Hike'; 'Attack'; 'Cougar'.

Lindsey read the first article. It said Randall Myers and his husband, Clayton Ellersby, had been camping when they encountered a cougar during an early-morning stroll. They tried to scare the cat away, but it wasn't deterred: it attacked Ellersby, knocking him over and biting his shoulder. Myers kicked at the predator, which responded with a forceful pounce.

As Myers fought from his back, he shouted for his husband to run. Bleeding heavily, Ellersby got back to the campsite and contacted rescuers. They arrived in time to tend to him, but not to save Randall Myers.

Officers tracked the cougar to a shallow cave, where they found it feeding on the victim's body. They shot and killed the cat.

Despite the summer heat, Lindsey felt a cold shiver. The most disturbing part of the attack was where it had happened: the same forest she'd hiked through the previous day.

She went back to the search results and found a social media post authored by Clayton Ellersby. In it, Ellersby wrote a fond remembrance of his husband: he discussed Myers's love of the outdoors, and how he'd always carry snacks to feed the squirrels; he mentioned the many peaceful walks the couple had shared alongside rivers and lakes. One passage, in particular, struck a chord with Lindsey:

Randall never let anything get him down, even when my family tried to keep us apart. In addition to his love, he gave me the best advice I've ever received: "You've only got the one life here on Earth – don't let someone else live it for you."

The post was a beautiful tribute to an obviously compassionate man. It ended with Ellersby asking for help in locating his deceased husband's wedding ring. Apparently, the cougar had mauled Myers's left hand before dragging him back to the cave, removing several fingers that were never found.

Lindsey looked into the living room, at her bone-shrine. She eyed her own ring-finger, contemplating its size.

For the first time since arriving at her grandparents' house, she considered going home.

No. No, there was no reason for that. There was *never* a reason to go back to that place. She'd enjoyed these few days to herself entirely too much, and wasn't going to give up her independence just because her imagination was running wild. Lindsey tossed the license into the mail pile without giving it another thought. She turned on the TV and watched a horror-comedy she'd seen a dozen times before; it always cheered her up.

When night fell, Lindsey went upstairs and got the bathwater going. Earlier in the day she'd had the idea to bathe by candlelight, and now that the time had come, she stuck with that plan – if not just to prove she wasn't afraid of anything. The night was warm, so she opened a small window and set up the leftover black candles. While the water ran, she went downstairs to snap pictures of the bone that had, undoubtedly, come from an owl.

She got out her phone and knelt by the shrine. Instead of feeling carpet against her bare knee, she touched something smooth – almost leathery. She moved her leg to inspect.

It was a leaf.

Small, green, oval-shaped. Lindsey held it up by the stem. Just another mess she'd dragged in. She added it to the shrine, behind the owl's left wing. She wished she had another, to make it symmetrical.

A scan of the area turned up just what she wanted: a second leaf. Then she found another. And another. They all lay around the base of the cabinet.

Something wasn't right. Lindsey could understand trailing a couple leaves in without noticing, but half a dozen? She set down her phone and got low, rubbing her palms over the carpet for stragglers. She extended an arm beneath the cabinet.

It was like reaching into a compost pile.

Lindsey jerked her arm out. A spray of dirt and leaves came with it.

"What the *fuck?*"

She stood and backed away, staring at the cabinet. Everything was silent – until the gnawing.

It was the same sound she'd heard in the pantry the night before, but this time it came from upstairs.

Lindsey rushed that way, eager to leave the living room. Why was there soil under the cabinet? Grandma kept potted plants throughout the house – had Grandpa dropped something and swept the mess away? That had to be it. It just *had* to.

On her way to the staircase, she grabbed a boot. She was going to put an end to that gnawing rat, once and for all.

At the top of the stairs, the bathroom's candlelight crept into the hall. The bathwater was still running, but it sounded different now: more like the trickle of a stream.

Lindsey reached the bathroom. There, perched atop the sill of the opened window, was a squirrel.

Relief washed over Lindsey. Somehow, just identifying the culprit brought her to ease. The squirrel nibbled a chip in its tiny hands.

"So you're the guy who's been keeping me up," she said.

The squirrel stopped. It stared at her.

"Okay," she said, entering the room and raising the boot. "I don't want to do anything drastic. I'm gonna give you one chance to turn around and vamoose."

The squirrel tensed up, nose twitching, beady eyes wide.

"Seriously," Lindsey said, "let's not—"

She noticed the bathwater.

It wasn't the clear fluid she'd seen filling the tub earlier. It was a dark, rippling mirror, adorned with loose pine needles and water-striding bugs. Lindsey thought she saw a bed of stones at the murky bottom.

A brown streak shot past her feet and out the door, nails clicking across the tile.

"Shit!" Lindsey said, sidestepping and dropping the boot. It bounced across the floor, leaving a muddy print.

No – there were two prints. A left and a right, positioned as though someone had been standing before the opened window, looking out.

Neither one matched her boot.

A low roar came from behind. Lindsey spun to find the hallway darker than it should have been; the bathroom's candlelight seemed to stop at the threshold, as if it'd hit a wall.

Somewhere in that black place there was a scuffle, like quick-footed animals fighting. The roar came again, followed by a pained squeak. Everything went quiet.

Two orbs like golden-green marbles shone in the dark, rising to waist-height. They angled toward Lindsey.

She slammed the door and clicked the lock. She stepped back, staring. The tub continued to fill, draining into the overflow slot. Mosquitoes buzzed around her head.

Something scratched the door: a faint, exploratory thing. Lindsey's heart pounded in her ears. Candlelight flickered; water flowed. The thing outside growled in a low, quiet rumble.

It darted off.

Lindsey heard it descend the stairs quickly, gracefully. Then came those four familiar words: "Run, goddamn it! Run!"

She recognized the subsequent commotion for what it must have been: man versus cougar, in a furious battle for survival. In her mind's eye she saw the cougar pinning Randall Myers down, biting at his flailing arms, ripping long red furrows down his face. During the struggle his hand entered the cougar's mouth, where fingers were torn loose and cast to the forest floor, along with a plain gold wedding ring.

Lindsey snapped out of the daydream when something on the bathroom floor caught her eye: a long, black band, shimmering in the candlelight. It slithered out of her boot, forked tongue tasting the ground.

The snake was huge: too long to have fit inside the boot. It just kept coming, shiny yellow eyes fixed on Lindsey.

She burst through the door and into the hall. Darkness stole her sight, but not her sense of touch: she felt grass beneath her feet, soft and cool.

There was no time to worry about where the carpet had gone. She needed to get out. The cougar continued its attack somewhere downstairs – where she'd left her phone – and it sounded like Randall's resistance was waning. Lindsey couldn't risk going that way. She felt her way to her grandparents' bedroom and flicked on the lights.

It was as if a forest had infected the place: big patches of bark grew on the walls like rough lesions; vines wove tight patterns over the windows; strands of moss hung from the ceiling like a swamp-hag's hair.

Lindsey ignored the madness around her and grabbed the bedside telephone. There was no dial tone; only static. No – not static. She listened closely. It was more like a flowing river. Beneath the noise, she heard a faint voice:

"Run, goddamn it! Run!"

Lindsey slammed the phone down. The vine-covered windows were inaccessible, and she couldn't escape out the second story anyway. The only option was to rush down the stairs and out the side door, hoping not to encounter the cougar along the way. She ventured from the bedroom, its light not penetrating the hall. Grass tickled Lindsey's toes. She wondered where the snake might be.

She eased forward. The downstairs struggle was no more, being replaced by sounds of tearing, chewing, swallowing. Passing into the dark, she stepped on something that wasn't grass.

With a surprised yelp Lindsey kicked her foot out, striking the thing. It tumbled to a stop in the bathroom's doorway, visible in the candlelight.

The squirrel lay there, lifeless and mutilated. From the looks of things, the cougar hadn't even taken a bite out of it. Lindsey's stomach churned at the sight.

She rushed to the staircase, descending as quietly as possible on the pebble-strewn steps. The side door came within reach. Lindsey grasped the knob in the dark.

It was sticky. Warm, too. Lindsey recoiled. She sniffed her hand: tree sap. She grabbed the knob again, but it wouldn't turn. Trying any harder would only make noise she couldn't afford.

She couldn't just let the cougar find her. She had to act. Upstairs offered no escape routes, and the side door was a lost cause. The only option left was to traverse the dark hall, farther into the house – toward the very thing that haunted her.

Lindsey listened to the sounds of messy eating. Her imagination supplied some grisly mental imagery: a cougar's gore-stained muzzle, digging ever deeper into the entrails of a wide-eyed corpse.

The activity came from the living room, where the front door was. Lindsey had to get to the kitchen, and the stairs to the basement; halfway down was the landing with the house's back door.

Down the dark hall she crept, not daring to turn on any lights. The walk seemed longer than usual, but in time the kitchen grew close. Eager to escape, Lindsey rushed the last few steps and tripped on a tree root.

She hit the uneven dirt with a heavy thud. The chewing stopped.

Lying stone-still, Lindsey shifted her gaze just enough to peer to the left, through the dining room. In the living room beyond, two shiny green eyes fixed on her from the darkness. A low rumble carried through the house.

Lindsey ran.

Into the kitchen she went, the sounds of agile pursuit behind. She made it down the stairs to the landing and reached for the back door.

Pain pierced her hand, forcing it back.

Thorns.

She clawed desperately, searching for the door, but found only thorns. Cuts opened across her hands and fingers.

She heard a tumbling in the kitchen, and envisioned the cougar taking too fast a corner around the table. It would be on her in a moment.

Lindsey rushed to the basement. The windows were too small to climb out, but they did let in some moonlight – just enough to reveal the tent Lindsey had found yesterday.

It was set up in the middle of the floor.

Lindsey dove inside and zipped the flap shut. Struggling to quiet her breath, she listened.

Paws touched down softly in the basement, stalking slowly. Lindsey tracked the deep, throaty growls as they circled her sanctuary. When her pursuer reached the window-side of the basement, moonlight drew a large, feline silhouette against the tent's thin material. It flowed past like a shark waiting for the right moment.

"Run, goddamn it! Run!"

The cougar stopped. Its silhouetted head perked up and turned toward the stairs.

"*Run!*"

The cougar took off, bounding up the stairs. Clouds must have moved to cover the moon, because everything went black.

Lindsey waited. She realized just how much her sap-sticky, thorn-shredded hands ached. No commotion from upstairs – the night was quiet.

Lindsey couldn't stay in the tent forever. Her best option was to leave now, while the cougar was distracted.

She unzipped the flap and stuck her head out.

The basement was gone.

Stars hung high above the tent, a billion bright pinpricks in the fabric of night. Huge ponderosa pines stood all about, spaced too widely to create a canopy. Everything shone with the blue-white glow of a full moon.

Lindsey stepped into the wilderness. A soft breeze slipped past. Up a small mound, at the base of a tree, she saw a table.

But it wasn't just any table: it was the small, round one from her grandparents' kitchen. Lindsey moved closer. The nearby tree's bark peeled like white paint, and on its branches stood a collection of salt & pepper shakers.

She was still in the house. But – she wasn't.

Lindsey wandered the moon-bright woods, her senses open. Fallen pinecones scraped her bare feet. She passed a familiar dining-room chair, its legs transitioning into roots as they met the ground.

A chirping drew her attention. It wasn't an animal sound – it was a ringtone.

Her phone.

Lindsey rushed through the wilderness. *Keep ringing,* she thought. *Just keep ringing!*

Maneuvering through a grove of small, shadowy trees, she emerged into a huge clearing. Before her, towering into the night sky, was her shrine.

The owl figurine stood big as a house. Arcing away from its outspread wings were pillars of smooth black rock, arranged in order of descending height. A band of shiny red liquid wound its way through the surrounding moss, shimmering like dragon's blood.

Propped against the owl's belly wasn't a bone, but a full human skeleton. The left hand was missing.

Lindsey spotted her blinking phone nearby. She rushed over, read the caller's name and answered.

"Mom!" she said. "I need help!"

"Lindsey, I've had about enough—"

"I'm lost, Mom! For the love of God, *help* me!"

A pause. Then, "I see. I'm glad you've come to your senses, dear. I'll be right over."

The call ended.

"*Shit!*" Lindsey said. She didn't even know where she was – how would *Mom* find her? Maybe she should call the police. But what would she tell them?

A low growl rumbled into the clearing. Lindsey's blood went cold. Slowly, she turned.

In the moonlight, across the way, stood the cougar.

"No..." Lindsey eased backwards. "Please..."

The cat advanced, head low.

Lindsey turned and ran.

Through the woods she sprinted, not even questioning which way to go. She just knew she couldn't stop.

The growls at her back grew closer, but Lindsey didn't dare glance that way. Her bloodied feet pounded the forest floor. She wasn't sure which would give out first: her legs, or her lungs. Neither would last much longer.

She plowed through some skin-scraping bushes and saw her salvation.

The lake was smooth and full of stars, like a great mirror to the sky. Lindsey had never been much of a swimmer, but the water was her only hope.

She kicked with everything she had left. Just before reaching the lake, she finally looked back.

The cougar burst through the bushes, teeth bared.

Lindsey jumped.

Splash.

She swam down and forward with tiring, inefficient strokes. Dirty lake-water stung her eyes. Her body begged for air, already exhausted from the run.

Lindsey didn't want to come up. She didn't want to find the cougar still following her. But if the cat didn't get her, the lake would.

When the stinging in her chest became unbearable, she clawed for the surface. Through the rippling murk, the stars blurred into a half-dozen flickering flames.

Lindsey breached the surface with a gasp.

She coughed, rubbed her eyes. She tried to tread with her legs, but kicked something hard and immovable on each side.

When she opened her eyes, she saw where she was: her grandparents' bathtub. A half-dozen candles flickered around her. The mosquitoes and boot-prints were gone, the bathwater clear.

"Lindsey?"

Her mother's voice, from downstairs.

"Mom! Mom, I'm up here!"

Lindsey spilled over the side of the tub, dripping and gasping.

"What in the..."

Lindsey looked over. There in the doorway, her mother stared at the mutilated squirrel on the floor. Her gaze moved to the black candles, then to Lindsey. Anger flooded her face.

"Mom," Lindsey said, struggling to her feet, "there's something here. It's—"

The palm struck her cheek with a clap like thunder. Lindsey fell against the tub, her legs too weak to resist. Her mother's hand came down again, and again. All Lindsey could do was curl up on the floor, covering against the blows.

"How *dare* you!" her mother shouted. "How *dare* you bring this sickness into your grandparents' house!"

Slaps landed around Lindsey's ears and neck. When she moved to block those, the kicks started.

Her mother's foot connected with her legs, her arms, her midsection. Not for the first time in Lindsey's life, she was stomped by the woman who'd raised her.

"Never again!" her furious mother yelled. "Never again will I allow—"

The words turned to a shriek as mother collapsed onto daughter. Lindsey felt the weight atop her immediately ripped away, and looked to see her mother being yanked into the dark hall, legs first, caught in the fearsome grip of a blood-splattered cougar.

The screaming woman disappeared into the void, clawing at the ground the whole way.

Lindsey scrambled to her feet. Her mother's desperate prayers pierced the night, filling the creaky old house. Bruised and broken, Lindsey rushed to the top of the stairs, grabbing the banister to stay upright. Somewhere straight ahead, her mother was fighting for her life. Down the stairs to her left, the house's side door stood wide.

Standing at the crossroads, Lindsey remembered. She remembered the teeth she'd lost against her grandmother's cabinet. She remembered the fractured arm, the taped-shut mouth, the icy showers. And she remembered the beating from just moments ago, when she needed her mother's love more than ever.

Powerful words sprung to her mind: *You've only got the one life here on Earth – don't let someone else live it for you.* Then came a voice, as if shouted by the house itself.

"Run, goddamn it! Run!"

And she did.

Down the stairs and out the door Lindsey went, hardly able to keep her footing. Bloody and aching, she just kept running – away from the screams, the horrors, and the lifetime of pain.

14 Oak Street

Morgan Sylvia

AMELIA ESCAPED this place through a slit in her veins, and rode to whatever heaven or hell she chose on a crimson wave of blood, a scarlet flow that soon congealed into a brown, sticky mess on the bathroom floor, beside the old claw-foot tub. Helen got out through a noose in a rope that once held the now-overgrown tomato plants in place. Rosanna fled through a needle. There is nothing more to tell of them, after that. Their before is cloaked in secrets, whispers, and cracked wishes. Their after is dust and bones. Their after is the after that you, too, will know someday.

Oblivion.

This house is not for the curious. It is not for the weak. The pale moon and yellow sun have crossed these cold skies thousands of times since I was summoned here. Years and wars have passed in the interim. The vortex is still open. It is eternal, as I am.

Such portals, once opened, are not easily closed.

As for the child? He watches silently, his eyes dark and filled with doom. One day, he will set me free. He has promised that.

This vessel, this flesh that holds me, is pale and weak and flabby. I look at the festering world through eyes clouded with cataracts. The skin on the hand writing this is paper thin and mottled with liver spots. The hand shakes. It spills the ink. It trembles, rendering my words into irrelevant splotches. The grandmother's heartbeats are thin and delicate. I feel them fluttering against the cage of fragile ribs like a sparrow beating its wings. Like this house, she is old and faded and weak, her once-vivid colors drained away into pallid, drab hues; her vein-shot eyes bleary with memory; her hair the color of bone. Like this house, she is worn and full of secrets.

I let her come forward, when occasion calls for it: when the doctors come, or the maids or landscapers. I give her the mornings, so she can tend the garden and see to bills and trivial matters. I rule the fourteenth hour, and it is always then that I return.

Soon, I must find another vessel. The grandmother – Martha – has half a decade left, at most, I suspect. Her flesh is old and weak. Her thoughts are scattered and erratic, squirrel-like. She is too thin. I try to remember to make her eat. But I live outside time, which makes this difficult: I sometimes sleep for weeks. I have taught the boy to nourish her with blended concoctions of fruit and vegetables and nutritional powders. He adds blood and raw meat for me.

My brethren often take up residence in gothic mansions, in old Victorian houses, in isolated farmhouses. One would not expect to find me here, in this ordinary, post-war dwelling, with its large porch and old, cavernous garage. It's one of a million similar houses.

But then, I did not choose this place.

Of the house? There is nothing remarkable about it at all, save myself. A keen eye might perhaps deduce that the shadowy interior is darker than it should be. Someone passing at midnight may notice unusual shadows moving across the grounds or settling in the trees. But humans walk past daily, and rarely give it a second glance. It is somewhat run-down, but that is not unusual in this old neighborhood. The gardens are overgrown, the driveway cracked and veined with weeds, the grey-blue paint peeling and chipping. The outdated floors and carpets are stained with years and use. In the kitchen, shiny new appliances stand out in sharp contrast against faded wallpaper: the fridge that orders food, the lights that dim at the clap of a hand. The smell of lavender and rose hangs in the air, above the lace doilies and antique glass pieces. These things belong to the grandmother's era, a time where my kind watched the tanks rumbling across Europe as the skies clouded with greasy smoke and broken dreams. Some of us wept. Some laughed. I only watched.

You wonder, perhaps, who I am. What I am. I could give you some of the names I have worn, if you knew how to ask. My true name will sear holes in your thoughts, and roar through your veins like rivers of lava. I've looked out onto the world through eyes old and young, through gazes clouded with tears and dry with bright sunlight. I've spoken through lungs clogged with smoke, and heavy with the scent of pine and sea air. I have worn scales and skin and fur. Beaks and black feathers have carried both my hatred and my blessings through vein-colored skies.

The child does not fear me. Nor should he: I have watched over him since he was born. I first showed myself to him when he was a babe in the crib. I was a teddy bear, then, soft and comforting. When he was a toddler, I made him laugh by making his toys dance or casting glowing images into his darkened room. I kept him safe from the ghosts that lurk in gloomy corners. Followed him to school, and stood beside him when he was nervous about class.

He knows me. He only sees his grandmother when he looks at me, but he is beginning to understand something of what I am. He knows I look at him through Martha's rheumy, watery eyes. He is strong in both mind and muscle, unlike his mother, Rosanna.

One evening when fireflies flit through the yard and snakes slither and twist through the trees, I take his hand. On wobbly legs, I bring him to the garden.

It is time for his lessons to start.

Amelia was curious about the occult, I tell him. She delved into the chaos magicks. She drank the words of Crowley and Solomon, and cast spells upon her lovers. She spent well over a year preparing for the rite to call me. Like most humans, she did not know the consequences of summoning one of us.

I suppose we all have roles to play.

As I speak, the dark star rises above the gazebo in the yard. Human eyes cannot see it, but it fills my thoughts with its terrible, beautiful song. I point the star out to the boy. "One day you will see it," I said, almost breathing its name.

"Is that where you are from?"

I nod. "It's a place where my dimension meets yours."

He doesn't know what a dimension is, but he nods anyway, his eyes filled with confusion.

"I came here through the vortex," I tell him. "The gate to breach it is closed now. Someday, you will open it."

The child is hungry. We go back inside. The setting sun shines through the picture window in the front parlor, painting the sky red. The body I wear moves stiffly in a faded patterned dress as it crosses the unswept floor and reaches into a cupboard, which Martha painted white decades ago. The boy watches, playing with a caterpillar, as I open a tin of tuna and another of peas, and then a box of buttery crackers. I let the grandmother cook for him until recently, when she almost started a fire. Now, it is microwaved meals, sandwiches and salads, delivery, or unheated canned goods. The boy doesn't mind. He eats, ravenous, and then gets himself a cookie from an antique jar.

The lessons continue. I bring the grimoire out from its hiding place in the wall. Its leathered pages are home to me. We delve once more into the occult. He is becoming curious. He wants to know more about my kind. I tell him what I am allowed to share, which isn't much. The lore of my brethren is not meant for him. Not yet, at least.

"There are others like you?" he asks. "Are they all helping boys like me?"

"There are only four of you," I tell him. "North, South, East, West. Two boys, two girls. Your children will rule the universe. They will open the four gates, and let the legions through. Then the world will collapse into perfect oblivion. We will all be one again among the stars."

He frowns. "But where is the gate?"

He is very curious about the gate. I found him lifting pebbles in the yard one day, looking for it.

I look at him. The old woman awakens for a moment. Her panic is exquisite. I crunch it down between her dentures, chew her rubbery tongue, taste her blood in my mouth. Absorb it. Energized, I meet his stare, letting my own eyes show through hers, black onyx replacing her faded grey orbs. "You know the answer to that already, Jacob," I say.

He pauses, thinking. "The cellar?"

I frown. "No. The cellar is foul, and tainted with dry bones and rotted souls. That is where the ghosts live."

Dead things stir in the shadows. One knocks a glass over, as if rebuking my words. They flutter away when I look at them, dissolving into mist and madness.

Jacob looks into the darkness clustered on the ceiling. "The attic?"

"No. The attic is full of relics. That is where you will meditate, and perform the rituals. It is not the gate itself."

He asks if the gate is in the garden. I tell him that the garden is filled with the beings that guard this place, stand watch around it, the beetles and the snakes and the crows, the rats and the feral cats with eyes that reflect sour moonlight and Enochian wisdom.

He sits back, sticking out his lower lip. "Where?"

"You are the gate, Jacob," I whisper. "You will bring my kind through the vortex, when it is time."

Dark flames flicker in his eyes. He looks happy.

It begins to rain, a soft grey veil closing out the world. The roses in the garden emit a strong perfume that wakes the old lady up. I let her have her eyes back, and she sits back in the cracked mahogany rocking chair. A spider scuttles across the end table beside her, a dark spot against a lace doily. I pick it up and pop it into her mouth, feeling it burst apart between her thin lips. Then I retreat, and let her enjoy a glass of iced tea and her favorite game show.

They spend the afternoon playing cards.

* * *

In the morning, the rain has cleared. The air is thick and heavy around the magnolias and the willow trees, and the smell of wisteria perfumes the golden sunlight. The maid comes, and quietly puts the house in order. The weekly delivery of food arrives in boxes. Jacob puts everything neatly into its place. I have let him and the fridge make the food selections recently. I've no care for such things. I've never truly gotten the hang of using the computer. Nor has Martha.

But when he reaches for a cookie, I stop him.

"You must learn to fast," I say. "No food until darkness. It clears the mind. You will need that later, for the rites."

He pouts. "But I'm hungry."

"When the sun sets," I tell him, "you can go online and order food delivery. Whatever you want. That is your reward."

He considers this. "Will fasting make me stronger?"

"If you do it properly. Too much fasting will only weaken you, especially at this age. Too little is useless. The point is to cleanse, not to starve. To clear your mind. To become a perfect vessel."

"Vessel for what?"

One of the dead things knocks a painting off a wall. Jacob is so used to these things that he doesn't even register them as abnormal. He is already stronger than the others, who went mad over such slights.

I do not answer.

"This isn't a punishment," I tell him. "It's training."

He accepts this.

We walk in the gardens, which are peppered with the statues of my brethren.

"Are these your kin?" he asks, staring at a granite cherub.

I nod. "They don't look right," I say. "But humans cannot truly capture our essence."

He pauses at one of the older statues. It is covered in moss. Despite what I just told him, I must admit that this one does faintly resemble Uriel. "Are any of these you?"

I consider his words. "None of them," I say. "And all of them."

He frowns.

I continue. "Our kind does not live in a reality humanity understands. We exist as energy, rather than flesh. Our thoughts become reality. Those who summon us shift reality, simply by inviting us into this realm. Some of us were born from the dreams and nightmares of your kind. Life and death follow our path."

Agathia appears as a flock of crows roosting in the trees. My brothers and sisters are often about, welcome or not. They are in large part responsible for driving Jacob's ancestors mad, and, therefore, for the bones in the cellar. "You will fail again," she says. "We are stronger. We will crack his mind and taste his thoughts."

"Begone," I tell her.

She laughs, and then speaks to the boy. "This place is very special, Jacob. It always has been. But now, it is time for you to learn to control it. This weak thing will not teach you everything. I will send you dreams, child."

Her words are blood in the sun. I blind her with a flash of light. She breaks apart into a cloud of gnats, and flies into the clouds, her laughter trailing behind.

Jacob watches the exchange calmly. Like any six-year-old, he is full of questions. "What do you want?" he asks, finally.

"Destruction," I say. "And then peace."

The old woman awakens, coughing and gagging. Her body fails for a moment. Startled, I release my grip a bit. "Take me inside," I croak, rasping breaths that wheeze out through Martha's false teeth. "It is not time yet for you to know all the answers."

At sunset, he orders Chinese food, and eats before the TV, watching the news. Apocalypse spreads across the land. The water wars are beginning. The southern continent is drying up, turning to dust. I smile through thin stretched lips. The grandmother stirs, but her fragile thoughts burst beneath my laughter.

* * *

The next day, we are in the garden, going over elements, when an ice cream truck rambles by, trailing distorted carnival music in its wake. "Go," I tell him, with the grandmother's wrinkled throat, her wrinkled voice. "Get yourself some ice cream."

He frowns. "I haven't any money."

I look at the ground, find a few fat, greasy worms and a shiny green beetle. I put them in his palm. He understands and closes his hand, concentrating, squinting with effort. In the trees, a seraphim watches, wearing the shape of a dove.

He opens his fingers. A few silver dollars sit in his hand. A grin splits his cherubic face, and he runs off after the truck. He buys a push-up cone and an ice cream sandwich. I let the grandmother savor the sandwich. It is cold and soothing on her throat. Her feeble hand shakes, drops the half-eaten treat into her lap. She turns her face to the sun and wishes for death.

Not yet, I whisper into her mind. *But soon. The dark will cover you like a veil, and there will be no more fear or pain.*

Watery tears seep from her eyes. I taste her sorrow, and realize that I have broken her dreams of heaven. I meant neither kindness nor cruelty, merely truth.

In the corner, the ghost of a dead thing watches us with eyes of smoke.

* * *

By that autumn, the candles jump when he laughs. When he is angry, clouds gather above the rustling trees. My brothers and sisters watch from the shadows, cloaked in fur and feathers and the forms of primal beasts. They fly, crawl, and slither into the uncaring night, come back and scold me for breaking the rules. I laugh, and turn them into flies. I am stronger here than I am in the ethos. Stronger than they are. Fed on ghosts and blood and smoothies, even this weak body can channel energy.

* * *

Before the next winter is over, I have taught him much of the esoteric. We fly the astral realms at night. We slip into forgotten graveyards and crack the bones of dead witches, drink memories from their skulls. He soaks up knowledge like a sponge, delving into the secrets of the kabala, the Enochian mysteries, the writing of ancient alchemists, the Avesta texts.

He still struggles with certain concepts.

"Are you good?" He asks. "Or evil?"

I laugh. My laughter turns to smoke, and curls around the roses. Green sparks fly from my eyes. I breathe a butterfly into being. And then I choke the grandmother, coughing out sharp pieces of words. "We were born with the sun and stars," I tell him. "We are dreams and nightmares that bound matter to them. We have seen the passing aeons, the ages of men. We've spilled oceans of blood and raised mountains of fire in the name of good. And in the name of evil, we have healed the sick and guided the lost. We are beings of light. But light is a spectrum. Some of its colors are too dark, too vivid, too beautiful for human eyes."

"How old are you?"

In answer, I point at the sun.

"I will free you," he says.

I am free in a way he will never know. I am trapped in a way he will never know. Martha's weak body cannot contain me much longer in its weakened cells of salt and fat. There are tumors growing in it now, disease spreading through the mottled, flaccid flesh.

"You will free everyone," I whisper.

I call a bat from the night sky, whisper burning dreams into its eyes when it alights on my finger. It flies off, diseased, to poison its colony. His laughter rings through the air like silver bells.

* * *

Years pass in the blink of an eye. Jacob is a boy one day and then suddenly a teen, dark hair, dark eyes. All at once, he has lost the cherubic innocence of youth, become somber and driven, intellectual. He, like me, is both ruthless and gentle. The shelves in his room overflow with books, movies, and CDs. He paints constellations on the ceiling, decorates his bathroom in black. In the mansions of the moon, my brothers and sisters sing his praises to the darklings.

Jacob is by now familiar with the vortex. He is strong and healthy. His time is approaching. He peers into the well, impatient to cast his tethered soul through the veil, where bones and flesh cannot pass. He paces the overgrown garden, and is annoyed when the landscapers interrupt his musing. He puts a basketball hoop up in the driveway. Joins the student council. Plants marijuana in the back yard. He orders the grandmother soft clothes and thick blankets. I let her sit by the fire in winter, soaking up the warmth, while the television casts a flickering blue glow onto her vacant eyes.

One night he wants to go somewhere with his friends, instead of studying with me. Anger bursts from my eyes in red sparks of fire. Inadvertently, I call a storm. The skies darken. A huge pine falls over the drive. He curses me. Rage seethes in his gaze, in his words. My rage. The rage of angels. This infuriates me. For a moment, I show my true form. I am foolish about it, and frighten the boy with my four wings. The ghosts shiver and flee to the cellar.

I realize that I am jealous of the things he has that I cannot experience: taste and sensation and smell.

"Go," I say. My voice scares the dog next door. "Taste your youth. Savor it. You will be dust soon. Even if you live to be a hundred, that is but moments away."

He takes the keys and rushes off into the night. He drives around the tree, gouging deep ruts into the lawn. I sink into the cellar, leaving the grandmother alone with her memories of beaches and dance halls. My tears burn holes in the death soil.

Later, something disturbs my rest. The grandmother is praying. Several of my sisters show up, but out of deference to me, they turn away, leaving the matter in my hands.

I go back to sleep. When I wake, months have passed. Winter blankets the house. The steps are unshoveled, the car missing. Jacob is gone. I find him in her memories. A crushed-up pill in his oatmeal before he drives to school. A missed stoplight. A twisted heap of metal. He is ashes in the garden now. She has put him in an angel urn, just to spite me.

I let the grandmother escape quietly through her failing heart. I have no use for punishment or vengeance: these things are the domain of Azrael and Kushiel, not mine. My brethren haul her soul towards the blinding light at the center of time. She is unmade and returns as a moth, fluttering around the porch light. Agathia, in crow form, eats her, snapping her out of the air. I sink deep into the earth, rooting among spiders and dead things, my thoughts volcanic and searing.

I must find another vessel.

* * *

I wait patiently for the house to sell. I survey buyer after buyer, frightening off one after another, until the right couple arrives. They are shiny with laughter and vibrant with color. I whisper a glamour into the young bride's thoughts, and then captivate her husband with a warm breeze and thoughts of a billiards room above the garage. She is a natural witch, and senses me immediately. I enchant her with butterflies and dragonflies. He looks at the cabinets, and tells her the kitchen must be redone. The wallpaper, he says, is hideous. Even the hardwood floors that creak beneath their feet need to be refinished.

Maliphias appears in peacock form, strutting his way around the garden. Charmed, the young bride wheedles, cajoles. The demon prince casts me a look. I nod, knowing he is repaying a favor I did him once, long before man crossed the churning oceans. Before he leaves, he turns a passing jogger into a finch. I retreat to a cloud of mist in the garden.

The sale closes quickly. The missing woman dominates local news.

I slip into the woman's body at the new moon. Her skin is firm and supple, her muscles strong, her thoughts silver and dazed. She fights me at first, until I discover her taste for wine. I sink through her fermented, alcohol-soaked thoughts, light her wishes on fire.

The young bride has a taste for magick and rituals. She is curious, not frightened, when the dead things break glasses or rattle cupboards. I lead her to the grimoire. The blood work does not faze her in the least. She remodels the kitchen, tears down the old wallpaper, paints everything red.

This angers the ghosts.

Her husband escapes through a bullet hole in his skull. There is nothing more to tell of him. He has joined the ghosts, with their secrets, whispers, and cracked wishes. He is dust and bones. He is oblivion.

Serena is born five months later. The cycle resets again. I play with her, creating flashing colors of light above her cradle, as I did with Jacob.

The house settles around us, a cocoon. Thick brambles and bracken close us in. In the daylight hours, kinder souls whizz past in shiny bright cars. Wildflowers erupt in the garden, growing from the skulls of fools. This place is filled with shadow and secrets, but they are sleeping now, in the summer daylight. The child laughs in the sunshine, and conjures one of the dialen, a lovely maiden with goats' hooves. She dances around Serena, and presents her with a black rose.

This child, I tell the crows and doves, *this is the one.* They carry my news on the wind as wars fill the streets with blood. I sense three more births. Time speeds up, even for me. There are blood dawns. Nuclear strikes. Extinctions. My kind emerge from rocks and pools and caves and clouds to witness the fall of mankind, drinking their fill of blood and souls. Some weep. Some laugh. I only watch.

My time is coming.

The child's laughter is bright beneath the low moon. In a moment of fecklessness, I whisper into her ears. "I am Adriel," I tell her, "an angel of death. One day I will slay all the living. But you, you will be safe. One day, you will bring my kin through the vortex."

Sirens toll in the distance.

In the garden, Maliphias puffs out his peacock tail, capturing the last traces of dark light from a galaxy where we once played among forgotten stars.

Pictures at Eleven

Mikal Trimm

"THIS IS a horrible picture of Leslie." George Parker stood in the living room, leaning precariously on his cane and examining the framed photo of his oldest daughter – a school-generic eight by ten, taken in third grade. "I mean, just *look* at it."

"What?" Laurel sat in the bedroom grading term papers by the glow of the computer screen. Her hearing always devolved as she worked. "What are you going on about?"

"This picture!" George stared at it, his hands ready to rip it from the wall. "She looks sick. She looks like a vampire or something."

Laurel came into the room, her eyes bloodshot, strands of hair slipping from the confines of her ponytail. "What's wrong, George? What are you talking about?" She glanced at the photo on the wall, sighed. "She looks great. She's just beautiful. What's wrong with it?"

"Just look at it. She's all pale and pasty, and she has dark circles under her eyes…I mean, did we pay someone to make her look like this?"

Laurel brushed her fingers across the back of his neck, then grabbed his shoulder and squeezed. "She looks fine, George. She's lovely. And be quiet, or you'll wake the girls up."

George tried to rally. "But just look, Laurel – she looks like she's embalmed or something."

"George." Laurel stood up, taking her hand away from his shoulder. She tucked a few stray hairs back into captivity. "I have seven more term papers to grade, and I'm tired as hell, and I don't need this right now. Go do something else for a while, okay? I don't have time for Photography 101." She gave a martyr's sigh and went back to her work.

George stared at the picture a moment longer, affronted. "It's just not right." He tried to go back to his crossword puzzle, but his mind was more interested in images than words. He rose and stalked around the living room, going from one photo to the next.

"Look at this one, for heaven's sake! Mattie looks like one of those UNICEF kids! All eyes and bones!" Mattie in flowery overalls, age five. "Didn't you take this picture? Why in the world did we get it blown up? We're talking *Amateur Hour* here!"

From the bedroom, Laurel hissed "George!" Her voice held a ragged edge, a serrated knife poised to maim.

Yeah. Okay. Sorry. George felt a pubescent urge to argue, to shout out some I-got-the-last-word epithet, but he thought he could hear Mattie upstairs, stirring in her sleep, and she was a holy terror when anyone dared interrupt her slumber. He could hear Laurel in the other room, the scritch of her pen on paper, the long sighs as she stumbled across yet another Hail-Mary jump of logic in the papers she graded. *And here I am, pissy because the weather is changing and my leg is throbbing. Nice reasoning, sympathy-boy.*

The pins in his thigh did cause pain when the weather turned cold. Fact. But he felt something else tonight, a restlessness that couldn't be dismissed by the familiar ache. He wandered aimlessly around the living room, his eyes drawn to every photo hanging on the walls. There was Laurel, looking pale and haggard; the girls together, smiling through lips that seemed stretched across barbed wire instead of teeth; finally, a family portrait: the girls in lovely dresses and ghoul faces, Laurel standing behind them wraithlike, and George himself, beaming with pleasure, his hair still thick enough to disguise his forehead, his face unmarked by scars.

"How old is this picture, dammit!" His voice echoed through the house, sharp and bitter. He held his breath, waiting for Laurel's comment, or the whine of one of his daughters, wakened abruptly. The house was silent, filled only with the sound of George's heartbeat. He went on in a whisper, "What was this, six," he did some mental math, "no, seven months ago? This is the newest sitting we have?"

Laurel's voice wafted from the bedroom, a shadow of itself. "What time is it, George?"

No, he thought, and the clocks started ringing the hour, the hodgepodge of antique timepieces that Laurel had collected for years. The chimes and gongs and whistles came together in mindless cacophony, and the clamor reminded George of the shrieks of children, the shattering of glass, the grinding of metal. He held his hands clamped over his ears until the echoes faded.

Eleven o'clock.

Bedtime. George took a last look at the family portrait, reached out to touch the faces of his wife and children, leaving yet more fingerprints on the glass. *This is not the way you look. This is not the way I remember you.* He touched his own face, barely noticing the scrimshaw of scars there, and hobbled into the quietude of his bedroom.

He stripped down, gathered his covers, and listened for the sounds of shifting bodies, gentle snores, the soundtrack of a sleeping family. All was silence.

This is wrong. Something is missing.

He rose, naked and cold, and turned on the computer. The gentle hum of its fans filled the room. Laurel always forgot to turn the damned thing off when she came to bed.

George lay down, closed his eyes, and fought to conquer the night once again.

* * *

He no longer had nightmares. Too much time, too many countless gallons of water under that particular bridge. Instead, his dreams celebrated minutiae: sweeping the floor with Leslie, doing dishes with Laurel. Tonight he dreamed about Mattie and her wild, untamable hair.

In the dream, he counted each strand, one by one, as Mattie sat quietly on a throne-like chair (*all little girls are princesses*, he'd told her and Leslie, so many times). As he counted, Mattie hummed something, a nonsense arpeggio of notes, and George cried, his tears soaking her hair so that he had to start over again, separating each wet strand. *One, two, three, four…*

He never made it past eleven, starting over and over again, again, until the alarm broke the spell.

* * *

George woke at six-thirty every morning, showered and shaved, ate a small breakfast – toast, some jam, maybe a grapefruit half if he'd remembered to go to the grocery – then drove around town, stopping to take a walk if the weather was good. He had a hard time remembering the day once he drove up the driveway. His thoughts were on his family during every waking moment. They needed to be.

He used to go to work, but he didn't really need that anymore. The insurance would cover him, at least for the near future.

After that?

George didn't think that far ahead anymore. *One day at a time* was his new mantra.

The girls appeared at three-thirty every afternoon, coming home from the bus stop and tossing backpacks, shoes and socks, and school gossip around them in a whirlwind of energy. George picked up behind them and gently reminded them of their duties: homework first, then chores, then dinner when their mother got home. No backtalk, thank you, and Mattie don't give me that look.

He started dinner once everything settled down and Laurel finally showed up, full of gripes about the day's classes, but holding it all in until the girls finished eating, took their showers, and went to their bedrooms for the night.

This was the routine. This was normal life, five days a week.

Heaven, George knew. Sheer bliss. Until the clocks chimed eleven and he slept.

Weekends were something else altogether.

* * *

But Daddy, you promised!

A Friday night, so long ago it seemed like part of another life.

You did tell them we'd go, George. You know they've been waiting for this.

Just a movie, no big deal, but George had three cases pending and he really needed to do some research, especially on the Marsden case which the police had mishandled so thoroughly, and even two hours seemed too long away from his desk, but—

You said we'd go, Daddy. You promised.

And so, unwilling to break a promise to his kids, he'd hustled the family into his wife's Ford Explorer and headed out to the multiplex.

Friday night. The movie ended at 10:42 – he knew because he'd checked his watch, wondering if it was worth trying to get some more work in before bedtime.

And at exactly eleven o'clock p.m., the world went black, and his girls, all of them, left him alone. For a long, long while.

* * *

George went to bed on Fridays a few minutes before eleven – never later. He turned off his bedside alarm. Not that it would wake him, but it felt *right* – something real people did on the weekends.

Then he waited. The few minutes before eleven stretched, stretched, and each time he wondered if this was the last time, if this was the end.

And right before the clocks went off all through the house, right before the pain started, he always prayed that it wasn't over. *Not yet, please give me a little longer with them!*

Then heaven became hell.

* * *

Friday night, at exactly eleven o'clock p.m.

The impact came from his right, unexpected, unbelievable in force. His airbag went off, burning his face, bruising his chest, then deflated; it held George in position just long enough to keep him from wrenching the steering wheel to the left, maybe enough to spin them away from the hulking shape bearing down on them, maybe enough to save—

Then the rollover, fast, incredibly fast, and George felt everything as if for the first time: the broken safety glass flying through the SUV like shrapnel, his driver's side window shattering as the vehicle bounced on its side, his face shoved against the glass hard enough to tear ragged gouges completely through his cheek and into his mouth. He chewed glass without thinking, trying to scream, trying to make the steering wheel do something, trying through sheer will to make the tires reach out for the pavement and grab it, trying not to notice how everything slowed down and how the blood misted around him in perfect globules. He heard another scream as well, Mattie, he thought, who was behind him in her seat, but there should be two others, right, two more? and then the Explorer flipped completely, what was it now two seconds two frigging *seconds* and Mattie shut up right in mid-scream and that's not good Georgie-boy, that is just not *copacetic*, dammit, and then something grabbed his thigh in jagged metallic teeth and *clamped down*, and that's all he could remember, he'd blacked out then and even God couldn't wake him up—

—but that was only Friday night, and the weekend was one unholy bitch.

* * *

During the weekdays, in the empty hours spent waiting for his children to come home from school, George tried not to remember those two days of agony, but flashes kept coming back to him, slices of life and death: the emergency crew using the jaws of life to rescue him from the jagged section of framework that had pierced his right leg clean through, snapping the femur on its quick passage through the muscles of his thigh; the ride in the EMT unit, with the oxygen and plasma and needles everywhere and stitches, God so many stitches, that they put in later in the emergency room, crisscrossing his face in mad variations on Frankenstein's monster; the steady chatter of the trauma doctors and nurses as they assessed the situation while he lay there – he was out, baby, shock and a massive head wound combining to put him in near-coma, so why whisper now, why go to another room, no point; and the real pain, the inner torture, more than the slice and dice they did to him in that damned ER, or later in surgery (and he felt it all on the weekends, every single cut and flay and stitch he'd missed the first time around, the unadulterated shitstorm of hellfire his body went through…).

The real pain came from words. Cold, professional, uninflected words.

Wife and the oldest child killed on impact.

Youngest girl died en route, maybe a blessing, considering.

Dead, dead, and dead again.

George felt it all, heard it all every weekend, as if for the first time.

And even then, he still prayed for more time.

* * *

George shaved. The temptation to just let everything go was strong, but it didn't add to the sense of *normalcy* he needed to get through the week.

When he shaved, though, he had to confront the mirror. *Bad thing*, his mind told him, *we don't need this bad thing, do we, George?* All the other mirrors in the house were gone now, removed or broken in anger. They didn't reflect the truth – his family around him, his utterly normal life, his *happiness*, damn it. Unreliable, they'd been banished from his perfect home.

But he had to shave, so he had to *see*. And the bathroom mirror showed him everything, every morning, in a harsh, unforgiving light.

Gray, listless skin, hanging around the hollows of his eyes, pulling the corners of his mouth down – not into a frown, but into an utterly neutral expression beyond loss, beyond life. He looked like the people in old photos from concentration camps, and he knew that if he took off his robe, he'd see his ribcage in bold definition, see his withered scrotum, his bandy legs, one of them twisted and scarred from the accident.

He left the robe on, finished shaving, and covered the mirror with a towel, so he wouldn't have to look in it again until the next morning.

Then he dressed, tried to eat, and went out to wander until it was time for the children.

* * *

Ten-thirty on a Wednesday evening, looking at the photos again. Just another weeknight, girls asleep, Laurel working. George found himself staring at the family sitting, himself surrounded by a woman and two women-to-be, everyone happy, dressed up, facing forever through the camera lens.

They look fine. They look wonderful. What's wrong with this family, what could ever be wrong?

A light caress across his back, Laurel's fingers touching him with a ghost's subtlety. "Why did you come back?" he asked her, not taking his gaze from the picture.

"I finished grading, George. I'm free. At least for tonight." She stroked his neck now, her touch still little more than a cool breeze across his skin.

"No, not now. In the hospital. Why did you come back to me? All of you?"

They'd been there when he came out of his little coma, waiting by his bedside as if they'd never left him, never – as if he hadn't known that they were – as if he hadn't heard the doctors and nurses talking while he was away, away...

But still he knew. Even then, drugged to the gills on pain medicine, he knew that they'd left him, his girls, his precious women, he knew he knew he knew.

And he'd pretended not to know.

Laurel laughed in his ear, then answered him in a delicate whisper. "Don't be silly, darling. You were hurt. You needed us."

Her fingers ruffled his hair, causing a few strands to blow softly across his forehead. "We love you, George."

"I love you too," he whispered back, wanting to touch her, wanting to hold her, wanting too much.

He heard the whirs and clicks of various clocks, knew they'd chime soon, and tried to hold on to another night, another week. He thought of the bathroom mirror, his own skeletal image mocking him in his memory. "Go to bed, Laurel. You have to get up early, remember."

A kiss on the back of his neck – moist air, a hint of pressure – and Laurel drifted back into the bedroom.

George watched the picture for a few minutes longer, daring it to change. *We will all be together. We will all be happy. We will all be a family. Forever.*

He stumbled into the bedroom, fumbled around in the dark until he found the power button for the computer and turned it on.

Then George fell into his cold bed and prayed for a few more days with his family. A few more days, that's all.

Let us keep living a normal life.

A Ghost Story

Mark Twain

I TOOK a large room, far up Broadway, in a huge old building whose upper stories had been wholly unoccupied for years until I came. The place had long been given up to dust and cobwebs, to solitude and silence. I seemed groping among the tombs and invading the privacy of the dead, that first night I climbed up to my quarters. For the first time in my life a superstitious dread came over me; and as I turned a dark angle of the stairway and an invisible cobweb swung its slazy woof in my face and clung there, I shuddered as one who had encountered a phantom.

I was glad enough when I reached my room and locked out the mold and the darkness. A cheery fire was burning in the grate, and I sat down before it with a comforting sense of relief. For two hours I sat there, thinking of bygone times; recalling old scenes, and summoning half-forgotten faces out of the mists of the past; listening, in fancy, to voices that long ago grew silent for all time, and to once-familiar songs that nobody sings now. And as my reverie softened down to a sadder and sadder pathos, the shrieking of the winds outside softened to a wail, the angry beating of the rain against the panes diminished to a tranquil patter, and one by one the noises in the street subsided, until the hurrying footsteps of the last belated straggler died away in the distance and left no sound behind.

The fire had burned low. A sense of loneliness crept over me. I arose and undressed, moving on tiptoe about the room, doing stealthily what I had to do, as if I were environed by sleeping enemies whose slumbers it would be fatal to break. I covered up in bed, and lay listening to the rain and wind and the faint creaking of distant shutters, till they lulled me to sleep.

I slept profoundly, but how long I do not know. All at once I found myself awake, and filled with a shuddering expectancy. All was still. All but my own heart – I could hear it beat. Presently the bedclothes began to slip away slowly toward the foot of the bed, as if someone were pulling them! I could not stir; I could not speak. Still the blankets slipped deliberately away, till my breast was uncovered. Then with a great effort I seized them and drew them over my head. I waited, listened, waited. Once more that steady pull began, and once more I lay torpid a century of dragging seconds till my breast was naked again. At last I roused my energies and snatched the covers back to their place and held them with a strong grip. I waited. By and by I felt a faint tug, and took a fresh grip. The tug strengthened to a steady strain – it grew stronger and stronger. My hold parted, and for the third time the blankets slid away. I groaned. An answering groan came from the foot of the bed! Beaded drops of sweat stood upon my forehead. I was more dead than alive. Presently I heard a heavy footstep in my room – the step of an elephant, it seemed to me – it was not like anything human. But it was moving from me – there was relief in that. I heard it approach the door – pass out without moving bolt or lock – and wander away among the dismal corridors, straining the floors and joists till they creaked again as it passed – and then silence reigned once more.

When my excitement had calmed, I said to myself, "This is a dream – simply a hideous dream." And so I lay thinking it over until I convinced myself that it was a dream, and then a comforting laugh relaxed my lips and I was happy again. I got up and struck a light; and when I found that the locks and bolts were just as I had left them, another soothing laugh welled in my heart and rippled from my lips. I took my pipe and lit it, and was just sitting down before the fire, when – down went the pipe out of my nerveless fingers, the blood forsook my cheeks, and my placid breathing was cut short with a gasp! In the ashes on the hearth, side by side with my own bare footprint, was another, so vast that in comparison mine was but an infant's! Then I had had a visitor, and the elephant tread was explained.

I put out the light and returned to bed, palsied with fear. I lay a long time, peering into the darkness, and listening. Then I heard a grating noise overhead, like the dragging of a heavy body across the floor; then the throwing down of the body, and the shaking of my windows in response to the concussion. In distant parts of the building I heard the muffled slamming of doors. I heard, at intervals, stealthy footsteps creeping in and out among the corridors, and up and down the stairs. Sometimes these noises approached my door, hesitated, and went away again. I heard the clanking of chains faintly, in remote passages, and listened while the clanking grew nearer – while it wearily climbed the stairways, marking each move by the loose surplus of chain that fell with an accented rattle upon each succeeding step as the goblin that bore it advanced. I heard muttered sentences; half-uttered screams that seemed smothered violently; and the swish of invisible garments, the rush of invisible wings. Then I became conscious that my chamber was invaded – that I was not alone. I heard sighs and breathings about my bed, and mysterious whisperings. Three little spheres of soft phosphorescent light appeared on the ceiling directly over my head, clung and glowed there a moment, and then dropped – two of them upon my face and one upon the pillow. They spattered, liquidly, and felt warm. Intuition told me they had turned to gouts of blood as they fell – I needed no light to satisfy myself of that. Then I saw pallid faces, dimly luminous, and white uplifted hands, floating bodiless in the air – floating a moment and then disappearing. The whispering ceased, and the voices and the sounds, and a solemn stillness followed. I waited and listened. I felt that I must have light or die. I was weak with fear. I slowly raised myself toward a sitting posture, and my face came in contact with a clammy hand! All strength went from me apparently, and I fell back like a stricken invalid. Then I heard the rustle of a garment – it seemed to pass to the door and go out.

When everything was still once more, I crept out of bed, sick and feeble, and lit the gas with a hand that trembled as if it were aged with a hundred years. The light brought some little cheer to my spirits. I sat down and fell into a dreamy contemplation of that great footprint in the ashes. By and by its outlines began to waver and grow dim. I glanced up and the broad gas-flame was slowly wilting away. In the same moment I heard that elephantine tread again. I noted its approach, nearer and nearer, along the musty halls, and dimmer and dimmer the light waned. The tread reached my very door and paused – the light had dwindled to a sickly blue, and all things about me lay in a spectral twilight. The door did not open, and yet I felt a faint gust of air fan my cheek, and presently was conscious of a huge, cloudy presence before me. I watched it with fascinated eyes. A pale glow stole over the Thing; gradually its cloudy folds took shape – an arm appeared, then legs, then a body, and last a great sad face looked out of the vapor. Stripped of its filmy housings, naked, muscular and comely, the majestic Cardiff Giant loomed above me!

All my misery vanished – for a child might know that no harm could come with that benignant countenance. My cheerful spirits returned at once, and in sympathy with them the gas flamed up brightly again. Never a lonely outcast was so glad to welcome company as I was to greet the friendly giant. I said:

"Why, is it nobody but you? Do you know, I have been scared to death for the last two or three hours? I am most honestly glad to see you. I wish I had a chair – here, here, don't try to sit down in that thing—"

But it was too late. He was in it before I could stop him and down he went – I never saw a chair shivered so in my life.

"Stop, stop, you'll ruin ev—"

Too late again. There was another crash, and another chair was resolved into its original elements.

"Confound it, haven't you got any judgment at all? Do you want to ruin all the furniture on the place? Here, here, you petrified fool—"

But it was no use. Before I could arrest him he had sat down on the bed, and it was a melancholy ruin.

"Now what sort of a way is that to do? First you come lumbering about the place bringing a legion of vagabond goblins along with you to worry me to death, and then when I overlook an indelicacy of costume which would not be tolerated anywhere by cultivated people except in a respectable theater, and not even there if the nudity were of your sex, you repay me by wrecking all the furniture you can find to sit down on. And why will you? You damage yourself as much as you do me. You have broken off the end of your spinal column, and littered up the floor with chips of your hams till the place looks like a marble yard. You ought to be ashamed of yourself – you are big enough to know better."

"Well, I will not break any more furniture. But what am I to do? I have not had a chance to sit down for a century." And the tears came into his eyes.

"Poor devil," I said, "I should not have been so harsh with you. And you are an orphan, too, no doubt. But sit down on the floor here – nothing else can stand your weight – and besides, we cannot be sociable with you away up there above me; I want you down where I can perch on this high counting-house stool and gossip with you face to face."

So he sat down on the floor, and lit a pipe which I gave him, threw one of my red blankets over his shoulders, inverted my sitz-bath on his head, helmet fashion, and made himself picturesque and comfortable. Then he crossed his ankles, while I renewed the fire, and exposed the flat, honeycombed bottoms of his prodigious feet to the grateful warmth.

"What is the matter with the bottom of your feet and the back of your legs, that they are gouged up so?"

"Infernal chilblains – I caught them clear up to the back of my head, roosting out there under Newell's farm. But I love the place; I love it as one loves his old home. There is no peace for me like the peace I feel when I am there."

We talked along for half an hour, and then I noticed that he looked tired, and spoke of it.

"Tired?" he said. "Well, I should think so. And now I will tell you all about it, since you have treated me so well. I am the spirit of the Petrified Man that lies across the street there in the museum. I am the ghost of the Cardiff Giant. I can have no rest, no peace, till they have given that poor body burial again. Now what was the most natural thing for me to do, to make men satisfy this wish? Terrify them into it! – Haunt the place where the body lay! So I haunted the museum night after night. I even got other spirits to help me. But it did no good, for nobody ever came to the museum at midnight. Then it occurred to me to come over the way and haunt this place a little. I felt that if I ever got a hearing I must succeed, for I had the most efficient company that perdition could furnish. Night after night we have shivered around through these mildewed halls, dragging chains, groaning, whispering, tramping up and down stairs, till, to tell you the truth, I am almost worn out. But when I saw a light in your room tonight I roused my energies again and went at it with a deal of the old freshness. But I am tired out – entirely fagged out. Give me, I beseech you, give me some hope!"

I lit off my perch in a burst of excitement, and exclaimed:

"This transcends everything! Everything that ever did occur! Why you poor blundering old fossil, you have had all your trouble for nothing – you have been haunting a plaster cast of yourself – the real Cardiff Giant is in Albany! – [A fact. The original fraud was ingeniously and fraudfully duplicated, and exhibited in New York as the 'only genuine' Cardiff Giant (to the unspeakable disgust of the owners of the real colossus) at the very same time that the latter was drawing crowds at a museum in Albany] – Confound it, don't you know your own remains?"

I never saw such an eloquent look of shame, of pitiable humiliation, overspread a countenance before.

The Petrified Man rose slowly to his feet, and said:

"Honestly, is that true?"

"As true as I am sitting here."

He took the pipe from his mouth and laid it on the mantel, then stood irresolute a moment (unconsciously, from old habit, thrusting his hands where his pantaloons pockets should have been, and meditatively dropping his chin on his breast) and finally said:

"Well – I never felt so absurd before. The Petrified Man has sold everybody else, and now the mean fraud has ended by selling its own ghost! My son, if there is any charity left in your heart for a poor friendless phantom like me, don't let this get out. Think how you would feel if you had made such an ass of yourself."

I heard his stately tramp die away, step by step down the stairs and out into the deserted street, and felt sorry that he was gone, poor fellow – and sorrier still that he had carried off my red blanket and my bath-tub.

The Staircase

Hugh Walpole

IT DOESN'T MATTER in the least where this old house is. There were once many houses like it. Now there are very few.

It was born in 1540 (you can see the date of its birth over the lintel of the porch, cut into the stone). It is E-shaped with central porch and wings at each end. Its stone is now, in its present age, weathered to a beautiful colour of pearl-grey, purple-shadowed. This stone makes the house seem old, but it is not old; its heart and veins are strong and vigorous, only its clothes now are shabby.

It is a small house as Tudor manor houses go, but its masonry is very solid, and it was created by a spirit who cared that it should have every grace of proportion and strength. The wings have angle buttresses, and the porch rises to twisted terminals; there are twisted terminals with cupola tops also upon the gables, and the chimneys too are twisted. The mullioned windows have arched heads, and the porch has a Tudor arch. The arch is an entrance to a little quadrangle, and there are rooms above and gables on either side. Here and there is rich carving very fancifully designed.

It is set upon a little hill, and the lawn runs down to a small formal garden with box-hedges mounted by animals fancifully cut, a sun-dial, a little stone temple. Fields spread on either side of it and are bordered completely by a green tangled wood. The trees climb skywards on every side, but they are not too close about the house. They are too friendly to it to hurt it in any way. Over the arched porch a very amiable gargoyle hangs his head. He has one eye closed and a protruding chin from which the rain drips on a wet day, and in the winter icicles hang from it.

All the country about the house is very English, and the villages have names like Croxton, Little Pudding, Big Pudding, Engleheart and Applewain. A stream runs at the end of the lower field, runs through the wood, under the road, by other fields, so far as Bonnet where it becomes a river and broadens under bridges at Peckwit, the country town.

The house is called Candil Place and is very proud of its name. Its history for the last hundred years has been very private and personal. No one save myself and the house knows the real crises of its history, just as no one knows the real crisis of your history save yourself. You have doubtless been often surprised that neighbours think that such and such events have been the dramatic changing moments in your life – as when you lost your wife or your money or had scarlet fever – when in reality it was the blowing of a window curtain, the buying of a ship in silver, or the cry of a child on the stair.

So it has been with this house which has had its heart wrung by the breaking of a bough in the wind, a spark flying from the chimney, or a mouse scratching in the wainscot. From its birth it has had its own pride, its own reserve, its own consequence. Everything that has happened in it, every person who has come to it or gone from it, every song that has been sung in it, every oath sworn in it, every shout, every cry, every prayer, every yawn has found a place in its history.

Its heart has been always kindly, hospitable, generous; it has had as many intentions as we have all had, towards noble ends and fine charities. But life is not so easy as that.

Its first days were full of light and colour. Of course it was always a small house; Sir Mortimer Candil, who helped to create it, loved it, and the house gave him its heart. The house knew that he did for it what he could with his means; the house suffered with him when his first wife died of the plague, rejoiced with him when he married again so beautiful a lady, suffered with him once more when the beautiful lady ran away to Spain with a rascal.

There is a little room, the Priest's Room, where Sir Mortimer shut himself in and cried, one long summer day, his heart away. When he came out of there he had no heart any more, and the house, the only witness of that scene, put its arms about him, loved him more dearly than it had ever done, and mourned him most bitterly when he died.

The house after that had a very especial tenderness for the Priest's Room, which was first hung with green tapestry, and then had dark panelling, and then was whitewashed, and then had a Morris wallpaper, and then discovered its dark panelling again, changing its clothes but never forgetting anything.

But the house was never a sentimental weakling. It was rather ironic in spirit because of the human nature that it saw and the vanity of all human wishes.

As to this business of human wishes and desires, the house has never understood them, having a longer vision and a quieter, more tranquil heart. After the experience that it has had of these strange, pathetic, obstinate, impulsive, short-sighted beings it has decided, perhaps, that they are bent on self-ruin and seem to wish for that.

This has given the house an air of rather chuckling tenderness.

Considering such oddities, its chin in its hand and the wood gathering round to listen, whether there should be anything worth listening to (for the house when it likes is a good story-teller), the eye of its mind goes back to a number of puzzling incidents and, most puzzling of all, to the story of Edmund Candil and his lady Dorothy, the events of a close summer evening in 1815, the very day that the house and its inhabitants had the news of Waterloo.

Sir Edmund Candil was a very restless, travelling gentleman, and all the trouble began with that.

The house could never understand what pleasure he found in all these tiresome foreign tours that he prosecuted when there was the lovely English country for him to spend his days in. His wife Dorothy could not understand this either.

There was a kind of fated air about them from the moment of their marriage. The house noticed it on their very wedding day, and the Priest's Room murmured to the Parlour: "Here's an odd pair!" and the Staircase whispered to the little dark Hall with the family pictures: "This doesn't look too well," and the Powder-Closet repeated to the Yellow Bedroom: "No, this doesn't look well at all."

They had, of course, all known Edmund from his birth. He was a swarthy, broad-shouldered baby, unusually long in the leg, and from the very beginning he was known for his tender heart and his obstinate will. These two qualities made him very silent. His tender heart caused him to be afraid of giving himself away, his obstinate will made him close his mouth and jut out his chin so that nobody could possibly say that his resolve showed signs of weakening.

He had a sister Henrietta, who was the cause of all the later trouble. The house never from the beginning liked Henrietta. It considered that always she had been of a sly, mean, greedy disposition. There is nothing like a house for discovering whether people are mean or greedy.

Chests of drawers, open fireplaces, chairs and tables, staircases and powder-closets, these are the wise recipients of impressions whose confidence and knowledge you can shake neither by lies nor arrogances.

The house was willing to grant that Henrietta loved her brother, but in a mean, grasping, greedy manner, and jealousy was her other name.

They were children of a late marriage and their parents died of the smallpox when Edmund was nineteen and Henrietta twenty-one. After that Henrietta ruled the house because Edmund was scarcely ever there, and the house disliked exceedingly her rule. This house was, as I have said, a loyal and faithful friend and servant of the Candil family. Some houses are always hostile to their owners, having a great unreasoning pride of their own and considering the persons who inhabit them altogether unworthy of their good fortune. But partly for the sake of Sir Mortimer, who had created and loved it, and partly because it was by nature kindly, and partly because it always hoped for the best, the house had always chosen only the finest traits in the Candil character and refused to look at any other.

But, if there is one thing that a house resents, it is to be shabbily and meanly treated. When a carpet is worn, a window rattling in the breeze, a pipe in rebellion, a chair on the wobble, the house does everything towards drawing the attention of its master. This house had been always wonderfully considerate of expense and the costliness of all repair. It knew that its masters were not men of great wealth and must go warily with their purposes, but, until Henrietta, the Candils had been generous within their powers. They had had a pride in the house which made them glad to be generous. Henrietta had no such pride. She persisted in what she called an 'adequate economy', declaring that it was her duty to her brother who drove her, but as the house (who was never deceived about anything) very well knew, this so-called 'economy' became her god and to save money her sensual passion.

She grew into a long bony woman with a faint moustache on her upper lip and a strange, heavy, flat-footed way of walking. The Staircase, a little conceited perhaps because of its lovely banisters that were as delicate as lace, hated her tread and declared that she was so common that she could not be a Candil. Several times the Staircase tripped her up out of sheer maliciousness. The Store-room hated her more than did any other part of the house. Every morning she was there, skimping and cheese-paring, making this last and doing without that, wondering whether this were not too expensive and that too 'outrageous'. Of course her maidservants would not stay with her. She found it cheapest to engage little charity-girls, and when she had them she starved them. It is true that she also starved herself, but that was no virtue; the house would see the little charity-girls crying from sheer hunger in their beds, and its heart would ache for them.

This was of course to some degree different when Edmund came home from his travels, but not very different, because he was always considerably under his sister's influence. He was soft-hearted and she was hard, and, as the house very well knew, the hard ones always win.

Henrietta loved her brother, but she was also afraid of him. She was very proud of him but yet more proud of her domination over him. When he was thirty and she thirty-two she was convinced that he would never marry. It had been once her terror that he should, and she would lie awake thinking one moment of the household accounts and the next of wicked girls who might entrap her brother. But it seemed that he was never in love; he returned from every travel as virgin as before.

She said to him one morning, smiling her rather grim smile: "Well, brother, you are a bachelor for life, I think."

It was then that he told her that he was shortly to marry Miss Dorothy Preston of Cathwick Hall.

He spoke very quietly, but, as the armchair in the Adam Room noticed, he was not quite at his ease. They were speaking in the Adam Room at the time, and this armchair had only recently been purchased by Edmund Candil. The room was not known then as the Adam Room (it had that title later) but it was the room of Edmund's heart. The fireplace was in the Adam style and so were the ceiling, and the furniture, the chairs, the table, the sofa, the commode Edmund had had made for him in London.

Very lovely they were, of satin-wood and mahogany, with their general effect of straight line but modified by lovely curves, delicate and shining. In the centre of the commode was a painted vase of flowers, on the ceiling a heavenly tracing of shell-like circles. Everywhere grace and strength and the harmony of perfect workmanship.

This room was for Edmund the heart of England, and he would stand in it, his dark eyes glowing, fingering his stock, slapping his tight thigh with his riding whip, a glory at his heart. Many things he had brought with him from foreign countries. There was the Chinese room, and the little dining room was decorated with Italian pictures. In his own room that he called the Library there was an ink-horn that had been (they said) Mirabeau's, a letter of Marie Antoinette's, a yellow lock cut from the hair of a mermaid and some of the feathers from the headdress of an African chieftain. Many more treasures than these. But it was the Parlour with the fine furniture bought by him in London that was England, and it was of this room that he thought when he was tossing on the Bay of Biscay or studying pictures in Florence or watching the ablutions of natives in the Sacred River.

It was in this room that he told his sister that he intended marriage.

She made no protest. She knew well enough when her brother's mind was made up. But it was a sunny morning when he told her, and as the sun, having embraced merrily the box-hedge peacocks and griffins, looked in to wish good-morning to the sofa and the round shining satin-wood table that balanced itself so beautifully on its slim delicate legs, it could tell that the table and chairs were delighted about something.

"What is it?" said the sun, rubbing its chin on the windowsill.

"There's a new mistress coming," said the table and chairs.

And, when she came, they all fell at once in love with her. Was there ever anyone so charming and delicate in her primrose-coloured gown, her pretty straw bonnet and the grey silk scarf about her shoulders? Was there ever anyone so charming?

Of course Henrietta did not think so. This is an old story, this one of the family relations greeting so suspiciously the new young bride, but it is always actual enough in its tragedy and heartbreak however often it may have happened before.

Is it sentimental to be sorry because the new Lady Candil was sad and lonely and cried softly for hours at night while her husband slept beside her? At that time at least the house did not think so. Possibly by now it has grown more cynical. It cannot, any more than the humans who inhabit it, altogether be unaware of the feeling and colour of its time.

In any case the house loved Dorothy Candil and was deeply grieved at her trouble. That trouble was, one must realise, partly of her own making.

Her husband loved her, nay, he adored her with all the tenderness and tenacity that were part of his character. He adored her and was bored by her: as everyone knows, this is a most aggravating state of feeling. He thought her beautiful, good, amiable and honest, but he had nothing at all to say to her. For many a man she would have been exactly fitting, for it was not so much that she was stupid as that she had no education and no experience. He gave her none of these things as he should have done. Nor did he realise that this life, in the depths of English country, removed from all the enterprise and movement of the town, removed also by the weather from any outside intercourse for weeks at a time, was for someone without any great resources in herself depressing and enervating.

And then she was frightened of him. How well the house understood this! It too was, at times, afraid of him, of his silences, his obstinacy and easy capacity of semi-liveliness, a sensitiveness that his reticence forbade him to express.

How often in the months that followed the marriage did the house long to advise her as to her treatment of him. The sofa in the parlour was especially wise in such cases. Long before it had been covered with its gay cherry-coloured silk it had been famous among friends and neighbours for its delicacy in human tactics.

There came a morning when Lady Candil sat on a corner of it, her lovely little hand (she was delicate, slim, fragile, her body had the consistency of egg-shell china) clenching the shining wood of its strong arm for support, and a word from her would have put everything right. The sofa could feel the throbbing of her heart, and looking across to the thick, stiff, obstinate body of her husband, longed to throw her into his arms. But she could not say the word, and the mischanced moment became history for both of them. Had they not loved so truly it might have been easier for them; as it was, shyness and obstinacy built the barrier.

And of course Henrietta assisted. How grimly was she pleased as she sat in her ugly old russet gown, pretending to read Lord Clarendon's History (for she made a great pretence of improving her mind), but in reality listening to the unhappy silences between them and watching for the occasion when a word from her to her brother would skilfully widen the breach. For she hated poor Dorothy. She must in any case have done so out of jealousy and disappointment, but Dorothy was also precisely the example in woman whom she most despised. A weak, feckless, helpless thing whose pretty looks were an insult!

Then Dorothy felt her peril and rose to meet it. The house may have whispered in her ear!

Yes, she rose to meet it, but, as life only too emphatically teaches us, it is no good crying for the moon – and it is no good, however urgent we may be, begging for qualities that we have not got. She had a terrible habit of being affectionate at the wrong time. A kind of fate pursued her in this. He would return from his afternoon's ride, pleasantly weary, eager for his wife and happy in the thought of a little romantic dalliance, and she, fancying that he would not be disturbed, would leave him to snore beside the fire. Or a neighbour squire would visit him and he be off with him for the afternoon and she feel neglected. Or he would be absorbed in a newsletter with a lively account of French affairs and she choose that moment to sit on his knee and tug his hair.

Dorothy was in truth one of those unfortunate persons – and they are among the most unfortunate in the world – who are insensitive to the moods and atmospheres of others. These err not through egotism nor stupidity, but rather through a sort of colour-blindness so that they see their friend red when he is yellow and green when he is blue. Neither Dorothy nor Edmund had any gift of words.

So, a year and a half after his marriage, Edmund, with an ache in his heart, although he would own this to nobody, went once again to foreign parts. The house implored him not to go: he almost heard its protests.

On one of his last evenings there – a windy spring evening – he came in from a dark twilight walk, splashed with the mud of the country paths, the sense of the pale hedgerow primroses yet in his eye, the chatter of birds in his ear, and standing in the hall heard the William and Mary clock with the moon and stars, the banisters of the staircase, the curtains of the long hall window whisper to him:

"Don't go! Don't go! Don't go!"

He stood there and thought: "By Gemini, I'll not leave this!" Dorothy came down the stairs to greet him and, seeing him lost in thought, stole upstairs again. In any case he had taken his seat in the coach, and his place in the packet-boat was got for him by a friend in London.

"Don't go!" said the portrait of old Uncle Candil.

He strode upstairs and Dorothy was reading *Grandison* by the fire, and although her heart was beating with love for him, was too timid to say so.

So to foreign parts he went again and, loving her so dearly, wrote letters to her which he tore up without sending lest she should think him foolish – such being the British temperament.

How the house suffered then, that Dorothy should be left to the harsh economies of sister Henrietta. Henrietta was not a bad woman, but she was mean, selfish, proud and stupid. She was also jealous. Very quickly and with little show of rebellion Dorothy submitted to her ways. If true love is in question absence does indeed make the heart grow fonder, and Dorothy thought of her husband night, morning, and night again.

She was snubbed, starved, and given a thorough sense of her insufficiencies. It is surprising how completely one human being can convince another of incompetence, ignorance and silly vanity if they be often alone together and one of them a woman. Women are more wholehearted than men in what they do, whether for good or ill, and Henrietta was very whole-hearted indeed in this affair.

She convinced Dorothy before her husband's return that she was quite unworthy of his love, that he found her dull and unresponsive, that he was deeply disappointed in the issue of his marriage, and that she had deceived him most basely. You may say that she was a poor-spirited little thing, but she was very lonely, half-starved, and her love made her defenceless.

The appetite grows with what it feeds on, and Henrietta found that 'educating Dorothy', as she called it, was a very worthy and soul-satisfying occupation. Dorothy began to be frightened, not only of herself and of Henrietta but of everything around her, the house, the gardens, the surrounding country.

The house did its utmost to reassure her. When she lay awake in her bed at night the house would hush any noise that might disturb her, the furniture of her room, the hangings above her bed, the old chest of Cromwell's time, the Queen Anne wardrobe, the warming-pan, the fire-irons that had the heads of grinning dogs, the yellow rug from Turkey, the Italian lamp beside her bed, they all crowded about her to tell her that they loved her. After a while she was conscious of their affection. Her bedroom and the parlour were for her the happiest places in the house, the only places indeed where she was not afraid.

She did not know that they were saying anything to her – she had not that kind of perception – but she felt reassured by them, and she would lock herself into her bedroom and sit there for hours thinking of her husband and wondering where he might be.

She became so painfully aware of Henrietta that she saw her when she wasn't there. She saw her always just around a corner, behind a tree, on the other side of the rose-garden wall, peering over the sun-dial, hiding behind the curtain. She became a slave to her, doing all that she was told, going where she was bid. The house considered it a disgusting business.

One evening she broke into a flash of rebellion.

"Edmund loves me!" she cried, her little breasts panting, her small hands clenched. "And you hate me! Why do you hate me? I have never done you any harm."

Henrietta looked at her severely.

"Hate! Hate! I have other things to do – and if he loves you, why does he stay so long away?"

Ah! Why indeed? The house echoed the question, the very floors trembling with agitation. The stupid fool! Could he not see the treasure that he had? Did he think that such glories were to be picked up anywhere, any day, for the asking? The fire spat a piece of coal on to the hearthrug in contempt of human blindness.

When the time arrived at last for Edmund's return, Dorothy was in a fitting condition of miserable humility. Edmund did not love her. He was bored with her too dreadfully. But indeed how could he love her? How could anybody love her, poor incompetent stupid thing that she was! And yet in her heart she knew that she was not so stupid. Did Edmund love her only a little she could jump all the barriers and be really rather brilliant – much more brilliant than Henrietta, who was certainly not brilliant at all. It was this terrible shyness that held her back, that and Henrietta's assurance that Edmund did not love her. And indeed he did not seem to. It was but too likely that Henrietta was right.

As the time approached for Edmund's return Henrietta was in a fine bustle and the house was in one too. The house smiled contemptuously at Henrietta's parsimonious attempts to freshen it up. As though the house could not do that a great deal better than Henrietta ever could! Bees-waxing the floors, rubbing the furniture, shining up the silver – what were these little superficialities compared with the inner spiritual shake that the house gave itself when it wanted to? A sort of glow stole over windows, stairs and hall; a silver shine, a richer colour crept into the amber curtains, the cherry-coloured sofa; the faces in the portraits smiled, the fire-irons glittered, the mahogany shone again. Edmund had been away too long; the house would not let him go so easily next time.

The night before his return Dorothy did not sleep, but lay there, her eyes burning, her heart thickly beating, determining on the bold demonstrative person she would be. She would show Henrietta whether he loved her or no. But at the thought of Henrietta she shivered and drew the bed-clothes closely about her. She seemed to be standing beside the bed, illumined in the darkness by her own malignant fires, her yellow skin drawn tightly across the supercilious bones, her hands curving over some fresh mean economy, her ridiculous headdress wagging like a mocking spirit above her small red-rimmed eyes. Yes, if only Henrietta were not there...

And the old chest murmured softly: "If only Henrietta were not there..."

The post-chaise came up to the door darkly like a ghost, for it had been snowing all day and the house was wrapped in silence. The animals on the box-tree hedge stood out fantastically against the silver-grey of the evening sky, and the snow fell like the scattering feathers of a heavenly geese-flock.

Edmund stepped into the hall and had Dorothy in his arms. At that moment they knew how truly they loved one another. He wondered as he flung his mind back in an instant's retrospect over a phantasmagoria of Indian Moguls, Chinese rivers and the flaming sunsets of Arabia how it could be that he had not known that his life was here, here with his beloved house above him, his adored wife in his arms. His head up like a conqueror's, he mounted the stairs, almost running into his wonderful parlour, to see once again the vase of flowers on the commode, the slender beautiful legs of his chair, the charming circles of his delicate ceiling. "How could I have stayed away?" he thought. "I will never leave this again!"

And that night, clasped in one another's arms, they discovered one another again: shyness fled and heart was open to heart.

Nevertheless there remained Henrietta. Would you believe that one yellow-faced old maid could direct and dominate two normal healthy creatures? You know that she can, and is doing it somewhere or other at this very moment. And all for their good. No one ever did anything mean to anyone else yet save for their good, and so it will be until the end of this frail planet.

She told Edmund that she had been 'educating Dorothy'. He would find her greatly improved; she feared that her worst fault was Hardness of Heart. Hardness of Heart! A sad defect!

During those snowy days Henrietta tried to show her brother that no one in the world truly loved him but herself. She had shown him this before and found the task easy; now it was more difficult. Dorothy's shyness had been melted by this renewed contact; he could not doubt the evidence of his eyes and the many little unconscious things that spoke for her when she had no idea that they were speaking. Now they rode and walked together and he explained to her how *he* was, how that at a time his thoughts would be far, far away in Cairo or Ispahan and that she must not think that he did not care for her because he was dreaming, and she told him that when he had frightened her she had been stupid, but that now that he frightened her no longer she would soon be brilliant.... So Henrietta's task was difficult.

And then in the spring, when the daffodils blew among the long grasses and the white violets were shining in the copse, a chance word of hers showed her the way. She hated Dorothy now because she suspected that Dorothy was planning to be rid of her. The fear that she would be turned out of the house never left her, and so, as fear always does, it drove her to baser things than belonged truly to her nature. She hinted that in Edmund's absence Dorothy had found a neighbouring squire 'good company'. And there had been perhaps another or two...*men*...At that word every frustrated instinct in Henrietta's body turned in rebellion. She had not spoken before she believed it true. She had this imaginative gift, common to lonely persons. She was herself amazed at the effect of her words on Edmund. If she had ever doubted Edmund's love for his wife (and she had not really doubted it) she was certain of the truth at last. Dorothy...Dorothy...His stout body trembled; his eyes were wounded; he turned from his sister as though he were ashamed both of her and of himself. After that there was no peace.

It was now that the house wondered most deeply at these strange human beings. The little things that upset them, the odd things that, at a moment, they would believe! Here, for instance, was their Edmund, whom they so truly admired, loving his Dorothy and entirely trusting her. Now, at a moment's word from a sour-faced virgin, there is a fire of torment in his heart. He looks on every male with an eager restless suspicion. While attempting to appear natural he watches Dorothy at every corner and counters in his mind her lightest word.

"Why," said the Italian lamp (which from its nationality knew everything about jealousy) to the Cromwellian chest, "I have never known so foolish a suspicion," to which the Cromwellian chest replied in its best Roundhead manner: "Woman...the devil's bait... always has been...always will be."

He attacked his sister again and again. "With whom has she been? Has she ever stayed from the house a night? What friends has she made?"

To which Henrietta would indignantly reply: "Brother, brother. What are you about? This jealousy is most unbecoming. I have suggested no impropriety...only a little foolishness born of idleness."

But it did not need time for Dorothy to discover that something was once again terribly amiss.

This strange husband of hers, so unable to express himself – she had but just won him back to her and now he was away again! With the courage born of their new relationship she asked him what was the trouble. And he told her: "Nothing....Nothing! Nothing at all! Why should there be trouble? You are for ever imagining..." And then looked at her so strangely that she blushed and turned away as though she were indeed guilty. Guilty of what? She had not the least idea. But what she did know was that it was dear sister Henrietta who was responsible, and now, as May came with a flourish of birds and blossom and star-lit nights, she began to hate Henrietta with an intensity quite new to her gentle nature.

So, with jealousy and hatred, alive and burning, the house grew very sad. It hated these evil passions and had said long ago that they ruined with their silly bitterness every good house in the world. The little Chinese cabinet with the purple dragons on its doors said that in China everything was much simpler – you did not drag a situation to infinity as these sluggish English do, but simply called Death in to make a settlement – a much simpler way. In any case the house began to watch and to listen with the certainty that the moment was approaching when it must interfere.

Jealousy always heightens love, and so, if Edmund had loved Dorothy at the first, that cool, placid anticipation was nothing to the fevered passion which he now felt. When he was away from her he longed to have her in his arms, covering her with kisses and assuring her that he had never doubted her, and when he was with her he suspected her every look, her every word. And she, miserable now and angry and ill, could not tell what possessed him, her virtue being so secure that she could not conceive that anyone should suspect it. Only she was well aware that Henrietta was to blame.

These were also days of national anxiety and unrest; the days when Napoleon jumping from Elba alighted in France and for a moment promised to stay there. Warm, stuffy, breathless days, when everyone was waiting, the house with the rest.

On the staircase one summer evening Dorothy told Henrietta something of her mind. "If I had my way," she ended in a shaking rage, "you would not be here plotting against us!"

So that was it! At last Henrietta's suspicions were confirmed. In a short while Dorothy would have her out of the house; and then where would she go? The thought of her desolation, loneliness, loss of power, gripped her heart like a cat's claws. The two little charity-girls had a time of it during those weeks and cried themselves to sleep in their attic that smelt of mice and apples, dreaming afterwards of strong lovers who beat their mistress into a pulp.

"Give me proof!" said Edmund, so bitterly tormented. "If it is true, give me proof!"

And Henrietta answered, sulkily: "I have never said anything," and a window-sash fell on his fingers and bruised them just to teach him not to be so damnable a fool.

Nevertheless Henrietta had her proof. She had been cherishing it for a year at least. This was a letter written by a young Naval Lieutenant, cousin of a neighbouring squire, after he had danced with Dorothy at a Christmas ball. It was only a happy careless boy's letter, he in love with Dorothy's freshness, and because he was never more than a moment in any one place, careless of consequences. He said in his letter that she was the most beautiful of God's creatures, that he would dream of her at sea, and the rest. Dorothy kept it. Henrietta stole it....

The day came when the coach brought the news of the Waterloo victory. On that summer evening rockets were breaking into the pale sky above the dark soft shelter of the wood; on Bendon Hill they were waiting for dark to light the bonfire. You could hear the shouting and singing from the high-road. The happiness at the victory and the sense that England was delivered blew some of the cobwebs from Edmund's brain; he took Dorothy into the garden and there, behind the sun-dial, put his arms around her and kissed her.

Henrietta, watching the rockets strike the sky from her window, saw them, and fear, malice, loneliness, greed, hurt pride and jealousy all rose in her together. She turned over the letter in her drawer and vowed that her brother should not go to bed that night before he had heard of it.

"Look out! Look out!" cried her room to the rest of the house. "She will make mischief with the letter. We must prevent her…"

"She has done mischief enough," chattered the clock from the hall.

"She must be prevented…" whistled the chimneys. Something must be done and at once. But how? By whom?

She is coming. She stands outside her door, glancing about the dim sunset passage. The picture of Ranelagh above her head wonders – shall it fall on her? The chairs along the passage watch her anxiously as she passes them. But what can they do? Each must obey his own laws.

Stop her! Stop her! Stop her! Edmund and Dorothy are coming in from the garden. The sun is sinking, the shadows lengthening across the lawn. One touch on his arm: "Brother, may I have a word?" and all the harm is done – misery and distress, unhappiness in the house, separation and loneliness. Stop her! Stop her!

All the house is quivering with agitation. The curtains are blowing, the chimneys are twisting, the tables and chairs are creaking: Stop her! Stop her! Stop her!

The order has gone out. She is standing now at the head of the staircase leading to the hall. She waits, her head bent a little, listening. Something seems to warn her. Edmund and Dorothy are coming in from the garden. The fireworks are beginning beyond the wood, and their gold and crimson showers are rivalling the stars.

Henrietta, nodding her head as though in certainty, has taken her step, some roughness in the wood has caught her heel (was it there a moment ago?), she stumbles, she clutches at the balustrade, but it is slippery and refuses to aid her. She is falling; her feet are away in air, her head strikes the board; she screams, once and then again; a rush, a flash of huddled colour, and her head has struck the stone of the hall floor.

How odd a silence followed! Dorothy and Edmund were still a moment lingering by the door looking back to the shower of golden stars, hearing the happy voices singing in the road. Henrietta was dead and so made no sound.

But all through the house there was a strange humming as though everything from top to bottom were whispering.

Everything in the house is moving save the woman at the bottom of the stairs.

Miss Mary Pask

Edith Wharton

Chapter I

IT WAS NOT till the following spring that I plucked up courage to tell Mrs. Bridgeworth what had happened to me that night at Morgat.

In the first place, Mrs. Bridgeworth was in America; and after the night in question I lingered on abroad for several months – not for pleasure, God knows, but because of a nervous collapse supposed to be the result of having taken up my work again too soon after my touch of fever in Egypt. But, in any case, if I had been door to door with Grace Bridgeworth I could not have spoken of the affair before, to her or to anyone else; not till I had been rest-cured and built up again at one of those wonderful Swiss sanatoria where they clean the cobwebs out of you. I could not even have written to her – not to save my life. The happenings of that night had to be overlaid with layer upon layer of time and forgetfulness before I could tolerate any return to them.

The beginning was idiotically simple; just the sudden reflex of a New England conscience acting on an enfeebled constitution. I had been painting in Brittany, in lovely but uncertain autumn weather, one day all blue and silver, the next shrieking gales or driving fog. There is a rough little white-washed inn out on the Pointe du Raz, swarmed over by tourists in summer but a sea-washed solitude in autumn; and there I was staying and trying to do waves, when someone said: "You ought to go over to Cape something else, beyond Morgat."

I went, and had a silver-and-blue day there; and on the way back the name of Morgat set up an unexpected association of ideas: Morgat – Grace Bridgeworth – Grace's sister, Mary Pask – "You know my darling Mary has a little place now near Morgat; if you ever go to Brittany do go to see her. She lives such a lonely life – it makes me so unhappy."

That was the way it came about. I had known Mrs. Bridgeworth well for years, but had only a hazy intermittent acquaintance with Mary Pask, her older and unmarried sister. Grace and she were greatly attached to each other, I knew; it had been Grace's chief sorrow, when she married my old friend Horace Bridgeworth, and went to live in New York, that Mary, from whom she had never before been separated, obstinately lingered on in Europe, where the two sisters had been travelling since their mother's death. I never quite understood why Mary Pask refused to join Grace in America. Grace said it was because she was 'too artistic' – but, knowing the elder Miss Pask, and the extremely elementary nature of her interest in art, I wondered whether it were not rather because she disliked Horace Bridgeworth. There was a third alternative – more conceivable if one knew Horace – and that was that she may have liked him too much. But that again became untenable (at least I supposed it did) when one knew Miss Pask: Miss Pask with her round flushed face, her innocent bulging eyes, her old-maidish flat decorated with art-tidies, and her vague and timid philanthropy. Aspire to Horace –!

Well, it was all rather puzzling, or would have been if it had been interesting enough to be worth puzzling over. But it was not. Mary Pask was like hundreds of other dowdy old maids, cheerful derelicts content with their innumerable little substitutes for living. Even Grace would not have interested me particularly if she hadn't happened to marry one of my oldest friends, and to be kind to his friends. She was a handsome capable and rather dull woman, absorbed in her husband and children, and without an ounce of imagination; and between her attachment to her sister and Mary Pask's worship of her there lay the inevitable gulf between the feelings of the sentimentally unemployed and those whose affections are satisfied. But a close intimacy had linked the two sisters before Grace's marriage, and Grace was one of the sweet conscientious women who go on using the language of devotion about people whom they live happily without seeing; so that when she said: "You know it's years since Mary and I have been together – not since little Molly was born. If only she'd come to America! Just think…Molly is six, and has never seen her darling auntie…" when she said this, and added: "If you go to Brittany promise me you'll look up my Mary," I was moved in that dim depth of one where unnecessary obligations are contracted.

And so it came about that, on that silver-and-blue afternoon, the idea "Morgat – Mary Pask – to please Grace" suddenly unlocked the sense of duty in me. Very well: I would chuck a few things into my bag, do my day's painting, go to see Miss Pask when the light faded, and spend the night at the inn at Morgat. To this end I ordered a rickety one-horse vehicle to await me at the inn when I got back from my painting, and in it I started out toward sunset to hunt for Mary Pask…

As suddenly as a pair of hands clapped over one's eyes, the sea-fog shut down on us. A minute before we had been driving over a wide bare upland, our backs turned to a sunset that crimsoned the road ahead; now the densest night enveloped us. No one had been able to tell me exactly where Miss Pask lived; but I thought it likely that I should find out at the fishers' hamlet toward which we were trying to make our way. And I was right…an old man in a doorway said: Yes – over the next rise, and then down a lane to the left that led to the sea; the American lady who always used to dress in white. Oh, *he* knew…near the *Baie des Trépassés*.

"Yes; but how can we see to find it? I don't know the place," grumbled the reluctant boy who was driving me.

"You will when we get there," I remarked.

"Yes – and the horse foundered meantime! I can't risk it, sir; I'll get into trouble with the *patron*."

Finally an opportune argument induced him to get out and lead the stumbling horse, and we continued on our way. We seemed to crawl on for a long time through a wet blackness impenetrable to the glimmer of our only lamp. But now and then the ball lifted or its folds divided; and then our feeble light would drag out of the night some perfectly commonplace object – a white gate, a cow's staring face, a heap of roadside stones – made portentous and incredible by being thus detached from its setting, capriciously thrust at us, and as suddenly withdrawn. After each of these projections the darkness grew three times as thick; and the sense I had had for some time of descending a gradual slope now became that of scrambling down a precipice. I jumped out hurriedly and joined my young driver at the horse's head.

"I can't go on – I won't, sir!" he whimpered.

"Why, see, there's a light over there – just ahead!"

The veil swayed aside, and we beheld two faintly illuminated squares in a low mass that was surely the front of a house.

"Get me as far as that – then you can go back if you like."

The veil dropped again; but the boy had seen the lights and took heart. Certainly there was a house ahead of us; and certainly it must be Miss Pask's, since there could hardly be two in such a desert. Besides, the old man in the hamlet had said: "Near the sea"; and those endless modulations of the ocean's voice, so familiar in every corner of the Breton land that one gets to measure distances by them rather than by visual means, had told me for some time past that we must be making for the shore. The boy continued to lead the horse on without making any answer. The fog had shut in more closely than ever, and our lamp merely showed us the big round drops of wet on the horse's shaggy quarters.

The boy stopped with a jerk. "There's no house – we're going straight down to the sea."

"But you saw those lights, didn't you?"

"I thought I did. But where are they now? The fog's thinner again. Look – I can make out trees ahead. But there are no lights any more."

"Perhaps the people have gone to bed," I suggested jocosely.

"Then hadn't we better turn back, sir?"

"What – two yards from the gate?"

The boy was silent: certainly there was a gate ahead, and presumably, behind the dripping trees, some sort of dwelling. Unless there was just a field and the sea...the sea whose hungry voice I heard asking and asking, close below us. No wonder the place was called the Bay of the Dead! But what could have induced the rosy benevolent Mary Pask to come and bury herself there? Of course the boy wouldn't wait for me...I knew that...the *Baie des Trépassés* indeed! The sea whined down there as if it were feeding-time, and the Furies, its keepers, had forgotten it...

There *was* the gate! My hand had struck against it. I felt along to the latch, undid it, and brushed between wet bushes to the house-front. Not a candle-glint anywhere. If the house were indeed Miss Pask's, she certainly kept early hours...

Chapter Two

NIGHT AND FOG were now one, and the darkness as thick as a blanket. I felt vainly about for a bell. At last my hand came in contact with a knocker and I lifted it. The clatter with which it fell sent a prolonged echo through the silence; but for a minute or two nothing else happened.

"There's no one there, I tell you!" the boy called impatiently from the gate.

But there was. I had heard no steps inside, but presently a bolt shot back, and an old woman in a peasant's cap pushed her head out. She had set her candle down on a table behind her, so that her face, aureoled with lacy wings, was in obscurity; but I knew she was old by the stoop of her shoulders and her fumbling movements. The candlelight, which made her invisible, fell full on my face, and she looked at me.

"This is Miss Mary Pask's house?"

"Yes, sir." Her voice – a very old voice – was pleasant enough, unsurprised and even friendly.

"I'll tell her," she added, shuffling off. "Do you think she'll see me?" I threw after her.

"Oh, why not? The idea!" she almost chuckled. As she retreated I saw that she was wrapped in a shawl and had a cotton umbrella under her arm. Obviously she was going out – perhaps going home for the night. I wondered if Mary Pask lived all alone in her hermitage.

The old woman disappeared with the candle and I was left in total darkness. After an interval I heard a door shut at the back of the house and then a slow clumping of aged *sabots* along the flags outside. The old woman had evidently picked up her *sabots* in the kitchen and left the house. I wondered if she had told Miss Pask of my presence before going, or whether she had just left me there, the butt of some grim practical joke of her own. Certainly there was no sound within doors. The footsteps died out, I heard a gate click – then complete silence closed in again like the fog.

"I wonder—" I began within myself; and at that moment a smothered memory struggled abruptly to the surface of my languid mind.

"But she's *dead* – Mary Pask is *dead*!"

I almost screamed it aloud in my amazement. It was incredible, the tricks my memory had played on me since my fever! I had known for nearly a year that Mary Pask was dead – had died suddenly the previous autumn – and though I had been thinking of her almost continuously for the last two or three days it was only now that the forgotten fact of her death suddenly burst up again to consciousness.

Dead! But hadn't I found Grace Bridgeworth in tears and crape the very day I had gone to bid her goodbye before sailing for Egypt? Hadn't she laid the cable before my eyes, her own streaming with tears while I read: "Sister died suddenly this morning requested burial in garden of house particulars by letter" – with the signature of the American Consul at Brest, a friend of Bridgeworth's I seemed to recall? I could see the very words of the message printed on the darkness before me.

As I stood there I was a good deal more disturbed by the discovery of the gap in my memory than by the fact of being alone in a pitch-dark house, either empty or else inhabited by strangers. Once before of late I had noted this queer temporary blotting-out of some well-known fact; and here was a second instance of it. Decidedly, I wasn't as well over my illness as the doctors had told me…Well, I would get back to Morgat and lie up there for a day or two, doing nothing, just eating and sleeping…

In my self-absorption I had lost my bearings, and no longer remembered where the door was. I felt in every pocket in turn for a match – but since the doctors had made me give up smoking, why should I have found one?

The failure to find a match increased my sense of irritated helplessness, and I was groping clumsily about the hall among the angles of unseen furniture when a light slanted along the rough-cast wall of the stairs. I followed its direction, and on the landing above me I saw a figure in white shading a candle with one hand and looking down. A chill ran along my spine, for the figure bore a strange resemblance to that of Mary Pask as I used to know her.

"Oh, it's *you*!" she exclaimed in the cracked twittering voice which was at one moment like an old woman's quaver, at another like a boy's falsetto. She came shuffling down in her baggy white garments, with her usual clumsy swaying movements; but I noticed that her steps on the wooden stairs were soundless. Well – they would be, naturally!

I stood without a word, gazing up at the strange vision above me, and saying to myself: "There's nothing there, nothing whatever. It's your digestion, or your eyes, or some damned thing wrong with you somewhere—"

But there was the candle, at any rate; and as it drew nearer, and lit up the place about me, I turned and caught hold of the door-latch. For, remember, I had seen the cable, and Grace in crape…

"Why, what's the matter? I assure you, you don't disturb me!" the white figure twittered; adding, with a faint laugh: "I don't have so many visitors nowadays—"

She had reached the hall, and stood before me, lifting her candle shakily and peering up into my face. "You haven't changed – not as much as I should have thought. But I have, haven't I?" she appealed to me with another laugh; and abruptly she laid her hand on my arm. I looked down at the hand, and thought to myself: "*That* can't deceive me."

I have always been a noticer of hands. The key to character that other people seek in the eyes, the mouth, the modelling of the skull, I find in the curve of the nails, the cut of the finger-tips, the way the palm, rosy or sallow, smooth or seamed, swells up from its base. I remembered Mary Pask's hand vividly because it was so like a caricature of herself; round, puffy, pink, yet prematurely old and useless. And there, unmistakably, it lay on my sleeve: but changed and shrivelled – somehow like one of those pale freckled toadstools that the least touch resolves to dust…Well – to dust? Of course…

I looked at the soft wrinkled fingers, with their foolish little oval finger-tips that used to be so innocently and naturally pink, and now were blue under the yellowing nails – and my flesh rose in ridges of fear.

"Come in, come in," she fluted, cocking her white untidy head on one side and rolling her bulging blue eyes at me. The horrible thing was that she still practised the same arts, all the childish wiles of a clumsy capering coquetry. I felt her pull on my sleeve and it drew me in her wake like a steel cable.

The room she led me into was – well, 'unchanged' is the term generally used in such cases. For as a rule, after people die, things are tidied up, furniture is sold, remembrances are despatched to the family. But some morbid piety (or Grace's instructions, perhaps) had kept this room looking exactly as I supposed it had in Miss Pask's lifetime. I wasn't in the mood for noting details; but in the faint dabble of moving candlelight I was half aware of bedraggled cushions, odds and ends of copper pots, and a jar holding a faded branch of some late-flowering shrub. A real Mary Pask 'interior'!

The white figure flitted spectrally to the chimney-piece, lit two more candles, and set down the third on a table. I hadn't supposed I was superstitious – but those three candles! Hardly knowing what I did, I hurriedly bent and blew one out. Her laugh sounded behind me.

"Three candles – you still mind that sort of thing? I've got beyond all that, you know," she chuckled. "Such a comfort…such a sense of freedom…" A fresh shiver joined the others already coursing over me.

"Come and sit down by me," she entreated, sinking to a sofa. "It's such an age since I've seen a living being!"

Her choice of terms was certainly strange, and as she leaned back on the white slippery sofa and beckoned me with one of those unburied hands my impulse was to turn and run. But her old face, hovering there in the candlelight, with the unnaturally red cheeks like varnished apples and the blue eyes swimming in vague kindliness, seemed to appeal to me against my cowardice, to remind me that, dead or alive, Mary Pask would never harm a fly.

"Do sit down!" she repeated, and I took the other corner of the sofa.

"It's so wonderfully good of you – I suppose Grace asked you to come?" She laughed again – her conversation had always been punctuated by rambling laughter. "It's an event – quite an event! I've had so few visitors since my death, you see."

Another bucketful of cold water ran over me; but I looked at her resolutely, and again the innocence of her face disarmed me.

I cleared my throat and spoke – with a huge panting effort, as if I had been heaving up a grave-stone. "You live here alone?" I brought out.

"Ah, I'm glad to hear your voice – I still remember voices, though I hear so few," she murmured dreamily. "Yes – I live here alone. The old woman you saw goes away at night. She won't stay after dark…she says she can't. Isn't it funny? But it doesn't matter; I like the darkness." She leaned to me with one of her irrelevant smiles. "The dead," she said, "naturally get used to it."

Once more I cleared my throat; but nothing followed.

She continued to gaze at me with confidential blinks. "And Grace? Tell me all about my darling. I wish I could have seen her again…just once." Her laugh came out grotesquely. "When she got the news of my death – were you with her? Was she terribly upset?"

I stumbled to my feet with a meaningless stammer. I couldn't answer – I couldn't go on looking at her.

"Ah, I see…it's too painful," she acquiesced, her eyes brimming, and she turned her shaking head away.

"But after all…I'm glad she was so sorry…It's what I've been longing to be told, and hardly hoped for. Grace forgets…" She stood up too and flitted across the room, wavering nearer and nearer to the door.

"Thank God," I thought, "she's going."

"Do you know this place by daylight?" she asked abruptly.

I shook my head.

"It's very beautiful. But you wouldn't have seen *me* then. You'd have had to take your choice between me and the landscape. I hate the light – it makes my head ache. And so I sleep all day. I was just waking up when you came." She smiled at me with an increasing air of confidence. "Do you know where I usually sleep? Down below there – in the garden!" Her laugh shrilled out again. "There's a shady corner down at the bottom where the sun never bothers one. Sometimes I sleep there till the stars come out."

The phrase about the garden, in the consul's cable, came back to me and I thought: "After all, it's not such an unhappy state. I wonder if she isn't better off than when she was alive?"

Perhaps she was – but I was sure I wasn't, in her company. And her way of sidling nearer to the door made me distinctly want to reach it before she did. In a rush of cowardice I strode ahead of her – but a second later she had the latch in her hand and was leaning against the panels, her long white raiment hanging about her like grave-clothes. She drooped her head a little sideways and peered at me under her lashless lids.

"You're not going?" she reproached me.

I dived down in vain for my missing voice, and silently signed that I was.

"Going going away? Altogether?" Her eyes were still fixed on me, and I saw two tears gather in their corners and run down over the red glistening circles on her cheeks. "Oh, but you mustn't," she said gently. "I'm too lonely…"

I stammered something inarticulate, my eyes on the blue-nailed hand that grasped the latch. Suddenly the window behind us crashed open, and a gust of wind, surging in out of the blackness, extinguished the candle on the nearest chimney-corner. I glanced back nervously to see if the other candle were going out too.

"You don't like the noise of the wind? I do. It's all I have to talk to…People don't like me much since I've been dead. Queer, isn't it? The peasants are so superstitious. At times I'm really lonely…" Her voice cracked in a last effort at laughter, and she swayed toward me, one hand still on the latch.

"Lonely, lonely! If you knew how *lonely*! It was a lie when I told you I wasn't! And now you come, and your face looks friendly…and you say you're going to leave me! No – no – no – you shan't! Or else, why did you come? It's cruel…I used to think I knew what loneliness was…after Grace married, you know. Grace thought she was always thinking of me, but she wasn't. She called me 'darling', but she was thinking of her husband and children. I said to myself then: 'You couldn't be lonelier if you were dead.' But I know better now…There's been no loneliness like this last year's…none! And sometimes I sit here and think: 'If a man came along some day and took a fancy to you?'" She gave another wavering cackle. "Well, such things *have* happened, you know, even after youth's gone…a man who'd had his troubles too. But no one came till tonight…and now you say you're going!" Suddenly she flung herself toward me. "Oh, stay with me, stay with me…just tonight…It's so sweet and quiet here…No one need know…no one will ever come and trouble us."

I ought to have shut the window when the first gust came. I might have known there would soon be another, fiercer one. It came now, slamming back the loose-hinged lattice, filling the room with the noise of the sea and with wet swirls of fog, and dashing the other candle to the floor. The light went out, and I stood there – we stood there – lost to each other in the roaring coiling darkness. My heart seemed to stop beating; I had to fetch up my breath with great heaves that covered me with sweat. The door – the door – well, I knew I had been facing it when the candle went. Something white and wraithlike seemed to melt and crumple up before me in the night, and avoiding the spot where it had sunk away I stumbled around it in a wide circle, got the latch in my hand, caught my foot in a scarf or sleeve, trailing loose and invisible, and freed myself with a jerk from this last obstacle. I had the door open now. As I got into the hall I heard a whimper from the blackness behind me; but I scrambled on to the hall door, dragged it open and bolted out into the night. I slammed the door on that pitiful low whimper, and the fog and wind enveloped me in healing arms.

Chapter Three

WHEN I WAS well enough to trust myself to think about it all again I found that a very little thinking got my temperature up, and my heart hammering in my throat. No use…I simply couldn't stand it…for I'd seen Grace Bridgeworth in crape, weeping over the cable, and yet I'd sat and talked with her sister, on the same sofa – her sister who'd been dead a year!

The circle was a vicious one; I couldn't break through it. The fact that I was down with fever the next morning might have explained it; yet I couldn't get away from the clinging reality of the vision. Supposing it *was* a ghost I had been talking to, and not a mere projection of my fever? Supposing something survived of Mary Pask – enough to cry out to me the unuttered loneliness of a lifetime, to express at last what the living woman had always had to keep dumb and hidden? The thought moved me curiously – in my weakness I lay and wept over it. No end of women were like that, I supposed, and perhaps, after death, if they got their chance they tried to use it…Old tales and legends floated through my mind; the bride of Corinth, the mediaeval vampire – but what names to attach to the plaintive image of Mary Pask!

My weak mind wandered in and out among these visions and conjectures, and the longer I lived with them the more convinced I became that something *which had been Mary Pask* had talked with me that night…I made up my mind, when I was up again, to drive back to the place (in broad daylight, this time), to hunt out the grave in the garden – that 'shady corner where the sun never bothers one' – and appease the poor ghost with a few flowers. But the doctors decided otherwise; and perhaps my weak will unknowingly abetted them. At any rate, I yielded to their insistence that I should be driven straight from my hotel to the train for Paris, and thence transshipped, like a piece of luggage, to the Swiss sanatorium they had in view for me. Of course I meant to come back when I was patched up again…and meanwhile, more and more tenderly, but more intermittently, my thoughts went back from my snow-mountain to that wailing autumn night above the *Baie des Trépassés*, and the revelation of the dead Mary Pask who was so much more real to me than ever the living one had been.

Chapter Four

AFTER ALL, why should I tell Grace Bridgeworth – ever? I had had a glimpse of things that were really no business of hers. If the revelation had been vouchsafed to me, ought I not to bury it in those deepest depths where the inexplicable and the unforgettable sleep together? And besides, what interest could there be to a woman like Grace in a tale she could neither understand nor believe in? She would just set me down as 'queer' – and enough people had done that already. My first object, when I finally did get back to New York, was to convince everybody of my complete return to mental and physical soundness; and into this scheme of evidence my experience with Mary Pask did not seem to fit. All things considered, I would hold my tongue.

But after a while the thought of the grave began to trouble me. I wondered if Grace had ever had a proper gravestone put on it. The queer neglected look of the house gave me the idea that perhaps she had done nothing – had brushed the whole matter aside, to be attended to when she next went abroad. "Grace forgets," I heard the poor ghost quaver… No, decidedly, there could be no harm in putting (tactfully) just that one question about the care of the grave; the more so as I was beginning to reproach myself for not having gone back to see with my own eyes how it was kept…

Grace and Horace welcomed me with all their old friendliness, and I soon slipped into the habit of dropping in on them for a meal when I thought they were likely to be alone. Nevertheless my opportunity didn't come at once – I had to wait for some weeks. And then one evening, when Horace was dining out and I sat alone with Grace, my glance lit on a photograph of her sister – an old faded photograph which seemed to meet my eyes reproachfully.

"By the way, Grace," I began with a jerk, "I don't believe I ever told you: I went down to that little place of…of your sister's the day before I had that bad relapse."

At once her face lit up emotionally. "No, you never told me. How sweet of you to go!" The ready tears overbrimmed her eyes. "I'm so glad you did." She lowered her voice and added softly: "And did you see her?"

The question sent one of my old shudders over me. I looked with amazement at Mrs. Bridgeworth's plump face, smiling at me through a veil of painless tears. "I do reproach myself more and more about darling Mary," she added tremulously. "But tell me – tell me everything."

There was a knot in my throat; I felt almost as uncomfortable as I had in Mary Pask's own presence. Yet I had never before noticed anything uncanny about Grace Bridgeworth. I forced my voice up to my lips.

"Everything? Oh, I can't—." I tried to smile.

"But you did see her?"

I managed to nod, still smiling.

Her face grew suddenly haggard – yes, haggard! "And the change was so dreadful that you can't speak of it? Tell me – was that it?"

I shook my head. After all, what had shocked me was that the change was so slight – that between being dead and alive there seemed after all to be so little difference, except that of a mysterious increase in reality. But Grace's eyes were still searching me insistently. "You must tell me," she reiterated. "I know I ought to have gone there long ago—"

"Yes; perhaps you ought." I hesitated. "To see about the grave, at least…"

She sat silent, her eyes still on my face. Her tears had stopped, but her look of solicitude slowly grew into a stare of something like terror. Hesitatingly, almost reluctantly, she stretched out her hand and laid it on mine for an instant. "Dear old friend—" she began.

"Unfortunately," I interrupted, "I couldn't get back myself to see the grave...because I was taken ill the next day..."

"Yes, yes; of course. I know." She paused. "Are you *sure* you went there at all?" she asked abruptly.

"Sure? Good Lord—" It was my turn to stare. "Do you suspect me of not being quite right yet?" I suggested with an uneasy laugh.

"No – no...of course not...but I don't understand."

"Understand what? I went into the house...I saw everything, in fact, but her grave..."

"Her grave?" Grace jumped up, clasping her hands on her breast and darting away from me. At the other end of the room she stood and gazed, and then moved slowly back.

"Then, after all – I wonder?" She held her eyes on me, half fearful and half reassured. "Could it be simply that you never heard?"

"Never heard?"

"But it was in all the papers! Don't you ever read them? I meant to write...I thought I *had* written...but I said: 'At any rate he'll see it in the papers'...You know I'm always lazy about letters..."

"See what in the papers?"

"Why, that she *didn't* die...She isn't dead! There isn't any grave, my dear man! It was only a cataleptic trance...An extraordinary case, the doctors say...But didn't she tell you all about it – if you say you saw her?" She burst into half-hysterical laughter: "Surely she must have told you that she wasn't dead?"

"No," I said slowly, "she didn't tell me that."

We talked about it together for a long time after that – talked on till Horace came back from his men's dinner, after midnight. Grace insisted on going in and out of the whole subject, over and over again. As she kept repeating, it was certainly the only time that poor Mary had ever been in the papers. But though I sat and listened patiently I couldn't get up any real interest in what she said. I felt I should never again be interested in Mary Pask, or in anything concerning her.

Mr. Jones

Edith Wharton

Chapter I

LADY JANE LYNKE was unlike other people: when she heard that she had inherited Bells, the beautiful old place which had belonged to the Lynkes of Thudeney for something like six hundred years, the fancy took her to go and see it unannounced. She was staying at a friend's nearby, in Kent, and the next morning she borrowed a motor and slipped away alone to Thudeney-Blazes, the adjacent village.

It was a lustrous motionless day. Autumn bloom lay on the Sussex downs, on the heavy trees of the weald, on streams moving indolently, far off across the marshes. Farther still, Dungeness, a fitful streak, floated on an immaterial sky which was perhaps, after all, only sky.

In the softness Thudeney-Blazes slept: a few aged houses bowed about a duck-pond, a silvery spire, orchards thick with dew. Did Thudeney-Blazes ever wake?

Lady Jane left the motor to the care of the geese on a miniature common, pushed open a white gate into a field (the griffoned portals being padlocked), and struck across the park toward a group of carved chimney stacks. No one seemed aware of her.

In a dip of the land, the long low house, its ripe brick masonry overhanging a moat deeply sunk about its roots, resembled an aged cedar spreading immemorial red branches. Lady Jane held her breath and gazed.

A silence distilled from years of solitude lay on lawns and gardens. No one had lived at Bells since the last Lord Thudeney, then a penniless younger son, had forsaken it sixty years before to seek his fortune in Canada. And before that, he and his widowed mother, distant poor relations, were housed in one of the lodges, and the great place, even in their day, had been as mute and solitary as the family vault.

Lady Jane, daughter of another branch, to which an earldom and considerable possessions had accrued, had never seen Bells, hardly heard its name. A succession of deaths, and the whim of an old man she had never known, now made her heir to all this beauty; and as she stood and looked she was glad she had come to it from so far, from impressions so remote and different. "It would be dreadful to be used to it – to be thinking already about the state of the roof, or the cost of a heating system."

Till this her thirty-fifth year, Lady Jane had led an active, independent and decided life. One of several daughters, moderately but sufficiently provided for, she had gone early from home, lived in London lodgings, travelled in tropic lands, spent studious summers in Spain and Italy, and written two or three brisk business-like little books about cities usually dealt with sentimentally. And now, just back from a summer in the south of France, she stood ankle deep in wet bracken, and gazed at Bells lying there under a September sun that looked like moonlight.

"I shall never leave it!" she ejaculated, her heart swelling as if she had taken the vow to a lover.

She ran down the last slope of the park and entered the faded formality of gardens with clipped yews as ornate as architecture, and holly hedges as solid as walls. Adjoining the house rose a low deep-buttressed chapel. Its door was ajar, and she thought this of good augury: her forebears were waiting for her. In the porch she remarked fly-blown notices of services, an umbrella stand, a dishevelled door-mat: no doubt the chapel served as the village church. The thought gave her a sense of warmth and neighbourliness. Across the damp flags of the chancel, monuments and brasses showed through a traceried screen. She examined them curiously. Some hailed her with vocal memories, others whispered out of the remote and the unknown: it was a shame to know so little about her own family. But neither Crofts nor Lynkes had ever greatly distinguished themselves; they had gathered substance simply by holding on to what they had, and slowly accumulating privileges and acres. "Mostly by clever marriages," Lady Jane thought with a faint contempt.

At that moment her eyes lit on one of the less ornate monuments: a plain sarcophagus of gray marble niched in the wall and surmounted by the bust of a young man with a fine arrogant head, a Byronic throat and tossed-back curls.

'Peregrine Vincent Theobald Lynke, Baron Clouds, fifteenth Viscount Thudeney of Bells, Lord of the Manors of Thudeney, Thudeney-Blazes, Upper Lynke, Lynke-Linnet—' so it ran, with the usual tedious enumeration of honours, titles, court and county offices, ending with; 'Born on May 1st, 1790, perished of the plague at Aleppo in 1828.' And underneath, in small cramped characters, as if crowded as an afterthought into an insufficient space: 'Also His Wife'.

That was all. No name, dates, honours, epithets, for the Viscountess Thudeney. Did she too die of the plague at Aleppo? Or did the 'also' imply her actual presence in the sarcophagus which her husband's pride had no doubt prepared for his own last sleep, little guessing that some Syrian drain was to receive him? Lady Jane racked her memory in vain. All she knew was that the death without issue of this Lord Thudeney had caused the property to revert to the Croft-Lynkes, and so, in the end, brought her to the chancel step where, shyly, she knelt a moment, vowing to the dead to carry on their trust.

She passed on to the entrance court, and stood at last at the door of her new home, a blunt tweed figure in heavy mud-stained shoes. She felt as intrusive as a tripper, and her hand hesitated on the doorbell. "I ought to have brought someone with me," she thought; an odd admission on the part of a young woman who, when she was doing her books of travel, had prided herself on forcing single-handed the most closely guarded doors. But those other places, as she looked back, seemed easy and accessible compared to Bells.

She rang, and a tinkle answered, carried on by a flurried echo which seemed to ask what in the world was happening. Lady Jane, through the nearest window, caught the spectral vista of a long room with shrouded furniture. She could not see its farther end, but she had the feeling that someone stationed there might very well be seeing her.

"Just at first," she thought, "I shall have to invite people here – to take the chill off."

She rang again, and the tinkle again prolonged itself; but no one came.

At last she reflected that the caretakers probably lived at the back of the house, and pushing open a door in the courtyard wall she worked her way around to what seemed a stable-yard. Against the purple brick sprawled a neglected magnolia, bearing one late flower as big as a planet. Lady Jane rang at a door marked 'Service'. This bell, though also languid, had a wakefuller sound, as if it were more used to being rung, and still knew what was likely to follow; and after a delay during which Lady Jane again had the sense of being peered at – from above, through a lowered blind – a bolt shot, and a woman looked out. She was youngish, unhealthy, respectable and frightened; and she blinked at Lady Jane like someone waking out of sleep.

"Oh," said Lady Jane – "do you think I might visit the house?"

"The house?"

"I'm staying near here – I'm interested in old houses. Mightn't I take a look?"

The young woman drew back. "The house isn't shown."

"Oh, but not to – not to—" Jane weighed the case. "You see," she explained, "I know some of the family: the Northumberland branch."

"You're related, madam?"

"Well – distantly, yes." It was exactly what she had not meant to say; but there seemed no other way.

The woman twisted her apron strings in perplexity.

"Come, you know," Lady Jane urged, producing half-a-crown. The woman turned pale.

"I couldn't, madam; not without asking." It was clear that she was sorely tempted.

"Well, ask, won't you?" Lady Jane pressed the tip into a hesitating hand. The young woman shut the door and vanished. She was away so long that the visitor concluded her half-crown had been pocketed, and there was an end; and she began to be angry with herself, which was more often her habit than to be so with others.

"Well, for a fool, Jane, you're a complete one," she grumbled.

A returning footstep, listless, reluctant – the tread of one who was not going to let her in. It began to be rather comic.

The door opened, and the young woman said in her dull sing-song: "Mr. Jones says that no one is allowed to visit the house."

She and Lady Jane looked at each other for a moment, and Lady Jane read the apprehension in the other's eyes.

"Mr. Jones? Oh? – Yes; of course, keep it…" She waved away the woman's hand.

"Thank you, madam." The door closed again, and Lady Jane stood and gazed up at the inexorable face of her old home.

Chapter Two

"BUT YOU didn't get in? You actually came back without so much as a peep?"

Her story was received, that evening at dinner, with mingled mirth and incredulity.

"But, my dear! You mean to say you asked to see the house, and they wouldn't let you? *Who* wouldn't?" Lady Jane's hostess insisted.

"Mr. Jones."

"Mr. Jones?"

"He said no one was allowed to visit it."

"Who on earth is Mr. Jones?"

"The caretaker, I suppose. I didn't see him."

"Didn't see him either? But I never heard such nonsense! Why in the world didn't you insist?"

"Yes; why didn't you?" they all chorused; and she could only answer, a little lamely: "I think I was afraid."

"Afraid? *You*, darling?" There was fresh hilarity. "Of Mr. Jones?"

"I suppose so." She joined in the laugh, yet she knew it was true: she had been afraid.

Edward Stramer, the novelist, an old friend of her family, had been listening with an air of abstraction, his eyes on his empty coffee cup. Suddenly, as the mistress of the house pushed back her chair, he looked across the table at Lady Jane. "It's odd: I've just remembered something. Once, when I was a youngster, I tried to see Bells; over thirty years ago it must have been." He glanced at his host. "Your mother drove me over. And we were not let in."

There was a certain flatness in this conclusion, and someone remarked that Bells had always been known as harder to get into than any house thereabouts.

"Yes," said Stramer; "but the point is that we were refused in exactly the same words. Mr. Jones said no one was allowed to visit the house."

"Ah – he was in possession already? Thirty years ago? Unsociable fellow, Jones. Well, Jane, you've got a good watch-dog."

They moved to the drawing room, and the talk drifted to other topics. But Stramer came and sat down beside Lady Jane. "It is queer, though, that at such a distance of time we should have been given exactly the same answer."

She glanced up at him curiously. "Yes; and you didn't try to force your way in either?"

"Oh no: it was not possible."

"So I felt," she agreed.

"Well, next week, my dear, I hope we shall see it all, in spite of Mr. Jones," their hostess intervened, catching their last words as she moved toward the piano.

"I wonder if we shall see Mr. Jones," said Stramer.

Chapter Three

BELLS WAS NOT nearly as large as it looked; like many old houses it was very narrow, and but one storey high, with servant's rooms in the low attics, and much space wasted in crooked passages and superfluous stairs. If she closed the great saloon, Jane thought, she might live there comfortably with the small staff which was the most she could afford. It was a relief to find the place less important than she had feared.

For already, in that first hour of arrival, she had decided to give up everything else for Bells. Her previous plans and ambitions – except such as might fit in with living there – had fallen from her like a discarded garment, and things she had hardly thought about, or had shrugged away with the hasty subversiveness of youth, were already laying quiet hands on her; all the lives from which her life had issued, with what they bore of example or admonishment. The very shabbiness of the house moved her more than splendours, made it, after its long abandonment, seem full of the careless daily coming and going of people long dead, people to whom it had not been a museum, or a page of history, but cradle, nursery, home, and sometimes, no doubt, a prison. If those marble lips in the chapel could speak! If she could hear some of their comments on the old house which had spread its silent shelter over their sins and sorrows, their follies and submissions! A long tale, to which she was about to add another chapter, subdued and humdrum beside some of those earlier annals, yet probably freer and more varied than the unchronicled lives of the great-aunts and great-grandmothers buried there so completely that they must hardly have known when they passed from their beds to their graves. "Piled up like dead leaves," Jane thought, "layers and layers of them, to preserve something forever budding underneath."

Well, all these piled-up lives had at least preserved the old house in its integrity; and that was worthwhile. She was satisfied to carry on such a trust.

She sat in the garden looking up at those rosy walls, iridescent with damp and age. She decided which windows should be hers, which rooms given to the friends from Kent who were motoring over, Stramer among them, for a modest house-warming; then she got up and went in.

The hour had come for domestic questions; for she had arrived alone, unsupported even by the old family housemaid her mother had offered her. She preferred to start afresh, convinced that her small household could be staffed from the neighbourhood. Mrs. Clemm, the rosy-cheeked old person who had curtsied her across the threshold, would doubtless know.

Mrs. Clemm, summoned to the library, curtsied again. She wore black silk, gathered and spreading as to skirt, flat and perpendicular as to bodice. On her glossy false front was a black lace cap with ribbons which had faded from violet to ash-colour, and a heavy watch-chain descended from the lava brooch under her crochet collar. Her small round face rested on the collar like a red apple on a white plate: neat, smooth, circular, with a pursed-up mouth, eyes like black seeds, and round ruddy cheeks with the skin so taut that one had to look close to see that it was as wrinkled as a piece of old crackly.

Mrs. Clemm was sure there would be no trouble about servants. She herself could do a little cooking: though her hand might be a bit out. But there was her niece to help; and she was quite of her ladyship's opinion, that there was no need to get in strangers. They were mostly a poor lot; and besides, they might not take to Bells. There were persons who didn't. Mrs. Clemm smiled a sharp little smile, like the scratch of a pin, as she added that she hoped her ladyship wouldn't be one of them.

As for under-servants…well, a boy, perhaps? She had a great-nephew she might send for. But about women – under-housemaids – if her ladyship thought they couldn't manage as they were; well, she really didn't know. Thudeney-Blazes? Oh, she didn't think so…. There was more dead than living at Thudeney-Blazes…everyone was leaving there…or in the church-yard…one house after another being shut…death was everywhere, wasn't it, my lady? Mrs. Clemm said it with another of her short sharp smiles, which provoked the appearance of a frosty dimple.

"But my niece Georgiana is a hard worker, my lady; her that let you in the other day…"

"That didn't," Lady Jane corrected.

"Oh, my lady, it was too unfortunate. If only your ladyship had have said…poor Georgiana had ought to have seen; but she never *did* have her wits about her, not for answering the door."

"But she was only obeying orders. She went to ask Mr. Jones."

Mrs. Clemm was silent. Her small hands, wrinkled and resolute, fumbled with the folds of her apron, and her quick eyes made the circuit of the room and then came back to Lady Jane's.

"Just so, my lady; but, as I told her, she'd ought to have known—"

"And who is Mr. Jones?"

Mrs. Clemm's smile snapped out again, deprecating, respectful. "Well, my lady, he's more dead than living, too…if I may say so," was her surprising answer.

"Is he? I'm sorry to hear that; but who is he?"

"Well, my lady, he's…he's my great-uncle, as it were…my grandmother's own brother, as you might say."

"Ah; I see." Lady Jane considered her with growing curiosity. "He must have reached a great age, then."

"Yes, my lady; he has that. Though I'm not," Mrs. Clemm added, the dimple showing, "as old myself as your ladyship might suppose. Living at Bells all these years has been ageing to me; it would be to anybody."

"I suppose so. And yet," Lady Jane continued, "Mr. Jones has survived; has stood it well – as you certainly have?"

"Oh. Not as well as I have," Mrs. Clemm interjected, as if resentful of the comparison.

"At any rate, he still mounts guard; mounts it as well as he did thirty years ago."

"Thirty years ago?" Mrs. Clemm echoed, her hands dropping from her apron to her sides.

"Wasn't he here thirty years ago?"

"Oh, yes, my lady; certainly; he's never once been away that I know of."

"What a wonderful record! And what exactly are his duties?"

Mrs. Clemm paused again, her hands still motionless in the folds of her skirt. Lady Jane noticed that the fingers were tightly clenched, as if to check an involuntary gesture.

"He began as pantry-boy; then footman; then butler, my lady; but it's hard to say, isn't it, what an old servant's duties are, when he's stayed on in the same house so many years?"

"Yes; and that house always empty."

"Just so, my lady. Everything came to depend on him; one thing after another. His late lordship thought the world of him."

"His late lordship? But he was never here! He spent all his life in Canada."

Mrs. Clemm seemed slightly disconcerted. "Certainly, my lady." (Her voice said: "Who are you, to set me right as to the chronicles of Bells?") "But by letter, my lady; I can show you the letters. And there was his lordship before, the sixteenth Viscount. He *did* come here once."

"Ah, did he?" Lady Jane was embarrassed to find how little she knew of them all. She rose from her seat. "They were lucky, all these absentees, to have someone to watch over their interests so faithfully. I should like to see Mr. Jones – to thank him. Will you take me to him now?"

"Now?" Mrs. Clemm moved back a step or two; Lady Jane fancied her cheeks paled a little under their ruddy varnish. "Oh, not today, my lady."

"Why? Isn't he well enough?"

"Not nearly. He's between life and death, as it were," Mrs. Clemm repeated, as if the phrase were the nearest approach she could find to a definition of Mr. Jones's state.

"He wouldn't even know who I was?"

Mrs. Clemm considered a moment. "I don't say *that*, my lady;" her tone implied that to do so might appear disrespectful. "He'd know you, my lady; but you wouldn't know *him*." She broke off and added hastily: "I mean, for what he is: he's in no state for you to see him."

"He's so very ill? Poor man! And is everything possible being done?"

"Oh, everything; and more too, my lady. But perhaps," Mrs. Clemm suggested, with a clink of keys, "this would be a good time for your ladyship to take a look about the house. If your ladyship has no objection, I should like to begin with the linen."

Chapter Four

"AND Mr. Jones?" Stramer queried, a few days later, as they sat, Lady Jane and the party from Kent, about an improvised tea-table in a recess of one of the great holly-hedges.

The day was as hushed and warm as that on which she had first come to Bells, and Lady Jane looked up with a smile of ownership at the old walls which seemed to smile back, the windows which now looked at her with friendly eyes.

"Mr. Jones? Who's Mr. Jones?" the others asked; only Stramer recalled their former talk.

Lady Jane hesitated. "Mr. Jones is my invisible guardian; or rather, the guardian of Bells."

They remembered then. "Invisible? You don't mean to say you haven't seen him yet?"

"Not yet; perhaps I never shall. He's very old – and very ill, I'm afraid."

"And he still rules here?"

"Oh, absolutely. The fact is," Lady Jane added "I believe he's the only person left who really knows all about Bells."

"Jane, my *dear*! That big shrub over there against the wall! I verily believe it's Templetonia retusa. It *is*! Did anyone ever hear of it standing an English winter?" Gardeners all, they dashed towards the shrub in its sheltered angle. "I shall certainly try it on a south wall at Dipway," cried the hostess from Kent.

Tea over, they moved on to inspect the house. The short autumn day was drawing to a close; but the party had been able to come only for an afternoon, instead of staying over the week-end, and having lingered so long in the gardens they had only time, indoors, to puzzle out what they could through the shadows. Perhaps, Lady Jane thought, it was the best hour to see a house like Bells, so long abandoned, and not yet warmed into new life.

The fire she had had lit in the saloon sent its radiance to meet them, giving the great room an air of expectancy and welcome. The portraits, the Italian cabinets, the shabby armchairs and rugs, all looked as if life had but lately left them; and Lady Jane said to herself: "Perhaps Mrs. Clemm is right in advising me to live here and close the blue parlour."

"My dear, what a fine room! Pity it faces north. Of course you'll have to shut it in winter. It would cost a fortune to heat."

Lady Jane hesitated. "I don't know: I *had* meant to. But there seems to be no other..."

"No other? In all this house?" They laughed; and one of the visitors, going ahead and crossing a panelled anteroom, cried out: "But here! A delicious room; windows south – yes, and west. The warmest of the house. This is perfect."

They followed, and the blue room echoed with exclamations. "Those charming curtains with the parrots...and the blue of that petit point fire-screen! But, Jane, of course you must live here. Look at this citron-wood desk!"

Lady Jane stood on the threshold. "It seems that the chimney smokes hopelessly."

"Hopelessly? Nonsense! Have you consulted anybody? I'll send you a wonderful man..."

"Besides, if you put in one of those one-pipe heaters.... At Dipway..."

Stramer was looking over Lady Jane's shoulder. "What does Mr. Jones say about it?"

"He says no one has ever been able to use this room; not for ages. It was the housekeeper who told me. She's his great-niece, and seems simply to transmit his oracles."

Stramer shrugged. "Well, he's lived at Bells longer than you have. Perhaps he's right."

"How absurd!" one of the ladies cried. "The housekeeper and Mr. Jones probably spend their evenings here, and don't want to be disturbed. Look – ashes on the hearth! What did I tell you?"

Lady Jane echoed the laugh as they turned away. They had still to see the library, damp and dilapidated, the panelled dining room, the breakfast parlour, and such bedrooms as had any old furniture left; not many, for the late lords of Bells, at one time or another, had evidently sold most of its removable treasures.

When the visitors came down their motors were waiting. A lamp had been placed in the hall, but the rooms beyond were lit only by the broad clear band of western sky showing through uncurtained casements. On the doorstep one of the ladies exclaimed that she had lost her handbag – no, she remembered; she had laid it on the desk in the blue room. Which way was the blue room?

"I'll get it," Jane said, turning back. She heard Stramer following. He asked if he should bring the lamp.

"Oh, no; I can see."

She crossed the threshold of the blue room, guided by the light from its western window; then she stopped. Someone was in the room already; she felt rather than saw another presence. Stramer, behind her, paused also; he did not speak or move. What she saw, or thought she saw, was simply an old man with bent shoulders turning away from the citron-wood desk. Almost before she had received the impression there was no one there; only the slightest stir of the needlework curtain over the farther door. She heard no step or other sound.

"There's the bag," she said, as if the act of speaking, and saying something obvious were a relief.

In the hall her glance crossed Stramer's, but failed to find there the reflection of what her own had registered.

He shook hands, smiling. "Well, goodbye. I commit you to Mr. Jones's care; only don't let him say that *you're* not shown to visitors."

She smiled: "Come back and try," and then shivered a little as the lights of the last motor vanished beyond the great black hedges.

Chapter Five

LADY JANE had exulted in her resolve to keep Bells to herself till she and the old house should have had time to make friends. But after a few days she recalled the uneasy felling which had come over her as she stood on the threshold after her first tentative ring. Yes; she had been right in thinking she would have to have people about her to take the chill off. The house was too old, too mysterious, too much withdrawn into its own secret past, for her poor little present to fit into it without uneasiness.

But it was not a time of year when, among Lady Jane's friends, it was easy to find people free. Her own family were all in the north, and impossible to dislodge. One of her sisters, when invited, simply sent her back a list of shooting-dates; and her mother wrote: "Why not come to us? What can you have to do all alone in that empty house at this time of year? Next summer we're all coming."

Having tried one or two friends with the same result, Lady Jane bethought her of Stramer. He was finishing a novel, she knew, and at such times he liked to settle down somewhere in the country where he could be sure of not being disturbed. Bells was a perfect asylum, and though it was probable that some other friend had anticipated her, and provided the requisite seclusion, Lady Jane decided to invite him. "Do bring your work and stay till it's finished – and don't be in a hurry to finish. I promise that no one shall bother you—" and she added, half-nervously: "Not even Mr. Jones." As she wrote she felt an absurd impulse to blot the words out. "He might not like it," she thought; and the 'he' did not refer to Stramer.

Was the solitude already making her superstitious? She thrust the letter into an envelope, and carried it herself to the post-office at Thudeney-Blazes. Two days later a wire from Stramer announced his arrival.

He came on a cold stormy afternoon, just before dinner, and as they went up to dress Lady Jane called after him: "We shall sit in the blue parlour this evening." The housemaid Georgiana was crossing the passage with hot water for the visitor. She stopped and cast a vacant glance at Lady Jane. The latter met it, and said carelessly: "You hear Georgiana? The fire in the blue parlour."

While Lady Jane was dressing she heard a knock, and saw Mrs. Clemm's round face just inside the door, like a red apple on a garden wall.

"Is there anything wrong about the saloon, my lady? Georgiana understood—"

"That I want the fire in the blue parlour. Yes. What's wrong with the saloon is that one freezes there."

"But the chimney smokes in the blue parlour."

"Well, we'll give it a trial, and if it does I'll send for someone to arrange it."

"Nothing can be done, my lady. Everything has been tried, and—"

Lady Jane swung about suddenly. She had heard Stramer singing a cheerful hunting-song in a cracked voice, in his dressing room at the other end of the corridor.

"That will do, Mrs. Clemm. I want the fire in the blue parlour."

"Yes, my lady." The door closed on the housekeeper.

"So you decided on the saloon after all?" Stramer said, as Lady Jane led the way there after their brief repast.

"Yes, I hope you won't be frozen. Mr. Jones swears that the chimney in the blue parlour isn't safe; so, until I can fetch the mason over from Strawbridge—"

"Oh, I see." Stramer drew up to the blaze in the great fireplace. "We're very well off here; though heating this room is going to be ruinous. Meanwhile, I note that Mr. Jones still rules."

Lady Jane gave a slight laugh.

"Tell me," Stramer continued, as she bent over the mixing of the Turkish coffee, "what is there about him? I'm getting curious."

Lady Jane laughed again, and heard the embarrassment in her laugh. "So am I."

"Why – you don't mean to say you haven't seen him yet?"

"No. He's still too ill."

"What's the matter with him? What does the doctor say?"

"He won't see the doctor."

"But, look here – if things take a worse turn – I don't know; but mightn't you be held to have been negligent?"

"What can I do? Mrs. Clemm says he has a doctor who treats him by correspondence. I don't see that I can interfere."

"Isn't there someone beside Mrs. Clemm whom you can consult?"

She considered: certainly, as yet, she had not made much effort to get into relation with her neighbours. "I expected the vicar to call. But I've enquired: there's no vicar any longer at Thudeney-Blazes. A curate comes from Strawbridge every other Sunday. And the one who comes now is new: nobody about the place seems to know him."

"But I thought the chapel here was in use? It looked so when you showed it to us the other day."

"I thought so too. It used to be the parish church of Lynke-Linnet and Lower-Lynke; but it seems that was years ago. The parishioners objected to coming so far; and there weren't enough of them. Mrs. Clemm says that nearly everybody has died off or left. It's the same at Thudeney-Blazes."

Stramer glanced about the great room, with its circle of warmth and light by the hearth, and the sullen shadows huddled at its farther end, as if hungrily listening. "With this emptiness at the centre, life was bound to cease gradually on the outskirts."

Lady Jane followed his glance. "Yes; it's all wrong. I must try to wake the place up."

"Why not open it to the public? Have a visitors' day?"

She thought a moment. In itself the suggestion was distasteful; she could imagine few things that would bore her more. Yet to do so might be a duty, a first step toward reestablishing relations between the lifeless house and its neighbourhood. Secretly, she felt that even the coming and going of indifferent unknown people would help to take the chill from those rooms, to brush from their walls the dust of too-heavy memories.

"Who's that?" asked Stramer. Lady Jane started in spite of herself, and glanced over her shoulder; but he was only looking past her at a portrait which a dart of flame from the hearth had momentarily called from its obscurity.

"That's a Lady Thudeney." She got up and went toward the picture with a lamp. "Might be an Opie, don't you think? It's a strange face, under the smirk of the period."

Stramer took the lamp and held it up. The portrait was that of a young woman in a short-waisted muslin gown caught beneath the breast by a cameo. Between clusters of beribboned curls a long fair oval looked out dumbly, inexpressively, in a stare of frozen beauty. "It's as if the house had been too empty even then," Lady Jane murmured. "I wonder which she was? Oh, I know: it must be 'Also His Wife'."

Stramer stared.

"It's the only name on her monument. The wife of Peregrine Vincent Theobald, who perished of the plague at Aleppo in 1828. Perhaps she was very fond of him, and this was painted when she was an inconsolable widow."

"They didn't dress like that as late as 1828." Stramer holding the lamp closer, deciphered the inscription on the border of the lady's India scarf; "Juliana, Viscountess Thudeney, 1818". "She must have been inconsolable before his death, then."

Lady Jane smiled. "Let's hope she grew less so after it."

Stramer passed the lamp across the canvas. "Do you see where she was painted? In the blue parlour. Look: the old panelling; and she's leaning on the citron-wood desk. They evidently used the room in winter then." The lamp paused on the background of the picture: a window framing snow-laden paths and hedges in icy perspective.

"Curious," Stramer said – "and rather melancholy: to be painted against that wintry desolation. I wish you could find out more about her. Have you dipped into your archives?"

"No. Mr. Jones—"

"He won't allow that either?"

"Yes; but he's lost the key of the muniment-room. Mrs. Clemm has been trying to get a locksmith."

"Surely the neighbourhood can still produce one?"

"There *was* one at Thudeney-Blazes; but he died the week before I came."

"Of course!"

"Of course?"

"Well, in Mrs. Clemm's hands keys get lost, chimneys smoke, locksmiths die…" Stramer stood, light in hand, looking down the shadowy length of the saloon. "I say, let's go and see what's happening now in the blue parlour."

Lady Jane laughed: a laugh seemed easy with another voice nearby to echo it. "Let's—"

She followed him out of the saloon, across the hall in which a single candle burned on a far-off table, and past the stairway yawning like a black funnel above them. In the doorway of the blue parlour Stramer paused. "Now, then, Mr. Jones!"

It was stupid, but Lady Jane's heart gave a jerk: she hoped the challenge would not evoke the shadowy figure she had half seen that other day.

"Lord, it's cold!" Stramer stood looking about him. "Those ashes are still on the hearth. Well, it's all very queer." He crossed over to the citron-wood desk. "There's where she sat for her picture – and in this very armchair – look!"

"Oh, don't!" Lady Jane exclaimed. The words slipped out unawares.

"Don't – what?"

"Try those drawers—" she wanted to reply; for his hand was stretched toward the desk.

"I'm frozen; I think I'm starting a cold. Do come away," she grumbled, backing toward the door.

Stramer lighted her out without comment. As the lamplight slid along the walls Lady Jane fancied that the needle-work curtain over the farther door stirred as it had that other day. But it may have been the wind rising outside…

The saloon seemed like home when they got back to it.

Chapter Six

"There *is* no Mr. Jones!"

Stramer proclaimed it triumphantly when they met the next morning. Lady Jane had motored off early to Strawbridge in quest of a mason and a locksmith. The quest had taken longer than she had expected, for everybody in Strawbridge was busy on jobs nearer by, and unaccustomed to the idea of going to Bells, with which the town seemed to have had no communication within living memory. The younger workmen did not even know where the place was, and the best Lady Jane could do was to coax a locksmith's apprentice to come with her, on the understanding that he would be driven back to the nearest station as soon as his job was over. As for the mason, he had merely taken note of her request, and promised half-heartedly to send somebody when he could. "Rather off our beat, though."

She returned, discouraged and somewhat weary, as Stramer was coming downstairs after his morning's work.

"No Mr. Jones?" she echoed.

"Not a trace! I've been trying the old Glamis experiment – situating his room by its window. Luckily the house is smaller..."

Lady Jane smiled. "Is this what you call locking yourself up with your work?"

"I can't work: that's the trouble. Not till this is settled. Bells is a fidgety place."

"Yes," she agreed.

"Well, I wasn't going to be beaten; so I went to try to find the head gardener."

"But there isn't—"

"No. Mrs. Clemm told me. The head gardener died last year. That woman positively glows with life whenever she announces a death. Have you noticed?"

Yes: Lady Jane had.

"Well – I said to myself that if there wasn't a head gardener there must be an underling; at least one. I'd seen somebody in the distance, raking leaves, and I ran him down. Of course he'd never seen Mr. Jones."

"You mean that poor old half-blind Jacob? He couldn't see anybody."

"Perhaps not. At any rate, he told me that Mr. Jones wouldn't let the leaves be buried for leaf-mould – I forget why. Mr. Jones's authority extends even to the gardens."

"Yet you say he doesn't exist!"

"Wait. Jacob is half-blind, but he's been here for years, and knows more about the place than you'd think. I got him talking about the house, and I pointed to one window after another, and he told me each time whose the room was, or had been. But he couldn't situate Mr. Jones."

"I beg your ladyship's pardon—" Mrs. Clemm was on the threshold, cheeks shining, skirt rustling, her eyes like drills. "The locksmith your ladyship brought back; I understand it was for the lock of the muniment-room—"

"Well?"

"He's lost one of his tools, and can't do anything without it. So he's gone. The butcher's boy gave him a lift back."

Lady Jane caught Stramer's faint chuckle. She stood and stared at Mrs. Clemm, and Mrs. Clemm stared back, deferential but unflinching.

"Gone? Very well; I'll motor after him."

"Oh, my lady, it's too late. The butcher's boy had his motor-cycle.... Besides, what could he do?"

"Break the lock," exclaimed Lady Jane, exasperated.

"Oh, my lady—" Mrs. Clemm's intonation marked the most respectful incredulity. She waited another moment, and then withdrew, while Lady Jane and Stramer considered each other.

"But this is absurd," Lady Jane declared when they had lunched, waited on, as usual, by the flustered Georgiana. "I'll break in that door myself, if I have to. – Be careful please, Georgiana," she added; "I was speaking of doors, not dishes." For Georgiana had let fall with a crash the dish she was removing from the table. She gathered up the pieces in her tremulous fingers, and vanished. Jane and Stramer returned to the saloon.

"Queer!" the novelist commented.

"Yes." Lady Jane, facing the door, started slightly. Mrs. Clemm was there again; but this time subdued, unrustling, bathed in that odd pallor which enclosed but seemed unable to penetrate the solid crimson of her cheeks.

"I beg pardon, my lady. The key is found." Her hand, as she held it out, trembled like Georgiana's.

Chapter Seven

"IT'S NOT HERE," Stramer announced a couple of hours later.

"What isn't?" Lady Jane queried, looking up from a heap of disordered papers. Her eyes blinked at him through the fog of yellow dust raised by her manipulations.

"The clue. I've got all the 1800 to 1840 papers here; and there's a gap."

She moved over to the table above which he was bending. "A gap?"

"A big one. Nothing between 1815 and 1835. No mention of Peregrine or Juliana."

They looked at each other across the tossed papers, and suddenly Stramer exclaimed: "Someone has been here before us – just lately."

Lady Jane stared, incredulous, and then followed the direction of his downward pointing hand.

"Do you wear flat heelless shoes?" he questioned.

"And of that size? Even my feet are too small to fit into those footprints. Luckily there wasn't time to sweep the floor!"

Lady Jane felt a slight chill, a chill of a different and more inward quality than the shock of stuffy coldness which had met them as they entered the unaired attic set apart for the storing of the Thudeney archives.

"But how absurd! Of course when Mrs. Clemm found we were coming up she came – or sent someone – to open the shutters."

"That's not Mrs. Clemm's foot, or the other woman's. She must have sent a man – an old man with a shaky uncertain step. Look how it wanders."

"Mr. Jones, then!" said Lady Jane, half impatiently.

"Mr. Jones. And he got what he wanted, and put it – where?"

"Ah, *that*—! I'm freezing, you know; let's give this up for the present." She rose, and Stramer followed her without protest; the muniment-room was really untenable.

"I must catalogue all this stuff someday, I suppose," Lady Jane continued, as they went down the stairs. "But meanwhile, what do you say to a good tramp, to get the dust out of our lungs?"

He agreed, and turned back to his room to get some letters he wanted to post at Thudeney-Blazes.

Lady Jane went down alone. It was a fine afternoon, and the sun, which had made the dust-clouds of the muniment-room so dazzling, sent a long shaft through the west window of the blue parlour, and across the floor of the hall.

Certainly Georgiana kept the oak floors remarkably well; considering how much else she had to do, it was surp—

Lady Jane stopped as if an unseen hand had jerked her violently back. On the smooth parquet before her she had caught the trace of dusty footprints – the prints of broad-soled heelless shoes – making for the blue parlour and crossing its threshold. She stood still with the same inward shiver that she had felt upstairs; then, avoiding the footprints, she too stole very softly toward the blue parlour, pushed the door wider, and saw, in the long dazzle of autumn light, as if translucid, edged with the glitter, an old man at the desk.

"Mr. Jones!"

A step came up behind her: Mrs. Clemm with the post-bag. "You called, my lady?"

"I...yes..."

When she turned back to the desk there was no one there.

She faced about on the housekeeper. "Who was that?"

"Where, my lady?"

Lady Jane, without answering, moved toward the needlework curtain, in which she had detected the same faint tremor as before. "Where does that door go to – behind the curtain?"

"Nowhere, my lady. I mean; there is no door."

Mrs. Clemm had followed; her step sounded quick and assured. She lifted up the curtain with a firm hand. Behind it was a rectangle of roughly plastered wall, where an opening had visibly been bricked up.

"When was that done?"

"The wall built up? I couldn't say. I've never known it otherwise," replied the housekeeper.

The two women stood for an instant measuring each other with level eyes; then the housekeeper's were slowly lowered, and she let the curtain fall from her hand. "There are a great many things in old houses that nobody knows about," she said.

"There shall be as few as possible in mine," said Lady Jane.

"My lady!" The housekeeper stepped quickly in front of her. "My lady, what are you doing?" she gasped.

Lady Jane had turned back to the desk at which she had just seen – or fancied she had seen – the bending figure of Mr. Jones.

"I am going to look through these drawers," she said.

The housekeeper still stood in pale immobility between her and the desk. "No, my lady – no. You won't do that."

"Because—?"

Mrs. Clemm crumpled up her black silk apron with a despairing gesture. "Because – if you *will* have it – that's where Mr. Jones keeps his private papers. I know he'd oughtn't to..."

"Ah – then it was Mr. Jones I saw here?"

The housekeeper's arms sank to her sides and her mouth hung open on an unspoken word. "You *saw* him." The question came out in a confused whisper; and before Lady Jane could answer, Mrs. Clemm's arms rose again, stretched before her face as if to fend off a blaze of intolerable light, or some forbidden sight she had long since disciplined herself not to see. Thus screening her eyes she hurried across the hall to the door of the servant's wing.

Lady Jane stood for a moment looking after her; then, with a slightly shaking hand, she opened the desk and hurriedly took out from it all the papers – a small bundle – that it contained. With them she passed back into the saloon.

As she entered it her eye was caught by the portrait of the melancholy lady in the short-waisted gown, whom she and Stramer had christened 'Also His Wife'. The lady's eyes, usually so empty of all awareness save of her own frozen beauty, seemed suddenly waking to an anguished participation in the scene.

"Fudge!" muttered Lady Jane, shaking off the spectral suggestion as she turned to meet Stramer on the threshold.

Chapter Eight

THE MISSING PAPERS were all there. Stramer and she spread them out hurriedly on a table and at once proceeded to gloat over their find. Not a particularly important one, indeed; in the long history of the Lynkes and Crofts it took up hardly more space than the little handful of documents did, in actual bulk, among the stacks of the muniment room. But the fact that these papers filled a gap in the chronicles of the house, and situated the sad-faced beauty as veritably the wife of the Peregrine Vincent Theobald Lynke who had 'perished of the plague at Aleppo in 1828' – this was a discovery sufficiently exciting to whet amateur appetites, and to put out of Lady Jane's mind the strange incident which had attended the opening of the cabinet.

For a while she and Stramer sat silently and methodically going through their respective piles of correspondence; but presently Lady Jane, after glancing over one of the yellowing pages, uttered a startled exclamation.

"How strange! Mr. Jones again – always Mr. Jones!"

Stramer looked up from the papers he was sorting. "You too? I've got a lot of letters here addressed to a Mr. Jones by Peregrine Vincent, who seems to have been always disporting himself abroad, and chronically in want of money. Gambling debts, apparently…ah and women…a dirty record altogether…"

"Yes? My letter is not written to a Mr. Jones; but it's about one. Listen." Lady Jane began to read. "'Bells, February 20th, 1826…' (It's from poor 'Also His Wife' to her husband.) 'My dear Lord, Acknowledging as I ever do the burden of the sad impediment which denies me the happiness of being more frequently in your company, I yet fail to conceive how anything in my state obliges that close seclusion in which Mr. Jones persists – and by your express orders, so he declares – in confining me. Surely, my lord, had you found it possible to spend more time with me since the day of our marriage, you would yourself have seen it to be unnecessary to put this restraint upon me. It is true, alas, that my unhappy infirmity denies me the happiness to speak with you, or to hear the accents of the voice I should love above all others could it but reach me; but, my dear husband, I would have you consider that my mind is in no way affected by this obstacle, but goes out to you, as my heart does, in a perpetual eagerness of attention, and that to sit in this great house alone, day after day, month after month, deprived of your company, and debarred also from any intercourse but that of the servants you have chosen to put about me, is a fate more cruel than I deserve and more painful than I can bear. I have entreated Mr. Jones, since he seems all-powerful with you, to represent this to you, and to transmit this my last request – for should I fail I am resolved to make no other – that you should consent to my making the acquaintance of a few of your friends and neighbours, among whom I cannot but think there must be some kind hearts that would take pity on my unhappy situation, and afford me such companionship as would give me more courage to bear your continual absence…"

Lady Jane folded up the letter. "Deaf and dumb – ah, poor creature! That explains the look—"

"And this explains the marriage," Stramer continued, unfolding a stiff parchment document. "Here are the Viscountess Thudeney's marriage settlements. She appears to have been a Miss Portallo, daughter of Obadiah Portallo Esquire, of Purflew Castle, Caermarthenshire, and Bombay House, Twickenham, East India merchant, senior member of the banking house of Portallo and Prest – and so on and so on. And the figures run up into hundreds of thousands."

"It's rather ghastly – putting the two things together. All the millions and – imprisonment in the blue parlour. I suppose her Viscount had to have the money, and was ashamed to have it known how he had got it…" Lady Jane shivered. "Think of it – day after day, winter after winter, year after year…speechless, soundless, alone…under Mr. Jones's guardianship. Let me see: what year were they married?"

"In 1817."

"And only a year later that portrait was painted. And she had the frozen look already."

Stramer mused: "Yes; it's grim enough. But the strangest figure in the whole case is still – Mr. Jones."

"Mr. Jones – yes. Her keeper," Lady Jane mused "I suppose he must have been this one's ancestor. The office seems to have been hereditary at Bells."

"Well – I don't know."

Stramer's voice was so odd that Lady Jane looked up at him with a stare of surprise. "What if it were the same one?" suggested Stramer with a queer smile.

"The same?" Lady Jane laughed. "You're not good at figures are you? If poor Lady Thudeney's Mr. Jones were alive now he'd be—"

"I didn't say ours was alive now," said Stramer.

"Oh – why, what…?" she faltered.

But Stramer did not answer; his eyes had been arrested by the precipitate opening of the door behind his hostess, and the entry of Georgiana, a livid, dishevelled Georgiana, more than usually bereft of her faculties, and gasping out something inarticulate.

"Oh, my lady – it's my aunt – she won't answer me," Georgiana stammered in a voice of terror.

Lady Jane uttered an impatient exclamation. "Answer you? Why – what do you want her to answer?"

"Only whether she's alive, my lady," said Georgiana with streaming eyes.

Lady Jane continued to look at her severely. "Alive? Alive? Why on earth shouldn't she be?"

"She might as well be dead – by the way she just lies there."

"Your aunt dead? I saw her alive enough in the blue parlour half an hour ago," Lady Jane returned. She was growing rather blasé with regard to Georgiana's panics; but suddenly she felt this to be of a different nature from any of the others. "Where is it your aunt's lying?"

"In her own bedroom, on her bed," the other wailed, "and won't say why."

Lady Jane got to her feet, pushing aside the heaped-up papers, and hastening to the door with Stramer in her wake.

As they went up the stairs she realised that she had seen the housekeeper's bedroom only once, on the day of her first obligatory round of inspection, when she had taken possession of Bells. She did not even remember very clearly where it was, but followed Georgiana down the passage and through a door which communicated, rather surprisingly, with a narrow walled-in staircase that was unfamiliar to her. At its top she and Stramer found themselves on a small landing upon which two doors opened. Through the confusion of her mind Lady Jane noticed that these rooms, with their special staircase leading down to what had always been called his lordship's suite, must obviously have been occupied by his lordship's confidential servants. In one of them, presumably, had been lodged the original Mr. Jones, the Mr. Jones of the yellow letters, the letters purloined by Lady Jane. As she crossed the threshold, Lady Jane remembered the housekeeper's attempt to prevent her touching the contents of the desk.

Mrs. Clemm's room, like herself, was neat, glossy and extremely cold. Only Mrs. Clemm herself was no longer like Mrs. Clemm. The red-apple glaze had barely faded from her cheeks, and not a lock was disarranged in the unnatural lustre of her false front; even her cap ribbons hung symmetrically along either cheek. But death had happened to her, and had made her into someone else. At first glance it was impossible to say if the unspeakable horror in her wide-open eyes were only the reflection of that change, or of the agent by whom it had come. Lady Jane, shuddering, paused a moment while Stramer went up to the bed.

"Her hand is warm still – but no pulse." He glanced about the room. "A glass anywhere?" The cowering Georgiana took a hand-glass from the neat chest of drawers, and Stramer held it over the housekeeper's drawn-back lip…

"She's dead," he pronounced.

"Oh, poor thing! But how—?" Lady Jane drew near, and was kneeling down, taking the inanimate hand in hers, when Stramer touched her on the arm, then silently raised a finger of warning. Georgiana was crouching in the farther corner of the room, her face buried in her lifted arms.

"Look here," Stramer whispered. He pointed to Mrs. Clemm's throat, and Lady Jane, bending over, distinctly saw a circle of red marks on it – the marks of recent bruises. She looked again into the awful eyes.

"She's been strangled," Stramer whispered.

Lady Jane, with a shiver of fear, drew down the housekeeper's lids. Goergiana, her face hidden, was still sobbing convulsively in the corner. There seemed, in the air of the cold orderly room, something that forbade wonderment and silenced conjecture. Lady Jane and Stramer stood and looked at each other without speaking. At length Stramer crossed over to Georgiana, and touched her on the shoulder. She appeared unaware of the touch, and he grasped her shoulder and shook it. "Where is Mr. Jones?" he asked.

The girl looked up, her face blurred and distorted with weeping, her eyes dilated as if with the vision of some latent terror. "Oh, sir, she's not really dead, is she?"

Stramer repeated his question in a loud authoritative tone; and slowly she echoed it in a scarce-heard whisper. "Mr. Jones—?"

"Get up, my girl, and send him here to us at once, or tell us where to find him."

Georgiana, moved by the old habit of obedience, struggled to her feet and stood unsteadily, her heaving shoulders braced against the wall. Stramer asked her sharply if she had not heard what he had said.

"Oh, poor thing, she's so upset—" Lady Jane intervened compassionately. "Tell me, Georgiana: where shall we find Mr. Jones?"

The girl turned to her with eyes as fixed as the dead woman's. "You won't find him anywhere," she slowly said.

"Why not?"

"Because he's not here."

"Not here? Where is he, then?" Stramer broke in.

Georgiana did not seem to notice the interruption. She continued to stare at Lady Jane with Mrs. Clemm's awful eyes. "He's in his grave in the church-yard – these years and years he is. Long before ever I was born...my aunt hadn't ever seen him herself, not since she was a tiny child.... That's the terror of it...that's why she always had to do what he told her to...because you couldn't ever answer him back..." Her horrified gaze turned from Lady Jane to the stony face and fast-glazing pupils of the dead woman. "You hadn't ought to have meddled with his papers, my lady.... That's what he's punished her for.... When it came to those papers he wouldn't ever listen to human reason...he wouldn't..." Then, flinging her arms above her head, Georgiana straightened herself to her full height before falling in a swoon at Stramer's feet.

Biographies & Sources

E.F. Benson

How Fear Departed from the Long Gallery
(Originally Published in *The Room in the Tower and Other Stories*, 1912)
The Room in the Tower
(Originally Published in *The Room in the Tower and Other Stories*, 1912)
Edward Frederic ('E.F.') Benson (1867–1940) was born at Wellington College in Berkshire, England, where his father, the future Archbishop of Canterbury Edward White Benson, was headmaster. Benson is widely known for being a writer of reminiscences, fiction, satirical novels, biographies and autobiographical studies. His first published novel, *Dodo*, initiated his success, followed by a series of comic novels such as *Queen Lucia* and *Trouble for Lucia*. Later in life, Benson moved to Rye where he was elected mayor. It was here that he was inspired to write several macabre ghost story and supernatural collections and novels, including *Paying Guests* and *Mrs Ames*.

Ambrose Bierce

The Spook House
(Originally Published in *The San Francisco Examiner*, 1889)
Ambrose Bierce (1842–c. 1914) was born in Meigs County, Ohio. He was a famous journalist and author known for writing *The Devil's Dictionary*. After fighting in the American Civil War, Bierce used his combat experience to write stories based on the war, such as in 'An Occurrence at Owl Creek Bridge'. Following the separate deaths of his ex-wife and two of his three children he gained a sardonic view of human nature and earned the name 'Bitter Bierce'. His disappearance at the age of 71 on a trip to Mexico remains a great mystery and continues to spark speculation.

Mary Elizabeth Braddon

The Shadow in the Corner
(Originally Published in *All the Year Round*, 1879)
Mary Elizabeth Braddon (1835–1915) was born in London, England. During her lifetime, Braddon was a productive writer, producing over 80 novels. Her most notable novel, *Lady Audley's Secret* (1862), brought Braddon much recognition and fortune. In addition to her tales of intrigue, Braddon wrote a number of works on the supernatural, including, *Gerald, or, the World, the Flesh and the Devil*, 'The Cold Embrace' and 'At Chrighton Abbey'. Beyond her literary endeavours, Braddon founded *Belgravia Magazine* (1866), showcasing the latest serialised sensation novels, poems and travel narratives alongside essays on fashion, history and science.

Rhoda Broughton

The Truth, the Whole Truth, and Nothing but the Truth
(Originally Published in *Tales for Christmas Eve*, 1873)
Rhoda Broughton (1840–1920) was born in Denbigh, North Wales. She was raised in an Elizabethan manor house and given a classical education, which influenced her later writing. Broughton quickly established herself as a writer of controversially frank portrayals of female

sexuality. Despite the consternation at her subject matter her novels were very popular and widely read. She also became known as a society wit that even intimidated Oscar Wilde.

Rebecca Buchanan
Sanctuary
(First Publication)
Rebecca Buchanan (North Carolina) is the editor of the Pagan literary ezine *Eternal Haunted Summer*. She has been previously published in a wide variety of venues, and has released two short story collections from Asphodel Press: *A Witch Among Wolves, and Other Pagan Tales*; and *The Serpent in the Throat, and Other Pagan Tales*. Her first poetry collection, *Dame Evergreen and Other Poems of Myth, Magic, and Madness*, has just been released by Sycorax Press.

Edward Bulwer-Lytton
The Haunted and the Haunters, or, The House and the Brain
(Originally Published in *Blackwood's Magazine*, 1859)
Edward Bulwer-Lytton (1803–73) was born in London, England. He was a politician, poet, and novelist. His works were highly popular and earned him a large fortune. Bulwer-Lytton also invented many well-known phrases that are still used today, including 'the great unwashed', and 'the pen is mightier than the sword'. He later suffered a sharp decline in his literary reputation, especially for his use of the opening line 'It was a dark and stormy night' in his novel *Paul Clifford*.

Ramsey Campbell
At Lorn Hall
(Originally Published in *Searchers after Horror*, edited by S.T. Joshi, © 2014 Ramsey Campbell)
The *Oxford Companion to English Literature* describes Ramsey Campbell as 'Britain's most respected living horror writer'. He has been given more awards than any other writer in the field, including the Grand Master Award of the World Horror Convention, the Lifetime Achievement Award of the Horror Writers Association, the Living Legend Award of the International Horror Guild and the World Fantasy Lifetime Achievement Award. In 2015 he was made an Honorary Fellow of Liverpool John Moores University for outstanding services to literature. Among his novels available from Flame Tree Press are *Thirteen Days by Sunset Beach* and *Think Yourself Lucky*.

Bernard Capes
An Eddy on the Floor
(Originally Published in *At a Winter's Fire*, 1899)
Bernard Capes (1854–1918) was born in London, England, and was one of eleven children. He was a very prolific writer and published over 40 books, including romances, ghost stories, poetry, and history. He won a prize offered by the *Chicago Record* in 1898 for his story *The Lake of Wine*. He died in 1918 during the Spanish flu epidemic and a memorial plaque was placed in Winchester Cathedral (where he lived for his last years).

Ralph Adams Cram
No. 252 Rue M. Le Prince
(Originally Published in *Black Spirits and White*, 1895)
Ralph Adams Cram (1863–1942) was born in Hampton Falls, New Hampshire, United States. He

wrote a number of fiction stories and was praised by H.P. Lovecraft for his horror. In addition to his work as a writer, Cram was also one of the foremost architects of the Gothic revival in the United States. His influence helped to establish Gothic as the standard style of the period for American college and university buildings.

B.M. Croker

'To Let'
(Originally Published in *London Society*, 1890)
Number Ninety
(Originally Published in *Chapman's Magazine of Fiction*, 1895)
B.M. Croker (1849–1920) was born in Kilgefin, County Roscommon, Ireland. In 1877 she moved to India where she lived for 14 years with her husband, who was an officer in the British army. Croker wrote many of her works there as a distraction during the hot season. Croker's first novel *Proper Pride* was published anonymously and, with the public believing that the author was a man, gained good reviews. Many of her stories are concerned with upper-class life in India and Ireland.

H.B. Diaz

The Patient in Room 96
(First Publication)
H.B. Diaz is a horror and mystery writer who also manages author and independent retail accounts for Penguin Random House. Her work has appeared in publications such as *The Sirens Call eZine*, *Danse Macabre Online Literary Magazine*, and Horror Tree's *Trembling with Fear*. Inspired by her travels through the abandoned places of America, her stories often explore the terrible beauty of decay, whether in architecture or the mind. She now lives with her husband in a historic (and likely haunted) Maryland town.

Tom English

A Handful of Dust
(Originally Published in Issue 37 of *Weirdbook*, 2017)
Tom English is an environmental chemist who loves reading comics, watching old movies, and writing supernatural stories. His work has appeared in such magazines as *Weirdbook* and *Black Infinity*, and several anthologies, including *Gaslight Arcanum: Uncanny Tales of Sherlock Holmes*, and *Bound for Evil: Curious Tales of Books Gone Bad*. His nonfiction includes *The Heart of an Angel*, an inspirational book written with his wife, Wilma, on the true meaning and significance of hospitality, which Publishers Weekly praised as 'impassioned' and 'deeply spiritual'. He resides with Wilma, surrounded by books and beasts, deep in the woods of New Kent, Virginia.

John Everson

The House at the Top of the Hill
(Originally Published on Horrorfind.com, 2002)
John Everson is the Chicago-based, Bram Stoker Award-winning author of *Covenant*, as well as the novels *Sacrifice*, *The 13th*, *Siren* and *The Pumpkin Man*, all originally in paperback from Dorchester/Leisure Books. His sixth novel, *NightWhere*, an erotic horror descent into dark desire, was released by Samhain in 2012 and was a Bram Stoker Award finalist. His tenth novel, *The House by the Cemetery*, was released in 2018 from Flame Tree Press. Over the past 25 years,

his critically acclaimed short fiction has appeared in dozens of magazines and anthologies. For information on his fiction, art and music, visit johneverson.com.

Joseph Sheridan le Fanu

An Account of Some Strange Disturbances in Aungier Street

(Originally Published in *Dublin University Magazine*, 1853)

The remarkable father of Victorian ghost stories Joseph Thomas Sheridan Le Fanu (1814–73) was born in Dublin, Ireland. His gothic tales and mystery novels led to him become a leading ghost story writer of the nineteenth century. Three oft-cited works of his are *Uncle Silas, Carmilla* and *The House by the Churchyard,* which all are assumed to have influenced Bram Stoker's *Dracula*. Le Fanu wrote his most successful and productive works after his wife's tragic death and he remained a relatively strong writer up until his own death.

Marina Favila

Haunting Christmas

(Originally Published in *Mythic Circle*, 2017)

Marina Favila is an English professor at James Madison University in Virginia. She has published essays on Shakespeare, poetry, and film in various academic journals, including *Modern Philology, Spiritus, Cahiers Elisabethains, Upstart Crow*, and *Texas Studies in Literature and Language*. Her published short stories include pieces in *Jersey Devil Press, Wraparound South, Fabula Argentea*, and Harvardwood's *Seven Deadly Sins* anthology. She has a story forthcoming in *Weirdbook*.

Shannon Fay

House Hunting

(Originally Published in Issue 1 of *Crowded Magazine*, 2013)

Shannon Fay is a manga editor by day, fiction writer by night. She currently lives in Nova Scotia, Canada. She is a graduate of Clarion West (class of 2014). She's had oodles of short stories published in a variety of genres and is currently working on a historical fantasy novel. She can be found online at @shannonlfay and ayearonsaturn.com. She is big on board games and bird facts. To the best of her knowledge, she has never lived in a haunted house.

Mary E. Wilkins Freeman

The Vacant Lot

(Originally Published in *Everybody's Magazine*, 1902)

The American author Mary Eleanor Wilkins Freeman (1852–1930) was born in Randolph, Massachusetts. Most of Freeman's works were influenced by her strict childhood, as her parents were orthodox Congregationalists and harboured strong religious views. While working as a secretary for the author Oliver Wendell Holmes, Sr., she was inspired to write herself. Supernatural topics kept catching her attention, and she began to write many short stories with a combination of supernatural and domestic realism, her most famous being 'A New England Nun'. She wrote a number of ghost tales, which were turned into famous ghost story collections after her death.

Adele Gardner

The Bones of Home

(Originally Published in a different and longer form under the title 'The Angles of Midnight' in *Zen of the Dead: Stories and Poems*, 2015)

Cat-loving cataloging librarian Adele Gardner (gardnercastle.com) hails from Tidewater Virginia,

USA. With a poetry book (*Dreaming of Days in Astophel*), 242 poems, and 45 stories published in venues like *Strange Horizons*, *Legends of the Pendragon*, and *The Doom of Camelot*, she's an active member of SFWA with a master's degree in English literature (thesis on William Morris). Adele loves the legends of the Round Table and recently guest-edited the Arthuriana issue of *Eye to the Telescope* (#27, Jan. 2018, eyetothetelescope.com/archives/027issue.html). She serves as literary executor for her father, mentor, and namesake, WWII veteran Delbert R. Gardner (8th Air Force, Rackheath).

Elizabeth Gaskell
The Old Nurse's Story
(Originally Published in *A Round of Stories by the Christmas Fire*, 1852)
Victorian novelist Elizabeth Gaskell (1810–65) was born in London, England, and is widely known for her biography of her friend Charlotte Brontë. In a family of eight children, only Elizabeth and her brother John survived past childhood. Her mother's early death caused her to be raised by her aunt in Knutsford, Cheshire, a place that inspired her to later write her most famous work *Cranford*. Tragedy struck again when Gaskell's only son died, and it was then that she began to write. All the misfortune in her life led her to write her many gothic and horror tales.

Charlotte Perkins Gilman
The Giant Wistaria
(Originally Published in *The New England Magazine*, 1891)
Celebrated feminist writer Charlotte Perkins Gilman (1860–1935) was born in Hartford, Connecticut. She is perhaps best remembered as the author of the short story 'The Yellow Wallpaper', which details a woman's descent into madness after she is cooped up in a misguided attempt to restore her to health. The story was a clear indicator of Gilman's views on the restraints of women and related to her own treatment for postpartum depression. She is also notable for having written the utopian novel *Herland*, in which three men stumble across a society composed entirely of women. Gilman's writings are not only engrossing in their own right, but also continue to spark discussion about gender and society.

O. Henry
The Furnished Room
(Originally Published in *New York World*, 1904)
O. Henry was the penname of William Sydney Porter (1862–1910). Porter was born in Greensboro, North Carolina, United States. He had a variety of jobs throughout his life as well as submitting his sketches, cartoons, and short stories to different newspapers. In 1898 Porter was convicted of embezzlement, after spending a brief period on the run in Honduras. He served 3 years in jail for the crime. He continued writing during his imprisonment and entered his most prolific writing period in 1902 just after his release.

William Hope Hodgson
The Whistling Room
(Originally Published in *The Idler*, 1910)
William Hope Hodgson (1877–1918) was born in Essex, England, but moved several times with his family, including living for some time in County Galway, Ireland – a setting that would later inspire *The House on the Borderland*. Hodgson made several unsuccessful attempts to run away to sea, until his uncle secured him some work in the Merchant Marine. This association

with the ocean would unfold later in his many sea stories. After some initial rejections of his writing, Hodgson managed to become a full-time writer of both novels and short stories, which form a fantastic legacy of adventure, mystery and horror fiction.

W.W. Jacobs
The Toll-House
(Originally Published in *Sailors' Knots*, 1909)
William Wymark ('W.W.') Jacobs (1863–1943) was born in London, England, and he is known for his deeply humorous and horrifying works. Drawing upon his childhood experiences, Jacobs wrote many works reflecting on his father's profession as a dockhand and wharf manager. His first volume of stories, *Many Cargoes,* was a great success and gave Jacobs the courage to publish other stories such as 'The Monkey's Paw' and 'The Toll-House'. Jacobs used realistic experiences as well as a combination of superstition, terror, exotic adventure and humour in each one of his famous tales.

M.R. James
Number 13
(Originally Published in *Ghost Stories of an Antiquary*, 1904)
The Residence at Whitminster
(Originally Published in A Thin Ghost and Others, 1919)
Montague Rhodes James (1862–1936), whose works are regarded as being at the forefront of the ghost story genre, was born in Kent, England. James dispensed with the traditional, predictable techniques of ghost story construction, instead using realistic contemporary settings for his works. He was also a British medieval scholar, so his stories tended to incorporate antiquarian elements. His stories often reflect his childhood in Suffolk and talented acting career, which both seem to have assisted in the build-up of tension and horror in his works.

Dr. Rebecca Janicker
Foreword: Haunted House Short Stories
Dr. Rebecca Janicker is a senior lecturer in Film and Media Studies at the University of Portsmouth and an editorial advisory board member for *The Journal of Popular Culture*. She is the author of *The Literary Haunted House: Lovecraft, Matheson, King and the Horror in Between* (2015) and the editor of *Reading 'American Horror Story': Essays on the Television Franchise* (2017). Her other publications have focused on the Gothic fictions of Robert Bloch, Stephen King, Richard Matheson and H.P. Lovecraft, including work on horror in film, TV and comics.

Rudyard Kipling
They
(Originally Published in *Scribner's Magazine*, 1904)
English writer and poet Rudyard Kipling (1865–1936) was born in Bombay, India. He was educated in England but returned to India in his youth, which inspired many of his later writings, most famously seen in *The Jungle Book*. He later returned to England, and after travelling the United States settled in Vermont, America. He was awarded the Nobel Prize for Literature in 1907, which made him the first English-language writer to receive the accolade. His narrative style is inventive and provides an engaging commentary on imperialism, making it no surprise that his works of fiction and poetry have become classics.

Gwendolyn Kiste

The Woman out of the Attic

(First Publication)

Gwendolyn Kiste is the author of the Bram Stoker Award-nominated collection *And Her Smile Will Untether the Universe*, the dark fantasy novella *Pretty Marys All in a Row*, and her debut horror novel *The Rust Maidens*. Her short fiction has appeared in *Nightmare Magazine*, *Shimmer*, *Black Static*, *Daily Science Fiction*, *Interzone*, and *LampLight*, among other publications. A native of Ohio, she resides on an abandoned horse farm outside of Pittsburgh with her husband, two cats, and not nearly enough ghosts. You can find her online at gwendolynkiste.com.

Bill Kte'pi

Drydown, 1973

(First Publication)

Bill Kte'pi ('kuh TEP ee', which he more or less made up when he changed his name, which technically means there are no incorrect pronunciations) has been publishing horror and fantasy short fiction for about twenty-five years, as well as two horror novels, *Low Country* and *Frankie Teardrop*. He's working on a science fantasy novel that he will be compelled to finish once he sees this in print. He lives in New England with his wife, Caitlin O'Brien.

H.P. Lovecraft

The Rats in the Walls

(Originally Published in *Weird Tales*, 1924)

Master of weird fiction Howard Phillips Lovecraft (1890–1937) was born in Providence, Rhode Island. Featuring unknown and otherworldly creatures, his stories were one of the first to mix science fiction with horror. Plagued by nightmares from an early age, he was inspired to write his dark and strange fantasy tales; and the isolation he must have experienced from suffering frequent illnesses can be felt as a prominent theme in his work. Lovecraft inspired many other authors, and his most famous story 'The Call of Cthulhu' has gone on to influence many aspects of popular culture.

Guy de Maupassant

The Apparition

(Originally Published in a volume of Maupassant's *Complete Short Stories*, translated by Albert M.C. McMaster, A.E. Henderson, Mme. Quesada, and Others, 1880–93)

Henri René Albert Guy de Maupassant (1850–1893) was born at the Château de Miromesnil in France, and is considered the father of the modern short story. His is perhaps known best for his short stories 'The Necklace' and 'Boule de Suif', which was inspired by his time serving during the Franco-Prussian War. Maupassant developed syphilis early on in his life, causing him to develop a mental disorder coupled with nightmarish visions, no doubt contributing to his skill in producing supernatural stories. He died in an asylum in 1893.

John M. McIlveen

Nina

(Originally Published in *Dark Hall Press Ghost Anthology*, 2013)

John M. McIlveen is the author of the paranormal suspense novel *Hannahwhere* and winner of the 2015 Drunken Druid Award (Ireland). He was nominated for the 2015 Bram Stoker

Award (HWA), and has penned two story collections: *Inflictions* and *Jerks*. Stay tuned for his forthcoming novels *Gone North* and *Corruption*. He is a father to five daughters, Editor-In-Chief of Haverhill House Publishing, and works at MIT's Lincoln Laboratory. He lives with his wife in Haverhill, MA.

Edith Nesbit
The Ebony Frame
(Originally Published in *Longman's Magazine*, 1891)
Edith Nesbit (1858–1924) was born in Kennington, England. Nesbit established herself as a successful author and poet, writing a variety of literature ranging from children's books to adult horror stories. She co-founded the Fabian Society and was also a strong political activist. Marrying young and frequently moving home, Nesbit made many friendships with other writers including H.G. Wells and George Bernard Shaw. Although she gained most of her success from her children's books, like the ever-popular *The Railway Children*, she was also a well-known horror writer, with such collections as *Something Wrong* and *Grim Tales*.

Kurt Newton
creak!
(Originally Published in *What Walks Alone: A Creative Tribute to Shirley Jackson's Novel 'The Haunting of Hill House'*, 2002)
Kurt Newton was born and raised in rural Connecticut where the creak of an old home is as commonplace as the caw of a crow. His short stories have appeared in numerous magazines and anthologies, including *Dark Discoveries*, *Weirdbook* and *Hinnom Magazine*. He recently won the 2018 Screw Turn Flash Fiction Competition held every year at www.theghoststory.com. His winning entry was included in the anthology *21st Century Ghost Stories*. He is the author of two novels, *The Wishnik* and *Powerlines*.

Vincent O'Sullivan
The Burned House
(Originally Published in *The Century Magazine*, 1916)
Vincent O'Sullivan (1868–1940) was born in New York City, United States. He was educated in New York and England. O'Sullivan led a comfortable life off the income from his family's coffee business until his brother Percy made a mistimed futures gamble at the New York Coffee Exchange in 1909. O'Sullivan remained destitute for the rest of his life. His works are known for dealing with the morbid and the decadent.

Margaret Oliphant
The Library Window
(Originally Published in *Blackwood's Magazine* in January 1896)
Margaret Oliphant (1828–97) was born in Wallyford, Scotland. As a young girl, Oliphant showed promise, dedicating her time to experimenting with story-telling. Success arrived in 1849 with her first novel *Passages in the Life of Mrs. Margaret Maitland of Sunnyside,* marking the start of a rich and varied literary career. She was later invited by the esteemed publisher William Blackwood to contribute to *Blackwood's Magazine,* a crucial partnership that was to last throughout her life. Calling upon the themes of history, domesticity and the supernatural, Oliphant's unique blend of ideas led to the creation of over 120 works including novels, books on travel, histories and literary criticism.

Edgar Allan Poe

The Fall of the House of Usher

(Originally Published in *Burton's Gentleman's Magazine*, 1839)

The versatile writer Edgar Allan Poe (1809–1849) was born in Boston, Massachusetts. Poe is extremely well known as an influential author, poet, editor and literary critic that wrote during the American Romantic Movement. Poe is generally considered the inventor of the detective fiction genre, and his works are famously filled with terror, mystery, death and hauntings. Some of his better-known works include his poems 'The Raven' and 'Annabel Lee', and the short stories 'The Tell Tale Heart' and 'The Fall of the House of Usher'. The dark, mystifying characters of his tales have captured the public's imagination and reflect the struggling, poverty-stricken lifestyle he lived his whole life.

Arthur Quiller-Couch

A Pair of Hands (An Old Maid's Ghost Story)

(Originally Published in *Old Fires and Profitable Ghosts*, 1900)

Sir Arthur Quiller-Couch (1863–1944) was born in Bodmin, Cornwall, England. He wrote under the pseudonym 'Q' and, despite publishing many works of fiction and verse, he is best remembered for editing *The Oxford Book of English Verse 1250–1900*. Quiller-Couch was a well-respected literary critic and professor at the University of Cambridge. Interestingly, Sir Arthur Quiller-Couch was said to be the inspiration for the character of Ratty in *The Wind in the Willows*.

M. Regan

Sparrow

(First Publication)

M. Regan has been writing in various capacities for over a decade, with credits ranging from localisation work to scholarly reviews, advice columns to short stories. In addition to pieces in a growing number of anthologies, she co-authored a collection of tech-based horror with Caitlin Marceau entitled *Read-Only*. Deeply fascinated by the fears and maladies personified by monsters, M. Regan enjoys composing dark fiction, studying supernatural creatures, and travelling to places with rich histories of folklore. She can be found and followed at facebook.com/mreganfiction.

Zandra Renwick

Gretel

(Earlier Versions Originally Published in *The Devil's Food*, 2009, and in Audio at *Pseudopod*, 2010)

Zandra Renwick's short fiction has been translated into nine languages, optioned for television, and produced on stage. Her genre-elastic stories have appeared under various mash-ups of her birth name in over one hundred magazines, podcasts, and anthologies including *Ellery Queen's & Alfred Hitchcock's Mystery Magazines*, *Asimov's*, *Interzone*, *Mslexia*, *The Year's Best Hardcore Horror*, and *The Baltimore Review*. When not in an urban swamp in Austin, Texas, she writes and lives near the downtown core of Canada's capital city in Ottawa's historic Timberhouse. More at zandrarenwick.com.

Charlotte Riddell

The Old House in Vauxhall Walk

(Originally Published in *Weird Stories*, 1882)

Charlotte Riddell (1832–1906) was born in County Antrim, Ireland. After the death of her father she moved with her mother to London in 1855. She is best known for her ghost stories with their atmospheric settings, which Riddell drew from her own experiences in Ireland and London. Riddell struggled to earn a living from her writing, despite being a highly popular author, and due to her poor circumstances became the first pensioner of the Society of Authors in 1901.

Zach Shephard
The Great Indoors
(First Publication)
Zach Shephard lives in Enumclaw, Washington, where he writes stories that are sometimes dark and sometimes humorous, and sometimes so maddeningly vague not even he understands them. His fiction has appeared in places like *Fantasy & Science Fiction*, the *Unidentified Funny Objects* anthology series, and three other Flame Tree publications: *Science Fiction Short Stories*, *Swords & Steam Short Stories* and *Endless Apocalypse Short Stories*. One of Zach's primary influences for dark fiction is horror-master Evan Dicken (evandicken.com), whose invaluable critique of 'The Great Indoors' helped produce the story you see in this book. For more of Zach's work, check outzachshephard.com.

Morgan Sylvia
14 Oak Street
(First Publication)
Morgan Sylvia is an Aquarius, a metalhead, a coffee addict, and a work in progress. A former obituarist, she is now a full-time freelance writer. Her work has appeared in several anthologies, including *Wicked Witches*, *Wicked Haunted*, *Northern Frights*, and Flame Tree's *Endless Apocalypse Short Stories*. Her first horror novel, *Abode*, was released in 2017. She recently released another novel, *Dawn*, which is the first book of a fantasy trilogy. She is also the author of *Whispers from the Apocalypse*, a horror poetry collection, and *As the Seas Turn Red*, an ocean poetry collection. She lives in Maine, and actually enjoys the snow. Usually.

Mikal Trimm
Pictures at Eleven
(First Publication)
Mikal Trimm has sold over 50 short stories and 100 poems to numerous venues including *Postscripts*, *Strange Horizons*, *Realms of Fantasy*, and *Ellery Queen's Mystery Magazine*. At one point he was an editor at the somewhat influential online 'zine *Ideomancer*. He resides in a small Texas town outside of Austin, where he finds himself always too hot and not nearly famous or rich enough. He keeps a shady presence on Facebook, where he is inundated with messages by virtually no one.

Mark Twain
A Ghost Story
(Originally Published in *Sketches New and Old*, 1875)
Mark Twain (1835–1910) was born Samuel Langhorne Clemens in Florida, Missouri. Twain's name is synonymous with his American classics *The Adventures of Tom Sawyer* and its sequel, *Adventures of Huckleberry Finn*. Twain was born shortly after an appearance by Halley's Comet, and he predicted that he would 'go out with it', too. As chance would have it, he died the day after the comet returned in 1910. Twain was a very influential author whose works are timeless pieces that are still being taught today in classrooms to students of all ages.

Hugh Walpole

The Staircase

(Originally Published in *Harper's Bazaar*, 1929)

Sir Hugh Walpole (1884–1941) was born in Auckland, New Zealand. He was incredibly popular and successful during his lifetime. As well as writing many novel and short stories, Walpole also conducted lecture tours of North America, and was invited to Hollywood to write scenarios for *David Copperfield* and *Little Lord Fauntleroy*. Walpole's reputation and popularity suffered after his death. Recently there has been a re-emergence in interest for the author.

Edith Wharton

Miss Mary Pask

(Originally Published in *The Pictorial Review*, 1925)

Mr. Jones

(Originally Published in *Certain People*, 1930)

Edith Wharton (1862–1937), the Pulitzer Prize-winning writer of *The Age of Innocence,* was born in New York. As well as her talent as an American novelist, Wharton was also known for her short stories and designer career. Wharton was born into a controlled New York society where women were discouraged from achieving anything beyond a proper marriage. Defeating the norms, Wharton not only grew to become one of America's greatest writers, she grew to become a very self-rewarding woman. Writing numerous ghost stories and murderous tales such as 'The Lady's Maid's Bell', 'The Eyes' and 'Afterward', Wharton is widely known for the ghost tours that now take place at her old home, The Mount.

GOTHIC FANTASY

For our books, calendars, blog
and latest special offers please see:
flametreepublishing.com